bluebirds fly

a novel
by
Robin Andrew

PigsFly Press
El Jebel CO, USA

bluebirds fly

CONTENTS

bluebirds fly

Robin Andrew

five preludes, and a nocturne

I

Seattle-Tacoma Airport
May 1, 2008

Elaine Gimbal hears her name crackling above the crowd and knows in an instant why she is being paged: Rodney needs something, and he's looking for her. Barely an hour until flight time and he is imposing himself upon her, once again. All his brave-arrogant-pompous talk about wanting her to go ahead and take her trip, live her own life, not get bogged down in his illness - all that talk, all that history - and *still* she is being paged.

"It's not actually Tahiti, you know," Elaine recalls herself saying only the day before. "It's the Marquesas. A whole different archipelago."

"The Marquesas then. Beside the point."

Rodney was buttoning a starched and pressed white shirt, fixing the French cuffs with a pair of gold disks imprinted with the caduceus; the winged staff of Hermes with its intertwined serpents, symbol of his calling. As he spoke, his thick lips pursed and released. Heavily-lidded eyes bulged from his face beneath eyebrows which rose and fell, one at a time, to emphasize the truth of his words. His was a face which did not bother to hide the mechanics beneath the flesh or the physical effort required to get those large features into motion. As if to assist them, his tall narrow frame pressed forward; back angled, neck projected, impatient to meet the world head on. A posture that had rarely failed to achieve what Rodney Gimbal wished to accomplish.

Doctor Gimbal was in a hurry.

Scheduled to perform a miracle in precisely two hours, he had made it clear that he could not afford to deal with this right now.

If Elaine wanted to go to Tahiti, the discussion had begun, she should go to Tahiti. There was no reason he had to go. It would not be the first time she went off someplace by herself. To each his own. Her own.

"No Rodney. That is precisely the point. To get us out of our lives long enough to remember something other than surgical schedules and what time the next benefit dinner is supposed to start." Elaine felt herself near tears. Not for the first time of course, not after thirty-nine years of marriage to this man. "It's not like we're going to have a lot of other opportunities."

Her husband finished with his cufflinks and selected a tie - a deep maroon silk, patterned with tiny silver diamonds in precise diagonal rows. Only when the tie was tied and tacked to his shirtfront did he circle around behind and place his hands on his wife.

Elaine felt those surgeon's hands kneading her neck and shoulders, carefully working the weary muscles. Trapezius. Infraspinatus. Supraspinatus. Sternocleidomastoid. His touch was warm and soothing. His words were cold.

"You'll have plenty of opportunities. More time than you'll know what to do with."

Dr. Rodney Gimbal was dying, you see; had been dying for some time, actually. Lymphoma cells running rampant through his bloodstream, metastasizing in nooks and crannies of anatomy so small a first year resident would be hard pressed to recite them. Nothing to be done about it, despite the progress he had witnessed over decades, the studies he had read, the lengthy conversations with his esteemed colleagues. Everything too far advanced to be stopped. Treated perhaps, a little time bought through chemo and the rest, but then there was the coronary history to contend with. Two open-heart surgeries had failed to correct the basic imbalance between muscle size and body mass which he'd inherited from a long line of Gimbals. That heart would never stand up to chemo, and no review board in the world would give him a new heart with the cancer coursing through his blood.

Rodney Gimbal had ceased to consider years. Years did not figure into it at all. Months were what mattered to him now. Months, and even weeks were the measure of what Rodney Gimbal had left, and in that time he proposed to save as many lives as he possibly could. That was why he was dressing for work on a Thursday morning when his wife had planned to start packing for Tahiti. Or the Marquesas. Whatever. There were no lives to be saved in the

Marquesas, no miracles for Dr. Rodney Gimbal to perform.

"I know," Elaine said, as he left her side and pulled a suit coat from its padded hanger. "I know how much time I'll have. That's why I want us to do this. Now. The two of us." She watched him in front of the mirror, checking his tie.

"It would mean so much," she added into the silence. "Walking on the beach. Nothing to do but talk, read a book, watch the sunset..."

He turned, tailored elegance in a wool so gray it sucked the very light out of the entire room. "I'm sorry," he said, without even trying to sound it. "The last thing I want is nothing to do. I don't see much point in my reading a book right now - it's not like I've got a lot of need for enlightenment - and I can't imagine sitting on a beach, watching my time drain away. Elaine..."

He had come to her then, face to face this time, with hands huge and firm yet gentle as feathers on her hips. "We've always known you'd survive me. Being younger. My family history. I say you should go to Tah... wherever. Go. See it. Take pictures, meet people, come back with stories. I want to hear all about it. I want you to do it, and enjoy it. I just can't go. I don't have the time."

One more try, Elaine thought as she pulled his hands from her, held them up in front of her chest. I'll give the son-of-a-bitch one last chance.

"It wouldn't be the same Rodney, without you. That's the whole point. At least it is to me. I don't want to go by myself."

"Even if I went with you, I wouldn't be there. I can't just forget who I am, or what's happening inside me. You'd be sitting on a beautiful tropical island and I'd be wondering about my platelet count and whether Mrs. Waters has recovered enough to have her respirator removed. Whether Ahmad has managed to close up correctly on a procedure that should have been mine. The truth is, we come into this world alone and that's how we leave it. I'm leaving and you're staying. Alone. I can't say exactly when, but we both know it's true."

Feeling something vital breaking down inside her, Elaine tried to turn away, but her husband held her there. "No, don't," he said, driving his will through her eyes and into her thoughts. "Don't get all teary on me now. I've got work to do. It's the only thing that makes sense to me, for the little time I've got left." He paused, eyes vacant for a moment as if distracted, then resumed, with even more certainty in a voice which had never, over all the decades Elaine had been listening to it, lacked for certainty. "We're all headed the same place in this life, Elaine, there's no denying that, but we each get there on our own schedule. As it happens, my life has turned into an express train, straight to the end of the line, but you've still got stops to make – lots of them I hope. Time is already moving differently for the two of us –what seems to last forever for me will be a blink for you; what I can only glimpse for the briefest instant will become your forever-after. You might as well start living with that today as a month from today."

Elaine hears the page now as she waits in line to go through the metal detector. Ahead, a wheezing man in shorts and tank top places a blue nylon backpack in one bin, his canvas shoes in another, as Elaine waits, trying to be patient. Ever since leaving the house she has fought the urge to go back. Has felt her stomach growing gradually more upset, her cheeks aching from the battle inside of her; the knowledge that of course she must go back, but then again she cannot go back, and will in fact never go anywhere *but* back if she does not go forward now.

In stockinged feet the man empties his pockets, placing belt, keys, wristwatch and change inside a small plastic tray oddly reminiscent of those Elaine uses to organize cooking utensils in her kitchen drawers. Behind them, people are talking merrily about their travel plans, sharing their anticipation in voices which seem a thousand miles away - and still too close. Elaine's hands tremble as she removes her shoes and places them in a bin, then sets it onto the moving belt, followed by her purse and tote bag. The floor feels cold to her feet damp with a trace of sweat as she puts her own watch, bracelet and rings in a tray and slides it too into the darkness. Her hand feels odd as she waits for a wave from the TSA attendant on the other side of the metal detector, as if so light from the absence of those tiny golden bands that it would rise up and float of its own volition. Stepping through the metal detector, its frame like a portal to somewhere no different, yet also not the same, she feels the TSA attendant's brief nod of approval as a message, a blessing even, for what she has just done.

A few steps and she is at the other end of the conveyor, purse and tote disgorged and waiting as she slips her feet back into shoes still warm with their own heat. Pulling her tray close, she places the watch on her left wrist, the bracelet on her right, to find herself transfixed by the two slender rings sitting in its depth; golden circles, diligently cleaned in anticipation of each anniversary, still shine as if new despite the decades of their wearing. Behind her a young woman struggles to lift a bag from the table, her shoulder bobbing against Elaine's with a message of urgency. 'Life is going on,' says that gentle touch, 'we are all in a hurry, get on with what you are doing;' and so she does. Taking the tray left behind by the wheezing man, she nests it on top of her own, consigning that glint of gold to darkness, then sets them both onto a stack awaiting re-use. Gathering her own bags, she turns crisply, and strides with sudden purpose down the carpeted ramp which, the signs assure, will lead her to 'DEPARTURES.'

II

The restaurant at Donaldson's always makes Chris think of Christmas.

Even in May, with summer fashions already taking over every mannequin, walking toward that faux-marbled archway fills her mind with images of snow-white angels and Victorian urchins, their mouths puckered in song. Of silver and gold garlands cascading from windows and door frames as ancient carols are resurrected once again for their seasonal half-life.

They used to come here every December, Chris and her mother, to do the shopping. A formal occasion, that was; Anne in tailored suit, pumps and evening make-up, Chris in velvet dress, white tights and Mary-Janes, hair curled and ribboned till she felt gift-wrapped herself. They'd cruise the departments for an hour or so, then stop for lunch among all the other well-dressed women. Anne would pull out a notepad and begin assigning names to the items she coveted.

"Aunt Edna would love that scarf we saw - the dark teal with the paisley border," she'd say, as Chris slurped whipped cream off the top of cocoa too hot to sip. Chris can hear her now and the memory brings forth a small bubble of indigestion, a seismic shudder which begins in her midsection, to rise and lodge in her throat, its acid breath wafting up and out her sinuses as she enters the dining room and is directed by the hostess to the table where her mother sits, in the fluorescent shade of an artificial ficus.

Anne McKloskey has chosen this place carefully - neutral ground, she would call it. After all, no one could possibly object to the restaurant at Donnie's, could they? The perfect place to ask Christina about her plans with that young man Anne saw at the opening a week before. Such a nice face. A nice suit too; well cut. Anne would love to have a name to go with that face and that suit.

"Hello mother," Chris says as she pecks at the powder coating Anne's cheek, careful not to touch the beauty shop curls which hover around her mother's head, her halo of respectability. "Sorry I'm late."

"No, no, dear, you're not late. I was early."

"Oh. Well then, I'll be sorry about something else." Chris

sits, holds out a hand in anticipation of the menu she knows will be pressed into it by an ever-attentive waiter. Donnie's likes to get its diners back out on the floor and spending.

"You're not sorry about a thing my dear," Anne says. "You never have been."

"Yes, it is a beautiful day, I'm so glad you brought it up Mother. I just love coming downtown to talk about the weather. It fills up my day so nicely."

Anne looks at the child she bore so late in life, the one and only fruit of her womb - twenty-one years old now, and quite possibly as unattractive as she can make herself. Face pale as death, port wine lips, eyes made up to suit a raccoon; and what, she wonders, could ever lead a girl to do that to her hair - chop it at random and tease it into a stylist's worst nightmare? For a moment Anne lets her eyes linger over the hit-and-miss bleach job which has left one side of Christina's head a thicket of variegated streaks, while the other retains just enough of her original jet to hint at what could be. She's too thin as well, of course. Dieting again, Anne imagines, or perhaps she has spent all her money on trash and now can't afford food. She certainly isn't spending it on clothes, judging from today's outfit.

"My day is filling up nicely too, dear - Oh, I've got all the time in the world for lunch of course, you come first, but then I'm going to meet with Mr. Green to go over some of your father's letters. He wants to include excerpts from several of them in a biography of Arnold Metzin. Father's correspondence with him is an essential element in explaining their collaborations. Mr. Green says they reveal just how the two minds complemented one another."

Chris makes no effort to conceal her boredom with this topic. She has been hearing about her father's achievements since before she can recall and is no longer the least bit interested in them. The river of life for Chris is visual, composed of color and light, concrete objects and tactile bodies, entwined in physical actions. Music and the lives of musicians are an ethereal tributary down which she does not wish to drift. Had her father been a photographer, a painter or a television repair man she might have retained some interest in him, but as it is, his world of tuxedoed maestros and sequined soloists was enough to drive her to tight-lipped silence at even the voicing of dinnertime grace. That his memory is still being dredged up to cast the rest of the family in its shadow does nothing to make up for the dismal selections on the menu she is perusing.

"There's not a thing worth eating, Mother. Why are we here?"

"I thought it would be nice to have lunch. A chat."

"When you want to have a chat, Mother, it's always for something very specific. Let's just have it out and you can go on over to Mr. Green's office."

Anne studies the menu, though she has been here so many times - and the menu changes so infrequently - that she could probably recite the selections from memory. She is not anxious to order, any more than she is anxious to get to the subject of her interest. Anne would much prefer to sidle gently up to the topic. To draw out the time with her daughter, despite the jabbing sensation which accompanies the girl's every comment. Faced with a full frontal assault however, Anne does what she has always done; she pretends to cave in.

"I was just hoping you'd tell me more about your life. What you're doing."

"My life is fine Mother. What I'm doing is going to classes, developing pieces, exhibiting them."

"And you're happy? You have friends?"

"I'm happy, and yes, I do have friends. Not a boyfriend, if that's what you're really asking."

"Oh yes you do."

Actually, Anne enjoys this part. The parrying. It brings out the youngster in her; being able to surprise her daughter with the secret knowledge she possesses. "I know, Christina. I saw you with that nice boy at the gallery."

Chris is astounded. She hadn't told her mother about the gallery opening the week before; the opening which included her performance piece "Three Lovers." The image in her mind is of herself, on stage, costumed as a ravaged housewife, interacting with her three lovers - television set, vacuum and food processor. She had not anticipated that her mother would see that. "You were there?"

Anne nods, happy with herself and with the surprise she has given. Her happiness lingers as the waiter arrives. A nice enough boy, Anne notices; Pakistani perhaps, with a single lock of hair gracefully bisecting his brow and a polite manner one sees only too rarely anymore. He takes her order of a Cobb salad - without onions - and iced tea - without lemon - then casts an inquiring glance at

Christina, who orders a Pellegrino water and whatever fresh fruit the kitchen can manage, then turns back to her mother before the boy has even left their table.

"You've been following me again."

"Oh no, dear. I simply read the newspapers. And the school newsletters. It's just me you know, wanting to keep up with things."

"That's spying mother. It's...it's...." Chris wants to say crazy, but does not. As much as she resents her mother's prying, she cannot bring herself to cruelty. The woman is just so... Listening with only half an ear, she searches for the correct word. 'Obsessive' seems too harsh, 'sad' not quite explicit enough. 'Desperate,' yes, but there's more. 'Pathetic' seems to suit it best, she concludes, wondering if there is a concept there – a piece entitled Pathetic Mothering, coupling tons of outdated beauty supplies with infant carriers and hi-tech monitoring devices. A good concept maybe, to let settle in the back of her mind. Gestate for a while and pursue next quarter, if it is interesting enough to rise above the flow of daily life and the conversation which seems to be continuing without her.

"...what a mother does Christina. It's what a mother does when she is asked to act as if her daughter who lives just a few short miles away from her does not even exist. Now be a dear and tell me his name."

"Jake."

"He doesn't look like a Jake," Anne muses. "I would have pegged him for a... Joshua. You wouldn't be trying to fool me would you? He looks like a Josh."

"I don't know any Josh. I do know a Jake."

"Christina," Anne wags a finger, "I'm quite certain I overheard him introduced as Josh."

"His name is Jake, Mother. When I sleep with someone I make it a point to find out his name." Chris waits a bit, but Anne ignores the bait. "And he's not a boy. He's twenty-seven and he's one of the founders of an E-bank that's going to go public next year."

"An E-bank. That sounds very impressive. What is it?"

"You don't care what an E-bank is, Mother. If it had any relevance to your life you'd know already. In answer to your *real* question, yes, Jake and I are serious. He's seriously considering marrying me and I'm seriously not interested. He's a great big hunk and balls of fun but he's also more than a little bit obsessive." Chris is distracted for a moment by the confluence this represents with the characteristics of her mother upon which she has so recently been musing. Why does she seem to be attracted to people who share this trait, she wonders, even as she continues on. "He's obsessive about his work and he's obsessive about making tons of money before he's thirty and I think he's getting obsessive about me. He asked me to move in with him and I said no and now he's leaving messages for me every hour."

"Oh dear. Perhaps you've confused the boy. Were you very clear in what you said?" Anne smiles up as the waiter delivers their beverages, making an elaborate show of pouring sparkling water from a liter bottle into an ice filled glass, both of which he sets before Chris, who immediately takes the bottle to her lips to sip the remainder of its contents.

"So," Anne asks when they are alone once again. "Are you all right otherwise? How is your apartment?"

"Oh, it's well Mother, just a few sniffles now and then."

"Christina. I am trying to have a conversation, there's no reason to make fun of me."

"Sorry. It's just a reflex to... My apartment is fine – and I really do enjoy having a place of my own. Classes are going well. My project has been accepted by the thesis committee and I've got the piece up at the Waverly that you saw. Lots of nice comments. I've got a wad of good friends from school and, like I said, Jake is fun when he's not trying to acquire the rights to the rest of my life."

Anne and Chris chat on for half an hour, as mother picks at her salad and daughter takes sips her water while consuming less than half the platter of sliced fruit which has resulted from her order. Finally the food is eaten, the check paid, and there remains no obvious excuse for either of them to linger any longer.

"It's always such a joy to see you dear," Anne gushes as they hug. "If there's anything you need, anything I can do for you..."

"That's ok, Mother. I don't need anything. I can take care of myself. Really I can."

"Of course you can, dear. Of course you can."

III

No alarm sounds. Despite the shiver in Elaine's spine, there is no command to stop and be searched, no demand that she explain to anyone why she is walking with naked finger toward the gate, heedless of her name broadcast throughout the entire airport. It is with something very much akin to surprise that Elaine concludes she can indeed do this. The concourse is long, and she walks slowly, granting the idea time to settle, to drape itself across her shoulders. To fit.

Taking her ticket the gate attendant notes the name.

"Mrs. Gimbal. We have a message from Customer Service. They paged you...."

"Oh that," Elaine interrupts, still not trusting herself to listen to what she knows is coming. The words come out sounding harsh; brittle and defensive, and so she pauses, swallowing and shaking her head just the slightest little bit to clear it before continuing. "That's already been taken care of," she says. "It's a very old message."

Walking by, into the boarding tunnel, she barely manages a polite smile.

IV

"I'm here, where are you?"

Kim Tree is talking into a cell phone from a table at The Good Cup, all the while sipping a double-espresso-97% cocoa-mocha frappe and listening to the conversation pulsing around her table of friends.

"No," she continues, "I said I was going to Angela's house and we were going to see if Terry wanted to go out so I said I would call you from wherever we went, but Angela wasn't there so Terry and I went to Fremont and we met Matt and Sonny, but they had Matt's brother's car and they were going to Northgate, so now I'm here with Kristl and Aubrey..." Short pause as she listens in apparent disbelief to the voice on the other end of her call. "Yes, Terry's here. And Mark; that's what I said," she concludes, with a brief roll of eyes around their shallow sockets for the benefit of those at the table.

With her smoothly-ovaled face, burgundy lips perpetually pursed and huge dark eyes, Kim Tree has the look of a streetwise waif. The impression is reinforced by her small stature and violence-prone hair – its original inky blackness bleached, dyed, streaked and chopped, then tousled into studied disarray - not to mention the miscellaneous clash of thrift-store garments she habitually wears. Allied with the self-assurance of one who seems never to have known disappointment and a figure worthy of a young dancer, her face makes Kim the star of nearly any company she keeps. This evening is no different, as her friends crowd in close, delighted by the prospect of meeting the mysterious boyfriend who, Kim says, has been pressing her for commitment.

"Is he coming?" asks Aubrey, a young woman sitting very close on Kim's left, dressed all in black, with black lips, bobbed black hair, and short, chipped, black nails. "Do we get to see him?"

"Shsshh," Kim snaps, clapping the phone to her chest for a moment. "I'm working on it." The instrument comes back to her mouth. "Yes. Right across from the theater. That's it. You too." She makes a kissing noise into the phone before snapping it shut with a look of triumph.

Seven minutes later, the table erupts into embarrassed laughter as a man walks in the door, wearing a business suit, though it is eight o'clock on a Friday. His tie is off, folded and stuffed in a jacket pocket, and the open collar of his shirt reveals a triangle of perfectly hairless skin at the base of a tree-trunk neck. Tall and straight-backed, he stands a head above the crowd. His arms and torso have the slightly inflated look of one who has spent countless hours in the weight room and his blond buzz-cut might read as a signal of conservatism, if it were not set off by a precisely trimmed goatee and the heavy gold ring in one ear. The overall impression is one of trendy success, a man riding the wave of the day. His eyes scan the room briefly, then land on the group, ignoring the men to quickly evaluate all the other women there before settling firmly on Kim.

"Hey Babe," Jake says as he reaches her, stooping down to plant a kiss on the cheek which turns up just enough for him to reach it. "Missed you at the Seashell this afternoon," he chides, pulling a chair from an adjacent table and squeezing it in beside Kim with a hand on her shoulder as, across the table, Mark Peterson holds both hands in front of his face and peers through a rectangle formed out of his fingers, framing the tender scene into the movie he is perpetually composing in his mind.

"We were up in the U. district," Aubrey offers, eagerly taking the blame for Kim's non-appearance. "I had to go to the bank," she says, then stops abruptly. "My bank," she inserts, as if correcting a major faux pas. "I mean... Kim says you...work in a bank. Right?" The girl on her right reaches over to squeeze her forearm and cast a look of sympathy, to which Aubrey responds with a glare, then turns her considerable powers of concentration to the serious business of running a finger round the rim of her coffee cup.

"Not *in* a bank," Jake begins, directing his words with an evangelical eagerness to the top of Aubrey's down-turned head. " 'In' implies that the bank exists physically. Bricks and mortar. We don't need any of that, because an E-bank exists only as a construct. It is what we think it is, where we think it is, when we think it is. You don't work *in* it or *for* it, you *exist* as a part *of* it."

"Jake's a *big* part of the bank," Kim says, imitating his pulsing rhythm and intensity but adding a conspiratorial lift of the eyebrows which brings smiles to the faces of her assembled friends. "One of the founding partners. If it scales up like they're projecting, he's going to be a zillionaire."

"Not if," Jake corrects, deadly serious as Peterson's imaginary camera rolls. "When."

V

"Ladies and Gentlemen," the pilot's voice drones over the audio system, somewhere over northern California. "I've just been informed that, due to severe fog in the Bay area, we will not be able to land immediately at San Francisco Airport. We're going to loop around up here for a while and see if the situation improves. In the meantime, we're encountering some turbulence so, for your own safety, I'm going to turn on the seatbelt sign."

Obediently, Elaine buckles the belt snugly over her traveling dress, a Delft Blue knit, amply cut and devoid of unnecessary decoration. Bought through the mail, from a catalogue filled with photos of gorgeous young travelers in exotic locales and fanciful drawings of garments designed with a level of care usually reserved for military hardware. One of the catalogue's multi-paragraph captions had detailed the dress's virtues at length: 'wrinkle-free and breathable, practical enough for trekking yet dressy enough for a four-star restaurant, with a hidden pocket for valuables.' The perfect garb in which to begin her new life. A life which starts today, if only she can maintain her resolve to overrule the sixty-one years which have come before.

The novel she has brought along is not engaging, and talk of delays, fog and turbulence lead her to seek other distractions. Lifting the emergency instruction card from the seat pocket in front of her, Elaine finds comfort in its plastic-coated durability, reassurance in its weight and stiffness and the precise way its three panels fold out from one another. She has taken it up with honest good intention, to study its diagrams and admonitions, its crimson arrows and cartoonish-figures sliding down balloon-yellow inflatable slides, so that she can be ready to save herself should the need arise...

But the need has already arisen, Elaine reminds herself, and she is - at this very moment - in the process of escaping a wreck.

nocturne

An hour after leaving The Good Cup, Kim and Jake lie on the mattress which fills one corner of her studio, their conversation no longer so casual.

"I don't know," she is saying, her naked back nestled against the arching curve of Jake's depilated chest, abdomen and thighs. "It's just..."

"It's absurd, that's what it is," Jake cuts in, arms tightening in unconscious emphasis of his words. "To have two apartments - when we spend practically all our time together. It's not like you'd be giving anything up, moving out of this dump." He pauses, one arm rising in a sweeping gesture, directing his lover to take a good look at the environment she has constructed.

Illuminated only by the crackling light of three television sets, the studio apartment is certainly not what most people would call homey. A nineteen-inch Magnavox on a tall stand faces into one corner, producing a hot-zone of cyan light that reflects back into the room. A twelve inch Sony on the dresser points up at the ceiling, casting its own rich splotch of magenta, and a tiny five-inch portable with a thumb-wheel tuner turns slowly on a wire in the middle of the room, its cord hard wired in replacement of the landlord's light fixture, its screen mutely displaying the perpetual snowstorm which is the fate of all who cannot find their proper station.

Stacks of magazines and library books cover the floor, but for a few narrow paths connecting doorways and destinations. The walls, doors and even parts of the ceiling are layered with posters, photographs and magazine tear-outs, all crudely pinned in carefully-overlapping mosaic. Clothes tossed in unruly piles cover every horizontal surface and the only visible items of any economic value are a tall stack of interconnected electronic components on a bare metal rack beside the doorway to the tiny kitchenette.

Snuggling against the warmth of Jake's chest Kim hesitates, debating the merits of various responses. They've had this discussion before, more than once, and she is not happy to be having it again. She could respond with anger - allow herself the pleasure of a good argument. On the other hand, the main reason she is not happy to be talking about their future is the degree to which it has intruded upon the athletic present they were enjoying only a few moments ago. A measured response, she concludes, seems to offer the best chance of replacing Jake's agenda with her own.

"Can't we just drop this?" she says sadly, reaching a hand around to rub the hollow just above his protruding hipbone. "I like things the way they are. Why do we have to change anything?"

"Because I love you," Jake answers, his own hand moving along her shoulder, up her neck and into the thicket of her scalp. "Because I want us to be together all the time. That's the logical evolution for our relationship. People start out alone, trying out connections until they find the one that fits. And when they manage to hook up with something that fits both of them - like we did - then they formalize it. By moving in together..." Jake's hand stops for a moment, and Kim supplies the words she knows from experience will come next.

"By getting married?"

"Yeah," Jake admits, somewhat taken aback by the reminder of his own predictability. "It's... what people do."

Kim snorts derisively, turning in his arms so their eyes can meet and her hand can move from hip to chest, fingertip tracing circles of decreasing radius towards one small nipple. "I know people who've been together for years without getting married. I don't see why we should. And even if we did, I still wouldn't give up my place. I need it for my work." The work to which she refers is, of course, her art. The 'new Art', always with a capital 'A.' Performance. Conceptual. Video. Electronic. Anything that doesn't involve canvas or marble; and the less traditional, the better.

"I love you." Jake insists, reaching out to grab Kim's hand and stop its motion, at the same time feeling a leg moving in between his, generating the warmth of friction. "I need you. I think about you all the time and I can't stand it when I'm not with you." Jake feels her movement stop, believes he has made some headway, and presses on. "We could get a bigger place together, set you up a whole studio. I can get great hardware from work, software too." Far from pleasing her, this seems only to increase Kim's resistance, as she worms her way from his embrace to sit against the wall, legs unabashedly spread, one hand draped casually across their intersection, the other resting on raised knee.

"We don't spend every minute together," she points out, fingers playing idly with her own narrow tuft. "I mean, first of all, we can only even see each other when you're not working – or working out - which is like maybe a couple of hours a week. And I spend a lot of time doing other stuff. When you're not around."

"Ok," Jake says, pulling himself into an upright position, a corner of the sheet draped modestly across his lap. One hand on Kim's nearest ankle, his other reaches out to grab her fiddling arm, stopping its motion. "You can still do that. I just want you to be there when *I* am. Not to have to chase around finding you in some weird hidden club or coffee shop."

"I like going to clubs," Kim says, pulling her hand back, and with it Jake's, which she begins to caress with cheek and lips. "Going out with my friends."

"We can go out with <u>my</u> friends. Parties. Trips. Peter is taking a bunch of us all up to Vancouver next weekend, to celebrate the new funding. He's chartering the old Nirvana tour bus and we're all staying in this hotel by the water. It'll be plush. Not hanging out drinking coffee with a bunch of lesbians and goths."

Pulling away sharply, Kim cannot believe her ears "Aubrey is not a goth," she points out. "She's just exploring an alternative to the full-color spectrum. Jeez. It's not a declaration of war, you know – wearing black. It's an artistic choice."

"Kimmie..." Jake reaches toward her but his hand is pushed firmly away.

"Don't call me Kimmie. Don't ever call me Kimmie."

"All right. Kimberley. I want us to be together. All the time." Kim's head cocks to one side, her look an explicit question which even Jake cannot ignore. "Whenever I'm not working, I mean. I need to be with you, it's like something that grows inside me whenever we're apart..."

"Except when you're at work?" Kim asks. She is leaning against the wall now, studying the man before her with the narrowed eye of one trying to see clearly through a thick fog.

"Well..."

"Which is practically all the time?"

"It's hardly all the time."

"Good. Tomorrow's Saturday. What are you doing?"

Jake takes a beat before answering, reluctantly. "Working." Seeing Kim's look of mock pity he attempts to make up for the point scored. "But I'm going in late, ten or so."

Kim throws her head back with a triumphant grin. "All the time."

"It is not all the time."

"You worked the last two weekends, and if you go to

Vancouver, that's work too."

"No it isn't, that's fun."

"It's work to me. Stuck on some moldy old bus with a bunch of arrogant geeks talking about partnerships and alliances and whose server is bigger. It's all your work. Your whole life is your work and it's not mine. I don't want to be a part of E-banking and I don't want to be part of your wardrobe." Kim stops, seeing she is not getting anywhere. She considers for a moment, then smiles. "I just want to do this."

Jake howls as her head disappears beneath the sheet.

An hour later Jake is asleep, droning the long deep breaths of one whose dreams are untroubled by conflict or doubt. Beside him, Kim lies staring at the ceiling, softly aglow in the Sony's light. Waiting. When, finally, the clock on the stove reads eleven she rolls carefully off the mattress and steps naked into the bathroom. Sitting on the toilet lid, she flips open a cell phone and dials a number.

"Yeah," she whispers as soon as the call is answered. "Is it on?"

A brief exchange follows; an address repeated to be sure it is correct and the name of the DJ for this night's after-hours dance party. A promise to be there, and Kim closes up the phone. In two minutes she has donned the clothes stacked earlier in the tub – pristine white Peter Pan-collared blouse, pleated plaid mini-skirt with matching dark green knee socks and a pair of oxblood-patent Mary-Janes - topped her hair with a raspberry colored beret, strung a tasteful gold crucifix around her neck and a Hello-Kitty lunch bag over her shoulder as purse, and is tip-toeing past the sleeping hunk taking up most of her bed. Closing the door behind her without so much as a glance at the room in which she lives, Kim Tree is casually certain she will return after a few hours of dancing and shouted conversations; the adrenalin rush of the exclusive, the illicit, the underground.

first movement

"Locked-in syndrome is a rare neurological disorder characterized by complete paralysis of voluntary muscles in all parts of the body except for those that control eye movement. It may result from traumatic brain injury, diseases... or medication overdose.

Individuals with locked-in syndrome are conscious and can think and reason, but are unable to speak or move... completely mute and paralyzed..."

> Information page of the National Institute of Neurological Disorders and Stroke (NINDS).

1

Nothing.

Not darkness, but the absence of light <u>or</u> dark.

Not quiet, but total lack of either sound or silence.

Not fresh air, not stale, but <u>no</u> air. No atmosphere, no breathing - and yet, no sense of suffocation.

Not stillness, or weightlessness or any 'ness', but a total elimination of touch, mass, up or down, movement or rest; no sense of anything at all.

I feel...

Nothing.

Dr. David Resor believes in miracles.

He witnessed one only this morning, as he sat trapped in traffic, slug-sliming its way across Lake Washington on the floating bridge. Michael Rabin, dead these thirty years, was playing his violin. From a long ago recording session, via a vinyl pressing plant, through a broadcast studio 3000 miles away and satellites above the stratosphere, the sound came to David in the electronically controlled micro-climate of his car, its dual rows of silicone-rubber weather-stripping effectively sealing out the rain and fumes and noise which surround it. Bright and fresh as the day it was played, the music of Paganini, absent far longer than Rabin, filled David's ears, spilling out in crystal clear full-spectrum sound from a dozen speakers hidden in the leathered interior. Two great artists who never met, collaborating to entertain a man on his way to work.

Not many decades ago, David remembers thinking as he sat in that traffic, such music in such a place would have been viewed as an impossible dream. A miracle. Today, it was entirely unremarkable, even commonplace. That's the way it is with miracles, David has come to believe; on any given day our understanding of the physical world says a certain event is not possible - we imagine it anyway, and say it would be 'a miracle.' And if one day we learn enough to make it happen, is it still a miracle? Not at all. The flood of experience simply absorbs it, washing over the event until it is taken for granted and we move on, imagining other, even more fantastic, challenges. The miracles of today, the everyday events of tomorrow.

The Applied Dialysis Laboratory is where Resor has come to seek his own miracle. A suite of rooms on Level Seven of Building 6 of Hilltop Medical Center, every inch of its four hundred and seventy square feet tightly packed with equipment, files and stacks of correspondence. He stands now in the middle of the largest room, staring at an object labeled 'Vessel # 2.' A tall steel cylinder, the vessel's top is sealed with a Plexiglas dome, clamped hermetically shut. Its base disappears into a painted metal box, or more technically, the Environment Stabilization Pedestal. Bundles of wires and plastic tubes snake from the vessel to one of the lab's specially modified artificial heart machines, to its trio of dialysis units and to the BEMS - the Biochemical Environment Maintenance System which is at the heart of Resor's research.

Through the dome a murky solution is visible; specs of proto-organic matter drift slowly, suspended in fluid tinted with the slightest touch of amber. At its center sits the subject of the current BEMS test, a lumpy pinkish-gray mass, festooned with wires and tubes, suspended in a fibrous cradle, motionless and inert. On the surface of the plastic, fragmented by the brighter reflections of the lights and monitors of his lab, Resor is confronted by his own haggard face - left eye focused straight ahead, right eye skewed as always in its own useless direction - surmounted by an unruly shag of dark, curly hair. The convex curvature of the dome doesn't just reflect the image though, but distorts it as well, rendering room, researcher and subject intertwined and collaged as if all one, in a world where the rules of proportion, distinction and identity have been thrown out the window.

Throwing out the rules is what this project is all about, as David has explained many times before, to many audiences. The rule that only the body can sustain the brain. That only 'Mother Nature' can manage the complex environmental controls which allow that critical organ to survive. "Too many times," Resor reminds the listeners to his prepared text, "the body fails in its responsibility to the brain. A blow to the head, a laceration of the jugular, a failure of the liver or kidneys, and the body's central processor is let down: its blood flow interrupted, its temperature allowed to swing wildly, its chemical balance disturbed beyond survivable limits. In the time it takes to correct that external damage, the brain, the seat of individual consciousness, is lost. What a waste," Resor has said, with all the sadness he can project. "What a terrible waste. That the critical component of a precious human life should be lost due to the temporary dysfunction of some far less crucial peripheral component."

With the new equipment on which he is currently working, David believes he has developed the ability to avoid some of that waste. His goal has been to artificially maintain the conditions necessary for the survival of the brain until such time as the body can be repaired and once again able to host its captain. Unlike others, who may have focused on replicating the function of one supporting system or another - the now-common devices to imitate the respiratory and circulatory function, or the kidneys' filtering action -

his strategy has been to identify all the factors necessary for the brain's survival and to connect them directly to it, first in this isolated vessel, but eventually within the cranium itself. If successful, he believes it will be possible to sustain the brain – unharmed - for as long as it takes to regenerate, regenerate or replace whatever bodily systems may have failed, and thus to restore full functioning to individuals who would otherwise have perished.

That is the medical miracle toward which he has worked for over two decades, and with a few more years of testing and approval he would have been ready to demonstrate its worth. On this morning though, despite having overcome every technical challenge, Resor is near despair. His project - and his very career - are in jeopardy, and today may be the day of judgment. Medical Holdings LLC, a health-care management company which has been growing faster than Ebola virus in a petri dish, appears ready to infect Hilltop Medical Center. If that happens, Resor is convinced it will mean the end of funding for his work. 'No immediate therapeutic applications,' he can almost hear some MH accountant saying, with a dismissive wave of his hand. 'Out of step with the current political mood as well,' he imagines his new Armani-clad masters pointing out; incompatible with the much-heralded return of 'traditional values' reflected in the growing prominence of religiously-defined political figures. The same climate which has respected academics unabashedly citing the 'Sanctity of Life' as justification for supporting or rejecting ethical positions on everything from reproductive enhancements to the types of care allowed for the terminally ill.

Resor has heard all the criticisms of his own work before, all the questions about whether it is proper to interfere so drastically with the workings of nature. Has answered them too. First to his thesis advisors at Charleston University School of Medicine, where his project began, then to the boards of four different hospitals where it was briefly housed before finding a more stable home at Hilltop. For seven years now, he has answered them to the satisfaction of the current Hilltop management and the baker's dozen of foundations and agencies from which he's cobbled together a marginally-workable funding plan. With each year though, with each election victory and each legislative roll-back, the project has become more tenuous. Without Hilltop to house it, under the current climate, the BEMS project would be impossible to pursue. And if Medical Holdings gobbles up Hilltop there is no way they are going to allow him to continue. It's not their style.

25

Staring into the vessel, imagining the conversation he will have when some sad-faced and pre-occupied MH executive calls him in for a first meeting, David Resor is thinking as hard as he ever has about the thin line between the possible and the impossible. It would take a miracle now, he is thinking, for his project ever to reach its goal.

Nothing.

I come not from sleep, but from something deeper and more secretive. An absence so profound it swallows me up and hides me from myself. I find myself here and wonder what 'here' this is; what time, what self. Whether this is life, or death, or something else completely. And the answer I come up with is...

Nothing.

The day after her lunch with Christina, Anne McKloskey wakes to a feeling that something is terribly wrong. She has had this feeling before, but not for a long time. Not since the day her husband's performance tour ended on a vine-tangled hillside in the Philippines, in a sudden compression of lightweight alloys followed by an even more abrupt expansion of petrochemically-based combustion gases. Finding herself a widow and a single mother had been the greatest shock imaginable, and she had not done especially well with it.

Oh, she coped admirably with the predictable events one had to live through - the phone calls from sympathetic friends and vulturous press, the documents which needed to be to signed in order to have his remains brought home. The beautiful, musical, memorial service at the cathedral on Capitol Hill, the concert that same evening in his honor. All of those she had handled with the aplomb of a woman used to the public eye.

It was after that, after all the attention had begun to fade, that Ann found herself adrift. Sean and his career had been the roadmap of her adult life. From the day they met - guided together by a friend who thought them 'made for each other'- she had lived by his schedule and his rules. Concerts here, a fellowship there, whom to have dinner with and how to raise their daughter; Sean had known exactly how to do everything. Without him, Anne found life's directives few, far between, and rarely satisfactory.

Their friends certainly tried, inviting the widow to dinners and luncheons, even to speak on her husband's behalf several times. That had felt so odd, to be up on some dais telling the world what she thought Sean would have said had he not been torn from them so unfairly. After the third one of those she had said 'no more' and begun instead to retreat into the safety of her home and child.

Sixteen at the time of Sean's death, Christina had never been an easy child. Perhaps because her father was so rarely present when she was small, she had never really accepted him as an authority in their home. Sean, for his part, treated his daughter much as he would a disappointing third-chair violin; with barely concealed contempt for her inability to perform at concert pitch. Their arguments were of mythic proportion; voices raised to the rooftops, toys and housewares thrown, hands raised for blows held back only at the cost of trembling will.

With her husband's departure, Anne briefly imagined she

would have more time than ever with her daughter. Time which she hoped would allow them to grow closer, to share their loss and bond more deeply, but instead, Christina acted as if his absence were a license to ignore everything he had stood for. Within a week she quit her piano instruction altogether. Slid the sheaf of music into a bookshelf between the world atlas and a volume of Beatrix Potter, never to be looked at again. If that had been the sum of it Anne might have been better able to cope, but her beloved daughter had more in store. Within a few months she had virtually ceased to relate to her mother, coming home as late as possible only to sleep and change clothes before disappearing again the next morning. Attempts to communicate grew more and more futile, as Christina accused her mother of interfering with her life, of alienating her friends and 'messing up every good thing' she ever tried to do.

When Chris moved out of the house, barely a month after graduating high school, taking a single suitcase with her, Anne experienced a surprising duality of emotions. The pain of seeing her daughter depart was paired with an almost overwhelming relief that the house was now her own, quiet and orderly, just as it had been years before, when it was only she and Sean living there. As Christina was establishing her independence - first taking a job as a waitress, then later getting admitted to the U W visual arts program - Anne was carefully rearranging her surroundings into a perfect re-creation of twenty years before. Recent pictures were replaced with faded images of the early years; fondly remembered pieces of furniture brought out from hidden corners of back rooms to retake their original places of prominence. Even books were appointed their shelves in honor of how long ago they had been acquired and read.

And – this was the most surprising part of it! - Anne still had Christina; could still visit her almost any time she liked. Once she found out where her daughter was living, it was easy enough to stop by in the morning and catch a glimpse of her moving past the window or climbing into her car. Such a blessing that there was a bus stop so near the apartment, with a convenient bench on which to sit and stare at the building; Anne had spent many hours there, an unrecognizable consignment-store coat wrapped tightly around her, scarf over her hair, watching that third-floor window, and the entry door below it. Later, when she discovered by riffling through the papers in Christina's car which classes she was enrolled in, Anne found it increasingly easy to keep in touch. Sometimes it was a matter of stopping by a campus classroom to glance in the door and see her daughter attentively taking notes. Other times it meant pausing outside a studio to watch her hard at work on some baffling assemblage of junk materials. With all those times and all those places, it was easy enough to remain involved in her life without the pain of confrontation.

So then. When Anne awakes shortly before seven one morning to the feeling that something has once again gone wrong with the watch-spring of life, she pays serious attention to the feeling. Dressing warmly against the early morning damp, she does not pause for a cup of tea, but climbs right in the car and drives to Ballard. Passing the three-story wood frame apartment building she is not deceived by the light burning in the bathroom window. Christina often leaves that light on at night; Anne has seen it many times when she has driven by, silently imagining her daughter asleep. Several times she has watched Chris arrive home and climb out of the little Civic hatchback, its red paint overlaid with a spider-web of blue-gray and daffodil-bright drip-trails - 'personalized' by the budding artist within a week after it came off the used-car lot. At least that paint job meant there was never any question whether it was the right car. In a University lot or parked on a First Hill street outside a loud party, Anne could drive by and recognize it instantly.

Ten past eight now, and Anne is driving the familiar street. Light on, the windows seem normal, but there is no red car. She drives around the block - perhaps Chris had trouble finding a space. Every street for several blocks around is traversed and checked, but no red Civic, and the fear is growing in Anne. Certainly she could just be spending the night; there had been that silly remark at lunch; 'when I'm sleeping with a man,' she had said, although Anne discounted that right off, as something said more for its dramatic impact on her mother than as any true indication of how often she did such a thing, and besides, Anne considers herself a woman of the times; she does not expect a twenty-one year old girl to remain celibate forever, especially not one as potentially-attractive as her own daughter.

Fortunately, Anne is rarely at a loss for information. Just now, for example, she has a name, the one she wheedled out of her daughter at lunch, one Jake Brindle, E-banker. And she has an address, the product of a search by Henry Green's secretary, while Anne and Mr. Green were reviewing the letters that afternoon. A West Seattle address, and a phone number. She will drive on over there and check the parking lot for automotive art. If it's not there, she will call this Jake, wake him up if need be, and see if he knows where her baby is.

As Anne is driving up the entrance ramp to Highway 99, the sun is making itself known, resolving out of the morning fog just lifting off Lake Union, and the mountain - Rainier - is visible in the glowing distance. Crossing the high Aurora Bridge, Anne feels she is on top of the world, her mind coiling tightly around an unshakeable conviction that her daughter will be all right.

5

Nothing.

A nothing so vast it takes the place of senses, so omnipresent it overpowers every thought. It has no form or features, and yet is solid as granite; impenetrable and unresponsive. So ubiquitous it could almost be missed, like atmosphere, like space itself, if only there were something more comprehensible to occupy one's attention. In the absence of which, it is The Nothing that I perceive. Absolute and pervasive, a nonentity so compelling I cannot possibly ignore it, and yet...

I surprise myself. Faced with this Nothing I should be impatient. Frustrated. I am not a person who deals well with being thwarted. I know this - remember this? - about myself, and I know that I am not the same now. There is a certain peace in total powerlessness.

'Nothing' has changed me.

"Dr. Resor," Katsas Disigurian calls breathily as he catches a glimpse of his mentor's back turning a corner of the seventh-floor corridor. As an intern on rotating assignment, Katsas has come to accept the floor as his entire world, for twelve to sixteen hours a day, six days a week minimum, and he knows every cramped turn of its passages. Besides being home to the ADU – as staff refers to Resor's Applied Dialysis Unit - 'Seven' also houses suites dedicated to Neurology and Hematology, disciplines with which Resor regularly consults. It is here that Katsas has found him, checking in with colleagues regarding several ongoing tests of equipment configurations.

"Mr. Kats," the doctor says, stepping back to wait for him. Less greeting than statement of fact, the pronunciation of the intern's nickname effectively communicates that the doctor's real attention is elsewhere. A moment later though, his mental jotting completed, Resor's brain registers Disigurian's attitude, reminds itself of the degree to which this intern has come to see him as mentor, and recalls the perpetual source of amusement which he himself has found the young man to be. "What mischief are you up to this morning?"

"I was just up at Admin."

Kats has caught up to Resor now and the two face one another in rough symmetry, each holding a clipboard in one hand, their other fists rammed into the pockets of their lab coats. The symmetry can never be complete however, if for no other reason than the disparity in their forms. Resor's face and body have a lean and drained look, his peaked brow furrowed from a history of deep thought. Katsas is shorter, wider, more sedentary it would seem, and bears the unmistakable stamp of innocence on his face. A face that tells the world its owner believes what he hears, marvels at what he sees, and has not yet begun to realize the extent to which the world will take advantage of those qualities. "Dr. Sugarmann called me in to discuss my residency options. I couldn't see her though, and I thought I should let you know."

"You thought you should let me know that you couldn't see Dr. Sugarmann?" Resor asks with mock concern as he steps back to allow a knot of people to pass, then sets off in their wake. "How kind of you."

"No," Katsas interjects, flustered. He is walking too now, keeping awkward company as Resor accelerates down the hallway, gracefully sweeping past parked gurneys, sidestepping circulating nurses. "I mean yes. I mean, I thought I should let you know, Dr., that Dr. Sugarmann and Dr. Bagley and all the rest of the big kahunas are in a special meeting. In the Board Room. With the board."

"And what, pray tell, is this meeting about Mr. Kats? The end of the world as we know it?"

"No. They're meeting with the people from Medical Holdings."

"Ah." Dr. Resor stops, taps his clipboard lightly on his assistant's head. "You see, I was correct after all. Thank you Mr. Kats, for your kind update. I shall prepare myself for departure. And you, I suggest, shall repair yourself to some far dim corner of this vale of tears we call workplace and home, and betake the opportunity to ally with another mentor. One whose professional prospects are measured in years rather than hours." Katsas' eyes are wide with disbelief, his interest in Resor's work having come, over time, to be exceeded only by his delight in the man's gentle urgency and teasing manner, a delight of which the doctor is well aware and not intolerant. "Anh, anh, anh," Resor chastises him. "No protests. Unlike me, *you* have a future to consider."

In the next instant, his mentor is gone, ducking into another suite of offices to leave Katsas alone in the corridor with his disappointment, which in no way even begins to approach Resor's.

I can remember though.

As The Nothing becomes more familiar, I remember the familiar more. I remember once, as a child, riding with my family to the top of a mountain. We parked at the end of the road and I raced to get out and dash up the slope to the penultimate peak before anyone else. There, beyond the rustle of tree or shrub, far from the omnipresent murmur of traffic or birdsong or babbling humans, I found a kind of quiet I'd never before experienced. No humming appliances resonating up from the basement, no gurgling pipes draining down from upstairs, no creaking building expanding or contracting around me as it perpetually warmed or cooled. In that quiet I heard my own breathing like a locomotive's roar, perceived the blood coursing past my ears like the current of a river within me.

But now?
Nothing.

A young woman sidles along the cafeteria line, tray scraping dryly on stainless steel rails. Without deliberation she gathers a green salad, an apple, a Styrofoam cup of hot water, a bag of Bengal Spice herbal tea and two small wedges of lemon. Showing her ID - Mary Antonias, Second Year Resident, Pediatric Care Unit, Staff number 043-773-2501 - to the checker, she turns to scan the tables arrayed six deep and twenty across in the low-ceilinged cavern buried beneath Hilltop's west tower. Staffers in scrubs and whites, non-medical employees in their work clothes, families of patients, and visitors in every possible variation of street attire – two-hundred faces or more she searches, in hopes of finding a sign of welcome.

Catching a glimpse of familiar yellow hair in a far corner, Mary's face relaxes a bit from the concentrated scowl into which it has cured over the previous fourteen on-duty hours. Making her way over, she navigates between the close-set diners, lifting her tray high and murmuring apologies when her hip or the hem of her lab coat brushes a stranger's shoulder. At her approach, Judith Baxter looks up and Mary sees a tight smile creep across her face.

"Hey Mare," Judith says, drawing the words out into something approaching a question, "How's it going? You know Marty Singer?"

Casting her own best smile toward a young man seated on Judith's far side, hidden until now from her view, Mary stands holding her tray before her.

"No, I don't," she says, and in the time it takes to say those words she experiences the familiar sensation of his eyes barely glancing over her face, her tray, her body, her clothes, before moving immediately back to Judith, where a flicker of recognition passes between the two. "Pleased to meet you," she adds anyway.

"Me too," Marty Singer responds without conviction, lapsing immediately into silence, his eyes moving distractedly about the room.

"Sit down," Judith offers, making a halfhearted motion as if to suggest she could, just possibly, remove the stack of files from the chair beside her, but Mary has already heard and seen enough to know this is not where she wants to eat her lunch. Making apologies, she wishes the young couple well and moves off to an empty table beside the busser's station. Careful to choose a seat facing away from Judith and Marty, still she is conscious all through her lunch of their presence; the private jokes and sheltered intimacy of their conversation together, the smiles and laughter she can feel passing between them. Never one to enjoy eating, today Mary finds even less pleasure than usual in that necessary act.

For all I know, I could be dead.

For some time I have told myself, and anyone who would listen, how well prepared I was for death. No fear, no regrets, no cowardly denial. Boldly acknowledging the inevitable, I have sincerely believed I would rise to the occasion with grace and objectivity. Perhaps this is my reward, this Nothing in which I now find myself - and yes, 'find myself' seems the proper way to phrase the thing.

For it is - after all and in this moment - the <u>knowledge</u> of <u>absence</u> which demonstrates my continued <u>presence</u>. If I am aware of things which are not here, then 'I' must still exist. I cannot locate my hands, my eyes, any part of my body, but still the idea of <u>me</u> persists.

Conclusion? Somehow, somewhere - some way - I am alive.

"It all seems positive at this point. Cops found a kids' lunchbox after they got the place cleared out and the lights on. Purse stuff inside it – phone, makeup, cash; couple of cards. And a driver's license, and the picture is definitely her, so our Jane Doe is now a Kim Tree - and it's got a donor endorsement, so bingo. That's all we know about her for now, but it should be enough if push comes to shove. Call me if anything changes." Jessica Bagley sets the phone back in its cradle, only to hear a voice from its speaker.

"Doug Taylor to see you boss," says Bagley's secretary.

"By all means," Jessica responds, leaning back and raising her eyes to witness the arrival of Hilltop's Head of Administration.

"Aren't you supposed to be chasing down some relative or something?" she challenges, before the visitor has even crossed the threshold.

"Oh, that may take care of itself." Taylor pulls a newspaper from under his arm and places it on the desk, folded back to reveal one half of page ten. "The press knows less than we do, but someone got hold of a cell-phone photo from someone at the club where she passed out," he says, then begins to read, quite fluently, though from his perspective the page is upside down.

"An unidentified young woman, approximately twenty years of age, remains in critical condition at Hilltop Medical Center following her collapse early this morning at an un-permitted pop-up club housed in a vacant warehouse in Renton. Reports indicate that the woman had been partying for several hours when she complained of a headache and went to a lounge area to rest. Some time later a passer-by found her unconscious and paramedics were called. The victim was taken by ambulance to Hilltop where she is reported to be in Critical Condition. Toxicology tests are pending to determine whether illicit drugs played a role in the girl's collapse."

Beneath that brief text reposes a grainy and somewhat fish-eyed photo of what appears to be a schoolgirl with streaky, spiked, hair. Amidst a jumble of blurred faces and heads, her untroubled eyes are open wide, seeming to stare up from the page in wonderment at Bagley and Taylor.

"Well," says the executive. "Looks like we have the entire readership of the P.I. investigating for us now. Shouldn't be long before we know whatever there is to know."

I am awake, in the darkness of The Nothing. A darkness deeper than the blackest night; than a basement with no windows and no lights on at midnight of the darkest starless moonless night of the year.

I used to sleep sometimes in the basement, when guests took over my room, but here there is no sound of distant celebration going on without me - no recent recollection of cheerful arrivals or the dinner table piled high with pot roast and dumplings on platters, gravy boat and pickle dishes and glasses sparkling with the chandelier's starry pinpricks of light - and yet the idea of some connection to those distant celebrations brings with it a warmth, a contentment.

There was a time when being helpless was the only reality. When the world could be trusted to care for one's needs, gently and predictably. Perhaps the reason I am so comfortable in this Nothing is that it provides a return to that blissful state, that time before time, before questions, cares and responsibilities.

Before everything that came
before I came
to be
here.

"Clinical," Elaine remembers saying after Rodney's speech about how little time he had left, her neck stretched and head thrown back to focus on his face, which hovered a good foot above hers as he held her at arm's length. "Meredith Phillips always told me she found you 'so clinical,' but I didn't know what she meant back then. It took me a few years I guess, to understand what Meredith knew in a minute. Did you ever really love me?"

"Of course I did. I do."

"No, you don't. If you did you'd see it differently, but you've never really let me in, Rodney. Never let your guard down enough for me to understand what it is that's driving you. All these years, and the longer we're together, the less I feel I know you."

"Say what you like, Elaine. I know who I am, and I'm not interested in changing. I don't have the luxury. It's what a man does with his life that matters, and I'm going to do as much good as I can in the time I have left. We had wonderful years together. I love you and I treasure those years, but I am not going to spend my last days on this earth worshiping them."

Elaine had watched his back striding down the hall then, straight and tall despite the pain and fatigue he claimed to suffer - and took a mind-boggling assortment of pills to combat. He would take a cab to the hospital; spend the day in surgery, consultation, whatever else he did when he was not remodeling hearts, and she would pack. Take her own cab to the airport. Turn in his ticket for an upgrade, perhaps.

Now, sitting buckled in her seat, she is glad for that upgrade, as the pilot announces that San Francisco is still closed and they have been re-routed to LAX, meaning she will miss her connection to Honolulu and beyond. With any luck, those extra inches between her and her neighbor will prevent him sensing the despair climbing up into her throat, the flush of heat across her face as she feels her independence in danger of defeat almost before it has begun, and wonders if, perhaps, that must be taken as confirmation that she is in the wrong.

I am standing in a line, singing. Suffused with comfort; the warm presumption that everything is as it should be. I hear the voices around me, rising parallel and true, like blades of grass laid back by the wind, like lustrous hair brushed smooth and straight, every strand in place beside every other one. Sound swells out of me and into me and fills the space around me and I am the sound, I am the space, the choir and the music. Joyous, fulfilled.

I wake into The Nothing, aware that I have just a moment before inhabited that perfect belonging. Aware as well that it has been a very, very, long time, in what came before, since I felt that peace. The Nothing has brought me back to a place and a time and a feeling I had long ago lost, and that, perhaps, is something.

Jake Brindle is staring. Through the glass of the fifth floor ICU he is staring at a face he knows as well as any in the world. Knows and loves, he is telling himself, with a love that consumes him and activates his fighting instincts.

Beside him stands Aubrey Maturin, Kim's best friend. It was she who saw the photo of an unidentified overdose victim in the newspaper, immediately tracking-down Kim's semi-demi-fiancé at his gym and telling him the terrible news that Kim had experienced some kind of seizure at the club, been taken by ambulance to this place, and ended up on life support. Aubrey's face is even more pale than usual, her eyes puffy from crying. Jake's face, by contrast, bears an expression not of sorrow but of anger.

The third person at the observation window is Bob Baker, the administrator to whom it has fallen to come up to ICU and deal with these two. The nurse on duty had called down for help after they insisted on being allowed to visit the former Jane Doe in bed number 5.

"So as far as you know," Baker is asking, because he wants to have it as clear as possible. "She has no living relatives?"

"No." It is Aubrey who replies, being as she seems to be the greatest available authority on Kim Tree's personal history. "I guess she might have...oh, like, a cousin or an aunt or something, but if she does, she never mentioned it. Her father died three years ago, just before we started school at the U. He was a steelworker in Pennsylvania, some little town near Pittsburgh. Killed in a mill accident. Her mother had died a few years before that, in a car-jacking. It was real tragic. Kim never got over it, and she didn't like to talk about it. She was really proud of how she was on her own." Here Aubrey's voice cracks slightly. "That was how she liked to be."

"And you, Mr. Brindle, did she ever talk to you about her family, any living relatives."

"We're her family. Aubrey and me. And her other friends."

"I understand," Baker says gently. "I understand, and we appreciate your concern. That is why I'm hoping you will understand and cooperate in her best interest. Miss Tree has suffered severe internal trauma, with high-degree cerebral impairment. The procedures she has undergone were not without risk, and the expected degree of improvement is not very great, but we've done the very best we could."

"Then why won't you tell us what you've done to her," Jake accuses. "What don't you want us to know?"

"We can't disclose details of a patient's treatment, except to family..."

"I'm her fiancée," Jake insists. "That's family as far as I'm concerned."

Baker inhales deeply, lets the air out in a puff as his head settles into his shoulders and his hands work at one another where they hang clasped in front of him. The discussion has been going on for nearly twenty-five minutes now, and still they will not see what is right before them. Their friend could get better, they say; they want to meet the doctors who have been treating her, call in specialists, get second opinions, more favorable opinions. All of which simply avoids the inevitable truth, that their friend is already gone. The machines are keeping her blood flowing and her lungs filled with air, but she is no longer alive in any meaningful sense.

"I'm very sorry for your loss," Baker begins. "But you are not entitled to any personal information, or to make these decisions for Miss Tree. In the absence of next of kin, we've had to make our best judgment as to the course of treatment and act in her interests."

As The Nothing becomes familiar, I have begun to formulate some conclusions, to believe I know things about it. One thing I now know about it is that in this place there is no pain. There is the recollection of pain, the thought that there might be pain, even the conviction that there should *be pain, but these are only shadows; the footprints of clouds which wash over and then pass, leaving in their place a gentle, painless, confusion.*

"Doug Taylor to see you again, Boss."

"By all means," Jessica Bagley responds, without even looking up from a stack of printouts detailing the financial health of Hilltop Medical Center.

Coming through the door, Taylor is mindful of his boss's state on this critical day. "Anything good in those?" He asks innocuously.

"Some good, some bad. What brings you back up here?"

"More information on the girl. A couple of her friends saw the photo in the paper and came in. They confirm no relations, no next-of-kin. SPD have been working with the folks at the U.; they think she might be a runaway from a few years ago." He places a thin file on Bagley's desk, open to an interior page. It contains a Seattle Police Department run-down on Miss Kim Tree. "Registration application said she was from Pittsburgh, parents deceased, no relatives. Same story her friends gave Baker."

"That's good. No relatives to be upset."

"Read on. None of the info she gave checks out - no record of a Kim Tree in the town where she says she grew up, and when she registered at the U.W., she submitted a transcript from Randall Cross Academy."

"Never heard of it," Jessica says, the words short and sharp, a directive to Taylor to get to the point.

"You wouldn't have, unless you've got a rich aunt somewhere," he jokes, oblivious to Bagley's growing impatience.

"Okay Doug. Where's this going?"

"Randall Cross is a top quality private school. Very expensive. Maybe a Pittsburgh runaway would choose to forge a transcript from there. But our girl didn't live like someone working her way through college either. There," he points to the file, "third paragraph from the bottom. She's got a part time job at an art gallery, takes classes, pays her own tuition - in-state, but still - plus materials fees, books. And an apartment all her own; small, but her own place, no roommates. Drives a Honda that the dealer's records show was paid for with a bank check not a loan, and SPD says when they followed up with the bank they find out she's got nearly seven-thousand dollars in the account."

"Pretty good for a twenty-one year old. So what do you think? She was a drug dealer or something?"

"Don't know. All I can really say is that our girl is likely to be a more interesting person than we thought. "

    "Well, I suppose that's MH's problem now, isn't it?"

Canceled.

Not just delayed, as Elaine had first read from the departures monitor, but canceled. The customer service representative is gentle in her explanation, but absolute. Due to an unseasonable tropical storm, the red-eye flight to Honolulu on which Elaine had gotten herself re-booked as soon as she touched down has now been canceled and there will be no other flights for at least sixteen hours that will take her any closer to the Marquesas. After an entire day of traveling with her doubts; after circling eternally over San Francisco and being rerouted to LAX, after half the night spent trying to divert her thoughts with an overrated best-seller, she is marooned; trapped in the endless concourses of an airport so devoid of anything remotely attractive or interesting, it might as well be a desert isle itself, albeit without the saving amenity of a waterfront. There are not a lot of choices, Elaine thinks as the representative speaks. She could make herself at home in the terminal, stretching out on a bench somewhere the way the college students do, or she could take a shuttle to one of the nearby hotels and lock herself in a rented box, but in either case she suspects her nervous state will not allow for sleep. On another hand, there are not many hours left until daylight; when it comes she could try to catch whatever sights LA has to offer, but it seems unlikely that racing around on a frantic-tourist scavenger hunt while a cab's meter ticks off landmarks would bring her any closer to the kind of solace she needs; and had counted on this journey to provide. Stepping away from the counter, its velvet-roped corrals nearly empty at this hour, Elaine feels herself adrift and on the verge of tears with the accumulated disappointments of her day and her life.

"Nothing is ever for sure when you're traveling, is it?" suggests a voice beside her. Elaine turns to find a woman, somewhere beyond her own age. Like her, the woman holds an envelope of tickets and baggage stubs in one hand. Very much unlike Elaine though, around her other wrist are draped several multi-colored scarves and over her shoulder, the strings of a loosely-woven drawstring bag serving in lieu of a purse. Exotic, deeply textured, the bag is clearly handcrafted; 'Bohemian,' is how Rod would have described it, with his forehead all wrinkled up in scorn.

"Oh," Elaine says, wondering just how much of her

consternation she has allowed to show, that a stranger should remark upon it. "Yes. That is... No, it isn't. I suppose."

"Your flight was canceled too," says the other, and the words are not a question, but a statement, delivered with such matter-of-fact acceptance that immediately Elaine feels a measure of her anxiety melt away. Looking more carefully at the stranger, she realizes that she had been mistaken; this woman is definitely her senior. It was the clothes that fooled. The crinkled broomstick skirt - tropical blossoms on an orange background - is ankle length and full. The billowing peasant blouse in matching orange silk is complemented by a paisley-print kerchief knotted loosely around her neck, and another tied around her head so only a few wisps of white hair show at forehead and ears, plus dangling silver earrings and seven or eight silver, brass and gold bangles looped upon each wrist. All in all, an outfit Elaine might have expected on one of those college girls sleeping on the benches, not on a woman in her seventies. Curiosity makes her look closer still as the two step side-by-side away from the counter, and in the woman's face Elaine sees something else. Through the amber glow and spider's-web wrinkles that speak of sun and wind lurks a sort of glimmer - a certain brightness which radiates especially from eyes the deepest green she's ever seen, peering out of deep and shadowed sockets. This, Elaine understands - though she is too harried at the moment to frame the understanding into thought - is a face accustomed to wonder.

"These things don't happen without a reason," the woman says, before Elaine has even had a chance to affirm that, yes, indeed, her flight has been canceled. "Our job is to discover that reason."

"Well," Elaine says, fumbling with her purse, which seems unwilling to accept her ticket envelope. It is difficult to carry on a conversation under the circumstances, she finds, the struggle with her purse seeming only to increase the weight of the bag on the opposite shoulder, which in turn brings up the subject of her other luggage, sitting somewhere, unclaimed and vulnerable, and then there is the hotel room, thousands of miles away, for which she has already paid, and her time in the islands, limited as it was and now evaporating steadily while she stands trapped in this awful concourse with its echoing trickle of stern-faced strangers, shuffling toward their own middle-of-the-night destinations, and then, there is Rodney...and still her purse will not cooperate, the envelope catching no matter which way she tries to insert it so that Elaine finds her hands beginning to tremble, her face to flush with an unfamiliar heat.

"I'm sorry..." she says, feeling obliged to hold up her end of a conversation yet unable to do so in a coherent manner; her words barely a murmur, the exertion of sending them out draining her of what little energy and optimism remain. Confused, exhausted, embarrassed, her eyes swing wide, searching for a way out of the moment until, remembering her manners, she turns to face the stranger and finds her looking back, eyes narrowed, but warm, and glowing with reassurance.

"You look as if you could use a cup of tea," the woman says, placing a hand gently on Elaine's elbow and starting her off across the concourse which has become, at just that moment, conveniently free of oncoming traffic. "And so could I."

18

I am wandering through canyons of color and light, their walls laid up in courses of brightly labeled boxes and cans and jars and bags. I hear the sound of leather soles slapping, see my feet moving across slick linoleum streaked with black shoe marks. From my viewpoint, close to the floor, I am privy to dust gathered in the recesses beneath shelf edges, cigarette butts crushed and swept aside, crumbled candy wrappers carelessly discarded. Ahead of me, a brighter light beckons and I teeter toward it. Coming to the end of the canyon, I am confronted with a glossy white wall, taller than my head, topped with gleaming metal, its grooved edge damp with dew. Lush green foliage hangs down from above, the leaves punctuated here with clusters of red radishes, there with orange carrots, purple and white beets. The radiant yellow of summer squashes calls to my eyes and fingers. Just as I answer the call, raising a hand to touch this vision of abundance, there is a sputtering squirting sound and a fine mist billows out from somewhere above. As it reaches me the mist is cold - no, frigid. Wet and frightening. My chest rises, sucking in a gutful of air, winding up to deliver a wail of terror and then, just as the fear engulfs me, I feel something take hold from behind, and I am lifted up, above the counters and bins and shelves. Up, where the narrow canyons of aisles give way to wider vistas and I can see the entire landscape of the grocery store, flowing with shoppers, carts and merchandise. I am lifted up and turned round and hugged close by my father, his overcoat dark herringboned and scratchy as he hugs me close.

"There you are," he whispers, patting me on the back of the head, nudging my face farther into the corner between his neck and shoulder where soap-spice and aftershave mingle with the musk of damp wool. "I've been looking all over for you."

I wake again to my Nothing. I say 'wake' but in truth I still cannot tell with any certainty whether I have been asleep, unconscious, or something else. Only that I am now quite certain of being here - wherever 'here' is - and that something about it has changed.

19

Anne McKloskey is standing in the lobby of a Denny's near Boeing Field. An entire morning - and now the afternoon as well - has yielded no clue as to her daughter's whereabouts, and that gentle feeling of assurance has drained away, to be replaced with foreboding. After driving all the way to Jake's apartment only to find no answer from the intercom and no Honda on the surrounding streets, she had began systematically checking out every place her daughter had frequented since leaving home. Now, mid-afternoon, she has stopped to use a restroom when the newspaper stand in the vestibule seems to call to her, communicating a message of urgency. Hands shaking, she places a quarter in the slot. Passersby jostle the elderly woman as she scans each page of the first section with elevating urgency, advertising inserts fluttering out to litter the floor around her. She doesn't notice them however, raptly scanning without knowing what she is looking for, until, at the bottom of page ten, she finds it.

"Christina," she whispers loudly, the consonants bouncing hard off the glass walls around her. "Oh, Christina. What have you done to yourself?"

I am watching a train circle round and round a small oval course. The track is nailed down to a table in a child's bedroom - some friend of mine it seems, from a certain time, a certain age, but his name escapes me, as does his face and any detail of his room or life. There is only the train, with its steam locomotive, long and narrow, black and sinister. It circles the track with desperate diligence and despite its small size it is belching real sooty smoke. There are cars behind the engine, passenger cars and freight cars and a long string of red cabooses, all bearing smudges of oily black soot. Above and around me is the noise of the locomotive, its pistons driving back and forth, back and forth, with a chuffing, tugging pulse which is more than just a sound, deeper than mere vibration. It is the raw expression of energy and as it persists the train grows larger, from something I might have concealed in my folded hands, up to shoebox size, then footlocker, refrigerator, and finally, to full and even fuller size, towering above me, black and hot and power-filled.

I am standing beside the engine now, watching as long steel shafts move back and forth, their ends disappearing into cylinders of enameled metal. With each movement the towering behemoth shudders and threatens to engulf me, its bulk rising higher and higher till it seems to tip outward and over me and I am consumed within in its boiling shadow, aware of the pressure building up inside of it, of steam trapped and contained against its will, striving to expand, explode, escape. 'Potential energy,' I hear a voice say, and then the word again, 'potential.' The voice has no source, does not come from any person I can see, and even as I hear it speak those words, the locomotive has become a car - the very car my father drove when I was small - and I am standing, staring down upon its engine in the shadowy triangle cast by its open hood beneath a summer morning's glare. That large round disk which lives on top of the engine has been removed and my father's hands are in its place, pushing and pulling at the guts of the engine while he shouts instructions to my mother at the wheel. The engine refuses to start and my father's frustration rises as he squirts fluid from a can into the open maw on top of it. As I watch him I hear the engine turning over, trying to start itself, and it is the same sound as the locomotive, chuff-tug, chuff-tug, chuff-tug. Over and over the sound speaks its name as my father - whom I never knew in all his life to work on a car, or an engine of any sort - pushes and pulls inside it, reaching farther and farther down until his forearms disappear, and then his elbows. Now he is bent fully over, both arms plunged to the shoulders inside the metal workings, and I see the outside of the car has turned from copper and white to a deep, rich crimson which glistens and pulses, liquid in the sun.

The sound is even louder now - chuff-tug, chuff -tug - and Father's arms are pulling out, and now they are my own arms, his hands my own hands, and as they appear out of the darkness I see in them a heart. Human and beating, steaming warm, I pull it from the steely recess and raising it high present it to the familiar figure standing now before me, who wears my own face and features and figure, all washed to translucence by the sun's bleaching light. 'This,' I say in my father's voice, 'is yours,' and here and now, outside of any imaginings, I know with absolute certainty the truth of it – that this thing I have begun to perceive, this sound/vibration/energy which has now nearly taken over all my thoughts, is the evidence of my own heart beating, the blood coursing through my very veins, and it tells me, with ultimate assurance, that The Nothing is no more.

Yucatan Charlie's, the concourse restaurant, could well be an hallucination. A generic white-box space dolled-up as imitation beach shack, with plastic palm trees and papier-mâché parrots, it is peopled at two in the morning by a sparse assortment of businessmen and pending-vacationers bearing sullen looks of silent desperation. Elaine and her new acquaintance have taken a booth, an avocado-vinyl retreat which gives them just enough elbow room and quiet to converse in peace and relative privacy.

The tea, when it comes, is weak and too hot to drink yet; it needs to steep. The stranger's name, as she quickly discloses, is Beryl, and she is taking care of some business in the states after an extended time overseas, and was headed to Minneapolis for a brief visit with a sister and her family before setting out again. Beryl, too, has missed a connection, but is fuzzy as to whether she has a few hours to kill at the airport, or perhaps longer. She is more definite when speaking of all the places she has seen, 'over there.'

"...then Cambodia, of course, because of the Wats. They're very special energy centers," Beryl says as she pours a bit of tea to check the color. Satisfied, she fills both cups, her hands cradling the metal teapot in a napkin as if it were fine china. There is a precision to her movements, Elaine notes, that makes each gesture stand by itself. As if everything she does has more significance than normal. Listening to this woman tell of travelling from country to country, Elaine pictures crowds of local people parting to allow her passage, revered holy men bowing their heads in respect to the powerful aura of rightness - that is the expression which comes to mind, odd as it might be - the sense of something profoundly on-the-mark in this exotic woman's every move and gesture.

"I've spent the last two months here, working on...well, it doesn't matter what exactly. Some work I do from time to time. And after I see my sister and her children, I'm going back to visit some places I know of. I never really know how long I'll be in any one place. It depends on what there is to learn there; how much good I seem to be doing."

Beryl stops, elbows perched on the table, teacup cradled in perfect symmetry between fingertips. There are rings on every one of her fingers, Elaine notes, and every one different. Some silver, some bronze; two carved right out of solid stones which might be jade. Along with the bangles on her wrists, pendulous clusters of links in her ears and several draping necklaces, they give her a defiantly gypsy air. Must take forever at the security scanner, Elaine thinks idly, immediately reprimanding herself for allowing such a mundane image to distract her from the moment.

"What kind of good?" she asks, conscious of how dearly she wants to keep this conversation alive. "Are you some sort of doctor?"

"Oh, nothing so grand as all that," the woman answers gently, though she seems then to ponder the thought at some length before continuing. "So many places in this world, it doesn't take much to make a contribution. One of the things I've learned," Beryl says, tilting her chin forward as if to indicate the arrival of an especially-important piece of information, "is that one always has more to offer than one realizes. Especially coming from here - the U. S., you know - we have so many limitations we've built up around ourselves here; qualifications and classifications, memberships and requirements to be met in order to do this or do that. When you find yourself in a...a less structured situation, you discover you can do a great deal more than you ever realized."

"Oh, perhaps that's true for some people," Elaine agrees, thinking of her own trip, and of the high hopes she'd had when first planning it. Visions of herself and Rodney in some beautiful tropical setting, talking intimately of the dreams they'd once had and how to recapture them. Thinking also of his response as the date drew closer, withdrawing into obsession with his vaunted work, his supposed service to humanity, which she had come to believe was really a means to avoid any whiff of introspection. Which brings her back to her decision to go it alone, to try something new and different, to break out of the box which their life together had become.

"I thought my trip would be a little bit like that," she says, hearing the colorless drone of despair in her own voice. "But....here I am, stuck in this horrible place. Perhaps I'm just not the type of person..." and it is at this moment that the day finally engulfs her. The sleeplessness, the lack of food, the wondering what is happening back at home and resenting her own concern about it, the fighting back of fears and tears, and suddenly there is not enough energy left within her even to finish a single thought.

"I think," Beryl interjects firmly as she reaches out a wiry hand and very softly touches three warm fingertips to the back of Elaine's, "that we need to talk a whole lot more. Don't leave this spot."

      With that the woman rises from her chair and strides off, jangling like a caravan in a windstorm, to converse with the restaurant's sole visible employee, a waitress taking orders at the farthest end of the room. Returning a moment later, Beryl's face bears the satisfied smile of one who has just resolved a major dilemma.

Something else is different as well.

*Memories, dreams, waking, sleeping; how does the mind
determine which is which, except by contrast? I have a memory of
having memories, I have dreams of having dreamt and now my
waking sleeping waking has composed itself into the semblance of a
life. Beyond the pulsing energy, the sound which is not sound, there is
another change, another signal of a world beyond one's own
imaginings.*

*I see a body on a table, covered in pale green cloth. Its head
is swaddled between pillows, its face obscured by tubes and towels as
a green-suited person alternately cradles it in two hands, then turns
to consult the screens and dials and dripping tubes beyond. We are
under a light so harsh and glaring I want to turn and hide my face but
the watching eyes of half a dozen figures in gowns and face masks
will not let me.*

*Looking down again I see my hand, latex-sheathed and
poised above naked flesh. Feel my index finger extended and pressed
against the narrow metal spine of the scalpel. So small in my grip, so
light and inconsequential if not for the sharpness of its edge. And it is
the honing-away, I recall, that makes an edge sharp, not the initial
blank steel. It is with absence that we cut, with nothing.*

*There is blood now, as edge touches flesh, and it is as if my
hand, gliding back across the surface, is drawing out that liquid life.
At first a single drop, pregnant and luscious, it swells and flattens
until it is a patch of crimson, then a starfish, legs spreading maroon
across swollen slopes of ivory skin. Soon the legs of the starfish reach
the torso's sides and begin to flow down, dripping off the overhang,
spotting sheets with rusty roses. My fingertip is inside now, the knife
pressed too deeply into hidden tissues and organs as the horror of
failure strikes me. I want to withdraw my hand but what is done is
done and it remains, as the red rivers flow outward, soaking the body,
the table, the watching figures and myself until the world is all blood-
red, glowing with the light of the operating theater. Theater, stage,
my greatest act.*

*This is the novelty, the reason I am so sure of a change. I see
it now, this blood red glow and like the pulsing energy sound
vibration, it is not of my dreams, my memories, my imagination. It is
there in them, but does not disappear when they end.*

bluebirds fly

This light and this pulsing are outside of me and that makes all the difference.

Surprisingly, after the cool reception he had previously given them, Jake and Aubrey have each been phoned by Bob Baker and asked to return to Hilltop for a conference about their friend Kim. When they arrive, the reception clerk directs them to a small, plain room off the grandiose lobby of Hilltop's main building. The room is not empty, but is occupied already by an elderly woman and Baker, deeply engrossed in conversation.

"Mrs. McKloskey," the solemn-faced administrator says, gently interrupting their conversation as soon as he sees the new arrivals. "These people came to see about your daughter as well. They're friends of hers." He turns to Jake and Aubrey. "This is Anne McKloskey. Christina's - Kim Tree's - mother."

Anne looks up, and though Jake sees only a stranger, the woman's eyes brighten with recognition at the sight of him, the corners of her mouth pulling themselves up into a smile of considerable warmth and pleasure, given the circumstances.

"Josh!" she calls out, fully confident in her miss-identification. "Thank goodness you're here." With surprising agility for one of her years she is up out of the chair and across the room, to wrap herself around the shocked young man. She speaks into his chest with a voice which is steady and strong – one might even say excited. "They've told me all about it," she begins. "Christina is all right. She's had an operation, but she's doing very well and everything is going to be all right."

Lingering near the doorway, Aubrey feels a headache coming on. The sense of loss she encountered upon discovering her best friend was in the hospital compounded now by the realization she had not really known this other person at all. 'Christina?' 'Mckloskey?' That defiant independence Aubrey had so envied, revealed as total fabrication. For an instant she toys with disbelief but cannot quite rise to it. Something in the woman's movements is so familiar, so 'Kim,' that Aubrey knows immediately that what she is being told is true. The rhythm of the dance has changed once again, the second time in as many days and - as always - it is Kim who has called the steps, even from the far remove of unconsciousness, and it is Aubrey who must roll with the punch.

A short time later, Anne, Jake and Aubrey are seated in a

Chinese restaurant a block away from the Center, nursing tiny cups of hot tea.

"It's unbelievable," Jake says as the others sip. "That they can't just come out and tell us what's going on. Let us see her. I mean we're her family."

Aubrey listens without saying much - she has heard more than she cares to already. From Jake, to start with, spouting on about his rights as Chris' fiancé - as if they were ever really going to get married! Aubrey remembers it differently, how Kim mocked his late night calls to check up on her, his insistence that they spend every weekend together. How she bristled at the confinement of it all. And then there's this Mrs. McKloskey....already widowed, and now grieving for the loss of her only child. You have to sympathize with that, right? But there's something else to this woman, because no matter how clearly the doctors tried to state it - 'your daughter has suffered severe brain damage Mrs. McKloskey. It is unlikely that she will ever regain even basic motor functions' - she's so happy just to have located her kid that she seems to think the entire episode will turn out beautifully if they just cooperate with the hospital's suits.

"Really, Josh," Aubrey hears her saying now, despite having been reminded at least twice in the last half hour that his name is not Josh, but Jake. "I think we need to work with them, not against them. I'm not interested in lawsuits or damages, or punishing anyone. No matter how badly they've behaved towards us. It's Christina I'm thinking of. I just want to have my Christina back."

"I understand, Mrs. McKloskey..."

"Anne," she suggests sweetly. As sweetly, Aubrey realizes with amazement, as if she were introducing herself to a new member at a garden-club luncheon, rather than discussing the fate of a child. "Please. We're practically related, you know."

"Anne," Jake agrees, and it occurs to Aubrey that he can hardly do otherwise. So complete is the woman's belief in the world as she sees it, that others find themselves compelled to act as if they share in that same vision. "What I mean is, they let you be with her for what, a minute? And now they won't let any of us get near her. They've got something to hide and they're in spin-control mode, measuring information out in tiny doses just the way they want it to come to light. You heard what he said - about that operation they did to relieve the pressure on her brain - he called it 'a reflection of ongoing research.' Like Kim is just some sample in a lab dish. Like she isn't even a person any more. That's where they're going with this. They have it all worked out, I could tell just by listening to that ass..."

"Mr. Baker?" Aubrey cuts in. The man from Admin. had seemed to her to be playing his cards reasonably straight, admitting right up front that there had been some 'adverse events' in the hours leading up to Kim's surgery.

"Yeah that's him," Jake answers. "He's a tap dancer. Knows a lot more than he's saying. Like about them not being able to predict her odds of recovering. They have to have some expectation, some reason to go to the trouble of this surgery, all that stuff she's hooked up to in there. None of that comes free you know..."

"But what he said... about her never being herself again, even if she did recover. I mean, that makes sense, if ..."

"Aubrey, my dear," Anne interrupts with a look of patient tolerance. "You're so young. Just like Christina. Josh and I have had much more experience with the way people in high places do things - we understand that they can't always tell everyone the whole story. What I think, is that there's been a terrible mistake. Your Mr. Baker didn't say it in so many words, but I think they made a mistake somewhere and they're afraid we're going to try to hold them responsible for what happened to Christina. So they've come up with this entire story, about research and experiments and all that rigamarole, to avoid letting us take her home and care for her because then we'll find out what happened. Isn't that right Josh?"

Jake appears about to speak, perhaps to remind Anne once again that that is not his name, but all he manages is a slight raise of the head before being washed over again by the flood of Anne's conviction.

"What we have to do is to keep reminding them that we're only concerned with Christina. We don't want to cause trouble; we only want to see her, to talk to her - sometimes just hearing the voices of loved ones can be the best medicine for a sick person, you know - and when she's ready, when she's able to leave the hospital, we want to take her home and to care for her ourselves. Whatever it takes, whatever condition she's in. We'll take her home and she'll be part of our family once again. That's all we want, isn't it Josh?"

For a moment Jake stares, open-mouthed, at the old woman, and Aubrey is certain he's going to try again to correct her on his name, but instead he sighs, that hope apparently abandoned. His lips close for a moment then, and when he does speak, it is with great care, and seriousness of purpose.

"I don't know, Mrs.... Anne. But what I do know is that we're all going to need to work together. With the whole of Hilltop Medical Center setting the agenda, we're all of us going to have to work together to make sure that Kim gets the very best care she can."

Watching the two of them, listening to their words, Aubrey is struck with the notion that they are bonding, their opinions and prejudices edging towards a closer correspondence. Not a correspondence with reality, mind you. More like a shared fantasy, it seems a denial-in-common of the reality which Aubrey has heard the hospital officials spell out so loud and clear.

It is becoming familiar now, this transition from nothingness to something. It begins with simple consciousness; the certainty that this is now, that there was something before, and that there will be something after. Overlaid on that is the inside and the outside. There are things outside of me - the blood-red light, the chuffing tugging sound-sensation which I take to be my own pulse - coming to me in some way that is not quite hearing, not quite feeling.

How many times this has happened, this waking into myself, I cannot recall, but it is becoming familiar. It is the way I live now, whatever the explanation.

I have come to believe that the scenes I see are not dreams at all. I believe they are memories, compressed and transmuted, and combined with bits and pieces from outside. Recently I have become convinced I can hear a sound from outside. A distant sound, like machinery humming away in the ceiling, or behind a wall. It was there when I awoke one time, and it has been there for several wakenings now. That is how I think of them, for there are no days or nights in this place I inhabit, only 'wakenings.'

That humming is my focus now. To clarify it, identify it. To lock onto it with all my attention and to gather as much information from it as possible. To revel in the solidity of it, the reality, the sensation of that one thing.

"I think," Beryl says, then stops, with a quick jerk of the head, as if her own words have reminded her of something vastly more important than what she was about to say. She continues a moment later, in the manner of one confessing a deep and private truth, a manner which Elaine finds at once compelling and also faintly amusing. "People tell me I start many of my sentences with 'I think;' and I say 'Yes, I do! I *do* think!' It's something many people avoid, and your husband sounds like one of them."

Elaine has been telling Beryl the story of her marriage to Rod Gimbal, as the two pick at a plate of rolls and fruit and cheese which arrived along with their second pot of tea. Beryl has listened, seeming absorbed in the tale of youthful exuberance, early hopes of a family, and the disappointment which grew and grew as pregnancy eluded the couple. As Elaine tells of her eventual acceptance of childlessness and the long slow slide into boredom which followed, she has seen Beryl's eyes narrow, her cheeks beginning to suck themselves in, as if Elaine's life has produced a bad taste in her mouth.

"I think," the woman begins, pausing to nibble a strawberry from its leafy stem and savor its taste, "that you are a person who is forever undervaluing yourself. No, don't," she says, waving the strawberry stem impatiently as Elaine begins to protest.

"In addition to the crime of thinking, I also make a habit of looking at people. I'm sometimes accused of staring, but what I'm actually doing is 'looking'. In capital letters. L-O-O-K-I-N-G. 'Looking' is how one sees things, but we tend to forget that. We think of looking as a way of avoiding: 'Look out for danger,' we say, 'Look out for trouble.' The problem is, whatever you 'look out' for - is what you are going to find." The more Beryl speaks, the more excited she becomes, emphasizing the words with large gestures, bangled arms rising up and spreading wide with tiny chiming sounds, face leaning forward towards Elaine, eyebrows hopping up and down. Expressions of joy, humility and astonishment flash across her features faster than scenes in a movie trailer.

"*Looking out,*" she continues, "is a negative, it saps the forces around us and burns up precious energy trying to avoid disaster when what we need to be doing is using that energy to see the opportunities - 'see' is the first part of 'seize', isn't it? - 'see' opportunities and then 'seize' them; that's the way we discover our soul's desire, the way we set our spirit free. 'Look in' is what we need to say, not 'look out.' 'Look in' to yourself. 'Look in' to another person's eyes, and see their soul. And when I 'look in' to *you* Elaine, what I see is a woman about to blossom. I see a life about to expand exponentially from what it has been. I see that this delay, this change of plans, is given to you by the universe - your universe - the universe of *your* making. If you listen *inside* yourself, you can hear it, imploring you to open your eyes to the world, to all the things you've been avoiding for decades. To choose a new direction for your thoughts. For your life."

'Look,' Elaine thinks sourly, as her companion stops speaking and settles back to pluck half a dozen grapes from the platter and pop them one by one into her mouth, bracelets clanking against the hard edge of the table. The words form clearly, as a dialogue inside her mind; Elaine speaking to Elaine. 'Look at yourself. Telling your life's story to a total stranger you've met in an airport. Some absurd character who traipses around the world in gypsy costume and half a ton of cheap jewelry. Listening to her foolish talk of the universe giving you opportunities. You are not the kind of person who believes in mystical energies, or predestination,' but as she hears that last thought Elaine realizes with a start that the voice in her head, the voice which tells her to dismiss Beryl as a kook, is not her own voice at all, but Rodney's. Oh, it certainly is similar to her father's, and any number of others she has known over the years who would have applauded its conclusions, but the particular strength of its conviction, the vehemence with which it denounces these insights, is one hundred-percent-pure-unadulterated Doctor Rodney Gimbal. After all the years together, it is as if he were right there inside of her, telling her what to think and how to react. She realizes suddenly the degree to which she has absorbed his views and allowed them to become her own, to color how she sees the world and everything in it. Instead of a guardian angel she is carrying around her own guardian cynic. Having realized that, and having recoiled from that realization, what Beryl is suggesting seems not so implausible after all; that some force has placed her in this situation as an opportunity, to exchange her broken view of life with a new one by turning off that voice.

Besides, her thoughts continue, trying the idea on for size, what better explanation is there for how she has come to be here, now? Accident is an unsatisfying justification for the expenditure of one's entire lifetime - the heart yearns for a better account - and what could be more rewarding than finding meaning at sixty-one; the resurrection of purpose in a life which has been stripped, gradually and systematically, over decades, of all other fruits? Meaning might be enough, Elaine concludes, with no voice inside her head now but her own. Meaning might just be sufficient return on what she has invested in this life.

26

Lord, how I have come to hunger for sensation, to seize upon the sight of that blood-red light, the sound of my own blood flowing on and on, these few small things which tell me I am alive.

That conviction - that I am alive - and that I am myself, is all the world to me now. It is not much, but it is what I have, and at least it is something.

Press release - to all Seattle media outlets, today's date, post also on all bulletin boards throughout Hilltop:

HILLTOP MEDICAL CENTER REORGANIZING

Recently appointed Chief Executive Officer Dr. Alex Martinez today announces a reassignment of staff aimed at "increasing operating efficiency and providing greater opportunities for our most talented physicians to advance their clinical and research work." Martinez, formerly of Oceanview Hospital in San Diego CA, was installed at Hilltop just last week, following the take-over of the prestigious research and treatment hospital by California-based Medical Holdings LLC, third largest private health care provider in the nation.

Following a meeting with the heads of Hilltop's major departments and research affiliates, Martinez announced the departure of Dr. Eldon Beckwith. Formerly head of Cardiology for Hilltop, Dr. Beckwith will assume the directorship of the Medical Holdings Foundation Institute for Heart and Lung Studies, in Rochester, Minnesota.

Dr. Howard Lembec, founder of the Lembec Plegia Institute, which has been associated with Hilltop since its founding in 1993, will assume the post of Director of Clinical Studies at Sherwood Hospital, a Hilltop affiliate in Boston with a worldwide reputation in rehabilitative care and research.

Dr. Yuri Rosen, Senior Staff Physician in Endocrinology, has been appointed to head a new Division of Infant and Embryonic Endocrinology at Miami University Hospital, the division to be supported initially by a generous grant from the Medical Holdings Foundation.

Dr. John Draper, a staff specialist in ICU care, has been selected to head the ICU and Critical care department at MH's newly acquired Institute de Medicine, a 100 bed hospital located in Katmandu, Nepal, first established nearly thirty years ago by French adventurer Francoise Petti.

Finally, Dr. David Resor, former head of the Applied Dialysis Unit at Hilltop, will assume the directorship of the Robert W. Service Memorial Trauma Center, in Fairbanks, Alaska.

This release, and the media articles which resulted from it, did not detail one related development, the departure of young Mr. Katsas Disigurian, an intern and sometimes assistant to Dr. Resor. Mr. Disigurian, following the announcement of those administrative changes, abruptly handed in his own resignation from Hilltop, his professed intention being to take a break from the intensity of internship and rethink his commitment to the practice of medicine.

28

"You're beautiful, did you know that?"

Mary Antonias stares down at the figure being prepared for transport. One more time she has been drawn to visit this room and stare at this youthful face, as if by studying its somnolent features she can better understand the miracle of their attraction. The girl's head is swathed in bandages now, bulbous and misshapen due to the surgery she has undergone, but even the little which is not covered is sufficient to convey that mysterious alchemical advantage which captivates Mary's thoughts.

Captivates them, as it has ever since the day an unconscious 'Jane Doe' was wheeled into Emergency Care and Mary was called down from Pediatrics, before the team stripped off the school-girl get-up and discovered a young woman beneath it. Later, when she stopped by out of curiosity to check on outcome, she learned the still-unidentified patient had been stabilized and shifted to ICU, where Mary caught another glimpse of her, hooked up to a respirator and a dozen other pieces of equipment to preserve the faint signs of life remaining beneath her loveliness. Mere hours later, after having been identified as Christina McKloskey, she had made an abrupt departure from ICU as well, whisked off for some ill-explained surgery which landed her here, in the Plegia Institute, connected to a new set of jury-rigged devices the local staff said were intended to avoid the swelling and resultant tissue damage which account for so many of the permanent disabilities associated with head injuries. To everyone's surprise not only did the girl regain a level of brain activity, but her vital signs had stabilized and she had begun breathing and regulating on her own. Now, a month later, though still in a coma, she is about to be transported from Hilltop and Mary has come by for one last look.

What is it, she wonders, that makes one nose more precious than the next? It has the same elements as any other proboscis, as Mary's own for that matter. Two nostrils. Flaring sides blending to cheeks, and a bridge connecting to the gentler plane of forehead above. Just as a nose by any other name is still a nose, this face has all the same elements as any other face, and yet...

Her own face, Mary is convinced, has none of the appeal of this one. Gazing in a mirror, she sees what she is certain others must

- a chin too square and too far forward, suggesting a belligerence she does not feel, beneath a 'Roman' nose which might fit comfortably on a hulking Legionnaire, but is substantially out of scale among its current surroundings. A forehead tall and wide, which no brushing-down of bangs can conceal, over heavy-lidded eyes that appear always on the verge of sleep and, holding the line between eyes and forehead, those brows of hers - thick, wide and dark. Unsuited to subtleties, they render surprise, welcome, and a dozen other emotions in almost identical manner. This child's brows, in contrast, are but a whisper of exclamation above lids as gently shaped and textured as petals of a rose, tipped with soft combs of lash. This face before her could signify a thousand different shades of emotion with ease, if only it would quicken.

It is these thoughts and a hundred like them which have led Mary to visit here several times since the patient came out of surgery. To stand over this bed and stare, and wonder what it would feel like to live behind that face, those eyes. To have the world react to you the way it does to those so blessed.

Obsession, Mary has told herself, in an attempt to rationalize these visits, may not be an unhealthy response, when one is confronted with an elemental mystery. Observing the success of others, she has always sought to measure herself against it, and found herself lifted in the process. Faced with the possibility of learning, discovery, the future, she has found the impulse to pursue it irresistible, and so been drawn forward into her own life. Here, confronted with a face which rings so many bells, Mary feels a gravitational impulse drawing her near. One last time she gazes upon that which she has been denied and wonders at the difference it makes.

"You're beautiful," Mary whispers softly to the static figure. Words she has never heard spoken of herself, even by herself. "Whatever happens, you'll always have that."

" 'Scuse me," mutters an orderly, all brusque efficiency as he squeezes in between Mary and the gurney. Grabbing a side rail he pulls it up and locks it into place, then moves around to do the same on the opposite side. Kicking wheel-locks loose with practiced disregard he leans into the weight and accelerates the rolling apparatus toward the door. In the blink of an eye he is gone, the girl is gone, and Mary is alone in the silent room; remembering.

second movement

1

Progress! Real progress. I have confirmed that my body exists.

This confirmation stems in part from what I experienced some time ago. An hallucination maybe, or a dream - or perhaps more particularly, the recollection of the memory of having had such a dream:

When I was a teenager I used to lie awake at night, eyes closed and body settled comfortably, but unable to drift off as my mind raced with the thousand worries which young people create for themselves. To escape this state between waking and sleeping I invented a game where I would pretend that I had left my body and was floating in the room, looking down upon my sleeping self. Though I had conceived it only as a game, the sensation of being outside of myself soon became quite convincing and so, once, in an attempt to determine whether what I was experiencing was real or not, I willed my disembodied self to float out into the hallway and around my house. To my surprise I was readily able to do this, to visit and view each room of my home as if plastered to the ceiling. In doing this I did not walk or crawl or flap my arms but floated quite naturally, without any locomotive action whatsoever.

This floating around outside of myself was quite pleasant, even exciting, and so I resolved to expand the testing regime. Imagining myself outdoors, I found I was there, hovering just above the front yard of our home. I then chose to rise a bit higher, until our yard was laid out beneath me like the playing surface of a child's board game. Over to my right I saw the lilac hedge which bordered the Sorenson's property, to the left the curving concrete walk which led to our front door, and by the door, that wire basket in which bottles of milk and cream were deposited each morning before any of our household had awakened.

Rising higher I viewed our house from a perspective I had never known before, as if I were a bird, or the pilot of a small plane. In the moonlight its shingled roofs made a beautiful geometric composition, some planes shadowed and bottomless, others outlined by highlights glinting off damp edges, sparkling like the crystalline aggregate I had seen up-close on a scrap of roofing that had blown off years before.

Willing myself to rise higher I saw our neighborhood appear, first one street, then several - winding in topographic curves to wrap around hillsides, here and there one of their number branching off to join the more-regular grids which occupied the flats between. Like a map, but with full detail and dimension. I could see the slope rising to the back of Deacon's Ridge, the flat plane of the school grounds, the blinking lights of a railroad crossing and, in the distance, the lake itself, a black hole without feature or scale until, far off, I noticed the red and green running lights of a small boat headed towards me. I think it was the size of those lights, their reminder of just how high I had floated, which turned my wonder into fear and caused me to snap instantly back to the conviction that I should be lying safely in my bed, and then - in that same instant - there I was. And once there, could not tell for certain whether what I had experienced had been entirely within my mind, or had in fact occurred outside, in that still and mysterious night. Though I did know that I had never been so scared in all my life.

I never again experimented with floating outside my body, nor gave much thought to what I had experienced. I suppose I had reached an age where the normal course of growth was to turn my attention more to the outside world. Just now though, in my dream/memory/imagining, I experienced a similar sensation of flying. Without willing it, I felt myself floating as once I floated over that old neighborhood, only this time, even as the sensation persisted, I remained within my familiar no-longer-quite-Nothing world. The same blood-red light, the same pulsing vibration/sound, but added to them, as clearly as if I had been able to see my surroundings, I knew that my body was moving. More specifically, I am convinced that I first felt myself travel in the direction of my feet. After a short time, that movement ceased and I experienced an impression that my head was moving one way and my feet another. Trying to picture this in my mind I reached the conclusion that my body must be spinning around its middle. Or being spun, since there was no sense of volition, of my acting in any way to cause these motions. In any case, I am certain that I had felt myself spinning, or rotating, about a center.

The more I have tried to picture this, the more convinced I have become that I must be lying down, for to be turned in this manner while standing up would be to cartwheel through space, an act I think I can safely assume improbable given my current incapacity. After smoothly rotating for a bit, I felt again that sense of motion, though now in the opposite direction, towards what my internal map imagines as my head. The motions went on for some time, starting and stopping in no pattern which I could discern, until a familiar sense of fatigue came over me and when I awakened again, from another comforting and familiar dream, I found the motions had ceased.

I conclude from all this that I have now some limited degree of spatial awareness, a minimal inner-ear function which serves to detect relative motion, and that my physical body - which I can neither see nor feel nor control - must have been moved from one place to another. Implicit in this is yet a stronger confirmation that I do in fact _have_ a physical body, meaning presumably, that I am not dead, nor in some ethereal cosmic limbo, but that I have merely – merely! - been physically incapacitated to a shocking degree.

There is an irony here, which I have been pondering ever since: in my youthful experiment a particular set of sensations – real or imagined – led me to believe I had separated my spirit - or more properly my intellect - from my body. Now, a not-dissimilar set of sensations has led me to conclude with some relief almost the exact opposite - that my intellect still inhabits that body! Exactly where my body resides, or how it got to be there, and my mind so poorly connected to it, is a question I hope to answer over time. In this hope I shall turn my attention forward and concentrate not on the dream/memories which have been my preoccupation since first awakening in my Nothing, but on the possibility of reaching out, of connecting once again to the world which I am now certain exists somewhere out there, if I could only reach it

Mavis Finch glances down at the bed. What she sees when she looks at her patient is a human being very much like herself, who just happens to be unable to take care of her own needs. Not the first such person for whom Mavis has cared, nor likely to be the last. Temporarily disabled, congenitally handicapped, terminally ill, it is all the same to her. Mavis has been hired to care for this one, and that is what she intends to do, so long as she is fairly paid and fairly treated and the little girl in the bed continues to need her care.

That Mavis finds herself referring to her new patient this way - as a little girl - is no doubt because that it is how Mrs. McKloskey thinks of her. Came through clear as a bell, from the very first phone call.

"My little girl is sick," the woman had said over the phone, "and I need someone who knows how to take care of her." Apparently she had gotten Mavis' number from one of the doctors involved in some sort of administrative review to determine whose responsibility it would be to care for the poor child. A not unfamiliar story: the heartbroken mother fighting an entire hospital's worth of doctors and administrators over liabilities and capabilities, projected costs and probable outcomes - all the crazy stuff the medical community and the insurance companies wrap around themselves to puff up their own importance. Mavis has no truck with that bureaucracy, as a rule, but it appears that in this case someone has at least had the good sense to follow a simple truth. However complex her treatment, however small her chances of regaining consciousness, this is Mrs. McKloskey's daughter, and her place, if at all possible, is with her mother.

This is an honestly held opinion, by the way, not the least affected by the fact that the call could not have come at a better time for Mavis Finch; Herman Gannon having died little more than a week before. Mavis had been old Mr. Gannon's visiting nurse for nearly four years. Had started out just spending the nights in the Gannon's spare room, to be on call in case he needed anything while his wife got the rest she needed. Mavis still had her day job at that point, over at Swedish Hospital, in the burn unit. Lord, how glad she was not to be *there* any longer. Like combat duty, that burn unit was; something even Mavis could only handle for just so long. Half the patients doomed to an agonizing death that even your best efforts could only prolong, the rest sentenced to an even longer and more painful recovery. The kind of work you had to take one day at a time, telling yourself over and over that you were doing some good even if you couldn't see it, and then get out before the tragedy of it all had destroyed any part of your self that you couldn't afford to lose.

Mavis was halfway relieved then, when Mr. Gannon's liver began to fail and he needed full-time care. The old man had done well over the years and his wife had no trouble paying to have Mavis come stay with them full-time and be his primary attendant. This current position appeared to be another version of the same story. Mrs. McKloskey had a big house in a big yard and enough money left from her husband to hire a full-time nurse. Unfortunately every bedroom in that big house was upstairs, so they had settled on putting the girl in this building out back. Used to be a workshop, Mrs. McKloskey said, back when the previous owners had the house. Converted to a studio when the McKloskey's moved in - Mr. McKloskey being a musician, as his widow was only too quick to tell you, who had played in orchestras and concert halls all over the world. Mavis had no use for that high-brow sort of stuff, but sat dutifully through Mrs. M.'s showing off the autographed photos and awards, the entire shelf full of recordings with her husband's picture on their jackets.

In any case, they had settled on putting the girl in here and for the first few weeks the place bordered on chaos as carpenters and painters and decorators made it over into the mother's fantasy of what a little girl's room should look like. It was pleasant enough now, if a bit fussy for a sick room, what with two layers of curtains edged in lace, a fancy carved headboard to dress up the motorized hospital bed, the dozens of stuffed animals pulled out of boxes in the basement and lined up on shelves along one wall. Mrs. M. referred to it as the guesthouse now, and it was plenty comfortable, with this big bedroom for the child, and a tiny one for Mavis behind.

The best arrangement Mavis has had in fact, since her own husband Tommy died and left his wife nothing. A far sight worse than nothing actually. After thirty-seven years of steady employment as a sheet-metal mechanic her man'd gone and had a heart attack, leaving her with nothing but a worn-out house he'd long told her was paid in full but which turned out not to be. The only way she found out why it wasn't paid off, why he had taken out a second mortgage when he said he was stashing money away for their retirement, was when she discovered a couple of shirt boxes full of worthless lottery tickets, betting chits and Vegas phone numbers, stashed in an old suitcase in the garage. Evidence of just how effectively Tommy had been deceiving her - and himself - for all those years.

So now here she is, her own five children grown and scattered across the country. A not-so-young woman herself, settled into this white clapboard cottage with the lacy curtains and flowered walls, fancy as a debutante's gown, watching over the girl in the bed.

A pretty girl, her mother can't help herself from endlessly pointing out, though Mavis has her own opinions about the issue. Foolish to talk about pretty when you're looking into eyes empty as marbles, or gazing upon a mouth as limp and unresponsive as two slices of uncooked ham, all connected to a body which is thin and only getting thinner, due to months of inactivity and intravenous feeding. Still there is something compelling in her looks. Some inherent trick of proportion - like the one that renders a puppy so much more cuddly than its grown-up parent – that makes a part of Mavis want to hug this girl close and protect her from harm. The gentle arcs that make up her eyes, the almost imperceptible way her temples wrap down into her cheeks into her neck, together create the optimistic impression of something freshly minted, never worn down by the pain and experience that carves up other, more experienced, beings. Mavis envies the girl those features. Her own have served their time and bear witness to every day of it. Ironic, it hit her one early morning when a beam of sunlight had struck the child just so, that the healthy person in the room should look so old and worn, while the sick one seems so untouched. The only place this girl shows any evidence of trauma is on her scalp, its ugly sutures and swollen bumps slowly healing as the hair which had been shaved clean for surgery grows out, long enough now to cover her ears and begin to drape its way across the pillow, jet black and silky straight.

The girl's skin does not really seem to go with that hair; it is fair, the slightest bit rosy, and, oh, so soft to the touch after being rubbed with moisturizer twice a day. Her neck rises like an ivory post from the Swiss lace collar of the nightgown as her hands lie folded where Mavis puts them each morning for two hours, then moves them to another position for the next two. A little thing that, but one on which Mavis prides herself, despite the ribbing she took when she worked up at the VA hospital.

"You're stirring the soup after it's all been eaten hon'," a brass-voiced nurse-supervisor called out one day as Mavis stopped at the floor-station after checking in on a stroke patient. "That old man doesn't care which way his hands are, he's already gone to a better place - if he's lucky - or else he's sittin' in hell thinkin' 'bout his sins if he ain't."

"We don't know what he thinks," Mavis had replied, in the careful enunciation she had learned from her Tennessee grandmother. "Do we? So until he can tell me what he thinks, I intend to treat him like I'd want to be treated in his place; and if I was in his place I wouldn't want to lie there exactly the same for all twenty-four hours of a day. I'd want to move around a bit."

"Next thing, you'll be standing him up on a handcart and walking him 'round the halls so he can see the sights," the brassy one challenged, then caught herself in mock surprise. "Ooh, maybe a handcart isn't good enough for one of Mavis's patients." She smiled a mile wide at her own cleverness. "Maybe you should pick him up instead, and give him a piggy-back ride."

"Well," Mavis had said then, boring her eyes into the other nurse's bloodshot orbs, "If that's what it takes to treat him like a human being, I just might do that someday." The two women lingered in silence for a moment, until the supervisor decided the charts in front of her were in urgent need of attention and Mavis found herself free to continue her duties, warmed by the knowledge that it was not she who had been first to turn her eyes away.

Mavis is proud of her eyes, careful that they never flinch, never shy away from anything. Talking to a supervisor, an administrator, or some hoity-toity doctor convinced of his own superiority to a lowly nurse, she has made it a point to lock her eyes onto the other person's and never let go. She can take a lashing, get fired for doing the right thing, listen to a banker explain how her retirement plans have been ruined by an unpaid note on the house, it's all the same. Mavis Finch's eyes will take it all in without fear or illusion, and toss it back at the giver with a challenge to see if they can stand up as well as she.

The girl in the bed has no such strength. In fact, her eyes, when they were pried open and examined with a doctor's penlight, showed as nearly nothing as any human being Mavis has ever known. Just stared straight ahead of her without reacting to anything. Movements, words, the changing light as her room drifted from morning to noon to night; none of it matters to those eyes. Same with the music Mrs. M. insists be played for several hours each day. Symphonies and violins and even - this seemed in questionable taste to Mavis - organ music. Her dead husband's music apparently. The same as has paid for this house and now pays Mavis' salary, much of that accumulating in the bank so that perhaps someday she can once again retire.

This is the background then, as Mavis enters the girl's room first thing each morning, mental checklist running before she has even washed her own face. Head position correct, airway unobstructed - check. IV, check. Meds current – check. Heart rate and BP...

Music!

Distant and muffled, like something filtered thru a wall, but unmistakable for all that, the sound of an orchestra comes to me. A symphony, I suppose, or a concerto...In truth I neither know nor care what it is called, only that I am hearing music and it lifts something inside of me to a degree I could not ever have imagined it would.

I can hear.

Like the other fragmentary sensations which have returned to me, my hearing seems to have come fully alive during sleep. Or unconsciousness, which I think is a better term for the periods between my awakenings. Sleeping is something a body does, and as I can sense so little about my body, I cannot really say whether I am sleeping some of the time, all of the time, or not at all. What I do know is that I have these periods of self-awareness, and that they often begin with a strong impression that something has changed while I was not paying attention - leading to the conviction that time has been passing by without me.

Enough. Enough analyzing and describing. My words defeat me. The more I try to explain and describe to myself what is happening, the more divorced it all seems from the actual experience. Experience. I realize now how much I have longed for something to happen; for any concrete sensory experience on which to focus my attention, instead of my own self-conscious rambling. This is the unexpected blessing of the music: that it is beyond my own control, for it seems now that only those things which are beyond one's own control can actually create anything new, can illuminate one's true situation. Who would have thought?

Those meds, Mavis thinks, as she rolls the girl to one side and pulls out the sheets, undressing the bed as she does every other morning. They are the one unsettling ingredient in an otherwise perfect situation. Mavis has never been one of those nurses to question her doctors. Not like Elizabeth Burden, back when they were at Swedish together. Lizzie was always going on about how the doctors had over medicated this patient, or given that one an interactive combination that she had learned of by reading back issues of some obscure journal she had found in the locker room. The girl got herself fired eventually, for telling some good ol' boy he had endangered her patient and she was going up the chain with it. Turned out Lizzie was right in the end, not that it got her job back for her, or anything else you could put in the bank.

Mavis has enough respect for doctors not to question the meds outright, even if she hadn't had Lizzie's story to caution her. Besides, at her age, a job like this is just too good to mess up. So she goes on administering what is on the chart, though it all makes no sense to her. In some ways it resembles an anti-rejection regimen, suppressing the body's natural reaction to foreign matter, in order to protect a transplanted organ. One of the doctors said the girl'd gone into kidney failure because of the drugs she took, the ones that put her into the coma in the first place. Said there had been a transplant, and that might have washed if Mavis hadn't seen enough patients with new organs to know that this was different. High doses for one thing, for a patient with such a low body-mass. Administered twice a day for another thing, instead of the once daily Mavis had seen before.

Plus mestatracine, an obscure neural-blocker which Mavis would not even have heard of if she had not done time on the burn ward. Those poor burn victims, tormented by the shrinking of flesh as their injuries scarred over, and by the compulsion to scratch at that new skin, which would tear its delicate surface. Mestatracine was administered to break the connection of mind to body and let them sleep without torment. An odd thing to prescribe here, for a girl with a transplanted kidney and no motor control.

Then there is the so-called enzyme drip. Mavis has never, in all her years of nursing, heard of any such thing as an 'enzyme drip.' Administered epidurally no less; the needle inserted directly into the spinal column just below the base of the skull - not down at the hollow of the back like a normal epi. Sounds to her like something out of a science fiction movie. Or a horror film. There's more too, a twenty page protocol she was required to read and sign that first day. Like working for the government it had seemed at first, though that feeling went away once the doctors had left and she was alone with her patient.

Still, doctors are doctors, and she only a practical nurse, so Mavis keeps her thoughts to herself on that whole medication issue. No need to worry Mrs. M., either. The poor lady has enough on her mind, a widow with her only child in such a state, and unlikely ever to come out of it.

She'll be along soon, Mrs. M. Nine o'clock sharp, she will knock on the door and Mavis will let her in. By then the girl will be sponge-bathed, sheets changed and dressed in a clean gown, her hair brushed and hands arranged just so. Mavis will leave for an hour and a half while Mrs. M. touches-up the unmoving face, her baby's lips and eyes painted until they shine like a magazine model. Maybe change the color of her nails too, she does that every week or so.

In the beginning it had seemed pretty weird, this desperate attention to the girl's appearance, but Mavis quickly realized where it came from, for Mrs. M. herself had to be the most carefully put-together woman she had ever encountered. Never a hair out of place, outfits always perfectly assembled and tailored. Clearly a woman who believed in the importance of image. Mavis had accepted it all on that basis, the mother still mothering after the worst had happened, unable or unwilling to admit that it made no difference anymore. Gradually she had even come around to understand that it did make a difference, in its own odd way. Mrs. M. was treating the child the way she herself would want to be treated, if it were her lying there. You could see that in her posture and poise - God forbid anyone should see Mrs. M. without her make-up and hair done. Once she had come around to that understanding, Mavis no longer even gave it a thought. She would return from her morning walk to find Christina propped up among the pillows, pretty as a wedding picture, perfectly ready to meet her public, such as it is.

5

Elaine and Beryl stumble up the slope as if in a dream, loose stones and gravel rolling like bearings beneath the soles of their sensible shoes. The air around them is thin and unsatisfying; breathing it is like sucking through a straw to quench a great thirst, one never gets enough. Ahead and behind them a river of pilgrims make the same journey, sandaled feet seemingly oblivious to the stony surface and near-freezing temperature, the pin-prick lights of their candles and battery-torches forming a snake which stretches far below, quivering and swaying with life as each individual moves at his or her own pace, stopping and starting, passing and intertwining all along the undulating ridge.

"How... much... farther?" Elaine asks, eyes searching ahead to see if by some miracle they have at last reached the final slope which will reward them with the summit. Beryl's face as it turns toward her is radiant as always, caught in a shard of light from the flashlight Elaine still wields, though the eastern sky has finally begun to glow just brightly enough to allow her to follow the path beneath their feet without it.

"No idea," Beryl answers happily. "Remember. It's the journey we're after, not the destination."

Among the few people who do visit the girl with any regularity are the doctors. Three of them, always visiting together and then stumbling around the bed trying to get out of one another's way. Excusing themselves for speaking their minds, then trying to appear deferential when underneath, you can tell they have about as much respect for one another as three dogs around a soup bone. Apparently this is something which was agreed to between Mrs. McKloskey and the hospital when she received custody of her daughter. In return for the Hearing Officer's certifying her guardianship of the adult patient over the hospital's objections that Chris needed specialized care, Mrs. M. and her lawyer had accepted that the girl's treatment would be jointly managed by a panel of physicians representing the different interests which competed over and around her.

First among these - at least when the mother is around - comes Dr. Carl Ayers, designated to represent Mrs. M. An old friend of her late husband's, he had called to offer his sympathies and services soon after Chris' true identity became known. That his true familiarity with Sean McKloskey was limited to sharing a table at one fund raising dinner for the Seattle Symphony has never actually been pointed out to Mrs. M., any more than the fact that he served on the board of East Side Children's Hospital for a four-year term leading up to and following that institution's acquisition by Medical Holdings, LLP.

Next comes Dr. Marty Sen, appointed by the hospital because of his familiarity with the case, though he is actually not the one most familiar. That would have been Dr. Howard Lembec, of the Plegia Institute, who had been responsible for the girl's care for the first weeks following her surgery, but by the time these arrangements were being negotiated Dr. Lembec had left Hilltop and in fact the entire US. Rather than Boston, as the initial press release indicated, he was now rumored to be setting up shop at an obscure clinic in Switzerland known as much for its clientele of Middle Eastern royalty and South American drug lords as for the excellent standard of care it offered.

The third participant was appointed by the court, supposedly to settle any disagreements which might arise between the other two, though from what Mavis has seen, Dr. Burton B. Smithson is singularly unsuited to this role. Despite over forty years of practice he manages to project the air of one perpetually surprised to find himself addressed as Doctor. He never volunteers an opinion, and when pressed (or at least on the few times Mavis has seen this occur) he manages to restate what the others have already expressed, though in even more convoluted and pretentious terms. Whatever summary suggestions he finally offers seem aimed less at improving the patient's situation than smoothing over the disagreement and allowing himself to get back to the commercial real estate portfolio which crops up often in his conversation.

Still, Mavis thinks for the umpteenth time as she tucks a fresh sheet beneath the slender limbs, the trio <u>are</u> physicians. Experienced practitioners with plenty of certificates and privileges. Members of a superior race. Whatever reservations she might have about their motives or judgment, she will keep to herself. Better to focus on her own job than to second guess those with more education and more expertise. Not to mention, more power.

Hearing the music now, so clearly not a memory or dream but alive and in the air around me, I realize I have been having impressions of sound for some time - a vague electronic sort of humming for example, and that pulsing which I take to be my own heartbeat, but they were indistinct and uncertain, with no impression of how near their sources were to me, how far, or in what direction. Now though, with each rustle or shuffle, each distant thud, I feel my attention drawn, the way one's head turns instinctively at a sudden movement caught out of the periphery of one's vision. It is that surprise, that unanticipated quality which is so different from all that has gone before it in this place, and which convinces me that all these impressions are real.

One of the first specific sounds I identified was a telephone ringing. At first I thought it another memory, of hearing a telephone in a dream. As it continued to ring however, I realized that was not the case. Then I heard a voice speak, not clearly, but as if from a distance, or through layers of heavy fabric. 'Guesthouse,' the voice said; a term which has no particular significance for me, and yet one which I cannot fathom my imagination creating of whole cloth. A moment later I heard the same voice say 'very well,' and the clattering sound of a phone being set down in its cradle.

Since that time I have been hearing other sounds as well. Footsteps, I believe, and the closing of a door. A rustling and crumpling which I cannot identify, and even a snatch of humming. Now that I am aware of these sounds outside myself, I actually believe I have been hearing them - dimly and without recognition - for some time. It was only the abrupt shock of the ringing which caused me to separate them out from my own thoughts and realize the sea change they indicate.

With this, I have begun to develop a theory. I suspect that these sounds are coming to me through some reconstructed neural pathway which my brain has managed to cobble together. Like an amputee learning to flex new muscles to operate a prosthesis, I imagine my brain mapping new pathways and recording them for future use.

Examining my sensations more closely, I believe I have also developed the ability to perceive a variance in the blood-red light. There are times now when it seems definitely brighter, more intense, and others when it is less so, when its color seems to shift, from deep red into an almost golden-yellow glow. Sometimes there are even patterns of flowing color, like some indecipherable Modern Art painting. These patterns seem consistent with the effect of pressure on the eye, perhaps applied from the outside, or by muscles contracting in some misguided attempts to focus. From this I infer that my eyes are at least partly functional, as well as the nerve pathway from them to my brain. That I cannot see more normally conforms reasonably well with the hypothesis that my brain is attempting to overcome some damage by forging new patterns of processing the information it is receiving. This is further reinforced by the limited return of auditory perception.

It seems most likely that I have suffered some major trauma to the brain. A stroke perhaps, or a ruptured aneurism. Given the correct location, the effect of such injury might well be to sever the connection between one's extremities and the cerebral cortex, such that the higher cognitive functions were able to continue, but isolated from the outside sensory world. The patient would exist then as if in a perpetual dream, inhabiting a world of memories and imagination without benefit of external stimuli or communication. Once again, this is consistent with what I have been experiencing.

If so, then what can I conclude from these recent changes in my condition? First, that I am, as I have believed for some time, alive. Second, that I have been injured in some way, but that the injury has not been totally destructive; a limited amount of stimulus is now - and has been for some time - making its way past the injury site. Third, that my higher functions are intact and beginning to make sense of the fragmented information reaching them through re-mapped neural pathways. My focus from now on must be to monitor this process, to make the most of what information I can glean. Therein lies my hope of somehow escaping this passive state.

Unless, of course, I am only dreaming all of this as well.

It has been nearly three days since Elaine Gimbal first met Beryl Nathanson at LAX. Sixty hours, more or less, since they shared tea and fruit and re-booked their flights to change the course of a life.

"There's a reason you're here," Elaine recalls Beryl saying, after they had been speaking and sipping for a couple of hours. "A reason why your husband didn't want to come on this journey, why your plane was diverted then canceled. Why we ended next to one another at that ticket counter, at that hour of the night."

Even now, somewhere on the face of this supposedly sacred peak, two hundred and twenty kilometers from the nearest airport, Elaine can still feel the way those words affected her. There *was* a reason, she had eventually agreed. There *had to be* a reason, for the way this woman's words struck chords inside her.

"The question is: are you willing to do what it takes to discover that reason?"

Beryl was certainly willing; willing to call her sister in Minneapolis - mercifully awake what with the time difference and a houseful of young children - and tell her that Auntie Beryl would not be coming after all. Willing to go back to the cursed customer service counter and talk her way throughseveral attendants until she found one savvy enough to convert their tickets into vouchers for standby flights on another airline. Willing to propel both herself and Elaine past dozens of sleepy-eyed travelers, and across two concourses to the International Departures area, and the gate listed for JAL flight 227, departing in twenty minutes for Tokyo's Narita airport.

"You don't have anything to go back to," she had said to Elaine somewhere along the way, when the younger woman's resolve seemed about to fail, her practical side ready to rise up and overwhelm the absurdity of what they were about. "You've said so yourself, and you have the resources, thank goodness, and your health; so the question is, why not? What is holding you back? And if you don't have a good answer for that question, then ask yourself this: if not now, when?"

All of which – and more in the days between - have led Elaine to this mountainside path, this early morning pilgrimage. Since two AM they have been walking, mostly in silence, insulated from one another by cold and darkness. Step after step Elaine has felt her feet propelling her up the mountain and every step has been, at the same time, a step back into herself.

9

Another sign of change in me, besides what I have been hearing, and the red light, which seems to come and go unpredictably. I woke this time to feel something resting on my stomach, though it was not so much that I was aware of the feeling itself, as it was of my mind forming a picture of what the feeling meant. I found myself conscious, and aware of something, and it confused me, and it was only after some time of being baffled and curious that it occurred to me that I was actually feeling touch, and then it was gone. As soon as I consciously addressed the sensation I couldn't find it. Like searching for a very faint star in the night sky, and if you look straight at it you can't see it due to the lack of photoreceptors at the optic nerve head, but if you move your eyes away, there it is. With this, once I tried to identify the sensation that had disturbed me, it was gone and I couldn't get it back. I'd almost think I had imagined it, except that it was so slight - not worth imagining. No, if I was going to hallucinate, I'm sure I'd come up with something more dramatic than an impression of weight on my abdomen. I resolve therefore, to wait for it to come back - or something like it - and to be more careful next time. To listen to the sensation for what it is, and not to drown it out with my analysis.

"How is she today, Mrs. Finch?"

"The same."

Mavis barely looks up from her magazine as Jake enters the room. It is Tuesday and it is quarter past one. He is on time, as expected, attired as always in a very nice and very expensive suit.

Mavis does not like Jake Brindle. She does not like the precision of his tailoring, or his body-builder's physique, both of which bespeak a self-consciousness she finds inappropriate in a man. Nor does she appreciate the fact that he is always so precisely on time, never so much as two minutes early, to visit the girl he says he loves with all his heart. Neither does she appreciate his slightly possessive way of speaking about her patient, or his casual familiarity with Mrs. McKloskey. There is something distasteful about it all, about the two of them doting on this child, speaking of her as if she were just recuperating from a head cold.

Still, Jake has the mother's permission to visit, even to spend time alone with her patient. Finishing a paragraph, Mavis folds back the corner of the page, closes the magazine and reaches for the plastic travel mug of Tetley Tea from which she sips throughout each day.

"I'll be in my room if you need anything," she says, and departs without a backward glance, though as always she does not close the door completely, but leaves it slightly ajar, the better to hear immediately if anything untoward should occur in her absence.

"Kimmie," Jake whispers as soon as he is alone with the sleeping figure. "How you doin' babe?" Sitting on the edge of the bed he reaches out, his wide hand easily eclipsing the pale ones which lie across her stomach, his thick fingers resting gently upon her slender ones, whose nails are so carefully shaped and polished - opaline punctuations for gestures never made.

"I got so much to tell you, kid," he continues, and commences to describe the past week in great detail. Conversations are recounted, potential deals related, even his meals served over again, as if he were a spy, debriefing to his handler after coming in from the field. Through it all the girl lies, motionless, her eyes shut, her face expressionless. The smoothly-brushed jet hair, the paper-white skin, the pitifully narrow ridges of her body beneath the bedclothes, all these could be waxworks, or sculpture, except for the steady shallow breathing which continues as he speaks, as he has done every Tuesday since she was brought here from the hospital.

"...and that's about it," Jake sighs eventually, as his recitation brings him up to the present moment, nearly an hour after he began. Conscious of the nurse in the next room, his voice softens and its volume lowers as he continues. "Except to say I love you. In fact, it's kind of a funny thing, but I think - since this happened - I think that I actually love you more now than ever before. I'm sure that must sound odd, but ... When I thought you were going to die, Kimmie, I realized how much I would miss you and I told myself I'd do anything to avoid that; to keep you with me. And then you didn't die, and I knew it was meant to be. So now, even though we can't be together all the time, it's you I'm always thinking of. When I'm working out, when I'm driving around, I'm thinking 'Kim.' Everything I do, I do it for you. For the hope that one day you'll get better and we can live the life I picture for us. I love you Babe, I'll always love you, no matter what happens, and that's what's going to make you get better. I'm certain of it."

With that the big man leans over, kisses his sleeping princess on the lips, and departs.

Several minutes later Mavis is back in her favorite chair, the one with the apricot-colored brocade upholstery, set into the window bay where her reading is illuminated by soft daylight falling through sheer draperies. Another hour will pass in quiet rhythm, before the next event of her, and her patient's, day.

'Blood pressure unchanged. Kidney function unchanged. Body-mass appears to have stabilized. Urinalysis... no significant deviations from previous data.'

A man's voice, flat and bored. He sounds mature; middle-aged at least, perhaps older – damned hard to tell without seeing. There is a nasal quality to his words that suggests a city background... somewhere in the east perhaps? Oh, hell, who am I kidding? I'm no detective, it's just a voice - but what a progress that is; from struggling to catch some distant music, to hearing an actual human voice!

There are others as well, three altogether, and together is what they always are, showing up periodically ever since my hearing became reliable. Physicians, clearly. Discussing a patient. 'Christina,' they call her sometimes, but mostly she is just 'the subject,' an indication perhaps that her case is something beyond the ordinary. An element of study perhaps, or research. 'Subject unresponsive to reflex stimulation,' they say, or 'subject exhibiting signs of cognitive functioning on a sub-autonomous level,' things like that. It is only when the women speak that the men call her by name. Make it sound like they care more about her. You can actually tell when the women come in, by the change in the doctors' voices, the sympathetic tone they take all of a sudden. I've never noticed that before, how doctors speak among themselves, when no one else is around.

There are two women. One has a strong voice, direct and certain. I know she is called Mrs. Finch because I heard one of the men shut her up once. 'That will be enough, Mrs. Finch,' he said, when she asked about the timing of the patient's medications. Damned rude, the way he treated her, like she had no right having an opinion about anything at all. I thought she had a good question.

The other woman is more problematic. 'Mrs. McKloskey,' she is called, and everyone treats her with respect. Deference even. She always refers to the patient as 'Christina', or 'my Christina,' and her voice is not nearly as strong as all the others; it has that quavering quality so many women have when they get older, like she's always wondering if she should even be saying anything. Still, there's a determination in her words, and when she speaks the men all respond. It's odd that a patient's relative, even a parent – if that is what she is - seems to be so much in charge here.

What I make of this is that I am in a semi-private room in a teaching hospital. These conversations I am overhearing must concern another patient in the same room, Christina, who is undergoing some sort of experimental treatment. Mrs. McKloskey is the girl's mother; the three doctors an evaluation team. Mrs. Finch has got to be a nurse, and a damned good one, from what I have overheard.

And there's another patient as well - named Kim. I know this from her visitor, a young man. A large young man, by his voice, big and beefy. I've heard him talk to her for long periods, pretty personal stuff, but she never answers back, any more than this Christina does. Or me for that matter. And I never hear anyone else talk to or about Kim; why I do not know.

In any case, it seems likely that Mrs. Finch and the three doctors are caring for me as well as those two, as I never hear any other staff come around. The fact that I never hear any of them discussing me suggests my condition is stable. Too stable. 'Immobile, unresponsive, vegetative.' As far as they are concerned, I am just a body, being maintained.

They have no idea.

"It was so long ago," Elaine says, staring out across the smoky vaults of Nanking's main railroad station. Bustling crosscurrents of traffic pass before her eyes; strange people, wearing strange clothes and carrying unfamiliar articles, trailing children behind, or carrying them - infants whose swaddled wrappings make them look like artifacts of another era. From every direction they come and go, concealing and revealing one another, like theatrical set-pieces shifting in ever-changing layers to indicate the passage of time. This place feels so unreal; the very notion of traveling by train - especially one pulled by a steam locomotive - seems torn from a different century, from a story not her own. But then, this entire continent is like that. It is, as Beryl pointed out in an earlier installment of seems now like one great extended conversation 'disorienting. Which,' she had gone on to admit, without in any way acknowledging her own pun, 'is precisely its value, to a couple of old ladies from the modern occident.'

They have come here to continue the journey begun in Los Angeles and Japan, a curiously-evolving itinerary whose goal appears to be for Elaine to experience 'a smidge' of what Beryl has seen in her long travels. Have taken a bus from the airport to this station where they are to board a train to the interior. Perched now on a straight-backed wooden bench between a woman cradling a naked sleeping child and a man in immaculate Madison Avenue business attire they wait, watching the clocks carefully, for Elaine at least has no confidence they will be able to hear or comprehend any announcement of their train's departure over the din of shuffling feet and shouted conversations, of creaking luggage carts and snorting steam and the street traffic which, though it is outside the station, still makes its constant throb and clatter heard through banks of open doors, the sounds streaming in along with the thickly-sooty air which seems to characterize this city. Of course Beryl may hear, and understand. In their few days together – can it really be almost a week already? – Elaine has learned to respect her companion's ability to pluck important information out of static, and to communicate with nearly anyone she chooses, despite apparent differences of language, culture or attitude. Even now, as Elaine answers her question, and Beryl listens with all the attention one could ask, there is the sense that a part of her is elsewhere, watching and listening to things which Elaine can neither see nor hear.

"I was young," she continues. "Younger than Rodney by nearly four years, though you wouldn't know it to look at us. He was so soft in those days, so...unfinished. The face of a boy, perched on top of this gangly man's body, all arms and legs and neck. Soft round eyes, dark as chocolate and a little lost. I suppose that was one of the things that attracted me to him, he looked lost, and I thought - silly me - I thought I could help him find his way. That was the teacher in me. You know, I wanted to be a teacher for years, when I was a girl. I don't know when that changed to nursing, but with Rodney, it was that impulse to teach, to guide - to open his eyes - that pulled me in when I first saw him, tagging along with a gaggle of other interns behind some pompous old fart of a doctor."

Another thing she has picked up from Beryl: irreverence. Elaine Franks, daughter of a Baptist deacon and a Sunday school teacher, who has never used a swear word in her life, has begun to appreciate the liberating effect of the well-chosen phrase. Indifferent bureaucrats, un-swayed by the most logical of pleas, seem more vulnerable to humor or even reprimand, if delivered with sufficient wit. She has seen this demonstrated over and over as Beryl has piloted the two of them through a succession of travel bureaus, visa offices, ticket counters and hotel front desks to reach this place. Piloted them so smoothly, in fact, she's beginning to think there is *no* circumstance the woman cannot negotiate.

"Christina, Christina, Christina. Look what I found!" Ann McKloskey begins as she enters her daughter's room

"I was looking at some pictures last night, Sweetheart, and came across this snapshot of you with your father, on that silly little airplane thing they used to have in front of the supermarket. Remember? You would climb inside it and put in a... I don't remember, it must have been just a penny back then, it's probably a quarter now for heaven's sake... and it would rock back and forth. You thought that was such fun."

Anne holds a photograph in front of Christina's face, its eyes as peacefully and gently shut as those of a babe in the depths of sleep.

"It made me think of the two of you. How much fun you had together, back...before...."

That woman again!

Telling Christina all about her father. Making all sorts of apologies for him, the fact that he was away so much, that the two of them didn't get along. I gather from what she is saying that he is dead now, that he died in some sort of accident, at a time when he and the girl were not speaking to each other. The mother seems to be trying to make amends - to smooth over that hurt and regret. As if words could do that. As if words could ever change anything.

Enough of that pointless distraction. Something else has happened. Something much more important than eavesdropping on Mrs. McKloskey's conversations with her daughter. I saw.

Not just the blood-red light, but true seeing. A glimpse of the room in which I exist. It happened while the doctors were here, examining Christina. I heard them reviewing vitals and then, just as they were examining her for ocular response, I experienced a flash of vision. For a moment I could see a wall, pale yellow with a painting of flowers and fruit in a heavy gold frame. There was part of a window as well, with gold-colored curtains and lots of green outside. A dresser or some such, cluttered with framed photographs and other junk which I did not have time to really comprehend.   It was all so bright, and I had only a moment to take it in, but I thought I also saw, to one side, a man, dressed in a blazer and tie.

The vision lasted only a moment. My supposition is that while the doctors were examining the girl someone came over to me and, on a lark, pulled one of my eyes open, just as the doctors were doing with her. I was so shocked by this, the brightness, the colors, just the fact of seeing, that I lost track of what they were saying about her, and next thing I knew they were gone.

At first, I found myself tremendously excited by the incident, which I take to mean that my mind has developed the ability to once again process visual data. This fits with my hypothesis of damage to peripheral regions of the brain, but not the cortex. It seems as if, during my sleeping times, the pre-conscious functions have been receiving sensory inputs and gradually re-learning to sort them out and deal with them again. Reconstructing neural pathways, or building new ones to replace those which were damaged. The blood-red light must have been a minimal visual impression, my very first interpretation of light penetrating eyelids perpetually shut due to loss of motor function.

It is now some time since this incident occurred and the initial excitement has changed to something else; the peacefully nostalgic dreams which had been my sustenance for what seemed like a very long time are gone now. Instead, I find myself constantly recalling that glimpse of my surroundings, mining it for details. Those photos on the table, what were they photos of? The man I saw, what was his face like? The light coming through that window - was it morning light, or afternoon? A rainy day or a bright one? Now that I have had that glimpse it is intolerable that I cannot have more. All it needs is for me to open my eyelids; even just one *eyelid. Such a tiny movement, an infinitesimal gesture of volition and control, and yet it is beyond me, as impossible as a buried miner moving tons of earth to regain the surface. This I find infuriating, and yet I have no way to act upon my fury.*

Damn, damn, damn, damn, damn it all. Even The Nothing was better than this; this something-but-not-quite-anything in which I find myself now.

"That was the first time I saw him," Elaine continues, "and the first thing that caught my eye. It wasn't for weeks though, that we actually spoke. And that, when it happened, was enough to seal our fate."

A Saturday evening in a long-ago May, some girl's parents' home, all antiques and artifacts. Doors thrown open to the garden as dozens of people mill about in couples and clumps, clutching cocktails of the era; Rob Roys and Manhattans, Whiskey Sours and the occasional hard drinker's Martini. Invited to tag along by a fellow nursing student who knew the hostess from high school, Elaine sits idly on a sofa near the glowing fireplace, desperately trying to warm arms exposed by the sleeveless cocktail dress she has borrowed for the occasion, when a young man plops himself down next to her with obvious intent.

"I'm Rodney Gimbal," he says, extending the hand not holding his highball glass which, she will later learn, contains nothing but straight whiskey and ice. The hand, when she reaches out to touch it, is soft and warm. It does not squeeze and challenge hers, as some men do, but gently wraps the ends of her fingers, seeming to savor their touch for just a moment then releasing them, to join its mirror image in cradling the glass as its contents are swished in rapid circles, the only hint of nervousness she can detect in his manner.

A conversation ensues – who do you know here, what do you do, how do you like it. The usual questions, the usual answers, but with a probing intent she has never felt before from a boy. He really *wants* to know these things, Elaine realizes, he really *cares* why I chose nursing, how I decided to go into pediatric care.

"That was so new to me..." Elaine relates to Beryl, as a runny-nosed toddler approaches them, hoping for a handout, or at least a smile. He is not disappointed in the latter, as the two women gaze with the softness of grandmothers, only to cringe when a teenaged girl in a close-buttoned blue jacket and crimson pedal-pusher pants scuffs up behind the child, grabbing one arm and wrenching it around to draw him away, squirming and twisting as he goes, trying desperately to keep his eyes on these ghostly strangers for as long as possible.

"...that a boy would actually be interested in what I had to say." Yes, there had been encounters with boys before; but always, Elaine had had the feeling they were operating on a sort of autopilot. Making the expected comments, saying the things they thought it fashionable to say, while all the while their true attention was elsewhere. She was a prop, an accessory, to their real interest, which was in themselves, their surroundings, their associates or their futures. With Rodney though, it was different. His questions probed - each answer leading to a new question, so that before she knew it she was talking to him about things she never intended to share with such a stranger. Not unlike Beryl, in that way - at least on that first meeting.

"That first glimpse in the ward was one thing but it was our conversation by the fire that truly made me want to be with Rodney. It was an impression that lasted...well, years actually. Long after it should have. Because that was the only time really, that he acted quite that way. Oh, I think we got into a certain mode of speaking to one another, and it was shaped by that evening, but it was never quite the same, and yet...I behaved as if it was. In retrospect..." she halts, wondering why she is speaking so formally, realizes it is because she is making these arguments not to Beryl, not to herself, but to some higher authority who lives within her. "In retrospect, it is as if I so much wanted that first impression to be the truth, that I never allowed myself to notice it was an anomaly. An 'unforeseeable atypical outcome,' as Rodney might phrase it. Attributable, I found out, to his medical training."

Another ancient evening, another sofa, this time Rodney and Elaine's own. Another gathering, this one professional, as the young couple pay down an installment on his social and organizational standing. Rodney at his most relaxed, sitting straight-backed, jacketed and neck-tied with another highball glass in his hand, when a colleague asks him how he met his 'beautiful wife.' Passing by on her hostess duties, a tray of finger sandwiches held carefully before her, Elaine pauses some distance behind her husband as he relates the tale, unaware of her presence. The story is the same one she has told, even to the same phrasing, until she hears him chuckle a bit, sees him lean closer to the obese Senior Supervising of Thoracic, a man Rodney has known for years.

"That was the same week I'd been called on the carpet by old Vigeborg, you remember him? Pulled me into his office and told me I'd never make it through the program if I didn't learn how to talk to patients. Said I had no 'manner.' Made me spend an afternoon with one of the psych. residents of all things, being told how to *involve* the patient in their treatment. Draw them out into a conversation, and make them believe I was concerned about their feelings, what they expected out of their treatment."

The party has gone silent for Elaine, the tray motionless and weightless in her hands as she listens.

"Mumbo-jumbo," she hears her husband say; "that's all it was to me; way to keep everybody happy so I could do my work. Anyway, that was the same day I met Elaine, that evening, and so I tried it out with her - my new bedside manner. Worked pretty well too, the way I see it."

For some time now I have been seeing, though not very consistently.

The first time was quite a surprise; I awakened from a dream of a hospital - obviously inspired by my overhearing conversations about this patient Christina. In fact, I have concluded that many of my dreams for some time have actually been inspired by fragmentary perceptions of the outside world. Bits of information rattling around in my brain until they find a hint of connection, then gradually assembling into semi-coherent explanations of themselves. In this latest dream I was one of several physicians discussing the care of a young girl, and I found myself having to tell her parents that she would not survive. I felt a measure of sadness of course, at the unfortunate death of one so young, but such things happen all the time; what was significant was that I felt I had not performed as I expected of myself, and that was excruciatingly painful. An intense regret filled my dream, a longing to go back and correct what could not be corrected, every bit as intense as the frustration I have been experiencing in my waking times, over not being able to act on even my simplest intentions. It was from that agony of guilt and powerlessness that I awoke to find myself staring into the face of a woman - an honest to God, flesh and blood, fussing-around-my-head-with-her-hands-in-my-face, human being. Something in the way she behaved – moving carelessly in and out of my field of vision, chattering amiably enough, but with clearly no expectation that I should respond to her words - made clear that she was real. Outside of my imaginings.

Once again, it is the lack of correspondence with my own thoughts that seems to prove a thing is not a fabrication - the limitations of a gift that assure me it is truly to be treasured.

Though it lasts for some minutes at a time, the perceptions bear a burden of unreality which I attribute to my inability to control just what I see. As much as I have tried to do so, I cannot seem to choose when my eyes open or close, nor can I move them. The woman I first encountered - obviously a nurse, apparently the one I've heard addressed as Mavis - will move in or out of my field of vision, and I cannot follow her. It is like observing the world through a hole punched in a distant wall. The picture changes as people move past the aperture, but the background is always the same - the same single patch of wall and window.

It is a blessing, this sight, a connection to the world, but also a frustration. To watch someone for minutes, only to have them disappear but still be in the room. I feel violated in a way, as I realize this woman can see and hear me every minute. That she must be caring for my bodily functions, changing my bedclothes, washing me, and I cannot even speak to her.

I have a renewed sense of time as well. Each time the darkness engulfs me again, I find myself waiting, anticipating sight's return. When it does not come I grow impatient. It is a good thing there is not a clock within my field of view, for I should find myself counting the minutes, the seconds, until something noteworthy happens. How many days have I lain here, how many weeks? Or is it months, maybe even years? I had thought myself about to die before all this, and later, for a time, considered the possibility I was already dead. Now I am convinced I am alive, but without understanding, without control, without any way to express myself or to act out my life.

It has been only a few days, as best I can guess, since this crippled-vision began, but already I am seriously wondering how long I can endure living in this fashion.

"This is a lovely house," Mary Antonias says, as the woman ushers her into the foyer, taking great care in the act of shutting the door - both hands pressing it softly into its frame with scarcely a sound other than the lock-bolt clicking into place.

Mary has parked her car in the driveway, quite careful herself to set the brake against the steep slope of the driveway which rises up from a curving stretch of Arbor Street. The house is more than gracious; some might even say grand, though with a slightly-neglected look. Nothing much, just a bit of peeling paint on a window sill, a cobweb at the corner of the porch roof above the front stoop. Just enough to distract her as she rang the bell, not knowing quite what to expect in the way of a welcome.

From their brief phone conversation, it had seemed to Mary that the woman was quite personable. Hardly the delusional fanatic suggested in those rumors which had flickered around Hilltop when the girl's custody was being determined. Neither did Mrs. McKloskey seem pretentious enough to be the widow of Sean McKloskey, revered leader of the Athos quartet, Seattle's famous contribution to the world of chamber music. Not a fan of the genre, still Mary recognized the name from public radio pledge drives and concert announcements scanned while browsing the Sunday Arts & Entertainment section, and that was enough to know that Sean McKloskey had been the real deal - world famous, eminently cultured, and used to swimming in the warmest waters of the social pool.

The woman who answered the door, on the other hand, seemed actually to be quite ordinary. The quiet, well-kept sort of neighbor anyone might live beside and never really get to know. A bit formal perhaps, the blue wool suit buttoned over a white linen top, the heels comfortably low - but heels nonetheless. Product of a generation or two before Mary's own, with all the differences of attitude which that implied.

The house itself, once inside, is more than nice - spacious and well decorated, with mementos of the husband's career covering almost every surface. Which is to say that Mary assigns Sean McKloskey's name to the man in a photograph on the foyer wall, his cello held casually across his chest. Sean McKloskey again, in an impressive painted portrait over the fireplace, staring off past the viewer like Meriwether Lewis about to set out for an unseen coast.

"My husband was an inspiring man," Anne agrees, seeing Mary's eyes drawn to the portrait. A natural docent, she touches the younger woman's elbow and gently guides her into the living room to view it at a closer distance. "He brought out the best in people, myself included. When I lost him it... it has taken me a long time to regain a sense of purpose."

For a moment Mary thinks the introduction will stop there, giving just that hint of what is going on in her life, as one might expect when speaking to a total stranger. But then she continues, speaking in the formal tone of one giving an interview, or reciting for the record facts which she has carefully prepared beforehand.

"A young woman like you might expect that a widow's life would center around caring for her daughter, assuming the burden of being both mother and father to her. But Christina would not have that, you see. She was just old enough to resent her father for dying; not mature enough to understand that it was not his fault. Or mine. Or hers for that matter. Instead of drawing the two of us closer, her resentment turned his absence into a wedge that...well...aside from what it did to her life, it left me rather adrift. I had always been so busy before - Sean was a very focused person, as you might guess. In anything that had to do with his music he was a perfectionist, and unbelievably capable; and financially as well - he understood money in a way I must confess I never have, but beyond that, well...he was really quite helpless, and so I took care of everything. The house... his clothes...his correspondence...even his personal needs – doctors, dentist, when to get his hair cut, when to take a day off. Now, so much of that was gone. Oh, at first after his death, there was even *more* to do; people to be notified and soothed, commitments to cancel, legal arrangements to revise; I thought it would never end. But then, slowly, gradually, it did. And I found myself with time to fill and Christina..."

The woman never stops talking as she makes her guest comfortable in the primly formal space, its wide windows filtered by sheer curtains, flanked by drapes which strike Mary as a bit too ornate in their heavily brocaded borders and tassels. Nor does she show the slightest curiosity as to why Mary has chosen to visit. Even as she steps into an adjoining room, returning instantly with a tray of tea things and an array of rather stale cookies, served on a cut-glass platter - elegant despite the obvious chip upon its rim - she continues telling the story of her struggle to shift the effort previously spent on her husband's life to that of her daughter, just as the girl's need for

106

independence was growing. All of her efforts succeeded only in driving mother and daughter ever farther apart - until the day Christina turned up in the hospital under an assumed name.

"Oh my, that was a day," Mrs. McKloskey almost sings, her eyes lighting up at the memory. "I positively flew into action then," and it is abundantly clear to Mary that the battle for her child has given Mrs. McKloskey a new reason for living. Just as she had cared for her husband, now she can care for Christina. Doctors, insurance companies, even the limitations of the patient's own physiology, these are not obstacles to Anne McKloskey, but opportunities. As the monologue continues, Mary feels herself developing a certain admiration for the woman. Small and wiry, her hands and wrists nothing but bone and skin, she yet manages to project an energy and power which would make her a formidable adversary for anyone, though Mary finds - to some surprise - that she herself is instantly assumed to be an ally.

She had been prepared for more resistance to her visit. Some reasonable degree of skepticism as to why a young doctor from sprawling Hilltop Medical Center, who had never even officially cared for the girl, would make the journey here, after all this time, to visit a patient who could not possibly be aware of her presence. A question she has asked herself many times of course; the ensuing debates a large part of the reason she is only now following through on what she has been drawn to do since she watched the orderly wheel that gurney out to start its journey. Those internal debates have clarified her feelings, given her a name for them, but have not removed them. Stepping back a bit, Mary knows it is not healthy - this obsession with one about whom she knows almost nothing - and yet the memories of those moments in the ICU will not leave her. She glimpsed something there, in that unconscious and unresponsive face, which will not be forgotten. How this girl could seem so blessed despite everything which had happened to her, is a question Mary cannot put down. It is the reason she is here; nervous, impatient, yet willing to put up with all Mrs. McKloskey's prattling to be admitted once again into the child's presence.

Nearly an hour of prattling, it turns out, before Mary is ushered finally through kitchen, out the back door and across the pool terrace, its chalky blue flagstones matted with soggy leaves smelling slightly of rot, to what Mrs. McKloskey referred to as 'our little guest house.' A one-story, shingled structure, it hardly fits in with the taller stone facade of the main house, though the exteriors of each, as well as the space between, are equally neglected, now that Mary sees them close up. Here a chair with upholstery faded and split from exposure, there a pot still overflowing with stalks and heads of long-dead flowers. The pool itself is brackish and scummy, a tea of brown leaves forming in the low end, as gray clouds skitter across the bit of sky visible above. Beyond that, overgrown shrubs enclose a yard which seems dark and cramped, more leftover space than garden.

"Mavis," Mrs. McKloskey announces as she enters the small house without knocking, "This is Mary Antonias. She knows Christina from the hospital. Mary, this is Mavis Finch, our nurse." The nurse greets Mary with crisply professional courtesy, then makes herself scarce as the two women approach the bed.

The patient Mary sees is much changed from the one she met at Hilltop. Gone are the bandages which swathed her head, replaced now by gentle sweeps of soft black hair which has been brushed and arranged to make the most of its still boy-short length. Her skin, which has not seen the sun's light for over two months now, has still a rosy glow, result of the carefully applied makeup which outlines her eyes and presents her lips, full and warm yet somehow artificial looking, so static and set are they. The face is thinner though, than she recalls it; zygomatic arches standing out in bold relief, the mandible visible against neck and cheeks, both of which have been edited down to nearly nothing. A human body, Mary knows, cannot thrive on intravenous nutrition, but only just survive. Nor can it maintain its mass - confined to a bed the muscles atrophy and shrink from disuse, even with regular manipulation.

While all these observations are expected, and readily explicable, there is another which startles Mary and chills her. The patient's eyes, she finds, are open. Truly-open that is; not the over-dilated pilot lights of the massively-traumatized, nor the sleepy sagging dim-bulbs of the drugged and indifferent. Admittedly immobile, they do not follow as she steps around the bed, nor react to a hand passed before them, but yet… These eyes, oddly azure against ebony hair, seem alive and alert. Mary cannot avoid feeling that something is happening behind their glistening surface.

"Mavis has to put an ointment on her, yes," Mrs. McKloskey offers proudly, and Mary realizes her shock has been taken for appreciation. "To keep them moist. She doesn't blink, like we do. Just opens her eyes now and then, and stares off into the distance for a while. Sometimes for a few minutes, sometimes for hours. Daytime, nighttime, it doesn't seem to matter. And then, we look back and they're closed again."

Suddenly Mary finds her entire purpose undermined. She had come here expecting a waxwork; had come, she now realizes, to put a final nail in the coffin. Everything she knew about Kim Tree's condition when she had been at Hilltop told Mary that the girl could only have deteriorated here, under what amounted to hospice care, her body progressing through the long slow decline to eventual shut down. She had expected the emaciated limbs, the hollow sunken features. Had expected really, to find the girl's mouth filled with a respirator tube, her arteries plumbed for feeding, her eyes taped shut. Mary had expected many things, but not this. Not the spark which seems to shine in those eyes, unblinking though they may be. From that first glimpse Mary is certain, against all odds, that there is a mind behind those eyes. The feeling is powerful enough that she finds herself whispering to Mrs. M., carefully holding her voice down in case those ears, with their pearl earrings peeking out from beneath her slowly-growing locks, are equally alive.

"What do the doctors say about this?" she asks, stepping off to the side, out of what might be the girl's line of sight.

"Dr. Sen tells me she can't actually see anything," Mrs. M. announces, sounding suprisingly-unfazed by that diagnosis. "He says it is simply an autonomic reflex. A random pulse of activity somewhere in her nervous system opens her eyes and they stay open until another random event closes them."

"And what do you think?"

"I think Christina is here with us," Anne says, ever the proud parent. "Whether she can see us or not, she's right here, and our job is to love her." Turning from Mary to her motionless daughter, Anne's face expands in a broad smile, her chin rises just a touch and her hands clasp in front of her chest. "Just the way she is."

Leaving the house a few minutes later, Mary takes only the slightest notice of the rusty brown sedan parked across the street, one skinny arm draped out the driver's window holding a smoldering cigarette. 'How can anyone still smoke, with all the information out there?' she wonders, before her thoughts turn to her upcoming floor shift. She is well down the block, headed for her bus stop, by the time Aubrey stubs her cigarette on the outside of the car's door and drops it to the pavement, rolls her window up against the possibility of rain, and climbs out for another visit to her lost friend. Aubrey has noticed Mary though, taken in the clunky shoes and briefcase. 'One of them,' is her reaction; one of the ones keeping Kim cooped up in that room, looking like the first installment in her mother's doll collection. Still, at least this one's a girl, and she's younger than the rest; it might be worth knowing who she is. 'Mrs. M. will tell me,' Aubrey thinks, as she crosses the street and heads up the steps to the front door. 'If I suck up to her real nice.'

On the train now, Elaine and Beryl pass through an industrial district as they head out of town, on the way to Luoyang. Gray factory buildings streaked by the downpour sit close by the tracks, their blocky masses alternating with muddy lanes bustling with traffic. Trucks and cars, yes, but so much more; pedestrians, bicycles, freight carrying tricycles, pushcarts, even oxcarts - handmade wooden apparitions fitted with motorcycle wheels and tires - appear and disappear as the train accelerates. At low speed, these lanes are scenes; visible for long enough that Elaine may notice an individual, a detail of signage, the color of a hat, but as the train speeds up they pass more quickly, like flashcards presented for quick familiarization, then faster still, until they are segments in a montage, impressions only, their meaning generated by the internal associations her mind makes, even before her consciousness can register the information her eyes are receiving. As the factories give way to neighborhoods of shops and residential buildings, the years with Rodney are flashing by too; days and weeks and months spent in work and housekeeping, get-togethers with friends, and then the occasional vacation trip to another city where Rodney would attend seminars and - eventually, when his expertise had grown - present them. The conversations she had with other women, wives of other surgeons.

"Rodney is wonderfully understanding," she recalls herself saying. "Not one of those doctors who are all wrapped up in themselves. He cares about his patients. Cares about me."

It was a well-rehearsed piece of marketing, she tells Beryl over tea accompanied by rice enhanced with egg and sugar and what Beryl tells her are osmanthus flowers. The power of that first fireside encounter proven by how long its effects lasted, despite all the contradictory evidence.

"It's as if I had formed this opinion of Rodney that first evening, and then put my mind on a sort of setting. Had defined how I saw him and how I saw myself based on that one conversation and then behaved as if that was the whole truth for... for nearly forty years. I just wouldn't let anything else change it, for the longest time. It was only when I reached a certain age, and I began to question...to *re-form* the *vision* I had of myself ..." - and here she understands she is using familiar words in new ways, learned in just the last few weeks from her companion - "...that I was even able to see it for what it was. I'd been projecting my desires onto the canvas of this person called Rodney, and refusing to see anything which didn't fit with what I wanted my husband to be."

Beryl eats the rice with her fingers - head bent forward as if by the years, bowl held close to it, a thumb and two fingers ferry small clumps of sticky grains to narrow lips where they are plucked perfectly, every grain captured, with airy little popping noises – and all the while her eyes are on Elaine's. Somehow, despite the bumps and jostles of the primitive roadbed, the swaying suspension which seems to send them rotating up and to the left, then down, then up again and to the right, her eyes remain fixed upon Elaine, just as her signature expression of slight amusement is fixed. The effect is one of otherworldly intensity, and Elaine feels these conversations, interspersed as they are between the mundane tasks of finding their way, accommodations, food and permits, are explorations into her unknown past, just as their journey is an exploration into unfamiliar territory. Or rather, unfamiliar to Elaine; for to Beryl everything seems known.

"That's what we do, dear, when we're filled up with the world. We invent our own shorthand for things, including people, and then the name becomes the thing. The fallacy is that we fix our visions - the names inside our heads - when the truth is that all the things in this world are changing all the time, but like clouds on a windless day, many of them change so slowly that we do not notice. We just wake up one day and are shocked to find them different. And if all we pay attention to is the *name* we have given a thing, we don't even do that. All we do is register the name, presume the thing is still what we understood it to be when we named it, and totally ignore all that has grown different in the interval."

For many years, Elaine recalls just then, her father wore a mustache, full and bristly. As a child sitting on his lap she loved to play with it, rubbing her forehead against its sharp ends, giggling and tickled and soaking-in the scent of his bay water and rum aftershave. Later, she went off to nursing school and came home for visits, a few days here, a week there. On one of those visits, she noticed her father's upper lip, clean shaven. 'Daddy,' she cried, 'you shaved your mustache!'

'Oh, princess,' he answered with a smile. 'I shaved it off months ago. I was wondering when you would notice.'

Ambushed by the memory, Elaine shakes her head to clear it.

Looking up, she finds Beryl beaming in her direction.

"We recognize the people most central to our lives by the expected," she says, wiping the inside of her rice bowl with a handkerchief, before replacing it in one of several drawstring bags between her ankles. "And if we see something unexpected, we pass right over it, because it doesn't fit what we've already decided we know about them." Reaching down between her feet she lifts from the floor a carafe filled with tea purchased at the most recent stop and pours into her tiny cup enough for just a few sips. "We petrify our concept of the ones we love, at the price of their growth." Brings the tea cup to her lips and sips, this time with a gentle slurping; polite acknowledgement that the tea is fine. "And our own."

Thinking the comment complete, Elaine nods and is about to speak when the other continues.

"We desire to build our lives on something solid and stable," she states, with utmost generosity. "But when you puzzle over how your life has turned out, you might ask yourself, which is the more enduring – those things which are firm and solid, or those which change and shift until they seem to have no form at all? When you ask that question, and understand the answer, you will understand more about yourself. And your Rodney."

Distraction. The new interns had been warned about it in orientation, an event which seems a lifetime ago. 'You cannot do this job with 90% of your attention,' a hoary old lecturer had droned. 'You cannot answer this calling with 98% attention. You must be 100% focused at all times. Your success as an intern depends upon 100% attention, your career depends upon it. Lives depend upon it.'

It is a lesson which Mary had always found easy to follow. Life on the floor was so intense, so full of the new and different, of challenges and surprises, that her mind had never wandered. Until, that is, she encountered the comatose Jane/Kim/Chris.

Mary had hoped the visit to Mrs. McKloskey's house would put an end to the distraction. That the sight of a terminal patient slowly fading into oblivious death would have consigned her obsession to history. Instead, she finds her thoughts returning even more frequently to the subject, and to its suddenly urgent corollaries: what could possible account for the sparkle behind those eyes, and why is her condition not deteriorating as her previous state would predict? Now, today, a new question has bubbled to the surface, as Mary sits quietly through a presentation on proper treatment nomenclature to facilitate Medicaid pre-authorization requests and her wandering mind returns to something the girl's nurse had mentioned - offhandedly just as Mary was about to leave - about the girl's medications. An anti-rejection regime, she'd said, for the new kidney. The medications Mavis described were correct, if atypically dosed and timed; it is the condition that now seems totally wrong, for, if the Jane had no neural activity upon arrival, as was the story around MH that day and ever since, there was no way the Transplant Board would authorize a transplant, or any funding source would agree to pay for it. Even in the unlikely event both those miracles occurred, the common waiting time for a Status 1 patient, the most urgent transplant candidates, was measured in weeks or months, and yet a match had been found for this patient, literally overnight.

Distraction is dangerous. Distraction causes mistakes as you zombie through your work, mind focused on one thing while your hands, your eyes, your voice, are occupied with another.

Feeling one's attention divided like this, Mary realizes - the self-awareness adding yet another strand of thought to those already competing for bandwidth inside her head - can drive a person to...distraction.

Early morning and the workroom is dim, overhead lights cut, only two monitors glowing silently to themselves as Mary enters. It is not that she has no right to be here that has caused her body temperature to rise; this is where she performs research and enters records every day. Rather, it is what she suspects she will find that calls up a slight sweat to moisten the small of her back and the palms of her hands as she sits at the farthest station, from which she will see anyone entering the room and have time to minimize a window on her screen before they come close enough to see the data it's displaying.

Transplants are a tightly regulated business. Money is one reason; these are expensive surgeries, with even more expensive follow-up care. Learning is another. Swapping organs is still a relatively young field of practice, and every transplant has the potential to teach something more about technique, treatment and outcome. But fear is perhaps the greatest incentive for the medical establishment to monitor transplants so carefully. Ever since the first surgeons began opening corpses to see what was inside, the public has feared them almost as much as it benefited from their work. Where did those early explorers of the internal find their subjects? Were those subjects really dead, and even if they were, could one be certain that medical curiosity came only *after* the fact, and did not play a role in soliciting - or even causing - their deaths?

It is those fears, and the related concern that organs might prove so precious a black market would arise and individuals be pressured to sell their parts - or others to collect them without, as it were, the prior owners' authorization - that has led every developed nation to enact laws governing the harvesting, transportation and implantation of human organs. From those laws has grown a body of organizations and procedures and with them, records, and it is those records which Mary wishes to access this early morning.

With a few clicks of a mouse, she enters the Patient Data Reference System, submitting her pass-code for authorization, and proceeds to make half a dozen routine inquiries. Regarding the Tumosky girl's new blood-thinning prescription, Mary checks for any other medications the child is taking and with which it might adversely interact. Timothy Allison is scheduled for a biopsy on his stomach tumor in the morning; no one will question her verifying that his insurer's pre-authorization has been received. Only after fifteen minutes of similarly mundane inquiries does she utilize the internal directory to find a link to Hilltop's Organ Transplant Program, one of the dozens of internal units operating within the hospital, and one with which she has never before had reason to deal.

As a resident, the patient registry is open to Mary, and there she finds her first surprise. An inquiry for Christina McKloskey yields a firm 'No Record found.' For Kim Tree the same, and the same again for Jane Doe, even with the date range set a two full weeks before and after the girl's admittance. Distracting.

There are more ways than one though, to scan a cat. A few key strokes brings her to the minutes of TAC, the Transplant Authorization Committee, which reviews every Transplant Authorization Request generated within, or submitted to, the Center. Here again, a search reveals no record under any of the familiar names. Search by date yields three TARs submitted on the date Christina was admitted; two males and one forty-seven year old woman, whose request was terminated when she herself terminated before the board could act.

Her curiosity mounting, Mary backs out of the Center's records folders and opens an internet browser. In a moment, 'www.optn.org' brings her to the Organ Procurement and Transportation Network website, national clearinghouse for the most vital component of any transplant. Here she is stymied, her Hilltop Resident's access code insufficient to get her past the usual introductions, boilerplate and FAQ lists, to view the voluminous organ allocation records she knows OPTN must maintain.

It s only after another half hour of fruitless searching for Medicaid PA requests, third party insurance contacts and other evidence of the approval process that she realizes she has overlooked an obvious starting point. While Christina's own daily treatment records will not explain the reasons for authorization, or the speed of locating a donor, they should at least shed light on why a patient in such grave condition was considered a candidate in the first place. Mary's fingers are nimble now, flying through territory familiar from hundreds of similar requests made over the years. With total confidence she enters first one, then another and finally the third, of the three names she has heard used for this patient and finds - once, twice and three times - no record at all.

Sitting back from the monitor, Mary Antonias sighs deeply, the fatigue of a long day finally settling in. There will be no relief tonight, from her 'distraction,' which - she strongly suspects - is about to become...an obsession.

Elaine studies her hands, gripping the top rail of the seat ahead. In truth, she notes, the knuckles are not 'white.' They are actually more striped; those areas of skin stretched directly over the bones and tendons shining a taught, pale yellow, while in the hollows between them, trapped blood pools to produce a bright hot pink; emblem of the effort required to hold herself upright against the jouncing-bouncing-rollicking motion the bus is making as it winds its way up, along some unnamed river, toward what might be the final pass, or might be just another in the seemingly endless succession of ridges and minor summits they have crossed in the past six hours en route to see the famous Dazu Rock carvings.

Beside her Beryl sleeps, wedged securely between Elaine's shoulder and the steel shell of the bus, the most prominent portions of its surface burnished by wear to a bright luster, the less prominent areas coated thick with decades' accumulation of dirt and grime. To Elaine's other side, across the aisle, a woman swathed in little more than rags nurses an infant, the two somehow managing to appear no more concerned about the bus's motion than they are about the eyes of this foreigner who has inserted herself into the midst of a busload of locals returning from whatever errands had taken them to the precinct's central trading town.

Whole families had boarded the bus in the pre-dawn darkness, and also women without men - alone but for the infants in their arms or the children trailing along by a hand twisted into skirt or sleeve, or the gaggles of offspring swarming around them like planets to their mothers' suns. Old men too, who could barely climb the bus's steps, and boys barely into their teens who appeared by themselves and behaved with all the authority and independence one could hope of adults. These people and more are her companions as this journey extends itself, and gradually Elaine is beginning to feel the early shoots of kinship with them. In a town where they stayed in Japan, she had bartered with an innkeeper to trade her leather purse for one made of the heaviest silk cloth she has ever seen, embroidered with cherry blossoms. In Nanking it was shoes; replacing her traveling pumps with a pair of lace-up oxfords, so as to be ready to walk for hours on a moment's notice. More recently, it was a full skirt of deepest indigo and a padded jacket with toggles in place of buttons. Looking in the mirror, when first she tried those on, she hardly recognized herself, a sensation which might also have been due to the whiteness spreading throughout her hair.

"It must be the stress of traveling," she suggested to Beryl one morning, as the two of them were dressing in the small hostel where they stayed for over a week while their applications for travel farther west were being masticated by yet another layer of the country's many-tentacled bureaucracy.

"Do you feel stress?"

"No," Elaine admitted with surprise. "Not really."

"What do you feel these days - your overall sense of yourself, that is, not just one moment?"

"I feel...liberated. Lighter. I feel free."

Beryl's mouth took on that wry twist which Elaine has learned signifies an impending teacher/pupil moment, a doling out of the wisdom which perhaps accounts for her friend's unflappable serenity, as well as her occasional lapses into a sometimes ponderous pedantry.

"You _are_ free. You have set yourself free to be who you are, and in so doing you have let go of some unnecessary baggage; and one of the pieces of baggage you have left behind - somewhere between Miyajima and Guangzhou, I would guess - is the desire to be younger than you really are. Your hair is turning white, Elaine, because you are ready to accept yourself having white hair. That is the way things work when things are working the way things are meant to work."

She called <u>me</u> *Christina!*

Another piece of the puzzle revealed and it only makes the whole solution more obscure. This morning - I have taken to estimating the time of day by the position and angle of shadows cast through the window; early in the day, shadows fall to the right of the window, stretching across the wall beside the dresser, and then as time progresses they grow more narrow, and more nearly vertical; then for a time there is no distinct shadow, and the window itself is at its brightest. Later still, the shadows return, cast now to the left, and sometimes a direct beam of sunlight enters to fall on the chair whose wingback I can just see at the corner of my eye. I have watched this progression, minute by minute for days now, noticing variations I would certainly have missed at any other time in my life, made consequential now by the fact I have so little else to notice, except when Mavis, or Mrs. McKloskey, or some other comes to visit. Then I am treated to the dumb show of people moving in and out of view, of faces thrust rudely into my own, tilting and turning, peering at me as if I were a freak in a sideshow; as if I were an object on display. Don't they realize that I can hear them? Don't they see my eyes are open?

I imagine myself screaming, raging at their ignorance, if only I had a voice to rage with. Yes, I know they do not understand, and I should have pity on them, but it is so...demeaning, this enforced passivity. This is not who I am; a person who lies around waiting, hoping. I have always believed in doing, *and now I realize just how central that is to my sense of myself...*

And then - this morning - that crazy woman, that 'Mrs. McKloskey,' leaned her flaccid jowls down into my face and addressed me as 'Christina'!

I wanted to twist and turn away - no, I wanted to reach out and grab her, to shake some sense into her. To scream at the top of my lungs 'I am not Christina!'

"The doctors don't agree with me, of course. I don't mind telling you - they are just as pessimistic as they've always been, but I reminded them how important it is to have a positive attitude, and they finally admitted it can't hurt, so I'm going keep playing your father's favorite music, and I'm going to keep on talking to you. Reminding you all about yourself, and about me, your father, and our family. All the things you used to love. You don't have to do anything, darling, you just listen. I'll do the talking for both of us."

Anne McKloskey is sitting on the edge of her daughter's bed, early on an April morning. As always, music plays softly in the room, this time a brass quintet trilling baroque fanfares in seemingly endless triumph. Outside the window, sunlight is peaking through a gap in the cloud cover, a single band of brilliance slicing across the laurel hedge and one corner of the swimming pool, its surface still littered with last fall's debris. The water has turned a deep tannin brown from the rotting leaves steeping in it for months and months; nearby, lawn chairs sit in disarray, their cushions bird-spotted and berry-stained and intermittently grayed by mildew spreading out from moisture perpetually pooling in seams and creases. An iced-tea glass rests on a table, in the same place it occupied on that May day when Anne first drove over to Hilltop to identify as her beloved Christina the Jane Doe whose photo appeared in the newspaper .

"I first met Sean during my junior year at Bennington," the tale begins. "I had gone to New York with several friends to visit the museums. One of the girls, Sally Batcheldor, had an aunt who had an apartment near Gramercy Park. The aunt was out of town so we could stay there for free; four young women, two of whom had never even *been* to New York City before. It was just glorious, Christina, glorious. We drove into town down the West Side Highway, with the river on our right, the Palisades across the water, and the city looming on the left. I had never seen anything so...all encompassing; a city that could swallow up every place I'd ever known before and hide it in a corner without anyone ever knowing."

Time passes quickly for Anne as she relives this pivotal moment of her youth. Happily she recounts to the silent figure in the bed how the girls shared the aunt's tiny apartment, littering it with dresses and night gowns, curlers and makeup, as they prepared themselves to blend in with the sophisticated Manhattan crowd. Describes also their eye-opening first experiences of the

Metropolitan Museum of Art, the Museum of Natural History, the Guggenheim, and others. For three days they soaked up the culture of a city which Anne, growing up in an engineer's home on the north side of Rochester, had only read about and dreamed of.

It was on the third evening that the girls attended the concert. Sally's aunt had suggested it, when the niece called to arrange the apartment.

"You *have* to go to a concert at the Chamber Academy," she had said. "It's a piece of the old world."

God save me, I am surrounded by delusionary maniacs.

The woman thinks I am her daughter, the man thinks I am his long lost love. The doctors are a trio of bumbling idiots and the nurse could care less about my condition, so long as she gets to read her magazines and watch her soap operas. And now this; this unbearable punishment of listening for hours on end to that woman recounting her life in my face.

A life which has nothing whatsoever to do with me. Hardly even a life, this endless drone of meeting and falling in love and birthing and raising a child - a whining woman's reflections and remembrances, regrets and recriminations. 'And then my husband did this and I went along and saw that.' As if holding his hand while he marches through life is itself an achievement.

Obviously she is deluded, calling me Christina, mistaking me for her daughter. But what of the authorities? There must be someone in charge in this place, someone who knows about her condition and is responsible to keep her away from the other patients. Or do they think my being mute and helpless gives license to cast me into her theater of delusion?

If even one person here were just a little less interested in their own talking and more in observing, surely they must see I am alive. Surely there has been some change in my appearance since I became able to hear and see. A different expression, a light in the eyes, something. Or maybe not. Maybe it's up to me then, to find some way to hit them over the head with it. I've been trying for days now, to move a muscle, to find something I can do, but it's like reaching out in the dark for a door knob you think should be right there, and finding nothing. You can't open the door until you find the doorknob, and I can't find anything. I imagine moving my hand and nothing happens. Try to open my mouth to speak, again nothing. The only thing that ever changes is my eyes being open or closed and I can't control that. Not that I haven't tried; good lord, I have tried again and again.. When I wake to find my eyes open, I imagine closing them, nothing happens. When I find myself in darkness, I imagine opening them, seeking to feel the right muscles, the particular sensation that will have an effect, but...nothing. Still, this is my best hope; to concentrate on opening an eyelid...

Jesus H. Christ! A lifetime of striving, of accomplishing every objective I ever set for myself, and I am reduced to hours of helpless listening to whatever idiot afflicts me while I struggle to move a single muscle.

I am here goddamn it! I am thinking and feeling. I have things to say.

Will nobody ever see that?

With a lurching swerve the bus rounds another curve and Elaine sees the road ahead drop away, leaving only sky visible through the windshield. 'I hope,' she thinks, 'that this bus's brakes work as they are meant to work.' Imagining Beryl's response to such a thought - 'the brakes will work if they are meant to work, at this time, for this load of passengers' - she feels the pull of a small, wry smile at her own mouth and wonders what would be the look on Rodney's face if he could see her now. White-haired, native-clad, dusty and sun burnt, her battered luggage lashed to the roof among all manner of cages, crates and sacks. Winding her way by bus into the central-China foothills to visit another ancient marvel of which she had never even heard as recently as ten days ago. A wellspring of joy flows up from somewhere deep inside her as she realizes she does not need his opinion to evaluate the changes she has been through; is still going through.

When Beryl, sitting in a booth of that synthetic LA restaurant, had proposed that they must set off on a grand tour, it seemed an absurd idea. There were so many reasons she had planned a trip of only a week. So many things she had to do when she got back. 'List them,' Beryl had demanded, and when Elaine did, with a pen from one pocket of her organizer tote, and a pad from another, the woman began, systematically, to demolish every item.
"Clean and re-stock the refrigerator..."
"I'm certain your refrigerator is already cleaner than the hospitals most of the world depend upon, and why does it need to be stocked if you're not there?"
"To make sure Rodney has what he needs."
"This man cooks?"
"Well, no," pause. "But he needs..."
"He's a grown man, Elaine. He can attend to his own needs, since he shows no sign of attending to yours." The words burned, but she found no ready means to extinguish them.
"My gardens then, I'd like to see what's blooming..."
"You've seen those plants already. Why not see what's blooming in Smoking Dragon Forest?"
"Oh, but if I don't keep up with my weeding..."
"If you don't keep up with your *living*, the weeds will choke that out and you will wake up one day to find you have already died

without even noticing it."

By the time they reached the end of the list, it was Beryl reading off the items and Elaine shooting them down with guilty glee. That left only one issue,; the critical component, the prime directive of a settled modern American life -

"I can't afford to do this…"

"Can you afford not to?" Beryl insisted, then immediately corrected herself, slapping her nearly weightless fingers against the edge of the table. "No! That's unfair and I apologize. Sometimes my ego gets the better of me."

Seeing regret threaten her new friend, Elaine hurried to assure her that no offense was taken. Indeed, she explained - feeling now a strong need to make things right - there were actually things she *could* do to afford such a trip, if she chose to. Rodney's salary was generous, and automatically deposited into an account from which he and Elaine each drew the cash they needed for day to day. Rodney could not care a whit about money or finances, so a bookkeeper had access to everything and took care of paying the bills, transferring money to or from various accounts as necessary. There was a substantial automatic transfer each month to retirement savings; if she directed the bookkeeper to cease that for the time she was away, it would help to cover her expenses, and the credit limits on her multiple cards would cover many, many weeks if she was not extravagant. The truth was, she could afford nearly anything she desired, if she could only permit herself the desire.

Releasing her hands from the rail, settling back against her own seat, its gashes stuffed with prickly straw and crumpled newspapers, Elaine catches another glimpse over Beryl's shoulder, down a thousand feet or more to where the muddy river grinds through a gorge of cliffs and boulders. Halfway up the opposite slope she glimpses a small farmstead, perched on a ledge which seems carved from solid rock. Beside its ramshackle house blossoms a single tree, while to either side a few small crop terraces glow green amidst their dun-colored world. 'An oasis of intention,' she voices silently, channeling her guide's perspective as the bus turns and the farm disappears from sight, 'in a desert of the accidental. Created of belief and trust.' Things working as they were meant to work.

Amazing. The emotions I have experienced over such an absurdly small achievement.

How does one blink one's eye? In my past life the answer was obvious: one simply does. The voluntary blinking of an eye is an action learned so long ago, so far back in the developmental years that it is impossible to break it into smaller units. Walking might actually be easier to relearn. Complex, but in a way the complexity makes it more vulnerable to understanding, because you can break it down. Can analyze the elevating of a foot, the bending of a leg forward from its hip, throwing off your balance until gravity takes over and you can't help but move. The toes pulled upward to allow first contact at the heel, then the fluid rolling forward along the sole until your center of gravity has moved far enough forward and it's time to lift the other foot from the ground and start the whole process again.

But the blink of an eye...

So small an action, we take it as indivisible; a singularity. Refer to it even, in our more poetic moods, as a minimal measure of time. This universal human act has been unavailable to my conscious mind, and yet for some time now my eyes have managed to be open most every time I awaken. Which means my brain is able to control the ocular muscles and, consequently, that I should be capable of electively replicating that same function. Knowing that, I resolved first to imagine myself asleep, to recreate the sensation of having my eyes closed, so that I might try to open them. In order to reach the world, I had to focus first on trying to obliterate it.

This I struggled with, for several of my awakenings. Stupidly, dumbly, in total isolation even as others' lives went on around me. Time and again I tried to capture the darkness, picturing my face with eyelids moving down until my eyes were covered. Hours of this, days perhaps, before suddenly, it happened. I had managed to bring the darkness on. I had shut my eyes, and I was still awake and instantly struck with fear. Ironic, Pyrrhic, victory! For now I was in darkness again and could not open my eyes. The same darkness which had been so peaceful and safe for so long was now my enemy.

Foolish despair, in retrospect, for just as I began to panic, I found my eyes open again, though my emotional perspective was hardly restored by the light. The fear of being stuck again in darkness was replaced by a new fear of the difficulties I was up against. I had no real idea of how I had accomplished the closing and opening, no control over when it occurred, and had nearly exhausted myself in motion-less - and yet emotion-filled - struggle. If this was what it would take to regain control of such a tiny portion of my world, there seemed no point in going on. Better to fall back into the darkness, take what came and accept it, than to struggle against my very being.

It was music which roused me out of my despair, the sound of a violin. Something quick and light, the notes dancing through the space around me, reminding me that one can learn to dance, to sing, to play the violin. That what was once so painfully difficult can become innate. I remembered singing in choir, long, long ago. Scanning hieroglyphic pages of musical notation, baffling and mysterious until I heard the melody playing, and something inside me knew how to imitate those sounds. Hearing, singing, hearing and correcting, it all happened as naturally as breath. If once, as a child, I could have done that, then surely I could master this.

With new resolve I tried to repeat the feat, this time imagining not just the darkness, but that peaceful place of dreams and memory in which I had lain, and there I was again, only this time, when I switched over to imagining the light, it returned in good time, with far less effort. Again I imagined the darkness and it came, then the light, and it came again and with it yet another sensation, of weariness. I was using muscles and capacities which had lain idle for so long, they quickly grew tired. One, two, three, no more than half a dozen times I opened and closed my eyes before the darkness of fatigue consumed me; rest and safety and Nothing.

I woke sometime later to the familiar static view of my world, but this time overlain with the knowledge that I had discovered a path to something more. God, it seems ridiculous; such a tiny, inconsequential parlor trick, and yet there I was, completely consumed with the thought that if I could only repeat this feat, I could control my world. With this one motion I would be again in charge of my own destiny. But then a doubt arose: what if I could not manage it? If I were to try and fail, that would confirm I had only dreamed my triumph. Or worse, what if I did manage to close my eyes again - but could not repeat the opening, and found myself stuck once more in darkness. The prospect was terrifying; so much so that I found myself putting off any attempt to repeat the act, even as I mentally berated *my own cowardice. Given the chance to escape my prison, I cringed in the corner for fear of failure. In memories of former life I paint myself a realist - rational and objective, with the ability to master whatever came my way - and yet, as I lay with eyes wide open, to go back into that blackness seemed impossible, like murdering myself.*

Pondering, my mind recalled an alternative, and suddenly there it was.

Not total blackness, but the momentary narrowing of view, and then its rapid restoration. It took a moment to realize that I had succeeded in blinking one eyelid alone. I had just thought of blinking and it had happened. Perhaps the primacy of one side of my brain made this an easier action than closing both eyes. Perhaps there is a physiological reason: one nerve damaged less than the other, one muscle toned more due to the tilt of my head where they have lain me, or to a reflexive squinting to resist the brightness of the sun. Whatever the explanation, my unconscious mind had retrieved the act of winking, a socialization gesture embedded deeply in the shared memory of my species, my inherited Human Survival Kit. Instantly I knew that was the tool I would manipulate, that one eyelid. My right, because the yellow chair, the farthest thing to the left in my vision, remained when I blinked, while the door jamb, the farthest thing to the right, disappeared.

Thus it is I lie here, anticipating with all my being a suitable opportunity to establish communication with the outside world...

"Oh. My. God."

The young woman leans closer, half afraid to believe what she has seen. Again it happens, this time quite clearly. An eyelid has fluttered shut for an instant, then opened again, and like the butterfly that flaps its wings halfway around the world, in Aubrey's mind this changes everything.

Heart racing, she dashes to the door of the adjacent bedroom, stealing a glance back at the patient even as she does so.

"Lady!" Aubrey shouts to the nurse, whose name she can suddenly not recall, though she has used it on a dozen occasions before. "Hey, Lady! Miss...nurse? Please can you come...?"

"What is it?" Mavis responds from her nearby room, where she had taken advantage of Aubrey's visit to 'rest her eyes.' Long experience and a highly developed sense of responsibility assure that her disorientation is only momentary; she is fully awake and ready to address the situation before Aubrey is across the threshold, hand outstretched as if to snatch her from her bed. "Something wrong with the child?"

"She blinked," Aubrey declares. "She blinked at me. She ever done that before?"

Mavis is upright now, sitting on the edge of her bed, head shaking slightly in knowing amusement. She would certainly respond differently if her patient had begun to choke, or ceased breathing altogether. If an intravenous tube had dislodged and was spewing fluid across the bedclothes, perhaps, or the body soiling itself with noxiously-odiferous waste. All these she has encountered, and seen less-experienced persons treat with panic. But here, now, she is confronted with the specter of an adult woman - though this Aubrey is only just an adult, and not a particularly exemplary one at that; far too trendy for Mavis' taste, with her metal-studded dog collar and belt wide enough for an ox harness, the pierced nose and multiple earrings, and the black jeans and t-shirt which from what Mavis has seen are the same ones the girl has worn on every one of her dozen or more visits. No, Mavis concludes, in reality this excitement is as much a consequence of Aubrey's hysterical nature as anything to do with the patient's condition, and it is in that light that she responds.

"Sure, she's done that before. Once in a while I see her eyelid blink. I asked the doctors about it. That Dr. Sen, he said it's just an autonomic reflex. An itty-bitty-little blip of energy trickling around inside her body, and once in a while it connects with a muscle and her eyelid goes flapping shut and open. I seen it a couple of times."

"No..." Aubrey insists, grabbing one of Mavis' hands in both of hers to draw her upright. "That's not it at all. It was an answer. I was talking to her, asking her questions. Like in this thing I saw on this You-tube video? About how to deal with people who'd been injured really, really, bad? It said you were supposed to talk to them as if they were listening, 'cause it could help them to get better. I was asking her about things we used to do together, like 'do you remember going to the botanical Gardens that time with Donny and Alana, when we...' She stops, a guilty look interrupting the flow of her words, then morphing into a broad smile, tongue rooting around in her mouth for distraction while she searches for a cover-up, and then concludes one is not necessary. "About old times we used to have. And then I was thinking about how hard it is, to keep telling her stuff and never have her say anything back, not to know if she's even hearing me, and what I said was, like, 'I wish you could talk to me, say something, do something – to let me know you're here,' and right then, just when I said that, she blinked one eye at me, and I'm sure it was an answer. Like she was telling me that she was there."

By this time Mavis has stood up, stretched her back and slid her feet into the white mules she wears inside the guesthouse, and crossed the few yards which separate her bed from the patient's. She stares into the child's eyes searching for a sign that anything has changed but, in all honesty, she can find none. Open for the time being, still they stare fixedly into the space before them. The carefully brushed hair remains draped like a storefront display across the pristine pillow. Placing her face in front of the girl's, Mavis sees no sign of recognition, no shying away from her direct gaze. Turning the poor thing's head slightly, her hands gentle as can be, Mavis notes that the eyes remain fixed within it, they do not swivel to stay locked on the same location on which they had previously been focused, if indeed they are focused at all.

"Coincidence," she says sadly to Aubrey, standing beside her now. "Plain old coincidence...."

"No. I know what I saw, and it was no coincidence. Here, let's try it." Aubrey leans in close, her head now next to Mavis', so that the nurse feels the heat of her excitement, smells the salty sweat breaking out across her brow. "Christina," she says, staring directly into the patient's face. "Can you hear me?"

Several seconds pass, marked by the ticking of a clock on the wall opposite the bed, its sound seeming louder in Mavis' ears than it has ever been before. From the stereo system a violin plays softly, its thin thread of melody dancing through the space around them. Outside the room a truck passes, its engine working hard to climb the nearby hill. Another second and then, unmistakable as the sun rising on a summer's morning, the girl's right eyelid, the one closer to the door, farthest from Mavis's room, the eye most fully exposed to the light streaming in through the curtained window, comes slamming down, holds for a trembling instant and opens wide again. Wider, it seems to Mavis, than it was before it began that momentous oscillation.

The two women glance at one another, Mavis now feeling a measure of Aubrey's excitement, though she is bound by professionalism to remain the skeptic. "Well, It might be something..." she begins, but Aubrey is already speaking to the motionless figure before them.

"Listen to me, Christina. If you can hear me, blink twice."

This time the first blink comes more quickly, almost as soon as Aubrey has finished speaking. The second takes longer, and it occurs to Mavis that this act - if indeed it is a voluntary act – seems to take tremendous concentration and effort, that fragmentary motion the equivalent of lifting a great weight, of Atlas hoisting the world up onto his shoulders. That is the impression she has of the second flutter although it is, when it finally comes, unmistakable.

"I think you may be onto something," she admits to Aubrey, whose excitement is now nearly hysterical.

"Something? Something? Shit lady, this is more than something; this is fucking everything! I mean... I mean, she's awake. She is fucking *there*.... All this time, that old woman - Mrs. McKloskey - she's been telling the Doctors her daughter is alive in there and they're like, 'no, no you're just a silly old woman who can't accept the truth,' and now we have proof. This isn't 'something,' this is a whole new fucking world!"

Returning to the bed, Aubrey places herself once again directly in Christina's field of view. "I'm going to ask you some questions. Blink once for yes, blink twice, for no. Ok?"

The eyelid flutters down and up, a single time.

"Can you see us?" Aubrey asks, enunciating the words slowly and clearly. The eyelid shuts and opens.

131

"Do you know who I am?" This time the eyelid flutters twice. Aubrey is undeterred as she turns only slightly toward the nurse. "Her memory could have been affected by all the shit they've been giving her. The drugs, the operations, the...the stuff." She speaks this last word like a foreign substance in her mouth, whereas 'drugs' flowed off her young tongue with a familiarity which Mavis cannot help but notice.

"Do you know who I am?" Mavis asks, stepping closer, into the patient's view. The eyelid flutters a single time.

"What can we do, to help you?" Aubrey asks, and then realizes the folly of such an open ended question. "I mean, do you want us to keep asking you questions?" 'Yes,' comes the response, in a single flutter and then, after a pause, a double wink, rapid and sharp and unmistakable. 'No.'

"What the fuck?" Aubrey mutters, recoiling in hurt and confusion.

"She must be tired," Mavis offers. "It's understandable. You got some poor person, been injured or sick, and they finally come out of it, and it's a real strain on them. To talk, to be talked to. They can't do very much at first. I think she's just tired, is all."

As much as Aubrey hears those words, her excitement will not let her hear their truth. "But this is such a fucking breakthrough. If we don't make her keep on working, she could be like, gone again."

"That's not up to us," Mavis cautions, her hand rising now to rest on the young woman's shoulder, steering her away from the bed. "We have to let these things take their course Miss. If that little girl there is waking up, she's going to do it on her own timetable. We got to watch and be patient. That's what you did, and look what happened. She told you she was listening, seeing. Now we got to let her get some rest. I think that's what she meant, when she said no. She meant no more questions, not right now."

"But..."

"No buts. I'm in charge here, and I say this visit is over. You understand?"

Aubrey nods, grudging.

"And another thing..."

As Aubrey takes the short walk from the guesthouse to the main residence, her excitement is tempered, though it will return later, when she recalls that incredible moment of connection. Passing through the house she thanks Mrs. McKloskey for letting her visit, telling her only, as Mavis has insisted, that she should come out to her daughter's room in an hour or so, to discuss with the nurse some thoughts she has on possible adjustments to Christina's care.

Days passed as I worked on my single motion. Seemingly endless days of frustration and rising anger. Like a freak in a sideshow I blinked at Mrs. McKloskey, who blathered on oblivious, as if it were every day in this place that a catatonic awakened into action.

Two days ago (as best I can tell) I was thrilled at the appearance of the doctors; that trio of self-important monkeys who see, hear and speak nothing of value. Now that my eyes are consistently open it is clear that there are no other patients named Kim or Christina, as I once thought. What I interpreted as overhearing them speaking about those persons' conditions was, in fact, their examining me. How to account for their shared delusions, I have no idea. Perhaps my incapacity has resulted in my being placed in an asylum, and these are not even real doctors, but inmates, allowed to play out their fantasies with me the helpless prop. 'Well, if I am in an asylum,' I told myself, 'let's see what kind of ruckus I can cause.' As soon as one of them put his face in mine I blinked.

"Hmm," the idiot muttered. I did it again; not once, but twice, then three times, as quickly and distinctly as I could manage.

"Autonomic reflex," he pronounced, as I felt myself exhausted from the effort and anticipation.

"Predictable random event," I heard another say, from out of view to my left.

Jesus H. Christ! If I could have risen from my bed I would have cut out their tongues, the only thing which could possibly make them any more dumb than they already are. Instead they concluded their show of examination and departed, leaving me again to my despair, which has been broken only by the arrival of the girl, this 'Aubrey.' I recall hearing her voice before, quite some time ago, and more recently have seen her, passing briefly through my cone of vision, but of them all she was the least interesting - an over-age juvenile with pierced lip and brow, her language full of casual obscenities. Her swaggering toughness miserably fails to hide the underlying insecurity. Where the others address me as if I were the child Christina, this one seems to think me someone else still, a friend and peer of hers named Kim. One more baffling ingredient in my curious circumstance, and totally irrelevant to my goal of establishing some form of communication, until....

"God," I heard her saying, leaning over me and looking in my eyes with all the lovesick passion of a teenage crush. "God, I wish you

could talk to me, Kim. If only you could say something, do something, to let me know you're there."

Blink.

"Shit!" she exclaimed and my heart sang at that scatological non-sequiter.

Blink, blink again, and she was reduced to silent disbelief. Slowly, glacially, her eyes narrowed and her brow furrowed with the dawn of understanding.

"CAN YOU HEAR ME?" she mouthed, like one talking to a stupid child, but I could not have asked for a better opportunity. I blinked again, and from her face I knew my world was changed forever.

So help me God, I hope I am correct in that - for I could not have endured much longer that helpless state, that being locked into myself, my shell, my impotence.

"I don't know..."

"Now don't you go all squishy on me, Mrs. Mckloskey. You know what you saw. She's doing it. She's talking to us."

Anne McKloskey's sparsely-tweezed brows are drawn into a tight vee over eyes which squint as if studying some alien phenomena, her crimsoned lips pursed as if to keep out some vile odor. All this Mavis sees, without consciously remarking upon it, though the impression is quite clear; she has brought her employer in to see the child demonstrate her newfound ability and Anne is decidedly not pleased by what should have been a remarkably upbeat turn of events. Not for the first time since taking this job, Mavis Finch wonders just what is going on with these people.

There are the doctors, of course, those ancient men in their black-and-white-TV-show suits who pretend to care for the child when really they are more concerned about impressing one another with their jargon and insight. Then the boyfriend, who professes to love Christina endlessly, when everything in his manner tells Mavis that he is more committed to the *idea* of having her to love than to any actual feeling, and at the top of the food chain is Anne herself, a real piece of work, with all the drive of a locomotive when she wants something done, the intransigence of a statue when she chooses not to see the obvious.

"She's answering our questions, Mrs. McKloskey. With her eyes."

"Dr. Sen said there was almost no chance she would ever recover," Anne responds, as if reciting gospel. "Next to zero, he said. That was why he wanted to put her in an institution. He told me if I brought Christina home I should expect to have to care for her for years. Unless she got some kind of infection or virus, in which case..." Her glance moves from Mavis to the prone figure, its eyes still firmly fixed upon their patch of wall. The mother's shoulders tighten just a touch, as if gathering strength to face the inevitable. "Her defenses are very weak, you know. Dr. Sen made it sound like that would be the best thing for her, if she just got sick and passed away quietly."

"She ain't going nowhere, Mrs. M. And she may be quiet, but she hears every word we say."

Anne studies her daughter's face and something changes in her own expression, surprising Mavis for a moment, and then reassuring her that yes, this is a mother, after all.

"I'll call the doctors," Anne says softly. "Dr. Sen will know what to do."

Mavis is gone. The one person who believed it when Aubrey brought her in and showed her what we could do, who after that treated me like I was really here; and now she's gone. Replaced by some pimpled brat barely out of adolescence who'd rather listen to the music blasting in his headphones than anything I might have to say, no matter how I say it.

The switch occurred two days ago - I am getting better at keeping track of them, now that I am awake through much of their duration. You never appreciate just how long a day can be, until you have to lie motionless all through one - or two, or three, or a dozen and more. Days which begin in the twilit dawn with the noise of birds and trash haulers, then progress through the stultifying sameness of sponge bathing and changing of linens - a process I believe I am beginning to experience in a tactile fashion, the lifting of my limbs, the sudden cool of a wet cloth on my flesh. I have seen my arms as well; spindly emaciated things that they are, so paled and softened by my existence here that I honestly do not recognize them as part of me.

Back to time, and its passage. My mornings begin with the taking of vitals. The new nurse, whose name is Desmond, can make even the taking of blood pressure a trial: wrapping and re-wrapping the cuff to get it right, usually having to pump and deflate it several times before successfully detecting the readings. Sampling blood for testing, which I gather is done weekly, becomes an epic search for a good vein, slapping and pinching to raise the surface, followed by repeated probing and twisting to get the needle just so and keep it in place while vials are connected and switched, then the final act: removing the needle and bandaging the puncture without spouting blood all over the sheets, which would necessitate another changing. For once I am grateful I have so little sensation. The idiot is so incompetent, the entire procedure would almost be comical, if it weren't an indication of the overall level of care I am receiving, and which could very well be affecting my potential recovery.

Following vitals I am left to my own devices for a while, after which Anne arrives. Although there are moments when her innocence can be almost charming, I find the visits more and more grating as she persists in her delusion that I am her daughter. Endlessly, I have been instructed in the details of Christina's life, from infancy to rebellion, all couched in Anne's opinions about what she, or

138

Christina, or the entire rest of the world, should have done differently to enhance Christina's thwarted emotional development. Spare me from amateur psychologists!

By the time Mrs. McKloskey has departed, it is midday, as I can tell by the lack of shadows cast from the window's light. Desmond makes another appearance, headphones securely fastened to his head to prevent any chance of the real world intruding on his thoughts. If there were any wonder why his faculties are diminished, it is made clear by the bass notes pounding his brain, which I can hear from before he actually enters the room until some time after he leaves. He bustles around for a while, I believe checking or changing the IVs which must be delivering my medications and nourishment, as I obviously cannot eat or drink anything myself – it's curious, by the way, how I do not miss that, the eating and the drinking. After a short time he disappears again, for what I take to be several hours, during which time I am left alone again.

I have taken to observing the minutest variation in my vista. One day I followed a spider's progress across the ceiling. Had he moved in a straight line I should have been entertained for only a short while, but fortunately, he meandered in seemingly aimless curlicues which stayed in view for some time. Eventually the beast chose to move diagonally, disappearing from my field of vision, and I found myself missing him terribly until, some minutes later, he reappeared from a slightly different angle. After that, I was tantalized as he moved in and out of sight for much of the rest of the day.

I frequently doze off for a while in mid-afternoon, about the time the shadow of the table lamp reaches the armchair. When Mavis was here she would sit in that chair and I could often see the side of her head. I would try to tell, by the angle of her neck, whether she was reading or napping, and though I formed opinions, especially on those days when she would bring a book into the room, I never could be certain. Desmond does not nap, I am quite certain, nor do I believe he would ever crack a book open unless it were required of him by some higher authority. A court order perhaps.

Twilight arrives eventually, the entire room dipping into shadowy coolness, and with it another round of vitals. Anne normally puts in another appearance, presumably after her dinner time, and tells me all about her day. This consists of an apparently endless round of visits to banks, doctors, the post office and other trivial errands, punctuated by shopping, which she describes to me as if it were an enormously challenging and worthwhile task. The search for a proper pair of dark gray socks to go with some new slacks assumes epic qualities as she ventures from store to store, mall to mall, trying on socks and rejecting them, sampling new varieties of cotton, agonizing over prices which have risen since some vaguely remembered pre-capitalist age, and finally returning to settle on an item she first selected hours or even days, before.

By the time Anne's evensong is concluded I am as tired as she professes to be. Desmond checks in after dark, sometimes as I am falling asleep, sometimes after I have gone off, waking me briefly. In any case, shortly thereafter I am consigned to dreams until early morning when I awaken and go through the same dreary rote again.

The only real variety, the moments I had looked forward to more than any other, were my visits from the girl Aubrey. Despite the appalling personal 'style,' I'd come to value her - for the simple reason that she asked me questions and listened to my answers. Where Anne seems to have blocked out the possibility of my consciousness and Desmond to be congenitally incapable of comprehending the phenomenon, Aubrey alone actually seemed to revel in it, but now, since Mavis' departure, Aubrey's visits, too, are no more.

"Me?" Beryl had answered on the first full day of Elaine's travels with her, her face and voice full of surprise that anyone would think her own history worthy of discussion. "There's not that much to tell. I loved being a pilot, but I can't do that anymore, so I travel as a passenger - on planes and trains and buses - and then I walk." Sitting in her appointed seat, sipping JAL's complementary tea, she had flashed one of those little smiles that said she didn't wish to talk about the subject any further, and in the slight toss of the head which accompanied the look, Elaine caught a glimpse of the young woman she must once have been; heart-shaped face perched on a long and eager neck, its wide, oval eyes perpetually a-pop at all the world had to offer. Add a leather helmet and you could well imagine her hopping down from the wing of a biplane, its engine coughing to a stop in a cloud of Serengeti dust.

The truth is not much different, Elaine has now learned, in bits and pieces over the weeks, though this particular pioneer didn't fly in Africa until quite late in her career; Nebraska was her territory, to start with. Daughter of a preacher, schooled at home by a farmer's-daughter cum preacher's-wife who nonetheless instilled in her only child the idea that girls could do whatever they put their minds to. By chance was treated to a ride in a barnstormer's airplane at age twelve and never looked back. Crop duster, mail-carrier, cargo hauler and bush pilot until the late '60s, when the rest of the world finally caught up to her and Miss. Beryl Nathanson became only the third woman captain of a commercial passenger carrier in the US. Retiring from flying when her eyes became a liability, she attempted to settle down on a houseboat in Sausalito but found it, in her own word, 'tiresome.'

"I'd gotten a glimpse of the east in my days with Pan Am, but you don't see much at 30,000 feet, and most of a pilot's ground time is spent sleeping or doing paperwork, so I put a few things in storage, sold the rest and headed for Hong Kong." Hong Kong led to Singapore, led to Sri Lanka, Nepal and Mongolia, then south again to Cambodia, Indonesia, Bhutan and India. A foray into China touched down in Beijing, Nanking, Changchun and Chongqing before taking her to a dizzying array of lesser locations not found on many western maps. Ultimately, even Beryl couldn't recall how many destinations she had visited, in a pinball odyssey which continued to this day.

Money was not an issue - there had been some property accumulated over her flying years, as well as a pension, and other than airfares her needs were modest. She was continually making new friends, and, when not actually moving from one place to another, spoke of staying for weeks or months in various homes, schools and monasteries as if they were no less public than a Holiday Inn.

'The family I stayed with in Quilon;' 'the monks in Shiquanhe;' 'the refugee camp outside Bitung;' these and dozens of equally obscure locations fell effortlessly from her lips. Tidbits of exotic worlds Elaine would never have dreamed of visiting on her own. With Beryl though, the world was all familiar; navigable and knowable, if one simply chose to take the journey.

Jake, Aubrey, Anne and Desmond have assembled around Christina's bed on a Saturday afternoon. Early-September sunshine streams around the edges of pleated shades, casting random rays of brilliance into a room lit otherwise by only the amber glow of a single bedside lamp. Mrs. McKloskey wears a burgundy coat-dress, many-buttoned and trimmed in blue satin piping, giving her a regal air which well accompanies the elaborate curls of her hair and the gold setting off her ears, neck and wrists. Desmond wears his requisite cargo pants, low-slung, tatter-hemmed and baggy, with a heavy silver chain linking a belt-loop to the trucker's wallet weighing down one rear pocket. His t-shirt is navy blue, with gold swoops beneath the armpits, as if it had been discovered too small and pieced with whatever fabric was at hand, while the sleeves of a thermal undershirt protrude and hang too long about the heels of his hands. The make-do appearance of his clothing is well suited to the barely-completed quality of his young features, which seem at odds with the brusquely-practical shaven scalp above them. Jake is, by any estimation, the most impressive of the four, his beefy form designer-perfect in pleated gray slacks and a long-sleeved navy polo shirt, buttoned to the Adam's apple. An alligator belt matches the buffed brown leather of his shoes.

Aubrey, as always, is in black.

"I made up this board," she is saying, perched on the side of the bed and holding up a sheet of neon-green cardboard on which are rudely printed the letters of the alphabet and, next to each one, a number. "A is one, B is two, C is three, and so on..."

"Is it some sort of a code?" Anne asks without enthusiasm.

"Like Morse Code," Desmond suggests, headphones draped around his neck, ready to be re-applied at the slightest need, though he has switched the music off for this demonstration.

Aubrey finds Jake's eyes, hoping he will signal a mutual frustration. Instead there is only the same cool calculation she always finds there.

"Yeah," she begins again. "Sort of like a code. So I ask questions, and Chris blinks out her answer. It gets us past just yes and no."

Aubrey has been preparing for this moment for several weeks. Ever since she returned for a visit and found Mavis gone.

Under the girl's gentle questioning Mrs. McKloskey had eventually disclosed that the doctors, upset at Mavis' claim that she could communicate with Chris through questions and blinks, had insisted on her immediate dismissal. Their reason was that Miss Finch had come to assume she knew better than they did what was in the patient's best interest, and was therefore a threat to her health. Desmond had been selected as replacement, in large part because he could be found on such short notice, though she suspects his added quality of being completely uncurious about any change in the patient's cognitive state may have been an added qualification, from the medical team's point of view.

Following that revelation, Aubrey had begun to work in secret with the girl, speaking softly enough that Desmond would not be likely to hear, and pretending ignorance whenever Anne was present. In scattered moments she had continued asking questions of the patient and had eventually hit upon this scheme, gleaned from a website which came up when she Googled 'blink' along with 'questions.'

"Do you know my name?" Aubrey asks, eyes focused on Christina's. Immediately the patient blinks once. "A," Aubrey announces, jotting the large block letter on a pad balanced in her lap. "Now watch this."

All eyes are on one flapping lid, its lashes thick and long as it moves up and down in rapid sequence. "...nineteen, twenty, twenty-one..." and once more before stopping.

"Twenty-two," Aubrey announces, with all the pride of a mother recording her child's first steps. "Twenty-two is U," she says, writing, as immediately the eyelid begins to flutter again, this time only twice before stopping. "B."

Short pause, and another eighteen flaps for "R," followed by five for "E," and finally twenty-five in quick succession.

"Y," Aubrey says very softly, printing the final letter and holding the pad up for all to see as her proud smile beams down at the girl's face before her, immobile and expressionless but for that one small feature.

"Awesome." It is Desmond who speaks first, the word issuing forth as if of its own volition, from a jaw dropped slack beneath eyes wide with vacant admiration for Aubrey. "How'd you do that?"

"She didn't do it you..." Jake answers, and for an instant he appears about to erupt in anger at the younger man's stupidity. The moment passes though, and Jake's manner softens as he moves closer to Anne and places a hand on her shoulder.

"Chris did it," he says then, "After all this time, our Christina's waking up."

"Christina," Anne begins, taking Jake's hand in her own as she moves forward to sit on the edge of the bed, looking closely in the staring eyes. "My goodness, I don't know what to say." Her head swivels, looking to each of the others in turn, as if they have an answer to her confusion. "To think that my baby can hear me, see me. After all this time, thinking she might never come back to me... it's, it's... I don't know what to say."

As Anne is speaking, Chris' eyelid has begun to flutter again, rapidly, endlessly. The mother does not notice, so rapt is she in her own excitement. Jake sees it though, and looks across at Aubrey, who bends quickly down to place her face in the girl's view.

"Stop, Chris. I wasn't counting. Stop and start again, Please."

The eyelid ceases, then begins again.

I am blinking furiously now, and counting. Close/open, close/open, close/open, close/open, laboriously working my one good muscle, then pausing.

"I," Aubrey pronounces, correctly, even as the idiot Desmond tallies eight blinks to my nine performed.

I blink again, one time, and wait.

"A," they say in unison as the letter is written down.

Thirteen blinks, then wait.

"M."

Fourteen.

"N."

Fifteen.

"O."

Twenty.

"S," Desmond says, proud of his speed.

"No," Aubrey corrects him, "Twenty is T."

"Yeah," the savant defends himself, "but that was eighteen. I mean nineteen - I counted 'em. Nineteen blinks is S, it says so on your thing there." He points a stubby finger, bringing with it the long sleeve of his white undershirt, frayed and grubby where it rubs against the table when he eats, against his body when he walks and who knows what or when else. I see this, from my vantage point trapped beneath their argument, my mind racing with the miserable few words I hope to communicate as they fumble and grumble over such a simple task as counting blinks and looking-up letters on a chart. It is the man 'Jake' who steps in - thank goodness - and puts an end to it.

"Chris," he says, in a voice which could part waters. "One for yes, two for no. Is the letter S?"

I blink twice.

"Is the letter T?"

I blink once.

"All right," Jake says, sliding as if by nature into control of the situation. If only there were a good strong man like him in charge around here, I might get the care I need to improve. "We have T. Go on Chris, we're listening."

Three.

"C," Jake pronounces, and the others are watching him now, deferring to his leadership. I can see Anne's face as they count and

listen and read the accumulating text, and it is filled with fear, the same fear I saw when I performed my feat for the so-called 'doctors.' Not the pride I see in Aubrey's otherwise belligerent eyes, not the proprietary satisfaction of Jake's face, as if he is actually responsible for all this; his own importance somehow validated by my action. Not even the innocent eagerness of Desmond, who I think would be just as entertained by a dog rolling-over or a bird squawking on cue as he is by my communication. Anne's eyes are wide with trepidation and her mouth is slack as her thoughts race ahead and away - where they are I do not know, but it is somewhere beyond this room as I finish my message.

Eight.

"H."

Eighteen.

"R."

Nine.

"I."

Nineteen.

"S."

Twenty again.

"T."

Nine again. And with each blink my frustration grows. They're all looking at the letters, can't they see where this is going? Do I really have to spell it all out for them?

"I."

Fourteen.

"N."

One final blink, and wait.

"A," Jake pronounces, with the air of one who has solved a great mystery. His face is close-above me, his eyes looking into mine with nothing but warmth, despite the message of denial I have spelled out to him, to the grieving mother, to the entire group of them who have been my whole world for these long weeks - or months, for all I know.

"Of course," the son-of-a-bitch calls out after a moment, the smile of satisfaction spreading across his face as he meets the eyes of the other three, reassuring them by his solid, stable presence, the air of authority which comes from a barrel chest, five-o-clock shadow at eleven in the morning and biceps big enough to stretch the sleeves of his shirt. "Of course," he beams down at me once again. "You're not

Christina anymore," he says gently, as if bestowing a precious gift upon a small child, then turns to the others. "She wants us to call her Kim. It's the name she chose for herself."

If I had a gun - and arms to hold it - I would shoot him dead this instant. I swear to God I would kill him, Hippocratic Oath be damned! I would kill all of them, these smug speakers and movers, walkers and eaters - inhabitants of a world that has been stolen from me. Kill them all and send them off to hell, just as they do to me with their damnable ignorance!

"If you don't believe in reincarnation, or heaven and hell and all that gumbo," Beryl lectured one morning as she and Elaine were packing their cases in a simple but exquisitely-peaceful room overlooking a seaweed farm on an island east of Zhanjiang, after Elaine had had the temerity to suggest perhaps they could spend just a few more days in one place. "If you don't believe in a life after this one – and I don't - then how can you not try to fit in as much as possible before it ends?"

More than simply accumulating visa stamps though, Beryl's odyssey does seem to have its own kind of direction. Each destination is linked to the last by desire to find something elemental. Whether historic – the seaside torii gates outside Miyajima - or spiritual – as when they visited Baima Si, the first Buddhist Temple in China – or social - as when Beryl insisted on entering a slum outside Osaka, to prove for herself that efficient, orderly Japan really did have lost souls sleeping on its streets - every stop on their travels has been selected to fulfill some curiosity of a woman whose curiosity seems to know no bounds.

"Seven Wonders my bunions," she scoffs some weeks later, as a government 'Travel Coordinator' in Shanghai attempts to coerce them into visiting the construction site of the Three Gorges Dam instead of their intended objective: the 800 year old temple of Zhang Fe - soon to be obliterated by said dam, which the official government brochure claims will soon be known as the Eighth. "There are more 'wonders' in this world than all the paper-stampers who've ever lived could count in all their lifetimes. My God, Elaine, every woman who survives childbirth is a wonder - not to mention the child itself. Every crop that's harvested before it can die of drought, every fish that's caught in a hand-thrown net, every sunrise after a frigid night – they're *all* Wonders of the World; and I intend to see as many of them as I can before I shuffle off to Buffalo."

I am drowning now, in numbers. Smothered in eye-blinks and suffocated with waiting for them to be counted and converted, my mind bursting with desire just as a man's lungs will burst, whose head is held underwater till his body screams out for oxygen, only what my mind is screaming out for is speech, expression - any independent action. I swear it will kill me, this waiting and hoping that they get it right. It is absolutely amazing, the capacity of human beings with all their faculties intact to yet be mislead by their own expectations and preconceptions. How difficult can it really be to count to twenty-six? I counsel myself to be patient, sympathetic, but it is no use. I am the one working under the handicap, for God's sake. This Desmond is a young man in the prime of his life and yet he wastes that potential on rock and roll and comic books. I'd give my right arm - albeit a right arm which I cannot currently feel or use - for half of his opportunities right now, and yet he imagines himself put upon, disadvantaged and generally the world's victim.

Still, I am communicating, in my own way. Every day I blink out a message to Anne McKloskey when she arrives for her morning visit. 'I am not your daughter,' I tell her, and am met with that same condescending smile. "Oh yes, dear," she says, without even trying to count up what I am really saying. "I understand. You want us to call you Kim now. That's fine, sweetheart, I just forget sometimes."

'Forget,' my ass. That woman has never forgotten a thing in her life. She's sharper than the sharpest tack, she is, despite the pitiful old widow act.

It is Aubrey for whom I save my real questions, my most important thoughts. She tells me that Mrs. McKloskey has banished her for believing in my recovery. Thank goodness she has little enough respect for authority to still sneak in now and then. Her visits are my only release, and as soon as one ends, I find myself desperate for her to come back again - and soon - no matter what name she has chosen to assign me.

On another note though, I have developed a new skill to add to my repertoire: I have learned to swallow. Like my other breakthroughs, it came about by tapping into some unconscious progress made in my sleep. I woke one time to a disturbing sensation of choking and just as I was noticing it I heard a popping in my ears and felt movement in what I realized to be my throat. The choking was still there but I did my best to direct my attention elsewhere - to the sounds around me, the light on my wall - and as I did so I heard again the popping, only this time I was able to identify that it started with an upward pressure of my tongue (another realization - I could feel my tongue, and in fact, had been able to for some time!) and I found that if I imagined the intention of pressing just that part of my tongue upward I could conjure the movement again. Suddenly I was in control, swallowing whenever I wanted to, feeling the movement in my mouth, the downward motion of whatever was clogging my throat.

That very day there was a new nurse attending me, and as she was changing my bedclothes I demonstrated this skill, making the swallow as obvious and exaggerated as I could and she immediately recognized it for what it was. If only that Desmond character would take more time off...

Since that day I have been able to swallow and now can also clear my throat with relative ease, giving hope that my retrieval of function may truly be progressive, in which case the possibilities are tantalizing; that with time I may be able to move a finger or raise a hand, to direct my own vision, or even - hope against hope – once again to speak for myself.

Now there is a possibility to fuel one's determination!

"Oh. My. God!"

Aubrey's face is a Greek mask of surprise as she enters the room, though her comments are whispered as softly as secrets in the night. The visit *is* a secret, after all; to arrange it, Aubrey had to corner a nurse named Rhonda, four days new to the job after Desmond was fired over a pint-bottle of rum found in his bedroom when Dr. Sen needed to use the toilet during one of the triumvirate's examination visits. Aubrey found out about this because she had been bribing Desmond with joints to let her visit Kim, and was, therefore, the first person he called to rant about the injustice of his being fired.

The very next Saturday, Aubrey parked her car down the block and waited. She knew that Anne gave the nurses Saturdays off, and sure enough, a little before nine, a tidy looking woman in her forties had made her way down the driveway and entered a blue-green Nissan parked there. Aubrey started her own car and followed the woman to the lot at Northgate, then into the mall and over to a coffee bar where she bought a cappuccino and sat down, clearly biding time till the stores opened. It was easy enough for Aubs to buy herself a cuppa, slide into a chair at the table next to the woman and start up a conversation. A friendly smile, a sad story of long friendship and parental misunderstanding - and maybe the fact that Aubrey had skipped her usual makeup and worn pastels for the first time in years - had smoothed the way for her to be let into the cottage early Sunday afternoon, without Mrs. McKloskey or the doctors being any the wiser.

Once inside, she finds Mrs. M. has been especially creative this morning, her daughter's face and hair and nails done up to suit an opening night.

"Look at you, all dolled up like Barbie on homecoming weekend. Jesus, Kim, if you could see yourself, you'd absolutely shit a brick. 'Course your mother would shit a brick, too, if she had any idea I was here."

Looking into those dark eyes, Aubrey is struck by something new and different. Wondering if it is in her imagination, she moves away from the bed, and the eyes follow her. Slowly she steps around the resting feet and comes up on the other side of her friend. Again the eyes follow her.

"You can see me, can't you?" She asks, and is rewarded by a single blink of the left eyelid. "You can, like move your eyes around now, right?" This time Chris's eyes shut, in unison, before opening again to reveal eyeballs swiveling first up, then to the right, then down, then to the left, before locking on Aubrey once again where, if they take in anything at all, they must see her face lighting up with a childish glee which is totally incongruous to the sinister look of her black and studded persona.

"Hot damn, sister, you know what that means don't you?" Aubrey says, practically dancing from one side of the bed to the other in her eagerness to come to grips with the progress. "It means you're getting better. Whatever-the-fuck they did to you, you're getting better! I mean, this may seem like piddly-shit: swallowing, blinking, moving your eyes, but it's fucking progress, you know?"

Plopping herself down on the side of the bed, Aubrey picks up her friend's hand and holds it between hers, rubbing gently, affectionately. There are tears forming at the corners of her own eyes, tears she wipes away with the back of a hand before her friend can notice them

"I'm gonna help you, Kim. I'm gonna come here every day if I have to, and I'm gonna talk to you and listen to you - whatever you say, however you say it - and we're gonna make the most of what you can do. That old lady - your mother? - she's fucking crazy you know? I mean, she's got those doctors and she keeps changing the stupid nurses, like she doesn't even really want you to get better, but I do. It's gonna be just like old times, girlfriend, and I'm gonna help you get there."

Chris's eyes blink once, twice, and continue fluttering until Aubrey notices.

"You want to tell me something?" she asks, jumping up and pulling a notepad from the messenger bag she carried when she entered. Pulls out a piece of cardboard as well - this one smaller than the original she had left here for the nurses to use, and which has been nowhere to be found since she began her secret visits, but with the same letters and numbers in black marker. Propping the piece of cardboard on the bed where both can see it she prepares to count and write. "Go for it, Sugar, hit me with your best shot."

Chris's eyes begin to blink rapidly now, sequences of flutters separated by brief but definite pauses. In each pause Aubrey checks her chart and voices the letter she thinks she has seen, Chris blinking once if it is correct, twice if not, in which case she must start over again, sometimes showing her frustration with several sharp swallows or a rolling of her eyes, once even by clamping those eyes shut for a time, as Aubrey apologizes and begs her to continue.

"I, a, m d, r, r, o, d, n, e, y, g, i, m, b, a, l," Aubrey reads from her notepad finally. Looking up she sees the face of Kim Tree staring directly at her. Kim, her friend of three years - fellow student and party animal, Jake Brindle's lover and sometimes fiancée, not to mention author of some of the freakiest performance art pieces the UW community has ever seen. Kim the joker, who turned out to have changed her name and history to hide the fact that she was actually the daughter of a famous cellist and had gone to great pains to hide her new life from her mother, despite the fact that the woman was supporting her with monthly checks.

"I am drro-dneyg...? Drrod...ney-gim-bal...Did I miss a letter or something?" Aubrey asks, and is rewarded with two blinks, for 'no'.

"OK, so...oh, I get it - the 'd' 'r' is for Doctor, right?" A single blink. "I...am...doctor...Rodney...Gimbal?" Another single blink, at which Aubrey cocks her head and purses her lips, as if faced with a most confusing choice. Shortly though, the smile returns to her face, genuine and innocent.

"Whatever you say, sister," Aubrey replies. "You want me to call you 'Doctor,' you got it. We can use all the doctors we can get right now, don'cha' think?"

"There are places I can take you, Elaine. Special places, where you will see miracles. It does no good to tell you where these places are - their names wouldn't mean anything to you - but I can take you to them - if you are willing to leave everything else behind. Are you willing to do that?"

Elaine is having difficulty recalling when it was Beryl made that particular speech. Was it that long first night at LAX, talking over tea, or the next day during their fifteen-hour flight across the Pacific? In any one of a dozen hotels, homes and hostels where they have since stayed together? Surely it must have been early in their travels, for it presaged everything which has come later. And yet, just as surely, she herself would have balked at such a threatening invitation, had it come before she grew to trust the woman. It must have been sometime after that first climb, when Elaine reached the mountaintop with the sun's first rays, and realized she had capacities she had never tested. Perhaps as they sat slurping a noodle breakfast following their descent, Elaine's muscles hardening into knots, her face burned from the sun, lips chapped from the wind, but her heart filled with the wonder of a new dawn observed from two miles above the surrounding plain, as mists dissolved and the world seemed to lay itself at her feet, to be viewed and comprehended as it never could be while standing on its flats.

Yes, she concludes, that must have been when the words were said. Except that they had stayed those two nights - and eaten that meal - in the guesthouse of a religious retreat where speech was forbidden, and Beryl had insisted on honoring the vow, refusing even to acknowledge Elaine's whispered asides. And so it could not have been there that the words were spoken...

Perhaps, Elaine suggests to herself as she settles down to search for sleep, she has only dreamed them.

37

These 'conversations' drain me.

A precious few questions and answers make my eyes ache and sleep suck me under, but each time I wake now there is a hunger to communicate, to ask the next question and the next.

Thank god for Aubrey, the only one who seems to want me to be anything other than an object in a bed. From her I've learned that I am not in an asylum but under Mrs. McKloskey's care and confirmed that she, deluded as she is that I am her daughter, rejects any notion of my condition being able to improve. The nurses she hires are no better. They come in and I blink in their faces and – when they finally happen to notice and raise a question - Anne says 'Oh, that's her little game,' like when an infant tosses a pacifier out of the crib. If the nurse disagrees, he or she is immediately replaced by someone new.

The doctors are no better, as they seem dedicated only to keeping me as quiet as possible. I have overheard their conversations, mumbled talk of reflex inhibitors and muscle relaxants, 'to protect me from harming myself,' but none of it makes any medical sense. Obviously they're hiding the truth of my condition from Mrs. McKloskey and the nurses and perhaps from the authorities as well. Why they cooperate with Anne's delusion that I am her daughter, when their own eyes must put the lie to it, is just one more bizarre twist in an altogether inexcusable clinical situation.

Oddly, even Aubrey, who seems the most competent of them all, when I tell her who I really am, pretends bafflement. She seems to think I am playing a game, 'punking her,' as she puts it. But at least she listens; without that, I would be lost. I might even go as crazy as they are.

Aubrey hesitates, pen a fraction of an inch above her note pad, where she has just printed out the last letter of Chris's latest request.

"Jesus, Kim, I don't know if that's such a good idea. I mean, you had, like, *brain surgery*... there were all these stitches all around your head, and they shaved off your hair - it's growing back in now, but it's, like, the way your mother does it, and all? Everything about you is the way she wants you to be, not...not 'you,' at all. I mean... shit girl, you are *not* going to like what you see."

Chris's eyes blink once, then lock on Aubrey again, the thin brows above them even seeming to furrow a bit, reminding Aubrey of the strong-willed way her friend has always approached life. With a shrug of resignation, she rises from the bedside and steps over to the dresser. Opening the first drawer, she finds if filled with underwear – panties, bras and lacy camisoles, all brand new. A second drawer contains socks and hose, a third blouses and sweaters, neatly folded. None of it them worn, and none of them what she is looking for.

She crosses to the closet, which has always been closed during her visits. Sliding the door open exposes hangers full of neatly pressed slacks, skirts, dresses and blouses. An entire wardrobe, fit for a homecoming queen, but not a single item Aubrey could ever imagine Kim wearing, even if she were able to rise up out of that sickbed.

"Damn, your mama has been busy. Looks like she's getting ready to send you off to fucking prep school." Moving into the bathroom Aubrey still cannot find what she wants. "Let me check in here," she says over her shoulder as she enters the nurse's room next door, to return a moment later, plastic-framed makeup mirror in hand. Sitting down on the edge of the bed, she pauses.

"You're sure you want to do this, right?"

The girl in the bed blinks once.

"Ok," Aubrey replies, still sounding highly skeptical of the wisdom of her actions. "Don't blame me if you don't like what you see." Unfolding the mirror's stand to serve as a handle, she reaches out to hold it a couple of feet in front of her friend's face.

I thought I was beginning to understand!

At least a part of it - what was a dream, what was memory, what was real. That I had been incapacitated, and somehow placed in the care of madmen; that at least made some sort of sense, but this?

To look into a mirror and see someone else's face? To blink and see their eyes blink?

I must be dreaming, but this has none of the quality of dreams. It is impossible, yet it feels as though it's coming from outside. The sights...the sounds... I try to tell myself it is only a dream I am having and it is time to wake up now, to step beyond the dream and banish it to memory, but I cannot stop it playing out in front of my eyes. Those same eyes I had been so proud of opening.

It cannot be, but, for the life of me, this feels real.

"You made a sound," Aubrey shouts, dancing away from the bed, jumping up and down only to stop in sudden embarrassment, hands to her face as she turns to look down at her friend in proprietary pride. "Oh my god, Kim. I mean, Chris... Rodney...oh, fuck... I get so fucking confused, but I heard you make a sound - like 'ahhhh.' Did you hear that? Did you fucking *hear* that?"

There are other words Elaine recalls as well, and these she knows she did not dream, but spoke and heard, long ago and far away.

"I want to go...I don't know where. Just someplace. Anyplace that isn't here."

Seventeen-year-old Elaine pushed her plate away, the food barely touched, well aware of the hurt this gesture brought to her mother's face. Relishing it, in fact, though at the same time she disliked herself for that. At the head of the table her father took it all in; the petulant girl, the mother's face frozen, the younger brother watching wide-eyed as if storing it all up for his own adolescence.

"And do what?" Henry Franks asked, the words projected out one side of his mouth even as he chewed a piece of beef with the other.

Perched in her ladder-back chair, the girl snaked one hand up to twist the end of a braid, careful to keep her eyes low. Fathers, she knew, were touchy beasts; as warm and huggable as they could be sometimes, they were liable to explode at any moment if you said the wrong words. Or even the right words, in the wrong way.

"I want to help people. Who need to be helped. Maybe sick people, or old ones, or... I don't know."

So far so good, she sensed, twisting tighter at her own hair until her head was pulled slightly off center by the tension, still not half as great as the tension inside her. 'Oh, why do things have to be so complicated,' she fretted to herself. There were so many wonderful places she'd heard of, so many exciting lives she'd read about. All the other girls seemed to have more interesting futures ahead of them. Boyfriends to marry, colleges to go off to, even Collette had her parents' restaurant to look forward to; at least Le Francais sounded glamorous and exotic - so what if it was just waiting tables. But Elaine? There was no place for a girl at her father's garage, and so far all her talk about wanting to go off and study nursing had met with nothing but silence from either of her parents. Her friend Mandy said it was because neither of them went past high school, and the idea of their daughter wanting more education made them feel inadequate. But then again, Mandy read textbooks for fun, which was where she got all her ideas and the big words she used to describe them, and no one really paid much attention to her because of that. Cynthia said her parents were the same way, and that it might be just about the money for them, or it might be because her older sister got pregnant in the middle of her second year of college and had to get married even though she had great grades, and because of that they figured sending a daughter to anything more than secretarial school was a waste of money. Then again, Elaine didn't have an older sister, or a boyfriend; so really, they couldn't be worried about that, if life were even a little bit fair. But life was not fair, as her father was eager to tell any of his family, any chance he got, and fathers are complicated beasts, so a girl had always to choose her words carefully, listening between each of them for a sign, a hint as to whether he was or was not willing to hear what her heart was telling her to say.

"Mandy Ashcroft is looking at a college in Virginia..."

A grunt from her father and Elaine concluded she'd stepped over the line, as he raised a grease-stained hand to wave his fork in derogatory circles before homing its tines directly on Elaine. "We are not the Ashcrofts," he pointed out, then paused, daring any of his family to disagree. When no one did, he continued. "We don't need to go halfway across the country to get an education. Not when they've got a perfectly good nursing school in Newark."

Afraid to disturb the moment, Elaine's fingers stopped their twisting. Hardly daring to believe her ears, she studied her father's face, looking for clues beneath the stubble. There, at the corner of his mouth, had a new wrinkle appeared just today, or was he hiding something? And that look in his eyes, just like when she was tiny and he'd come crawling across the floor toward her, hands slapping the carpet like giant cat's paws, eyes locked onto hers in playful earnest. How thrilling that had been back then, to be watched with hunger, stalked and then captured, gathered in his strong arms and rolled over and over across the floor. Tickled into screaming, then hugged again - nearly smothered with his strong affection until both of them collapsed in mock exhaustion, breathing deep and slow as her mother stood in the doorway, wearing a contented smile to complement her apron. The same smile she was wearing now, Elaine realized, as her own eyes searched for confirmation of what she thought she had heard, and were rewarded to see her father's composure weaken more and more until finally it broke completely, a wide grin coming over his face as well.

"We've been talking this over," he said, reaching out to take his water glass in hand, pull it toward his face. "Your mother and I."

"Don't let him fool you, dear," Grace Franks corrected, her

face a beacon of pride and joy. "Your father's the one who had the idea. He called Aunt Meredith, and she says she'd be happy to have you come stay with her. Then you'd be a New Jersey resident, and that makes the tuition a lot lower, so..."

"Jake," Aubrey begins breathlessly, even before her bottom touches the seat cushion opposite his. "You gotta hear this: Kim's talking." She pauses, hoping for a flood of questions, or at least an exclamation. Instead she hears only the buzz of conversations around them as Jake's oversized paws toy with an equally enormous cup of mochachino. "She's talking again."

Around them The Liquid-Air cafe is crowded with men and women eating lunch or just loading up on caffeine for the downtown afternoon to come. Voices mingle in a constant hum, nearly drowning out the soft jazz playing through carefully exposed speakers. Each time the door opens the rush of traffic intrudes just enough to remind the clientele that they are at the center of something busy and important.

Jake's eyes seem to be avoiding her as he ponders what she has said and Aubrey feels the tension rising up between her shoulder blades. For the first time since calling his office number to say she wanted to meet and give him some very good news, it occurs to her that this might have been a mistake.

"You've seen her?" he asks eventually, and his tone reaffirms her innate suspicion of men with massive arms and expensive suits.

A waiter approaches, a young man about Aubrey's own age, but with the tailored slacks and excessively neat goatee of one more anxious to be accepted. He asks if she would like anything, but all the time she feels his energy focused on Jake, sizing him up. Two seriously-buff guys, she thinks, and wonders if the clichés are true. Not that she has any problem with that - Jesus, no - it's just so...predictable. She orders a double espresso and watches the boy walk off, Jake paying him no attention at all.

"Once," she offers, but knows it is not a convincing answer. "Well, a couple of times. Since..." Jake's hand shoots out to where her wrist rests defenseless upon the table between them. His grip is not tight enough to cause pain exactly, but more than firm enough to prevent her pulling away. The width of his palm covers halfway from hand to elbow, lying upon her forearm like a lead weight to convey a very effective message of power. Looking around, Aubrey sees that none of the other customers has taken notice of the gesture, almost indistinguishable from one of great affection; a handsome man reaching out to one he cares for, holding her arm in deep emotion.

"*Since* her mother told you never to come to her house again? *Since* she threatened to call the police if you so much as set foot in the same room with her daughter?" Jake's words leave it at that, but his face makes it clear that he agrees with Mrs. McKloskey about the importance of Christina not being disturbed in her 'rest.' That he will be telling Mrs. M. about this conversation, and also, perhaps most importantly, that if Aubrey ever goes near Chris again he would not consider it out of line to use bodily force against her. As if on cue the man's cell phone buzzes, audible even from inside his jacket. As he pulls it out and answers the call, Aubrey rubs her arm, feeling resolve growing stronger with every bit of blood that returns to her flesh.

Jake had been there, after all, had been given a perfect opportunity to speak up for Chris the day Aubrey invited him and Mrs. M. to see her communicate by blink-code. Despite his professed love for 'Kimmie,' he had gone along with Mrs. M., agreeing that the doctors must be consulted before anyone pursued the information further. Later, when Anne called Aubrey to tell her not to visit any more, she had been very specific in saying that she and Jake had talked it over with the doctors and they had all agreed that Aubrey's visits were harmful to Christina. Overstimulation, Mrs. M. said the doctors had told her, could lead to frantic random activity which might appear to the ill-informed to be conscious actions. If allowed to continue, that nervous tension would increase her risk of high blood pressure and even stroke, a condition to which Christina was congenitally predisposed - as evidenced, they reminded one and all, by the aneurysm which was now known to have precipitated her collapse at the club that night (rather than the drug interaction which was first reported, and which, Mrs. M. added firmly, she had never believed of her Christina). 'Continued over-stimulation' posed a great risk to her daughter, a risk which could not be justified by some small change in her condition, though the physicians were careful not to concede that there had been any such change. In their professional opinion - arrived at jointly, and after extensive consultation, Anne had pointed out carefully - Christina should be left as still as possible, with the least possible stimulation, and that meant no visits from hysterical young women who thought they could communicate with her, no matter what good friends they had once been.

Aubrey has heard all that, and knows that Jake is onboard the train shipping Kim back into silence, but she does not understand why. It is that uncertainty, as much as anything, which has led her to make one last attempt at changing his mind. As soon as his call is ended, even as he snaps the phone shut and places it back in his coat with an expression of faraway confusion, she makes her final pitch.

"I just thought…I mean, you knew Kim. She was all about action. Mixing it up, breaking the rules. Shit, she would never lie there and keep her mouth shut, if there was even a tiny little chance of getting back into things. Protect her from herself? That's the last thing Kim would want anybody to do."

"Look, Aubrey," Jake says, back in the present, and apparently not pleased about it. "I want Kim back, just as much as you do. After all, I'm the one she was going to marry, not you. But as her fiancée I have to look out for her best interests, not just what I want, and if the doctors say she needs time and rest, then that's what I'm going to see she gets."

Even as he says the words, Jake is rising from his seat, pulling out his wallet. Dropping a ten on the table next to the cup of coffee he has not even sipped since she arrived, he leans down toward to her, the broad drape of his suit coat practically curtaining off their booth from the rest of the room.

"I'm sorry I can't stay longer kid, I've got a thousand things to do. Anne and I, we appreciate your interest in Christina. You were her friend, after all. But she's family to us, you see, so we have a different level of concern, a higher purpose, kind of. And if I ever- " here he leans even closer, so the scent of Old Spice fills her nostrils as his meaty hand clamps down once again on her wrist, "ever - find out you've been near her again without permission, I'll have my lawyers on you so fast it'll spin the studs right out of your eyebrows."

Without leaving her time to reply he turns, striding out of the shop as several sets of eyes follow appreciatively, their looks of approval turning to something less complimentary once he disappears and they glance back at the girl he has left behind, rubbing her wrist till it turns red. She is so obviously wrong for him, they think, not at all what he deserves, despite the look of determination slowly dawning over her moonish face.

Another dinner, a different table, a different man speaking as he chews, and Elaine hanging, just as before, on every word.

"It's *unnecessary, Elaine,"* her husband said one night in the early years of their marriage, as if the applicability of that adjective must certainly be obvious to any intelligent observer. "We do not need the money, and I need you to do the things you do already. Besides, I work with nurses all the time, as you well know, and believe me, there's nothing rewarding in what they do. Taking vitals, giving meds. Prepping patients and checking up on them around the clock. Cleaning up after them. It's not medicine, it's grunt work pure and simple."

'You would think that,' Elaine imagined herself saying, though she did not open her mouth. She'd been around her husband long enough to know his thoughts on this subject, and deep inside the more-real truth; that his comment did not so much reflect a low opinion of the nursing profession, as it did his high opinion of himself which made *everyone* else pale in comparison. Not just nurses, but administrators, and shopkeepers; car salesmen, the plumber who came to their house to fix a clogged toilet, the neighbor boy who mowed their lawn while Rodney worked through the weekends, and the broker who handled their investments. None of them could measure up to his own stature - this man who stooped his body to pass through doorways and stooped his ego to speak with patients before slicing into their flesh to fix what time and biology had put amiss – and neither could she, though she kept his house just the way he said he wanted it, prepared the meals he said he liked, and was in every way the model wife he seemed to desire.

In every way, that is, except this wanting something...more. Perhaps their life together would have been enough if children had come along, but they had not, and her husband was not about to subject himself to personal questioning by a Urologist - or an Ob/Gyn; heaven forbid! - to find out see why not. That discussion had ended almost before it began, with Elaine feeling her face flush and her stomach contract into a knot that took days to disappear. The same flush and the same knot she was feeling now, the same fear – and yes, it really was fear, ashamed as she might be to admit it. Fear of his disapproval, of the possibility that she was not being the wife he needed. If only, she imagined, he could have used a different word. 'I'd *like* you to do this, or that,' he could have said, or 'I don't *want* you to go back to school... back to work,' or whatever. Phrased that way perhaps she could have disagreed, but Doctor Rodney Gimbal did not ever *like* or *want* something, he only *needed*. He *needed* things done the way he said, and he *needed* them done the way he said *right now*, because he was a man with a mission to do the impossible: to save lives which would otherwise be lost, and if, in the process, his wife felt her own life being lost, well, she should take pride in the fact that she was helping him accomplish his mission. That was the way these things worked, after all, when one had been raised properly.

'He is so certain of himself,' Elaine thought that evening, as they ate the rest of their dinner in silence. Sitting ramrod straight, with those arms that could reach half the length of the table, those hands so large the silverware seemed in danger of disappearing into them. Every so often as he ate, his head would nod up and down, witnessing his own agreement with some thought he'd been having, all to himself. Not that there was any doubt of that, Rodney always agreed with Rodney. Was always sure, always strong; so forceful, and so very, very intelligent, and his wife so unsure of herself - of whether what she wanted was really right, or just...just her 'being Elaine,' as he put it.

It was no wonder, really, that things turned out the way they did. No wonder at all.

44

A rust-rimmed Oldsmobile the color of potting soil sits in the farthest row of a Safeway parking lot, three-quarters empty at ten AM. The girl in the front seat is smoking a cigarette and nodding to the beat of an old Eurythmic's tune. Annie Lennox's bleach-white boy-cut hair and hollowed eyes fill her mind, only to vanish when Mary taps on the window. Aubrey motions her around to the other side and reaches across to pull the handle of the passenger door which groans mightily at the indignity of being opened, at its advanced age.

"Is this really necessary?" Mary asks. "The cloak and dagger stuff?"

"Cloak and dagger?" Aubrey replies, genuinely baffled. That just shows, Mary thinks to herself, how far we've come. A kid who can probably program your computer with her eyes closed, or recite the plot line of a hundred movies from heart, but doesn't understand a simple figure of speech. The interior of the car, as she looks around, seems to hold the accumulation of years of daily errands. Newspapers are strewn across the back seat, some fresh and white, some yellowed with age. Several paper bags are visible, crumpled into balls, with golden arches or the Taco Bell logo peeking out of the creases. The captured air, as she settles in and shuts the door, is redolent with fragrances of cigarette smoke and French fries, and maybe just a hint of mold.

"Just an expression. Means spy stuff. Meeting in parking lots, sneaking around. Is it really necessary?"

"You think I do this just for fun?" Aubrey's look combines genuine hurt with the wounded pride of one carrying serious responsibility. "That Mrs. McKloskey, she's a son-of-a-bitch, I'm telling you. Kicked me out when I tried to tell her Kim was talking with her eyes, was all like 'you're interfering with my daughter's medical care'. Said if I ever came around again, she'd have me arrested." She lets that sink in a bit while she takes another drag, then blows the smoke out in a long thin stream, with a James Dean tilt of her head. "She's switched nurses at least four times now. Which is just fine, actually, 'cause she finally got one I can work with. June. Lets me come in for a little while in the mornings while Mrs. M. is out shopping - Jesus, you know that woman shops more than anyone I've ever heard of? Goes to Northgate Mall about three times each week..."

"So about Christina?"

"Oh, yeah." Aubrey casts a long questioning glance at Mary, then turns to examine her cigarette, nothing more than a butt now, though still smoldering. Cranking the window down a few inches she flips the thing out into the drizzle with a practiced nonchalance and reaches inside her leather jacket for the pack of Viceroys, from which she extracts another stick, placing it in her mouth before offering them to Mary, whose face wrinkles up in reply. With a shrug Aubrey replaces the pack in its pocket and presses the lighter into the dashboard.

The Oldsmobile is ancient, probably older than its driver, Mary realizes as they sit in silence. Its beige upholstery is caked black at the wear points, from all those soiled bottoms sliding across its seams and high spots. The top of the dashboard bears a map-work of lines zig-zagging across it – from hairline cracks to deep fissures that expose the foam core, all visible through a sticky layer of dust and dirt that nearly obscures the original tan color and leatherette texture.

"She started talking last Saturday, when I put a mirror in front of her and she got a look at herself. I mean, she didn't actually talk then, just made a sound, like 'ahhh,' which was really like 'what the fuck,' and then I came back the next day and she managed a few real words. Told me she was not Christina, which I already expected, 'cause from the spelling out stuff, and all. We had got from that that she didn't want to be called Christina. Which was ok with me of course, 'cause I'd always known her as Kim. Except that one time she blinked out that she wasn't Kim either, but this doctor guy. Rod something."

"Gimbal?" Aubrey had already spoken the name on the phone, asking Mary to see if she could find out anything about a Dr. Rodney Gimbal, prior to this meeting.

"Yeah."

A click signals that the lighter has heated up sufficiently and Aubrey pulls it out, pressing its glowing coil to the end of her cigarette and inhaling deeply. Mary brushes away the smoke as Aubrey exhales, then opens her window several inches, only to scoot herself closer still to Aubrey in order to get way from the drizzle which makes its way through the opening. With a shrug and a sigh Aubrey cranks her own window down far enough to blow the next puff out into the wider world. "How'd you know that?"

"You told me," Mary answers. "When you called."

"Oh." Aubrey stares for a moment at the woman next to her - a doctor herself, or close enough. Dumpy clothes, like out of some catalog or something. 'Practical' haircut. 'Practical' shoes. 'Practically' too boring to even notice, if not for her connection to Kim.

"I guess maybe I did. Anyway, it took me a while, but I got it figured out now - that this is like, a performance she's doing. Kim's been cooped up inside of herself so long, and she came up with this bit, that she's going to pretend to be someone else now. You didn't know Kim, did you?" Mary shakes her head and Aubrey realizes how absurd the idea is, Kim and Mary might as well have come from different planets. "Course not. Well, she was a real artist, and that was her thing - Performance Art. Jesus, for Kim, every day was a 'performance.' I mean, I thought so back then, before all this started, but I'd say it even more now - now that I know about her mom and everything. She would do those pieces of hers, she'd be so into it...I mean nothing could shake her. Like this one time, she was doing her homeless person in front of Nordstrom's, right downtown, and a cop told her to move along and Kim pretended to flip out and get all angry at him, calling him a communist and a Nazi and stuff. Well, the cop doesn't know she's an artist and all and next thing he's taking her to the police station in handcuffs. Professor Daniels had to go down there and explain it all and get her released and she still didn't break character, even then."

Mary says nothing, waiting for the girl to get around to her point.

"Anyway, that first day, when she got a look at herself, she could only make a few sounds, but I guess she was awake all night working at it, whispering to herself, and by the next day, when I came back, she was starting to actually say words. But only just barely, like one of those retarded people, you know; the way they have to work so hard to make the words come out?" Mary nods in understanding, and Aubrey takes a drag, blows it out the window, and continues. "So ever since then, I've been sneaking in and let me tell you, she's getting it down. She just wants to talk and talk, and she has all these details she's made up about this guy. Who he was, what he was like, but mostly she's just full of questions, like where is she and how did she get there, and that's why I thought of you - I saw you coming out of the house once, back when I was still allowed to visit her, and Mavis told me who you were and when I asked June the last time I was here she told me how I could leave a message for you and... and so, I was wondering if maybe you could talk to Kim. Fill in some of the details about what went on in the hospital, bring her back to reality. Can you do that?"

"There are wonders in the world," Beryl says, as she and Elaine wait for a truck to pick them up at a small airfield outside Tam Dao village in the highlands north of Hanoi, where they have come to visit a man who lives among cobras without fear of being bitten. "Things we believe cannot exist, and yet they do. I've seen a living dragon, you know." The woman's face assumes that slightly smug expression which Elaine has learned to recognize as meaning she desires prompting.

"A dragon?" she asks then, with what she hopes will be the correct attitude of wonderment.

"A dragon," the other repeats proudly, raising her water bottle to her lips and taking a long sip. "A living dragon which has been inside the same cave for at least two hundred years. The local people worship it, bring it offerings, and some even say they have seen it breath fire..."

The roar of an airplane taking off again, after just having delivered them here, sweeps through the corrugated steel walls of the shack which serves as a terminal at this small airstrip, roiling Elaine's stomach as its propellers tear through the atmosphere. "Well," she admits, once the sound has moved away, "I have to agree with you. My education would tell me that is not possible."

"And if I told you I had seen a woman hold fire in one hand, and ice in the other, and be neither burned nor frozen? Would you say that too, was impossible?"

"Absolutely."

Beryl's face blossoms then, the sparkle in her eyes brightening to lunatic level, excitement seeping from every crease and fold.

"If you travel with me," she whispers, then stops and corrects herself – a rare occurrence, in their acquaintance. "*As long as* you travel with me, Elaine, you must not use words like those. 'Absolutely.' 'Impossible.' Words like those will not serve you where we are going."

"If there's nothing else?" Alex Martinez' eyes circle Hilltop's most impressively-panelled conference room. Seeing no hands raised or mouths creeping open, she slaps shut her leather folio and declares the morning's Executive Staff Review closed. "I'll see you all on Thursday. Marty, you wanted to speak to me?"

Marty Sen kills time gathering his papers as the nearly two-dozen department heads and service directors make their way out a pair of monumental walnut doors to the corridor. Beyond the room's enormous window, a steady drizzle beats across lower downtown and, beyond that, the cranes of the freight docks. Still farther off, the water of Puget Sound is dull gray beneath a sky only slightly less dark than its surface. When finally the others have left, he rises and heads down the long, gleaming table toward Martinez, whose wool suit, he notices with little amusement, is an exact color match for that sky.

"I had a call last evening," he begins, as she thumbs something into her Blackberry. "From the girl's fiancé."

"Bear with me," his boss instructs. As always, her voice betrays little emotion, only the clear instruction that they must speak softly. Without looking up she finishes with her electronic minder, places it in a recess of her small tote, and only then begins to move - gracefully and in full control despite tall shoes whose slender heels sink deep into the thick carpet which gives Hilltop's executive suite the look of an expensive corporate headquarters, which, in all important respects, it is. Folio clutched to her chest she leads Marty out a smaller door at one end of the room, into her own front office, where an assistant sits at a walnut work station, headset buzzing as calls come in with machine-like frequency. "Thomas," she calls as they pass, "I'm on my way to Finance. Let them know I'll be there in four minutes." Without missing a beat she drops her folio on Thomas' desk and picks up another which has been sitting there, heads for the door opposite the one through which they have just entered, and continues speaking at Dr. Sen. "So. The fiancé?"

Marty struggles to keep close to Alex as they move down the corridor. "He says the girl is actually speaking. To this other girl..."

"Maturin." Alex's face bears no indication of interest as she stops outside a bank of elevators and presses the call button for 'UP.'

To the constant flow of passersby in this busy hallway she could be hearing a report of Marty's latest tennis match, or a drop in the price of barrels of oil. Only the fact that she has not struck up a conversation with anyone else - or pulled the Blackberry out again - tells him she is, as expected, quite concerned.

"Yes. The weird one. She's been sneaking in to visit and the girl's been saying things..."

"But only to this Maturin girl; not to our team?"

"So far..."

"Good. I like that."

For a moment Sen is perplexed, until he catches his boss's drift.

"We have no direct knowledge," he agrees, as an indicator light flashes green to announce a car's arrival and Martinez' silent nod confirms his understanding. "Only what some un-credentialed friend of the family heard from some low-life girl who isn't even supposed to have been there."

Stainless steel doors open with a whisper as the elevator arrives. An orderly and two women in street clothes step out and Alex glides in as Marty follows closely. A woman in scrubs approaches but Alex fends her off with a glare, her finger already pressed to the 'Door Close' button. With another whisper the doors shut, leaving the two executives alone in a steel box, as beautifully-lined as a gentleman's humidor, the mechanical humming of its workings barely audible, no vapid music to disturb their thoughts.

"We've got to consider the mother in this," Alex begins, for the first time turning to look in her employee's face. "She's elderly; she's had a great shock, her daughter being struck down like that. She does not deserve to have her hopes elevated for nothing. Are we in agreement?" Marty nods. "Good. She needs to keep this other girl away. Maturin. And we need to get the patient on a blocker ASAP. To prevent her causing herself harm, correct?" Again Marty nods. "If the nurse makes any noise, replace her. Him. Whomever."

And that is it. No long involved debate about what the girl's responses might mean. No agonizing over whether perhaps there had been mistakes made in the past, or the possibility of detection in the future. Once again, Marty marvels at his boss's ability not just to avoid obstacles which would make others cringe, but to forge-on without even seeming to acknowledge their existence. Able to pass through endless crises without being harmed, as if the very rules of physics were different for her; she is pure goal-oriented energy and that is how she has risen so far, so fast. Truly, the rules *are* different for some people - Alex is one of those people, and Marty can learn from her, had better learn, in fact, if he wishes to continue his own rise in the MH hierarchy. She had told him as much at their first meeting.

Still, Marty Sen is not Alex Martinez, and the whole affair has got him worried and fearful enough that he cannot help calling for one more life raft.

"What about Parry," he asks, as the doors begin to open. "And Ayers?"

"They're your responsibility, Marty," Alex says breezily as the doors open on a corridor bustling with business suits and buzzing with conversation. For a brief moment her face shifts into a sly grin. "I trust you'll bring them along," she says, and disappears into the flow, leaving Marty nothing to do but press the L button and wait as the cab fills with people and noise.

"...not a damned thing," one man says softly to another as they squeeze inside the now-crowded elevator cab and turn to face the anonymity of closing doors. "We watched the game, had a drink after, and then all she wanted was to go home. Alone."

"Story of my life," says his companion. "Eighty bucks for tickets and what does it get you?"

"So where we going for lunch?"

Beside them, Mary Antonias wonders at the idleness of their talk. Where do they get the hours to go to games, out to lunch? She herself has barely time between shifts to get home, sleep half as much as she really needs and get cleaned up before heading back to the hill. It's taken several weeks of waiting for a quiet hour so she could make this trip to the fifth floor and innocently request the correct ID number to submit a leftover billing code on the account for one Christina McKloskey.

To her surprise there was no confusion, no missing records in Accounting. A clerk pulled up the name, gave her the patient ID number and even answered her question about the funding, which he was not, strictly, supposed to do. No, he explained without hesitation, there wasn't any insurance code to include. Christina's costs were being (not 'had been,' she noted) posted to an operational account and, though the clerk did not say it, Mary understood enough about the business end of medicine to understand what that meant: Hilltop Medical Center had absorbed - and was continuing to absorb – all costs of the girl's treatment on its own, without even trying to be reimbursed. Not something a hospital would do for no reason, especially with the hawks from MH looking over their shoulders.

Pondering this as the elevator descends, it takes Mary a moment to realize that she has seen one of its occupants before - the one who remained inside the cab when its doors opened to disgorge the 'Hefe,' as Alex Martinez is known to the less reverent staff. Where has she seen him before? Not on rounds, his face doesn't reflect the constant, critical tension that comes with active practice. No, it must be somewhere else. She does not read newspapers or magazines, so that cannot be it. A bulletin board perhaps, or a newsletter circulated to all the staff. That's it, a bulletin in her mailbox sometime back, boasting about Hilltop's recent accreditation in pharmacological treatment of emotional disorders. Marty somebody or other, she remembers; high up in the management. He could probably tell her why the center would be paying for Christina's care. Of course she'd have to explain to him how she knew that - and why she cared, in which case she'd probably not learn a thing, and maybe get herself fired in the process. Still, if she had the nerve...the right approach. Maybe talk him up a bit. Flirt. Distract him with her eyes, her hair, her figure, like they do in the movies or on TV. If only this were a scene from Charlie's Angels.

It's not, of course, and Mary Antonias hasn't entertained that fantasy in a very long time. Not since Wednesday evenings in seventh grade, watching her favorite show in Mom's bedroom, and so she keeps her mouth shut as the cab stops at the ground floor, doors opening to the bustling lobby, where pages and ring tones bounce off soaring plaster walls and spotless glass storefront. She lingers a moment, watching as Sen strides confidently toward an open corridor. Only when other passengers begin entering does she realize it's time for her to move, making her way against the in-flow of bodies. Move out the doors and down the hall - back to work, back to her questions, her doubts. Her obsession.

Barely ten minutes later, Marty Sen is back at his own desk, on the speaker phone with Dr. Carl Ayers, Mrs. McKloskey's representative on the three-man board of oversight. "We've got to consider the mother's emotional well-being," he begins, and hears Carl murmur in agreement. "I trust you'll come along with me on this...."

June Hirschfeld, CNP, strides down the sidewalk through a watery mist which promises to last all morning. Mrs. McKloskey has delayed her departure with questions about Christina's night.

"How did she sleep?" the woman wanted to know.

'Like she'd been drugged,' the nurse wanted to say, but phrased her thought instead in a more politic manner for her employer. "The same as always."

"Did she seem troubled by her dreams?"

No more so than your ordinary log.

"Any change in her condition?"

Only towards the end of each cycle of her medication, June pointed out, to no avail. Each time the time for her next round of medication approached, there seemed to be an increase in the small hand and leg twitches which she has found in other patients to be an early sign of sensation returning to a numb and damaged limb. But it is no such sign to Mrs. Mckloskey, nor to the girl's doctors. No, June fumes, as she stretches out her paces to ensure she reaches the stop before her bus does. From their reactions you'd think it was her 'fault' the patient was exhibiting signs of possible improvement.

Even as June is turning the corner onto Hamlin Way, a battered brown sedan weaves across to the wrong side of the pavement and to take up a stretch of curb in front of the house which once belonged to the great Sean McKloskey. Aubrey's heart thumps in her chest as she climbs out of the driver's seat, shuts the door and makes her way up the steep walk. Her legs feel naked and vulnerable, their freshly-shaven flesh brushing the hem of the skirt she's borrowed from Mary. Her toes complain as each step presses them into the narrow confines of the matching pumps, their unaccustomed height a constant reminder to stand straight and walk with care. Reaching the stoop she pauses to tug at the jacket of her suit, shift from right hand to left the stupid little purse which Mary has insisted she carry, and, finally, after several deep breaths, reach out to press the doorbell.

"Look, Mrs. McKloskey," Aubrey rushes to explain as soon as the door is opened, even as she can see the frown spreading across Anne's face. "I want to apologize. For sneaking in to see K...I mean Christina."

The older woman's face is impassive, the door still held open hardly more than a crack. Aubrey pulls the jacket more closely around her neck in imitation of someone chilled and in need of mothering.

"I'm sorry I got on your bad side or whatever...that we got off to a bad start, I mean... Actually, we should be friends, 'cause we both really care about what happens to Christina. You do see that, don't you? That we have that in common?"

Anne considers for what seems a long time, and Aubrey's heart sinks. This is not going to work, she is thinking, there is no way this woman is going to fall for me apologizing. Even in this get up.

"I thought," she begins again, "maybe you could give me another chance. If I could tell you how much Chris meant to me, about the good times we had together before... Well, maybe you'd understand..." Looking around, at the street, glistening black and wet, shivering her shoulders, Aubrey brings puppy eyes back to Mrs. Mckloskey and finds something there which she has not noted in any adult's expression for a very long time.

"We're letting the heat out," Anne says. "Why don't you come inside for a minute?"

As soon as she sees the front door close Mary climbs out of the Olds and scuttles across the street, then makes her way up the sloping lawn and along the side of the house. At the back corner she steadies the fence gate with one hand while she thumbs the latch, wary of the slightest sound. Closing the gate carefully behind her, she hugs the edge of the bushes to round the pool, its surface almost completely covered now with soggy brown leaves. Stopping at the guesthouse door she knocks very softly. Hearing no response, she knocks again and then, very carefully, turns the knob and opens the door.

The room is just as she has seen it on her earlier visits. Same lily-dotted wallpaper, pale-gold curtains with sheer liners, their lacy edges scalloping the windows into storybook fancies. Pictures on the dresser of young Christina and her mother, young Christina and her father, young Christina, Christina, Christina. The patient sits up in the bed now, back supported by several pillows. The face is familiar from Mary's previous visit, but there is a very different quality to the expression she sees as she closes the door behind her and stands, hand still on the knob.

"Christina?" she calls softly. There is no answer. The eyes are only half opened, pupils dilated slightly. Mary moves to one side of the room and the head remains fixed, eyes still aimed at the opposite wall. The face is made up, as on her last visit, hair carefully brushed and laid out, a bit longer than before. The delicate hands still deathly pale, resting in her lap, tips of two fingers barely touching one another. Beautifully perfect at first glance, then provoking, just as Mary has always found her, and no, what it provokes isn't anything as easy as curiosity - Mary has seen enough patients already that she does not ache to know every suffering individual's story. Envy might be closer to the truth perhaps, but who could be envious of one so incapacitated?

"Kim?" she calls out, chasing such thoughts from her head, and then again, a little louder this time, though the room is still and there is no doubt her voice would already have carried the few feet to those pearl-hung ears. Again, no response. Just what one would expect of a patient with complete loss of brain function. A body in a bed, breathing, beating, but nobody home. Still, something inside Mary fights against accepting that. Perhaps her commitment to healing, or her own ego; the conceit that she, with all her training, ought to be able to do something to save this child from her fate. Or perhaps it is something else, something less intellectual. The sixth or seventh or eighth sense that one develops after working with patients long enough.

"Dr. Gimbal?" she asks softly of the motionless face, quite embarrassed at the absurdity of this last-ditch question. "Can you hear me, Dr. Gimbal?"

By the time she leaves, Mary has spent less than five minutes in the room, but it is all she needs. No verbal. No reflex in any extremities. Vitals strong, but no sign whatsoever of directed motor activity, and certainly no speech. Nothing to justify Aubrey's frantic claims and conspiracy theories.

Absolutely nothing.

It is like some ancient myth, some horrible play-acting written by an evil-hearted pervert. To have felt my capabilities returning - to communicate - for so short a time. Oh, the relief they brought me, those few minutes of being able to speak and move; to act. And then to have it taken away, disappearing over – what? not overnight; my waking and sleeping are not day and night in the usual sense, but my own private damnation of losing the world and finding it again, over and over and... I digress. With no reality to hang on to, no anchor point, I lose track of my own thoughts; what is and was and never was and perhaps could be again sometime in future...

To have had that taste of catching hold of the world, and then to have it taken away and to realize myself once again being handled like a piece of freight, manipulated however they wish and now comes this one; obviously an intelligent young woman with some degree of medical knowledge, from the way she took my pulse, the focused look in her eyes as she extended my fingers, tapped my arm. CALLING ME BY MY OWN NAME and me not able to acknowledge, to react in any way. For the life of me I CANNOT STAND THIS ANY LONGER. I feel my mind slipping away, thoughts racing around... do this, try that... but nothing makes any difference.

I shout inside my head, but there is no welcome reverberation, no one cringing in fear at my soundless voice. I beat imaginary fists against the walls of my own mind, but there is no reassuring pain in the flesh, no resonating thump to prove I have an effect, quixotic though it might be. Empty visions are all I have, bringing no release to the pent up energy, the need to make a difference. Helplessness is one thing, powerlessness is another, but total ineffectuality is yet a higher plane of frustration and despair.
THIS IS THE WORST.

"I'm speechless."

Anne McKloskey is sitting on her living room sofa, her salon-perfect hair backlit by the June sun, hands folded carefully in her lap, legs cocked slightly to the right, knees together. Just as she was taught to sit by her own mother decades ago. A proper woman, her mother was, Virginia Arbaney, who taught her daughter to sit properly, enunciate clearly, and behave as a lady was supposed to. Unlike these young women today.

"I'm speechless," she repeats, as deeper thoughts compose themselves inside her. "To think that this has been going on in my own house. Right under my nose. Conspiring against me..."

Mary Antonias lowers her eyes. Despite her suspicions about the mother's state of mind, she has to admit a degree of shame about sneaking around as she has done, though at this moment she knows she is in the right. As soon as it had become clear there was no truth to the reports of Christina's miraculous recovery, she marched herself right over to the main house and burst in on Aubrey's diversionary conversation. Oddly enough, she found the two of them having what looked like a pretty good time of it. Chatting away over flowered bone china, tea and cookies flowing like the proverbial peace pipe. Not surprising that Mrs. M. was enjoying herself, but Aubrey was either a helluva a good actress or she had found herself appreciating the older woman's company in a way Mary never would have guessed. It almost seemed a shame to break up the party with the disappointing truth.

"You're right, Mrs. McKloskey," she resumes, with all the humility she can muster. "We had no business going behind your back, but I can assure you it won't happen again. I believe Aubrey truly cares for your daughter, and she just let her imagination run away with her."

"What do you mean my imagination?" Aubrey practically shouts, sending the cookie dish flying as she rises to her feet, only to have one ankle fold atop a carelessly-placed heel. The stumble adds embarrassment to anger and her face flushes bright pink as she struggles to disengage her other foot from the legs of the coffee table. "Are you saying you don't believe me, after you've seen it, heard it with your own ears?"

"I didn't hear anything Aubrey. And what I saw is the same as before. A young woman with extensive and profound loss of brain function. No motor capabilities beyond simple reflex response to local stimulation. No evidence of consciousness or autonomy. She can't talk, she can't *do* anything..."

"She can so talk. She's talked to me on Sunday." To Mary's surprise Aubrey is almost hysterical, clearly near tears as she moves about the room as if looking for an exit. Stumbling again, she kicks off first one tall shoe and then the other, to stand stocking-footed and diminished, her lower lip trembling slightly as she looks from Mary to Anne and back again to settle her eyes there, an expression of understanding gradually consuming her face. "Oh, I get it now - this is some kind of fucking conspiracy and you're in on it, too, aren't you?"

"I will not have that language in my home," Anne scolds, only to have Aubrey's attention snap back over to her.

"Fucking, fucking, fucking," she repeats, bending forward with both arms extended, middle fingers flashing in the elderly woman's direction. "You're keeping your fucking daughter like a fucking prisoner and now you've got everyone else playing along with you. Well I'm not buying it lady. I'm not buying any of it, and you..." Turning to Mary she begins shucking off the borrowed jacket, "can keep your smart-ass objectivity and your fucking polyester suit..." Tossing the jacket in Mary's face she twists around, nearly losing her balance as she searches for the skirt button. Feet moving in a tight spinning circle to keep from falling over, her fingers fumble ineffectually until, with a grunt, she rips open the overlapping waistband, sending the button flying to clatter against a lamp on the nearby end table. Stepping out of the skirt she flings that too in Mary's direction.

"You may not give a shit about what happens to Kim, but I do, and I will find a way to help her, I swear I will, if it's the last fucking thing I do," Aubrey shouts before turning to leave the room, even as her hands tear at the buttons of her blouse.

"Well," Anne remarks, several seconds after the slam of the front door has died out. "It's just as well Christina won't be exposed to *her* attitudes in future."

182

"Your husband's life is like a hollow tree; its center has been eaten away. A hollow tree gives no fruit or blossoms; it cannot dance with life's breezes, only resist them, and when the strong gusts of misfortune come along - it will snap and fall."

Elaine looks down at her friend.

"Parting from him was a necessary step for you."

Beryl's bony fingers are caressing the tail of an enormous carved dragon whose coils nearly fill the cave in which they stand. Reaching it has taken three days' journey from Phnom Penh, two of them spent on one of those rickety buses which seem to be Beryl's preferred method of transit, the third a wet and insect-ridden trudge through a forest of towering ebony and teak trees, over ground most remarkable for its abundance of tripping roots lurking beneath a carpet of leaves both dead and alive, and for the frequent rustling of snakes and who-knows-what other creatures, similarly hidden from sight.

They have spoken little along the way. For some time now Elaine has noticed Beryl's verbosity retreating, her conversation dwindling into short bursts. At first she felt herself alarmed by this, wondering whether she had done something to disappoint her friend, but after a time she came to understand it as a sign of acceptance. Arriving in a new town, it was now Elaine who would ask for directions to a place where they could stay. Haggling with a hotel proprietor, chattering with the woman cooking one of the many indescribable meals they had taken to eating; it was Elaine who navigated the pair through these and other day to day events, while Beryl's attention seemed focused inward, attending to the outside world only when they reached some destination, or were ready to embark on a new chapter of their journey. She had become less a person, it seemed, than a reference. A living, breathing itinerary for the journey on which she intended Elaine to travel.

"How do you think this got here?" Beryl asks, voice raised slightly over the hiss of propane lanterns carried by their two guides, whom the innkeeper had insisted must accompany them to the cave. His insistence had been firm, buttressed by a hand gesturing toward his own groin as he explained in fragmented English the dangers which might befall two 'lovey women,' alone outside the village.

Elaine looks carefully at the beast. Its body and wings,

covered with scales tipped in gold paint, twist oddly in the space; a tortured writhing that leaves barely enough room to walk around it. Certainly the cave's narrow entrance would not have allowed it to be brought inside as it is.

"It must have been brought up in parts," she answers, though she can make out no seams. "Carved down in the village in pieces I suppose, then carried up here to be put together. Painted afterwards to conceal the seams."

"The people in the village say the dragon grew here. You don't believe that though, do you?"

"It didn't grow; it was carved. Out of wood. By people."

Breathing audibly, Beryl moves around a bit, making a show of examining the rock walls which bear clear signs of having been worked themselves – chips and scrapes and gouges repetitive enough to certify them the work of human hands. Finding a suitable spot, she settles herself, sitting precariously on a small ledge. For some time she is silent, and when she speaks again, her voice is soft, forcing Elaine to lean far forward to hear her words.

"When one thinks one *knows* something, it sometimes prevents one from seeing what *is*," Beryl recites, her expression in the flickering lamplight an infuriating mix of serenity, smugness and good humor. Her eyes seem focused on the reptile's head, which protrudes out of its massive coils, piled almost to the top of the space. There, near the top, the head presses against the cave's roof, its rippling gold tongue flicking out into the air, as if frozen in motion. As Elaine studies the scene, eyes straining against the shadows, she gradually makes out that the beast's head is not free of the ceiling, but rather is fused to a dark mass squeezing out from a fissure in the overhanging slabs of rock. The mass appears different than the surrounding rock, softer edged and without the quartzite sparkle. A warm brown tone, and if she allows her eyes to stray off-center she can make out, with the sharper perception of peripheral vision, dangling shreds of a papery thin reddish-brown outer layer and beneath it, the lighter, smoother sheen of hard, moist wood.

"It's a root," she concludes softly. "Sent down by some tree above this cave. It must have grown here for a hundred years, twisting around in search of water. Skinny where it reached into a crevice in the rock, fatter where the space allowed. Someone found it and carved it into this dragon." Without looking she knows that Beryl's smile will have coalesced at this, spreading across the wizened face in satisfaction.

"So you see, the villagers are correct. The dragon is alive. And it did grow here."

"But it isn't really a dragon."

"Really? What means – 'really'?" For a moment Beryl sounds as if she is making fun of her own attitude. Elaine looks over and sees an impish smile flash upon on her friend's face, confirming the touch of humor, but immediately her expression grows serious again. "When you entered the cave, your eyes recognized the form of a dragon, but your education told you such a thing could not be alive, and so you concluded that it was not 'real.' Then, when you looked at it with wonder, you realized that it *is* alive. Has been alive, in fact, longer than you or I. And it acts, too, though more slowly than you and I can perceive. For decades this messenger grew downward, searching, following - exploring. Reaching out to explore the earth with a force that can split rock, to bring back precious moisture which would sustain the tree above. Many years ago, that tree was struck by lightning, and caught fire - if you look closely, you can see where the charring reached all the way down here, to the dragon's head. The people who observed it said the dragon was breathing that fire. After the flames died out, and the smoke finally ceased, the people thought the dragon had died, and they mourned for it, but eventually a new shoot sprouted from the charred stump, and once again there is a leafy tree growing from this same root; a tree which blossoms and bears fruit."

Once again Beryl falls silent, appearing deep in distant thought. When she speaks again, it is in a voice of utmost seriousness, the same voice one might use to confide some dire news: the loss of a fortune, the death of a loved one. The sort of voice a well-travelled woman uses when she has glimpsed the approach of her own mortality.

"The dragon *is* real, Elaine, but with a different reality than that which you expected. A reality you could only see after you had opened up your mind and begun to question what you thought you knew. There is more wisdom to be found in questioning, my dear, than in knowing. More wisdom in wonder than in all the lessons ever taught, all the books ever written."

Even at midnight, streetlight glare streams in through the thinly-curtained windows of Aubrey's inheritance: an algae-green Monopoly-house of a bungalow, jammed-in tight between a derelict gas station and the three-story brick mass of the Eddystone apartments, home to retired merchant seamen and never-married stock-clerks. The thumping beat emanating from her stereo is more successful at closing out the audible world than stapled beach towels are the visible one; it easily overpowers the shuss of tires from the nearby highway as she methodically strips clothes from hangers on a closet rod, gathering jeans, shirts, sweaters and whatever else is there among them. When her arms are as full as she can carry she moves rapidly through the bedroom and across the living room. Pushing the screen door open with her hip she steps to the porch rail and heaves her load onto a rapidly growing pile which nearly fills the narrow strip of dying weeds and gravel which passes for a front yard, towered over by the concrete lanes of Interstate 5, whose pole-mounted lamps cast an uncompromising light on all who come and go in this stretch of Forty-third Street. Without remark she turns back into the house and gathers another load.

  Once she has finished with the closet, she starts in on the tall dresser, hauling each drawer out through the rooms to dump its contents onto the pile. After that there are food items from the kitchen cupboard, boots and jackets from behind the door, and two posters from the wall above the narrow kitchen table. After half an hour's hard work she surveys the ravaged rooms with a suspicious eye, before stepping quickly over to the TV, pulling cables from the VCR and hauling that as well to the pile outside. Leaving the front door open – no sense making this more difficult than it needs to be - she switches off the stereo, stretches out on the couch and closes her eyes.

  Just after 1 AM she is roused from a sound sleep by a shout outside the door.

  "What the fuck?" calls a voice, young, male, and well-lubricated. A moment later the screen door is pushed all the way open to admit a smallish man dressed in black jeans and a motorcycle jacket, black leather with crimson inserts on the elbows and shoulders and 'Bultaco' writ large across the back. Beneath his arm is a matching helmet, its mirrored visor sparkling as he teeters through the door. His hair is matted with sweat and his eyes have the rheumy look of one long overdue for a pillow. Fumbling around the door jamb he locates a switch and clicks the room into brightness.

"What the fuck?" he repeats to Aubrey's blinking face. "What the…"

"Stop," she cuts him off in a stage whisper, "and keep your fucking voice down." Rising from the couch she stands as straight and tall as she can, her eyes coming nearly even with his. "I've had enough; I know about Rachel, by the way, and that you've been selling again. Which means you've got no excuse for being two months behind on your room rent."

The man is rubbing his eyes now, head wobbling from side to side, as if trying to convince himself that this is all a dream. He places the helmet on a table only to watch as Aubrey picks it up ceremoniously in two hands and marches, holding it out at arms' length, to drop it atop the pile outside.

"You can't do this Aub, it's the middle of the fucking night…."

"Keep your voice down," she says again as she returns. "There are people sleeping."

A look of confidence erupts on the drunken man's face as he first glances - and then begins moving - toward the door of Aubrey's larger bedroom. "So that's it, hunh? You found yourself someone else, so you throw me out on my ass in the middle of the…" The thought is stillborn as he flips on a light to find the bed empty. Confusion replaces the earlier expression and is itself replaced by weariness as he slumps back against the wall and slowly slides to the floor.

With surprising tenderness, considering her earlier actions, Aubrey steps to his side and squats, pulling his chin up so he is forced to look her in the eye.

"That's not it," she whispers gently. "I'm just sick of your stupid face and your stupid screwing around and me feeling like your stupid mother." With a look of rage the man reaches up and grabs her wrist, holds it for a long beat, then smiles broadly. Aubrey smiles as well and the two break into laughter, at first nervous and restrained, then louder and more sincere, the sound of great relief. Aubrey settles down onto her haunches, rolls over against the wall and very slowly slides down, until she too is sitting on the floor, their two hands clutching one another softly.

"In that case," the man says after they have exhausted their laughter. "You're not kicking me out. I'm kicking you out. Out of my fucking life, you stupid little bitch."

A few minutes later he is gone, with a plan to flop at a friend's house and a promise to return in the morning for his things. As Aubrey settles into her bed for what is left of the night she is pleased to conclude that Step Number One was not nearly as painful as she thought it might be.

Dark. Silent. Still.

The agony of another long awakening, as I ponder the black hole of my Nothing.

That room, those people – were just one more of the many illusions to which I am prey. Dreams, memories, imaginings. Random chemical interactions.

Seeing other persons... their hands, their faces...hearing their voices and even my own; of course it was not really real. Just another trick of what is now my life...no, not life; my <u>existence</u>. The dream contained a kernel of truth and the truth is that this is what comes after life, this waking from Nothing into memory and dreams and hallucinations. Into imaginings which are meaningless because they have nowhere to go. Useless. Pointless, without a life in which to live them out.

I suppose this is the punishment for my sins, whatever they were. To travel perpetually between memory and emptiness, never again to move forward. To find myself now wishing only for it to end once and for all. For the peace of less than Nothing.

Dark. Silent. Still.

No breeze stirs the rhododendron bushes as three black-clothed figures creep past walls of peeling whitewashed brick. A thick coating of debris lies still on the water's surface, no current moving its leaves and twigs, its moldering blossoms and wind-blown seed pods, no ripples disturbing their scalloped shapes, drifted and massed into every corner. Footsteps from the figures sound as soft as the falling of leaves; barely-audible sonic signatures progressing across the concrete patio to approach the door of the small cottage-like building.

"Wait, I've got to change my grip," a voice whispers. A shifting of fabric, the tiniest creak of metal, and then "OK, that's better. Jeez, this is so noir, I can hardly stand it. "

A hand grasps a doorknob, turning it slowly. A scraping movement inside the wall, bolt sliding against strike-plate, then a soft click as the door is pushed out a fraction of an inch by the energy stored in compressed rubber weather-stripping.

"You first," whispers the voice again, a young man's, as the door swings wide to the inside, revealing in pale-green nightlight-glow, a bedroom. Beyond that, in the smaller room of the cottage, June the nurse lies in her own bed, eyes carefully shut, thoughts consumed by a new mantra, cycling through her head like a folk song sung in a round. 'I never heard a thing; they must have been so quiet; I can't believe I slept right through it. I never heard a thing.'

The tallest of the three figures advances toward the bed where a young woman lies, motionless. Surgical tubing runs from an IV stand beside her, curving down to the side of her neck where it disappears beneath a patch of tape.

"So, what's this thing here?" asks the tallest of the three, his voice, cocky and confident despite his obvious ignorance of the situation. Mark Peterson had the good fortune to be sucking down a cinnamon-apple frappe at the Good Cup when the others of this unlikely band met to discuss their plan. An aspiring screenwriter, the opportunity to experience a possible plot development firsthand was more than enough inducement to recruit him to the team.

"That's an epidural," answers the first voice, also male. Though its owner is clearly fluent with medical jargon, his tone communicates tension, doubt and Desmond's very real desire to get this over with, as quickly and quietly as possible. "Dripped directly into the spinal fluid. Causes complete shutdown of motor control, reflex and sensation below the point of insertion. June said that was part of the new regimen. Put in as soon as the docs realized she was getting back some sort of motion."

"Awesome," offers Mark, and his hands reach up to remove the plastic bladder from the rack.

"Careful," Desmond says now, his face revealed in the soft glow of the night light as he moves near to the bed. Worry lines are etched around his eyes, the bags of sleeplessness deepened over the last few weeks as he has struggled to find a new job with Mrs. McKloskey's negative reference following him to every interview. There is no hesitation in his actions though, when it comes to the patient's care. He knows what needs to be done here, at least the medical details. "Don't kink the drip line. We won't disconnect until later. Till we decide if we're going to bring her out of it."

"How, not if," reminds a third voice, coming from the smallest of the three. It carries neither the giddy excitement of Peterson's, nor the tentative worry of Desmond's, but a grim determination. Aubrey Maturin is the author of this little drama, the one who decided action must be taken, recruited the others, and insisted that they follow a carefully-developed game plan. Besides that, the night is her element, far more so than it is for either of the others.

"Open it up now," Desmond instructs, and metal scrapes briefly against metal as his two companions extend and lock the legs of the wheeled stretcher they have been carrying between them.

"Mark's on the shoulders, Aubrey, you get the feet." Rubber soles scuffle along the carpet as the figures take their places. "Blanket off," comes the command, and four hands pull the blanket and top sheet free and toss it aside. "Corners," and all four corners of the bottom sheet are pulled out and gathered close around the sleeping patient. "And on my count... one, two, three and *go*."

The inert figure makes not a moan as it is hoisted clear of the mattress. The two novice orderlies have no trouble lifting its slight mass across onto the stretcher, where it is quickly secured with nylon straps tightened and double checked.

"I've got the chart," Desmond calls out as he grabs a clipboard from the bedside table and places it inside a nylon duffle. He lifts a tray from its place on the dresser and dumps its contents into the bag as well. The clatter of bottles and utensils rings like a carillon in the otherwise silent room. "And the meds."

191

"Perfect," Peterson whispers approvingly. "A little noise boosts the suspense."

"Fuck the suspense," Aubrey corrects him. "Let's roll." With a tip of her head and a surge of her shoulders she sets the stretcher in motion toward the door, which Peterson just manages to open wide-enough in time for it to pass. Crossing the threshold there is a loud clanking and the front legs of the stretcher collapse, dropping that end to the concrete with a scraping thud.

"Shit," Aubrey exclaims, "I...."

"It's OK." Desmond is there, one hand holding the drip-bladder high while the other lifts the end of the stretcher and rests it on his raised knee as he reaches down and locks its legs into place. In the time it takes him to do this Aubrey has made a discovery.

"Shit," she hisses, her voice returned to its loud stage-whisper. "A fucking light just came on."

The others follow her gaze to an upstairs window, the amber glow of which definitely was not present when they crossed the patio, short minutes ago. Three sets of nervous eyes watch as a form appears, silhouetted against the yellow glow. As if in slow motion the window slides upward and a voice rings out, shattering the night.

"Who's there?" Anne McKloskey calls, not the least bit groggy. The parent's reflex, instilled decades ago, has brought her instantly to waking at the first sound from the direction of her sleeping child. "Is somebody there?"

"Move," Aubrey urges, more exhalation than speech, and the stretcher begins to roll, its hinges clanking with every joint in the flagstones.

"Oh, my goodness," Anne shouts as the gate closes and the back yard returns to its customary vacancy. "My goodness, no! They've taken my Christina." Her tone rises from uncertainty to urgency as her eyes turn helplessly toward darkened roof-scapes barely visible over intervening hedges and shrubberies. "Stop them, someone stop them! They're stealing my baby."

"I like that," Peterson mutters cheerfully as the trio come out onto the front lawn and accelerate toward his van, waiting at the curb with its back doors already splayed open. "Distraught mother catches them in the act, summons neighbors. Maybe one has a shotgun. Yeah, one impotent blast as they disappear around the corner. That's the way Frankenheimer would have done it. Tarantino would have, like a whole platoon of urban-rednecks, zombie-ing in from all directions..."

third movement

1

"Calm down, Mrs. McKloskey. Get a grip on yourself."

Carl Ayers speaks softly to avoid disturbing his own wife, sleeping a dozen feet away. He is leaning against the dresser, one hand combing through his thinning gray locks as the other holds the cordless to his ear. Draping folds of his pajamas glow cobalt in the narrow moon-beam falling through the skylight of their dressing room; otherwise all is midnight darkness as his mind catches up with the circumstances. He has just been awakened by the ringing of his phone. It is that girl's mother, the questionable one. Her 'baby girl' is missing – 'stolen' is how she put it, an expression which strikes him, at this moment, as oddly apropos. Immobile, uncommunicative, requiring constant support and maintenance, yes, she *is* more object than person. A 'thing,' which can be considered to have been 'stolen,' rather than the more dire 'kidnapped' which would apply to the same crime against the living. So it seems, away from the light of day, and so it must stay.

"No," he continues in response to her flood of questions. "Do <u>not</u> call anyone else. I'll be right over – as soon as I make a couple of calls. I'm sure there's a rational explanation for this."

Minutes later, phone calls made, Ayers is directing the questions at himself as he pulls on brown slacks and a black polo shirt, the combination he long ago settled upon as appropriate attire for dire after-hours consultations. He has no answers yet, though several possibilities are forming in his mind. There are a finite number of people who even knew the girl was there, an even smaller number who have any reason to care about her situation, and there is a reason the girl was taken - just as there is a reason he got himself tangled up in this mess with Alex Martinez and the rest of the Hilltop crowd. Relationships come with both benefits and responsibilities. With privileges and with confidences. Grown-ups can handle that, he reminds himself, dragging a hand to lightly touch his wife's sleeping foot beneath the mounded duvet as he passes toward the door, and Carl Ayers is nothing, if not a grown-up.

UNTITLED
A Screenplay by Kelvin Marcus Peterson
Draft - 001

(Note to self - put one of those disclaimer things at the beginning
that says "this film is based on a true incident, some of the
names have been changed to protect the innocent," etc., etc.,)
Talk to Prof. K. about which names to change (besides me =
Francis), whether I really need to change any others, so leav for
now.

Act II (Act I will be the rescue and all the stuff up to it – get
Aubrey to help me with more detail on that, after I have an
outline for it.)

scene 1: Interior, small hours of the morning: The rescuers have
brought the girl to Aubrey's house, a cramped, dingy set of
rooms in a neighborhood dominated by the overhead ramps of a
freeway interchange. Traffic sounds pervade everything, as does
the clutter and mess of a depressing bohemian poverty, like Rent
without New York City. or music. Clumsily they shift her from the
gurney to the bed, IV tubes tangling in the process.
Aubrey: Can we disconnect this thing now?
Desmond: Not yet, we'll reduce the flow gradually over the next
few hours, see what happens.
Francis (me): You mean you don't know what will happen?
Desmond: Well... I have a pretty good idea. But it's always...
(Francis is giving him a hard stare, Desmond gets more nervous
by the second) you've got to...every patient is different. You've
got to take it one step at a time. You don't want to go barging in
and...
Francis: Isn't that what we just did?
End of scene 1.

Scene 2: Interior: Aubrey's apartment, bedroom, later that same
morning. The girl is obviously waking up from a drugged state.
Her eyes open and close at random, her arms and legs twitch and
jerk. The kidnappers (change this to conspirators?) are becoming
concerned.

Aubrey: Is this what's supposed to happen?

Desmond: Not exactly.

Francis: So, exactly what *is* supposed to happen?

Desmond (as he tries to get control of her arms and pin them beneath the sheet): She should just... I don't know, wake up and... If it's like Aubrey said, that she can talk and all, she'll be, like, really grateful to us for getting her out of there, and then we go to someone to get the old lady and the docs in trouble and say that we're the heroes for saving her from them.

Just then the girl swings a leg up and kicks him in the back of the head. Desmond goes flying and Aubrey steps in to try to hold her down. Francis moves quickly, tearing a spare bed sheet into strips and begins to tie her limbs to the corners of the bed (a four-poster? No, Aubrey wouldn't have that kind of bed. Find an old metal frame that he can tie things to)

Francis: Well you're supposed to know about this medical stuff. You better figure out something quick, before someone gets hurt.

end of scene 2

scene 3: Interior, the bedroom, several hours later. The girl is wide wake, eyes scared and darting around the room. The conspirators are gathered around her, eyes baggy from lack of sleep. Desmond is agitated, Aubrey very worried. Desmond: I just don't know. Her vitals say she should be fully conscious and communicative. Her eyes are alert and responding to light. It's like, she's there and all, but she can't control what her body is doing.

Only Francis, of the three, seems in command of himself and the situation. Sipping coffee from a mug, he assesses the situation coolly, speaks with a voice of authority.

Francis: Could it be an after-effect, from being on the neural blockers for so long? You said they're really powerful.

Desmond (at a loss, stumbling over his own words): Yeah, it could be. It could also be...

Aubrey: The truth is, you don't fucking know do you?

Desmond averts his eyes, shuffles his feet.

Aubrey: You haven't got a fucking clue what to do have you? Kim's been drugged up the ass for weeks (as she's speaking, cut to the girl's eyes, opening and closing, then focusing on each of them in turn) and now we brought her here to get her clean and

195

you haven't got a fucking clue what to expect or how to take care of her. We could be doing all the wrong things, and on top of that, we could be arrested for, like, kidnapping and shit and... (throws up her hands in frustration) I can't fucking believe this. While she's been talking, Aubrey has been moving closer into Desmond's face, ignoring the girl. Cut back and forth between their confrontation and the girl's face where we see her lips begin to move, forming words without sound. Background noise of traffic rises up, drowning out the argument, becoming like the rush of water in a river, the sound of blood pumping, insistent, exciting, suggesting something to come.
end of scene 3

Scene 4: Interior, the living room, many hours later, Aubrey asleep on the couch. Sound of conversation from the bedroom, tight shot on Aubrey's eyes opening, closing, opening, trying to shake off sleep (make it clear this is an echo of what is happening in the other room). Slowly, stiff from exhaustion, she rises and moves to the bedroom door. In the background, we see Desmond asleep in a chair.
Francis: ... so we dropped the drip rate to half of what it was, then a quarter, and then a few hours ago, we stopped it completely.
The Girl (she speaks very slowly, one word at a time, like somebody just learning to talk after a stroke or something. Her arms and legs are still tied down, but not jerking around any more. Her face is weird, no real expressions. The eyes are alert, focusing where they should be, but they are the only part of her that seems to work the way it should. Note – her voice – it's the girl's voice in pitch and tone (not the old guy's voice, but maybe use that later, when the audience hears her thoughts) and all, but even as she stumbles through the words, she's got this really superior thing going. Like she knows more than the rest of them put together and thinks they're all a bunch of jerks, right from the moment she first wakes up. She says: "Spastic (something, something, something; medical words I can't remember. Look stuff up and add them later). "
Francis:....it's a commonly encountered residual effect. A sedative would be indicated if the patient's circumstances suggest a possibility of self-inflicted trauma, but contraindications usually prevail. (insert more jargon).
Aubrey, from the doorway: Kimmie!
The girl (to Desmond): What's she doing here?
Desmond : Aubrey? She's the one who organized this, who got

us all together to rescue you and bring you here to her house.
She's also your best friend.
The girl: Best friend? I'm old enough to be her grandfather.
end of scene 4

Scene 5, Interior: The small bedroom of Aubrey's place, shortly
before seven PM. Just as the day's light is leaving the window, a
pair of eyes open. Cautiously they scan the space, taking in its
yellowed ceiling, the palm tree picture beach towel pinned across
the single window and the three concert posters tacked
carelessly around the walls. Alerted by Desmond, who has been
watching and waiting in the corner chair, Aubrey enters from the
living room, where she has been napping on the couch.
Stepping slowly into the patient's field of view she is careful to
wear an expression of calm reassurance.

Aubrey: Welcome back to the world of the living,
Camera cuts back and forth as the two women stare at one
another, and Aubrey has a sense of connecting, of catching a
glimpse of the individual behind those eyes. At the same time
we are struck by the lack of movement in the patient's face.
Where we expect to see a smile of recognition and eyes widening
with wonder, or at least narrowing in suspicion, there is nothing.
The eyes have opened, they are staring and then, just as
suddenly, they are closed more tightly than ever, an act of
conscious shutting out rather than falling back into sleep.
        This is the impression with which we are left; that The
Girl/Patient has not 'fallen' back into anything, but has actively
chosen isolation over connection.

Tea again. An infusion of herbs, actually, this time.

A handful of unidentifiable leaves dumped bare-fisted into the pot by a tanin-complected old man in a sarong the rich, dark color of a fine Malbec. Elaine and Beryl are sitting beneath a raffia canopy overlooking Kaptai Lake, in the Rangamati region of Bangladesh. Rain drips from the canopy's edges; it has been raining for days now, a steady rain, neither shower nor downpour, but constant as the flow from a faucet. Yet it is not the sound which has been wearing at Elaine, nor the challenge of staying dry. Rather, it is the images which that sound conjures that do so. Images which seem to drain something from her, by reminding her...of home. Of sitting quietly in her front room with a cup and a book, surrounded by all her possessions, in rooms she has decorated so they look just-so. Of regular schedules and cooking her own meals in her own kitchen and sleeping in her own bed beside her own husband and of knowing just who it is she is supposed to be.

The fact is, Elaine Gimbal is exhausted. Physically, emotionally, spiritually – in any way she considers the situation, she feels that her resources have been used up. For weeks, it seems, they have been travelling - by plane and train and bus and truck, but mostly by foot. Walking up a mountain, then down. To a temple, and back. Then across a mountain, to get to a temple, then another mountain, to see a snake charmer, to see a snake, to see a woman do tricks with fire and water which must have been tricks, though Elaine cannot imagine how she could possibly have faked such things, with a hundred people watching, some close enough to have their faces flush with heat emanating from one hand, to catch on their tongues the melt-water dripping from the other. Through cities and countryside they have walked, through hotel lobbies and crowded streets to find their meals, their tickets, their inspirations. It is certainly true, as Beryl keeps reminding her, that her strength has grown, her endurance increased, but for every increase in ability, her fearless leader has ratcheted up the demand.

Here and now, listening to the pock-pock-pocketa-pock dripping of rain, Elaine is struck by her own desire for the familiar. After all that newness and unpredictability, there is great peace in hearing the same sound minute after minute. In fixing her eye on a bulbous, glowing droplet. Watching it swell and stretch, dangling longer and more precariously until finally it can hold on no longer and must let go, to disappear down out of sight, leaving in its place the confidence that soon enough, another will form, and another, and another. This she imagines, is how her days once were; glowing droplets glistening round the edges of the life she had chosen, the decisions made long before. The decision to set her sights on Rodney – young, driven, inspiring. To accept his proposal, and be married, a wife, and have a home. Decisions following one another and days following decisions naturally - or at least so it felt at the time. Beryl, she imagines, would say otherwise; and yes, even when her friend is nowhere to be found, Elaine has added that steady voice to the chorus of others inside her head,. Never before, in fact, has she heard so many voices in her own thoughts: her mother's, the authority on how to live and how to look (although she's pretty-well ignored that one recently - her current attire would not have served on Fifth Avenue, which was her mother's standard, though her life was spent on the sidewalks of Carteret, neither would the lengthening silver locks which frame her sunburned features, nor the bracelets and amulets she's accumulated). Her brother Tony's voice too, visiting them in Seattle a few years out of college: "You guys have done pretty well," he had said, looking around the house in Wallingford, which was nothing compared to where they ended up later. "Guess the doctor business isn't bad."

The voices of friends as well: Shirley Melton, whose schoolgirl crushes gushed forth in hours of whispered confidences, leaving a young Elaine feeling woefully inadequate without a beau; Rebecca Dupuis, haughty in her Hollywood-fueled determination to escape to the 'real' world of Paris, London and Vienna, to leave 'all this' behind her and, in the process consign Elaine and all her other classmates to the status of also-rans before the starting gun had even gone off.

And then there is Rodney's voice, louder than any of those, thanks to its booming confidence, its lack of qualification. 'Doubt is a sign of failure,' she had once heard him say, a captured snippet of a conversation with some smug old man at a professional function – a hotel ballroom, perhaps? She wonders for a moment where that was, but then dismisses the wondering. It no longer matters where the conversation happened, or with whom, or what it was about. All that matters out of that moment, after weeks of trudging and climbing and rubbing aching ankles, is Rodney's voice and how it looms in her memory. 'This is what I do,' he said, that last morning, 'this is who I am,' and something inside her had wanted to wrap around that thought and hold on for dear life. To remain safe in the certainty that it was her life, too - being there for him, backing him up and supporting his work. There is no question, sitting here in the middle of nowhere, that a large part of her had wanted to stay there in that comfortable house and do the things she had done for so long; and yet some other part would not let her. Another voice, not shouting or angry, not arguing, nor even rising to be heard; a voice which differed from the others precisely because it was so quiet and patient, yet always, always there. Yes, Elaine thinks, that is it: like the dropping of rain, this last voice has always been present and that is how it was ignored for so long. We tune out what is consistent and focus on what changes - the new, the unexpected – and where does that leave the voice that is always inside us, that has always been there? If we are not careful, we forget that voice even exists - until something happens to allow us to hear it once more.

What happened? What was it that caused her to hear her own voice again – to plan the trip that led to the confrontation that led her to this place that she could never directly have conceived of visiting? It had been a morning, like any other morning. Rodney getting ready for the day, Elaine sitting down to tea – again my blasted tea, she thinks, reaching for her present cup; can I never have enough of the stuff? - leafing through pages of magazines when something stopped in the world around her. The rain perhaps, or the traffic on Montlake Bridge, blocks away. Or the hammering of workers installing a new roof three doors down. It could have been the ticking of the hall clock, its spring winding down after days of perfect synchronization.

Syn. Chron.

A clock slowing down just enough to make itself noticed. Or stopping altogether.

Si. Lence.

Silence then, and an almost inaudible voice floating up from where it had been waiting. Wafting in to wind around her unprotected heart, drowning out the everyday and reminding her that even grown women had dreams once.

'Silence has a voice,' she imagines Beryl saying, 'silence is louder than the boom of a cannon, eruption of a volcano, the big burst of the Big Bang which started it all - or ended it all, if we think in simultaneous opposites,' which - the woman has made clear before - she highly recommends.

Across the table Elaine sees her friend writing, as she often does in the mornings. Precise movements of an almost comically-fat silver pen across pages of cream colored paper which she will fold and place in matching envelopes. What it is the woman writes, Elaine has no idea, for when she asks she receives the merest of explanation, accompanied by that knowing smile. 'My work,' is always the response, as if that dismisses the subject, work being of little importance compared to life and death and knowledge and wonder. In contrast to Rodney, on whose lips the words 'my work' meant everything. Oh, how tall he stood when he spoke of his 'work,' how straight his spine and steady his eyes - oh, damn the man! How she hated him for it; for having his 'work' and lording it over everyone and everything else for all those years. 'His god-damned work,' her perfect gentlewoman of a voice whispers, in the instant before she notices the rain has stopped. A single drop catches her eye, suspended from the tip of a single jagged frond, gathering all the light filtering down through thirty-thousand feet of saturated air to sketch a crystalline crescent and hold in its center a brilliant highlight. Feeling something of herself drawn out to a great length, Elaine perceives the drop more closely, magnified a hundred times, and in it the world reflected, refracted and illuminated for an instant, as clear as the cup perched between her outstretched fingertips. Smells the tea, and the scent of the plant growing in a pot at her feet, infused moisture rising up through the humid air and drifting into her nostrils. The air is inside her even as she is inside the air; the drop is before her and around her and she is inside it looking out and feeling herself drop from the end of the frond as Rodney closes the front door of their house behind him on his way to work, only the sound the door makes is really the sound of Beryl closing her address book.

"Shall we go?" she asks, in a voice brimming over with patience. And sympathy.

Scene 6: Francis sits beside The Girl, tipping a cup of cool water to her lips. The room is dim, lights kept low during the night to avoid attracting notice from neighbors. We can clearly hear the slurping sound when the girl drinks, and the steady ticking of a wall clock (find something silly for this, like a kid's Elmo clock or something, left from when aubs was a kid). The Girl is clearly conscious now, eyes dilated normally, they follow the others as they move around the room. Just like Aubrey said, she can speak, it's kind of mumbled and stumbling, but understandable nonetheless.

The Girl: It... doesn't... matter. (sips, swallows, with big effort) Rod. Christina. Kim. Whatever you ...choose to call me. You're not real anyway. This is all another goddamned dream and... sooner or later it's going to end... and I'll be right back where I was. Wherever that is.

Scene 7: Francis and Delvon are standing in the kitchen drinking a Dew and a Monster, Aubrey has just returned from her waitress shift at the Turkey Trot Restaurant and is asleep on the couch.
Delvon: Maybe it's the drugs. Maybe that inhibitor they were giving her made her, like psychotic or something.
Francis: That was so weird, when she said about those not even being her arms and legs so why should she care? I think, it's like, she woke up so many times before to stuff that turned out not to be real - hallucinations, visions, whatever shit the old lady's doctors put her thru, that she's given up making sense of it all and instead she's convinced herself that it's all just a dream. She'll get over it after a while. Give her time.
Delvon: Speaking of time, it's been nearly a week. Shouldn't something have happened by now, on the news? I mean, it's like, a total media blackout. Didn't the mother even call the cops? That's, like, the first thing I figured she would have done.

(flash back to Delvon and Aubrey and others planning to liberate the girl from her mother's house. It's afternoon, at the Good Cup. Lots of people around, they lean in close to talk to each other, speaking in whispers)

Francis: So, after we rescue her, there's this big hoopla, cops all over the place dusting for prints, CSI teams combing the city for clues, and what we do is, see, we call one of the news stations and say we're Chris friends and we didn't kidnap her, we *rescued her,* from her crazy mother who had her locked up and drugged. We get interviewed and go on the talk shows and all, and then it's the old lady and her doctors who have to answer a million questions. (everyone agrees, high fives all around)

(back to the present, in the kitchen)

Delvon: We're all out of the epidural drip, but as far as I can tell, that was just to tranquilize her, keep her looking like she was comatose (check this out make sure it's the right tech. thing to say, I don't trust his words). It's the other stuff I'm worried about. We're running low on that mestatracine stuff (spelling?). It's not anwhere in any of the drug indexes on the net but from the name I'm figuring it's a modified growth hormone, to speed up healing, except what would still be healing this long after she left the hospital, I have no idea. (the more he talks, the more panicked he gets) Everything's running out, and there's no one to talk to to get more. We need a new plan, and soon.

Francis (suddenly inspired, excited, he moves out of the kitchen and Delvon follows him, thru the living room, to the bedroom door): They're afraid of something. (quick cut to the girl's eyes, she is listening, interested in what he is saying) The sons of bitches are afraid of what she'll say to the cops, so they're waiting for *us* to come to *them.* (He's even more excited now that he's got it figured out, puts his Dew on the table, doesn't even notice as it tips over and spills on the floor, he runs to the sofa where Aubrey sleeps under a blanket, TV glowing softly. With both hands he shakes her into waking, then pulls her up from the couch and steers her into the other room, flicking the lights into full brightness and causing both women to blink and squint for a moment before their eyes connect.)

Francis (to sleepy-headed Aubrey): They didn't call the cops because they don't want her talking to anyone. (points to the girl) They wouldn't give a shit what we say about the drugs and stuff, 'cause we're the guilty ones. But her, she's got no reason to lie, so she's the one they must be afraid of. All this stuff about her not being Chris, not being Kim. There's something there! Something they don't want anyone else to know, so they're waiting for us to come to them. (getting more excited now) We need them, to get more medicine for her, but the thing is, *they* need *us* too, and that's what we've got to work with. She knows something they don't want getting out and *knowledge is power* man.

Aubrey (mumbling, shaking his hand off her shoulder and rubbing her face till the skin turns red): OK. Knowledge is power. So how do we use this 'power' to get some help taking care of her?"

Francis (still wired with excitement, pacing back and forth between the girl and the others – I need to figure out the set, he can't be in both rooms at once? maybe it's a big studio apartment instead – maybe find a real location, like in a warehouse or something – anyway, he has his hands up in front of him, fingers alternately clenching and pointing, like he's examining possibilities in the air around them. Delvon and Aubrey's eyes follow, Chris's expression becoming more animated as his performance becomes more exaggerated.

Francis: I'm thinking, thinking. Ideas…. ideas gotta come. We're like… three days of the Condor, we're on the outside and we've got to get in. Like Jack Ryan….no, like Jason Bourne. We need someone on our side, but with respect. We need… our own doctor that's what we need. We need a doctor to talk to the hospital for us and make a deal. They help us, and we won't…. we won't embarrass them, whatever it is they don't want you (he looks directly at the girl, she looks back at him like she's totally tuned in to his words) to say.

Delvon: What about that other lady you said was interested in her. The one from the hospital, who came to visit?

Aubrey: You mean Mary? (he nods) Hell, she's the one who messed everything up. Told the mother I'd been visiting when I wasn't supposed to. She's, like, the last person I need to talk to right now.

Francis: No, Aubrey. She's *exactly* who you need to talk to. And *right* now.

"Jesus, you sound like you just woke up or something?"

"As a matter of fact," Mary answers. "You did just wake me up. I work shifts." She goes on to explain about rotation and thirty hour shifts, is just getting into the subject so near to her heart, when the girl on the other end of the line interrupts.

"Yeah, well I work late too sometimes, so I know how it feels. Sorry I ruined your sleep and all, but I thought you'd like to know that Kim – or Chris, but I guess you probably call her Christina and all – is awake and talking and everything."

It takes a beat for Mary to understand who they're talking about. Kim, Chris, Christina, Jane Doe: the girl from ICU. Of course, it makes sense. That's the only connection between her and Aubrey; but Mary knows better than anybody that Mrs. McKloskey has insisted that Aubrey have no more contact with her daughter since their disastrous visit together. In the next few words that too is explained, as Aubrey relates how she and her friends 'liberated' the patient from her mother's care.

"You've got to be kidding," Mary responds, fully awake now, turning on a table lamp against the heavily draped darkness of her room. "That girl needs round the clock care, she's...."

Again Aubrey interrupts, describing in detail how she and the others have been caring for Kim. There's a tone of pride in her voice which Mary has not heard before, and it strikes her that the bristling angry adolescent she last encountered in Mrs. M.'s living room has been growing up a bit lately. Responsibility can do that, as any resident knows, especially the life and death responsibility for a sick person's care. Those thoughts are cut short as she realizes what it is Aubrey has called her for.

"I can't do that," Mary tells her flatly. "First of all, I can't just walk into the pharmacy and take whatever I want. It doesn't work that way. I write a scrip and the nursing staff put it into the system to get it recorded and filled and then they administer it; and even that's only for admitted patients who are on my roster. Second, I would never treat someone for an existing condition without her full medical records and communication with the physician who'd been treating her previously - in this case three of them - and third...You kidnapped her! And now you want me to help you and become a kidnapper too?"

Mary is out of bed by now, portable phone shifting from

hand to hand to shoulder as she pulls an old flannel shirt on over her nightshirt. Less than two hours till her shift begins, she might as well get a cup of coffee, because she is certainly not going to get back to sleep after this. In the meantime, Aubrey is full of reasons why Mary 'absolutely has to' help them with their problem child.

"Look," Mary says finally, exhausted by the flow of Aubrey's arguments. "There is one way I might be able to help you." One of the less typical learning experiences during her internship had been involvement in a lawsuit. The family of an assault victim claimed that the care at Hilltop's ER, where Mary was taking a rotation in critical care at the time, had contributed to his death. Mary was required to give a deposition regarding the length of the attending physician's initial examination of the victim, and whether the internal bleeding which would eventually kill him was more readily detectable than the Dr's. notes suggested. She is surprised to find her palms beginning to sweat at even the memory of that day; the opposing attorney's office, bustling with hard-faced men and women, every one of whom exuded a confidence in imminent danger of slipping over into arrogance; the conference room a tomb of dark wood, its surfaces polished to perfection and every sound diminished by the heavy carpet and the thick drapes drawn over the windows; how small and tentative her own voice sounded, compared to the row of grim-faced men assembled on the other side of the table; and the powerful doubts which began to consume her the moment the grimmest-of-the-grim began to question her.

"He can be a real asshole," she advises, placing the kettle on a burner and twisting the knob to 'HIGH.' "He's got no shame and he doesn't care if people hate him, but I got the sense that he loves going after big guys. My guess is, if we make it sound like it's us against the whole of Hilltop, he'll jump right on it."

It is only later, mulling over the conversation during her bus ride to work, that Mary realizes she had said 'we' and 'us.' Putting herself on the opposite side from her employer cannot be a good idea, she realizes. There's years of work and study to be considered, against what? A couple of young crazies and a comatose invalid whose wealthy mother will probably do everything she can to oppose them. Still, there's that weird business of the missing records, the mystery transplant, Hilltop paying out of pocket and the absurdly excessive setup with three doctors watching over her. Something is going on there, and it does not seem right....

Don't get involved, Mary is thinking, as the bus pulls to a stop and she gathers her things to get off. You've got your hands full just keeping up with work; you've invested years getting to where you are today, and there's still a long way to go. Don't screw it up just because you find something compelling in a sick girl's face. Just because you see yourself in her eyes – or, more to the point, wish you could. Do. Not. Get. Involved.

Wheeling the chair through the entry doors at Sullivan, Krebs, Miklemas and McNair, Aubrey feels as if she is entering enemy territory. The wood paneled elevator was stuffy enough, but the lobby onto which it opens seems to have come from another century, with its mustard-yellow leather chairs and massive paintings of alpine peaks and waterfalls looking like backdrops for some Rocky Mountain Gotterdammerung. The receptionist only reinforces the image, with her hair curled wide around a powdered face, half-glasses precariously balanced at the tip of a knife-sharp nose and secured with a silver chain around her neck, the very picture of a stern librarian - if librarians could afford cashmere suits and silk blouses and wedding rings large enough to snag a catfish.

"We're here to see Jim Auster," Aubrey announces from several steps away. The words strike even her as weak and unconvincing, which is maybe not so surprising, given the sense she has that this place is somehow geared for battle, and she inherently a member of the other side.

Un-phased, the receptionist continues the careful examination which had begun as soon as the elevator doors opened. Beneath furrowed brows, her eyes scan Aubrey, in leather jacket and boots, then move on to Kim, bundled in her wheelchair and wrapped in a tartan blanket of day-glow tones. They seem to settle for some time on the limp hair which, without Mrs. McKloskey's careful styling, is not quite long enough to fully conceal the lumps and scars beneath. 'Yeah,' Aubrey realizes with some satisfaction, 'that might be of interest to an ambulance chaser.'

Kim is playing it up well, she notes, as she tries to see her friend through a stranger's eyes. Anyone could read the appreciation warming her complexion as she gazes around the walls. Yeah, if some old doctor guy was brought in here after coming back to life in her crummy apartment, he might have just that reaction. That look of quiet satisfaction, that rising of the shoulders as he soaks in the atmosphere of male power and privilege. An old boy, back inside the Old Boys Club. So caught up is Aubrey in her friend's performance, she is taken totally by surprise when they reach the desk and Kim takes the character one step further, abandoning her recent 'none of this is real' stance to fix the woman in her eyes as she speaks up, louder and stronger, it seems, than she has at anytime since her recovery began.

"I am Dr. Rodney Gimbal," she says to the astonished receptionist, "And this young lady is Aubrey Maturin, and we have an appointment at this hour with Mr. Auster, arranged by a past client of his. Dr. Mary Antonias."

Aubrey will say later that she wished she had Mark's camera at that moment, to record the waves of expression which passed across that old lady's face. For an instant, it seems, she is startled - intimidated by the tone and directness of Kim's approach - but in the next moment, a puckering between the brows and a slight vacancy in her eyes suggests she is trying to remember if any of those names mean anything to her. Next comes resentment, as if she has decided she is being diddled, before finally a small, wry smile appears at one side of her mouth as she concedes that, yes, even this comes with the job. Pressing a button on the console in front of her she speaks softly, and only now does Aubrey notice the discreet microphone suspended from a headset nearly hidden by all that carefully fluffed and sprayed designer hair.

"Mr. Auster," she says with an excess of politeness. "There are two," the tiniest of pauses, yet unmistakable to one as sensitized as Aubrey, "ladies" – the word with a falling inflection that communicates quite clearly the cultural gulf between speaker and subject - "here for your ten-fifteen."

Another pause, this one long enough for the person on the other end of the line to have said something substantive, or perhaps asked a question, since the receptionist pronounces a smug "Oh yes," then listens for several more seconds before a final "Yes, I will," leads to her eyes once again meeting Aubrey's, with no more warmth than before.

'If you'll just have a seat," the woman says, a patrician hand directing their attention toward the sofa opposite, "Mr. Auster will be out shortly."

"I thought we agreed," Aubrey whispers furiously once they are seated and the secretary's attention seems to have migrated elsewhere. "You weren't going to play that crap here."

"It got us in," Kim answers, her words halting once again, and carefully calibrated to appease. "Didn't' it?"

It takes several minutes, as they are waiting, for Aubrey to convince Kim once again of the need to keep their appeal simple and direct, but eventually her friend agrees, if not very convincingly.

Robin Andrew

As is his custom with new clients, before coming out of his private hallway, Jim Auster gives the pair a good looking over through the one-way mirror behind Ruth's reception desk. His eyes quickly settle on the one in the wheelchair, sitting there wrapped in a gaudy Mexican blanket with a look on her face that says she owns the place. Intriguing, Auster thinks, that someone with so much against her - the wheelchair, misshapen head, butchered haircut, outcast companion - still has that much presence. There's a quality there that might prove persuasive, if not exactly sympathetic, under the right circumstances. It's actually not a bad face, he realizes, after watching for a while. Cute little turn-up to the nose, wide eyes that look like she might have a Japanese grandmother hidden somewhere. Pleasantly exotic, though the lips could use a little more color. Yes, he concludes; let the hair grow out, get her some decent clothes, and she might clean up into something, if she's got a decent figure hidden beneath that blanket. The other one, the one who made the appointment and brought her here, is hardly worth a second glance as she pretends to scan magazines, fanning their pages in her lap before setting them on the seat beside her. Last month's Business Week is hardly sufficient camouflage to hide who she is: a loser and proud of it. Defiantly impolite to anyone who doesn't instantly applaud her for being 'different.' A poor candidate for the witness stand, and not the kind of person with whom he wants to spend any more of his day than necessary.

Observations over, the attorney steps around the partition into the waiting area and introduces himself. As he pushes 'Rod's' wheelchair down the corridor to his public office, Auster's mind wanders a bit, noting how the thick pad he specified beneath the carpet lets the chair sink in, making pushing it a definite piece of work. How he can feel the strain in his shoulders and thighs; he worked out yesterday and today is a skip day, so his muscles are slightly tight, just enough to make him feel extra fit, extra powerful. Casting a sideways glance as they pass the floor-to-ceiling glass of a conference room, the person he sees is satisfyingly trim, his stride powerful in a charcoal worsted with a blue pinstripe just bright enough to start a conversation with his shirt and tie, and bring out his eyes as well. He is feeling very comfortable with the image he projects, as they turn into the small space occupied by his secretary, Gwen, and pass, after brief introductions, into the spruce-green enclave of his office. Jim Auster chose that color himself, along with the worm-wood furnishings, the antique yacht models on the credenza, the paintings of racing boats in full sail which adorn three walls, and the shelves stacked with legal volumes along the fourth. All calculated to convey an image of establishment success, a subtle indication of the horsepower he can bring to bear on his clients' behalf, though it seems like overkill with this particular pair.

"I understand from Ms. Antonias you need help with some sort of guardianship dispute," the attorney begins, cutting off the small talk as soon as they are all settled into place. It is Aubrey who responds, launching into a convoluted recapitulation of her relationship with the one-time Jane Doe, who turned out to be Christina McKloskey. As she moves into the details of the girl's recovery and attempts to communicate, Auster notes that the girl herself seems impatient, even angered by the telling. There's another dynamic going on here, his experience tells him, though what it is he cannot guess as he listens to Aubrey's flood of anecdotal data – there's an old boyfriend in the story, suspicious medications and an obvious resentment of the other girl's mother which seems clearly related to Aubrey's own self-image problems, but why this Christina - who he is now certain could be a keeper if she got herself back to health and made the effort - should even be hanging around with such a loser is another puzzle entirely to him. It is not long before Auster feels his time being wasted and interrupts the flow.

"Let's cut to the chase Miss. What you want is for someone in authority to determine that this girl," he nods toward the other, who seems to bristle at the words, "is competent to make her own decisions about where she lives, who cares for her, and so forth. Is that right?"

Up to this point, Christina has maintained a tense silence, though her eyes have been darting between Aubrey and Auster, as if measuring the words of the one and reactions of the other. Now she begins to speak, though at first only a croaking whisper comes out. With a shake of her head and an almost spastic flapping of hands above her lap, she clears her throat loudly then takes a deep breath before trying again.

"There's. One. Other issue," she says, hands settling again into her lap as if one were capturing the other and holding it hostage, after which the words begin to come more freely. "I am not...Christina McKloskey. I am Dr....Rodney Gimbal."

"Oh, shit," the tough one jumps in. "We said we weren't gonna get into that with him."

211

"We're here...now," Christina shoots back, and Auster finds himself amused by the flash of spirit across her young face. "And I will tell the truth." With that she launches into a painstaking explanation of how 'he,' an elderly and terminally ill man, struggled to understand the isolated state in which he found himself, gradually regaining his capacities only to find himself under Mrs. McKloskey's care and somehow, impossible as it appears, living in this young woman's body.

"Well," Auster says with exaggerated precision, once the girl's story seems to have run its course. "That's somewhat more interesting than your average competency judgment." There is a long silence as he stretches his arms in front of him, fingers entwined, while his neck and head arch back in the manner of one taking a well-deserved break from some very hard work. "I don't think you need an attorney, ladies," he continues, casting his glance back and forth between the two. "I think you need a shrink. And I think you are wasting my time and yours." With that Auster begins to rise from his chair, stopping only when Aubrey addresses him in a tone of righteous suspicion fulfilled.

"Yeah," she says, rising to match his pose. "That's what I figured you'd say. Like why should you help us anyway? We're just a couple of punk kids with no money, and you're a big high-rise lawyer and all." Before Auster can reply, she continues. "I knew this would happen. You think I'm some kind of freak, and Chris - you don't have a clue what to do with her. But there's one more thing you might be interested in, see? That doctor lady, Mary, she says you like to go after big guys; that you don't like hospitals and big companies and stuff, right?" Auster nods, conceding that might be true. "Well...Hilltop Medical Center has been footing the bill for all of Chris's care ever since she got out of the hospital."

"You're sure of that?" Auster asks, settling back into his chair with more interest than he has shown at any previous time during the entire interview.

"Yeah. We can prove it. Mary says she can get photocopies of some papers that show it. And then there's the drugs," with which Aubrey resumes her explanation of what they found in Chris's medical records and how they have been unable to come up with a rational explanation for the types and amounts of various medications which have been given to Chris, some of which they cannot even find mentioned anywhere on the net. The fact that Mrs. M. has apparently not reported Chris' disappearance to the

212

authorities is the final card she plays and it has the anticipated effect, appearing to trigger a change in Auster's attitude.

"Well," he says again, as he swivels his chair a bit toward the window and lets his eyes roam the peaks of the Olympic Mountains, just visible above a layer of cloud which has settled in the bowl of Elliot bay. His hands form a tent, elbows pegged to the upholstered armrests, as he considers this latest bit of information. A man in his position keeps up with many sorts of news, so Auster is well aware that Hilltop was vacuumed-up a few months back by Medical Holdings. Knows also that MH is a very big fish, with over twenty-thousand direct or indirect employees, tens of thousands of beds in the facilities it controls, billions in assets, and a reputation for aggressive management which leaves no dime unaccounted for. That they should be paying the bills for a woman who left one of their facilities comatose can only mean that something questionable – at the very least – happened to that girl while under their care and that someone at a responsible level of the MH pyramid is not anxious to answer questions about it. Just as a small boy cannot resist prodding a sleeping dog, Jim Auster cannot resist the opportunity to prod MH, if only just to see how it will react. This morning, he thinks as his gaze returns to the women in his office, has just gotten a whole lot more interesting.

In the next few minutes, Auster lays out the bare bones of a plan. Step one is a simple court filing, he explains; a request for determination of competency, supported by sworn and notarized statements from Chris and an examining psychologist. That will start the ball rolling. File the request, put a notice in the newspaper of record, and then sit back. If no one objects, in thirty days they have a brief interview before a judge, and Chris will be free to live anywhere she chooses. "If someone objects – your mother, Hilltop, or anyone else, we listen and ask questions. Maybe we find out what they're hiding, and figure out how to use it to our advantage."

"Your simple...filing," Chris asks, as Auster finishes describing his strategy. "Will it also say...that I am...Doctor Rodney..."

"No," Auster answers, smiling like a tolerant parent who knows his child's antics. "There is no way..."

"But I am who I am. That's what I need..."

"Look, young lady..."

Hearing these words Christina bursts into a flurry of motion, wasted arms rising up from their place in her lap to twitch aborted gestures in the air. "I. Am. Not any...young lady," she says, with total conviction and not a trace of irony. "I am. A grown man... and I...resent... anyone saying otherwise..."

"I don't care who you think you are, sweetheart. There is no way any court is going to rule that you are a sixty-year-old man. Not with a face like that and a bo... Never happen. And if you insist that you are somebody else..."

"Not somebody else," she demands, struggling to push herself up out of the wheelchair. "Look; I know it's...difficult, but...I...swear..."

Before Christina can finish Auster cuts her off, rising once again and addressing Aubrey in the strongest tone he has taken yet. "Your job," he begins, "will be to keep her in line. If she insists on this act in front of the judge, you can forget about it. She'll be ruled incompetent and placed back in her mother's care in a second and - if what you've been telling me is true - MH will have gotten away with whatever they are trying to get away with."

"Then you can't help us," Aubrey says flatly.

"I didn't say that." Auster grins the grin of a man who loves being in control; who loves having answers when no one else does. "I said we can't expect to establish this person is someone other than she appears to be. But getting her out of their hands? That should be easy enough, *if* she'll cooperate. All we have to do is get in front of a judge and demonstrate that she," he nods in Rod's direction, "is conscious, competent and does not wish to be under Mrs. McKloskey's care. Then we present a reasonable medical alternative, and bingo, your patient is a free woman. Or man," he adds, with a curiously covetous glance at Christina.

"So when do we get in front of a judge?"

"I'll have the request drawn up and filed by this time tomorrow. In the meantime, you need to get her back in line and presentable."

With that, Auster rises again from his chair and steps to the door. Turning as he pulls it open, he makes it clear that he is addressing the one girl out of the pair who walked in on her own two feet. "If you want to go ahead, let Marjorie know, at the front desk. She'll take all the information and get it scheduled; all you have to do is show up." Turning to the one in the wheelchair, his expression changes. "You show up looking your best, sweetie, and I'm sure we can make this all work out. On the other hand, if you don't want to follow my instructions and get this resolved, it's still been a pleasure meeting you. Whoever you are."

214

"I don't want to go."

Embarrassed by her own petulance, Elaine sits on the bed beside her packed travel case. For the first time in weeks she feels old. The fact that she has spoken the words out loud, in a room she alone occupies, is not the issue; that is a practice to which she has become quite accustomed - speaking words in order to give them a chance; to find out if they have a life of their own. Some words, she has learned, fall flat to the floor when spoken out loud. Those are words in which one does not truly believe. Other words though, take wing as soon as they leave the mouth; they have a life of their own, and meaning is that life, and so, she has learned, we must sometimes speak our thoughts out loud: to see if they have wings.

"I will not go."

There are alternatives, after all. There are always alternatives - another of her friend's lessons, recalled from a week before, or two, or any number, for all it matters any more. "Even when there is no physical choice," Beryl said, as the two women faced bowls of soup with pickled vegetables, placed before them by a woman who seemed ages older than themselves. "There are alternatives in how we deal with that lack of choice. In fact," she continued, raising a deep wooden spoon to her mouth and slurping the substance from it before finishing her thought, "that is the most important choice of all; how we deal with what we cannot change."

The soup looked awful. Greenish gray, and murky, its consistency more than liquid, but not quite solid. 'Gelatinous'- with all the creeping sensation which that word can conjure. Bubbles of oil dotted its surface, and where a bit had slopped onto the rim of the wooden bowl, the cold air seeping in around the tattered door-curtain quickly congealed it into pasty white grease. The bits of meat hovering beneath the potion's surface glistened with gristle and membrane - lord knows what part of what animal they might represent, certainly not any cut on the chart in the butcher shop her mother used to take her to, back in Carteret. Still, the women had not eaten since just after dawn, the sun was past its zenith, and they had been walking the entire time. Walking. Again. Putting one foot in front of the other takes a toll, and bodies must be sustained - though much less often, one had found, than one used to believe. Still there were times when fuel was needed, and this was one of those times, and so one dipped one's spoon into the scary liquid, taking a conscious vow to do so without expectation, without predicting how it would taste, or feel, and when one did that, when one approached the soup without preconception, one might actually find it hot and sweet, just salty enough to feel at home inside one's mouth, sliding down one's throat to fill the body with warmth and nourishment, the muscles with energy, the spirit with hope.

Elaine cannot change the fact that Rodney is dead. Nor the fact that she knows it. She *can* conclude that it was a mistake to call the States, to succumb to that nagging voice which had been claiming for some time that she had some sort of responsibility to inform him about her journey, her plan to continue travelling with Beryl. A mistake also, after she failed on three attempts to find him at home in the evenings, to call the hospital. The greatest mistake though, she may conclude as the guilt and shame close in upon her, was in allowing herself to believe over these last weeks that nothing would be changing back there, even as so much was changing here, inside of her.

It is two days since she received the news.

"I am so sorry..." Doug Taylor had begun, with a sympathy she'd never heard him use in all the times they'd met with her at Rodney's side. "Your husband...." and the rest is all a blur. How she ran into the other room intending to tell her friend then realizing there was no need, as Beryl's eyes seemed to know the only important fact in an instant. The tears, embraces, the quiet walk later along the riverside, talking about death and surprise, loss and pain and how time flows, like the river's water, and one can choose to float along with it, or to stand and let it swirl around one, but either way the water will flow.

Flowing forward or eddying back, staying or going. She can travel back to Seattle, where his remains have already been cremated, in accord with the will opened by their attorney when Elaine could not be reached following his death. Can put her affairs in order, behave like a normal spouse – 'widow' now, though that descriptor still feels alien to her. She could, conceivably, stay here and ignore it all, though the attorney says that would be a mistake, could cost her thousands and tie up Rodney's pension, her survivor's benefits, a dozen other plans and programs of which she is a part even at ten thousand miles remove. Or - as he admitted under some pressure, after Beryl had taken the phone from her trembling hand and spoken with a firmness which brought Elaine back to the present - she can find a local legal office to print out the power of attorney which he will prepare and transmit and to witness her executing it, then transmit it back to him so he may act in her best interest.

"Act in your best interest."

One meaning of the word 'interest,' Beryl pointed out as they discussed the options after hanging up the phone, is financial. A trickling compensation for assets put on hold; in the same way people sometimes put their lives on hold, investing years of quiet desperation in hope of golden years to come. But interest also means involvement - to 'have an interest.' To be 'invested' – to continue twisting analogies around one another - in an outcome. Which Elaine is, in all those plans and programs, whether she chooses to be or not. And finally, it could mean curiosity and wonder – to be 'interested in' the thing - a meaning which itself suggests the promise of the unknown.

The word 'interest,' it seems, is just another question.

"What you need to decide, my dear," Beryl had said, just before she stepped out of the room to allow Elaine some private time in which to gather her things and prepare for the arrival of the taxi for which their hotel's desk clerk had sent a boy, "is which form of interest is your *best* interest?"

"I do not want to go," Elaine says to her empty room, the words repeated several times to see if they will fall or fly.

Going back means standing still. Staying here means moving forward. Seeing new places, new people, new things. Tasting ugly soup, without preconception, and finding...whatever one may find.

"Kim-babe, I'm back," Aubrey calls as she elbows through the back doorway, arms strained by plastic grocery sacks dangling like a bumper crop of synthetic fruit from pinched fingers. Immediately she senses something different in the house, some as-yet-unidentified sound or look, a balance rearranged. Setting the parcels down on the kitchen table she creeps around to the back room only to find the bed empty - the first time, to her knowledge, that Chris, as she's been trying to think of her, has been out of it without assistance.

"Hey, all right, you're up," she calls toward the bathroom, its door hanging slightly ajar. Nothing like a full bladder, Aubrey thinks to herself, to get a girl out of bed.

"You could at least close the friggin' door," she adds as she steps across the room, though she hears no sound of water running, no greeting called back. No answer, in fact, but an odd clicking sound and some soft grunts. Reaching the bathroom door, she calls again and when still there is no answer, only more of that muffled clicking, presses the door gently inward, eyes cast to the floor. Seeing a pair of pajamaed legs not on the commode but standing before the sink, she presses the door fully open.

"What the fuck?" she shouts then, as the picture comes into focus: Christina's form, hips braced heavily against the counter, the blue-striped fabric of her pajamas sprinkled with tufts of dark hair, scissors held unsteadily with two hands, about to chop another hank from her head. Blood drips from the top of one ear, bright and glossy as it makes its way down the side of her neck. A smear on her arm is darker, with bits of hair glued into it.

In an instant Aubrey reaches her friend, seizes the shears and tosses them, clattering, into the tub.

"What the fuck do you think you're doing?" she scolds. "You could...let me see..." Chris tries to fend her off but those arms, after months of inactivity, are no match for Aubrey's, toned from nights spent carrying dishes and trays at the restaurant. In an instant she has her friend pinned despite the resistance, and is able to assess the damage. "Just a little cut, but Jesus, girl, you could have taken your ear off."

Chris's look is full of resentment as she wriggles, trying to get free, and Aubrey feels her own features flush with heat. The body she holds is thin and bony, wasted from months of lying in bed, yet despite that frailty it is warm, and soft where a body needs to be soft, and Aubrey finds a sob welling-up inside of her. A sum of all the times she has watched Kim laughing and smiling in others' arms, all the times they have said goodnight and gone their separate ways. Now, to be living in the same apartment, day after day, night after night is almost more than she can bear. Aubrey holds on tight, her hands desperate to explore the myriad contours of spine and ribs, shoulder blades and hips, all too easy to find beneath the thin skin. So easy, to touch and hold, to...

With a start, Aubrey releases her grip, and steps back. The two stand inches apart, eyes locked. Looking for anger, or embarrassment, outrage maybe, she finds herself disappointed. Wiping her own eyes in hopes the tears have not been seen, she feels an overwhelming impression of distance; as if, despite their physical proximity, she and this other person are living in different worlds. It's the same thing she's felt since the girl came back to the surface weeks before, the same thing that's been missing through sponge baths and muscle rubs and stretching and the words which seem to come in fits and starts, but only now is it clear: Chris might as well be living on another planet, for all the connection she has with her once-best friend.

"I want it off," the girl says now, as if nothing had happened between them.

"What?" Aubrey asks, "Your hair?" She reaches out to brush a tuft of it from Chris' cheek. "You got beautiful hair, babe. I wish I had hair like..."

"I want it off. And I am not your babe - I'm a grown man and I am going to look it."

Seeing Aubrey's baffled look, she continues, in the over-patient tone of one forced to go over and over what should be obvious to the naked eye.

"*For my hearing*. And I want a suit; if I'm going to have a hearing in front of a Judge, I am going to look my best, like Jim said."

For a moment Aubrey is puzzled, until she realizes 'Jim' means 'Auster', and that when Chris says that about looking her best, she means as Rodney Gimbal.

"I don't think that's what he had in mind, babe," she says with a chuckle as she brushes off another tuft of hair which has transferred itself to her own arm. "Didn't you see the way he was looking at you? When he says look your best, he's thinking short skirt, make-up and maybe a bit of the old boobs exposed." The look on Chris' face is of such horror at the prospect that Aubrey finds herself laughing out loud. "What, you think an old prick like him can't have horns for a girl in a wheelchair?" she asks, only to see her friend's face cycle rapidly from shock to disgust to anger, before it goes pale and her petite frame crumbles toward the floor as she grasps at her stomach and begins to convulse. Scrambling, Aubrey gets her to the toilet and the lid off in time for most of the meager contents of her stomach to land inside.

A few minutes later the two sit together on the bathroom floor, surrounded by scattered wads of toilet tissue blotting up what missed the bowl. Gently, Aubrey draws a damp washcloth across Christina's forehead and face. The girl is weak, still shaken by the bout of nausea, but her words come out as clearly as any she has yet pronounced.

"I want this to stop," she says. "I want this all to go away so I can have my life back."

As patiently as she can, Aubrey explains how she sees the situation. As much as Kim - whatever name or identity she insists on using - may want to go back in time, they can't. What's more, the meds they got during the rescue are nearly gone and Mary has been no help replacing them. Even with the progress she's making - speaking, walking a few first steps, there's still a long way to go for her to be able to live the kind of life she remembers; they need doctors and medicine and maybe even more help for her to recover as fully as possible. And then there's money – Mrs. M. may be able to pay for night nurses and food and clothes, but Aubrey's waitress gig barely keeps *her* in Ramen, much less the two of them, especially with no renter in what has now become Kim's bedroom. They need to get the legal thing sorted out, and Auster is the guy who can do it for them and like he said, the worst thing that could happen would be for them to show up in front of the Judge claiming Chris is Rod. Regardless of whether or not that is true, it would certainly result in a judgment of non-competence and returning to the guardianship of her mother.

"What's more important, honey? Now. Today. Your name, or getting control of your own life so you don't get dumped right back into your mother's little dollhouse?"

Despite Chris' insistence that Mrs. McKloskey is not her mother, she grudgingly agrees. Given that, Aubrey continues, the first step in getting her life back is to do as Auster says. Show up for the judge as Christina. Let him rule that she is competent, and can stay here in this house – 'our house,' Aubrey hears herself saying, with an unfamiliar mix of pride and longing – and maybe get the docs to help with the medicines, too.

"Once we get that much done, we can start to put your life back together. You can get your hair cut as short as you want it – hell, you can shave your friggin' head for all anyone will care. Call yourself Rod or Rambo or Ragnar-From-Planet-Nine if that's what you want."

Struggling to her feet, legs wobbly, Chris is the very picture of determination in a small package.

"What I want," she says as she begins to move out the door and across into her bedroom, "Is to get my life back. The way it was before…before whatever this is that has happened to me. Before I ever heard of Jim Auster or Christina McKloskey or her god-damned mother or you."

With that she slams the door and Aubrey is left alone on the bathroom floor, legs splayed among scattered scraps of hair and traces of vomit, wads of toilet tissue, and the memory of how alive she felt when she held her friend so close.

Alive is certainly what Elaine feels as she squats in the shade of a steeply overhanging rock wall, two days after her decision to continue travelling with Beryl. Especially if, as the followers of the Buddha say, life is suffering. Her feet are bruised from battling the rocky trail. The muscles of her legs ache, half of them from going up an endless procession of hills, the rest from going down the other side of those same hills. A duality which - Beryl has been kind enough to point out - is of serious significance; seeing the other side of a hill, she says, is a reminder that everything in life encompasses its opposite. Or some such thing; lately, Elaine is having a difficult time keeping up with all the insights her friend imparts, what with the dust kicked up by their own feet, the confusion of exchanging greetings with passers-by who seem each to be speaking a different language, and the sensory overload of trying to appreciate an otherworldly landscape while one's mind is being constantly pulled into the past by memories of her life with Rodney, and tempted into the future by projections of what her life will be without him.

At present though, they have stopped near the bank of a tumbling, roaring dragon of water. In another geology this might be a small stream, but here - where massive snowfields thousands of feet above are melted by the roasting sun to carve their way down through young formations devoid of buffering forest - it is a raging cataract, twisting and thrashing over boulders and ledges as it descends a sharp crease between the hill they've just descended and the one they must climb next. Even from a safe distance, she can feel the milky melt-water sucking heat from the air around her. To cross this force of nature, a pair of heavy ropes have been strung between log pylons set in either bank. A series of more slender lines, their hand-twisted fibers punctuated with lumps and tangles, suspend from these ropes a walkway of rough wooden treads, some flat as boards, others still half-rounded as the tree limbs from which they came. The reason the women have stopped is that the approach to this swinging bridge is blocked by a dozen or so pack animals, their backs piled high with cargo, their heads bent down in search of stray vegetation as their masters busy themselves around the bridge.

Halfway across the span, one man hacks at a plank he has untied from the ragged spider web of ropes which form both support and handhold. Closer by, two men are securing a second guy-rope from the top of one pylon to a huge steel ring embedded in the nearby cliff, apparently intending to reinforce the old rope, its fibers frighteningly few where passing animals have rubbed against it. The fourth man has climbed high into the rigging, where he is tying a string of prayer flags, their colors fresh and bold in contrast to the welter of faded, tattered flags already hanging there.

All around this scene the landscape, from bedrock to gravel, from boulders to dust, presents a single hue: a dusty, beigey gray, which hardly rates the compliment of being called a color. The few small trees lodged in crevices on the surrounding hillsides seem faded by the heat until they, too, are more anomaly than greenery. A thermal breeze pushing up the streambed combines with the cataract's noise and the water's radiating chill to create a sort of curtain between Elaine and the men, their movements and sounds an artificial tableau, separate and distant, though only a few yards before her eyes.

Pulling a water bottle from her daypack, Elaine takes a short swallow to see how thirsty she really is, then follows with a deeper draught. With the long sleeve of her blouse she wipes a bit of sweat from her forehead, grateful for the shade of overhanging rock, and watches as Beryl clambers past the beasts to join the men working at the bridge. On the way her friend reaches down and picks up a rock, larger than Elaine would have thought possible for one of her age and size, then staggers awkwardly up the pile to the pole's base where she deposits it, neatly filling a gap between several even larger stones. She gives the slightest of bows toward the bridge, exchanges a few words with the men nearby and makes her way back as the two men continue their rigging.

"The local Department of Transportation, out fixing the highways?" Elaine asks facetiously, as Beryl settles beside her, taking the water bottle she offers. Drinking her usual small amount the woman hands it back.

"Just traders, dear. They may come this way now and then, or they may never have been here before. May never come this way again."

"So they just take it on themselves to fix up someone else's bridge?"

Somewhere in her things Beryl has found a Junar orange purchased several days and many thousands of feet of elevation before. Small and shrunken and well-past its prime, but an orange nonetheless. Turning it in her hand, she examines its skin, then bites into the top end, her prominent front teeth peeling back the thickest skin, where its stem once lodged. With a knobby thumb she begins to remove the rest of the peel, exposing white rind and shining sections in practiced motions that seem to absorb her full attention for some time. Only when the skin is nearly all off, hanging in a spiral beneath her juice-damp hands, does she answer.

"No one owns this bridge, dear; it's been here longer than any person has been alive and certainly none of the people who live in these parts would claim to own such a thing. As far as those men are concerned, it has always been there, and for that they're grateful and so before they pass over it, they add a few stones, make a small repair if it's needed, string some flags. In gratitude, and to honor those who built it."

A thought comes to Elaine then, which has not come before: that these trails they walk on surely took enormous effort to carve through such a rugged land. Likewise, the many other bridges they have crossed. "Back home we pay taxes for things like that. Or tolls. It makes me feel guilty, like I'm taking something I shouldn't, using these trails and bridges for nothing."

Digging in her pack Beryl pulls out a cloth-wrapped chunk of bread, torn from a loaf baked that morning in the small lodge where they spent the night. Tearing it in two she takes a tiny bite from one piece then offers the other to Elaine. "Every day of our lives we depend on those who came before. One cannot live without crossing bridges one did not build, warming oneself at fires one did not light. Sometimes we have the opportunity to light a fire for someone else, sometimes the most we can do is drop a few stones as we cross. It's part of being alive, unless one chooses to be a hermit. And I, for one, have no intention of becoming a hermit."

From her own pack Elaine pulls a bottle of sunscreen and begins to coat the backs of her hands, her forearms and the exposed areas of her face.

"We all have an obligation then, to the people who came before us."

"Those men," Beryl points with her bread as the four return to their animals and proceed to check their loads. Though their clothes are ragged, their hands and faces filthy, the men's expressions are bright, their voices full of energy as they tug on the crisscrossed ropes, here and there untying and retying this one or that. "Do they seem obligated?"

"No. They seem…" Elaine searches for a word to describe the way in which the men move and communicate. It is not as simple as happiness, though they do seem to smile quite a lot. Certainly not laziness, though they show little evidence of effort. No sign of strain as they gather up tools and tuck them into the animals' burdens. "Comfortable," she concludes. "They seem at ease in what they're doing. Natural."

Their gear properly stowed, one of the men swigs water from a goatskin as the others muscle their animals into line, preparing to get under way again,

"Those men are doing what they believe they are meant to do, Elaine. Going where they are meant to go. Their ancestors wore trails and built bridges and then passed on, leaving trails and bridges and space for these men, who will pass on someday and leave it all for their children, and their children's children. That's the way it works."

With loud whistles and clapping of hands the men set their livestock moving. The animals cross the swaying, creaking bridge with great reluctance, drovers tugging at their harnesses and slapping their buttocks. For a few minutes the span is a hive of activity; shouting men, snorting beasts and creaking boards oscillating high above the roaring river, and then they are across, blending into the dusty trail beyond, their fading sounds soon lost beneath the water's roar, leaving the bridge still and clear. An empty space in which Beryl and Elaine can move forward on their own journey.

Gathering their packs they rise and thread arms into straps. Before heading for the bridge though, Elaine selects from the side of the path the largest rock she will be able to manage, carries it a few yards to the pile at the base of one bridge-pylon and places it carefully into a gap among the others lying there.

'Interesting,' she thinks a moment later, as she sets a careful foot upon the first plank. The rock, once she actually got her hands on it, was not nearly so heavy as she had imagined it would be. She could have done much more.

"Auster here," answers the attorney at twenty-past-six, on the same day he's received confirmation of the date for Christina's hearing before Judge Bartenieff. "What can I do for you?"

Over the years, Jim Auster has observed that certain calls are made at certain times of the day. Morning is for introducing new subjects; setting the stage, taking the pulse of the other side, but the real business gets done late in the day, when all the alternatives have been weighed, all the maneuvers maneuvered, and all other options ruled out. That is the time when people reluctantly accept the reality of what has been going on and make the call which will really resolve a situation, in a way that offers something for each side.

That in mind, he listens patiently while the party on the other end speaks.

"You know me," he interjects after a few seconds. "I've always been attracted to the outlaw types." The sly smile which accompanies that crack remains on his face, as he listens some more.

"No," he says abruptly, after listening a while a longer. "I wouldn't agree with that." Affecting a tone of irritation, he gathers steam and lets his volume build. "What I would agree with is that your clients fucked up and my girl has spent the last few months trying to put her pieces back together. Now, we're all big boys, Kurt, and we know that anyone can fuck up once in a while, so we're not trying to bring the roof down or anything, but actions have consequences, and in this case, I'm one of those consequences. So you tell your client to do some hard thinking in the middle of the night, will you?"

After six is the time for settling, Auster muses, as his eyes return to the papers on his desk. Unless, that is, you intend to win.

The girl is sitting up now at the Formica table in Aubrey's kitchen, a bowl of Rice Krispies in front of her, and a glass of milk. The threadbare folds of an old dish towel drape across her chest and lap, not quite concealing the cartoon dragster and NHRA logo on a sweatshirt grudgingly loaned by Desmond, its rolled-up sleeves making Michelin-sized life-rings around the slender sticks of her wrists. A spoon is in her left fist, gripped awkwardly and desperately, like someone holding on to a lifeline.

"That's it," Mark coos, hands on the lower and upper parts of that arm, guiding its motion while providing just enough resistance to steady the trembling limb even as his eyes stray once again to the notebook on the counter, where he would much rather be jotting down impressions for incorporation into his screenplay. "Now we just move it straight up," he says, employing that exaggerated enunciation usually reserved for small children and young dogs. Trembling noticeably, the spoon begins to rise, both his and Christina's eyes tracking intently, watching as it takes on a few degrees of tilt, the first tiny pods of cereal sloughing off into the bowl, onto the table, into the lap of her sweat pants (also borrowed, though from Mark's little brother, without his knowledge). Higher it rises, the arm crooked at the elbow, the wrist swiveling uncontrollably. Leaning her face forward, the girl opens her mouth only to find the spoon nearly empty by the time it reaches her lips.

"Son-of-a-Boston-barman," she spits, fist opening to drop the spoon, which clatters to the floor as the flattened hand slams down on the table with enough force to send bowls and glasses hopping into the air, coffee spilling from Mark's cup and running toward his waiting lap.

"Well," the helper says, rising wearily to fetch a roll of paper towels. "At least your anger reflexes work well enough." He has only begun wiping up the spills when a knock comes at the apartment's front door. "You expecting anyone?" Mark asks with a mischievous smile, then answers his own question. "I'm not expecting anyone. 'Cept maybe Publishers Clearing House..."

The only reaction he receives from Rod – as she now accepts being addressed, along with the more formal 'Rodney' or 'Dr. Gimbal' - is a stony silence, her eyes glaring with the look of accusation to which all her friends have become accustomed, along with her refusal to wear any clothes belonging to Aubrey or any other woman.

Those glaring eyes follow as the filmmaker makes his way through the small living room, stepping around piles of books and clothes which have been accumulating ever since the rescue. At the door he pauses, casting a glance back toward the kitchen, then checking to make sure the safety chain is hooked before pulling the door open only an inch or two to reveal a narrow view of what is clearly a very large man, standing on the shallow stoop. "Yeah?" he asks, as the man's eyes quickly scan him before moving on to focus beyond, searching the interior of the house.

"I'm a friend of Miss McKloskey," the stranger offers in explanation.

"I don't know any one by that..." Mark begins, only to be interrupted.

"Listen kid," the man insists, "I'm her fiancée and I've got a right to see her." The voice and the words it carries click now, taking Mark back to an evening at The Good Cup, waiting for Kim's current squeeze to show, and the raunchy jibes which followed their departure together. Turning toward the kitchen he calls out to Rod.

"Hey, Doctor," he calls over his shoulder. "You want to talk to your fee-ance-ey?" Before Rod can answer, the man in the hallway thrusts his shoulder against the door, straining the chain to its limit with a rattling, clanking, sproing.

"Kim," he shouts as he does so, his face thrust into the narrow gap between door and frame, eyes wide with excitement. "Kimmie? It's me honey - it's Jake."

His shouts have two distinct effects inside the apartment. For Mark's part, the sight of a large man trying to force the door triggers a myriad of cinematic memories. Just as he's seen on a hundred TV episodes, he throws his own body against the inside of the door, slackening the chain somewhat, only to have it snap back immediately as the other responds. A minor struggle ensues, with Jake pushing from outside and Mark from inside, the door leaf moving back and forth an inch or so as first one and then the other thrusts their weight.

In the kitchen however, the effect on Rod is less of fear than of curiosity. Rising slowly from the chair, her hand bumps the cereal dish, sending it to the floor with a shattering crash and the sodden slog of wet spill. Oblivious, she reaches for the thrift-shop walker Aubrey picked up to ease her transition to full mobility. Two clumping shuffling steps behind its metal frame bring her into Jake's field of view.

"Kim," the young man shouts, even more excited than before. "I knew you were here. Tell this idiot to open the door."

Completely absorbed in the effort of making her way across the room, Rod ignores the man's urging. Head bent, hands gripping the rubber handles, she proceeds to lift Christina's right foot and move it forward a few inches, then do the same with the left. Mark and Jake both watch now, their jousting interrupted by the spectacle of this young woman investing such mighty effort in crossing the short distance between her and them. Jake, for one, seems quite appalled at what he is seeing.

"Kimmie, Babe. What have they done to your hair?"

His question goes unanswered as Rod continues to make her way closer, eventually stopping several feet from the door, leaning heavily on the walker and fixing her eyes on Jake's stubbled face.

"Who are you?" she asks, in the manner of one accustomed to receiving straight answers to her questions, the gradual improvement her speech has shown over the weeks culminating now in a cadence and tone which belies Christina's small stature and disheveled appearance.

"It's me," answers the young man at the door, "Jake." Reaching a thick arm through the wedge of opening he stretches toward Rod, open fingers grasping. "Jesus, Kimmie, tell this idiot to open the door. I've got to see you, sweetheart. Got to talk to you."

"You want me to open the door, Doc?" Mark asks with a knowing smile, his shoulder still braced against the wood. "You want me to open the door and let this wild man in?"

Rather than answering, Rod lurches her walker even closer, till she stands just out of reach of the grasping fingers. Squinting hard she studies the face, half in shadow, half illuminated by the apartment's own feeble light through the sliver of opening. Young and chiseled, it exudes the sort of untested boldness often associated with salesmen and politicians, rather than the well-earned confidence of those who have worked long and hard to know their field. Still, she pauses, face crinkling in concentration.

"There's something familiar," she says firmly. "I've heard your voice before. That hospital or whatever it was?"

"You can't fool me, Kimmie," the man responds, excitement twisting his words into a wail. "You've gone too far with this act. It's time to call it off. Come with me; I'll take you back to your mother's house so we can help you get well again."

The mention of Christina's mother's house causes a

229

connection in Rod's mind, a memory echoing through the confusion. Early days of waking and sleeping. Voices talking about a girl in the next bed. Multiple voices speaking in clinical detachment as Rod struggled to understand.

"You were there," she says now, one hand coming slowly up to point in accusation. "You were there when I was in the Nothing." The effect of this recognition on Jake is immediate and profound. What had seemed angry now becomes prideful, what had been a frantic panicked energy becomes more calm; a patient and paternal pleading.

"I've always been there, Kimmie. Since the first day I met you, I've been there for you." Mark sees the man slumping with something very like fatigue, the despair of a long fruitless wait taking over his frame as he leans into the narrow opening, outstretched arm draped over the security chain. "I'll always be there, because I love you - you've got to believe that, Babe - that I love you like nobody else ever can and as soon as you are well enough, I want us to be married, just like we were planning before. Before all this happened."

Watching this scene unfold, Mark is thrilled at the dramatic possibilities. Two young souls, nearly destroyed by her horrible affliction, somehow managing to find one another and be reunited. Not the same demographic as the action/rescue plot he's been pursuing, more of a Nicholas Sparks chick-flick sort of thing, but maybe even more financeable. Afraid to disturb the moment by going back to the kitchen for his notebook, he instead makes notes in his head: the hired nurse witnessing the reunion, a smile creeping over her world-weary face to symbolize the joy of hope rewarded and love triumphant, now that this girl and this boy can make a life together. Certain that his picture is coming together, Mark hears the words form and flow, as Christina realizes she's been deluded, breaking down to accept her man's love, accept herself for who she obviously is, the truth of her body, her face, her voice and every other physical fact. Instead what he actually hears is Christina's voice bursting forth in strangled fury.

"I am not your Kimmie," she says, arms rising from her sides, like a preacher entreating the congregation to believe. Teetering without the walker's support, still she is defiant, head swiveling to target both Mark and Jake with her words. "Not Kimmie, or Kim, or Chris, or Christina, or your little girl, or any other name you can make up for me. I am Dr. Rodney Gimbal. I have a life and a home and a wife, and as soon as she gets my letters she is going to come and straighten this all out... "

"Oh, man," Mark begins, the intensity of the girl's commitment overruling his artistic vision just as his voice is overruled by Jake's, shouting from his side of the door.

"Stop it, Kim. For God's sake, please stop this crazy act. Don't you know you're breaking my heart?"

"Go away," Rod says, her voice rising as well, to a high pitched desperation which catches all three up short even before she slams the walker against the door jamb and turns away, hands flailing at the air around her. "I don't give a damn what anyone says, I know who I am and I don't ever want to see any of you again." Halfway back to the bedroom door the weakness of legs unused for months catches up with her and Mark and Jake both watch helplessly as the small figure sways, then topples, crumbling to the floor with an angry expulsion of air, somewhere between a growl and a sob.

"I am me," she says softly between heaving breaths. "Whatever is going on, whatever has happened, I am who I am. And always have been."

scene XX: Interior, Municipal Court, downtown justice
center, Auster (definitely use his real name, he'll love the
publicity), walks ahead as Aubrey wheels The Girl into an
elevator. They are rushed, late, Aubrey apologizes; The Girl
was not cooperating with getting dressed, and we can see
why – per Auster's directions she is in a prissy blouse,
overdone make-up, hair brushed and tied with a pink ribbon.
Legs hidden beneath a blanket, she wears a look of distaste
through the entire scene.

Aubrey: Sorry about the blanket, I tried to put a skirt on her,
but she wasn't cooperating, and I...
Auster (speaking out side of mouth as he taps text into
Crackberry): Not to worry. It makes her more sympathetic.
(elevator door closes, he looks at berry in disgust, it has cut
off inside the elevator. Then to the girl) You ready for this,
Miss?
Girl: I am not Miss, I am Doctor...
Auster: Hold it right there. (pushes Stop button and elevator
jolts to a halt) You are going to listen to me and you are
going to do what I say, do you understand? (She just glares at
him) I had a call a couple of days ago, from an attorney
who's going to be here representing the hospital and your
mother. (the girl starts to react but Auster shuts her up with
a wave of his hand) They've got her and one of the nurses
who worked for her ready to testify that you have been
deranged since you first recovered from the coma – claiming
to be some eighty-year-old doctor guy when they can show
pictures from the day you were born till the day you left her
home that prove beyond a doubt you are Christina
McKloskey, so if you say *one word* to that judge about being
Rod Gimbal, she's going to conclude you're a loon and re-
affirm guardianship by your next of kin, which is that old lady
you're so enamored of. You want that? (the girl just glares)
OK. So what you're going to do is, you're going to say you are
Christina...
Girl: I will not say that. It's not true and I will not perjure
myself. (she's still talking with difficulty, slow and slurred. I'll
need a real good actress for this part – or maybe use an actor

and dub his voice over hers, like it's her Rod voice that she hears inside her head because she believes..... OK, so figure out later how to get that across)

Aubrey: Kim…

Auster (he's reaching the end of his rope): Who the hell is Kim?

Aubrey: I explained that in your office. Kim Tree is the name she was using when I knew her, at school.

Auster: Right. (sarcastic) Has she got any *other* names I should know about?

Aubrey: Oh yeah. She used lots of other names, when she was doing her performance pieces? Like the time she got arrested for being June, her bag lady character…

Auster: (To Girl) You got arrested?

The Girl: That wasn't me.

Aubrey: Look, I'm sorry. I mean, fuck, it just never….

Auster: No. No, actually…(looks at his watch, distracted, thoughtful) She got arrested – really arrested?

Aubrey: The whole deal, took her to the station, booked her in, took her pictures and all, and she never once broke character. (Auster looks distracted, like he's not even listening any more) Look I'm sorry I didn't…

Auster: No., no, it's…(punches the elevator button again like he's just decided something, the car starts moving, shot of floor indicator going up, twelve, thirteen…no, that's so cliché, find another way to indicate that)…actually, that's better. (to the girl, really firm) So, I get that you won't say you're Christina. But will you go along with me if I don't say you're really this Gimbal guy?

The Girl: You can say or not say whatever you want, but I know…

Auster, interrupting very bluntly: That's right. 'I can say whatever I want and you're not responsible' – we agree on that? You'll stand by that in that room up there?

The Girl: Yes.

Auster: OK. So here's the deal: I ask the questions, you answer honestly, but you say as little as possible; yes or no if you can, otherwise keep it short, and I'm not asking you to lie so long as you don't object to anything I say. All right? (the girl looks puzzled but eventually gives a faint nod). Good. (The doors open and they exit the elevator, and Auster begins tapping on his Blackberry again as he mutters to himself) This is fine. This is very fine.

Scene XX: a generic looking court room with lots of people coming in and out – crooks, lawyers, family people – give it lots of color and diversity, kind of chaos-with-arguments. Lots of big flabby cops standing around looking bored and sleepy. The Judge (what should judge look like? Google says the real Bartenieff is 53, mother from Chicago, father French, from a family of professors that fled Russia just before the revolution, moved to US after WWII, met at Northwestern. Hard to find an actor as good as the real thing – imposing, exotic, unexpected – maybe just see who shows up for cattle call and figure it out then) Judge is talking to a couple of people standing in front of her bench as Auster and Aubrey maneuver the girl's wheelchair to an open spot at the end of the front row, but there are no open seats there so he and Aubrey have to sit two rows back. Auster glances at several suits sitting in the very back row, including Doug Taylor from MH. They nod in recognition. Next to them are Mrs. M. (in one of those nubby thick suits like women politicians wear and her hair all perfectly curled) and Jake (Armani suit of course, but in a really bad mood, like he's about to bust someone's chops). Mrs. M. sees girl, smiles a Mayberry smile, then blows her a kiss)

Indicate some time passing as Judge hears a bunch of other cases and deals with them, very quick-like; not taking any bullshit from anyone. Cases are about real low-lifes, in orange jump suits and shackles. More people and cops coming and going, backing up in the aisles, bailiff putting more files on the bottom of judge's stack. All the time The Girl is looking around like she can't figure out what any of this is. Aubrey's very quiet, like she's freaked-out just by being here. Mrs. M chatting happily with Jake, both trying to catch The Girl's eye but she won't look at them at all. Auster texting furiously on Blackberry, then looking at it and pushing buttons now and then as the scene goes on. After she gets rid of another case, the Judge gathers a new file from her stack, looks briefly at the papers inside and calls out 'Christine' McKloskey. Auster waves a finger to the Judge, taps Aubrey on the knee and the two move up close to the bench, gathering Chris in her chair as they go. At the same time we see the suits all rise and file like soldiers around to where they can stand in front too, but off to the opposite side from our three. (use the MH guys real names too, if they raise a stink it's good promotion). Mrs. M. starts to get up but Jake puts a hand on her arm; he's telling her not to worry, they've got it all covered.

Judge: All right, ladies (a nod toward Aubrey and The Girl) and gentlemen. This is a hearing to determine the competence and, if necessary, guardianship, of this young lady here (another nod toward The Girl, at which she starts to speak but Auster puts a hand on her shoulder and makes some sort of signal to the judge, who nods back, all in an instant). Mr. Auster, you're representing the respondent? (Auster nods, judge turns to the suits) Mr. Kunzig, what is your interest?

Kunzig (the head suit, and a real straight arrow.) Big and square, so you can't believe he's ever done a thing wrong in his entire life. Think that guy from star trek next gen – not the captain, the other guy - Roker was it? starts out very precise and proud of how well prepared he is, where Auster is loose and relaxed): Your Honor, in the matter of...

Judge: Gentlemen, as you can see, this court is very busy, so let's cut to the chase. We are all aware as to what matter we're discussing.

Kunzig (a bit taken aback by that): Yes Sir...I mean, your Honor. The respondent, *Christin-a* Mckloskey (judge's face puckers up at being corrected by him) suffered a drug incident several months ago, during which she suffered severe neurological damage, for which she was treated at Hilltop Medical Center, whom we represent. (reaction shot: Judge is visibly anxious to get to the point) Since recovering the ability to communicate, she has been in a delusional state, apparently believing that she is one Dr. Rodney Gimbal which is the name of a senior practitioner who passed away in an unrelated incident while she was a patient at Hilltop. This claim to be Dr. Gimbal is prima facie evidence that she is incapable of managing herself or her affairs by reason of persistent delusional behavior and therefore....

Auster (almost under his breath, looking bored and

distracted): We stipulate that the respondent is Christina
McKloskey.
Reaction shot of Mrs. M. pleased and Jake, suspicious
Kunzig (surprised; Looks at Auster, then the judge, then back
at Auster.): You what?
Auster: You heard me. (to Christina) Do you object to my
stipulating that you are Christina McKloskey?
The Girl (thinks for a second, then answers, a bit tentative):
No.
Judge: Stipulation is accepted. (another reaction shot of Mrs.
M. again, pleased about this. she pats Jake's arm, he's not so
sure) Mr. Kunzig? (Kunzig didn't answer immediately so
Auster jumped in)
Auster: You're over eighteen years of age?
Girl (beginning to smile): Oh, yes. I am way over eighteen.
Kunzig: Wait a minute... Your honor....They can't do this.
Judge: What? Agree with you? Opposing counsel can't agree
with you on respondent's identity?
Kunzig: No... I mean, yes. (to Auster) I mean, that's not what
you said in conference.
Judge: Parties were in conference prior to this hearing?
Auster: (again, jumps in real quick, but also really laid back,
like he's telling her it's no big thing) By telephone, your
Honor; contact authorized by both principals. Mr. Kunzig's
client offered to provide for all Christina's medical expenses
for the duration of her convalescence if she agreed to remain
under her mother's care. Without characterizing their
position for them, I would say there was an appearance that
they accept some measure of responsibility for her current
disability.
Judge looks suspicious: Mr. Kunzig – is this true.
Kunzig (looks at the other attorneys and MH execs. beside
him, they make various small gestures of agreement, but are
clearly not pleased). No, there was no accession of
responsibility, but yes, your honor, due to her delayed
recovery from the drug overdose, we offered – without in
any way admitting any liability, and conditioned upon a full
release and waiver – my client agreed to provide medication
and supervision for Christina, in her mother's home and
under the care of a physician or physicians satisfactory to our
professional review...

Judge (growing more impatient): Interesting, but hardly pertinent. Mr. Kunzig, other than what name she wants to use, do you have any evidence to demonstrate that the respondent is not competent to make her own decisions?

Jordan (one of the other MH attorneys): Your honor, we didn't anticipate...

Judge: Mr. Kunzig?

Kunzig: We expected....

Judge: Any other grounds, Mr. Kunzig?

Thompson (another of the MH lawyers, steps in over Kunzig): Your honor, we have provided to the Court this Affidavit of Examining Physician by Warren Phillippe, a registered psychologist who examined the respondent during the first weeks of her convalescence and again less than a week before she was forcibly removed from our care....

Auster: And we have an affidavit from our own equally-expert witness (waves a file in the air), which describes the marked difference between that description of respondent's condition and what she observed only a few weeks after Ms. McKloskey's *voluntary departure* from your care. Oh, but I'm not certain Mr. Taylor really wants that affidavit entered into the record does he? (puts the file back in his folio) We also have documentation from the University of Washington (waves some more papers around) substantiating that during a period of several years while living under the name of ...(makes a show of looking thru papers and finding the name)... Miss Kim Tree...that during that time she carried a full load of classes - earning a 3.7 GPA, by the way - produced artwork which was highly regarded by faculty, held a student assistantship for two semesters, paid all her fees on time and lived independently off-campus. All of which conclusively demonstrate her ability to manage her own adult life, regardless of what name she might use. (to Girl) How many meals should a twenty-three year old woman of your size and weight eat each day?

The Girl (after a pause, apparently a bit disoriented by the question): Three.

Auster: And what should they consist of?

The Girl: Well...a balanced diet would include all food groups, but with less than 30% of calories from fat, red meat no more than twice a week. Heavy on vegetables and fruits,

237

with plenty of fiber and...

Judge (holding out wrist to gaze at a prominently-jeweled watch): Is this really necessary?

Auster (stalling): We are simply trying to establish the respondent's competence to care for herself. How many times a day do you brush your teeth?

The Girl: I brush after every meal.

Auster: Do you know right from wrong?

Judge: Enough, Mr. Auster...

Kunzig: Your honor...(at this point, a woman entered the court room - definitely <u>not</u> trying to be inconspicuous about it. Model-pretty and dressed to kill in skinny red skirt-and-jacket outfit, but with eyes as hard as granite, she walked right up to Auster, put a hand on his shoulder and whispered something with her lips practically inside his ear. She handed him a thin file which he didn't even look inside of, as she turned and walked out, every eye – including Auster's - following her until the doors shut and he, in an entirely different tone, like suddenly he couldn't have cared less what happened next.)

Auster: OK, Kurt, your turn (Kunzig and the other suits exchange glances. Taylor, visibly irritated with them all, takes a step toward the Girl)

Taylor: Are you Dr. Rodney Gimbal?

Auster (puts a hand out to the girl to make sure she does not respond): We have already stipulated the Respondent's identity.

Taylor: Your honor, ever since she began to communicate she has been maintaining she is Dr. Rodney Gimbal...

Auster: That's absurd, Doug. Dr. Gimbal - if he were not deceased - would be in his sixties. Your honor can see that this is a young woman, ergo, this cannot be Dr. Gimbal. (throughout this speech Auster gathers speed and momentum, like Alan Shore building to the climax of a Boston Legal summation) Christina McKloskey, on the other hand, is a vibrant young performance artist, with a history of taking her characters to heart. This (holds up the file the woman just delivered) is an SPD Record of Intake showing that she once performed one of her pieces with so much commitment that she was arrested and booked without ever breaking character – a youthful indiscretion which will not be repeated, I'm sure? (he looks at the girl, who puts on a serious face and shakes her head emphatically) But it illustrates that her personality – the behavior which is normal *for this individual* - has remained consistent even as she recovered from a very serious injury. The fact that she may from time to time *perform the character* of Dr. Gimbal, or anyone else she chooses, is actually the best evidence of all that this young lady is indeed Christina McKloskey, a fact to which we have already stipulated.

Judge: Gentlemen, enough. I trust I don't need to remind any of you that under the law of the State of Washington, an individual may use whatever name he or she chooses, so long as there is no intent to defraud. If this young woman wants to call herself Rodney Gimbal, she may do so. If she wants to make that her legal name, paperwork is available at the Clerk's. If she attempts to represent herself as a doctor without proper credentials she would be subject to administrative and civil action and if she attempted to claim the assets or property of the deceased Doctor Gimbal by reason of having the same name, she would be guilty of fraud. Does the Respondent understand all that?

Auster: Yes, your honor. (Judge ignores him and stares at the girl, who eventually answers with her first smile of the entire proceeding).

Girl: Yes, your Honor, I understand what you said.

Judge: Good. Now let's get on with it. (to girl) To the degree that you require assistance during your convalescence, do you wish to be in the care of Mrs. Mckloskey? (reaction shot, Mrs. M. tense, hand to her mouth)

Girl: No. (Mrs. M. bursts into tears, Jake comforts her)

Auster: Do you wish to be in the care of this woman here (pointing to Aubrey, who looks like she's just about to win the lottery)?

Girl: Yes. (reactions all around)

Auster: Your honor. Counsel requests that the Respondent be confirmed competent and of legal age, in which case she will choose to live with Miss Maturin until such time as she feels ready to live on her own.

Judge (to the Girl): Miss McKloskey: is that what you want?

The Girl: I am not...(a sharp motion of Auster's head catches her eye; he looks about ready to take a swing at her) Yes, I am...yes, that is what I want, your honor.

Judge: So ruled. Clerk will please issue and record.

Thompson, Kunzig, Jordan and Taylor all begin to protest but are silenced as Auster launches into what is obviously a well-planned speech.

Auster: As to the unspecified mistreatment which my client suffered at the hands of Hilltop Medical Center, we submit this agreement (pulling a document from the folio he's been holding the whole time, he hands it to the nearest MH guy and they pass it from one to the other till it gets to Taylor, who squints at the small type, then fumbles in his pockets for reading glasses) in which we agree to limit and hold harmless - yadda, yadda, yadda - in exchange for their providing necessary medications and services via a physician of our choosing - medical certifications to be to their satisfaction of course - we don't want to vitiate their professional liability coverage. Gene, (to Taylor directly) this is basically the same offer you had previously made to us except for that silly stuff about remaining under Mrs. Mckloskey's care. We've been so intimidated by your incredible legal maneuvering that we have no choice but to knuckle under, provided such agreement is executed here and now. Oh, and we've added something to cover legal fees, which have been substantial, due to the need to defend against your team's complex and extensive arguments.

Judge: Gentlemen – and ladies – that agreement is between the parties. This hearing is concluded and adjourned. Next is... (places Chris's file on the stack behind her and lifts top one off the stack in front, then begins looking around the room as she speaks) ...Mr. Thomas Hardy?

(Auster and the girls move toward the back of the room, followed by the clump of MH guys, one of whom takes the agreement from Taylor and begins scanning it rapidly. Mrs. M. is in tears, Jake looks about to fire one off at the MH guys. Aubrey leans over to flash a triumphant smile at The Girl, who seems quietly satisfied with the situation, as if she never expected anything else, while Auster smiles - just the way you'd expect of a man who's having the time of his life.)

end of scene

"I've lived so many lives. Which one do you want to hear about?"

Elaine looks over at her friend, face barely visible in the fluttering glow of a butter lamp. Beyond her the hut's walls are soot-stained and indistinct. Periodically the dancing flames pick other faces out of the room's shadowy perimeter – a farmer, his wife, their five children who appear to range from a few months to perhaps ten years in age. Despite the poverty of their home these people have taken the two trekkers into it without hesitation, sharing dust-tea and doughy balls of fried millet and cornmeal as if they were an offering.

The day had begun well enough, Elaine and Beryl setting out from their lodging in the village of Birethanti in company with a kindly young New Zealander named Andy, who had arrived just before dark the night before, having walked in one day what had taken them the better part of two. Over morning tea the three discovered they were headed for the same destination and Andy offered to help them find their way. Supremely unconcerned about their age, he assured them that the journey to the Golden Flower monastery was actually very easy. If they had made it to the top of the Sacred Mountain, and all the places since, surely they would have no trouble with the walk – he did not even call it a hike - to the Golden Flower.

Within the hour though, the trail began to wind more steeply upward, Andy disappeared ahead, and it was clear to Elaine that the altitude would make for a long day. By lunchtime, when she had not seen another westerner besides Beryl for nearly four hours, she began to feel some apprehension. As always, her companion took the situation totally in stride.

"We are at a point, on a path between two other points," she said as she carefully sectioned a Singh Durbar apple during one of their infrequent rest stops. Cutting each section in turn into bite-sized chunks she placed them on the handkerchief laid out upon her lap. The sun of central Nepal beat down upon them. Not the untempered torchlight sun of the high Himalaya though, for here, deep in the Pokhara Valley, the light was less brilliant, diffused by remnant subtropical humidity to render the distant panorama flat and indistinct, as if one were staring at an aged painted copy, rather than the real thing.

"What matters is that we continue along the path. It is not necessary that we move rapidly, or that we know the distance ahead of us, only that we trust the trail and continue along it."

'What if we get lost?' Elaine thought. 'If the trail peters out, or forks? What if there are other paths to choose from?' She knew better by now, though, than to ask those questions. Three months of traveling with Beryl had taught her that her friend would have an answer, always delivered in the patient, knowing tone of a teacher. Sometimes the answers were practical and realistic, like the evening at Je Ngor, in Bangkok, when Elaine had realized her purse was missing: Beryl had bartered one of her bracelets to pay for the meal and a samlor ride back to their hotel. It was only after Elaine had found her purse on the bed where she'd left it that Beryl admitted she'd had plenty of Thai Bhat the whole time. She'd simply preferred to get the two of them out of the situation without resorting to the money belt beneath her skirt. A test of her traveler's prowess, her tone seemed to suggest, and, perhaps, of Elaine's nerves.

Other times the answers were more difficult to fathom, as when they had emerged into a clearing at Preah Vihear to behold a secondary temple only recently discovered under its centuries of Banyan trunks and creeper vines covered with orange trumpet-flowers. "It is just as it was," Beryl had whispered in Elaine's ear, though she had previously made clear that this would be her first visit to this region of northern Cambodia. Later, when asked about the comment, she explained that a feeling had come over her there, a feeling as distinct as hunger or pain, but of a different sort. "I felt yellow," she said, as if that would make things more clear. "I always feel yellow when I come home to a place I've never been before. It is the color of belonging," she added, as if that proved her point.

So Elaine had learned to keep her questions to herself, and when they finished their snack she dutifully followed in her friend's footsteps as the trail wound its way between stone-walled terraces, past the clustered houses of several tiny hamlets with priceless views of the Annapurna massif peeking over a hanging cloud which had been above them earlier in the day but now was nearly at eye level. Only when the sun dropped below a ridge and the temperature lowered precipitously, had she dared to venture her concern.

"Andy will come back along the trail for us," Beryl said then, "and if he doesn't, we'll find a place to spend the night. These mountains are actually quite full of people; in fact, they've been settled far longer than North America. Did you know - Siddharta Gautama, the man who became the Bhuddha, was born 500 years before Christ, right near Katmandu? Think about that – what most of our friends and neighbors would think of as an undeveloped society has actually been going on for longer than our entire European culture. Traditions, rituals, stories; all older than virtually any of the things we were taught to believe in. It's not mechanized or industrialized - not prosperous, by our definitions, at least - but those qualities have nothing to do with how advanced a culture is. Real advancement comes from understanding, and that is often most plentiful in places the commercial/institutional/technological world thinks are the most backwards."

Not long after that, as the last glow of the sun silhouetted the ridges of Dhaulagiri high above, their trail began to descend again, and soon they had come upon a small plateau, where two drainages intersected. Set back a little from the trail was a low square house, a thin streamer of smoke rising from a gap in its thatched roof. A trio of mongrel dogs challenged the trekkers well before they reached the house, the chorus of barks and howls tapering off only when a man emerged. Dressed in multi-patched trousers and a sun-bleached Puma warm-up jacket, with a scrawny black moustache like catfish feelers, he watched as they came closer, setting down the bowl held in his blackened fingers as the dogs swirled around his legs.

"Namaskram," he greeted them each, "Namaskram aamai," bowing slightly with hands held before him. Elaine listened as Beryl and the man exchanged a few words and very soon the two women were inside, listening to the dung-patty fire crackle as a rising wind searched for gaps in the walls.

"They have so little," Elaine whispers, using the smallest of gestures to indicate the children, whose soiled clothes and smudged faces make them appear more like features of the hut's well-worn interior than inhabitants of it. The father's eyes are heavy, his head drooping, the mother is attentive and busy, eyes darting constantly from visitors to kerosene lamp, to father to children who, for their part, lie comfortably across the packed earth floor and one another, as if it were nothing at all to have two pale women sitting around their fire speaking a foreign language while the family settles in for the night. "I feel guilty, eating their food. And I feel like we should at least strike up a conversation with them, wouldn't that be more...polite?"

Beryl's face takes an odd turn at that, and Elaine wonders if she has lost her appetite, until the smile returns and she realizes her friend was actually suppressing laughter. "But we are being polite. We've come into their home, accepted their food, soon we'll sleep beneath their rugs. By doing those things, we honor them; confirm that they are prosperous and benevolent. What would you have us do - ask them all about their lives? Their hopes and dreams? These people don't talk about such things with strangers; they open their homes, share their food, but their thoughts are their own. 'Do not ask about what you do not know, do not tell about what you <u>do</u> know;' in their world, that's part of being polite."

Elaine knows better than to pursue the issue. She will finish her tea and when it is done she will lay her head on her pack and cover herself with the blankets the woman hands her. In the morning they will all rise, share tea, and the two women will take their leave, bowing and smiling before heading off toward the Golden Flower. Somewhere along the way they will find Andy - or not - and in the meantime, they will warm themselves at a fire they did not build and be sincerely - and politely - grateful.

"You really believe this, don't you?" Aubrey asks one morning as she works a slender leg back and forth above the bed. Prescribed by a therapist sent over from MH as part of Auster's agreement, the exercises have become part of their daily routine, along with a dozen or so pills and serums. Twice a day the patient's limbs are manipulated, and already the movements of her arms have become stronger and more controlled. Her hands remain weak though, and too uncoordinated to do much more than hold a glass of water, but they can feel things, like her own face, and the reality of her body beneath the sheet. "This Rod stuff?"

"Who do you think I am?" Christina's lips ask. Her eyes implore an explanation.

"You're Kim," Aubrey answers, without hesitation. "I've known you for three years. Longer now. We were students together. At the U., before...all this."

"Tell me about me."

For nearly an hour, as legs bend and straighten, as arms are stretched and pulled and the petite torso is bent upward to a sitting position then lowered to the pillows, Aubrey explains it all. How the two girls met, the classes they took. How she watched as Kim's artwork became ever more bizarre and conceptual. The good times they had; with boys, with parties, with wine and drugs, with each other.

"You're my best friend," she concludes with a broad smile, as Kim lies back, exhausted by the workout. "My best friend in the entire world. I don't care what you say, I can see who you are, and I don't care what name you want to call yourself, or what that old lady wants to call you. To me you'll always be Kim Tree, and it hurts me when you say that everything I remember never happened."

Kim seems to consider this for a time, deeply and carefully. Her look is faraway, but her words, when they come, are as steady and clear as any she has uttered since regaining consciousness at Mrs. McKloskey's guest house.

"I do not pretend to know what has happened to me. I do not know how I came to be here, or to look like I do. For the life of me, I don't know if I am dreaming, or dead, or just stark raving mad, but I do know, with every thought that passes through my head, who I am. I am my mother's son and my father's son and for all my life I have been and I always will be Rodney Gimbal, and I am going to find a way back to the life I had before all this, even if it's the last thing I ever do. Do you understand that, young lady? *Do you understand that?"*

It seems to Elaine that she has been sitting here for hours, in this dim cavern of a space. A space that wears the chill of ancient underground, though its entrance was at the highest level of the Golden Flower Monastery, a collection of stuccoed buildings perched on the most-nearly-level bit of land in the valley where the rivers Tatopani and Ghorepani meet.

Approaching the temple after four days trekking, Elaine was struck by how small it was, hardly worth the journey. There might be some magic though, in how its gold-capped roof shimmered in the sunlight; until they came closer and she saw plainly that the shimmer was only the perfectly explicable result of water directed from a small tributary stream thru wooden pipes, to sluice constantly down its bronze-shingled surface.

A wide, ring-like basin surrounded the small conical structure, capturing the runoff in a welter of floating lilies and grasses. Birds that might have been swallows swooped and dove above this cultivated marsh and several larger waterfowl could be seen wading among the blossoms. Some local variety of heron, Elaine supposed, feeding on whatever creatures lived in the murky water. Around this, stretched a promenade along which a scant few fellow-travelers walked, mostly silent. Even the usually voluble Beryl seemed hushed by this place they had labored so hard to reach. Pressed for an explanation of its origin and significance, she had little to offer.

"The names you have heard - Temple of The Golden Flower, Temple of Reflection of the Center - are only my poor attempts to translate some of the many ways it is described. Other than that, this place has no text. You enter. You see. You hear. The rest is...well; it just is."

With those words she directed Elaine toward the portal, a narrow slot in an otherwise featureless wall, and turned away. On her own, confused and somewhat hurt, Elaine entered, to discover that the opening was only the beginning of a narrow passage which soon began to slope steeply, curving around and down until it felt as if she were spiraling not into a temple but into the very hill upon which the monastery rested. More and more dim the passage grew, as she went, until finally she was reduced to placing a hand along the outer wall to guide herself along its ever-widening arc. Feeling her apprehension grow, Elaine was about to turn around when she began to perceive a faint glow ahead. Walked on, the glow growing stronger, eventually she reached what she took to be the Temple itself; an expansive space whose rough earth floor glowed dimly in the light from one small central opening high above and the flames of perhaps a dozen tiny butter-candles burning in niches around the outer wall.

Far larger than its visible roof had suggested, the room was well over a hundred feet across, and nearly as tall.   What she had taken from outside to be the temple's roof, she quickly realized, was in fact, only its very apex. The entire 'hill' on which that smaller structure appeared to sit, the whole circular pond and promenade, were actually the temple's roof, the difference between exterior and interior geometries allowing space for that descending passageway. Despite the room's great size, she found the atmosphere close and somewhat stuffy – a blend of loamy earth, oily butter smoke and the exhalations of twenty or so persons sitting lotus-style at apparent random around the floor, each staring toward the unoccupied center of the space. Barely visible in the shadowy light, not one of them gave any sign of noting her arrival. Indeed, there seemed nothing going on at all, until, without warning, an orange-robed man some thirty feet away made a small huffing sound and began stiffly to unfold himself. Once more-or-less vertical, he bowed deeply toward the center of the room, then strode with great precision toward a barely discernable dark spot on the far side, into which he disappeared without another sound.

For several minutes Elaine stood, hoping that her eyes would accustom themselves to the light and reveal some other features, but her waiting brought no reward. The continuous surface which formed both wall and ceiling bore no decoration but the few faint streaks of soot above the candle niches. Reflection seemed exactly the wrong term for this space.

'Think,' she imagined Beryl telling her. 'Listen.'

'Look,' she told herself.

Feeling perhaps that imitation might lead her aright, Elaine stepped over to where the robed man had been sitting and took his place, legs crossed as best she could, though nowhere near full-lotus. Hands in lap, body facing center, her open eyes found little on which to focus as she resigned herself to waiting for something – anything - to happen.

At least now - six weeks after the hearing, ten after the rescue and the weaning her off of that Mesta-shit - Kim can take care of her own body. That had been the worst of it for Aubrey, though also, oddly, the best. Having to wipe up the messes when she started taking food, handling those god-awful plastic sheets and adult diapers had made Aubrey nearly sick to her stomach. On the other hand there was the opportunity to see her friend's body up close, to explore every inch of it. Secretly she had to admit to herself there had been some...something...in that. There was a time, back when Kim was still awakening into her self - whatever self this new Kim was - that the two had shared tender moments. During a sponge bath for example, Aubrey supporting those bony shoulders as she gently wiped Kim's back with warm soapy water, feeling the cloth glide over rounded curves of muscle and bone, the shoulder blades like sleek, wet fish beneath her touch. Kim would make small noises then, hints of pleasure as she admitted that her muscles hurt from the therapy; that she longed to get up out of the bed and move around.

Wiping her legs too, with their downy covering of unshaven hair. Not long, Kim's legs, but slender, especially after months of disuse. Her calves felt full and liquid in Aubrey's hand, like bags of precious fluid, her thighs as smooth and white as ceramic, with a secret map of shadow-blue veins beneath their surface; country roads meandering within sight of the private geography hidden at their confluence, which Aubrey carefully cleaned, since her friend would have nothing to do with it.

"That's not me," Kim had said, the first time Aubrey suggested she wash herself. "I don't know how it got there, but that's not me."

Aubrey can only imagine how 'Rod' gets along now, as she insists on taking her own showers and dressing herself; about the only time 'he' lifts a finger to get through the day.

Early morning. Rod rises slowly from the bed, head groggy after hours of late-night channel surfing, body a bit stiff, but nothing like that of a sixty-three year old man, in which the act of climbing out of bed must resemble the unfolding of an ancient manuscript - careful not to tear the shrunken muscles and tendons before they've had a chance to warm up and regain whatever remains of their elasticity. Compared to that, this body rises quickly to its feet and wanders into the bathroom with only the slightest difficulty – walking at least, has come back to him pretty well these days. He does not turn the light on though; that would not help matters at all. By dim glow streaming in beneath the bottom of the door he reaches out a hand to locate the sink and for a moment his mind is filled with the picture he should see in the mirror above it: a tall figure, in a thick brown bathrobe, eyes drooping with weary resignation as the familiar hang-dog face is lathered above a sinkful of steaming water in which he will dash the foam from his razor. One look at the mirror, he knows, would put a lie to it all. In its impassive reflection he would find instead borrowed blue pajamas, buttoned to the neck, and staring back at him, a pair of wide eyes in a face so young, so unlined, that its expression reveals nothing of what is going on inside his mind. Even after these months, he cannot correlate what he would see there with what he knows. Turning from the sink without taking that one look, he reaches around the bath curtain to turn on the shower, then steps to where he knows from experience the toilet sits, deep in the darkest corner of the room. He drops his pajama trousers without looking, sits and lets his bladder void itself, the shower's waterfall blocking out its splashing gush - so different from the narrow strangled stream to which he had grown accustomed over the years. Finished, he keeps his eyes straight ahead as he pulls the still-buttoned pajama top over his head and lets it fall to the floor, tests and adjusts the shower's temperature, then steps around the curtain and into the steaming spray which, in sleepy visions he has imagined will wash away all that is wrong with this flesh, will cleanse all that has gone on and return him to himself.

Now, awake, the reality is that showering entails a careful dance with his own perceptions, if he is to avoid the reality of body-parts he will not view. It takes concentration even to grasp the washcloth in this unfamiliar left hand, the one he finds most useful. Equally challenging to load the slithering bar of soap in the right, and scrub the two together. The motion works up a credible lather though, and Rod feels a small glow of reward, that this at least he can do for himself. No more ignoble sponge baths from fawning nurses or that overgrown teenager Aubrey. From now on he will establish some independence. The soap slips from his clumsy fingers, clattering to the surface of the tub, where it skitters around his ankles, thunking the porcelain loudly enough, it seems, to wake the dead.

Without changing his grip on the cloth, for fear of dropping it as well, Rod runs it first across his face, unable to avoid feeling how small the surface is, the features carved with almost no relief, the flesh soft and giving over a jaw which barely protrudes from the smooth contours of neck and cheeks. Rounding the curve from neck to shoulders he cannot avoid picturing their narrowness; though youthfully squared and erect, they have none of the thrusting power he remembers, the broad mass which used to arch down and forward, making visible to every uncomprehending listener the power of his words, his arguments.

Armpits, Rod has found, must be washed very carefully, reaching out and turning the hand back in a broad arc, so that his forearm does not accidentally brush the flaccid lumps of flesh hanging from his chest, does not accidentally scrape across the darkened tips with their over-sensitive nerve endings anxious to announce a world of difference. There is hair now, beneath his arms, a welcome thought, but only scrawny patches, so fair and fine as almost not to count. Running the cloth over his stomach presents little problem, the region neither so firm as it was in his youth, nor as flabby as in his aging, but pleasantly absent of disturbing anomalies, unlike the region to which it leads, that other patch of private hair in which resides his greatest dismay. To distract himself he has taken to calling up the words of old familiar songs.

"*Chi-ca-go,*" he starts softly this morning. It is the act of singing he desires, the actual sound of it sufficiently hidden by rushing water that he can ignore the disturbing question of whose voice this really is. The words feel good in his mouth, that first syllable like a whisper that gathers momentum until it has enough energy to clap the hard C from his throat. The '*go*' that echoes out in natural reply. "*Chi-ca-go,*" he sings again, and immediately the rhythm in his brain catches hold. "*That toddlin' town,*" comes easily as he scrubs washcloth against soap again and reaches down, eyes shut as he consciously pictures a tiled shower wall, its careful regimentation of lines and squares so predictable and reassuring. One single swipe brings a symphony of sensations, but he blots them out - "*Chicago, Chicago, I'll show you around,*" - as he runs the cloth more safely across his lower back and bottom, making the necessary passes with as much detachment as he can muster. Down his legs Rod's left hand progresses, his right steadying against the dependable solidity of ceramic wall as he sings about betting your bottom dollar and losing your blues. These legs are firm and slim but all too smooth. A faint fuzz is all that has cropped up there in all the time since Anne's nurses last took a razor to them.

He's singing louder now, the beat of the song strong in his head, remembered from what seems a very long time ago. *"On State Street, that great street,"* swabs tiny feet, fleshy and unveined, with perfect clear nails in place of the horny yellow-brown things he remembers. Of all his features, it is the hands and feet with which Rod has made the most progress toward some sort of tenuous peace. Hands which look so fine and capable, fingers apparently strong enough to grasp a scalpel if he could only coordinate them. He can even imagine advantage in their tiny dimension, compared to those clumsy implements he used to employ, which fit so poorly into cavities that he was often forced to work with only two fingers where three or even four would have been optimum. These hands, he thinks, as he struggles to rinse the cloth and wring it out, these hands could work wonders if they would only respond properly to his commands. Instead their graceful flexure seems almost random, clumsily perpendicular to his intentions, as fingers fail to close, or closing, refuse to open again, their intended concert dissolving into an argument of independent motions; try as he may he cannot even snap his fingers to the beat of his own song.

"You'll have the time, the time of your life,"

Water off, out of the shower into the dim room where a towel awaits, the thick cloth an insulation between his hands and all that he does not wish to see or touch as he carefully pats himself dry.

"Chicago, Chicago,
my...home...town."

"Well listen to you," Aubrey's voice rings out as she pushes the door ajar. Instantly, Rod reaches for the bathrobe he knows is hanging on a hook nearby. Red velvet, with pink piping, it would be far down on his list of choices, but still preferable to being caught in the altogether. "I'm impressed."

"Don't be," Rod deadpans. "Any adult can take a shower with his eyes closed."

"No," Aubrey attempts to explain, she meant the voice, so clear and bright, but Rod will have none of it. Even at this early hour her surliness is a wall between them, resentment evident in every word, in every movement, as she brushes past and begins gathering clothes to put on. Aubrey knows from experience that she is expected to withdraw for this, is not welcome to watch her houseguest/friend/patient don ill-fitting boxer shorts and double undershirts – one tight to bind what 'Rod' refuses to acknowledge, one loose and baggy to complete the camouflage. White shirt and gray slacks complete the look by the time Rod emerges from the bedroom and shambles toward the kitchen.

"Breakfast ready?" Rod asks, and Aubrey feels the thud of disappointment crashing down upon her. This shave-headed apparition, insisting on being called a ridiculous name, pretending knowledge of things she could not possibly possess while issuing endless demands for care - for service, just like the customers Aubrey already serves six or ten hours a day. What happened to the beautiful, spontaneous Kim she used to know? That's the problem with people, Aubrey realizes as she reaches for a box of cereal; as soon as you get them figured out and learn to like who they are, they fucking go and fucking change into someone-fucking-else entirely.

As the minutes pass and nothing changes in the Temple of Reflection of The Center, Elaine feels her attention drifting to the other visitors who sit around her, their faces hidden and their garments drained of color by the dimness which surrounds them. Each time she catches her eyes wandering so, she reprimands herself, redoubling the effort to focus straight ahead, on nothing at all. For a time she is struck by how the space, despite its large dimensions, seems to confine her; like being inside a giant vase or bottle - a genie in a lamp. As for reflection, even after a substantial time, it seems singularly devoid of any physical reflection, or anything on which the mind might engage itself. Every worshipful impulse seems stripped away, absorbed by this featureless void, whose chill she feels penetrating farther toward her bones.

After the heat of the trail, this place is really more than cool; it is down-right chilly, and the longer she sits, the more chilly it seems; she can readily envision the energy of warmth radiating away from her folded legs, her bended arms, her tipping head. Eyes drooping, she feels even her breathing slowing down, and shakes her shoulders to fight off sleep. After all their effort to get here, surely it would be a waste to fall asleep. A sin even, a violation of whatever code governs this place.

In an effort to combat that drifting, she tries to concentrate on the concrete sensations of the moment, nearly all of them unpleasant. The hard floor, deforming her buttocks as her weight rests upon them, and highlighting the presence of her pelvis within. The stiffness of her heavy shoes, where they press upon ankles forced into odd angles by her splayed and bended knees. A lock of hair, touching one ear, and the resulting impulse to reach up and brush it away, countered by the fear of disturbing the stillness all around.

Yet not still, when one has little to do but listen. With time she finds she can hear the breathing of the person to her left. Now a slight rustle to the right as another visitor rises, bows quickly toward the empty center, and leaves. Far below those sounds, there is a slight humming, the barest hint of hearing a far-off voice chanting something. Constant and droning, once identified, it grows in her imagination until it underlines her thoughts and frustrations and she turns her mind forcefully away, searching for a hint, a clue, to what is supposed to happen here.

'Temple of Reflection of The Center,' Beryl has called this place, suggesting perhaps she might focus her attention upon its center. The unavoidable fact that there is nothing *at* the center of the temple was not discussed, of course, nor how long she is to focus on it, nor what it is she might hope to gain by doing so, and so Elaine sits, feeling the dust and grit of the floor grind beneath her as she adjusts the position of her legs, searching for some slightly different arrangement which would be more comfortable. Imagines the dust clinging to her skirt and working its way beneath her fingernails as she stifles a yawn, feeling the weariness of the trail creeping up inside her as it did on her first adventure with Beryl, when they climbed the sacred mountain to be rewarded by the expansive sensation of standing atop its summit in the glow of a new day's birth. Finding her chin resting upon her breastbone, she makes an effort to pull it upright, and discovers her perception of the space around her revised. No longer is it enclosed by a wall, but instead her eyes perceive only a surrounding darkness; an endless expanse in which those few candles have lost their substance and appear now as nothing more than pinpricks of light floating in dimensionless void, a void in which something else is realizing itself - directly in front of her, in the previously empty center, is a slight but unmistakable brightening; a faint, glowing shaft that reaches from skylight almost to floor, and in which swirl myriad motes of dust, flickering like stars themselves, as each captures for an instant a tiny measure of the brightness from above and casts it out upon the void. This virtual object, materialized of light and dust, swirls in obedience to invisible crosscurrents, themselves the after-effects of movements long past, while around it the candle-pricks of light seem to move as well, floating up from their niches to dance and flicker then disappear, each one in its own time, only to be replaced somewhere else in her field of vision, by another. It is as if the space before her has come to life - *is alive;* a swirling column of light, of dancing stars in endless space and then, just as she feels she is beginning to understand something incredibly important, Elaine is startled by a shiver, snaps her head upright, and finds herself still sitting in the temple, its center empty, its candles flickering in breezes of their own convection.

'This,' Aubrey says to herself, as she closes the door and hangs her shoulder bag on the knob behind her, 'is not what I signed up for.'

She has just returned from yet another shift at the restaurant. Ten hours of serving and schlepping and putting up with an endless menagerie of rowdy students, picky faculty and don't-rush-me tourists agonizing over what's the perfect menu selection while keeping their waitress – Aubrey – standing over their shoulder when she has a million other things that need doing *right fucking now*. Her feet hurt, her back hurts - even her frigging eyelids hurt! - and the one thing she truly wants to do is lie down and turn into a vegetable but instead, there is her new roommate, 'Rodney' perched on the sofa with a glass of scotch in 'his' hand, watching a god-damn boxing match. Dressed in a pair of Mark's slacks and one of Desmond's shirts, hair combed and oiled into perfect order that does little to conceal the map of suture lines across his scalp, he sits with legs carelessly wide as he cheers for the big man to knock out his opponent.

"You've got him," Kim's voice calls out, and for a moment there's a trace of Aubrey's old friend in that enthusiasm, her lust for life, until in the next instant the same voice hollers "pound him, pound him while you got him," and Aubrey finds herself turning away in disgust, looking for somewhere, anywhere, to hide. In her own home.

It was not supposed to be this way. Grabbing a 2-litre Pepper from the fridge, Aubrey recalls how different it all felt back at the start. Plotting the 'rescue' was a whopping rush, like being part of a movie, and that same high had continued for days afterward. Even later, when they realized they needed help, calling in Mary, and the legal stuff with Auster; the hearing and all had served as a distraction from the day-to-day efforts of caring for a total invalid. Oddly, it was only as they were getting things straightened out - medications resolved and Kim's condition improving every week - just when it should have gotten easier – that the real frustration had begun for Aubrey. Yeah, things were better in some ways; Kim could communicate now, and was able to do more things for herself. But instead of resuming the easy familiarity and shared attitudes she and Kim had found when they first got to know one another at the U, there was this 'Rod' thing. The more Kim regained her abilities, it seemed, the more deeply committed she became to inhabiting this fucking bullshit character day and night, without ever admitting that it was an act, or what a burden her act imposed on those around her.

Mark, for example. Once the aspiring filmmaker disclosed to Rod his plan to make a screenplay about her rescue, the poor sucker found himself trapped into endless hours of his subject's personal history: growing up in a tough neighborhood during the war, working through college in the mystical Eden this 'Rod' character made the nineteen-fifties out to be. Then his glorious progress thruugh medical school and all that shit, how hard the work was and how well he did. Sometimes it felt like Kim was using the whole trip to rub it in all their faces what slackers she thought they were. She could go on for hours, apparently improvising all this stuff from out of thin air, or more likely, late night movies and reruns; that's what it sounded like to Aubs. At first, Mark had eaten it up, thinking it could be boiled down into a few good bits of background, but after filling his drive with over twenty hours of the shit, even he'd had enough.

"Can't you get her to break it off ?" he asked Aubrey, "I mean, this is OK, but we need to get to the part where Kim comes back and admits who she really is. I've written scenes around that, and I want her to help me make it real, show what she's really like."

That would have made Aubrey laugh, if she weren't so angry already - 'What she's really like?' - as far as Aubrey could see, what her old friend was really like now was a lazy pig; a character from a bad sitcom. Staying up till all hours watching TV and drinking. Expecting the others to cook and serve for her, on the grounds 'he' had no idea how to do it himself. "Elaine took care of all that," he had the nerve to say one evening, as Aubrey stirred Rice-a-Roni while he stood by impatiently, without lifting a finger. "Yeah right," she had shot back, thinking herself clever. "And I'll bet 'Elaine' did the cleaning too. And ironed your shirts and darned your socks?"

"Yes," Rod answered, apparently oblivious to the sarcasm. "And took my suits to the cleaners, remembered birthdays, all those things. She was a very good wife." The only thing which prevented Aubs from tossing the entire concoction over his damned head right then and there was the hint of a sob in his voice and the watery look in his eyes as he said it all. Goddamned Kim; she was one hell of an actress when she wanted to be. Even half drunk.

The drinking had started as soon as she could hold a glass steady. In a way, Aubrey felt that was her own fault. Seeing a few bottles of beer her ex roommate had left in the back of the fridge, she mentioned them to Rod, suggesting a beer might calm his nerves, relieve some of the muscle-trembling that made it so difficult to do even small tasks. At first he refused, but then she came home one night to find two empties on the coffee table and Rod zoned out in front of the tube. Beer did the trick for a week or so, taking the edge off his resentment, and Aubrey thought the relaxation might lead to the return of her beloved Kim, so when he asked if she could maybe pick up some scotch - 'I like a little sip, now and then' - she was more than willing to grab a bottle of something cheap on the way home. When that bottle was gone, and the next one drained in only three days, however, she began to wonder if self-medication was such a good idea.

"It dulls the pain," Rod said when she asked, as if that were the end of it. When Aubrey tried to find out more, whether there really was some pain they should tell a doctor about, all she got was anger.

"I didn't ask for this, young lady," he shouted back at her. "I didn't ask to be here, like this. If having a drink now and then helps me fill the time until this...whatever it is – is over, that's my choice, not yours."

Maybe it was fear of his unpredictable anger, or maybe an expression of just how much Aubrey cared for her old friend, even submerged beneath this new façade. Whatever the reason, she found she could not deny Kim the one thing she seemed to really want, so from then on there had been regular trips to Discount Liquors to keep them in scotch, though Aubrey had at least held the line in one sense; Rodney would have to live with the cheap stuff. There was no way in hell she could afford the expensive single malts to which 'he' claimed to be accustomed.

'How embarrassing,' Elaine scolds herself. 'To fall into a daydream, after all that effort spent getting here.'

If there is something to be found in this place, it has escaped her. Perhaps all those years of modern-living, of comfort and predictability, have left her incapable of seeing it. Perhaps she herself lacks some innate quality necessary to...perhaps, perhaps, perhaps.

With great weariness, Elaine unfolds legs which cry out in protest, and rises, back bent and aching. Making a modest bow as she has seen the others do, she sets off, skirting the empty center to make for that portal she has seen them use to exit. 'Nothing,' she thinks to herself as she passes through a series of dusty ante-chambers which eventually disgorge her upon a lower terrace of the complex, eyes cringing at the light of a day at once familiar and as foreign as ever. 'Nothing there at all.'

Later, sitting beneath an awning on the temple promenade, the two women sip dudh chia – milk-tea - purchased in finger-searing brass cups from a mantis-thin vendor who squats, elbows on knees and chin perched on one palm, in the shade of a pear tree, tending a small charcoal brazier.

"I don't know what I felt," Elaine offers, speaking around her true feelings, unwilling to admit she found so little when she was supposed to be experiencing something monumental. "It was...impressive."

Embarrassed, knowing herself undone, she stops, only to find Beryl's eyes gazing at her with great tenderness.

"How is the tea?" she asks.

"Hot," Elaine replies, grateful for the foothold in a firmer reality. She sips, the cup held loosely between extended fingertips. A young woman walks by, child wound into the folds of a golden sash draped intricately over, under and around the woman's arms and neck and body. Despite the child's weight, Elaine notes, the woman moves with quiet grace, as natural and inevitable as the swaying of trees in wind, or the rippling of water over a shallow gravel bed. After they have both watched the young woman disappear around a corner, Beryl begins to speak again.

"In the temple you listened to what was outside you. Next

time you have such an opportunity, you must listen to what is inside you. That is the way in which one reflects the center source in one's consciousness."

A few sips later Elaine asks if there is a way to study this... her words stumble for the correct noun; religion carries too much baggage, philosophy seems dry and impotent – this *idea* then, of the Centersource. Are there teachers, a school to go to, or books to read to understand it better?

"Writing," Beryl responds, "would kill this thing. The truest knowledge is living knowledge; putting it down in words on paper only limits it, in the same way that writing the story of one's life limits it. The words we put down are soon taken as the entire story, when actually, they are only a tiny fraction of what went on: what we saw, heard, felt, imagined. At any moment in your life, you could choose to spend the rest of your life writing the story of what has gone on before, and you'd never get it all, and in the process, you'd miss the rest of what might have happened. Live, linger, listen. That is the only way to learn the lessons which are truly worth learning."

"I'm hungry," Kim's voice calls out from the sofa, as if that news must be of great importance to the rest of the world. "Is there anything to eat?"

As if she cannot just walk into the kitchen and open the refrigerator door to see for herself, Mark thinks, but does not say. No, apparently that's everyone else's job - even now that she can get perfectly well from room to room, can stand upright without the walker and can even carry small objects. None of those things is a problem for her anymore, so long as the object at hand is a glass, or a bottle, or a dish of food that *someone else* has prepared. Oh, no, self-service is fine there, any hour of the day or night, but ask her to make her own meal, or even to clean up her own dishes, and it is as if you are asking the fucking President of the United States to fight his own war.

It is Mark's turn to deal with her this particular afternoon, with Aubrey at the restaurant, Desmond off at the new gig he's just landed in some chiropractor's office, and no temp from Hilltop on Thursdays. He's set up his laptop to work at the kitchen table while Rod sits around complaining about the books Aubs brought him from the library. 'Not current,' he said, of the last medical textbook, whose shiny cover and cracking spine seemed brand new to Des. 'Speculative dead-ends,' he accused of another, tossing it on the floor after scanning only a quarter of the way through it.

Saving his file, Mark minimizes his own work and opens an internet connection. In a few seconds he has located the medical library at the U and called up their catalog.

"Here," he says to Rod, who is now standing at the window and staring out. "Find what you want and one of us can pick it up the next time we're on campus. You can use my ID to reserve it."

Mark makes up a sandwich from the cold cuts in the fridge – roast beef and provolone, per Rod's shopping directions - and one for himself too. In the time it takes to do that he twice has to come over and help the girl navigate the website as she insists on pretending she's never used the net before. Finally the two sit down to eat.

"When can you get my books?" Rod asks, Kim's mouth full of food. For a character who's supposed to have been so particular about his appearance, Mark thinks, it's an odd choice to make his table manners so gross. He makes a mental note to address that in his character description. Of course the answer to the question - that he will be over there on Saturday morning - isn't good enough. It has to be today. Rod is wasting time, falling behind current practices. Can't they go today?

Mark explains his own schedule. A paying job at REI, a new film he promised to see with some friends, even the pile of dirty laundry back at his own apartment, but Rod is persistent. Finally they reach a compromise. If Rod promises not to tell the others, Mark will lend him his transit pass and Student ID, and the library's self-checkout kiosks will avoid any question about why the photo doesn't match the user. On top of that, he will start asking around to see how she can get her own fake ID, to use the library whenever she wants.

Half an hour later Rod is on the #23 bus, Christina McKloskey's face exhibiting a new level of energy as her eyes watch the Wallingford world go by.

A watery moon peeks out from behind the Seacliff Condominiums as Jake's black coupe rounds the corner and heads for the garage ramp. Gliding to a stop at the card reader he presses the window button then reaches into the console for his card key as tinted glass slides silently down. Reaching out into the cool night, he slices the card through a slot in the metal stanchion and unconsciously revs the engine in anticipation of the gate's motion. Tonight though, unlike every time he has approached this gate in the four years he has lived at Seacliff, it does not move. Instead, a small red light next to the card slot begins blinking and, a few inches higher up, green letters scroll across a small window in the steel card-reader.

"ACCESS DENIED," read the words, not once, which would have been irritating enough at a quarter past one in the morning, but over and over again, repeating a message which, Jake has to admit even as he pretends amazement for the benefit of the blonde who has pulled up behind him and will now have to back her car into the street to let his car out, he knew damn well was going to come up any day.

Tomorrow, Jake thinks to himself as he searches the nearby blocks for an open stretch of curb, first thing in the morning, he will talk to that little shit of a superintendent, and explain that he will have his condo fee paid any day now. Just as soon as Digibank starts moving in the right direction; just as soon.

"Tell me whatever you know," Rod asks, one early morning when Mary has chosen to use her day off for a visit to find out how the person she sometimes still thinks of as 'Jane Doe' is progressing.

"What I *know* or what I *think*?"

"Whatever will make some sense out of...all this."

"That might be too much to hope for. I mean, I've been doing some poking around, but it doesn't make much sense." The girl listens intently as Mary recounts what she has learned in several weeks of casual questioning: that Rod Gimbal was in surgery, performing a quadruple bypass involving a complex aortal shunt due to accumulated tissue damage and an individual complication by way of thin-wall flexure. In the middle of the surgery, he had a coronary himself, not that surprising as it was well-known that he had a history of heart trouble. What was not widely known until later was that Dr. Gimbal had been self-medicating in order to be able to keep working despite the fact that he had multiple malignancies in his liver and colon – conditions sure to prove fatal in the near future. A number of powerful pain killers and stimulants were rumored to have been found in his blood stream.

"I would never perform surgery if I was not one hundred percent up to it," Rod huffs. "The only medication I administered for myself - would do, I mean, if I had done anything like that – would be properly prescribed and dosed medication to moderate symptoms so my own physician wouldn't get himself all twisted around and question my abilities."

Looking into those suddenly-fierce eyes, Mary is definitely impressed by the girl's performance, the stone-face practically daring her to go on, which, after a long moment, she does.

When Dr. Gimbal collapsed, she explains, Dr. Jorgendern stepped in but somehow in the process the patient's left ventricle was punctured, and the team had to scramble to deal with that. By the time another team got on the scene, it was too late for Dr. Gimbal. The new Attending attempted resuscitation, even put him on a respirator, but the EKG showed no activity so eventually he was pronounced, and his chart coded for organ removal. This was happening on the very same day MH was taking over, so there was a certain amount of confusion all over Hilltop – distraction, as Mary ruefully remembers her own use of the term in relation to this girl.

"That was late on the day before the morning you were

brought in as a Jane Doe. I was called down to the ER from Pediatrics, when they still thought you were a 'peed,' and I... I just had a kind of emotional reaction. To the way you looked, and how tragic it was, that you would never recover. Then, later, I heard how your condition had stabilized, and even if you weren't exactly dancing and singing, just the fact that you were still vital was pretty miraculous, so I came up to the Dr. Lembec's Plegia unit, which is where you were. That didn't make much sense, until they said you'd had a cranial expansion to mitigate for extreme swelling of the brain - on top of a kidney transplant. A few weeks later, I heard that you were transporting out – I knew your name by then, Christina McKloskey – and I came down to see you one last time. Only, it wasn't one last time, was it?"

The afternoon following their visit to the Temple of Reflection, Elaine finds herself at the top of a switchback, staring down into a narrows where the sluicing brown waters of the Kali Gandhaki, frustrated by a collection of enormous boulders, have worked themselves up into a mosaic of frothing white waves which fold and spread and oscillate, perpetually reborn. The sting of the previous day is still strong upon her, and here she sees an opportunity to diffuse it.

"Which is more enduring?" she calls out-loud, knowing Beryl to be close by her shoulder as she picks up this topic from one of their earlier conversations. "The earth seems solid, permanent. You can hold a rock in your hand. See it. Feel its weight. But water is elusive. It has no shape of its own, running over things, being absorbed. It changes state from vapor to liquid to solid ice so easily, so naturally, we take it as ordinary weather. It doesn't seem permanent, it flows, evaporates, rains down again, and along the way it picks up some of everything it encounters, uses what it has acquired to change the world. You can barely hold water in your hands - it leaks right out - but run it over solid granite, and you have all this."

"And yet," Beryl adds, sounding quietly pleased, "whichever of its forms it inhabits - water, ice, vapor – it's still H-two-O. Wherever it goes, whatever it looks like, whatever baggage it acquires..." The two women's eyes meet and both chuckle at the thought of what baggage *they* have 'acquired' over the decades. "It is still itself."

For some time they stand, shoulder to shoulder, peering into the void and listening to the distant roar of water reshaping earth, content to share the answer to Beryl's question without speaking it, but there is another thought on Elaine's mind as well, one which does need to be spoken in order to be shared.

"I wanted you to know," she explains, very softly. "I do understand. Some things at least. I know you were disappointed with me... back at the temple."

"Disappointed?"

"Because I didn't see. Didn't discover whatever I was supposed to discover there."

Silence. Turning her head slightly, Elaine seeks out Beryl's expression, finds it to be one of amusement, sympathy, pride. Maternal almost. So little does that word suit her friend's life, and yet so well her attitude at this moment, that the thought produces its own quantum pulse of amusement and awareness in Elaine.

"Oh, my goodness," she bursts out. "I just realized. It wasn't you who was disappointed at all, was it?"

Perched on one of the hard wooden dining chairs, the heel of her left oxford lodged precariously on the edge of the seat, Kim's body seems folded into a knot of arms and legs. Small fingers grab at skinny black laces as she attempts once again to tie them. Pinkly-crescent nails, clipped to their quick, flicker over a field of eyelets, around plastic tips; searching, slipping, grabbing again. The battle has been going on for several minutes and Aubrey, slouched against the counter with both hands cradling a cup of instant coffee, has already been told in no uncertain terms that her assistance is not required, desired, or welcome, though her money is.

"What for?" Aubrey asks, desperate to get her friend talking, to make any real contact with the thoughts behind that concentration.

"I'm going to make myself useful," Kim says, enunciating each word very precisely, the way one might speak when explaining relativity to a four-year old while disarming a nuclear weapon. "The bathroom light burned out. I'm going to get a new one to replace it." Her right foot rests on the floor, its shoe tied awkwardly, one lace hanging long enough that it has become caught beneath the sole already, before she has even taken a step.

"I remember..." Aubrey suggests gently, as she watches the thumbs collide and the fingers lose their grip on a loop of lace which refuses to be wrapped around another. "In freshman studio. We had to draw stuff from life." Kim ignores the comment, now working just as intently to untangle the rat's nest she has created in preparation for another attempt. "Simple stuff, like a spoon, or a piece of fruit. A brick even. The thing is, sister - you sucked. You were so bad it was, like, embarrassing. I mean, you'd draw an apple and it'd come out looking like something from outer space. The teacher – I don't remember what his name was - that skaggy grad student who was always looking down all the girls' shirts? He'd stand there telling you different ways to hold the charcoal, turning the paper to match the angle of your head. The only reason he kept trying so much was he had a fucking hard-on for you, but finally even he had to admit you were, like, the worst drawer – is that a word even? Draftsman, I guess... Whatever you call it; you were the worst he had ever seen. He's the one who suggested you start working on performance pieces, 'cause that way you could explore your ideas without people making fun of your drawing."

Shoelace finally tied, Kim has now stood up from the chair, brushing hands across thighs to smooth the pleated front of her slacks. In the practiced gesture of a dandy she reaches up to the tie around her neck and snugs its knot a little bit tighter, then runs a flattened palm across the slicked-down top of her head.

"That," she says firmly, "was not me. I have always had excellent physical skills." She stops, a look of great dismay come over her face, like one who has just been reminded of a death in the family, or a judgment passed down against her. For a moment it appears she is about to say more but then, with a slight snort directed not toward Aubrey, but toward the ceiling, she turns and removes her suit coat from where it has been draped across the back of another chair. With only modest difficulty she places an arm in its sleeve, then reaches behind herself to insert the other; the copious dimensions make donning the jacket an easy exercise, just as they make the end appearance comical. 'A kid in her father's clothes,' Aubrey thought when Chris first tried it on in the thrift shop. Aubrey hadn't laughed though, hadn't said anything about how butch it all looked, so obvious was her friend's pleasure at being dressed at last in the style in which she claimed she had always dressed herself. Perhaps it is that absurdity of appearance, the childishness of it that leads Aubrey to conclude that this is it. Time to settle this thing for once and for all.

"Look," she says, "I can understand wanting to get away from your mother. She's a bitch sometimes, most mothers are. So, fucking A; you left home and changed your name to Kim and..."

"No," the smaller girl insists. "That's not what happened. That's not me. That's someone else's story and you're the ones who've got it wrong. Somehow...somehow, I look like this, but inside I am who I have always been, Rodney Gimbal. I am an adult male, older than I care to admit, an accomplished physician and..."

"But you're not. I mean, look at you..."

"Listen, young lady. I do not pretend to understand how I came to be here, looking like this, but I do know that when I dream, I dream the dreams of Rodney Gimbal. When I think, I think the thoughts of Rodney Gimbal, and I have memories - a head full of memories - of a time when my life was entirely different than this life. When everything was as it should be and I didn't look...like...." She stops speaking for a moment, surprised at something, some possibility her own words have raised inside her. Focusing again on Aubrey's face her eyes are threatening, accusing, as a finger rises to drive her point home.

"How do *you* know *you're* you?" she asks, and Aubrey realizes the battle is lost. Any answer she gives will be inadequate, drowned beneath some god-damned 'logic.' Just like old Mrs. what's-itz in junior year Social History class, she'll have some complicated philosophical explanation that proves Aubrey is just assuming herself out of thin air, when the truth is very simple. She is Aubrey because she has always been Aubrey and when she looks in the mirror she sees herself and knows herself, which is exactly what Kim would do if she were not so wrapped up in this stupid masquerade of which Aubrey has had just about enough.

"OK, fuck it," she responds, reaching out to grab that flailing finger tightly in her fist. "Be whoever you want to be. Rod or Rob, or Albert fucking Einstein for all I care. Cut your fucking hair and wear your stupid clothes and I'll use whatever name you want, OK, but just don't go getting all stuck up about how you know everything and everything I say is wrong." Struggling, Kim wrests the finger free, and holds it up once more, as if about to state a point, then thinks better of it, shakes her head in pity and turns. In three stuttering steps she is at the door and fumbling with the knob. "You're no better than me," Aubrey accuses the retreating back, her own voice rising in pitch and volume, becoming thin and screechy; a sound she hated when it issued from her mother's mouth and yet here it is, flowing from her own. "I took care of you when you couldn't wipe your own ass. You need me, Kim," she shouts, though by this time there is no one left to shout at, only the silent door, completing the wall between them as her friend walks away, visible through the window for just one moment - a shadow of gray among the raindrops - before passing out of view.

"You need me," Aubrey says softly, anger congealing rapidly into loneliness. Sipping halfheartedly at lukewarm coffee, she looks around herself. An hour till she leaves for work, four days till her break, and who knows how long till Kim decides to drop this stupid game. So much for having her old friend back. For making herself useful so Kim would understand how much Aubrey cared for her, that she was the best friend a girl could ever have; better than Kristl, Matt, Sonny, or Desmond, and definitely way better than that dumb stud Jake. Such a good idea it seemed, when she was stuck there all pimped out in her mother's guest house. Escape her from the demon lady and bring her here so the two of them could live together, just the way it should be. Such a good idea, goddamn it, if only it hadn't turned out this way, if only...

"Fuck," Aubrey mutters, dashing the last of her coffee into the sink. "Fuck me."

Late that evening, Aubrey is bone weary as she returns from her shift; she has her key in the door before the sound registers. Music. Coming from inside her house. Not her own music though, not the steady beat of NarciSus, or Jennyboy's wailing delivery, nor the therapeutic waves of electronica rising and falling like a sleeper's respiration. This is sappy and melodic, one of those slow motion voices you get stuck listening to while you're waiting for some appointment you didn't want to make in the first place. 'Grandma music,' she and Kim would have called it, back in the day.

Opening the door she finds the living room bathed in light. Instead of slouching by the glow of the TV set, her roommate is sitting casually on the floor, back resting against the sofa, half a dozen CD jewel cases fanned out around her.

"Hey. Rod," Aubrey offers, trying the name on, and finding it fits better than expected.

The figure looks up from the liner notes she has been reading, a slightly embarrassed smile crossing Kim's face as she grabs the remote and punches a button, silencing the crooner in mid verse.

"You're early," she points out, with less accusation than Aubrey has come to expect. A dinner plate sits on the counter, crusted with remnants of something unrecognizable, the suit jacket hangs over one spindle of his usual dining chair, a plastic bag with the Wal Mart logo lies nearby. That's unusual enough, for one who is ordinarily so particular about her things, but on top of the mess there is something else different about the place, an unaccustomed impression that Aubrey needs a moment to decipher. It comes to her only after she looks again at Rod's face, where it is impossible to miss. It is cheerfulness. For the first time in a long time, her old best-girl-friend appears to be enjoying herself.

"The crowd thinned out," Aubrey says, removing her own coat and pointedly throwing it on the floor. If Mr. Clean is going to let down 'his' hair, she will damn well do the same. "I only had two tables and one looked like they were going to be there forever so I asked Jude if she would cover them for me. I'm bushed." In two steps she crosses the small room and slumps to the floor next to Rod, picking up a jewel box as idly as possible, though she makes a point to scan the title before tossing it back on the pile with a gesture of total unconcern. "Sammy Kaye? Who the hell is Sammy Kaye?"

Without a word Rod picks up the remote again, punches a button, and Aubrey hears the CD player cycling through to a new disk. In a few seconds a swell of strings rises from the speakers and after the first bars a voice joins them, singing *"Don't warm your hands, in this cold heart, Cause this cold heart, won't play that part, the choice is yours, to hesitate... he threw his line, and you took the bait..."* Rod beams, as if this answers the question of who Sammy Kaye is in the most exquisite fashion, but Aubrey only shrugs.

"Sammy Kaye," Rod implores emphatically. "Careless Hands?" Aubrey shrugs. "Four Winds and the Seven Seas? Lavender Dilly? I can't believe you don't know him. He had a whole string of hits when I was....well..." Rod's face begins to droop, back to the hangdog look Aubrey has been seeing for so long. "In '49, I think. He was right there at the top. "

Despite her frustrations, Aubrey feels sorry for this person. Hears the longing in her voice for something apparently lost and irretrievable. As the music plays on, she picks up another case, and another, eying the ancient clothes, the dated hairstyles and archaic graphics of a world she has never known.

"Where did you get these," she asks, "you win the lottery or something?"

Smiling once again, Rod rises to her feet and heads for the jacket hanging on its chair. "They're free," she says proudly, fishing for the inside breast pocket and pulling out a small white card. "I am now the proud holder of a card at the Seattle Public Library, in the name of one Rhonda Fishbeck. Get you a Pepsi?"

Aubrey nods and takes the card as Rod heads for the refrigerator. Sure enough, it is a public library card, grimy round the edges, its surface dimpled and pocked as if embossed by a printer with an acne fetish.

"I found it in the street," Rod says, popping open a soda can and handing it over, as her other hand stretches out to take back the card. "I was walking over to Ole's to get some light bulbs - the one in the bathroom burned out - oh, I already told you that, didn't I? - and I saw a piece of paper lying on the ground. I picked it up to throw it away, but then I saw what it was... Would probably have thrown it in a trash can anyway, except I knew a girl named Fishbeck back when I was in junior high school. Her name was Judy though, not Rhonda. Still, it was kind of an interesting coincidence. Made me wonder how you would get to a library from this neighborhood and just about then there was a bus coming up to the stop down the corner, so I got on and asked the driver; and when I got there I didn't find anything worthwhile in the periodicals but they were right next to the music collection, and something caught my eye. They've got some great stuff, you know. Sinatra and Cole, of course, but not just them, the *real* hits, too; the ones I remember hearing when... well, I found this one," she picks up a disk emblazoned with the name 'Art Mooney' in flowing script, flashing it with all the pride of a gangsta' showing off a roll of hundreds. "And this - Johnny Ace. I remember when he died." Rod pauses, as if considering something important. "I had a hard time keeping it to six. That's as many as you can take at one time. But you get to keep them for a week."

Aubrey listens as the music swells, strings sawing away, the voice outlining all the trouble 'Careless hands' can make. A little later she goes to use the bathroom, only to find the ceiling light has been taken apart, the lens lying in the sink, the lamp socket still empty. Bathed in the music of her supposed youth, Rod seems cheerfully oblivious to the unfinished business, and Aubrey decides it is not worth asking if she ever got the light bulbs for which she had gone out. If she can shower in the dark, well, Aubrey can pee in it too.

"This gets you off?" she calls out afterwards, drying her hands with the door open. "This is the stuff that gets your juice going?"

Rod looks puzzled as she enters the room, and Aubrey imagines Kim reviewing her character. Kim would have understood, and Christina too, judging from how she ran away from her old mother, but this Rod character? Sixty-five year old heart surgeons probably don't talk about 'getting off' on stuff, or what 'gets their juice going.' They're too busy proving how much better they are than anybody else, with their journals and their suits and their degrees and certificates and shit.

"Yes," Rod replies, the puzzlement on Kim's face replaced by something like surprise, which itself surprises Aubrey. "Yes, I guess that's right. Hearing these old songs, remembering how it felt to listen to them when they were new; it makes *me* feel new again. Like there are...possibilities. Instead of just being..." Even as she speaks, Aubrey can see the emotions taking over; her features dissolving from hope to sadness, regret and then despair as her eyes cast down at the smooth hands rising in front of her face, at the body she claims is not hers. "Here...Like *this*. With no idea how I got this way, or how

I can ever...get back...to being...me."

In a moment, Aubrey is across the floor. Kneeling, she takes her friend in her arms and hugs her as close as she can, feeling the sobs as if they were her own.

"Jesus, Kim. No, damn it - I'm sorry - Rod. You..." She looks him in the eyes, this strange and awkward person who mixes a little of her old Kim and some of Mrs. M's fantasies with a whole world of other stuff, and she searches in those dark eyes for anything that recognizes her and the history they share. She does not find that recognition, but something else instead. A willingness - momentary perhaps, but no less real for that - to be held and comforted. In that moment Aubrey flashes on what it must mean to be a stranger to one's self, and what it could mean to have that self accepted by another. She feels that deep inside her, and knows it is a gift she can give.

"Look," she begins again, holding her friend's face in both hands, their eyes just inches apart. "You get to be whoever you need to be, OK? If you need to be Rod, that's who you'll be. You're still my best bud."

"Look," Mary begins, unsure how what she has to say will affect the girl, who is, after all, still recovering from a great trauma. "Not that I believe any of what you are saying or anything. But I've done some checking, just to... Just to put some things to rest, OK?"

The girl nods her acceptance of that conditionality; even seems appreciative - for once - of the effort Mary has put in by seeking out information and by giving up part of another precious day off. The fact that 'Rod' has come all this way, from the house in Wallingford to this worn-out but still bustling Taco Bell a block and a half from Hilltop, is another indication of the changes going on inside her. 'Just had to get out of that place,' she'd said during their phone call, when she asked Mary to suggest a meeting place. 'I can't stand the shabbiness, the dust and grit of it.'

"Okay," Mary begins again. "So I asked around the hospital till I found someone who was sort of friendly with Dr. Gimbal. Believe me, it wasn't easy." Most everyone Mary had talked to was surprised when she said she was looking for his closest friend, because apparently, he was not the kind of guy who had friends. In fact, she had gotten the clear sense that lots of people felt like, well, like he got what was coming to him, dropping dead in the middle of a procedure. The general opinion seemed to be that he was an arrogant son of a bitch who pushed himself and everyone else past their limits, and treated his patients primarily as a means to prove how good Doctor Rodney Gimbal was.

Once more the girl nods, though this time her eyes seem far-away. Mary can see a small muscle twitching on one side of her neck and wonders if it is a sign of emotion, or just another of the many ticks which seem to come and go as her body works to accommodate itself to whatever damage remains from her illness, the lingering effects of the heavy meds she was on at Mrs. M's., and the capabilities she's regaining at a surprising rate.

"So anyway, I did eventually talk to a Dr. Ahearn, an internist who had known Gimbal for years, sort of socially. He suggested I talk to their lawyer..."

"Whit Thiessen," the girl interjects, much to Mary's surprise.

"Yes. How did you know that?"

In lieu of response the girl simply stares back, as if the answer were too obvious to speak. "Just go ahead," she says after a while. "Tell me what you found out."

Mary continues, explaining how she contacted Whitney Thiessen and what he told her - that Elaine Gimbal had been out of the country when her husband passed away. After Thiessen had tried and failed to reach her, he had handled much of the paperwork necessary upon Rod's death, including arranging for cremation per the terms of the man's will. Several months later, when Elaine contacted him from overseas after learning the news from Doug Taylor, Whit had been given power of attorney to put the house on the market for her and to handle whatever affairs her bookkeeper and accountant couldn't.

It is here that she notices the girl's eyes filling with tears, which comes as something of a shock, given the stolid manner Christina normally affects as Rod - the commanding and judgmental way she treats Aubrey, Des and the others. Now, for once there is a trace of vulnerability, a bit of what one might expect in a young woman recovering from a long illness.

"So that's it," the girl says softly, barely avoiding a sob. "My home is gone, my wife and friends have written me off for dead. Well, at least I have my skills, my knowledge. At least I can practice medicine."

"There's more," Mary says, feeling absurdly sorry that she has to drop this other shoe – as if it actually had anything to do with the girl in front of her – and so all the more committed to telling what she knows. "When you...when Dr. Gimbal had his coronary and died, there was a PM, of course. To determine the circumstances, particularly since it occurred in the middle of a procedure. Toxicology revealed tramadol and buprenorphine in his system. The hospital's investigation turned up evidence that he had been taking drugs from the pharmacy under false scrips and possibly even performing surgery while under the influence of narcotics. If Dr. Gimbal hadn't died, and those things had come to light, he would certainly have been brought up before the medical board and lost his privileges and certifications. His career would have been over and he would probably have faced criminal charges."

"So, even if I could somehow convince you all to believe I am who I am, I have no life to go back to. Is that what you are saying?"

"What I'm saying Christina, is that Rod Gimbal was not a very likeable person. By the time he died, he had burned his bridges pretty well. If I wanted to inhabit someone's life, he's about the last person I'd choose. You, on the other hand... The first time I saw you, you were in Trauma unit, everybody frantically trying to get you stabilized, but even then - and even later, after they'd practically disassembled your skull to relieve the pressure on your brain, and your head was all wrapped in bandages and tubes coming out of everywhere, there was something.... I don't know what it was about that girl I saw there, but I've heard it from the people who knew her before – Jake, Aubrey, Mrs. M.   They all say the same thing: that young woman was...is...special. Full of life. If I were you, I'd be working to rebuild my life as Christina McKloskey, not trying to make myself over into some old dead guy nobody liked even when he was alive."

Elaine and Beryl are walking.

By evening, the plan goes, their journey to the temple-of-whichever-name-it-seems-to-be-wearing-today will be over. Back at a comfortable Pokhara hotel they will order their Dal Bhat from a menu, bathe in abundant hot water, sleep in soft beds beneath crisp cotton sheets while electric fans spin silently overhead. For now though, they are still walking. Winding up cruelly steep switchbacks to a ridge, then picking their way down an even more precipitous slope into a wet and muddy gully and struggling up the opposite side, only to find before them one more ridge, one more gully. As the day draws on, Elaine feels herself stooping lower and lower under the weight of even her modest daypack. Leaning forward into an uphill slope, her field of view narrows, from wide and distant vistas to just the nearby slopes, from the nearby slopes to just the path which is visible ahead, from the entire path to only the next few yards, the next few feet, the very next step. To that convenient rock by the side of the trail - the perfect rock on which to sit for just a moment, to catch her breath and say to her indefatigable companion the words she has wanted to say for the past hour, at least.

"I can't go on any more, Beryl. I'm exhausted."

With a patience at once soothing and infuriating, Beryl stops beside her. Taking in a deep breath, she speaks with the same energy and good cheer she had when they set out early this morning.

"I've warned you dear. Be careful of words. We use them to describe a thought, and from that moment, the thought takes on the shape of the word. If a task is difficult, that is one thing; but once you say 'I can't,' your mind has made the difficult impossible. Yes, your body is tired, but if you say you are exhausted, then your conscious mind closes off the possibility of going on."

Elaine leans upon the slender Sal-tree branch she carries as a walking stick. Looking about her rock she sees a verdant landscape, with emerald terraces stepping endlessly down toward a valley floor, narrow streams inhabiting the deep recesses of twisting canyons, their rock ledges lipped and undercut into fantastical shapes that seem about to come to life. Where the terraces intersect and overlap, tangled brush crowds the trunks of trees whose limbs stretch as if pointing out the distant Annapurna Range, its frozen peaks shrouded in cloud, though here all is sunshine and warmth. It *is* beautiful, she thinks, if only it did not go on forever. Just as Beryl sometimes seems to do; going on forever with her philosophy, if you can call it that. The current favorite topic, it seems, is words and how, once one has been successful in moving beyond an existence defined by objects, one must then seek to move beyond words. Must learn to entertain ideas themselves, without the words that describe them. Must experience the being tired, for example, without putting a name to that experience.

"Exactly," Beryl says, and her satisfied grin makes Elaine wonder if she has simply spoken aloud without meaning to, or whether indeed, her very thoughts have been read. "Words are slippery things. But then, ideas are slippery, too. You have an idea in your mind and, if you are not careful, if you have not trained your mind correctly, that idea crowds out others which might be – which *are* – just as true. I said a dragon was alive, and you pictured an animal moving around on all fours. That obvious meaning crowded out any other possibilities. But if you can keep your mind open to meanings beyond the obvious, you will find that everything exists somewhere and anything is possible, as is its opposite; and when you reach that place where your mind embraces *both* a thing *and* its opposite, simultaneously and equally, without prejudice between them, you will be ready to understand yourself. Comprenez?"

Elaine's thoughts turn back to her initial encounter with Beryl. LAX is so very far away. A different world, entirely, from this land of endless paths and numberless small valleys. Except that, just as she imagines that contrast, she is reminded of how endless the delay had seemed while her plane was circling over San Francisco, or later, as she waited in the airport, as their plane the next day had taxied around to find its runway, a peregrination in some way not so very different from this endless wandering with Beryl in search of … of what, she does not really know. So long ago, so far away, and yet the weeks since landing in Shanghai are actually a very short time, compared to how long she has been alive, or Beryl, or the cave dragon.

"Yes," she hears herself answer, and feels a smile rising out of the understanding. Looked at with one side of her eyes this place is completely different from the world she has known, yet in another view, they are one. This time is apart from the years she has lived before, yet they all exist together, mixed in her memory, and the memories carry the places, embedded within them, in her behaviors, and her dreams of what might come. "I do believe that."

"Which calls for even greater care," Beryl responds solemnly. "*Belief* is more slippery than either words or ideas. 'Belief' is the most difficult thing in the world to pin down, because when you believe in something, what is it you are believing? The words? The ideas those words attempt to express? The past events that led you or someone else to formulate the ideas and the words? Or are you believing in the world and the life and the 'you' which will result from choosing that belief?"

For a moment, Elaine 'believes' the lesson is over, her friend's pronouncement completed; but then the voice resumes, in a tone as deeply thoughtful - as solemn even - as at any time in their long, brief, acquaintance.

"Belief, my dear, creates the world in which you live. One cannot change one's beliefs and go on living the life one did before - heavens, no! If you truly change what you believe, you must be ready to become a new person. To let the old 'you' die and a new one take her place -and are you ready to do that? Are you ready to become someone new, perhaps a person you would not recognize – don't answer that, by the way, it's rhetorical. I have an easier question: are you ready...to walk a little farther?"

"Yes," Elaine answers, feeling oddly refreshed. Standing tall to stretch her aching back, she sees that her resting rock marks a crest, which had escaped the pinpoint focus of her fatigue. Beyond it, the trail winds gracefully downward, through country more gentle than any they have seen in days. "I am ready."

It is unclear whether Beryl even hears the response, however, for she has already started off, down the trail.

"Are you Mary?" asks a voice, hushed despite the mid-day hour and the absence of anyone else within earshot. Mary has been busy recording notes of her morning's rounds and was not aware of anyone else in the room, though she realizes belatedly that not only has she a visitor, but that the sound she disregarded a moment ago was that of the door to the Resident's Recording Room shutting, which it rarely does.

"Yes," she answers cheerily, grateful for the interruption. It has been a long night and even the simple task of reading notes and data into the recorder is draining. Turning, she finds herself face to face with a woman some years younger: dark-haired, caramel skinned, with wary eyes that seem uncertain of their purpose in being here. She wears employee ID on a lanyard around her neck, but the slim-fitting slacks and plush pullover tell Mary she works behind the scenes, away from Hilltop's precious public image of total professionalism. Pulling a chair over from the nearest recording carrel, the woman sits, crosses her legs demurely, and leans close to Mary.

"I heard you were asking about Dr. Gimbal. The day...the day he..."

"Died?" Mary offers, concluding her visitor is a civilian, for sure. One could not get very far in any medical field if one couldn't even speak the name of that affliction. All the people Mary works with are on first name terms with Death.

The woman nods, and Mary realizes that she is scared. Way more scared than she should be, discussing the death of an elderly man months ago, unless... The thought occurs to Mary that the woman may have had some relationship with Gimbal. The old dog had a reputation for young flesh, she's learned, despite his crustiness. The idea disappears however, as she sees the girl hold out a mini-cassette, the same kind Mary herself used to record lecture notes back in school. The small device has been hidden in her balled fist and is now offered, like precious currency, on a hand which trembles visibly.

"It was recorded the same day he died. By a Dr. Resor, but he's not here anymore; I checked. Anyway, I found it in an old recorder - my boss gave me a box full of them that were turned in when IT made the last holdouts exchange them for digital. She told me to find a place to recycle them, but I saw this one had a tape in it and I wanted to make sure it wasn't something important, and when I heard the name, I remembered someone saying you had come around asking about him."

Without waiting for response the girl drops the cassette on the desk beside Mary's files and rises from her seat.

"Wait," Mary calls. "What's your...?"

"You don't know me," the girl says, her hand already on the doorknob. "And if I see you, I don't know who you are. You don't know where that cassette came from, okay? I'm a single mom and I like my job very much and I really need to keep my job. Okay?" Mary nods and, for the first time, a trace of a smile crosses the girl's lips. "The other voice on the tape is Dr. Rosen, Yuri Rosen. I know his voice, from..." the girl smiles more broadly now, indicating amusement with herself, purses her lips and dips her head to indicate she will say no more, and is gone. As the door closes Mary finds herself smiling as well and realizes that some bond has been formed between them, though she herself has given only the slightest nod of assent.

Listening to the tape in the privacy of her own apartment - after digging through three boxes of old textbooks to find her own recorder and a trip to Rite-Aid to get new batteries for it - Mary's first reaction is one of total boredom. Re-wound to the beginning, it seems a perfectly proper recording, starting with the speaker identifying himself, his staff position and specialty. Date of shift as well, time the recording was begun, and then the familiarly-tedious recitation of patients visited, conditions observed, comments noted and actions directed. Each patient a unique individual; each consultation potentially a life-and death drama, and yet, distilled and accumulated like this, all blending into a mind-numbing sameness - exactly like what Mary herself has been recording every day for years. Given that the tape was begun after eleven PM, and how long it has been going on, with various stops and starts indicated by audible clicks, it could well have been near midnight when the longer silence occurred; a period devoid of speech, its only content the oral respiration of a deep, fatigue-induced, slumber. From experience, Mary knows just how it must have come about: Resor sitting at his desk to dictate, or perhaps even lying back on the couch in his office, then drifting into a doze, the notes falling from his outstretched hand, the machine still recording for some minutes before pausing itself, then starting again when Rosen's knock on the door jamb or the desktop caused it to awaken. As did Resor, whose ingrained reflexes would bring him upright and awake in a moment, despite the heaviness of his state.

"Mind if I disturb your slumbers, David?" says a voice which must be Rosen's, and Mary finds herself visualizing the scene as if it were happening before her eyes, rather than issuing forth from tiny earbuds connected to an electronic device.

"Not at all," Resor says, and she pictures him rubbing his eyes into action before looking at his watch. "I've got to check on a patient soon anyway. What can I do for you?"

"Howard and I had an interesting conversation earlier this evening. In the cafeteria men's room."

"I've always had my most interesting conversations with Howard in men's rooms, Yuri. What was this one about?"

"Frankenstein's monster."

There is a slight pause, and Mary imagines David carefully examining his friend's expression, wondering what he means, but when Resor speaks again it seems he has understood something quite clearly.

"How serious was he?"

"I can never tell with Howard. No, that's a cheap shot. I believe he was totally serious."

"And you, Yuri - how serious are you?"

"I'm leaving for Geneva in a few days. I don't want to do anything that would upset that. On the other hand, it's going to happen sometime. I don't believe for a minute that the possibility will not come up again, sometime, someplace. There are too many people making too much progress on too many fronts. Your work, of course. Mine. Howard's - and we all know he's not even the most advanced in his area. The Chinese've made great strides. We've all been doing hearts and lungs for decades, then heart/lungs, now heart/lung/liver; that complete GI tract in Argentina last year; re-attaching hands in France. Faces. There's no question it will come sooner or later. The thing is, it could be delayed for decades if we let the politicians and preachers worry about whether we're playing God or not."

"Hell, we play God every time we put a patient under the knife. Every suture. Every cold-fucking compress at an accident scene. We've been playing God since before Hippocrates."

"You want to say that in front of a congressional inquisition?"

"No," Resor responds immediately, his tone dismissing the

idea as absurd before turning more thoughtful. "What we're talking about would be the biggest news a medical researcher could ever hope to make. Brings words like Nobel struggling to the surface of a man's mind. Struggling to the surface," he repeats quietly. "That's how I imagine him."

"Howard?" Rosen asks.

"No. The subject. In there. I imagine him struggling to make some sense of what's going on. Or rather, of everything that's not going on."

"From what I've seen of Rod Gimbal, I wouldn't want to be around if he ever found out something like this had happened."

"Now that's a picture," Resor says, and the two exchange rather guilty-sounding chuckles.

Those last few lines are lower in volume, difficult to discern amidst what Mary interprets as the rustles of Resor rising and straightening his clothes, then a gentle scraping and clunking as he gathers some personal items from the desk before the clearly audible sound of a door closing, followed by more silence, until the machine shuts itself off once again.

"I do not understand," Rod is saying, as Aubrey places five plastic sacks of groceries on the kitchen counter and stretches out her fingers, cramped from their hanging weight, "how you can live like this."

"Live like what?" Aubrey replies, pulling two boxes of instant mashed potatoes from a sack and shoving them into an upper cupboard. Almost shouting, in order to make herself heard over the music; an unfamiliar voice calling out *'be mine again'* to some lost lover or other. It is another grim, gray day in November, and the Olds is out of commission, parked beside the Blue Moon Garage until Aubrey can come up with the money for a new water pump, which is the reason she has just walked the eight blocks to the grocery store and back, an expedition which has left her hair wet with sweat and her emotions extra-sensitive to the vision which greeted her return; her long-term guest sprawled on the living room floor, surrounded by her music and her drink, making no effort to help with the unpacking.

"This." Standing in the kitchen doorway now, Rod swivels her head around and raises a hand to indicate the entire house. "This place is so…. squalid. Everything you own is old; there are piles of dirty clothes all over the place, and there's dust piling up in the corners of the baseboard."

"Squalid," Aubrey repeats softly to herself as she pulls apples from another sack and places them in a bowl beside three browning bananas and one withered orange. New word, familiar theme. The more Rod's vocal abilities have recovered, the more Aubs has found herself enduring 'his' pointed criticism of not just the food she prepares, but the cleanliness of her floors, her hand-washing technique, how often his pajamas are laundered and even which toiletries to buy. Yes, Kim's got this character down so well, he's now demanding just the right toothpaste – Arm & Hammer, which he claims is the only one to neutralize 'aphoristic acid' or some such shit, which is supposed to contribute to 'something-or-other of the esophagus' which in turn increases the chances of getting some other disease she's never heard of. Well aware that he's nursing a glass of scotch already, though it's only two PM, she chooses not to reply as she gathers cans of soup and stacks them along the back of the counter.

"Tomato?" asks Kim's voice, though the dismissive way the words come out has nothing of the joy and wonder that timbre once expressed   "You know what I think of…"

"Enough!" Aubrey shouts, sweeping her forearm across the counter to send the rest of the groceries crashing to the floor with a clatter that drowns out the music – but only for a moment; its preeminence quickly reestablished by a bleating pulse of horns. "Jesus, I've had it with you," she continues, moving out into the living room to the stereo where it takes three stabs of a finger to find the power button. "This fucking game you're playing. When are you going to get real?"

The sudden quiet does nothing to quench Aubrey's anger, for though her friend's face projects sadness, on top of that and embedded in her voice is the now-familiar contempt of one who knows so much, is so much older and wiser, that he can sit in judgment of everything Aubrey says or does; of her whole stupid boring life.

"Get real?" Kim's lips pronounce in slow and measured cadence, as if it is a strange new language they are speaking, full of curious, exotic expressions. "Get real about what? Myself? About who I am? Am I to gather then, despite that excellent speech you made and the weeks you've been calling me by my name, you still don't really believe me?"

"This isn't about what I believe or don't believe, Ki…Rod. Jesus, I told you before, I've got no problem with who you want to be, it's just… You sit around all day listening to your goddamned music and drinking like a frigging fish, and then when I come home all you do is bitch at me about what a pit this place is. So why don't you do something about it, okay? Get up off your fucking ass and do something."

"Don't you think I want to do something?" Rod accuses, eyes bulging as the tendons of Kim's slender neck stand out like buttresses beneath her ovaled face. Shoving aside assorted jewel boxes, disks and newspapers, he struggles to gather legs beneath him and rise stiffly from the floor to stand, body stacked off-kilter in awkward balance, hands twitching oddly, as if they don't know where they want to go. "Do I need to remind you that I've been working all my life? I worked harder when I was in school than any of you kids work today. I worked through four years of college and three years of medical school and then I worked even harder through internship and residency and specialty and once I was doing what I'm trained to do, I kept working as hard as any man I ever met."

Maybe it would have worked if Rod had just stopped there.

Maybe the act would have held together. After all, work is something Aubrey understands; it's universal when your father left early and your mother had so many 'troubles' after that she could never hold a job more than a few months. If all Rod wants is work, hell, there's never been any shortage of that in Aubrey's world. Only, instead of stopping there, he has to go on, has to raise the stakes absurdly high and make her feel, in the process, like nothing she does is ever good enough for him – her - for Kim, the girl who always had to have it all.

"I'm a surgeon," he says, like it's the password to something glorious, and in those words Aubrey sees where this is going and sets herself to stop it.

"Well, if you think that any amount of acting and spitting out medical facts is going to get them to let you be a doctor, you're crazy, bitch. Doctors - man, if a doctor fucks up, it's really real. People get hurt. I mean, that's, like, life and death."

"Which is precisely what this is for me," Rod answers, not the least deterred, in fact encouraged. "It's about life and death. *My* life, that *I* have to live. And being as good as dead if I can't. If I have to go around being this...ridiculous little girl that you and everyone else want me to be."

"Oh yeah, I get it. The old 'nobody takes me seriously because of my looks'..."

"You think I care what I look like?" he shoots back, in a fair imitation of sincerity. "I care what I can do, and I can't *do* surgery with these hands." Rod pauses dramatically, holding out his arms; slender, pale and – at least to Aubrey - perfect, except for a slight trembling which could just as well be emotion as the residue of his long recovery. "A surgeon has to have perfect coordination, control, strength, but these...." His voice trails off and Aubrey marvels at the acting she is witnessing, for if she didn't know so much better, she could very well believe her friend is truly in despair. Even her own body believes it, for there comes a tingle up her spine, a melting at her center that wants to hug and comfort this afflicted soul, which only makes her anger rise in opposition as the improbable speech goes on. "There's no way I can ever do the one thing I'm good at. You wouldn't understand this, but... A man's work is everything; it's how he justifies his place in the world. His food, his home, everything...and if I can't... After all I've been through over the years, all I've accomplished, to have to be dependant on some nasty little waitress..."

It takes a large heart to bear a hurt and not strike back. Aubrey, young and insecure, has not that sort of heart, as much as she might wish it. The fact that Rod has been doing nothing himself to improve their quality of life might also have a lot to do with the flood of words which she unleashes. The word 'drunk' crops up in her first attack, along with 'lazy,' followed by 'crazy,' 'stupid' (which she immediately admits to herself is far from true) and that old standby 'fucked-up.' Rod, for his part, exercises a wide vocabulary of terms derogatory to the young, the counter-cultured and those who favor any lifestyle alternative to his own professional establishment. Voices are raised and fingers pointed, feet stamped on the floor and at one point even a sofa pillow tossed across the living room before both realize deep down that there is nothing to be won here, and Rod gathers up his canes to take himself out for a walk, leaving Aubrey to flop into a chair as tears of shame and fatigue sting her eyes. After he is gone though, she finds herself looking at her home with different eyes, though whether newly opened or just more seriously jaundiced, she is not certain.

Nearly an hour later Aubrey is mopping the kitchen floor, the empty fruit bowl soaking in a sink full of suds, when she hears the front door open. There is no greeting as footsteps cross the floor and stop at the kitchen doorway.

"Where you been?" Aubrey asks in the silence which follows. Allowing herself no more than a quick glance at the dripping, slouching figure, she is careful to frame the words gently, with no hint of challenge or reprimand.

"Walking."

The mop squeaks slightly as it moves across linoleum scratched and spotted from years of use. Soapy humidity fills the room, as the two women avoid one another's eyes.

"It's cold out there...and raining again. I got myself...chilled," Rod says softly, the words sounding as near an apology as any Aubrey has ever heard from him. "I... I'm going to take a hot shower."

As she continues cleaning, Aubrey hears the water come on, the splash at first quite harsh as it dashes unobstructed from nozzle to floor, then muffled and varied, its pitch rising and falling as the bather's body diverts the stream higher or lower on the wall. After a short while she hears something else as well; not loud enough to catch words, but unmistakably Kim's voice, toying with a song. A jazzy rhythm, brisk and choppy. What she cannot hear, and cannot know to picture, is the way Rod's hands are moving as the hot water drenches Kim's face and splashes against her shoulders, cascading down her back, buttocks, legs and feet. Forward and back those hands dart, fingers scrunched into tiny fists - a left and then a right, then left again, twice, followed by another quick right; punching an imaginary bag. Eyes closed in a darkened room, transported by movement and melody to another time, another place, another self.

The amazing thing, Elaine is thinking to herself as she takes the envelope from the desk clerk's outstretched hand, is not that the letter has found her, but rather the way she feels about it.

It has been over four months since she left the states; two-and-half since she learned that Rodney had died, and decided she would not go back to deal with the fallout. Nearly half a year of the most incredible adventure she can imagine. Not the cheap adventure of rafting down rapids or racing some souped-up off-road vehicle; she is after all, a mature woman – but adventure of a more internal sort. The adventure of seeing the world made new again by its unfamiliarity. Valleys lush with jungle, rice paddies quilting the very earth into a plush comforter, and mountains which tower so high and go on so far that flat land seems a distant memory. Rivers so wide and slow they beat with the pulse of time itself, and sea shores coved and pointed into unimaginable complexity, facing out toward islands whose forms she would not have believed if an artist had painted them. Cities that seem without end, and only a few days travel away from them, villages so extravagantly isolated they transport one immediately into realms of myth and legend, of ancient times and mythic forces. Ingenious temples and breathtaking artifacts and the even more astounding devotion and faith of the believers they attract. Beryl Nathanson's 'Cooks Tour' of places known and the unknown, the famous, the hidden and the obscure, accompanied all the time by hints and suggestions of the deeper meanings beneath them all. Sights, sounds and ideas she had never known existed but now, having experienced them, cannot imagine having lived her life without experiencing. For something has happened to Elaine on this journey, something unexpected and yet exactly what she was looking for when she planned that little vacation to the Marquesas. She had tried to describe it a few evenings before, sitting here in the lobby of Pokhara's Hotel Barahi, with Beryl and Mr. Ludower, the modest Indiana University professor she met while Beryl was busy disappearing for the day to do some of her 'business.'

"When I stepped into the room," she recalled, referring to the sanctuary at an obscure monastery she and Beryl had visited just before leaving Kathmandu, "the first thing I felt was that I had been there before. There was a rush of familiarity, like putting on your favorite sweater on a cold winter morning. If I looked around me, everything was strange and exotic - the incense, the sound of the chanting, the golden walls and fabrics, the monk..."

"Lama," Mr. Ludower had corrected, but gently, offering her a piece of information, not demanding she get it right, as her husband had done throughout her adult life if ever she made even the slightest factual error.

"Yes. It was all so exotic and foreign, and yet the feeling it gave me was familiarity. And then, when I saw him, his eyes looking at me, it was as if I had seen those eyes before and this whole trip - coming here; to Japan first, and China, Vietnam, Nepal - as if the whole thing had been a prelude to seeing those eyes."

Mr. Ludower smiled gently, an expression which said yes, of course he understood. She could see from his face that he had had a similar experience. Not that day perhaps, not in that place, but somewhere, sometime, he had experienced that same sense of coming back to a place he'd never been before.

"I don't need to explain it, do I?" Elaine remarked, her own smile growing from a place deep within her. A smile not just of the face, but of the entire body, the self, the soul. "You already know."

"Yes," Mr. Ludower had said then, almost too softly for Elaine to hear. "And what is more Elaine, you already know. What really matters, what you came here to learn? You already knew it before you arrived. We all know everything we really need to know, before we even go looking for it."

All we need to know. She settles into a rattan chair, her tote bag jammed behind her, for security - as Beryl has counseled - and for lumbar support - as the miles have taught.

"Ellie," the letter begins, the familiar nickname transporting her immediately from the hotel's lobby to memories of years gone by. Tender memories, some of them, like sitting in Rutler's Delicatessen while the floor was being swept around them, the lights already dimmed for closing, the two youngsters unwilling to let the evening end. More complex memories as well, of the times that followed; of promise and hope as the brutal schedule of Rod's residency gave way to the only slightly-less-inhuman schedule of a practicing surgeon, and, later still, images of how their life together had turned out; those years of steely concentration, Rod's on his patients, papers and profession, Elaine's on her home and garden. Most recent of all, the glossy, stop-motion-snapshots of her own loneliness, calling up the ashen taste of a life grown pointless. All this comes flowing back over her as she reads and rereads those five characters, scribbled in a hand she does not recognize, can barely decipher; as foreign, in their way, as any inscription on any stone she has seen in all her travels.

"I cannot say I understand why you have stayed away so long. Obviously, you must have your reasons. Nor can I begin to tell you all that has happened since you left. Some of it I do not know, much of what I do know, you would not believe..." Even as she reads that far though, Elaine feels herself drawn back to the salutation. 'Ellie,' the letter begins. No 'Dear,' or 'Darling,' or even 'My,' and in its brevity she finds all the message she needs. It is that simplicity which penetrates into Elaine's heart; that all too familiar aura of certainty. The implicit assumption that he can, with no preface, no softening offer of conciliation, command her attention and her life. She must read no further to know how the letter will conclude. Rod needs her, it will say. Right up to the end he needed even more from her than what she had already given. No surprise there.

And no surprise either that the letter has taken this long to reach her, what with the way she and Beryl have been travelling - off the tourist track, changing direction at a whim, staying as far as possible from hotel chains and tour groups. Nor has Elaine made more than the most cursory effort to keep in contact. A monthly check-in call to the bookkeeper, less frequent conversations with her attorney's assistant. The few pieces of mail which she actually does need to see bundled up and forwarded, sometimes taking three or four skips before they reach her. What is curious, though, is the letter's date – only three weeks ago, which puts its origin several months after Rodney's death. A mistake perhaps - her husband was never good at keeping track of anything other than his professional responsibilities, though he could certainly be trusted to know what month it was. Perhaps - and as soon as this thought arises, a mere few sentences into her reading, this seems much more likely than her momentary flash of believing - perhaps this is only a hoax of some sort; somebody using Rodney's name in a twisted prank or even a scam. She's heard of such things it seems, way back in a distant past when a newspaper article or evening news item about the latest effort to defraud the elderly might have been worthy of her attention. Certainly the handwriting bears no resemblance to Rodney's; curious that a forgery would be no more convincing. Curious, too, how out of place its scribbles look among the stack of formal legal and financial correspondence forwarded to her by the attorney's office. It is all mildly curious, in the way one might be curious to hear that a new acquaintance happens to have a distant cousin in another country who has a name similar to one's own, though there's no other reason to suspect she might be a relation.

Looking up from the paper, Elaine sees people moving about her, with clothes and faces which would once have struck her as strange. For all this time she has been among people who speak unfamiliar languages, live unfamiliar lives, inhabit worlds completely alien to the one to which she is being called back, but they are inscrutable no more; she has begun to understand these people, to absorb their way of looking at life and themselves. This is the journey on which she travels; to discover that which she already knows - about herself, about the world. To transform what remains of her life into something different from what went before. It is a journey she has grown to relish, and one she will not abandon easily.

With slow, deliberate motions, her eyes idly roaming the far, dim recesses of the lobby, Elaine folds the letter back along its own creases. Gently, almost affectionately, she runs pinched fingers over the folded edges to perfect their precision, then slides the missive back inside its envelope and rises from her seat. The steps she takes across the hard tiles are steady and even, with no sense of urgency or emotion; simply steps - away from one spot and toward another. The kind of steps she has learned to take at the beginning of a long day's walk - setting a pace which can be sustained for as long as necessary, neither fast nor slow, but simply moving, inexorably toward one's objective. Nearing the door her path veers slightly, bringing her close to one of the hammered brass cylinders which function here as trash container, ash tray and spittoon combined. As she makes the last few strides her hands come together in front of her heart, grasping the letter and slowly tearing it, just once. The crudely-squared sections do not flutter, but fall decisively, layered edges of their torn and folded sheets calling to mind the scalloped pages of an antique book - its uncut-pages never opened, its messages forever silent - as they disappear into the container's open mouth. By the time they have settled among the detritus, Elaine is already gone, out the door and onto the streets of a city she has seen before, but never with these eyes; a city which has no place in her history, and where, therefore, her past will not rise up in ambush of her present.

"Rhonda, I'm home," Aubrey calls, trying to set a lighter mood as she opens the door, two days after her confrontation with Kim. For once the music is silent, though a pile of CDs and cassettes attests to Rod's activities of the day. Tossing her coat on the sofa, she stoops down to paw through the stacks: Rosemary Clooney, Buddy Clark, Louis Prima, Kick Haymes... Some of the names are familiar to her, many she's sure she has never heard before. There are tapes of more recent music too; rock bands she recognizes from Oldies radio, but those are only raw material. Rod has been picking them up at second hand stores for twenty five cents apiece and taping-over the little security notches so he can re-use them, copying his favorite loaners from the library to create his own music collection. Finished cassettes sit in a neat row along the mantle of the apartment's long-defunct fireplace, their labels scrawled in Rod's virtually illegible hand.

She knows how he spent his day; the same way he has spent nearly every day since discovering Rhonda Fishbeck's library card in the gutter. Listening to recordings of fifty-year old hits. Playing them over and over as he picks and chooses which ones to keep, painstakingly calculating which songs will fit on one side of a tape, then, as the machine rolls, copying the titles and times onto sections of notebook paper cut and folded to fit inside the cassette boxes. It reminds her of her brother who, as a teenager, developed a fascination with off-road motorcycle racing. He read magazines devoted to the sport, cut out pictures and built bulging scrapbooks recording the season's victories and losses for men he had never met. Rod has that same intensity about his music, like he believes he is really accomplishing something by making all those cassettes so nearly identical. Stacking them in rigid precision along the shelf. Like her dad too, arranging the tools in his garage onto pegboards screwed to the wall, each tool carefully spaced from the next, with outlines drawn onto the pegboard so there could be no mistake about which one went where. Must be a 'guy' thing, she says to herself, and in the next instant realizes that, yes, she has begun to think of Rod as a guy. Just goes to show what you can get used to, she observes, if you live with it long enough.

Over the last few weeks Aubrey has grown used also to the sound of big bands and small orchestras, of jazz trios backing singers and of belters fronting groups. She has listened as Rod explained who had a big hit when he was ten, who was top of the charts when he reached thirteen, and whose sounds on the radio had fueled late night studying during his college and med school years.

Picking up one of the borrowed cases lying in a pile, she glances over the liner notes. Jimmy Dawson, the words say, had risen to the top of the pack in July of 1956, with his hit, Holding You. Flipping over another she finds a paragraph recounting how the career of Eddie Muncie had slumped as the new sounds of rock and roll began to attract the young audience. One CD is immodestly labeled as a compilation of lost treasures from the last days of the swing era, the next claims to contain 'the most indispensable music' from the post-war years. Pawing through that stack, it is quite suddenly clear how Kim can seem so knowledgeable. All she has to do is read the liner notes and string the narratives together. A little history here, a little nostalgia there, and anyone could become an instant expert on the music of the forties and fifties, of any era for that matter, especially to an audience who knows even less.

"The more I read," Aubrey tells Anne over tea a few days later, "The more it hit me. This has got to be something, like, really big, inside her mind. That she would choose to be this Rod person, all day, every day." Anne nods quietly, her face composed as always into a look of gentle good nature. Hardly the face you'd expect on a mother discussing her daughter's pathological deception, but Aubrey has given up trying to understand that. "It's like, this Rod person has taken over her entire life, her whole fu... her whole brain and everything. She even tried... I don't know if I should be telling you this, Mrs. McKloskey; it's kind of gross."

"Oh, Aubrey," Anne warbles, "I'm Christina's mother. If you're ever lucky enough to be a mother yourself, you'll find out there's nothing left to be embarrassed about after that."

"She tried to pee like a guy," Aubrey confides, putting the thing as politely as she can. When Anne seems not to understand, she elaborates. "I mean, I came home from work and found the floor all wet around the toilet, and when I asked her if it had flooded or something, it was like, there was this weird silence and she acted all, like, pissed-off at me, if you'll excuse the joke. Finally I figured it out, when I found a pair of her pants in the wash smelling like the ladies room at a gas station. She must have dropped her drawers and tried to stand over the toilet to pee like a trucker, only it got all over and she was too embarrassed to say so."

The two women chat for a while more, Aubrey filling Mrs. M. in on the latest news about Christina's behavior in her character of Rod, careful to omit any mention of her rising alcohol consumption. Anne listens attentively, happy to hear any news of her daughter, serenely un-judgmental about the tack their lives have taken. Sooner or later Aubrey senses it is time to go, thanks her for the tea, and rises to leave. Inevitably it is then that Anne reaches into the purse she seems always to keep close at her side and presents Aubrey with a few folded bills.

"Just to tide you over," she had said, the first time Aubrey visited, so sheepish and afraid of being turned away. "To help out with expenses, because I know how hard it must be to get by with an extra person to feed."

It had taken Aubrey quite a while to work up to this, knowing how much Chris hated her mother's attention. She'd be absolutely furious if she ever found out, of course, but it wasn't like they had much choice. Food, clothes, haircuts, and liquor – there was no way Aubrey could keep up with Rod's expenses herself, and since he refused to get any real job, she felt justified getting the money from the one ready source: Christina's mother. (Well, there was also Jake, maybe; but Aubrey had her own reasons for not wanting to give *that* relationship any ground in which to grow.) That first phone call had been a bit awkward, what with her and Mrs. M.'s previous history – the arguments, the rescue, that little court thing - but once she came to the old lady's house, it was almost like they were family. Anne seemed always glad to see her, always gracious and happy, and she dispensed the money like it really did give her pleasure. At first Aubrey had been surprised and grateful, though it certainly wasn't enough cash to make things easy; but by now she had come to expect it - payment, she figured, for putting up with Christina's charade. This day she feels just the slightest guilt at that, wonders if it might not be good to offer something in return, some extra tale to feed the mother's endless curiosity. The two women are standing in the doorway as she speaks, a light drizzle dripping from the porch roof.

"Oh yeah, I meant to tell you something else; she's been singing. Singing these old songs to herself when she thinks I can't hear it."

"Oh, that's wonderful," the woman replies, her face taking

on that same satisfied glow it gets whenever the subject of her daughter's childhood comes up. Like she's gone back to a 'happy place' in her mind. Aubrey finds herself envying that look, so confident and serene. "Christina always had a beautiful voice. Sean wanted her to study, you know, but she wouldn't have it. Oh, they had such a terrible fight, and Christina swore she would never sing another note. It nearly broke her father's heart. I'm glad to hear she's gotten over it."

Yuri Rosen. Harvey Lembec. David Resor. With each name Mary finds herself more frustrated, as her search of Hilltop's website leads her nowhere: 'Page Unavailable,' 'URL Invalid,' 'Site No Longer Maintained,' are just a few of the ways the world of IT has of saying she is SOL – shit-out-of-luck. That the men no longer practice there, she already knows, the staff directory told her that in a few seconds, but this succession of dead ends is something else. They *had* worked there once, and by rights there should be the typical boastful descriptions of positions held, citations for publications under the banner of Hilltop, at the very least some forwarding information for patients or colleagues who need to contact them. Instead? Nothing. Like they had all disappeared into a black hole. Which is exactly where she decides to go - the department affectionately known as the Black Hole, in honor of what happens to any scraps of paper or pages of notes which have the misfortune to be sent there.

The graveyard shift, Mary reasons, would be the best time to approach someone in Information Technology, with its weird mix of young wiz-kids grooving on the technology and ancient clerks marking time till their pensions kick in. It is one of the former that she finds at his basement terminal, well after midnight on a Tuesday in early December.

She'd actually scoped the guy out several evenings before, as he reinstalled a balky utility on the computer in a sixth floor Pharmacy station. Had asked a few questions of a female tech in the cafeteria as well, before deciding for sure to make her approach. Twenty-three or -four as best she could tell, Jason Privet appeared married to his work. Ten-hour shifts six days a week setting up workstations as the hospital constantly remodeled itself, whipping up program add-ons and subroutines to accomplish whatever esoteric cross-referencing some research associate might need, freeing locked-up computers in the middle of the night when Admitting faced a forced shutdown due to operator error. Word was - if Jason couldn't do something in the IT domain, it couldn't be done.

Despite the difference in their ages, or maybe because of it, Mary actually found Privet sort of cute. Only barely taller than her, and skinny - in an out-of-shape but not quite wasted-bird sort of way that made him seem unthreatening. Dark hair manhandled into a faux-bedhead peak, too-long pant legs pooling around his ankles, and shirts which had never caught a glimpse of an iron; his air of studied neglect suggested a comfortable lack of ambition which was actually quite appealing after nine years of high pressure education and apprenticeship. Standing in front of her own closet, Mary had spent a few minutes guessing what might make a good impression on him, before pulling from its far reaches a pair of dark green cargo pants her sister had sent two Christmases ago and a low-cut top with empire waist and back tie in a stretchy cotton blend. Both had the store tags still attached but, surprisingly enough, fit reasonably well. Coupled with her clunkiest walking shoes and a pair of plastic hoop earrings, the image which greeted her when she had dressed was decidedly un-professional. Just the thing, she thought, to fly beneath Jason Privet's cultural radar.

The nameless sanctuary is dim, nearly dark, so that all Elaine can really say she has seen, as she sits on a ledge composing her thoughts, is a shadow; an indistinct form that seemed to move like mist along the wall. Not far away, a voice murmurs, chanting one hundred prayers, and the shadow seems related to that, so perhaps it was not really anything she saw, but only some impression of the sound. Her mind has been playing tricks like that lately, the interior images it creates often seeming more real than the ones it receives from outside. Ever since they reached Kolkata - with its jumbled buildings filling the lowlands flanking the Hooghly River, its streets and sidewalks jam-packed at every hour of the day, and nearly as crowded in the wee hours of the night, when swaddled sleepers stretch across every available flat surface - she finds her inner visions competing directly with the world outside. As if her spirit, grown accustomed to more open, more natural, surroundings, refuses to accept the reality of this city, its people, what it means to the future of humankind.

'Business to take care of,' Beryl had said when disclosing her intent to visit the sub-continent's infamous hive of poverty and devotion, though what that business consisted of, she was loath to explain. They arrived by ferry from Howrah, disembarking into a terminal thronged with people, only some of whom seemed to be travelers. A goodly number of them appeared instead to be actually living in the terminal, their few belongings stacked in piles beside them. Charcoal fires burned in cast-iron braziers, smoke rising to a gothic-vaulted ceiling painted with murals of the Raj; cooking smells mixing with incense but still not powerful enough in these close quarters to mask the nose-pinching undertones of rotting garbage and waste. Beryl had hustled her through; their baggage gathered up and carried by a startlingly skinny boy who materialized out of the crowd as soon as their feet touched solid ground. A battered van was found at the curb, and the boy paid off with a single coin, for which he thanked the women repeatedly, bobbing like a water bird before disappearing into the flowing mass of humanity as Elaine and Beryl were whisked, horn honking and tires squealing to dodge a succession of seemingly-inevitable collisions, to the front of a run down, colonial-looking house, in two small rooms of which the women were to make themselves at home for what Beryl said would be their longest stay yet in any one place.

　　The long stay was definitely due, Elaine realized when first she woke in that room, her body stiff and sore, her mind unsure how much time had passed but certain it had been considerable more than eight hours. The fact that Beryl has not appeared since that awakening makes it seem unreal to Elaine that she is even here, in a city of which she knows nothing, surrounded by people whose words she cannot begin to understand. Not that they are unfriendly; quite the opposite, she has been treated with great respect by the several women who bustle about the house. As soon as they realized she had awakened she was shown to a bathing room whose chipped-enamel tub they filled and refilled with hot buckets. Fed her as well, on dishes of sweetened curd, grilled flat bread, roasted lentils with chilies, crunchy/spicy pancakes stuffed with green peas and plates of melon cut in star and flower shapes, the whole accompanied by a strong green tea, with which she felt her strength return. Two days passed in soothing quiet, since none of the people around her seemed to speak any English, and few words were said between them in her presence, though she sensed this was more politeness than secrecy. The silence allowed her mind to fill itself with all manner of scenes - recollections from the past, snapshots of her journey, and other images, which came from nowhere she could recognize and which she felt certain she had never lived.

　　Early one morning - the time apparent from the sun's low angle and the birdsong filtering through wooden shutters - Elaine attempted to thank one of the two women who had been bringing her food. Having no words in common, she improvised with gestures, miming herself taking food from the bowl beside her bed, smiling broadly, then pointing to her hostess and miming an attitude of gratitude, hands pressed together before her breast as she dipped her head and lowered her eyes. Clucking small sounds of understanding, the woman smiled back, exposing a sparse grove of stained teeth sticking at odd angles out of blackened gums beneath sparkling ebony eyes, and a few minutes later appeared at the door once again, with more fruit - this time on a shallow woven platter. She did not enter though, but made as if to leave, and beckoned Elaine to come with her. Hard-won muscles no longer complaining, but even eager for activity, she did so, senses alert with the tingle of impending discovery.

　　The street outside the house's rear door was barely wider

than the room in which she had been sleeping, and so filled with traffic that it took great effort to keep up with her guide. There were handcarts to squeeze by - laden with crates and cardboard boxes - bicycles with baskets on their wheels and passengers on their handlebars, and every remaining meter filled by people on foot, moving as if at random, some rushing, some dawdling, some standing in rapt conversations or sitting with their legs folded beneath them. Dust assailed her nostrils, overlaying the drifting scents of foodstuffs - baking bread, pungent spices and mouth-watering grill-smoke - all struggling to compete with the less pleasant fragrances of sweated bodies and the foul-looking drainage running down a stone gutter at the pavement's center. Keeping one's feet out of that gutter added a layer of difficulty, as she shuffle-stepped along the rough surface, cadence constantly shifting to suit the traffic, ears alive to the myriad conversations, shouts and noises which constituted an aural landscape every bit as dense as the visual. Coming to an intersection, the chambermaid darted to the right and Elaine hurried to stay with her. One street led to another, some wider, some even-more narrow until, eventually, they reached a modest building, into whose stucco mass was set a wide wooden façade, remarkable first for the bleached and weathered quality of its woodwork, which spoke of centuries in the sun. Coming closer, Elaine saw its columns and lintels were covered completely with intricate carved moldings - pyramids and dentils, linear reveals and ogees, and among them, slender tendrils of leafy vegetation. Likewise, the panels infilling between those columns were attended in every inch by faux latticework and checkerboarding, the whole bearing faintest traces of bright blue, red and gold polychrome, nearly lost to the decades. At the center of this ghostly memory of splendor, between the largest columns, stood a narrow doorway and here it was that the woman stopped, her platter held high with satisfaction.

Perhaps Elaine's long weeks of travel constituted an informal education in the ways of this new world, or perhaps she had simply become accustomed to following directions, but either way, she found herself entirely comfortable with the implication of her hostess' gesture. With a sincere smile and a double bow, she took the platter and thanked the woman before stepping from the brilliance of a side-street into the darkness of this ancient artifact.

"Dean Malloy can see you now Miss..." Linda Vesteers hesitates, "er, Mister, er...."

" 'Doctor' seems to work pretty well," the visitor suggests, the professional title a handy way to skirt the gender confusion which has filled the small reception space ever since he first introduced himself to her.

"*Doctor* Gimbal," the administrative assistant repeats with exaggerated labor, as if working her mouth around a too-large bite of something whose texture she does not trust. She holds the door to the inner office at arm's length, her body as far as possible from where Rod must pass, then leaves it open wide, standard school policy when an official meets with a visitor of the opposite sex.

Jim Malloy has done well for himself. As Dean of Academics and University Affairs at East Pacific College he rates a corner office in the converted mansion that houses the school's top administrative staff. Wood paneled, the walls lined with framed certificates, awards and photographs, his office has the look of a country gentleman's den; the sort of place where one might once have encountered a cloud of cigar smoke upon entering. Jim himself furthers the cliché expectation, dressed as he is in gray wool slacks and fisherman's knit sweater beneath a tweed jacket.   The only thing out of place as Rod enters is the look on Jim's face: a look as if he were seeing a ghost - and a particularly distasteful one at that.

"Good morning Jim," Rod says, when the silence has gone on as long as decently allowable. He holds out his hand.

"Good morning," Jim manages, grabbing the tips of the fingers in a perfunctory shake, then withdrawing his own hand quickly. "I... uh, come on in, sit down. Please." His eyes are buggy as the visitor moves and sits, carefully positioning one leg with her hands before leaning her cane against the arm of her chair.

"Left leg doesn't seem to be part of the same team. The cane helps me remain vertical."

"Staying vertical is a good thing, I suppose...." Malloy stops before he completes the innuendo; his jokes have gotten him in trouble more than once, and he is schooling himself to stick to the agenda when meeting intriguing young women. "Linda said Rod Gimbal was here to see me. What is this, some kind of practical ...."

"Linda," the visitor calls, loud enough to be heard in the next room, though her eyes are squarely on Jim's. "Would you mind closing the door?" The assistant rises, and comes to the door, leaning politely around the door frame, from which she searches her employer's eyes for direction. Again, it is the girl who speaks. "It's all right, Linda; Jim and I are old friends. I'm quite sure that once I say what I have to say, he won't try to do with me what I know he has been doing with you for a very long time."

Malloy's face flushes at this, as does his assistant's, and the door is quickly closed, leaving the two alone. Jim Malloy feels suddenly warm in his jacket but since taking it off is now out of the question, resigns himself to that physical irritation, which is small compared to the mental irritation of knowing that this visitor is aware of his long-standing affair. Instead he waits, anxious to find out what she intends to do with that knowledge. Flashing him a reassuring smile, the girl jumps into the void he has left.

"One rainy day in the early sixties, you and I went to a small hotel on lower Third Street. A very seedy hotel. I remember there were two old men sitting in the lobby; one had tobacco juice dripped all down the front of his undershirt. As we stepped into the elevator - it was quite small and it stank of beer and piss - I said what we were about to do was probably the dumbest thing we had ever done and you said no, the dumbest thing we had ever done was taking that stupid Music Appreciation course. Supposed to be a breeze, but we - two guys who aced all our pre-med courses - ended up copying Al Valentine's paper on Verdi's Requiem just so we could pass." Jim gives a grunt, whether of amusement or simple acknowledgement is not clear, but either way it does not halt Rod's story. "When we got off the elevator we went to the door number you had gotten from some guy over at Phi Delt - was it Richie Carson?"

"Phil Carlson," Jim offers, sitting down now, behind the protective bulk of his mahogany desk. In the chair opposite, Rod struggles to cross his gabardine-clad legs in square, manly fashion.

"Phil Carson," he agrees. "We went in and paid the girl - I use the word girl loosely, she must have been thirty-five at least – we paid her fifteen dollars each. I went into the bedroom first, while you waited, and when I came back out, she called over to you; 'I had to give your buddy here half his money back. Think you can do any better college boy?'"

"And I said, 'I'm not a college boy,' Malloy interjects quickly, caught up for a moment in the memory of a much simpler time, "I'm a college *man*."

He laughs, as does his visitor, and for a moment the

atmosphere is easy, until Malloy remembers to whom he is speaking, and what pressures he is under since being hauled in front of the Regents' Committee over an alleged - but thankfully unwitnessed - improper advance to a young faculty member. His face tightens and the pencil with which he has been idly fidgeting is suddenly gripped tightly in his fist. "How do you know about..."

"Jim," the girl interrupts, very seriously. "You knew Rod Gimbal for a long, long time. Do you think he would ever admit to anyone that he couldn't make it with a hooker when he was twenty-one years old? Is there any way I would be telling you that story except that I know it from experience, and know that you were the one person who had been there with me."

Malloy rises from his chair, paces behind the desk, looking sideways at his visitor. A young woman of obvious assets, yet dressed in a man's suit, her bristle of hair combed severely from a side part, and glistening of Brylcreem. No make-up, no jewelry that he can see, nails cut to the quick, feet shod in black wingtips. Altogether the image of a girl in serious denial. And yet, what she says rings true. Rod Gimbal was a ferociously proud man who guarded his image as tightly as anyone. The idea that Rod would have told anyone about that incident seems incomprehensible... unless that someone were very close to him.

"You're his daughter, are you?" Malloy blurts out, proud himself, for figuring this out. "Rod had a daughter he never told anyone about, and you're her, and you're here for...."

"Look, Jim, it's okay. I understand this is difficult to accept, but I'm me. Rod Gimbal, only I look different. I won't bore you with the explanations I've postulated, the bottom line is: I know who I am and who I have always been, and if I have to go around looking like this, that's what I have to do. I'm not asking you to... it's not like we're going to pick up where we left off, go out for a drink and talk about old times."

"Hell no," Malloy laughs, relieved, "My wife would be furious!" Too late he realizes what he has implied; a look of consternation taking over his features like muddy water filling a dry riverbed after a sudden rain. The girl seems unperturbed, however, responding with just the right note of polite curiosity.

"And how is Adrienne? Well, I hope?"

Malloy launches into a description of his famously suspicious wife's latest doings, careful to insert that he hadn't meant anything with his comment. The girl brushes off any suggestion of offense, then goes on to recall for Jim a comment he'd made years ago about his penchant for younger women. The two share a laugh over that and Malloy is struck that her words are exactly what he would expect from Rod Gimbal. The same confident control of how a conversation flows, that slightly arrogant assumption that everything she says will be accepted, because of the source. One thing leads to another and soon the two are reminiscing just like the old friends his visitor claims them to be. He is still chewing on this idea, and wondering at his own gullibility, when the subject shifts to the purpose of her visit.

"The thing is, Jim," Rod says sadly. "I want my life back. I want my work back. I know I can no longer perform surgery - my hand-eye coordination is not what it was, and I can't stand for long periods, but I was thinking there might be a place for me, in academics. I have years of experience, diagnostic knowledge, technique, and I want to put them to use." She waits and when Malloy doesn't respond, adds, "That's what a man does, after all, isn't it?"

She sits, suit jacket lying open just enough to disclose the curve pressing against the thin fabric of a white dress shirt, a detail which draws Jim Malloy's roving eye. Carefully Rod pulls the jacket tighter, just as Malloy jerks his head away, annoyed at himself, and suddenly annoyed at this person, this girl who has come into his office on such a wild pretense.

"Look Miss...whoever you are - I don't know, and it doesn't really matter - but if you think you can come in here and gain some advantage by pretending to be Rod Gimbal..." Malloy stops in mid-rant, short-sheeted by his own memory. "It was Miller, wasn't it? Arnie Miller told you that story about Rod and me? I should've known better than to trust that nitwit; and then he went and put it on that internet-blab thing of his he's so proud of, and now anyone in the world can..."

The look on the girl's face is, truly, priceless. Mouth dropping open, eyes wide, the flesh draining of color as Rod Gimbal realizes one of his greatest personal secrets has been casually passed around by a man he had counted among his closest friends. Yes, the Dean thinks; it looks just like that. Or it could be the shock of a con-artist who's just realized she is not going to get away with her con. Either way, that expression of abject disappointment - on that pretty little face - cannot help but complicate the anger of a man like Jim Malloy.

"Look," he begins, choosing a new tack. "Rod Gimbal was a fine surgeon, and a friend of mine, but he had his faults as a human being. The fact is, if it weren't for his technical skills, he'd have been eased out years before he passed away. You said something before about the bottom line? Well, the bottom line is this: *if* you could somehow convince anyone that you were Rod Gimbal - *if* you could somehow get over that *incredible* hurdle - you'd find it was not such a great thing to be. So I suggest you figure out some other scam to push. And someone else to push it on. Do I make myself clear?" By the end of this speech he has risen out of his chair, crossed the room and opened the door which, he now indicates by a nod of his head, he expects the girl to use.

Sitting at her desk, Linda Vesteers has overheard her employer's voice rising and recognized another interview gone wrong. She looks up now, as the door opens, to observe his visitor's halting progress past her desk, only to stop at the outer door and turn, the young face a striking combination of anger and despair, though her words are anything but defeated.

"Thanks for nothing, Jim," she says, looking back at the man who stands just inside his own office, glaring. "I came to you as an old friend, looking to make myself useful. Thought you, of all people, would be able to see through this...appearance, but I guess that's just too much to ask." Malloy opens his mouth as if to say something, but stops, shaking his head in denial of whatever it is she is claiming. "And yes," the girl continues, "it's a good thing you didn't try any of your usual tricks on me. I'm not interested in men and I wouldn't hesitate for a minute to report you to Adrienne. Or better yet, the Faculty Oversight Committee. I testified for you once, but I've got a different perspective now." She turns, hand on the doorknob, and fixes Linda with a glare. "Maybe a little more of Linda's perspective, don't you think?"

A few minutes later the secretary is surprised to see Malloy heading out of his office, canvas bag in hand.

"I'm going over to the gym. Be back after lunch."

"Dean Malloy," Linda asks as he passes. "That girl who was here; should I know who she is? For your contacts list, I mean."

"She's nobody Linda. She claimed to be someone but..." Malloy pauses, at a loss to explain the encounter he has just had. Catching his assistant's worried look, he smiles back, wishing to reassure her. "Don't worry, kiddo, she's nobody."

In contrast to its neglected-looking facade, the interior of this holy place seems untouched by time or wear. The air is still, and the scattered hints of daylight soft, as they filter in from narrow windows hidden high above ledges, in alcoves or around corners, their actual openings never directly visible even as the light they admit renders surfaces solid and alive with detail. On the stone-slab floor, the narrow lines of mortared joints meet and branch, forming mosaic patterns of almost snowflake complexity, interlocking with such ingenuity that it is impossible to distinguish which shape is the object depicted, and which the space around it. On walls, columns and soffits, plaster of a single creamy tone is bordered in curlicues and vine motifs. Within these boundaries, tendril patterns interweave and repeat in perfect symmetry, disguising planes and volumes so that distance and geometry seem to dissolve, and space to become indefinite. Overhead, supported by concentric rectangular arrays of stone columns, blue-painted vaults mimic the night sky with sparkling golden dots for stars. Here and there the flames of votive candles and butter-lamps cast their rich and golden glow. All the more surprising, then, that the center of the temple, inside the smaller rectangle of columns, is occupied not by some precious-metal marvel, but by a simple figure carved of monochromatic gray granite. The figure of a woman, standing on a plain, square base, her sturdy legs covered by a long and heavy-looking skirt incised with a few faint lines to suggest waistband and folds, and no other garment - no sign of jewelry or excess. Above maternal hips her waist narrows to an almost dainty torso, bare, its small breasts held close and high, suggesting youth with all of its potential. Both arms are missing; one broken off above the elbow, the other just below the shoulder, but any hint of violence which those absences might suggest is contradicted by her face, and here it is that the meaning of this place comes clear, for on her strong features - the relaxed lips and gently closed eyelids, the slender nose beneath brows which arch just enough to suggest amusement with the world - is a look of such profound serenity that Elaine finds her breath at first sighting caught between in and out, on the cusp of awe and of submission.

For several minutes she stands, inhaling the tangible peace of this place, so unexpected amid the vibrating energy of Kolkata. From recognition - clearly, this must be some ancient shrine to the female Buddha, the 'Goddess of Transparent Wisdom,' as Mr. Ludower had described her over chicken Tikka Bhuna back in Kathmandu - Elaine's thoughts scatter to recollection: of all the many bridges, trails, fires, friends, hosts and hostesses which have brought her here. This simple, even crude, statue touches something deep within her, and she feels moved to honor it; not from belief, or disbelief, but for the act itself. Consciously directing her mind to fill her heart with gratitude for life's wonders, she places the platter at the feet of the effigy and, murmuring thanks in her own language, bows her head while backing off into a far corner where a narrow ledge beckons. Her intention, to the small degree she has formed one, is to sit for a few minutes, not meditating in any strict sense, but perhaps cogitating, as her grandfather used to call it. True to that intention, she soon loses herself in thoughts of other times, imagining this holy chamber consecrated by the softly murmured prayers of generations of believers, but even as she tries to imagine the sound of such a chant, a dusty scraping alerts her to the fact that she is not alone. Glancing over, her eyes catch the flicker of a shadow, disappearing behind a column on the far side of the space, beyond the silent statue.

Moments later, the shadow reappears on the other side and Elaine is reassured that her mind has not been playing tricks, at least not in this regard. Curious, she watches as the distant figure reaches the column nearest the Goddess's statue and stops. For sometime it watches and waits, just as Elaine is doing, the stillness of the chamber seeming to grow even deeper, as if a spell has been cast over this darkened volume and the two figures, immobile in their opposite corners.

It comes as a shock then, to see the shadow materialize into a stick-thin figure, clad all in maroon, who steps calmly to the smoky center, picks up the basket of fruit and commences striding boldly toward the entryway and street beyond.

"Stop," Elaine calls out, expecting the figure to burst into a run. Instead it does exactly as she has requested, stopping short of the doorway to turn, silhouetted by the narrow shaft of light working its way past the wooden door, and bow deeply in her direction.

"That's mine," Elaine says sharply.

The shadow does not speak immediately, but seems to consider before responding. "If you offered it to the goddess, then it is no longer yours."

Opening her mouth to disagree, Elaine realizes the shadow is correct. If the point of an offering is to give back for that which one has received, then, once offered, the gift is no longer the giver's. Not to mention the fact that the old woman had presented it to Elaine in the first place. 'Nothing we have is ours,' Beryl has pointed out, at some unremembered moment, and it occurs to Elaine that the shadow knows this better than she does, though still - there seems something not quite right about stealing from a temple. "But I gave it as an offering. To show my gratitude."

"Now I will be the grateful one."

"But that's stealing."

"Goddesses do not need to eat. Or statues."

"Of course they don't," Elaine finds herself agreeing, intrigued by the shadow woman's total lack of guilt or inhibition. "Leaving it is a gesture. A symbol."

"Then I will eat it as a symbol of the goodness of Prajnaparamita. See, the statue's belly is full, mine is empty." Instead of sounding shamed, her tone is patient and gentle, almost childlike in its careful pronunciation, though the English words come easily, not at all like one struggling with a foreign language.

"But that was not what I had in mind when..."

The shadow steps closer, and in the change of angle Elaine begins to see her better. A narrow nose separates wide eyes, pupils indistinguishable from the black irises which surround them below long, thick teardrop-shaped eyebrows. The lips, too, are dark; more brown than red, and pursed softly when they rest between words. A face, this is, which oscillates between being brilliantly alive at one moment, and peacefully on the edge of sleep the next. Her long, thick hair is haphazardly braided, and her sari and blouse, though beautiful in color, are matted and soiled, like garments worn both day and night. This vagabond appearance does not prevent her from speaking with authority though, as her voice rises to scold. "My teacher says, 'to make an offering is to return what has been loaned to you.' Yet you act as if you own what was not yours before you borrowed it - and is no longer yours, since you have given it away? Perhaps you are not yet ready to make an offering."

The shadow's mix of innocence and pedantry is rather sweetly compelling. Realizing that she wants to hear more, and deeply certain this tiny thing can be no danger, Elaine invites the young woman back to her hotel. A good thing, for when they reach the street Elaine realizes she has no idea of the way to where she is staying. A brief description elicits a nod of recognition and sets Sparrow - a name the girl offers readily, but only when asked – off through crowded streets and alleys, the feather-light fabric of her sari swaying gently to her measured pace, which causes Elaine no trouble to keep up as the throng seems to part at their approach. Soon the two are back in the Lodge's cozy room, gorging on sacred fruit while Sparrow proceeds to try on every item in Elaine's wardrobe, setting aside in a pile those things she covets.

It is some time before the subject of the teacher comes up again, and Sparrow is at first reluctant to provide any information.

"I had a teacher," is all she says, when Elaine asks how a person in her position speaks with such certainty about spiritual matters. When pressed for more detail, the girl commences to tell her entire life story, beginning with her birth in the Chetla slum to an impoverished teenaged mother - the truck driver responsible for conception having disappeared the night he was informed of her impending birth. A childhood in tin-and-cardboard shacks was followed by teenage years as a taxi-dancer in bars, a weak cover story for the prostitution which was the real intent of those on both sides of the lights. All this, she suggests in the telling, was itself only a prelude to the encounter which changed her life, when an American, an economic-development assistant at the US consulate, had taken a liking to her and set her up with a room of her own. Though only a low-grade civil servant, he was rich in comparison to the world she had known, and for the first time in her life the slum-girl knew a full belly and a clean bed. It was this man, Corbin Mintz, who taught her English beyond the few words she had been given by the bar's owner to do her business and he, also, who gave her the name Sparrow - for the way she ate: picking tiny bits of food for hours on end, savoring the act of eating as if it were a ritual. For three years she was his woman, and it was during those years that she had need of medicine to prevent the reenactment of her own origin and was directed by another girl to the Teacher.

"He wouldn't allow me to have a...what you call it, a... an..."

"An abortion?"

"Yes," Sparrow agrees, her voice betraying no emotion, only reassurance at having the proper word to use. "An abortion. Instead he told me to pray, and he prayed with me. For two days and the night in between we prayed, never stopping for food, or drink. He said it was a prayer to release the child within me, so it would not have to suffer this life, but could remain where we all come from. He said because the life within was so new, that it had not yet formed an idea of itself as apart from all that is, and so it could choose to wait until a more suitable vessel arose. After those two days of praying, there came a point when I felt myself getting lighter, so light my head seemed about to float away from my shoulders and I must rise to my feet to avoid losing it. The monk rose too and together we walked out into the light. The next morning my body flushed itself and I was no longer expecting. Anything. The prayer had changed something inside of me and since that day I have lived without expecting anything else. I drift and I take enough to sustain my body. When Corbin, my boyfriend, was transferred to Thailand he said he would send for me, but then he stopped writing or calling, and I learned from a woman at his office that he had gotten another girl pregnant. Her skin was not so dark as mine, perhaps, or she was younger, and so he married her instead."

Sparrow pauses and gazes toward the window, a rising quarter-moon just visible over the roof of the next building, which bristles with satellite dishes and antennae. For the first time in their talking Elaine senses sadness in Sparrow's voice, and wonders if she is longing for her lover. Her words though, make clear it is for something else she pines.

"You are going to do what I did," Sparrow says, the nodding of her head making clear that this is not a question, but a confirmation, though Elaine has voiced no thought to be confirmed. A slight smile passes across her features, before they settle into much the same serene and certain expression that graced the statue which brought them together. "You will find the Teacher," she says, in little more than a whisper, "and he will give you what you need. When he does, do not thank him, for that would show you are still attached to self and believe him to be, as well. You must seek another way to express your feelings."

Outside the University's Admin. building, Aubrey busies herself looking bored as she leans against a stone balustrade. Cigarette dangling from pursed lips, hands jammed into the narrow pockets of a battered motorcycle jacket, her attitude is enough to make passersby bend their paths to the far side of the monumental stair, seeking the comfort of distance. Those few who have the temerity to glance at her face are discouraged from any closer approach by a scowl of resentment and belligerence.

     Her inward climate, though, is more complex than that look suggests. Accompanying Rod on this errand to his old crony has called up a whole stew of conflicting emotions. There is the rush of adventure, like watching a high wire act; a rush which itself brings back welcome memories of student days with Kim, when bold and reckless actions seemed commonplace and nourishing. That feeling roots for success; to see her come striding out of the building with a great broad smile on her face. Another vector of feeling - one which Aubrey senses equally clearly, and does not shy away from admitting to herself - is actually hoping for failure. A total, dismal failure, so this 'Rodney' act can be put to rest and Kim - or Christina, or whoever she may choose to call herself next - will be that much more dependant on Aubrey's assistance and support.

     Which leads to the other track playing in her head, beneath those two conflicting strains: a more tender melody of affection which has been growing, despite the friction, during the months the two have been roommates. Back in the day - when Kim was only Kim and Aubrey one of the many friends and acquaintances who buzzed around her - there had been a certain unreachable quality in their friendship. As if Kim were so much in demand that any one person could have only a small part of her time, her attention, her affection. Now that they are living under one roof, Kim's physical disabilities forcing her into dependence, Aubrey has found herself in the position of favored courtier. Watching 'Rod' struggle to regain her physical abilities has wakened a nascent maternalism in Aubrey - though god forbid anyone say that word out loud - and this infuses her wait with something very like apprehension. Imagining the certain failure of this errand, she imagines also the crushing blow to her girlfriend's hopes, and feels the pain which she will surely feel. True to her strongest traits, Aubrey's reaction to this sensitivity is to bottle it up in crystalline reflections on all the little frictions generated by two women living in a small space, on a limited budget, with a paucity of introspective capabilities. Thus the scowl, the huddled shoulders, the all-in-all very fine imitation of a nineteen-year-old James Dean at his sullen best.

It rewards Aubrey's mood, therefore, when she sees one of the chrome and glass doors at the top of the steps snap abruptly open, as if captured by a hard wind, though the morning is still, and when she sees the space created by its movement fill immediately with Rod's bustling form, head bent, eyes crimped, and mouth set against questions, as she makes her cane-syncopated way down the gray granite stair which sets the Admin. Building on its high pedestal. She casts no glance around at the russet and auburn highlights still present in a few dead leaves clinging to limbs, the damp ground, the cotton-white puffs of clouds dotting a wintry sky striking in the depth of its blue, nor the youthful faces of students padding this way and that on their own private timetables. Reaching Aubrey, she does not even stop to acknowledge her presence, but stumbles right past, down the last few steps to the sidewalk, where her gait, still awkward and asymmetrical, picks up speed as she heads off toward the street and the city beyond.

"Went well then, did it?" Aubrey calls after the departing figure. Dropping her cigarette to the ground she crushes it out with a twisting motion of one boot then sets off, quickly catching up and settling into step just offshore of Rod's right shoulder. Along the curving promenade they walk, oncoming pedestrians parting to avoid Rod's glare - or Aubrey's leather, or perhaps the combination of the two - then across the courtyard of the Chem. Lab before reaching the gate which gives on to Seventeenth Street and the commercial district beyond. When they reach the intersection with Union Street and must wait for a traffic signal before crossing, Aubrey inserts herself into Rod's silence.

"We going anyplace in particular," she asks, eyes straight ahead, "or just out for a walk?"

The light changes and Rod steps off the curb, sun glistening from the oiled bristles of her dark hair. A girl crossing in the opposite direction casts a glance at them, and from the way her eyes quickly shift away Aubrey intimates judgment - a dismissal of her and Rod as just another pair of dykes having an argument in public. Suddenly the girl's pretty student blondness seems an insult, and Aubs finds herself erupting.

"You got a problem with me?" she asks the stranger, whose

314

eyes instantly widen. "You looking at something you don't like to see?"

Before the scene can go any further Rod steps between them, her demeanor instantly commanding.

"Leave the young lady alone," she says, eyes meeting Aubrey's as a parent fixes on a child to gain its attention. Coming from Kim's soft features, though, the effect is more comical than commanding. Despite the crew cut, the dark suit, the sensible wing-tip shoes, Aubrey cannot accept this paternal tone emanating from the vessel of Anne McKloskey's daughter.

"Don't give me that shit," she replies as the student hurries on, grateful that the two strangers are turning their wrath on one another, not her. "Don't give me that older wiser 'I'm above all this emotion' act. I'm not the one who just walked three blocks without saying a word about what happened after you brought us all the way over here on my day off. I'm not the one who's acting like the whole fucking world has ended."

A horn honks, highlighting the fact that they are standing in the center of the street and the light has changed. Grabbing the sleeve of Aubrey's jacket Rod tugs the stiff leather, urging her toward the curb.

"No," Aubrey says through clenched teeth, as another horn honks, its tone deeper and more threatening than the imported squawk of the first. "Not until you tell me what happened."

"We're in the middle of the street, for God's sake," Rod says, her voice still rational and level. "We're holding up traffic."

"And you're holding up me." Aubrey tugs her arm away and flops to the pavement, settling cross-legged, her face directed at the nearest vehicle, a furniture delivery van, whose flattened windshield collages the faces inside among swirls of reflected cloud and building tops. Traffic is backing up now behind the truck, and horns honk irregularly as the seconds drag on. The driver eyes the scene before him: two mismatched women, the standing one kind of cute, despite her butch attire, the other dark and tough in camo pants and commando boots and sitting square in the middle of the crosswalk. 'Another spoiled college kid fucked up on drugs,' the driver concludes, thoughts moving on quickly to the schedule he is expected to keep. In the seat beside, his helper briefly imagines himself leaping out to defuse the situation, then walking off with the dark one, whose angry face seems to reflect just the way he feels most days: mistaken, misjudged and alone. It is only a fantasy, however, as he hears impatient breathing in the seat beside him and sees the girls oblivious to any but each other.

"All right," Rod gives in, "you were right. They didn't exactly laugh at me. But it was close. I'll tell you all about it but not here, not in the middle of the road. You must know someplace we can go, around here - get a cup of coffee and talk it over like two adults?"

Relieved that he can keep his schedule after all, the driver watches as the smaller woman reaches out, offering a hand to the seated one. Touches her elbow with the other hand as she rises, too. Just the way a gentleman would, to help a lady rise to her feet. Kids these days are strange, he thinks, letting-off the brake and tapping the gas as they move out of his path. So very fucking strange.

The Greek restaurant to which Aubrey leads Rod is a bland box of a room, its décor limited to a few potted plants and a smattering of faded travel posters on that part of its walls not taken up by floor-to-ceiling windows. Student traffic fills the sidewalk outside, while inside, the dining room buzzes with late breakfasters and coffee suckers, conversation mixing with the nasal drone of bouzouki and laouta, klarina and daouli. Here, among the crowd of students, professors and those who simply frequent the university district for its cosmopolitan feel, Aubrey and Rod attract no attention but that of the waiter who takes their orders with a grunt then leaves Rod to tell the story of his interview.

Watching her friend toy with the silverware as she speaks, Aubrey finds herself remembering other restaurants, other times she has spent with Kim, and how it was never just the two of them. Always there were others: usually a whole crowd of boys and girls - classmates, friends, friends-of-friends and ex-friends of ex-friends. Sometimes even a favorite prof or instructor. The girl just attracted action and attention. Some of them might have hung around for what was being said; Kim was, after all, a bit of a star among the art students, what with the controversy of her pieces. Some were there just for fun, to be part of the pretty, confident clique she traveled in – Erika Watkins, model-thin and tall; Raisa Cohn, with her exotic accent and shy way of admitting she knew nothing about almost anything; Dom Petri, who played both football and the saxophone, and Mark, of course, perpetually reminding them he was in the *Professional* Film Program, as he prospected for dialogue and scenes he could steal. Plus the endless succession of boyfriends and hopefuls, more often than not making fools of themselves as they tried to engage the girls with jokes and conversation, seldom finding any common ground. In the center of it all would be Kim; the brightest star in any constellation, calm and often quiet, never appearing to ask for attention, but constantly receiving it all the same. Necessary and central to the group's energy, as if the others had all been captured in her gravity.

Aubrey's own place had never been that certain. As an artist, she showed some promise, but never made the front wall at school showings, never had her own pieces featured on the Division newsletter, as Kim had three times. Nor was she a target for the buzzing bees, male or female; they tended to give her room, whether put off by her looks or her defensive bristling. Though Kim would give her a quick hug now and then, it was more likely to be in parting than greeting. She felt herself more tolerated than welcomed, her interjections into conversation rarely met with the full round of laughter or endorsement which Kim's seemed so effortlessly to elicit.

That was the way it had been, and so now, to sit in Costa's, just the two of them, with Kim all to herself in something like need, makes for a good feeling. A satisfying picture as she imagines how they must appear: two close friends sharing their troubles, helping each other through it all. Aubrey wants to be there for Kim, the way she was able to be while Kim was ill and silent, before this Rod thing got so in the way. Kim's distress allows her for once to feel older, in a good way – something she would never have thought possible. Stronger, too; as if, in dealing with a friend's frustration, her own ability to cope has been released.

The first cup of coffee comes and goes, refills are poured and still Rod is going on about the inability of others to accept her as who she feels she is.

"It's so ridiculous," she is saying now. "Being…this…" With damp eyes she stares across a cup held unsteadily, the fingers smooth and feminine, despite their quick-cut nails. "I did everything I could to convince him. Told him things no one but me could possibly know and yet he wouldn't believe me. Hell, I'm not sure I believe me." For a long time she stares across the room, then continues, more decisively. "It's not that teaching is so important to me. It's a poor substitute for practice. But…" Again that long stare, again the sense she is changing tracks. "After the Nothing, when all this…stuff…started happening, there was a time I thought I could simply ignore it and it would go away. 'This can't go on,' I told myself, 'it's just a dream; a delusion of some sort,' and I thought as long as there was a part of my mind that could see that, then sooner or later that part of my mind would win out, reality would reestablish itself and I would be myself again. Now... I'm not so sure."

'Reality is overrated,' Aubrey remembers Kim saying, somewhere back in their common past. She does not repeat the quip, though, but waits, sensing – hoping - that her friend is finally tiring of the masquerade, that maybe this is her idea of giving herself an out, a way back to herself.

"There are times lately," Rod continues, fixing eyes on Aubrey's, "when I wonder if it's me that's got it wrong. If perhaps all I've got to do is accept what I see when I look in the mirror, and somehow it would all make sense again. All my memories would fade away and I'd just be this Christina person. Or this Kim - what did you say her last name was?"

"Tree," Aubrey answers softly, hope spreading as she reaches out and lays one hand upon Kim's.

"Tree." The response is tentative, as if trying the word on for size. "Kim Tree. Christina McKloskey, Jane Doe - that's how Mary says they identified her when she was first
admitted - but the problem is, none of those names means anything to me. Every memory I have, every dream I dream, is a memory of me: Rodney Gimbal. I remember being a boy, I remember growing up, going to school. I remember classes, procedures, diagnoses and pharmacopoeia. A million memories that this person you all want me to be could never have, and they are as real to me as you sitting across this table. More real, actually, because they make sense. The things I remember are more real to me than the things I can reach out and touch, the food I eat, the coffee in this cup.., and yet I cannot imagine how that could possibly be. I can't..."

Aubrey knows this feeling, this disconnect between who you are and who the world believes you to be. Her mother, for example, when they would argue, seemed always to be talking to someone else. Confidently and emphatically answering a different question than her daughter had posed, offering suggestions that had nothing to do with what Aubrey needed or wanted. Friends described the same thing, during conversations held in drizzly smoking knots around the side of some convenience store, or slumped in the backseat of a borrowed car passing a bottle in a paper bag. No one understood them then, no one would accept them for who they were, and it drove them all crazy. Literally crazy, if you were Danika, who had lived down the street from Aubrey for a while, then had to go away after she cut herself. Crazy in less obvious ways more often, like the kid who joined the Marines at seventeen to escape the teasing he got for being named Romeo David Valentine. One way or another, they all went away, Aubrey recalls, feeling the old bitterness rise up like a morning-after stomach.

"People are always telling me I fight too much," she says, not sure how it fits, but certain it's a piece of the puzzle. "Put up walls around myself and don't let anyone get in. That's what my therapist told me, anyway."

"I don't need a therapist."

"I wasn't saying that, it's just...like, a 'what if,' " Aubrey suggests carefully, aware that she is asking her best friend to do exactly what she has so long refused to do herself. "What if you did just pretend you are Kim?" As she speaks those words the idea becomes more clear and she corrects herself. "No, better yet, Christina. Pretend that that's really your name. Like trying it on to see how it fits. Instead of fighting it all the time, try it on and maybe, after a while, it will feel more right."

In the pause Aubrey sees Kim's lips compressing, her eyes casting about the room in search of something. Softly, she sets the cup upon its saucer, bottom mating in the corresponding recess, china to china, just as their maker intended. Something in the fitting of those two pieces appears to intrigue her, as Aubrey sees her eyes focusing there for a time, fingertips withdrawn only a few inches. Gently then, they settle, the hands laid flat on the table, as if bracing for a jolt.

"I am Christina. I am Christina McKloskey, a young woman with a mother and a friend..." Here Rod looks up at Aubrey, a question in her eyes, a look which Aubrey feels deep inside, warming and rewarding her. "Is that what you want? You want me to say those words?"

"Yes," Aubrey answers hopefully, confusion setting in as she sees Kim's expression change in response. "I..."

"I knew it. You've never believed who I am, have you?" The words come not as a statement, nor even a question, but an accusation. "Despite that pretty speech you made, calling me by my name all this time, you've never believed me for a moment."

"I..."

"I will not lie to anyone, young lady. I will not play pretend.

There's nothing of this Christina or Kim or Jane Doe in me and there's nothing in any of them that I want. I want my self, my name, my life; and anyone who wants anything else for me is not my friend."

By the end of this speech, Rod is out of his chair and headed for the door, napkin still tucked into the belt of his trousers. Few around them react, though in a far corner the young waiter makes a mental note. He will give the left-behinder a few minutes to get control of herself. Let her cry it out before he brings her the check. He'll keep a close eye on her though, that's for sure. Dumped girlfriends are among the most notorious check-skippers, and this one's depressive look does nothing to reassure him. Oh yes, he'll keep an eye on her; because no matter which of the thousand possible ways it is that she's just been screwed, it's no reason for him to accept the same.

"I don't understand," Jake says, fighting to control the emotion he can hear creeping into his voice. "You said we had a bulletproof business plan."

The man behind the desk gives a deep sigh, rolls his eyes toward the ceiling and swivels in his chair, a fifteen-hundred dollar confection of cast aluminum and ribbed leather identical to the one in Jake's office next door, although this one has actually received some use in the year and a half since the two men went into business together. Colin Seacrist carries the title of Chief Executive Officer for DigiBank PR, as the stationary, web site and marketing materials all title their creation, but in reality he *is* DigiBank. Visionary, technocrat, ceaseless schmoozer and perpetual optimist, it was he who conceived the idea that two young men without any banking experience could use the internet to seek out borrowers and connect them with willing lenders, collecting a small percentage in both directions as their own commission.

It was Colin who had searched the net and come up with the idea of an overseas charter, to avoid those fussy legal requirements and certifications necessary to do business in the states. Far better, he'd explained, to operate in the overseas markets where they could concentrate on the numbers of their deals, not a lot of government paperwork. Colin, too, who had hired their first and only employee, lovely Roxanne, who even now sits at her desk outside his office, answering the rare phone call, ready to greet any visitors who might accidentally find themselves in front of her. And Colin who had expressed enormous pleasure when Jake suggested they purchase a series of photos and props documenting one of Chris's performance pieces, Sinking Woman, and display it in the lobby of their offices, conveniently located on the twenty-second floor of a black glass shaft at the corner of Second and Hope, a very prestigious, not to mention expensive, location.

"It is bulletproof," Colin answers, the words flowing off his lips like money from a gambler's fingertips. It was that glibness which had appealed to Jake from the start. He admired anyone who was fluent in business, who could rattle on about rates of return and point spreads and overnight discount rates as easily as Jake could move from one weight station to the next. Jake was, in fact, in awe of Colin's command, when they had sat for over an hour in the study of a mutual friend's house on Mercer Island and discussed the infinite potential of the web to change their lives.

"You can reach anybody in the world," Colin had said at one point. "Whatever you have to offer, you can find the person who wants it the most and is willing to pay the most for it. Instantly, all by yourself, without middlemen, without a huge organization, with virtually zero capital. Twenty years from now, anyone who didn't get in early, is going to be kicking themselves."

Those words had resonated strongly with Jake, whose father had made his own modest fortune during construction of the Alaskan oil pipeline decades before. Dan Brindle had been in the right place - Seattle - at the right time - 1975 - to lease his two broken-down barges to an oil extractor desperate to transport equipment and supplies to their new base of operations in Port Valdez. As the multi-billion dollar construction effort got under way, he had used the lease proceeds to expand DanCO from a freight and salvage operation to an equipment provider, ready to offer whatever the contractors needed - a fleet of heavy overland trucks to transport the gear inland from Valdez along a swath cut with tree-felling tractors, some of which DanCo had bought cheap from loggers caught in the squeeze of cheaper overseas lumber, and DanCo-payrolled teamsters to drive both trucks and tractors. By the time the pipeline neared completion, DanCo had nearly a hundred-and-fifty employees and an inventory of equipment which would soon become worthless when its sole customer switched from pipeline construction to billing by the thousands of barrels of oil transported. Fortunately for Jake, his father'd had the sense to sell off a good part of his ownership at the height of the boom, with the fortuitous effect that all the family's own holdings were actually in blue-chip industrial stocks and bonds by the time DanCo's business volume dropped seventy-three percent in the course of a single year.

Dan Brindle had lived well off the fruits of his opportunism, and Jake had heard at a young age that a man had to be ready to jump on board when he saw his ship come sailing through. By the time he encountered Colin, his father was four years beneath the ground and the estate had been divided among four kids, two ex-wives and the IRS, leaving Jake with a livable but not particularly impressive portfolio in search of rapid growth. Listening to Colin's enthusiasm that night, as the lights of Seattle glistened across Lake Washington's waters, he felt a small shiver of excitement. This, he imagined, was what his father must have experienced as he sat in their tired bungalow a block away from the boatyards of Lake Union and read in his morning paper that the pipeline had been approved for construction, and Jake had resolved then and there not to miss the boat on the potential bonanza of internet banking.

It is with more than a little chagrin, therefore, that Jake listens today as Colin outlines the state of DigiBank's finances. Apparently the cost of establishing their operation has been significantly more than they'd allowed for, and the pace of closing on loan contracts significantly less. Detailed financial statements don't mean much to Jake, whose education has extended only as high as a few courses at Seattle Community College, and those in areas far afield of finance - Art of the Film, Fundamentals of Nutrition, Cultural History of Bodybuilding; the sort of courses taken by a footloose young man who never expected to have to earn a living for himself. The stacks of paper Colin trots out may as well be printouts from some other bank's archives for all Jake knows (and in fact, that is exactly what many of them are). What does hit a home run on his attention meter though, is his partner's request for an additional infusion of cash, to keep the operation going for another month or two.

"I can see the light at the end of the tunnel," he explains to Jake. "We are at the top of the hump and in just a short time I am certain that we will begin showing regular operating profits of a substantial amount."

This sounds awfully familiar to Jake, who has, over the last few months, developed a sinking feeling in his stomach whenever his attention turns to the office. Mornings, on his way to the gym, he'll call in and ask about the overnight inquiries, nearly always hearing that there were numerous strong prospects, but never any closings. He has asked about other investors as well. If this business plan is so awesome, shouldn't there be others eager to invest, as he has done? Colin's answer to that was reassuring at first - that he hoped not to dilute Jake's ownership stake by taking money from any of the others clamoring to get in - but now, as the calls for more capital have added up, and Jake's assets have been drawn down, the idea of sharing the stakes seems positively appealing.

"So go to Dave Fergusson," Jake says when the subject of operating funds comes up, a not so subtle reference to the mutual friend in whose home they had hatched this partnership. "Or Vicki Ito. Trudy Limelite. Mort Ziegler. Al Bender," he continues, naming a few of the wealthy people to whom Colin has introduced him over the last year and a half; a varied collection of friendly beauties and tired-eyed executives with whom they've lunched at clubs on the top floors of skyscrapers like this one, cheerfully discussing the growth of international lending and the enormous sums to be raked off the top as electronic money flows through the night skies above the broad Pacific.

"Jake," Colin soothes now, his voice at once both caring and disappointed, as if his friend were being enormously naive, "Jak-ey. If we bring those guys in now, they'll take us over. Hell, I could go to Paul Allen today and get all the capital we could ever use but you know what? He'd own this whole operation lock, stock, and barrel, and when the money really rolls in, it would all go to him, nothing left for the little fish like me and you."

Jakes face through all of this remains frozen, but in his lap the broad hands are fidgeting, rubbing together, knuckles popping ominously. There's an air about him of a gathering storm and Colin is enough the salesman neither to miss it nor to confront it directly. Instead, he places his hands on the desk before him, palms up to show he's hiding nothing and lets his face slacken to show the depth of his own emotion; just how much this situation pains him, too. For a few moments he appears to consider something very deeply, to be torn by his own thoughts before he swivels his chair away and gazes for a long moment toward that wonderful view.

"Look," the banker announces emphatically when he swivels decisively back to focus once more directly on Jake. "I wasn't going to tell you this, until it was a done deal. But I can see you're sincerely concerned, so, here goes. This is absolutely hush-hush, you understand?" Jake nods, always flattered to be included in something confidential. "The truth is, Jake, I've been concerned about our situation, too. Just like you have. Even more, because, I mean, I'm the one who got you into this, aren't I? So I have a responsibility - a *fiduciary* responsibility – to make sure you get what's coming to you. Right? So I've been talking – for some time, but especially over the last week or so – I've been talking to some big money out of Shanghai. These guys are anxious - no, I'd say they are desperate; *desperate* - to get a piece of the kind of action we are looking at, and the beauty part is, they don't want to take things over! In fact they can't, because their own laws – in China it's a whole different ball game, but I don't need to tell you that, right? – in China their own laws mean that, if they were to take a controlling stake in something like DigiBank, then the state could come in and take it from them! Can you believe that? And they would, too, the big guys in Beijing would see the potential and want it all for themselves and then where would our guys be? So the beauty of this, Jake, the beauty is that these guys I've been talking to are ready to invest, and they also have borrowers lined up, in Shanghai and other places on the mainland, and they need our organization to keep it out of the government's greedy little hands. Now like I said, this has got to be absolutely confidential, just between the two of us, because these guys run pretty scared – of their own government that is. They hear any word that anyone knows about this, and they head for the door, you got me? And they need just a little more time, a little more coaxing. In fact Jake, I'm scheduled to go over there," Colin pauses to consult his 'Berry, working the tiny buttons faster than Jake can rattle a hanging bag in the boxing room at his gym. "Thursday, the sixteenth. Overnight red-eye - economy class of course. We just need to keep operations at full speed long enough to get them under contract, and then," Colin makes a gesture with his right hand, starting flat against the desk, then moving slowly forward and sweeping faster upward until his arm is fully extended, fingers pointed directly at the ceiling, "we are off, like a jet from the deck of a carrier. Another thirty thousand, thirty-five at the most, to see us through to that milestone, and we will be raking it in like you never imagined. I am absolutely certain of this, Jake, it is the surest thing I have seen in all my years, but I'm asking you to trust me on it. I'm begging you to give me just a little more line to catch this fish and you'll see; it will all work out, just the way I told you it would."

Colin pauses, his face a question, but Jake's face is still, his thoughts unclear. With a small inhalation the banker dips his head, shaking slightly from side to side, and his own mask as he rises from his seat, is one of disappointment. He is the trainer now, the coach whose star player is not performing and is in danger of being benched, and his voice is full of the power of positive thoughts as he paces, dodging and weaving around the desk.

"It's like when you're lifting a new weight, Jake, when your body tries to tell you it's too much, but your mind knows you can do it, and you gotta call up something from deep down inside yourself?" Instinctively, Jake nods his eagerness to go that extra mile, then realizes what he is doing and goes still again, both signals readily recognized by Colin, who drifts around behind his guest, placing both hands on those magnificent shoulders and kneading the dense tissue with all his fingers.

"You gotta keep your mind in control, Jake; you gotta find that belief in yourself. You've done it a hundred times in the gym - I've seen you do it, man; I can't believe the things I've seen you do in the weight room, buddy - and all I'm asking...no, I'm not even asking, I'm begging...I am *begging* you to do the same thing here, just this one time. Are you with me Jakey-boy; are you game for one last lift?"

"You are such a fucking bore," Aubrey blurts out one evening after another sullen attempt at dinner together. In the aftermath of his failed efforts to connect with the outside world, 'Rod' has withdrawn ever further into himself and his bitter, self-pitying, isolation. His mornings begin later and later, his drinking begins earlier, fueling late idle nights, about which he has nothing to say when his house-mate tries to engage him in conversation the next day. The only thing in which he seems truly interested is his music, which he has taken to playing incessantly.

"You used to be the most un-boring person in the whole world. Christ, you would try damn near anything; that's what got you into so much trouble."

Rod simply stares back at her, idly pushing food around the plate, his fork emitting a scraping sound that makes her hair stand on end.

"That's it," Aubrey says, pushing her chair away from the table. "I'm going to find us something to do, before I fucking kill myself. Or you."

Still, for several days she can come up with nothing, until she hears him in the shower again. That unexpected voice rising through the water's rush reminds her of an evening several years before, when she and Darcy and Manny and Peter Maxwell had all wandered half-drunk into a diner up near Northgate, to find some old lady with blue hair playing the organ, singing hokey old songs to a bunch of grandmas and grandpas. They took a table near the front, ordered more drinks and later, as the evening wore on, watched some of the grannies and grandpas stuff a bill in a jar on top of the organ for a request, then sing along as the woman played, clearly lost in fantasy of another time and place. Drunk as a pack of skunks, Aubrey and her friends had listened to the old folks wail their hearts out, becoming stars in their own minds. That place would be a perfect fit for Rodney-fucking-Dr. Gimbal.

Aubrey picks up the phone book, but nothing she finds there rings a bell, not surprising given her chemical state that night. Instead, she decides to consult the good old *Weekly*, that proudly alternative newspaper, which boasts an entire Classified category just for 'Karaoke,' including one listing advertizing an open sing every Wednesday night. Seeing the name in print, Aubrey realizes she's heard of it before – the Swedish Social Club is a favorite weekend party bar for some of her campy gay friends – the nitrous-oxide and Brandy-Alexander bunch. Perfect place to take old grandpa Rodney – she'll blend right in.

The RANWEI LOUNGE – so proclaimed in lemony neon that easily overpowers the faded Bangla script of its proper name - is brightly lit, in contrast to all the other places Elaine has visited over the past three nights. As at every one before, she does not ask the muscular bouncer lurking just inside the door, or the speedy-eyed bartenders busy shoving glasses of beer and whiskey at customers. Instead, her eyes seek out the corners of the room, the shadowed periphery, where girls sit bored and bleary-eyed, hoping to be chosen for a dance, or more. It is these Elaine approaches, always choosing the most sorry-looking girl; the one with the darkest circles around her eyes, most ill-fitting halter, most needy smile.

"I'm looking for a teacher," she says in her own language, trusting Sparrow's assurance that any working girl worth her salt will understand that much at least, especially with the addition of a few local words which the beggar also provided. "DikSaka? The teacher who is also a doctor – abaidya? Who helps girls when they are garbha," she adds; the Bengali word for being with child.

More than one girl has burst out in scornful laughter, to think of this gray-haired old-one searching for help with a pregnancy. Others simply stare at her, the presence of an elderly American woman as unexpected in their world as an alien spaceship would be in hers. Twice she has been grabbed by bouncers, and hustled out back doors where she was accused of trying to steal the bar's girls, or worse, reform them. In one dark hole though, a haggard child with a bleached-blond pageboy and a slender cigar took her by the arm into a curtained alcove. There she whispered directions to the Landing District, a group of especially tough bars tucked-up against the fence that encloses the runways of Subhash airport, where every few minutes huge airliners and cargo jets roar overhead, low enough to drown out any conversation. The RANWEI - or RUNWAY, as she guesses it must have been intended - is the third Landing bar Elaine has entered, and it is there that she finds the lights burning brightly, as two men attempt to revive a patron passed out in the middle of the postage-stamp dance floor.

"Fucker's not breathing," shouts a heavily-built man wearing sunglasses, thick mustache and a 'Marylin' Manson t-shirt. He proceeds to slap the motionless figure repeatedly on the sides of his face, with no apparent result.

The other man, a slight Bengali in tailored slacks and a

spotless white shirt, begins shouting, a rapid fire of words directed at the girls who have gathered round. Two of them run off in opposite directions, platform shoes clunking concrete floor and in the distance, Elaine hears the sound of doors banging as the big man continues his clumsy attempts at revival and the remaining girls whisper among themselves, one crying silently while her fingers fondle a cap which Elaine guesses might have come from the injured man. Several long minutes pass before the sound of a door-slam somewhere behind the bar signals the return of one of the girls, followed by a small figure clad in a deep-red sweat-shirt with the cuffs cut off, baggy brown pajama pants and flip-flop sandals, and Elaine knows she has found her dikSaka. Not by the clothes, certainly, nor even by his shaven head, but by the way he moves, seeming to glide across the floor without effort, and by the way the crowd parts at his entrance - just as waters part when they flow around a boulder.

Kneeling beside the body, the Teacher's hands move rapidly, touching several spots around his torso, neck and head; each for only an instant though, until, abruptly, he stops, placing two fingers of one hand upon a spot just beneath the man's left armpit. Holding them there, he begins to make a sound, a smooth stream of unintelligible syllables, as near music as speech. Several of the girls move their mouths as well, though no sound comes from their lips. Overhead, a jet approaches, its auditory signature accelerating swiftly from distant whine to freight train rumble to full volcanic roar. It is at the peak of this sound that the prostrate man begins to move, his body first giving a great shudder, then kicking both legs, the heels of his work-boots sounding drumbeats on the wooden floor as the monk holds his fingers pressed deeply into the flesh beneath that arm.

Bar glasses shake and ring to the airplane's pressure wave and chairs vibrate their own feet against the floor as the jet passes directly overhead, its sound drowning out all thought in Elaine's mind and causing her to shut her eyes for a moment. When the noise begins to recede she opens them again, to find the customer lifting his head from the floor, a dazed expression in his eyes. The Teacher stands back as the other two men help him to his feet and hustle him unceremoniously out the front door. Almost instantly, the lights dim and a juke box begins playing, scratching over a thunderous beat. "Gimme' mo' bling-bling," raps a raw and angry voice, "gimme' mo' bling..." as girls drift off to dim corners and patrons back to their tables. Elaine catches the Teacher a few steps outside the back door, in a puddled alley bounded by chain link fence and ramshackle buildings, its darkest corners occupied by hulks of several long-abandoned vehicles. A feral cat winds around her legs; in hope, perhaps, of scraps.

"Wait," Elaine calls out, and he stops, casting a worried eye in her direction. "A girl named Sparrow told me to find you," she offers, suddenly feeling very foolish. "She said you were her teacher."

The man's lips purse tightly as he examines Elaine from head to foot then begins walking again, an offhand wave inviting her to follow him. Some distance down the alley he approaches the rear of a camouflage-painted ambulance perched on stacks of wooden cribbing in place of wheels long since removed. Pulling aside a thick blanket which serves as its rear door he reveals an interior glowing with the light of a single candle and the ember of a joss stick. The space is low, requiring both to stoop as they move into it, and very nearly filled by a sleeping mat jumbled with throws and pillows, a wooden crate serving as table and a wire-mesh bench which hangs by steel cables from the side wall, the only visible remnant of the vehicle's original equipment. It is on that bench that Elaine sits, as the Teacher pulls the blanket closed behind them, then settles cross-legged on the mat and begins stroking the head of another cat which has appeared from somewhere among the meager furnishings.

The atmosphere in this confined space is thick with incense, a sweet mixture of flowers and spices. There is a human component, too: the sweaty musk of men's things, which Elaine has not encountered, or thought of, since leaving home. Thinking of her home she feels immediately a sense of loss, of life gone by so fast it cannot be grasped, only remembered, and that without precision.

"Sparrow told you something," the Teacher states, his words so soft and casually spoken, they are nearly lost in the cat's purring. "And so you came."

"Yes."

"What are you looking for?"

"I don't know that I'm actually 'looking for' anything," Elaine answers, surprised by the note of defensiveness which shows up in her own voice. As if she were concealing something – though she has no intention of hiding anything, nor any idea what she would be hiding if she had. She is here, she imagines, because Sparrow spoke so highly of this person. Because the girl told her she should seek him out. Because, she realizes, she has become used to following Beryl, and now – the thought comes with some consternation - she

331

has followed even the words of an impoverished street person to this broken down carcass in a back alley, several worlds away from any place the old Elaine Gimbal could have imagined herself arriving. Life flying by at its own speed, on its own itinerary.

"Everyone's life is a journey, and everyone who journeys is looking for something. Your European legends call it the Grail, but even in that tradition it's not so much the object that matters, but the idea." The Teacher is silent for some time, eyes fixed on Elaine's as the cat stretches and rolls onto its back. Without looking, his hand goes to its belly and rubs there, where the fur is thin and its skin shows through, buff and pink and vulnerable. The creature's most tender and defenseless part, yet eagerly exposed to this person. "So what is it you're looking for?"

"I don't know," Elaine answers, though the question has raised something inside of her. Discomfort of a sort. Guilt perhaps, though why she should feel guilty in the presence of this person, who looks so...normal. Except that he is not normal. Indeed, despite the thrift-store clothes and a manner of speech that would be perfectly at home in any suburban community college, the Teacher seems to demand a high standard of honesty. He sits so very still, his eyes so calmly observing hers, that she feels she is not so much conversing with a person, as sharing her thoughts with another mind, all the rest of each person dissolved into incense, candlelight and the tender way his fingers still rest upon the motionless feline's belly. "Are you really a guru?" she asks, without knowing why it should matter. "A dikSaka?"

"I am a person," he answers, "who lives and learns. Anything else is...distraction."

Elaine feels her leg tightening, circulation cut off by the metal bar at the edge of the seat. She is conscious of an impulse to move, to stretch it out, but also of a stronger desire not to disturb what feels like silence – feels like it, not because there is no noise penetrating from the world outside this metallic space, but because that noise is, so clearly, irrelevant. Things are folded-in upon themselves here; silence within noise, a space which is not a room, a teacher who is just a person; a journey she did not intend to take but is pursuing, for reasons she has never really understood. "I am not looking for anything actually. I... " Even her own words seem conspired to trip her up, to complicate what should be simple.

"All right then," the Teacher agrees, with no hint of irony or skepticism. "You are not looking for anything. But what you are missing?"

The Teacher's eyes hold Elaine's for a moment longer, then turn away, toward the door, though Elaine has heard nothing to attract attention. The cat makes a snorting noise, raises its head to squirm from beneath his hand, and rises, stretching its back in a high arc before darting with a snarl past the edge of the curtain and out into the alley. As if in response to the cat's actions, the Teacher extracts his feet from under himself and starts for the doorway, his back bent nearly horizontal, well below even this low roof.

"What happened in there?" Elaine asks as she follows him out into the night, where the layered noise of traffic and air-conditioners, fans and circling planes assaults her ears, and fragments of light from all directions and angles do the same to her eyes. Reluctant to lose what she has searched for days to find, she knows her question is as much to hold his attention as for whatever answer it might elicit. Something has moved inside her over these few minutes, something has changed in a way she does not yet understand, and this odd little man is her only lifeline to where that change is leading. He is *her* Teacher now, as well as Sparrow's. "You didn't really bring that man back from the dead, did you?"

The cat is back, or perhaps it is the stray from outside the club - or another altogether - that is curling around her ankles this time, and meowing, loudly. A distant whine deepens and accelerates, warning that another airplane will soon be declaring its dominion overhead, screaming out the raw power of petroleum-fueled fire and the wealth of nations. The Teacher stands in total relaxation, hands at his sides, back straight, face a single smoothly curving plane from lighted forehead to shadowed chin. It is a simple face, Elaine sees, with no beard to smother its expressions. A face stripped to essentials; slender slit for a mouth, nose hardly more than a bump, protruding just enough to admit air. Eyes which seem set directly at its surface, not sunken into deep recesses like a European face, the eyebrows no more than an afterthought. Unwrinkled, though not youthful. A face, she thinks, which is unmarked by all that is around it, by all that so affects the rest of us. In the midst of noise and stink and glaring lights, in the midst of the messiest, cruelest parts of life this Teacher stands untouched by it all.

"Bring that man back from the dead?" he replies, pronouncing the words as if he had never heard them before and must consider each one individually in order to grasp their meaning. "It *is* possible the man was actually dead. Or, it's possible he was not. But to bring a man back from the dead? Such a thing is impossible, is it not? In-con-ceivable?" The round head nods several times to confirm its own judgment, then abruptly stops, to settle cocked a bit to one side and back, eyes aimed up toward the stars. "And yet...?"

Elaine watches as a smile, growing slowly from within, appears to consume the Teacher's face, creasing the flesh beside his eyes and lips, stretching the skin of his cheeks until they shine, highlighted with reflections of the random points of light which interrupt the night around them, and she feels her own smile growing in response.

"Inconceivable," she repeats, bowing slightly, hands pressed together before her chest. "Ab-so-lute-ly."

"No can do," the young man responds, leaning back to swivel his chair rapidly from side to side. A toothpick protruding from one corner of his mouth flaps up and down as his jaw muscles work continuously. Though Jason Privet's body is draped across the seat and arms of the chair as if dropped there from a great height, Mary cannot help but feel the energy coursing inside him, eager to talk about his systems, even as they frustrate her once again.

"No digging around Personnel if it isn't in the open fields. Big 'no-no' - access levels, authorization codes, cookie'd up the wazoo; we'd leave a trail from here to Pittsburg and I'd be back at Burger King. What'd you say that other name was?"

"Yuri Rosen." Tap, tap, go the fingers, and once again, Privet shakes his head. "Either you've got the wrong name, or else...I don't know what else, but if he'd ever worked here, there'd be a public record and a forward."

"I know he worked in pediatric endo," Mary repeats without hope. They've been going on for ten minutes, and for each name Privet draws the same blanks she had. So much for her James Bond fantasies; this is getting nowhere, and she's due back on her own floor in five minutes.

"So why is it, exactly, you want to know about these guys?" Privet fixes her with amber eyes peering out from beneath two sparse and scrubby brows. The toothpick has gone still all of a sudden, his chair too, and Mary is aware of a quality she had not noticed before, a critical capacity normally hidden beneath the boy's nonchalance, but which makes sense - if he is as good a trouble-shooter as his reputation suggests. It might be giving too much away, but something inside her says it is OK to trust him more than she'd planned.

"There's a girl," she begins, and proceeds to administer the short-form version of her involvement with Christina McKloskey, from that initial encounter in ICU, to their recent conversations. All her suspicions about the girl's release and subsequent treatment, the odd mix of meds, everything, that is, except her claim to be Dr. Gimbal. Privet takes it all in, pursing his lips now, smiling a bit then, with an equanimity that suggests he hears such stories every day.

"Dates?" is all he asks, and Mary is stumped for a moment, as to whether he is asking about her social life, or Christina's. Privet reads the confusion, smiles like it was his mistake, and corrects himself. "When did all this start?"

"Last May," she recalls, with a mix of relief and disappointment. "I don't remember exactly, but she was admitted the day before that big deal up in Admin; when the new people took over..."

Privet's widening grin stops her in mid sentence. Without comment his fingers begin working, one hand palming a trackball, the other expertly skimming the keyboard to type as quickly as she could do with two. Screens flash too rapidly for her to catch their content until the movement stops on an image of a document, headlined, in bold type, 'MEDICAL HOLDINGS, LLC. FOR IMMEDIATE RELEASE.' As quickly as Mary can read that, the image changes again. Like a bird pecking for seeds, the document scrolls and stops, scrolls and stops, and each time Mary recognizes a name – Rosen, Resor, Lembec – they're all there, along with several others. All leaving Hilltop for impressive-sounding posts in far-away locations: professional exile.

"May twenty-second," Privet reads proudly, when the image settles again on that title page. "MH took over and cleaned house. Typical turn-around behavior. New wigs come in the front door, bunch of pee-ons get shuffled out the back; costs go down, revenues up, and some middle-manager back in New York or Cleveland gets a fresh Mercedes. I'm guessing your guys got axed right away, so, technically, they never worked for MH, and since our current data base is an MH proprietary, anyone who never worked for MH isn't there. As to what they did to get the bosses so pissed off at them...I could go back and look at an archive, see what we have for the old admin, except I'd still have to get my boss's authorization to do that, and she'd want me to have a legitimate reason, which we don't really have, right?"

Sadly, Mary shakes her head. There's so much more to this than she had imagined. She'd expected to find herself studying a medical chart, reviewing symptoms and diagnoses, not press releases and business deals. Standing, she's about to thank Privet for his time when he goes on.

"If you want someone to tell you what really happened back then," he says, a hint of mischief in those eyes, "Jessica Bagley is your man. Woman, I mean."

That name is certainly familiar to Mary, though explanation into which Privet launches adds entire new dimensions. Bagley had been the head of Hilltop for two years before Medical Holdings' takeover; the sea change which commenced right around the time

Christina McKloskey was admitted. The first thing the MH folks had done was to remove Bagley in favor of their own executive, Alex Martinez, who arrived like an invading general, cutting off careers as casually as she cut budgets and re-worked staffing allocations. Within three months the hospital was operating with 9% fewer professionals and 13% fewer non-professionals, despite an average heads-on-beds rate 4% higher than the year before. Bagley had virtually disappeared, Privet says with an odd sort of pride; no one in a position of responsibility around Hilltop has spoken of her since the day she packed up her personals and was driven off in the same limousine that had just delivered Martinez.

Jason laughs as he begins searching again, then squints to scan a new page, filled with headlines and sidebar ads.

"Hell, Doc," he concludes after a moment. "Looks like Jessica Bagley is the one person who *can* afford to talk to you. Just make sure her husband doesn't know you're coming." Mary's bafflement must show on her face, for Jason's voice takes on a patronizing tone as he disgorges information from the screen. "William D. Seivers, nickname: Three Dollar Bill - I guess for how cheap he is - CEO and COO of the Honeycomb Fund, which he began in 1987 as an investment vehicle for successful farmers in central California. Had the good luck to invest in a couple of early Silicone Valley start-ups, so by the late '90s the Fund had assets over a billion, all under his personal control. Moved his operations from Fresno to San Francisco in '96, then when his piggy bank got too big to invest in real estate he branched out into corporate acquisitions. Medical Holdings was just a local San Fran operation when he snapped it up, but within five years Seivers turned it into one of the largest operators of private care facilities in the western states."

"So Jessica Bagley is now married to the head of MH? I'd think that makes her the last person who would talk to me."

Once again Jason sighs loudly, as if the entire world pains him - its slowness of understanding, its naïveté and ignorance of facts which are so obvious to a clever young IT technician. "Maybe so. Maybe Bagley and Seivers just saw each other across the board room and fell in love at first sight." He fixes an eye on Mary, head cocked a bit to one side, toothpick protruding from a mouth puckered sourly around it. "You believe in love at first sight?" he asks, but before Mary can answer he goes on again.

"MH isn't afraid of people like you, Mary; they can buy you off or ruin your credibility before they've ordered their morning latte.

It's the higher-ups they worry about, the people who could be hauled into court to testify against them, who can demonstrate a chain of knowledge up to the board room. The kind of people an Attorney General would be trolling for; a Rudy Giuliani, back in the days when he was still a prosecutor, not a revolving door."

"But Bagley is one of those people," Mary protests. "Or at least she was, before MH came in."

"Was," Jason repeats, with as much emphasis as a simple linking-verb can bear, then goes on talking as he taps the keys and reads from a succession of pages. "Before she got the boot. And before she became the wife of the top man, which is just too much of a coincidence for my little brain to stomach. Bagley gets a velvet cushion - unlimited wealth, for all practical purposes - freedom to travel and do whatever she wants – anything except pursue her career or talk about whatever happened before she got the boot. Fancy homes in who knows how many places, but New York is the base camp. And Seivers got the one thing he maybe needed."

Jason stops, obviously enjoying the riddle he has posed, and Mary finds herself smiling at the kid, enjoying his cockiness. That a twenty-something who spends his work-week in a windowless basement can be so knowledgeable about people far older, richer and more apparently successful than himself, seems to open a myriad of new possibilities. As if the flimsy panels dividing the world into a hundred million little cubicles have just begun to dissolve - cardboard under a hard rain. If Jason can show her the path to whatever MH is hiding, then anyone has the potential to do anything, and even as she is thinking these thoughts, the young man's hands begin moving again, left hand rolling the trackball in abrupt bursts as the right taps quickly back and forth across the whole width of the keyboard.

"A prime witness to *something*, and she can't ever be forced to testify against him," he says proudly, though his tone in the next moment turns to disappointment. "No listing," he says sadly, fingertips perched around the trackball like a cage around a rabbit. "Unpublished address, unpublished phone, Facebook locked off, no Bizz-link, no blog. This lady does not wish to be found."

Mary feels herself heave a deep breath of disappointment, but before she can say anything, Privet tosses over a smug smile and begins keying once again, narrating his own progress in the monotone of one either working too hard at what he is doing to pay attention to how his words come out, or so under-utilized that he can't be bothered even sounding interested. He's checking the MH server, he explains as the screen flashes from one page to another, to confirm how they've set up individual e-mail accounts; verifying there are no tracking cookies on hits to each user's individual list of contacts. A muttered 'dipshits' confirms there are none and with a few more keystrokes the two are looking at a long list of names. These, he explains, are individuals whose folders of contacts and addresses - identified out of several hundred thousand files by recurring letter combinations in their file paths - have been backed up on Hilltop's shared server drives. Having filtered them out, he can now search them all at once for key words and see what comes up. Privet types in 'Jessica,' clicks the cursor, and in less than a minute the screen shows a list of over one-hundred persons named Jessica, none of whom sport the last names of Seivers *or* Bagley.

"OK," he sighs, fingers pausing for only a couple of seconds before they begin flying once again. "Should've known it wouldn't be that easy. Besides, the serious players wouldn't have their on-board drives backed up on the server; too much chance of someone finding out what underwear stores they use to buy their secretary's birthday presents. Still, everything's available if you know where to look. Who do you think, in all of MH, would be the most likely to keep in touch with a disgraced ex-honcho?"

Mary thinks for a minute. Other administrators? Personnel department? "Legal," she answers with a start and a smile.

"Annnh," Privet responds, in the nasal tone of an electronic buzzer. "That's the dark side - their own local network; separate storage devices, separate access codes; all maintenance and updating done on the spot, nothing remote. Same with finance. Got to be someone who doesn't really have any say in things, someone who doesn't have a real reason to keep in touch, but wants to anyway."

"Public relations?" Mary offers, and leans close to Privet's shoulder as he brings up a list of media, community and family-relations staff and they agree on one which sounds familiar. Several screens flash by as Jason types in maintenance authorization codes and passwords, but very shortly they are staring at a typical desktop arrangement, fifteen or twenty icons superimposed on a photo of Bob Baker's family on vacation at the Grand Canyon. Click, wait a few seconds, click again and type, and Mary watches as a highlighted box on the screen fills up with fancy faux-cursive lettering.

"So glad to see Mr. Baker keeps up his Christmas card list,"

Jason remarks, handing Mary a pen and a post-it. "I know," he apologizes as she copies down the address and phone number. "It's primitive, but printers leave tracks. Make sure you get the address; you can try calling, but I doubt you'd ever get her to talk on the phone - too many ears that way. Get her face-to-face though, you might find she's got something to say. Worked with me, didn't it?" Privet gives her that smile again, the one that says he's just a kid with nothing to hide, and then he asks the question he's apparently been holding back for the last half hour. "You ever play paintball, Doc?"

A few minutes later Mary is in the elevator, headed back to her own floor, wondering how she can get to New York any time soon and - equally compelling - what one wears to a paintball exercise.

"Let's go then," Aubrey, says, nearly exhausted before they even leave the apartment, due to the endless encouragement and cajoling necessary to get Rod to put on his clothes and a bit of food in his stomach. Finally though, they are in the 'Old-mobile' and joining the late evening traffic which is only now winding down from the rush of wage-slaves hurrying home to their wage-caves.

The Swedish Social Club, when they arrive, appears to be nothing more than a dark doorway in the blank face of a brick commercial building. Situated mid-block between a State liquor store and a commercial fishing supply warehouse – this is Ballard, after all - the door is lit by a neon green sign, the name written out in mechanically-dull block letters, the windows to either side of it blackened so thoroughly that no light escapes them.

Entering, Aubrey forks over several bills for the cover charge and the two are waved in past a goateed hulk whose function seems limited to dumbly monitoring the flow of newcomers - acne-scarred, dressed in K-mart khakis and an undersized black polo shirt, he gives these two barely a glance. Once inside, the thump of techno is inescapable, as is the crush of people moving this way and that or just standing and talking right in the middle of a narrow hallway which, once they push their way through, gives-on to the great barn of the club room, its peaked roof supported on age-darkened timber trusses from which dangle an eclectic assortment of string lights. Japanese lanterns in Easter pastels, crimson chili peppers, multi-colored cowboys and blue-gray sharks blink on and off at random, shedding cumulatively just enough light to disclose the dozens of patrons who've made themselves at home among the round tables and mismatched wooden chairs. Artificial palm trees dot the perimeter and the far end of the space is dominated by a raised platform and its backdrop, a crudely painted tropical beach scene, complete with thatch-roofed beach shack. Overall, the effect is one of festive shabbiness; a high school prom décor set-up in – oh, maybe 1962 - and never taken down.

"This used to be some kind of sailor's meeting hall," Aubrey explains over the music and voices. Steering them past the bustling bar toward a small vacant table off to one side, she continues the story learned two days before by chatting up a couple of customers at Sylvio's whose looks seemed to fit what she'd already heard of the place. "It was vacant for, like, twenty years or something, until the whole disco thing started, in the seventies. Then when that died out – you do know disco is dead, right?" Kim's blank stare suggests 'Rod' never knew it had been alive, and his furtive glances at the rest of the trade make her wonder just how this place and crowd must look through the character's antiquated filters. "Anyway, since then it's been...well kind of a party club on the weekends, and somewhere along the way they got the idea to do this karaoke thing to pick up the midweek, and it really caught on. Now it's just, like... anybody who wants to come, comes. And sings." Seeing that this last has seriously raised his shields, she quickly adds, "Or not."

Once she's confident Rod is going to stay put for a while, Aubrey offers to go to the bar and get drinks. Her best bet, she knows, is to get her friend buzzed before she can freak out and insist on heading home. Thus, Dr. Aubrey's prescription: a healthy dose of alcohol to release those carefully rehearsed inhibitions and let Kim's true nature shine, in a setting that would have totally grooved her before all this shit with Rod and Christina and the rest. Getting through the crush takes a few minutes, and by the time Aubrey returns, Rod is wearing a look of high disapproval.

"This is a gay place, right?" he asks, eagerly taking the scotch from Aubrey's hand.

"Not only," she offers brightly. "Lots of people come here, all types."

"It's not that I'm offended," Rod explains, swallowing a good part of the drink in one gulp. "But it would have been better to warn me."

Looking around, Aubrey tries to imagine how she might have phrased such a 'warning.' Sure, some of the tables are occupied by men whose presentation suggests they might be gay, or women who might be lez, but they're hardly the rule. For every obviously queer cluster, she can point out plenty which defy easy classification. Mostly it's just a complete mash-up of all kinds of young people, in every possible variation on club attire. Still, given her worries about keeping Rod here long enough to relax into the spirit - or spirits - it is a relief when the table to their right empties out and its initial occupants are replaced immediately by five men in jeans and work boots, several with more than a day's growth of unshaven beard. Their well-worn flannels are layered over t-shirts and long-sleeved thermals, and they have the ruggedly-un-fit look of men who do physical work for a living, eat cheap food and drink religiously. Sure enough, two of them carry pitchers of beer along with handfuls of glasses. Factory workers, Aubrey concludes quickly – if there even are such things as factories any more. 'Real men,' - just the ticket, she figures as she takes a sip of her own beer, a beverage carefully-chosen to make Rod's male character feel more at ease.

"It's all right," he confides, leaning close. "You may have assumed, given my age and background, that I'd be uncomfortable around this kind of crowd. But actually, medical training conditions you to treat everyone equally. You learn to look past a patient's personal problems," he says, apparently unaware of the contradiction in his wording, "and treat them just as you would if they were normal."

Perhaps to show how emancipated he is, when it's time for another round, Rod offers to go to the bar himself. When he comes back, his face bears the look of one with a great story to tell. "The bartender was really pretty friendly," he says, placing Aubrey's beer in front of her and taking his seat close by. "From the back, I thought it was a guy, but once she turned around, I realized it must be a woman." Rod laughs at his own mistake, then continues, clearly just getting to the good part. "Because she was wearing a t-shirt that said - in great big letters right across her bosom - 'Yes, these are breasts. But have you seen my *eyes*?'"

He shakes his head in a mixture of wonder and amusement, and Aubrey is relieved to think the evening might not be a total failure, if only her companion can maintain that sense of amusement. She does not notice the look of disgust thrown their way by one of the men at the next table, who then whispers something to another of his buddies as he re-fills both their glasses while his cohorts continue drinking and talking. Steelworkers; part of a crew brought up from San Francisco by an outfit called Downtown Erection to speed up construction of a nearby condominium tower, each of the five has worked at least sixty hours in the last five days and all are more than ready to blow off some steam at what their motel's desk clerk told them was the most lively bar in walking-home distance. Talking and joking easily amongst themselves, their radar is nonetheless on the lookout for female companionship; every now and then one of them casts a disappointed glance at the table to their left, where they see a tough-looking girl in black sitting quietly with another chick dressed in men's clothes.

"The one in the suit," Eddie 'Whiskers' Halfert says to the

man beside him, "She must have just come in on one of them boats we saw - she drinks like a fish."

'Gimp' Delinsky smiles at his friend's joke. He had noticed the little butch woman as well. She doesn't interest him much though - his eye is on the other girl, the taller one with the sour look on her face, like she's worried about something. She has a decent body, what he can see of it, and after two weeks in this town where he doesn't know anyone but other steelworkers, she's looking pretty good to him.

The rest of the table is filled out with Al Berger - the head of their crew and, at forty one, the oldest, hence his nickname 'Papa Al' - Earl 'Sandy' Carter, a Montana boy who claims to be half Indian (*not* Native American, he says with anti-PC relish), despite his blond crew cut; and John 'Robo-Cop' McCraggen. 'Robo-Cop' is actually only the public version of his nickname, which started out as 'Robo-Cock' after the story got around that he had made it with a Nevada whore four times in one night at his own bachelor party. Even among this crew, though, that was just a little too explicit to be hollering across the jobsite or into a two-way radio, so it had devolved into 'Robo-Cop,' or just 'Robo,' for most occasions.

Robo and Gimp are watching the short one return from the bar with her third drink, when the background music fades to silence and a heavy-set woman in a tuxedo steps out onto the small stage. With a carnival barker's pomp she announces that the entertainment is about to begin.

"Don't be shy," she urges the crowd, which has thickened around the back and sides of the room, knots of people standing together wherever they can be out of the circulation. "No judges here, no door prizes, except the ones you give each other."

Somewhere a voice chimes in. "Hey, Carol," it calls, "How about you be the prize?" to which the emcee responds cheerily, "'Cause I don't want to get us closed down again," and the crowd reacts with laughter and calls of support, clearly a lot of these people have been here before and share at least a bit of common language and stories.

"Some prize she'd make," one of the steelworkers moans to his companions. "She sat on your face, she'd probably break your nose."

"Bullshit, Robo," Sandy replies. "You'd take her in a minute if you thought she'd have you."

"Busted nose'd probably improve your looks anyway," Gimp

adds, his voice loud enough to carry to the neighboring table he is eying. "Maybe make you pretty enough for that little freak to take a tumble with ya'." Robo sneers back at him and Sandy, while the other two enjoy his discomfort and Aubrey feels her temperature rise just a bit.

"This is all pretty simple," the Emcee continues. "There's a song list here," pointing toward a thick stack of pages sitting atop a small table in a pool of light at one side of the stage. "And a prompter here," she slaps her hand onto a video monitor which faces up at her from a small dolly sitting near the front of the stage. "When it's your turn, introduce yourself and tell us what song you want to do. Give Elliot a second to cue it up from his 'always-hard' drive," - somewhere in the back a patron shouts out 'Ell-i-ott' and a number of faces turn and hands wave toward a lighted control booth at the rear of the room - "and when the music starts..." the strains of the old Broadway classic, *Another Opening, AnotherShow* begin to issue from speakers discretely hidden around the stage - "you just follow right along. Oh, and put your lips real close to Mike here," the emcee says, seductively caressing the microphone, to another round of laughter and cat calls, "otherwise nobody'll hear a goddamned thing."

Even as she speaks, a line several people long is forming at the table, ignoring the list of songs. These eager participants clearly know the ropes, acting totally sure of themselves.

First up is a middle-aged woman who approaches the mic with all the seriousness of a prospective diva making her debut at Carnegie Hall. With stiff back and squared shoulders she waits through a long string introduction before belting out the first notes of a lover's ballad in full vibrato.

"Give me a break," Sandy cracks to his friends, "I hope we're not gonna sit through a bunch of opera?"

"Not likely," Papa Al reassures him. "That line of fucking freaks up there don't look like any opera lovers to me."

Sure enough, even as polite applause for the diva is dying down, the second singer, a precisely coifed man in tight khakis and crew neck sweater, reaches the mic, accompanied by the rising rhythm of a Latin tune with an upbeat tempo. Pulling the mic free from its stand and shuffling his feet during the intro, he has the crowd on his side from the start.

"*Turnin' the beat around,*" he sings, over and over, each time turning himself around and projecting his backside at the crowd, which roars its approval.

"Guy's a fucking queer," Whiskers announces to his table in disgust.

"Look around you, old man," Papa Al points out. "This place is full of 'em."

"Yeah, Whisk," Sandy offers generously, "You can take your pick."

"Screw you, asshole," Whiskers shoots, his anger mostly pretended, but with a hint of old resentment lurking somewhere along its edges.

"They would, too," Gimp pipes up, and the entire table roars with laughter at how Whiskers set himself up for that one.

Nearby Aubrey overhears the banter and begins fuming. If those guys want to be Neanderthal, she wants to tell someone, they should stick to their own turf, not come here, where the whole point is to let people be themselves. "Shake it, honey," she yells out over the music, pumping her fist in the air. It is just one of many encouraging calls thrown in the singer's direction as the number winds into its percussive finale, but the glares exchanged between Aubrey and Gimp confirm to both that her words carry other intention as well.

As the evening goes on, the crowd reaches full swing, calling out to the singers with suggestions alternately helpful and humorous; cheering those who manage to hit the notes, cheerfully booing those who fail. It is all good-natured fun, lubricated by plenty of alcohol, and the room has melded into a happy party. Not quite the entire room though; as the table of five grow progressively more pointed in their criticism and, nearby them, a table of two simmers with a more complex brew.

One effect of this evening, for Aubrey, is to remind her just how good it feels to be out among people again. Over these months of caring for Rod, she has almost forgotten what it is to be part of a crowd, sharing the energy of common laughter, relaxing into the moment. It's not the music that matters, or this place in particular, it's just having people around, feeling like she belongs. The recollection of how much fun this could be if she were with her old crew - Darcy and Ellie, Kristl and Terry, Mark, Willie, Jodie - and Kim too; if only she would go back to *being* Kim - grates up against the reality of noisy assholes at the next table, and a companion who seems to have decided firmly not to have any fun tonight. Hunched over his drink, one slender finger running almost constantly around its rim, Rod gives each new singer a single glance, then lowers his eyes in apparent boredom. True enough, none of them are singing songs from his pretended era, but there are some good songs. Hell, she thinks, they're not what she would choose to listen to either, but, come on, you can still have a little fun, can't you? When she tries to engage him with a comment about a singer, or a song, the monosyllabic responses remind her of nothing so much as herself at an earlier age, thirteen perhaps. She feels herself growing furious with his lack of gratitude, furious with herself for expecting anything more, and decidedly ready to take her anger out on someone, anyone, who gives her an excuse to do so.

It is nearing 11:30 when a skinny guy in straight-leg jeans and snap-front shirt reaches the microphone, an outlandish white cowboy hat perched on his head. His boyfriend has literally pushed him onto the stage, ending with a quick pat of the butt before scuttling back to a front table, where he joins several more pretty-boys, cheering eagerly before the music has even begun. Visibly nervous, the singer grips the mic stand with both hands as a country guitar starts in, to a schizophrenic mix of rowdy hoots and disappointed groans from the audience. Stumbling over the first few lines, it is only on the chorus that he begins to capture the rhythm, singing 'Mamas don't let your babies grow up to be cowboys,' in enthusiastic but tuneless baritone. Behind him, several others wait their turns to sing

"That ain't no cow-boy..." comes a yell from the steelworkers' table. It is Gimp, his voice strong enough to carry over the music, and harsh enough that the singer stumbles, his attention diverted. "Maybe more of a sheep-boy," Gimp delivers, and his table roars, oblivious to another dirty look tossed in their direction by Aubrey. Rod, who seems finally to have been distracted from his own funk, whispers calming words to her, touching his fingertips to her wrist, but the gesture has no effect as her blood boils more with every remark the roughnecks make.

"Bring on the girl," Sandy shouts out a few measures later, in apparent reference to a buxom blond who is next in line to perform. As the song moves into its second verse and the young man struggles to regain his way with it, the taunts become more insistent. "Bring on the babe," Sandy calls again, louder than before.

"Yeah," agrees Gimp, who has already downed two shots of tequila in between his beers. "Bring on the one with the tits." His friends burst into raucous laughter, slamming beer mugs onto the table and generally congratulating themselves on their buddy's audacity.

"Hey, cut it out," Aubrey calls across the aisle between them. The cracking in her voice suggests nervousness, but there is a menacing angle to her head and shoulders and her eyes are fixed straight on Gimp, whose face goes red at the public rebuke.

"I wasn't talking to you," he answers loudly enough for several tables to take note. "Fucking dyke," he adds for good measure, the words directed to his own table, but only a little less loud, and the five roar with laughter, raising mugs and clashing them together in self-congratulation even as Aubrey stands, knocking her chair back in the process.

"You got a problem with me?" she challenges, and in an instant Gimp is up out of his own seat, their eyes just about even despite his far greater bulk. The cowboy has finished his song and a new tune begins as the blonde takes his place, but more than a few sets of eyes are turned away from her as Gimp's tone turns mock serious.

"You're the one's got the problem, lady."

"Yeah," Sandy chimes in, as the music continues and heads turn in their direction. "A problem figuring out which bathroom to use!" Again the five erupt, slapping hands and rocking back in their chairs as the music keeps pulsing around them and the rest of the audience tries, with varying degrees of success, to ignore the distraction. Aubrey bristles, exhaling an angry breath, but before she can say anything, her companion is out of his chair, placing a hand on her arm as he addresses the others.

"You're out of line, fellows," Rod says, Kim's reedy voice level and calm, though her eyes have the slack look of someone who's been drinking hard for hours, her jaw the set of one ready to be troubled-with.

"And you're out of uniform, soldier," Gimp shoots back, convulsing his friends yet again.

"Where'd you get that haircut," calls Sandy, "Dykes Are Us?"

"I've had this haircut all my life," Rod retorts without hesitation. "Since before you were in diapers."

Sandy jumps up at that, shoving his chair well out of the way as he rises. At the same time, Aubrey, suddenly worried about what Kim might do, places her own hand over the one on her arm.

"Let's just go Rod; they're not worth our time."

"Rod?" Sandy hoots out in surprise, his head turning to bring his four friends in on the joke. "I thought her name would be Butch," he implores them in mock confusion. "Or Buster, or maybe Ah-nold. But Rod? Jesus Christ, is that pecker envy or what?"

"You ignorant son-of-a-..." Rod snarls, taking a step to bring himself face to face with Sandy, who stands at least a foot taller, and whose chest alone is wider than Chris's shoulders. By now much of the rest of the audience has noticed the altercation brewing and is focused on it. Up on stage the blonde is going through her motions without conviction, her eyes also on the two women and five men who have all risen from their seats.

"Whoa," Sandy answers in mock fear. "Save me, Mommie, the little cocksucker's gonna hit me. I am so scared..." Before he can finish Rod moves forward and takes a swipe at his chin, but the guy sees the blow coming and ducks away from it, at the same time that Papa Al brings his hand up to grab the offending arm and hold it tightly.

"You're out of your league, Miss," he says softly as Rod struggles to break free.

"I'm not *Miss*. I'm *Doctor* Rodney Gimbal, Sherman Street YMCA Golden Gloves Champion, Light Heavyweight Division, 1953, and I'll take this match any day of the week." With that, he slips out of Al's grip and takes another swing, a smoothly executed right hook which catches Sandy full on the chin, sending him tumbling down in a tangle of chairs and table. Instantly the scuffle spreads, as Aubrey steps forward and shoves Gimp, sending him back against the table and overturning several pitchers. Taunts and insults fly in both directions as the startled men struggle to regain their feet and the two women strike out at anyone they can, Aubrey with reckless abandon, Rod adopting the formal stance and careful aim of one trained to fight before a referee. Up on stage the blonde gives up her singing as the music is sharply cut off and the lights turned up. All around the room people have risen from their seats, some to move away from the ruckus, some seeking a better view, and some casting their eyes about in search of anyone in authority who will halt the disturbance.

It is a paunchy man in turtleneck and cardigan who actually steps forward, grabbing an empty pitcher from the men's table and slamming it down violently against the wooden surface with a sound that rings like a hammer blow. This brings the combatants' attention to him long enough to notice the black wallet he is holding out at arm's length, folded open to display a silver badge with gold and blue highlights.

"Cut the crap right now," he says, in a voice of calm confidence.

"Yeah, break it up," adds an equally assured bass voice from the other side of the table, as Sandy and Rod each feel a heavy hand settle on one of their shoulders. Turning, the two find themselves facing the enormous bearded man they had passed at the front door. The bouncer's expression is one of high seriousness and now that his arms are flexed, the short sleeves of his polo reveal the bulging biceps of a muscle builder. With the music stopped and the lights turned up, every eye in the room has turned to focus upon this little knot of people.

"What seems to be the problem?" asks the man with the badge, his glare virtually daring any of them to speak. It is Aubrey who finds her voice first.

"These assholes," she says, with a little snap of the head which sweeps her hair out of her face at the same time it incriminates Sandy's crew, "were making a lot of rude cracks that just don't belong here."

"That one's a pretty rude crack herself," Gimp quips under his breath to Big Al, who promptly cuffs him on the shoulder and tells him to cool it.

"Hell, officer," Whiskers responds for wider consumption, his face and back as straight as any wrongly accused man could be. "We were just having a little fun; enjoying the show, like everyone else. These two freaks here, they're the ones who were looking for a fight."

"Who threw the first punch?" asks the officer, and all eyes settle on Rod, defiantly rubbing one fisted-hand into the palm of the other, Christina's face a study in righteous belligerence as he sees the officer's expression turn quizzical. "And who did...she...hit?" Sandy's chin gives a sullen jerk forward, identifying himself as the initiator, without quite admitting he has been knocked down by this little woman.

"All right," says the cop, clearly more amused than concerned now that he understands the nature of the fight. "Looks like you two get to come with me."

Unnoticed by Aubrey or Rod, another person has been making her way through the crowd. A strikingly-tall woman, well-dressed and made-up, though a little over-formal for the setting, she appears older than most of the crowd, and her expression is not the idly-curious stare of voyeuristic amusement which predominate on their faces, but the determined look of one with a job to do. With soft 'excuse me's' and a 'let me by please,' she makes her way to the inner circle just in time to hear the cop's directive.

"I have another suggestion, officer," she interjects. "If I could just speak to these two for a second?" Seeing the cop make no move to stop her, she first turns Sandy aside, whispering something softly for his ears alone. 'I will if she will,' the others hear him answer quickly. The woman gives him a grateful nod, and one to the cop as well, then approaches Rod, looking him straight in the eye with an occasional quick glance toward Aubrey, as if to make sure she isn't going to start something on her own.

"You ever been in jail?" the woman asks, and her voice, though slightly husky, is gentle, almost motherly. Seeing him shake his head, she continues. "Well I have, and I can tell you, you don't want to go there, even for a few hours. People like you and me, we don't get along too well when they throw us into a cell with a bunch of drunks and head-bangers. So what I'm saying is, if I can keep you from going to jail, will you work with me a little bit?"

Aubrey is still wondering who the hell this woman is to butt in like this when, to her surprise, she sees Rod nodding in agreement. He seems, in fact, to have warmed to this old broad, with her plastic earrings, polyester blouse, and the strappy heels which add several inches to what would already be an impressive height. It is that height in part, which makes her next move so successful as, raising a hand in the air and placing two fingers of the other in her mouth, she produces an ear-splitting whistle which brings the crowd to something like attention.

"Listen up, folks," she calls out to the room in general, "We got a dispute going on here. What do you think we should do, let the police settle it?"

A smattering of 'Nos' and catcalls greet this. Clearly the Swedish Social Club crowd have little sympathy for the legal process.

"Maybe we should send them into the alley for a catfight," she suggests next, to be answered by a mixed bag of boos, catcalls, whistles and hoots. Aubrey gets the clear impression that the audience knows what is coming, that they are, in fact, enacting a familiar ritual. Sure enough, the woman's next question, a mock-helpless "What should we do then?" is answered immediately.

351

"Diva Duel," call several voices almost in unison. Immediately, others echo them, followed by still more, with ever-increasing confidence. The policeman - who, it is now clear, has been in-on the game for some time - breaks into a smile and turns to Rod and Sandy, speaking quietly, but with clear authority.

"The People have spoken. You two can duel it out - loser buys a round for the winner's table - or I can take you both to the station and book you in for disorderly conduct, public drunkenness, malicious mischief and whatever else I can come up with by the time we get there. What'll it be?"

Behind and around them, the crowd has taken up the call in rhythmic unison. "Diva-duel, diva-duel," they chant, and the sound is like the breathing of a great hungry beast as the stranger-woman explains to the two just how this will play out, Rod looking severely confused, like one struggling with a foreign tongue, while Sandy's smile broadens.

"I'll go first," he says, with a confidence that makes clear he thinks this a fine way to determine the pecking-order between them. Rod gives a theatrical shrug of Christina's narrow shoulders, and plops all hundred and fifteen pounds of her frame into his chair, where he takes one sullen look at the glass of scotch before him, then tosses it down in a single gulp.

As the bouncer steps back into the shadows at the side of the room and the cop returns to his table, Sandy shares high-fives with several of his companions before striding to the center of the stage without even glancing at the songbook. "In honor of our friends," he calls out loudly, nodding in the direction of Rod and Aubrey's table as he adjusts the microphone stand to his height, "I'm gonna do a little number...by the King."

"Ohhh," roars the crowd in response to this gladiator's challenge. A smattering of applause rises around the room, as voices settle into conversation, the whole exuding a palpable sense of relief at getting back to entertainment, after the recent dramatic interlude.

"You just listen to Sandy," Whiskers interjects, as the lady peacemaker borrows Sandy's chair to make herself at home next to Rod. "I seen him do this at a party once. Gets the chicks in the palm of his hand."

"This is ridiculous," Rod mutters down toward his empty glass. "I'm no performer."

"But you've got a great voice," Aubrey reminds him. "I've heard you in the shower."

For a moment Rod appears shocked, as if a great secret has been revealed. "That doesn't count," he points out, with total conviction. "This is…getting up in front of a bunch of strangers…this is not the kind of thing that a man in my position does. It's…un-professional."

To Aubrey's surprise it is the stranger who responds to this, placing a hand on Rod's shoulder as she fixes him with a look of great seriousness. "I came here tonight for a good time," she says, in the tone of one threatened with great injustice. "Not a bar brawl. If you're any kind of a real gentleman, you'll do this. For me. My name is Stevie, by the way." Straightening his shoulders, Rod reaches out to give a gentle shake to the hand she has offered, and once again Aubrey is struck by the sense that these two, despite their apparent differences, already share some common ground.

Before she can consider this any further, her attention is drawn to the stage, where the lanky steelworker has positioned himself, square in the crosshairs of the angled spotlights. Taking a wide stance behind the microphone stand, he grabs its shaft with brutal confidence, hunching slightly and tipping his head forward so a lock of hair hangs down, nearly covering his tight-shut eyes as his body goes all still, one arm and hand held halfway out, palm down in mute command for quiet. It takes a moment, but soon enough he has his silence and then, without cue to the booth, without any music to back him up, without any preamble at all in fact, but a one-sided, twisted, smirking hint of a smile, he swings into action.

"*Well since my baby left me,*" he sings, the words emanating from far inside his own deep throat, yet somehow coming out clear and strong through the microphone he holds so close it is almost part of him. Two snaps of his fingers establish a counter-rhythm which is quickly recognized, since most in the crowd have heard this tune countless times since they were little babies.

"*I've found a new place to dwell,*" Sandy adds, winking at the crowd as they eat up his pose of absolutely confident raging testosterone. "*It's down at the end of lonely street at,*" – the vowels of 'end' and 'lonely' almost yodeled in their quivering anticipation. Another 'snap; snap' and the voice swallows itself once again on "*Heartbreak Hotel.*"

The next few lines are almost whispered into the mic, the pain of the first "*I get so lonely…*" writ large across the singer's face. When he repeats the same line though, the tone turns intimate and seductive, aiming the words right in Rod's direction, causing the audience to nearly drown out *"I could cry,"* with laughter, applause and every other possible form of verbal encouragement for this dead-on impersonation. By this time, the techie in the booth has found the track on his hard drive, cued it up, and somehow managed to fast-forward it into sync so that the walking-bass line rises gradually until it forms an audible compliment to Sandy's impersonation.

From that point on, the performance is as much about movement as it is about voice. From swaying hips, to arching back, to the iconic pelvic thrusts, Sandy has it all down. He might get a little lost on the lyrics of the third verse, but his new-found fans are quick to forgive that as he undoes three buttons of his shirt and replaces the mic in its stand so that one hand can cup the back of his head while the other rubs his visibly hairy chest in mock ecstasy. By the time Sandy delivers the last *"...Heartbreak Hotel,"* - accompanied by a totally-anachronistic Michael Jackson crotch-grab - there are people on their feet, calls for his phone number from several tables, and even a pair of highly questionable Y-front underpants flying in from somewhere off stage.

With a fist pumped over his head, the new star strides proudly from the stage, high-fiving strangers all the way back to his table, which he reaches just as a barmaid arrives with two more pitchers of beer and the crowd begins to turn its eyes to the girl with the crew-cut.

"Let's see you top that, little big man," Sandy smirks, his swaggering bravado accentuated by the friends and strangers still eagerly congratulating him.

'Little' is certainly how Rod looks, as Stevie takes charge, gently urging him up and out of his chair, hoots and hollers surrounding the three as Aubrey follows her friend's unsteady legs toward the side of the stage, where the songbook lies.

"I'm no singer," she hears him protest, then turn as if to leave the stage, but Stevie is having none of it.

"This is just for fun," she says, placing one arm firmly round his shoulders while with the other she reaches out to the songbook. "And to keep you out of jail," she reminds, "So look; there's got to be something here that's familiar." Following her finger, Rod scans the titles, quickly shaking his head. Stevie flips a page, Rod shakes again, and Aubrey is aware of the crowd's impatience, the hollers bubbling and feet stomping in anticipation. Stevie turns another page, and another, until finally Rod makes a grunt and reaches out.

"That," he exclaims, jabbing Kim's slender finger at the title. "I sort of know that."

"Perfect," announces Stevie, as she slaps the list closed. Before Aubrey has a chance to see what song has been selected, the woman is leading Rod, amid a smattering of applause, to center stage. Gazing toward the booth at the rear of the room, she speaks softly into the microphone, "Number two-sixty seven," and around the audience quite a few heads bob or murmur 'ooh' in approval, as if the number has some special meaning. With a gentle pat on his shoulder she steps aside, leaving Rod standing alone at center stage, eyes casting about like one lost in a strange and threatening wilderness. Alone only for a moment though, as Stevie returns with a tall four-legged stool which she manages to shove beneath his bottom so he won't fall down - or perhaps more, to discourage him from running away. This done she proceeds to adjust the microphone's height with the ease of a professional, pat him gently on the back and whisper 'Good luck' before stepping gracefully to the side of the stage where she disappears in shadow.

Standing in those same shadows, seeing the glare of spotlights on her best friend's face, Aubrey feels for him. She can see, as he must, scores of faces aimed his way, every one expecting something from him; something special, something 'entertaining.' She has known that expectation herself - at home, in classes, at other times a whole lot more personal - and knows that, for her, it is poisonous. Her own most frequent response to that kind of expectation has been to bristle and deny, to clam up in silence, or push back with anger in order to avoid the test - and the disappointment - that she is certain will be her due. In his place, she knows, she would be frozen, as the horns pulse into the first bars of number two-six-seven. Up here near the stage, the music is louder than at their table; a pounding surf which cannot be escaped as, behind the horns, a melody emerges, woodwinds rising in a soft and comforting tune which Aubrey finds vaguely and fondly familiar, but just out of reach to identify. She feels her pulse quicken, as the all-too brief intro ends and the monitor in front of Rod comes alive, its gray-green simmer replaced by a deep blue background across which white words quickly begin streaming. "You can do this," Aubrey whispers softly, remembering her girlfriend Kim, who could always do anything she wanted.

As if to deny that optimism, the music and lyrics seem to have no effect on Rod. For several lines he simply stares at the screen, Kim's hands rising slightly from his lap in search of something to do. As the crowd reacts with hoots and comments, once again his head begins to swivel, looking all around, searching for a way out until, moving surprisingly swiftly on those teetering heels, Stevie is at his side, her focus entirely on him, as if the crowd did not exist. "*Skies are blue...*" she speak-sings with just a hint of melody, over-enunciating each word like a mother teaching her child a new vocabulary.

"*And the...dreams that you dare to...*" she sings next, still for his ears only, and is rewarded as Rod mouths the next few words just behind her. With '*Someday I'll wish upon a star,*' he manages to find the rhythm and the tempo, his lips moving at the right times, though still no sound escapes them. Finally, on '*...wake up where the clouds are far behind...,*' Rod begins to sing, and as he does, Aubrey sees his back straighten and his body relax into itself until, on "*That's where you'll find me,*" she hears Kim's voice singing out with strength and clarity that send a shiver up her spine. In that moment, time loses its meaning as Rod perches on his stool, where Christina's dis-obliging legs no longer matter as her shoulders sway just a little to the rhythm and her open hands sweep tiny arcs through the air. Aubrey hears the voice rising out of that gabardine-clad figure, and it is as if her friend has come alive once again. Except that she had never once heard Kim raise her voice in song - not in any of her performance pieces, not at the wedding of their good friends Susan and Montoya, nor at the late night parties which morphed into all sorts of performance and parody - never, in all those times, has Aubrey heard a single song escape those pursed and pulsing lips. Experiencing it now, so unexpected and yet so obviously natural, fills her with joy and heartfelt pride as her beloved Kim pulls this crowd to its feet.

For that is what she is doing, the audience responding not - as they had expected - to some awkward brat struggling to follow the music, but to the audible legacy of Sean McKloskey coursing through his daughter's body, testifying to the value of early exposure. Mrs. M. has pointed out more than once, even in Aubs' limited conversations with her, how Christina McKloskey was schooled in the art of music; marinated from birth in the greatest melodies the world can offer, filling her home before she could separate them from her own thoughts. Was taught to sing like others learn to ride a bicycle, at an age so young that her body has apparently remembered it, even if her mind chose to gallop in the opposite direction at the first opportunity. As the words stream out – lyrical visions of rainbows and blue skies, of dreams coming true and waking up upon the clouds - there is a waking in Rod's eyes as well, a look of something melting *"...like lemon drops, away above the chimney tops..."*

"Somewhere..." I sing now, and feel my body rise weightless from the stool and take the microphone stand in its hands. "Over the rainbow," the chorus continues, and I cannot help but snake my head back and to the side, spine curling all the way down to my sacrum. I am possessed by the swaying sound and an intuition that now, for the first time since I woke inside my Nothing, something feels correct. "Blue-birds fly..." is like a column of air expanding from within me. "Birds fly over the rainbow," emanates not from my mouth or my throat, but from somewhere farther down, a place below my chest even. A place inside me which is now so full it wants to spill over, to push the boundaries of this room outward and upward with waves of sonic pressure. The sight of a hand - apparently my own - rising up before my eyes, draws moist tears to their surface and 'Why then, oh why, can't I?' seems the most important question in the world, and one which I have been seeking to answer for a very long time.
"If happy little blue birds fly..." I sing, "...beyond the rainbow..." every muscle, tendon and ligament of this unfamiliar body for once cooperating. All my inconsistent memories submerge beneath this one unmistakable present, and this time when I sing "...why, oh why..." it is no question at all; for in the instant of that fluid power escaping, I understand that I am made to do this, an understanding just as real, just as definite, as the feel of my chest heaving to gather breath for the final phrase. "...Can't I..." I sing, and for all I can feel, I am flying; soaring on the strongest breeze above a rushing river of sound; brass and strings and this miss-appropriated voice flowing out to wash across the audience in harmonics that are as real and as meaningful as anything in this whole sweet world; a world which it seems I am perceiving clearly now for the very first time.

It seems a different Rodney Gimbal who bows his head, exhausted, as the dying strains of music are smothered by the sound of applause. Aubrey and Stevie rush from their places in the wings to shower him with hugs and kisses, bringing even more delighted howls from the audience. One tentative bow, and then they are helping him, weak-kneed and drained, off the platform, between the fawning tables and back to a seat beside his recent adversary, the policeman and bouncer nowhere to be seen.

"I give," the pock-faced Sandy concedes cheerfully, raising his mug in tribute. "This round's on us."

"Thank you," Rod mumbles, his entire demeanor suddenly vague and uncertain. To his friends he seems confused, shaken even, as Stevie steps in to fill the void.

"You did a great job yourself," she tells the steelworker. "You got it down, that Elvis thing."

Leaning across between the tables, Sandy speaks softly so his buddies will not hear. "Lady, that's nothing. A fuckin' party trick. But her," he says, swinging an elbow in Rodney's direction. "She's the real thing."

An hour later the trio says farewell to their neighbors, Stevie even reciting a phone number when Gimp asks for it, though she confesses to Rod and Aubrey moments later that it was a phony. A call from him, she suggests, would require more introduction than he could probably stomach. To Rod though, she gives a business card which, she takes trouble to emphasize, carries her correct information, saying she'd be happy to hear him sing again, any time.

"When that cop threatened to send us to jail," Rod asks on the sidewalk outside the club, "it sounded like you were speaking from experience?"

The woman's eyes crinkle a bit, her mouth screwing up to one side. "Yeah," she answers. "I've been to jail. Twice, if it matters." She looks down at the ground, slickly shiny from the night's gentle rain. Red, yellow and white lights reflect in its sheen and from the enameled metal and dampened glass of cars streaming by. "When you...when you don't fit into the little boxes people make in their heads, you sometimes end up in awkward situations."

Glancing over, Aubrey studies Rod's face for the expected signs of judgment and disapproval. Instead what she sees is sympathy, and real concern.

"Well," he says softly, taking Stevie's hand in his smaller one and raising it toward his face. "I suppose we can forgive that." With the slightest hint of a bow he kisses the back of her hand, surprising both Aubrey and Stevie, who pulls away reflexively, then pauses, the hand upraised between them, as if it were somehow injured, or suddenly quite precious. Embarrassed, the three exchange polite 'good nights' and walk off, Rod and Aubrey in their direction, Stevie in her own.

The auto-rickshaw driver who brought Elaine to the Landing District had shown zero interest in waiting while she searched for her DikSaka, and no cabs cruise its derelict streets; nor are there any busses or trams in the early morning hours; as a result of which circumstances, the eastern sky is beginning to glow by the time she makes her way back to the guest house. When finally she does recognize its weathered wooden doorway, the night shutter is in place across the barred opening, yet her first knock brings an almost instant response. As soon as she is inside it is apparent that something unusual is going on - lights burning in the hallways, the kitchen in full swing, and women scurrying all around. Seeking the source of the commotion, she follows the lights upstairs to find Beryl's door open and her friend in the middle of the room with all her modest belongings spread out upon the bed.

"Oh, there you are," Beryl exclaims, placing a hand to her own breast in relief. "I was afraid I'd have to leave without you, and then you'd have to catch up with us and who knows what that might entail, and...Well. You're here now; that's what really matters." Apparently satisfied with that exposition, the woman resumes her task, folding each garment precisely, then stacking some inside a nylon rucksack, while the majority go in a pile to the side. A moment later she looks again at Elaine, as if quite surprised by something.

"Shouldn't you be packing?" she asks, then, before Elaine can speak, answers her own question. "Ah, but you don't speak Bengali, do you? So they won't have been able to tell you. Well, my dear. The long and the short of it is, things have come together a bit more abruptly than I might have wished it, so...we are leaving again."

"Today?" Elaine asks, thinking of the sleepless night she has just spent and the events of the past hours - which she would dearly love to discuss with her mentor. Apparently though, these will have to wait, as Beryl launches into more of her fragmented explanation. Some 'arrangements' have been made, it seems, for travel to one of her 'special places,' and these 'arrangements' are only good for a very short time, which means that not only are they leaving Kolkata today, they must actually be on a plane before noon, and what with the traffic coagulating even now in the city's streets, they need to be packed and out the door within the hour.

"No, no," she concludes, waving off all further discussions. "No questions. The ladies will bring your tea, you just get yourself washed up and packed and we can discuss it all on the plane."

Air India flight 9853 takes off from Netaji Subhash Chandra Bose International Airport right on time, at 11:53 AM, Asia/Kolkata time zone, bound for Bangkok. For the first few minutes of the flight, Beryl Nathanson is occupied: organizing and stashing away travel papers and receipts from their stay in Kolkata, tallying the cash changed from Indian Rupees to Thai Bhatt during their mad dash through the airport, along with various other mundane necessities of globe trotting. It is not until after the captain has advised her passengers over the intercom that they may leave their seats, and the attendants have begun their beverage service, that she turns to her companion in seat 27 C. Outside the window and far below, the green waters of the Bay of Bengal glisten and ripple like a living beast. Somewhere beneath its surface, Olive Ridley turtles glide, and Irrawady dolphins dart, but Elaine is not looking for these. Right leg draped across her left, hands folded peacefully in her lap, head slouched against a tissue-paper-cased pillow, she sits with eyes comfortably shut and the steady, unselfconscious breathing of one deeply and deservedly asleep.

Explanations, as it happens, will have to wait a bit longer.

"I..."

"What you're doing is moping. Sitting around like a spoiled teenager who doesn't know what she wants to do with her life and won't risk getting involved in anything because it might not turn out just like her Barbie-doll fantasy."

"Where do you get this, young lady? This pseudo-psychological babble that you come up with? Some supermarket magazine plucked from the rack between True Romance and the Racing Form?"

"Well at least *I* get out *to* the supermarket," Aubrey shoots back, her focus blown by the unfamiliar references and being spoken to once again as if she were a child in her own home. "At least I..."

Aubrey feels her frustration peaking once again - a feeling all-too-familiar these days. It had been better - for a little while. For two or three days after the club there was a hint of brightness in Rod's attitude. She'd even caught him singing once, when she came in from work, though of course he stopped as soon as he realized Aubrey was there. Said he was self-conscious about his voice, because it sounded so 'feminine' – the very word pronounced like it was a foreign object, like it stuck in his throat even to say it. Kim's acting again, laying it on; thick as the makeup on a Capitol Hill drag queen.

The change had been short-lived in any case. Within the week he was back to his old routine, sitting around listening to ancient music, drinking scotch all day while complaining about the noise from the highway, the size of her place. Advising Aubrey what foods they must eat and how to cook them, though he wouldn't admit to being able to tell a tablespoon from a soup spoon or a sauce pan from a fryer. It was like, the more helpless he claimed himself to be, the more certain he was of how other people should be doing their own things.

Even worse was this whole parent-child bit, 'Rod' talking down to her just like...she can't say exactly who it's just like, but it sure as shit jabs at someplace deep inside her. Like when she made the mistake of mentioning that she'd popped a little vitamin-S to get her through a shift one Saturday night and he made it sound like a federal offense - half an hour's speechifying on possible side effects: tissue damage which was documented to result from prolonged use, the neural mechanisms that facilitate physical addiction and the incredible burden which 'the drug-abusing general population' placed upon 'responsible practitioners doing their best to serve those who truly require medication.' It was enough to make a girl throw up her hands and growl in frustration, which, she realizes as the recollections wind and rewind through her head, is precisely what she is doing right now.

"All right," Rod shouts in return, slamming his hand against a stack of CD boxes, sending them flying across the floor like cards being dealt across a poker table. "I'll get out of the house, if that's what you want me to do, I'll get out of your precious little slum of a house."

Watching how difficult it is for the character to get his legs beneath him, to lever his body up with the aid of the sofa arm, Aubrey wonders if at least that part of it all *is* real: if maybe Kim's body really *is* fucked up some way, from the medications they used to keep her quiet back there; or the brain stuff that happened while she was in the hospital; or maybe even whatever drugs she took that night at the club. The idea makes Aubs feel guilty all over again, that she is giving her friend such a hard time when maybe the girl can't help it.

"Where you going, then?" she asks, softening her voice as much as she can.

"Out," is all the answer she gets, delivered in full 'Rod' mode. No compromise, no suggestion he has noticed her attempt at peace-making. Taking a cane from where it leans in the corner, he is at the door, hunched over and bitter-faced. "Just out," he says, and is gone.

Elaine squats by the side of the trail, wide skirt hiding her business from the porters loitering not ten paces away. Something she has learned to do quite comfortably in all this journeying, where plumbing is a distant memory and the most basic privacy so often seems a bourgeois luxury. Other things she has learned: the Customs inspection upon entering Bangkok from Kolkata is at least as stringent as that from San Francisco into Tokyo; one night in a very cheap and uncomfortable hotel is not sufficient time to recover fully from even a mild case of food poisoning; and a day spent on the district bus system is no better. Travelling overland from northern Thailand into the extreme western corner of Laos following a truck loaded with crates labeled in multiple languages and alphabets, on the other hand, *can* be reasonably comfortable - if one is seated in an air-conditioned Range Rover with an official of an Australian company that holds a major bauxite concession straddling both sides of the border. And, perhaps the most memorable lesson of all: crossing the border from Laos into China is not at all comfortable when the remote and ramshackle border post appears totally deserted upon approach, and one must leave both Ranger Rover and Australian on the Laotian side and walk across the freshly-limed line to climb up into the cab of the truck as its cheerful Thai driver is replaced by an un-smiling Chinese girl of no more than seventeen who slams the vehicle into gear as soon as the doors are shut and takes off without any introductions, then proceeds to check the rear-view mirror every three seconds for the first two kilometers before heaving a great sigh and spitting out the window. Twice.

For the first few days after leaving Kolkata, Elaine found herself given only bits and pieces of information as Beryl was repeatedly interrupted by calls on the cell phone she had unexpectedly adopted, or was pulled away for a succession of meetings with what were described only as 'old acquaintances.' Indeed, the recent days have created in Elaine a whole new regard for this woman, who appears to have organized, at some remove, the acquisition and shipment of what must be a ton or more of supplies. She has also overseen the dispersal of those goods – in a very small hamlet west of Jinghong in the province of Yunnan – among their trail party (several of whom Elaine takes by their appearance to be ethnically Chinese but most of whom look more akin to the Nepalis of Elaine's limited acquaintance, leading her to surmise that they may well be Tibetan), and has, by uttering an astounding string of pidgin-Mandarin one misty early-morning, set the whole apparatus into motion on a generally westward heading.

"I apologize for not telling you before," Beryl said in one of their trailside conversations, the sincerity of her remorse all the more affecting coming from one so habitually free of regrets of any kind. She had been explaining to Elaine the reason for their companions, the seventeen prune-faced little men with bundles and boxes lashed to their backs who have accompanied the women ever since they set out from that hamlet. 'Supplies,' she had said, the first time the subject came up, shortly after their departure from Bangkok. When Elaine raised the subject once again, later in the same day, she had admitted the 'supplies' were not for the two of them, though the very magnitude of the cargo made that quite obvious.

Huffing along another stretch of trail two days later, Elaine puzzled again. She had never known her guide – which was how she had come to imagine Beryl in these days; a guide, as Humphrey Bogart was guide to Katherine Hepburn, piloting the African Queen on an apparently endless journey through a mysterious swamp to an unknown destination for an unfathomable purpose – she had never known Beryl to be at a loss for words, or the source of an idea. Now though, the closer they came to her destination and the more she purported to share their purpose, the more she seemed to be hiding something.

This woman, who had always seemed so transparent, her joy in life as clear as day, had abruptly become opaque and secretive. Observing her huddled with the porters one morning, Elaine had seen her hand the lead-man a mass of currency, wadded up and rubber banded, without counting or receipt. On the trail there were several anxious moments when a porter would come running back from ahead to chatter nervously with the head man, who would then confer with Beryl, their faces turned to the ground, eyes away from one another as they spoke in muffled voices; postures that reeked of shame, or worse, dishonestly. Once, Elaine had seen the man pounding a fist into the palm of his other hand, a gesture of frustration which required no translation.

"For some families in a remote valley," Beryl admitted another time, as the human snake progressed along a foot-wide track carved into the side of a narrow valley, the walking surface completely hidden by a knee-high tangle of wet vegetation beneath the canopy of sixty-foot trees so closely spaced their branches nearly blocked out the sun. 'Some families,' in a village she had visited before and to whom she had taken a liking - 'developed a sympathy,' as she blandly put it.

"They had so little," Beryl added, beaming as if that lack were in fact a great achievement. "I felt, as soon as I arrived there, that I had reached a destination, though on the map...well, it wasn't even on the map. Not my map anyway. Nor any I have seen since. Blank space; empty land; and yet, people were living there, raising crops, children. 'Far from the sight of God.' Not my words, by the way; that's a quote. From...somewhere. I don't know."

Their fifth day along the trail now, and something seems to have changed once again, a bit of the old Beryl coming back to the surface as the two take a break under a sky roiling with cloud. Perhaps it is the weather; for the atmosphere has definitely turned cooler. For some time they have been climbing, and the vegetation changing - from semi-tropic vines and fronds, to more of a forest feel. The trees' trunks are thicker, their leaves smaller. Beneath the canopy, rather than the complete tangle of the lowlands, individual seedlings and shrubs are now visible, some with seductive purple berries. The cover is still dense, patches of direct sunlight rare and clearings rarer still, but it is apparent that the trail is heading for higher ground, which explains why Beryl had provided them both with warm jackets before setting out from steamy Bangkok.

"I don't like secrets," Beryl says, as Elaine stands, her business completed, and removes a plastic vial from her pocket to squeeze a bit of its sanitizing gel onto her hands. As always, the two smile at this lingering touch of American fastidiousness so far away from home. "One does not ask a friend to keep one's secrets. It is not fair to the friend. Nor is it, generally, very effective."

Elaine, finished with her hand-cleaning, is about to speak in her own defense, when a wave of Beryl's hand tells her it is not necessary.

"The time for secrets is over," says the older woman, her face for once devoid of its usual good humor. "It's time you knew where we are really going. And why."

365

44

"Singularity Bytes," Stevie answers into the air of her car. She is steering across the floating bridge on her way back from meeting at a client's shop in Kirkland. Traffic is light, the day gloriously clear, and her mood upbeat. Bluetooth allows her to keep both hands on the wheel as she waits to hear who is calling her this time.

"Miss Margulies?" a voice asks - female, and youngish. Vaguely familiar but not instantly recognizable, its attitude an odd mix of timid timber and commanding cadence. "This is Rod. Rodney Gimbal, from the club last week?"

Oh yes, Stevie recalls, and says as much. She remembers the young transman, with his lovely voice and hands, his belligerent attitude and weakness for Scotch. Intrigued, she listens as the voice explains he's hoping to see her again.

"I'd like that, Rod, I'd really like that." Stevie swallows hard, as she always does when this part comes. "Only there's something I need to explain first. Just so we're all on the same page."

A too-short time later, cruising up the connecting ramp onto I-5, Stevie consoles herself with the assurance that she has done the right thing. Better to be up-front from the start, she is certain, than to shy away from the truth and add deceit to the list of her lifetime's sins. The boy's reaction was not totally unanticipated; Stevie has encountered it plenty of times before, and accepted that she will encounter it many times again. It's just a little surprising, coming from him.

Over the last few years, following her own descent into anger, doubt and despair, it was largely thanks to the help of strangers that Stevie found a way through. These days she believes the world has allowed her a place; has opened up much wider than expected and made a bit of room in which she can be herself. Her hope, when Rod explained who he was, was that she could return the favor, could help him learn to be more comfortable in his own skin. That would have been very gratifying, and maybe even fun. What a pity then, that one so obviously trying to find his own special place in the world, should deny others theirs.

A pity, she thinks, as she merges into the main stream of traffic, but hardly unexpected.

"Before I tell you though, I want to know - what happened when you went to see the Teacher."

Elaine hesitates. Her visit to the odd little monk has left unsettling shadows on her mind. His suggestion that she had come on her journey for a reason seemed, at first, plainly incorrect. Certainly she *had* had a reason for leaving her own home and heading for the Marquesas: a simple desire to get away, to take a break; relax. To see something different than the walls of her own home, her usual errands and friends. The fact that, in doing so, she was actually leaving her husband of so many years, well...that had come about by accident, hadn't it? It was Rodney who decided not to come with her, all she had done was to stick to her plan. It was not as if she had ever actually specifically decided to leave him, it just...happened.

In any case, if there was a deeper reason for her journey - either the one she originally intended to take, or the more extensive one she was upon by the time of that night in Kolkata, or the even more surprising one on which she now found herself - it was to *get away* from things, not to find them.

"He asked me what I was searching for," Elaine answers, as if the issue were of no import. "He said every life is a journey, and everyone who journeys is searching for something; but I don't know that I agree with that. It is one way of looking at things; but it doesn't apply to me. I'm not looking for anything, I just wanted to get away from my life...from my normal routine."

"Well," Beryl says with a laugh, "You have certainly done that." In the pause which follows, her face gradually adopts an expression of great seriousness. "Is that all he said?" she continues. "All you have thought about?"

Uncomfortable, Elaine does not answer immediately. Certainly she has thought about their conversation. About the Teacher mostly, why he seemed so...not sinister exactly; he was clearly not evil - but just as clearly privy to something to which others did not have access. Perhaps it was the setting, that odd little space off a back alley in a foreign city. Perhaps she was simply overloaded with the new, the different, the challenges of travel. Suddenly Elaine finds herself longing to be home - in her own rooms, her own bed, eating the food she knows and doing the ordinary household tasks which would be so familiar and so safe; which would reinforce her notion of who she is - rather than here, where everything seems to challenge that notion, urge her to consider and reconsider and possibly to change. Suddenly she does not want to change a thing about herself. Not one thing.

"He said: to learn what you are seeking, ask what it is you want and do not have. I have - or, at least, when I was at home I *had* - everything I wanted or needed."

There is no immediate response. For some seconds Beryl seems frozen, neither moving nor speaking, and Elaine feels a breeze touch her cheek, carrying a scent of something sweet. Looking up she sees a bush a few yards away, its branches punctuated with enormous coral-colored flowers. Perhaps that is the source of the scent. Perhaps she should get up and walk to that bush, lift a blossom between her fingers and hold it to her nose, to drink in the sweet fragrance. Perhaps...

"Not true," Beryl declaims, like a schoolmarm admonishing a disappointing pupil. "What you do not have is quite obvious and has been since the first evening we met."

Flowers forgotten, Elaine looks at her friend and is struck for the first time by how much she has in common with that Teacher - a certain tightness in the corners of her eyes, a particular erectness of posture, a way of speaking more softly the more important the words, all suggest the two share a common understanding of the world, and so Elaine waits.

"We were sitting at our table in that horrid airport café. I was pouring tea. You may not even remember it, because for you this was a normal occurrence, one I suspect you have repeated innumerable times and so its meaning has been lost to you, but for me it was new and striking. A young woman came into the restaurant, only for a moment. She asked the hostess a question, received directions to something - somewhere - and then she left; but the important thing was, she was not alone. In her arms was an infant, all wrapped up in a soft blue blanket and a matching cap - hand-knitted, Delft-blue with five-petaled yellow flowers." Beryl's eyes are closed now, her body still, and as she speaks her head rises slightly, neck arched back, as if she is straining to focus upon the scene being replayed on the inside of her eyelids.

"She had another child, a little older, trailing behind by the hand. Dressed in a corduroy jumper - navy-blue - with a white cotton blouse underneath. Frilled cuffs and princess collar; tiny ebony buttons right up to her chin, and dark hair tied back with two white ribbons. The girl looked exhausted, as did the mother - it was the middle of the night after all, and she had a bag slung over each of her shoulders. Some people would look at that scene and think, how terrible, to be travelling alone with two small children in the middle of the night. How hard that woman's life must be, how glad I am that I am not her. But what I remember most - the reason, Elaine, that I remember the incident at all - is the look on your face. Your eyes came to life when you saw that young mother. In that moment all your cares disappeared, as you watched that mother with her children, and when they left, the radiance persisted in your face for several minutes, until your cares came back again, stuffing the light down underneath the surface, where you hide it nearly all the time. So do not tell me there is nothing missing from your life, my dear. Nothing you are searching for. I know better."

Had those last words been spoken harshly, as an admonishment, Elaine might have found them intrusive, even threatening. Unfortunately for her, they were delivered with the utmost gentility, the way one might say, reaching to another, 'here, let me help you up,' or 'may I give you a hand with that.' An offer rather than a threat; and so Elaine has no easy way to reject them, no superficial reason to dismiss her friend's contention, and so she does the only things she can do at that moment and in that place. Feeling her hands' desire to rise toward her face, she clasps them in her lap, pressing the flesh of one against the other until both ache. Feeling the emotion boiling up within herself and making for her eyes, she shuts them as tightly as the muscles of her face will allow, and presses her lips together so they do not tremble as she waits for composure to return, burying impossible longing once more beneath the landslide of the ordinary.

Moments later Elaine opens her eyes to find the porters stirring, Beryl speaking softly to one and then another, her words received without visible response. As they hoist their burdens once again, she returns to Elaine's side.

"Enough secrets," she says, giving Elaine's arm a reassuring squeeze. "We walk, we talk. We understand."

"What the fuck is this?"

Aubrey holds a plastic bag at arm's length, the purplish contents crushed in her fist. Behind her the refrigerator door hangs open, revealing a jug of orange juice, half a watermelon, a family-sized bottle of ketchup, and precious little else. She has just returned from a shift and, driven by hunger, scoured the cupboards and refrigerator for something to eat.

"Prosciutto," Rod answers with a shrug.

"No. Not *what* is it; I mean, what the fuck *is this*? I mean," Aubrey continues, reading off the package's label, "nine-ninety-seven a pound for lunch meat? It's like, come on! I can't even pay my god-damn phone bill and you're buying fucking prosciutto at fucking Andre's Mediterranean Deli?"

Rod is standing, slumped against the kitchen door frame, a short scotch in one hand, clad only in a fraying beach-striped bathrobe which reveals skinny legs grown-in with fine brown hair. Red-rimmed eyes and the uncombed friz on his head reflect a succession of late nights and poor sleep.

"I was passing by," he begins, with the bored air of one lecturing a slow pupil, "and a poster in the window reminded me of something. A place Elaine and I went once – Moltacino. In Tuscany. We had lunch in the courtyard of a restored stone farmhouse, under a green and white striped awning, looking out over hillsides covered with acres and acres of olives, and grapevines, and long lines of fruit trees - pears and peaches and lemons. There were goats wandering right between the tables and they served us pieces of green melon wrapped in prosciutto, with some sort of vinegar drizzled over the top. When I saw that poster in the deli yesterday, I had the strongest urge to experience that sensation again, the cold sweetness of the melon standing up against that tart vinegar, and the prosciutto, salty and chewy as taffy, wrapped around them both. But when I got home and put a rolled-up strip of prosciutto in my mouth, I couldn't taste it. Nothing. Like cardboard in my mouth." He takes a pull on his scotch. "I didn't even bother cutting up the melon. It's there somewhere, in the fridge."

Aubrey sighs, long and deep and loud enough that Rod cannot possibly miss it, or its meaning. They have had these conversations before, her sigh says, and she is fed up with them. Ever since she brought Kim to her apartment, money has been tighter than a Republican budget. Food for two, new clothes for one, medicines, and now scotch - all the time more scotch - have eaten up Aubrey's take-home. Even with the extra twenties from her visits to Mrs. McKloskey, the little she'd ever had in the bank has dribbled to almost nothing, and her old friend/new roommate has not shown any sign of seriousness about bringing in her share.

"Kim," She begins only to be cut off before the syllable is complete.

"I am not Kim," the girl reminds her. "I'm not Kim and I'm not Chris. I'm Rodney Gimbal."

This time Aubrey does not sigh. Reaching back farther than is really necessary to cock her arm she rockets the bag of meat as hard as she can, across the room and into the kitchen sink where it knocks down several glasses and mugs that have collected there. The shattering of glass rings through the small space, followed by a long and rather shocked silence which lasts until she speaks.

"Baby, you are my best friend in the whole wide world and I am trying to remember to call you how you want me to, but I have had it up to here with this game. Acting like you're so much better than me; better than everybody. You are not a fucking doctor. You are not sixty years old, you were never married to a woman named Elaine and I'd bet my sorry ass you have never been to Tuscany. You're a twenty-three year old punk with a chip on your shoulder the size of Tennessee because of I-don't-know-what and until you admit that, I may just not say another word to you."

To Aubrey's great surprise though, her speech elicits not the expected angry response, but a sly smile on her friend's face.

"What?" Aubrey responds, frustration raising her voice to near-scream level. "You think this is funny? You think this is some sort of a game we're playing here?"

"I was just thinking," Rod answers genially, the smile still there, even growing a bit. He takes a sip from the glass he seems always to have near at hand, looking very relaxed as he settles back against the door jamb. "About something Stevie said." Pause - a long one this time - then a slight cock of the head as he pretends to question whether to speak, and then decides to go ahead. "About you. And me. About why you get angry sometimes."

"I get *angry* 'cause you do stuff that *makes* me angry. Like leaving your shit around, and eating all the food and making me spend money I don't have and...who is Stevie, anyway?"

"Stevie Margulies. We met her at the club that night?"

"That..." Even as she stops herself from saying what she is thinking, Aubrey feels the need to sit down. Resting an elbow on the kitchen table, she rubs her forehead, remembering. The woman and Rod had hit it off pretty well after all the ruckus died down. She remembers coming back from the bathroom to see them sitting there, heads tilted together in a conversation which suddenly stopped as they saw her approaching. The guilty looks on their faces, like a couple of high-school chicks caught gossiping.

So they were talking about her, were they? Then again, who the hell *was* it that was talking about her – was it good old Rodney, sixty something and pining for his lost wife, striking up a conversation with some new woman he met in a bar? Or was it her old friend Kim forgetting her cover-story long enough to make contact with the kinky... No, Aubrey decides, quite consciously, I am not going to stoop that low.

"Ok," she asks instead, arms crossed firmly as she eyes the smirking figure in its second-hand bathrobe. "Exactly what did your new girlfriend – if we can call her that – say about me?"

"She said," Rod answers, "that you were right. I do need to get out more. She said I should come visit her at a restaurant where she plays background music. The Dogpen or something like that. And she said I should try getting some kind of a job, even if it has nothing to do with medicine."

That can't be all, Aubrey is thinking, as Rod inhales a long, slow breath, Kim's head rolling slightly in apparent relish of the pregnant pause. He's getting too much pleasure out of this for a conversation about job prospects. Unwilling to give him the satisfaction, she waits, unfolds one arm as if to take a puff...and realizes there is no butt in her hand to puff on...then waits some more, her foot tapping impatiently.

"And," he says, drawing the word out as long as possible. "She said it was obvious to anyone with two eyes that you've got a crush on me. That the reason you get so angry all the time is because you've got this idea in your head of who you want to love, and when I don't live up to that, you turn it all around into anger at me, for being myself."

"Being yourself?" Aubrey shoots back. The need of that cigarette grown suddenly irresistible, she rifles through her purse, finds the pack and taps one furiously out, then lights it. The hot smoke is reassuring; its swirling wisps give her something to watch as she quips, "You wouldn't know your 'self' if you ran into her coming through the door. Ever since you came out of that fucking hospital you've been…"

"You see?" Rod breaks in as he turns away, switching on the oven fan and opening the window, something he insists on doing whenever she lights up in her own kitchen. "Just like Stevie said…"

"There's something you need to know about your friend Stevie," Aubrey begins, and once again is caught off guard as she sees Rod's face change in an instant.

"Yes, I know what Stevie is," he says, looking and sounding every bit as defeated as he has in all the months she has known him. Silently, she waits and soon enough he goes on.

"That night at the club? I enjoyed her company. Talking together like two grown-ups." Aubrey snorts a puff of smoke out her nostrils. Rod ignores the comment.

"The kind of woman I could be comfortable with. And she seemed to understand about me, how I feel."

Stubbing the suddenly-unappealing butt into a cereal bowl left over from some other day's breakfast, Aubrey rises to pace the small room, anger and resentment rising up into their accustomed place; familiar and safe. Anger is a good place to go, actually, when you find yourself tripped up and cheated. When, after all you've done, after all you've been though for months and months, you finally see the handwriting on the wall.

"So, when did you…

"I called her up a few days ago; I thought maybe we could meet. Of course when she told me…what she was…is…naturally, that meant we couldn't."

"You couldn't? You mean to say you'd be fine to go off with some old woman after all I've tried to do for you, but now that you know she's a trannie…? Oh, no - Mr. High and Mighty Doctor Rodney Gimbal could never stoop to that, could he? Girl, you are so fucked up, do you know that? You are so fucking fucked up I can't believe it. I…"

For a brief moment Aubrey is still, arms tightening around her own chest, watching as the smile which has been on her friend's face through all this recedes into a look of quiet disappointment. Outside, traffic shushes by; a distant horn alerts someone to something, but in the kitchen there is silence. She takes in a large breath, about to go on, but none of the words that come to mind can possibly communicate the jumble she is feeling - of bafflement mixed with betrayal, anger alloyed with need, and tension competing with a fatigue that is of its own causing - and so eventually she lets the breath out again, feeling the deflation of her lungs like something precious oozing away forever. On the table, the pack of cigarettes beckons, promising distraction. A welcome pause in which to find her words, except that right there beside the pack sit three dirty glasses and a cereal bowl with one amber-filtered butt nose-down in a sea of milky dregs, like the sunken wreck of some movie starship. She can actually smell that soggy mess, the bite of stale milk mixed with wet ash; one whiff sufficient to make her entire life seem like a soggy stinking fagged-out butt, and in this moment Aubrey wants nothing to do with any of it. Scooping up the cigs with one hand and grabbing her purse with the other she steps into the next room, gathers up the sweater she had tossed across the arm of the couch only minutes before, crosses the space in two long strides, and is out, slamming the door hard enough behind her that several of the sweatshirts, jackets and other garments hung upon it bounce right off their pegs, hanging briefly in the air before falling to the floor with a desultory 'whump.'

Still standing in the kitchen after the door's slam has died out, Rod speaks softly but aloud, Christina McKloskey's shapely mouth and sonorous voice rendering the words at once both wistful and dismissive.

"Women," he says to no one but himself, "I'll never understand them."

"You should understand my dear, that when I first visited this part of the world, it was a very difficult time. The entire region was just beginning to open after the war and the reprisals that followed it, so there were not many foreigners around, even fewer foreign women. I came to search for my brother Anthony, who had been reported missing in Laos years before and was presumed dead. Of course he was never officially there, even before he went missing - no Americans were supposed to be there at the time he disappeared, but everyone knew they were. The local people. Their government. Our government. Reporters. That's another reason I don't like secrets: they're a form of discrimination. The 'right' people get to know the truth, the rest get lied to."

The crew of porters are ahead, sometimes visible, mostly not, and so the women move along the trail encased in their own bubble of conversation, two souls drawn together by circumstance, their closeness cemented by their distance from all that went before and is still going on elsewhere. Close on Elaine's heels, Beryl's face is unseen, her words meted out to suit the cadence of steps and breaths, their syllables just audible above the competing buzz of insects, swishing underbrush and slopping wet suck of earth grabbing at the soles of their boots.

"My parents never got over losing their son, and I hoped that, if I could find out where he died and how he died, perhaps it would help them. It just didn't seem fair, after all they had done - raising a son, seeing him go off to service - that their lives should be dragged out in endless years of loss and wondering.

"In any event, I came as soon as it was possible - never mind particularly easy or legal, and I followed what few clues I had. There were lots of dead ends, disappointments; and eventually I realized I was unlikely ever to find out what had happened to Tony. War leaves many traces, but generally they're just fragments, all jumbled together. People die, or they live. Other people forget, or pretend to. Places change their names, are abandoned, destroyed, and new places are created. Things begin to grow again, and become something other than what they once were. Even borders change, move around."

"Borders," Beryl repeats, a few strides later, working the word round in her mouth as if to taste it, to find its essence. Finding nothing there, she huffs a bit, shifts the daypack higher on her back and continues her monologue.

"Lines we draw on maps, and then foolishly believe they actually exist. In wars people cross borders all the time; to hide, to strike, to get supplies or find a place to rest and heal their wounds.

"As I searched around where I thought Tony might have been, I heard tales of places even more remote, in what was then called Burma, and beyond that even. The tales said that people who really truly needed to escape just kept going west until they disappeared. I never actually decided to cross any borders, but somehow I did, and eventually found myself in one of those places. A valley which was not really part of any country. Small enough that the military didn't fear it and therefore acted as if it did not exist; remote enough that the commercial interests couldn't be bothered to spoil it; and without either of those...well...basically, the government - such as it was - had no reason to take any notice of it. The valley, the villages, the people themselves.

"Those people were quite curious about me; this pale woman – old, even then, to be traveling as I was - and when I told them why I had come, they...they said they knew nothing of Tony, but they offered to find me a new brother."

Elaine halts for a moment, casting a glance behind her to see if this is meant to be humorous. It is not, and so she starts walking again.

"They were refugees, you see. Generations ago the first of their people had fled from somewhere else and come to that place where now their descendants live. Others had arrived more recently, but all of them had fled from something, and left behind most of what made up their lives, so they had acquired a habit of constructing new lives out of whatever they could, just as people in war zones construct shelter from whatever is at hand. I thanked them for the offer, but said I had no real need of a brother. I told them I had only wanted to know that Tony was at peace, and that if his end had happened anywhere near that place, then I was sure he was.

"After I had been there for some time there was a small ritual - not religious exactly, at least not that I recognized. More...domestic. At the end of it I was declared a member of their people, a citizen of the valley, and it struck me very deeply. I don't know that I could ever explain what it meant to me, and so I won't try, except to say that I knew then that we are all refugees in one way or another. Some of us seek a new place, some a new start for a broken life. Some seek a whole new identity. The luckiest among us seek only another soul or two or three in whom we can take refuge."

"Only," Elaine remarks, immediately regretting the sarcasm in her tone. Though she considers apologizing, she says nothing, worried she may already have broken the spell these thoughts seem to cast upon them both.

"Only," Beryl repeats softly, and chuckles at her own word. "You asked once why I go off by myself in some of the places we have visited. Well, in Delhi, a woman I know arranged the acquisition of a quantity of baby formula, at much lower cost than it would have been elsewhere - powdered formula which can be transported readily and used to nourish young ones when their mothers are sick, or died in childbirth, or simply have too little food to feed themselves, much less a new mouth. In Calcutta, I visited a man who sells outdated medicines; surplus from European aid agencies and the like, but still good, or at least better than no medicine at all. In Kathmandu, a whole range of items were available, that western doctors would not call medicines at all, but which the people who suffer the diseases which exist in some remote places believe will cure them - and so they often do. In Thailand, I purchased paper and pencils. And school books in a language the people of the valley can understand, so that children can be taught to read and write, and to know something of the world outside.

"And from America?" Elaine asks, beginning to catch on. "When we first met, you said you had come back to the U.S. for some sort of work?"

"From America, what America has the most of: money. To buy all those things, and to pay the porters to carry them. And especially to pay the guards and the smugglers, because it is not legal to cross foolish lines, so crafty men demand exorbitant sums of money to help one do so. And demands for exorbitant sums of money must always be paid.

"Since that first visit I have returned four times to the valley, each time bringing what I can to make their lives a little more secure. The population of the valley is growing, and as it grows so does the need, and so has my sense of belonging there. I've never found any trace of my brother and at this point I no longer look for him. What I have found instead is a feeling, wider and deeper than any other feeling I've ever had, except maybe when I was flying."

Elaine can tell by the absent noises that her companion has stopped, and so she does as well. Turning, she sees Beryl's face twisted in thought, searching inside herself for something very important.

"There were times, back when I was flying, that I felt I understood for a moment how infinity could actually exist. Ahead of me, to the left, the right, above - especially above - there was no end to possibility. Only when I thought back to what I had left behind me, or looked down to the earth below and remembered the suck of gravity, did I feel any limit to where I could go, what I could become.

"Belonging is like that as well. There is no limit to where it can take one, so long as one focuses on going forward. Or upward, or any new direction. So long as one does not attempt to go back, or allow oneself to be pulled down by the gravity of what has been left behind, there are no limits."

"So we are going to your valley?" Elaine asks, after another period of silence.

"It's late," Beryl says, less an answer than an aside, as if pre-occupied with her own thoughts. "Summer was short this year, autumn seems...impatient. Very soon the snow will start – yes, it actually does snow this far south, if one is high enough - and once it does, the passes will be closed until spring. A long time to live off only what one has managed to grow, especially in such stony soil. So, the answer is 'yes,' I am going there with what small gifts I have been able to assemble. But you..." Beryl stops herself and fixes Elaine's eyes with deadly seriousness, "Things are getting complex. It could be dangerous; or just more than you care to get involved with."

"I already am involved, aren't I?"

"You could still go back. You get to decide for yourself."

"Yes," is all Elaine replies, though she understands the word to carry a heavy freight of meanings:

'Yes, I get to decide for myself.'

'Yes, I will go with you to your village.'

'Yes, I will cross foolish lines, though I know it will likely cause me trouble.'

'Yes, I will go forward, upward, to one side or the other - anywhere but back or down.'

"What happened to her hair?" Sylvio asks, when Aubrey brings Rod in one Saturday to fill the gap left by a busser's abrupt departure into I.C.E. custody.

The two women have been doing an uneasy dance around one another ever since the comment about Aubrey's feelings, with Rod acting guilty and keeping out of her way more than usual, and Aubrey, without quite realizing it, taking great pains to avoid saying or doing *anything* that might suggest the trannie's guess was on the mark. She might, however, have been willing to admit gratitude to Stevie for one thing: that a single offhand comment from her about Rod needing to get a job had more impact than all Aubrey's jabs about how tight her finances were getting. It was clearly the only reason he would even consider giving the restaurant a try when the opportunity arose. The fact that one hint from some drag queen meant more to him than her happiness, though, tempered that gratitude quite a bit.

In any case, Aubrey had told Syl on the phone that she was bringing a friend in to help out, but had not even thought to mention anything about his appearance. It was only when she saw her boss staring at that butchered butch-cut and the clumps of extra waistband gathered under the belt of his Dockers, and saw also Rod's belligerent stare back, that Aubrey realized how accustomed she had become to her roommate's curious mix of attributes.

"It's a long story, Boss. Besides, she'll fit right in with this place."

Sylvio ignores the slight as he looks the new recruit over again; this tiny girl brimming with attitude. It is obvious to him that she has never seen the inside of a kitchen before, the way her eyes scan the stainless, the racks of knives and pans, the tubs and bins of prepped ingredients set out for the evening's rush. He's seen that look before, in kids whose parents pushed them into taking a job when all the kid wanted to do was hang out with his friends and party. The kind of kids who knew they'd eat well whether the job worked out or not. Sylvio'd much rather have someone hungry for the opportunity, even if they had no skills or education. Immigrants were the best; they expected to work hard for whatever money they got. Single mothers too. They're good workers, usually; except when they come begging to move their shifts around to deal with their brats. Still, Aubrey isn't an immigrant, or a mother - that he knows of - and she's worked out OK, so maybe...

"She's a hard worker, right?" he asks Aubrey, but it is Rod who answers.

"If you call three six-hour surgeries in one day hard work," she says, and Sylvio feels himself pinned by the threat in her eyes, like she's daring him to disagree with her.

"Ok," he admits, sidestepping the challenge. "So...the girls can tell you what to do." Turning back to his own work, he still makes a point to give half an ear as Aubrey introduces Rod to the rest of the staff and instructs her in the specifics of bussing tables. The kid seems to pay decent attention, even asking a few questions, but there is always still that attitude, as if her mind is really on something altogether separate from the proper placement of silver, the right way to pour from a pitcher without dumping a load of ice on the customer's lap. Sylvio doesn't have much time to worry about it though, as the tables soon began filling up and the kitchen to buzz with activity. By six-fifty it is a typical Saturday evening, the swinging door barely settling from one passage before being shoved open by the next foot or elbow. From the little Sylvio can see, the kid seems to be doing okay, despite being slowed by the way one foot drags behind her, and her left hand, which Aubrey tells him was injured a while back and is still a little weak.

Seems to be doing OK, that is, until Syl hears Theresa holler at her to stop hassling table seventeen about asking for more butter. Not long after, Attencio the dishwasher comes to Sylvio in a lather, complaining that the new busgirl is bringing plates and silver back to be washed again.

"She is seeing things," he tells Sylvio, shouting over the din of a kitchen in full swing. "You want to know why the counter is backed up and we don't have glasses for the water? Because she," he points a soggy towel at Rod's back as it disappears through the door to the dining room, "she looks at every plate and glass and every stinking spoon and she is seeing things that are not there, so she is bringing it back to me and telling me to wash it again."

Sylvio has a word with Rod after that, but the impression he takes away is that she's merely humoring him by listening. That impression is reinforced when Sylvio makes his round of the dining room around 7:30, shaking hands and asking each table if they are enjoying their dinner.

"The food is great," says the man at the Number 6 two-top. Gray haired and dressed in an expensive looking tweed jacket, Sylvio is pretty sure he's been in before, though not often enough to be a true regular. The woman he's with wears a dowdy brown dress, her heavy array of costume jewelry tinkling as she nods in agreement when he adds, "But if I want medical advice, I get it from my doctor, not the girl who clears away my dishes."

Sylvio laughs, and quickly sees that the customer is not amused. Chatting further, he learns that Rod had seen the man testing his blood sugar before his meal, had taken that to mean the guy was diabetic, and had then proceeded to chastise him for ordering a Coke. Sylvio smoothes things out, comps them two desserts and praises the woman's hairstyle to score a few extra points, then continues around the room. It is some time before he manages to corner Rod, busy scraping plates into a trash can near the back door.

"Hey kid," he calls as he approaches her, only to receive a perplexed look in return. "Yeah, you. I hear you've been giving the customers pointers on their diets?"

Rod continues to scrape plates, placing them on a tall pile as if she had not heard a word.

"I'm talking to you," Sylvio says, a little louder to make sure he is heard over the competition of Megan calling in an order behind him. "One of the customers says you gave him a hard time about ordering a Coke..."

"That man is killing himself," Rod responds indignantly, dirty plate and spoon held before her like a gladiator's sword and shield. "He's going to leave that woman a widow, and there's no need for it. Diabetes is a controllable condition and I would be remiss if I didn't say something when I see behavior like that." Her tone is so calm and sure of herself, it takes Sylvio a moment to remember who he is talking to. The clatter of a pot onto a hub of the big gas range, a muffled 'shit' from Attencio at his dishwashing station, and a bead of sweat trickling down his own temple remind him quickly enough.

"I don't care if he wants to drop dead the minute he's out the front door," Sylvio shouts at Rod, grabbing the spoon from her hand and waving it in front of her face. "Inside my restaurant he's a paying customer and he's free to make his own choices without getting any shit from a stupid busgirl, understand?"

"I can't believe you got fired from Sylvio's," Aubrey begins, just minutes later, shaking the wet from her hair after a mad dash across the parking lot. The sounds of the dining room are still fresh in her ears as Rod sits slouched at the far end of the seat, Kim's face all red and tear-streaked. It is after nine and a hard rain beats on the Oldsmobile's roof, threatening to drown her voice, already hoarse from an evening of shouting orders into the kitchen, where she just heard the news - and where someone is going to notice her absence any minute. "Nobody gets fired from Sylvio's unless they're…like…doing fucking drugs in the dining room or something. I mean, how can you screw up bussing tables?"

Rod does not respond, allowing Aubrey time to search the pockets of her apron for a pack of cigarettes, shake out a straggler and light it up. 'Fucking A,' she thinks to herself as the smoke fills her lungs, a slender wisp rising from the fag's tip toward the sagging fabric of the headliner. 'No paycheck for Rodney-boy after all, and Tuesday is a new month, meaning rent, and electric, and….'

"Goddamn it, Kim," she blurts out, feeling herself about to burst into tears as well, which will not help matters one bit, with hours still to go till closing. "This is fucking bullshit. We haven't got enough money to pay the bills and you go and fuck up your one chance to help out by acting as if this stupid fucking character of yours is for real."

Once again, Aubrey is reminded of the change in her friend. Kim - the old Kim - would have answered that emotion with her own; would have risen to the challenge, shouting right back in her face. This new person seems to absorb the anger without effect. Her voice as she speaks is level, serious and deadpan, though it does quaver a bit. The voice of someone badly beaten at their best game, and deeply disappointed.

"I am real, Aubrey. I am really Doctor Rodney Gimbal and I can't turn that off just because other people don't believe it."

Aubrey takes a long drag on her cig, knowing there's bound to be a table calling for her by now. Any minute Sylvio will be banging on the car window and it'll be her job on the line, too. She's just about decided to give up arguing when Rod interrupts her thoughts.

"For that matter," he says, sounding just like one of those counselors they used to send her to at school. "I've been too silent on the subject of your smoking. We both know…"

"You know what, kiddo?" she shoots back, the words carrying a puff of smoke with them. "I can't take this anymore. You pretending to be this other person, that you don't remember me or anyone else. Fucking lying around drinking and moping and me wondering when the hell you're gonna' snap out of it and be the girl I remember, the girl who was fun and wired and…" Aubrey struggles to find the right word; the one which will finally break through the façade of Rod and make Kim realize it's time to quit, but cannot come up with anything she hasn't said already. "Fun," she repeats, helplessness swamping her even more deeply as she hears the futile wimpiness of that word as accusation.

Once again, Rod doesn't answer, and Aubrey feels the frustration boiling up inside her. All the things you do for someone, and all you get in return is silence? It's not fair, she's thinking, it's not fair even from your best friend.

"You're not a fucking doctor, Kim. You're not that old man's health-class teacher and you're not my long-lost father figure, and the honest truth is, no one is going to believe a word you say about anything until you give up this fucking game and start acting like yourself."

"Someone will," Rod answers, with a finality that tells Aubrey he has been thinking a lot about this. "I'm going to keep telling people who I am until someone believes me, and then…"

"Give it up girl. No one is going to buy this bullshit. You can be Christina McFucking-whatever-that-old-lady's-name-is. You can be Kim Tree, the best girlfriend I once had. You can be lots and lots of things, but one thing no one is ever going to believe you are is some old doctor guy - who died a year ago, anyway - so if you want to keep this act up forever and ever, you can count me out. You said once you want your life back? Well, I want my life back too. I want my house to myself and I want my paycheck to myself and I want my friends and my nights out."

"All right," Rod replies with a weary shake of the head. Aubrey can see the effort it takes him to form the words against the rising tide of emotion. "I'll leave."

Seeing a hand reach for the door handle, Aubrey leans across and grabs it, only to find it is Kim's hand, small and soft in her own. Like a child's, almost, in the way it yields to her grip. Suddenly conscious of the cigarette in her other hand, she goes to toss it out the window only to find that avenue closed. She reaches for the crank, for the door handle, finds them both too far away. The car's ash-tray long-since disappeared, she finally just tosses the burning butt on top of the dash, where its smoldering tip immediately warms a circle of windshield, mist receding rapidly as Aubrey reaches around and pulls Kim's unresisting head onto her shoulder and finds herself obscurely gratified to gather in the sobs racking that precious body. For some time the two women sit, holding on to one another, as rain pours down upon the aged Olds, the splatters on its windows creating Fourth of July starbursts out of red taillights and yellow floodlights as the parking lot life goes on around them.

"I'm sorry," Aubrey mutters finally. "Jesus, Rod," she says, careful to use the preferred name. "I'm sorry I got mad at you. I want to go along with you - really, I do. It's just... sometimes it's so hard, you know?" In her arms she feels no nod of agreement, but at least the sobs have stopped, and in their absence her own direction seems clear.

"Don't go anywhere," she says, "OK? Just hang out here. I've only got a couple of tables and it's getting late - I'll tell the girls I've got the runs or something and they got to cover for me - and I'll take you home and we'll... I don't know what we'll do, but we'll figure out something... all right?" When there is no response she tries again, shifting around so she can see her friend's face; those gentle eyes staring off as if focused miles beyond the dashboard where the cigarette, still smoldering, has begun burrowing a new mark into the dusty vinyl; acrid, toxic smoke rising above it in twisting, swirling tendrils.

"We'll figure out something."

"Jake, dear," Anne's voice purrs into the phone. "You're not going to believe what I heard this morning."

Jake Brindle pulls the phone from his ear to check the time. Eight minutes past one, thanks to downtown traffic, and that incredibly slow attendant in the parking lot. It is a warm day for February, but not so warm he can blame the weather for the beads of sweat on his forehead. Putting the phone back to his ear he tucks his father's ancient leather briefcase under his arm to free up a hand, but before he gets a grip on the office building's massive door, it swings open, forcing him to step aside and make way for the outward flush of somber-faced workers, till one of them takes pity and holds the door open a moment, allowing him to move upstream into the lobby.

"This is not really a good time," Jake cautions into the phone as he scurries past the security guard behind her counter. "I'm just going into an important meeting."

"Of course you are," Anne coos back at him, "You are so industrious."

"I can't talk now, Mrs. McKloskey," Jake interjects as he approaches the elevator doors, the burnished leather of the briefcase slipping farther and farther down the smooth worsted of his suit coat. Twisting and stooping, he gets a hand beneath it, then shifts abruptly to catch the handle in mid-air. To the young woman sidestepping to avoid him he looks for a moment like a dancer, moving to some internal music, but there is no melody in it for Jake. His internal image - if he were so introspective as to characterize his activity of the moment, which he is definitely not - is closer to that of a boxer, bobbing and weaving to avoid blows coming at him from every direction. That is what this interview really amounts to, in fact: a desperate attempt to avoid the financial blows coming at him from every direction. "I'm going to lose you, Mrs. M.," he says as he presses the 'UP' button with an elbow. "I'm going into an elevator. I'll call you later." Across the vestibule a green lamp blinks as a chime rings and Jake dodges around an exiting pair of young lovelies to take his place at the rear of the cab.

"I had a wonderful conversation," he hears, as the doors begin to close, "with that young Miss ..." then silence, and the cab jerks into motion, its destination the twenty-fifth floor of the Second and Hope building - three stories directly above the now-empty offices which once housed DigiBank PR.

Moments later the elevator lurches to a stop, its doors opening with what seems to Jake a deliberate lack of urgency. Stepping into the corridor, he takes a moment to wipe a sleeve across his wet brow and straighten his tie. A glance at his watch shows eleven minutes past one - eleven minutes late. With a shake of his head and a deep inhalation he straightens his back and strides confidently through the open doors of North Coast Trading Company, whose owner, George Sawson, was a good friend of his father, back in the Alaska days.

"I'm Jake Brindle," he offers to a weary-looking receptionist a minute later, "I've got an interview with George."

"I'm sorry, Mr...Brindle. But Mr. Sawson had to leave for his next commitment. Your appointment was for one, you know. If you'd like to reschedule..."

Back home, Anne settles her phone into its receiver with a sigh of concern. The boy seems so harried these days, not at all his old self. And she had so wanted to give him her wonderful news. 'Imagine,' she planned to say, 'our Christina taking vocal lessons. After all those years of denying it, she's finally acknowledging her gift. Her father would be so proud.'

The fact that it was Aubrey who told her about this, not Christina herself, is of little consequence to Anne. Getting information through her daughter's roommate is, after all, still more direct than having to drive around town searching for her car. And there is the prospect of Aubrey's visit later this afternoon, when she comes to pick up a check for the first month of lessons - a bit more than Anne thinks appropriate, but it is for Christina, after all - and surely there will be more information then, more word of Christina's recovery. Perhaps she is drawing again as well, Anne imagines, as she heads into the kitchen to see if there is any cake mix on the shelf. Something light yet refreshing; lemon would be best, to go with their tea.

Mary Antonias does not carry a cell phone during her work day; as soon as MH took over Hilltop an edict came down from Risk Management, prohibiting their use on all floors of all buildings, due to the possibility (apparently miniscule from all the data she had found on the Internet) of interference with sensitive medical equipment. Nor does she cradle the handset of the nurse's station land-line between shoulder and ear, for at least three reasons. First, because her calls are usually not long enough in duration to require any such accommodation; second, because it can lead to neck pain due to over-contraction of the sternocleidomastoideus; and third - and most importantly - because she has seen what people look like when they do that, their necks disappearing as head and body conspire into one anatomically-inappropriate mass. No, when Mary needs to speak for more than a few seconds she stops whatever else she is doing, flips the hair back from one side of her head, and holds the phone properly to her ear, as she is doing now, waiting for Jessica Seivers to pick up.

"Blaaat...' she hears on the other end of the line, a graceless electronic irritant as a nurse reaches in front of her to grab a pen from the holder on the station counter. "Blaaat..." again as that skanky old Dr. Thomas raises an eyebrow in her direction, headed down the hall toward Mrs. Patrino's room, where he will see Mary's notes on the progression of the woman's sub-dermal streptococcus infection, which threatens to take the better part of her left calf muscle if it is as resistant to Dispermox as it has so far been to penicillin V, amoxicillin, and Veetids. "Blaaat," again, as another nurse coughs obtrusively behind her and Mary gathers her own files, turns and steps as far from the counter as the coiled cord allows, careful at the same time to avoid the oncoming wheelchair bearing an elderly man in a bathrobe and plaid slippers.

This must be the tenth time she has called, Mary muses, as the answering machine finally picks up. "This is Jessica Seivers," the familiar voice intones, "I'm not able to come to the phone right now but I check messages every day, so leave your name and number and I'll get back to you as soon as I can."

For the tenth time then, Mary leaves her information, explaining as she has each time before, that she wants just a moment of Ms. Seivers' time to ask about a mutual acquaintance. It's a bit of a stretch, but not exactly a lie, she tells herself. And much less likely to scare the woman off, it seemed to Mary at the start of this particular quest, than saying she needs to ask about a patient, with all the liability flags that would immediately raise. Once more she ends her call and once more she places the phone back into its cradle, only this time, she resolves, she will not bother calling again. Either the woman calls back, or not. Enough is enough, and Mary has more than enough to keep her busy, without trying any longer to follow up her nagging suspicion that something decidedly curious happened while that girl was here at Hilltop.

"Boyfriend?" asks a voice behind her shoulder, as Mary leaves the station. Turning, she finds Judith Baxter close on her heels, a purse upholstered in LV logos slung over her shoulder and a superior smile splashed across her tastefully-painted face. "I was just visiting Steve," the Center's most notorious gold-digger continues, with an air of triumph. When Mary does not react, she gives a little wriggle of excitement and explains. "Steve Sharpton? You must have heard of him Mare; he's been in all the papers. Got his leg broken in the game last Sunday and now he's here. I had a little time so I thought I'd cheer him up...."

Judith's conspiratorial smile gives Mary an idea. Always on the make, Judith does have an uncanny ability to learn what's going on in far-flung corners of the center, and it never hurts to ask.

"No," she begins, in answer to Jude's original question, adding a little flip of the head that spreads her hair across one shoulder. As expected, the girly-girl gesture signals just the sort of conspiracy Judith cannot resist, and the woman leans a little closer as Mary continues. "No boyfriend. Just trying to get some information." As the two stride down the wide corridor she gives a brief summary of her inquiries regarding Christina McKloskey. To her surprise, Judith shows enough interest to stop walking and urge her into a nearby alcove, standing between several parked equipment carts as the story concludes.

"So I've been trying to call..." Mary hesitates, thinking perhaps Jessica Seivers' name might be too much information. "People. People I thought might have been around at the time, might remember something."

For a moment Judith is silent, eyes scanning the traffic passing by with a focus which seems quite foreign in her. When she speaks, the excitement of her initial greeting to Mary is gone, replaced by a businesslike tone which would not be nearly so alarming, were it coming from almost any other person.

"No," Judith answers, to the question Mary has not even asked yet. "No," she says again, as if pronouncing sentence. "I don't know anything about that. But I'll let you know. If I... If I hear...," she pauses, apparently confounded as to how to proceed, until a shrug indicates decision, the brilliant smile returns to her face and her closing is delivered as if it were a great gift. "Well...anything."

Rod Gimbal moves at a moderate pace, lightly swinging the cane he
carries now as much for the dapper way it makes him feel as for any
real need, the progress of his recovery having made it almost
unnecessary, though his body still gets quite tired on these long
walks. Eleven blocks he has come, perhaps a mile and a half, by his
reckoning. Made his way up the steep hill past all those stores and
offices without having to stop even once to catch his breath, after
which he turned left for a block and a half and to where the concrete
widens and a single bench sits, facing west, over a grid of narrow
streets and tiny houses boxed side-by-side, to the open water of
Puget Sound. It is the fifth time he has made this journey to what
he's come to think of as 'his' bench, each time arriving a little less
worn-out.

      Pleased with today's exercise, he takes position on the
wooden slats, acknowledging the slight inflammation of joints
stressed beyond their habit, the tightening of muscles as the heart
rate slows and blood flow returns to normal, the slight ache from
lactic acid build-up and those pesky enzymes stimulated by calcium
leaking out thru cell membranes to eat away the muscle fibers
themselves. Mildly uncomfortable, the anatomist in him would
readily admit, but all part of the building process, and hardly enough
discomfort to outweigh the knowledge that he is gaining strength
with every step.

      A glorious winter afternoon. One of those infrequent days
when the westerly flood of oceanic air has halted briefly, allowing
Seattle's horizons to clear. Here and there a puffy tuft of cumulus
dots a sky so blue it seems painted overhead. Beyond the streets
and houses of Ballard, a forest of masts rise above roof ridges,
announcing the docks of the fishing harbor, and way off beyond
them the Olympic Mountains rise, their blue-green masses edged
and rent by the streaks of snowfields which are visible more as an
absence of color than a presence of anything else. Angling his head,
Rod positions his face to soak up the sun, which he can already feel
baking his chest as well, through his customary shirt and t-shirts. As
always, the clothes are a poor fit, slacks pulled tight by the shape of
his rear, while pleats of excess material around the narrow waist are
cinched together with a belt whose length escapes from its loops to
hang long, like a snake's half-shed skin. The shirt hangs loose across
his shoulders - purposely large so as not to show off the figure he

prefers to hide, and its sleeves bunch clumsily at the wrist. Once again he is reminded that nothing these days ever fits him quite right - fits both his mind *and* his body, that is. One or the other is achievable, but the two of them together...

These idle thoughts are halted now, by the sudden awareness of someone standing near, and a flush of irritation at the thought of encountering yet another stranger. Aubrey, for all her faults, at least *attempts* to make herself accept him for who he really is, but strangers these days, no matter how well intentioned, all seem to reveal something else in their eyes. Curiosity is the least of it; the most-benign reaction to his hybrid appearance. More often there's a sort of dismissal - or even revulsion - in the faces of those who read him as a misfit, a weirdo, a non-conforming outcast. From the first days at that woman Anne's home, to the courtroom with Auster, to his fruitless encounters with old associates and new acquaintances, every individual he has encountered seems to have their own template in which they try to make him fit. There seems no one anymore, with whom he can simply be himself.

With a slight turn of the head, he glimpses through the corner of his eye the person whose presence he has sensed. A tall man, broad shouldered in a sport coat and slacks. Shirt unbuttoned at the collar, the jacket creased and rumpled, the face in need of a shave, he stands ten feet away and turned halfway aside, as if he's no more certain he wants to meet than Rod is. For a few moments Rod pretends to study the view, then, when the other has not left, begins to rise from his bench.

"Don't go," says the stranger, giving the impression of one forming his words with great care. Crossing quickly, he sits on the far end of the bench, then continues, in a voice that is distantly familiar. "It's okay," he says. "Everything's okay."

"I was just about to go," Rod says, clearing his throat between words to bring down the plaintive tone of this new voice he's wearing – its feeble timber another reminder of how vulnerable he is these days, and a hint of what it must be like for them. The women, that is. To feel this thread of threat, woven through the most ordinary encounters. Through all his decades Rodney Gimbal would have thought nothing of it, secure in his own ability to deal with anyone who came along, but not today; not anymore.

"No. You weren't about to go," says the stranger, "you just got here." That simple truth is tossed out as a challenge - for Rod to leave now would be an admission of fear - and has its desired effect, compelling him to remain. "You're getting pretty fit these days; hardly even need that," the stranger adds, one hand flipping out to indicate the cane, then pulling back into his lap, to nestle with its other, rubbing away as if fighting against cold, despite the beaming sun.

"Oh, that's not for walking anymore," Rod offers, semi-seriously, "but it'll come in handy if I need to fight a duel." Raising the cane, he flashing it in a figure-eight through the air then, realizing the effect is far more comical than threatening, looks around for passersby, or traffic, and finds none. Only himself and this stranger, with his square jaw and broad shoulders...and that casually-resonant voice - where has he heard that voice before?

"Oh, you're a fighter all right, know that," the stranger agrees, a remark which Rod realizes could indicate the man has any of several associations with his various histories. Some Gimbal family connection perhaps, with knowledge of his childhood athletics - but that seems unlikely in this time and place. Absent that, the comment could be a reference to his early medical career; the persistence and intensity with which he drove himself might well be described as combative.

"When the work requires it," Rod agrees, inviting contact with any such strand of his past, but another glance at the man reveals him far too young to be a part of Dr. Gimbal's training years. The connection must be more recent then; from his work at the Center, but this man is certainly not a colleague, judging by the disheveled - almost desperate - look of him. Maybe, then, a patient, someone whose life he fought to save? Naturally there are far too many of those for him to remember every face. "It sounds like you speak from experience."

"Of course I do. Let's not play this game anymore, okay? You know exactly who I am."

"I'm sorry...I don't seem to remember as well as I should. Things have gotten a bit...muddy...in here." Rod points to his head as he stalls, eyes and mind searching to define a vague connection he's feeling, to that voice, that chiseled face and hulking bulk - to something back in the early days of this existence, when everything was so new and confusing.

The stranger is looking straight at him now, eyes roving over Rod's face and body. Scanning his chest, his legs, his shoes, and back again; examining every inch of flesh and fabric, as if looking for signs of disease. Despite long sleeves and slacks, despite buttoned collar and solid oxford shoes, Rod feels almost naked before those searching eyes, which seem to strip the clothes from his body, revealing private secrets he himself is loath to look at.

"I remember," the stranger says, "how you walked. Like a rooster, with your tits pushed out and your ass up high. Proud of yourself. Proud of being Kim Tree."

Which clinches it, of course; this is not anyone from *Rod's* life after all, but another envoy from that other history he does not recall, who believes he is talking to the girl they all seem to remember and Rod does not, and then it comes together – it's one of those voices from outside the Nothing. This man was there, then. And later too, at the apartment door, the wild one who tried to get past the chain; Rod only glimpsed part of a face that day, contorted and straining at the opening, and one long arm, reaching through the narrow gap, but is sure now that it was him, and at the courtroom as well, sitting with Mrs. McKloskey. Leaning close to her, murmuring, then festering in anger as Jim Auster worked his magic. Sent here now perhaps, by Mrs. M., to try to bring her 'daughter' back by force? Surely she wouldn't stoop that low. She may be loony, but not criminal. Not a woman of their generation.

"These days you look like you have something to be ashamed of," the stranger continues, accusingly. "It's not right, you know. You should be proud of who you are."

"I'm not..." Rod begins, only to have his words cut off.

"You can't fool me. I see it in your eyes. You can cut off your hair and wear men's clothes. You can do anything you want, but I know when I look in your eyes that it's you and that you know me." Again, Rod begins to interrupt but is halted, waved off with a dismissive hand, washed over by the larger voice, so fluidly emitted, so comfortable in itself. "I don't know why you're doing this, but you can't fool me. I know it's you and I'm not going to let your girlfriend Aubrey or any high-priced lawyers take you away from me."

Another detail comes back, from conversation with Aubrey; a puzzle piece whose shape has suddenly materialized before him. Proudly, he pushes it into place. "You're Jake, aren't you?"

"See, you do know me." The stranger's voice is triumphant. Vindicated and more sure of himself than ever.

"No. I mean...yes. A little bit. You tried to visit us once. And from before; I remember hearing your voice. And I've also been told...Aubrey told me, that she...that girl, had a..."

393

"How could you not know me? After all the things we've done together, after all we've been to each other."

As they've been speaking Jake has moved closer, in little shifts and twitches, till now his thigh presses against Rod's. His arm comes up and around Rod's shoulders - heavy, like a bag of wet sand pressing him down. Rod begins to rise but the arm holds him down, the hand clasping his shoulder. Not gently.

"You're hurting me. I want to go."

Without slackening his grip, Jake pulls him round so they face one another. "I don't want to hurt you," he pleads. "I want to hold you. Jesus, babe, I see you, walking, sitting here. I hang around that stupid house hoping for a glimpse of you and it kills me not to be together. Look, Kim – or Chris, Christina; the names don't matter; not yours, or mine, not any names - I've learned things like that, these last few months...I'm trying to get a job, not that E-bank thing, that's over now, but a real job, but...it's hard you know? Really hard, 'cause for so long I didn't really 'do' anything, you know? But when I do, when I can get myself set up, I'll be able to take care of you. I love you Kim and I need you, and I need you to come back to me."

"I'm not Kim," Rod states emphatically, struggling to push away the arm. "I'm Rodney Gimbal and I do not know you, any more than I know why I'm here, looking like this, living like this, but it doesn't matter. What I look like, who you think I am - none of that matters. There's no one here for you to love, so get your arm off me," Rod concludes, "because I'm leaving." He tries to rise, but the arm is strong, far stronger than Chris's body can resist. Jake must outweigh him by eighty or a hundred pounds – or more; an ever-present denominator when one is small, in a world where size is still a form of power.

"Don't go, Kimmie," Jake's voice is pleading, even as his hands grow more forceful. They are in motion now, across Rod's back, on his thigh, pressing and tugging. His face is close enough for Rod to see every pock and pore and prickle of stubble, every twitching muscle; the mouth a wide rift, the nose all cartilage and bulging nostrils, eyebrows a forest, bordering the great flat expanse of forehead which stretches to a hairline in the early stages of recession. Close enough to radiate its heat, and the moisture of exhalation. "You don't know what this has done to me," the voice is saying. "I'm a wreck. All those weeks of worrying by your bed - not knowing if you'd make it. And the doctors, with all their bullshit explanations and evasions...and then to see you waking up, lying there in your bed." He grabs a pinch of hair in his fingers, his expression nearly frantic with these memories. "I watched as your eyes opened, as your hair grew back. You were so beautiful then, Anne made sure of that. So beautiful I felt my heart swelling till I thought it would burst. And then you left and I didn't know what to do."

The man has practically collapsed now, his head leaning on Rod's, his arms pulling them together into embrace, as Rod's heart races, chest straining for a full breath, all other functions overwhelmed by the need to escape. To run and be free of this clinging monster. He struggles to push away the encircling limbs, but manages only to rise part-way, twisting and straining against the greater strength.

"Get off me," Christina's voice screams. "Go away. I'm not who you think I am." They are sliding off the bench now, halfway upright and squirming as Jake's arms work and Christina's form struggles against them.

"Kimmie, it's me. I can help you; I'll remember everything for you. I can help you."

"Get your hands off...," Rod shouts, "Or I'll... I'll..."

"You'll what?" Jake asks, changing tone abruptly. The bland certainty in his voice only heightening Rod's fear. "Hit me? I love it when you hit me. Come on, Kimmie, fight back. Hit me and slap me - just like old times. Be my feisty little babe again. I love it when you do that. I love you, I love you, oh god, I love you so much."

Rod is nearly off his feet, lifted and locked in those tentacles, when he hears another voice.

"Hey, you kids! Why don't you take it inside? This is a public walk, not a drive-in."

Jake's moment of surprise is all the opening Rod needs. Tearing himself free he trips and stumbles, teeters uncertainly, then crumbles to the ground, as both he and his assailant take in the figure before them: a short and scrawny man, white haired and stooped, holding two retractable leashes with Schnauzers at their ends, the dogs sniffing, sniffing, sniffing in erratic movements along the ground.

"Are you all right, Miss?" the dog-man asks, offering Rod a hand.

Jake steps back a bit, looking stunned as he runs a hand across his hair. "I didn't mean to hurt her," he stammers. "We were just talking."

"Well try doing your talking with your mouth instead of your hands, why don't you." Despite his age and small size, the elderly man's attitude yields no ground as he turns back to Rod, helping-hand still extended. "Do you want him to leave you alone, Miss? Do you want me to call the police?"

"No. No," Rod insists, accepting the hand to pull himself up. "I'm okay. I just want to go home." He grabs his cane from where it has been leaning against the bench, holds it ready to use now, as he catches his breath.

"I know how it is to get around with one of those things. Had to use a walker for a couple of months before my hip surgery. Got better though." The old man is proud of himself, throws out his chest as his smile beams warmly. "I'll walk with you. Just to your door," he assures, with a glance toward Jake. "Don't want your neighbors to think there's anything improper, right?" He laughs, making clear that the idea is quite a stretch - that anyone might imagine *him* having improper motives toward a young woman, much less this buzz-cut weirdo.

"Thank you," Rod answers. "I'll be all right." He turns toward Jake, the bystander now, dazed and embarrassed. "Don't you talk to me anymore. Don't ever come near me again. I'm not your 'Kim,' your 'Kimmie.' I'm not your anybody."

With that he begins moving slowly along the walk. At first the old man's hand hovers near his elbow, ready to assist if needed, then it moves away, redeployed to leash-handling, as the dogs snuffle and shuffle around the pair's feet in perpetual threat of entanglement. Rod is silent as they proceed.

Awkwardly, the man tries to generate a conversation. "Old boyfriend?" he asks.

"Certainly not," Rod answers vehemently, then reconsiders, his voice turning more conciliatory. "He's just confused me with someone else," he offers, the truth of that statement a welcome bit of reason in a world gone mad. "Someone he knew, a long time ago. Not me at all."

As they turn the corner Rod chances a backward glance. Thirty yards away, Jake still stands before the bench, one hand limp at this side, one caressing his scalp, eyes squarely on the two departing figures. Eyes which are, even at that distance, hollow with anger and tightly-focused intention.

The two women speak little after Elaine's commitment to what is now *their* journey; for long periods they walk alone, sometimes in sight of the string of men, sometimes not. Time and again the lead porter comes hurrying back to speak to Beryl, and each time his agitation increases. With heads close, the two talk; the man's hands gesticulating wildly, Beryl reaching out as if to touch him - a fingertip toward the shoulder, a hand about to clasp his wrist, but only just for a moment and never actually making contact. After one of these conversations Beryl says she must go forward to talk to the porters, who have stopped a short ways ahead, though unseen due to the vegetation which fills this broad basin; the largest and darkest stretch of forest they have seen for some time as the trail has led them up and down – but mostly up – a series of ridges and swales, with only the barest sign of human habitation. Elaine offers to come but her friend says no, she is to wait there. The men are refusing to go on any farther, and Beryl cannot offer them more money to change their minds because she has already given them all she has, as well as the last of her jewelry. Instead, she must play on things less tangible: the honor of the agreement they made before setting out, their courage as men - not to be afraid of going where a mere woman is willing to go. It is a touchy business, a woman telling men their duty, and the conversation will go more easily without yet another female watching. In a few minutes, she assures, she will be back and they will start moving again.

Without waiting for agreement, Beryl and the lead man are gone, disappearing up the shadowed path as surely as if a door were closing behind them.

Time passes slowly after that, punctuated only by the sounds of birdsong, random and ever changing, and therefore always the same. As dark and chilly as it is in the brush, a mere three steps off the trail take Elaine to where a small patch of sunlight falls upon a bit of exposed earth and rock, its heat a welcome relief to her face and shoulders, though she had not previously been aware of feeling cold. 'Sun and shadow, light and darkness, heat and cold,' she muses, 'contradictions and opposites, nested, one within the other.'

"How's the food these days?" asks a voice behind Mary's shoulder, as she deposits her tray and heads toward the cafeteria doors on the morning after her encounter with Judith Baxter. Turning, she is surprised to discover that the smile surrounding that voice belongs to none other than Doug Taylor, Chief of Admin for all of Hilltop; a man she knows primarily from publicity photos, though also from gossip among the female staff. To make things even more uncomfortable, Taylor, true to reputation, is standing just a little too close; the intensity of his gaze suggesting his interest in this young resident is more than administrative. "The new offerings, I mean. Any improvement?"

Vaguely, Mary recalls that the cafeteria's menu has been changed recently; standard comfort foods like mac-and-cheese replaced with entrees whose labels tout their organic ingredients and back-to-the-future slow-food seasonality. Never having ventured beyond the salad section, she feels somewhat at a loss to give an opinion, though intuition tells her that's not really what Taylor is after anyway. Mary has never spoken to the man before, nor ever expected she would, and the fact that he is here, talking to her, sends a stitch of tension through her body as she wonders whether it is truly an accident. Taylor, after all, is one of the most powerful persons at Hilltop, with the ability to affect any employee's position. He is also, it comes to her, one of the few who managed to remain in a position of authority through the transition from independent operation to MH ownership of the Center.

"I suppose," she answers, concealing those thoughts as Taylor settles into step beside her. "I've always found the food...fine. I'm not a picky eater, unfortunately."

The man is good with small talk, and he keeps the words flowing as they make their way out of the cafeteria and across the lower lobby to where a steel and glass stair flanks the bank of elevators. Packed at meal times, the broad two-story space is nearly empty at this hour, light streaming down from high windows as glass, plaster and polished-concrete floor imbue a hard edge upon the sounds of voices and scuffing shoes. Without realizing how, Mary finds herself steered toward a group of sofas and chairs tucked between the grand stair and a low-walled planter housing two towering ficus trees; one of the numerous 'decompression zones' which have been installed around Hilltop by the new management, ostensibly to reduce staff stress (though the real intention is to capture the resulting increase in productivity projected by their V.P of Industrial Relations). Taylor's introduction, however, does nothing to help Mary's stress level.

"I understand," he begins, after glancing around to make certain there is a healthy distance between them and any other set of ears. "That you've been making some inquiries."

For a moment Mary is confused, wondering how he could have heard, but quickly it occurs to her that Judith, with her ready eye for well-positioned men, is not an unlikely point of contact for a senior administrator with an equally ready eye for pretty young women. The thought is no help in formulating a defense.

"I..." she stammers, desperately trying to think of a response that will neither lie nor incriminate herself. Taylor, as it happens, is in no mood to wait for explanation.

"Miss Antonias," he begins, as he takes one of Mary's elbows in his hand, gripping it a little too tightly for her taste.

"It's Doctor."

"*Doctor* Antonias," Taylor corrects himself, dropping the elbow with no hint of apology. "If I were you, and if I valued my position here at Hilltop, I would cease any efforts to pry into confidential information which does not concern you or your patients."

"But..."

"No 'buts,' Doctor," Taylor interrupts, voice rising as his complexion shifts into the purple range. "Our patients entrust us with the details of their care. Their lives. They have a right to expect that information to remain confidential, even from other staff. The fact that you have been going around asking questions about a patient who is not in your care reflects badly on this entire institution and I will not have it. Do I make myself clear?"

Apologies, promises, soothing words; all these Mary knows how to use, from dealing with patients and their families. By the time she and Doug Taylor part ways, the flush has cleared from the man's face and he seems once again his politic self. Mary, on the other hand, finds her composure difficult to regain. The man's reaction was just too big, she repeats to herself as she turns away from the elevators, choosing instead to head down one of the many tunnels which connect Hilltop's buildings. Checking her schedule for the next stop on the day's rounds, her mind is still on that reaction.

Too big, too quick, too self-righteous by far. The nervous system, after all, is largely autonomous, only remotely subject to its owner's conscious control, and despite Doug Taylor's attempts to seem reasonable, the overwhelming impression which Mary takes away from their encounter is that she has, in fact, touched a nerve. A very large, very raw nerve, where, by rights, there should have been, if anything, only the most minor sensory branch.

Mary's quick agreement not to search any further in Records seemed to assuage his worries though, as did her assurance that she had found nothing there anyway. His demand that she not talk further to any Hilltop staff about Christina McKloskey was easy enough to accept as well. The staff to date had been a total dead-end anyway, and that fortuitous wording, as it turned out, left Mary with one very large loophole; a loophole large enough, in fact, for an airliner to fly through.

"Oh, crap," Aubrey whispers under her breath.

Rod is standing in the alcove outside the rest rooms when she spots him. A tray with four entrees in her hands, she passes by without another word, then catches several furtive glimpses of him as she deals out the plates and takes requests to bring the table ketchup, Splenda and two more glasses of water. Even from a distance - and in between smiling politely at a customer's 'you know you're a redneck...' joke - she can see there is something very wrong, but the lunch crowd is thick this day, lots of big parties squeezing a meal in before heading to the Huskies game, and it is some time till she can make her way over and drag the protesting figure into the women's room, where the handicap stall provides room for two with a modicum of privacy.

"If Sylvio sees you," she begins, then stops. It is clear her roommate is in no shape to appreciate the boss's easily predictable reaction to her presence in the restaurant. "Oh baby," she says, more gently, touching a hand to that stubbled head. "What happened?"

It takes a while for the story to come out, and just about the time Aubrey thinks she understands the gist of it she hears the ladies room door open and Theresa's voice call out to ask if she is in there.

"Stay here," Aubrey says with a roll of her head and an apologetic grimace.

"But what if someone needs to..."

"Just lock the door and stay in here." The look on Rod's face reminds her of his professed inexperience with Women's Room culture. "If anyone hassles you, start crying," she offers gently. "It happens all the time."

Another table's food delivered, orders taken from a two-top who bear all the awkward signs of a blind date, and one snarly look from Sylvio all conspire to make it ten minutes before Aubrey can return, call over the partition for Rod to open up and enter the stall again, all to the bemusement of a middle-aged woman fluffing her salon-hair at the mirror.

"The guy," she asks, as Rod sits, fully clothed, on the toilet. "He was a real hunk; a body-builder type?"

Rod nods.

"And he called you Kimmie?"

Another nod.

"No bullshit, then," Aubrey says, a wry smile taking over her features. "It *was* Jake. Your old flame."

Rod protests that *he* has no old flame, and no interest in any hunk, until Aubrey finds herself suddenly short of patience.

"Don't give me that innocent act; you let him think you were going to marry him for god's sake, and all the while you couldn't wait till his back was turned before you put the guy down," to which Rod only stares, as if in shock. "You led him on babe, remember? He was your 'Big Chunky,' 'The Ticket?' Your 'One-a-day daily-lay?' How do you think he'd feel if he'd heard some of those names?"

"Aubs?" comes a voice from the doorway, Virginia's this time. "Table six is looking restless, and you've got orders up."

Exiting the stall, Aubrey makes for the door, only to hear a woman at one sink clear her throat loudly while pointing her hairbrush toward the sign on the wall that reminds employees to wash their hands before leaving. Feeling caught, Aubs stops and gives her hands a perfunctory rinse, then wipes them on a paper towel which she conspicuously drops just short of the trash can before heading out to the noise of the dining room and kitchen.

"Hey girl," Sylvio calls a couple of minutes later, as Aubrey struggles to translate 'bacon mushroom cheeseburger without the bun' into words one of the kitchen boys will understand. "You got the runs or something? I seen you go in and out of that little-girl's room half a dozen times this past hour."

"No," Aubrey shoots back, swinging her tray up to counter height and placing dishes on it as quickly as she can.

"So..." Sylvio begins, but before he can go on she blurts out the one answer she knows he won't pursue.

"That time of the month," she stage whispers, loudly enough for the entire kitchen to hear. "You know how that is, don't you, Sylvio? You're always on the rag." Several faces look up with broad smiles as their boss cringes.

"All right, all right," the head man admits, flapping his hands and shaking his head as he turns toward the cooler, then tossing back over his shoulder, "Just make sure you keep your tables happy."

"Look," Aubrey begins, as she enters the stall again a few minutes later, to find Rod slumped against a side wall while three sorority types wait outside for the two toilets which are actually in use. "I happen to know that Jake really does love you. Your Mom tells me he's been totally busted up about how you won't even admit you know him. He's, like, lost his job or something, and he's broke and…"

"Wait a minute," Rod interrupts, but before he can continue, is himself interrupted by a voice from the other side of the partition.

"Are you going to let anyone else use that stall, or what?"

"Fuck off," Aubrey answers, "Can't you see my friend's upset?"

"No I can't see, bitch," comes the answer, not at all amused. "There's a wall in the way."

"You've been talking to that woman?" Rod asks, his eyes opening more widely as the women outside talk loudly among themselves about the rudeness of some people.

"Well, duh," Aubrey mimics, her patience with the whole scene rapidly dwindling. "Who else could I go to when you wouldn't get a job?"

Rod is on his feet now, straddling the commode, as Aubrey sees a head peering over the partition from the next stall.

"I thought so," shouts the head before disappearing. "She's got a guy in there," the voice continues unseen, and the three sisters commence an argument over whether Rod is indeed a guy, as their quick glimpse of his haircut suggests, or a butch, as her voice implies - and what kind of perversion might be going on in the stall in either case.

"You went to that woman," Rod demands, "and you took money from her? Don't you see what a difficult position that puts me in?"

"Hey slut," calls one of the sisters. "I don't want to know what position you're in. I just need to take a pee, OK?"

"Who you calling a slut?" Aubrey hollers back, but before the conflict can escalate further, she hears the ladies-room door open and a shuffling of feet followed by Virginia's voice again, advising that table six is asking her for service and that Sylvio says he doesn't care what time of the month it is, people gotta eat, don't they?

"Stay here," Aubrey demands of Rod, then exits, taking time to flip the sisters a bird in lieu of a hand wash. Two of the three stick their tongues out in response, leading Aubrey to toss a sideways bump of her ass in their direction as she squeezes past Virginia's disbelieving face.

The next time Aubrey manages to get a break, she needs the rest room for real. There's no response when she calls Rod's name at the end stall, and looking underneath the door she finds a pair of stockinged feet jammed into a pair of chartreuse pumps which neither Rod, nor Kim nor, she suspects, even Christina, would ever choose to wear.

The afternoon sunshine here is stronger than any Elaine can remember. Sitting in a cleft among the rocks where the wind cannot reach her, she feels the light baking her muscles, bathing her in warmth from the heavens.

When Beryl does not return in the promised few minutes, Elaine decides to have a snack from the small daypack her friend has insisted that each carry whenever they trek. Just a few things in there - a light jacket for warmth, a soft Pashmina shawl for versatile comfort, a bottle of water, some dried fruit and bread. Cheese; chocolate when it is available. Matches - though where she would find anything dry enough to burn, Elaine has no idea, nor how to build a fire, for that matter, though she has seen it done many times.

It is not until after she has eaten and taken some water that Elaine begins truly to worry. If only she had thought to note the time when Beryl and the head porter went ahead, she thinks, but she did not. Certainly it has been more than a few minutes, but how much more? Fifteen? Twenty? It hasn't been half an hour, she feels certain. But then again, perhaps it has.

A slight shiver down her back suggests the world is moving on. Looking around, Elaine sees that her patch of warmth is disappearing, the shadows of surrounding trees closing in as the sun's position shifts westward, its vertical angle lowering. Surely, she thinks, it has been more than a few minutes. Something must be going on up ahead with the porters; the conversation taking longer than expected. Or perhaps they would only go on with Beryl among them. Yes, she thinks, that must be it. And if they are moving, she must move with them, in order to catch up. In any case, the shifting sun means evening is coming, and the last thing in the world she wants when the sun goes down is to be here, alone, in the middle of nothing.

Donning her pack Elaine begins moving up the trail, certain she will find the rest of her party soon. Her way, at least, is obvious: a swath several feet wide, trodden by multitudes of feet, with here and there a branch cut sharply out of the way, a fallen sapling crudely chopped to ease passage. There is clearly no other route they could have taken, and so for a time she feels energized, liberated even, to be walking by herself. Beryl's pronouncements have become, if she is honest, a bit infuriating. Always some message to be read out of coincidence and commonplace; some lesson to be drawn from the most frustrating of circumstances. Walking alone is actually a relief - and besides, if ever she wonders what Beryl might say about this or that, she has only to imagine her friend's face and her own mind supplies the words she knows would issue from it. So long have they traveled together, so much time have they spent in one another's company, that she is sure she can channel Beryl Nathanson's voice at any time.

After several minutes walking, Elaine comes to a modest-sized clearing, the trees and brush interrupted for perhaps forty feet by a gently-sloping plane of hard, trampled dirt and sparse grasses. Off to one side, away from the center, she spies a topless plastic water bottle, its label torn away until just a few traces of white paper and adhesive remain. Around it, a patch of earth appears perhaps more beaten and compacted than the rest. This, she guesses, must be where the porters loitered when they refused to go on any farther.

Stopping in the middle of that empty space she considers for a moment, then turns, slowly, studying the scene, careful to examine every gap in the trees, every change of color or pattern, every detail or hint of difference. Making a full circle, her heart sinks more and more deeply, for as her eyes scan she hears only the buzzing of insects, the trilling of birds, and sees only that one piece of trash - no other sign of human presence, recent or not.

"Hello?" she calls out, only to feel immediately embarrassed at the sound of her own voice in this emptiness. There is no answer and, despite feeling so foolish, she tries again. "Is anyone out there? Beryl?" The name, when shouted out, seems oddly-shaped, its drooping inflection more suited to soft conversation, or perhaps that is just a legacy of its owner's perpetual composure.

In any case, her words bring no response. No voices drift back to her from beyond the clearing, no figures burst forth from the fierce green wall which surrounds her, and worst of all, as she listens, she can see no gap in that wall to mark from which direction she entered. Silently she examines the space in which she stands, shuffling only the slightest bit to turn herself incrementally around, and with this second circuit she grows more confused than ever. Perhaps that is where she entered, there, between that slightly darker green bush and the tall tree, for the plastic bottle was to her right when first she noticed it. Or had she already walked partway across the space and turned back when she saw it? The harder she tries to remember, the less certain she is of her recollection.

She does not recall pushing any brush out of the way to enter the clearing, so surely there must be a gap in the foliage through which she came in, and yet no gap is visible now that she is inside. She feels her heart beginning to beat as if with exertion, though she is standing still, and idly wonders how long it takes for justified concern to rise to the level of true panic.

'The center,' Beryl's voice returns to tell her, 'is not a thing itself, but the source of things. A circle is defined by its center, but to truly comprehend the circle one must leave the center, which is why we precious souls live in a world of hard and dirty objects.' This clearing certainly qualifies as a hard and dirty object, and so, swiftly and with determination, Elaine strides from her spot to where the plastic bottle lies. Picking it up, she continues until she reaches the edge of the clearing. There she selects a projecting branch and slips the mouth of the bottle over its end. Now she has a marker, a set point which can be seen from all around the clearing, and, moving slowly in a clockwise direction, she begins examining the ground and brush. Sure enough, only a few paces away, her eyes discern a pattern to the earth, the dusty layer scraped somewhat consistently in one direction, a rock peeking through the surface, its top burnished bright by wear. Pushing aside the nearby branches she finds one which has been recently broken and hangs unnaturally, filling-in what would otherwise be visible as a gap, and beyond it a clear footpath into the now-darkening forest. Glancing back into the open, she imagines herself entering here, the bottle lying... Well, she cannot pinpoint exactly where it was, now that she has moved it, but yes, that seems right; entering from here, seeing the bottle about there, and that spindly tree across the way as she came out into the brightness...

"I must have been distracted," she says to no one but herself, "by finding the clearing, and not even noticed as I pushed that branch aside." The sound of her voice seems alien and out of place, with no one near to hear it. Still, there is great satisfaction in having located the path by which she entered the clearing, and it is with confidence that she continues along the perimeter, looking for another patch of shiny rock, another broken branch, any sort of signpost to mark the way out, for certainly there must be one, since the rest of the party did not come back past her.

A little more than half way around the perimeter Elaine finds what she is looking for. This patch of packed earth is not as clearly defined as the one upon which she entered, the scuffing less uniform in its direction, but again there are stones scraped clean by the passage of feet and as soon as she looks up from them it is clear how the shape of the clearing has fooled her, for it is not completely a circle, but here stretches out around a dense bush. Just as an ocean bay might wrap around a hill to reach the mouth of a river, the space curves around the bush to form an alcove, at the back of which she now sees it tapering down into a narrow slice through the forest, where ridges of thick mud nearly lost in shadow tell of many feet passing, and the start of another trail.

So pleased is Elaine with herself, so certain she has found the answer to her worries, that she sets off down this new trail immediately. From her first steps, the very unfamiliarity of what she sees, the fact that she does not recognize any rock or bush or tree, seems confirmation that it must be the right path. Surely just a short way along she will find the rest of her party: Beryl, the head man and all the grumbling porters. She is several minutes along when a thought occurs which stops her in her tracks. Should she not have continued, she wonders, all the way around the clearing? Marked this trail perhaps, to be sure she could find it again, but checked the rest of the perimeter to make sure there were not *other* paths as well to consider?

Could there have been more than one trail leading out of such a small clearing? It seems unlikely. No, this must be the way; it feels so right. 'And one must learn to trust one's feelings,' she imagines Beryl's voice telling her. Taking comfort in that philosophy, and bolstered by the clarity of the path ahead, she sets out once again, moving quickly in hope that she will soon catch up with her companions who must, surely, be right around the next bend.

"It's lucky for me you were still at your office," Rod says, as his host hoists the two grocery bags of clothes and tapes from the car's shallow trunk and leads the way up several stone steps.

"Don't mention it," Jim Auster responds generously, his voice sounding quite sincere, though one could wonder at that; after all, the two had not exactly gotten along back when Auster represented him, and that whole strategy of agreeing to be identified as Christina still rankled Rod, but the reality was that Jim Auster was the only mature male with whom he had formed any sort of relationship since awakening to this whole sorry mess, and right now what he wanted more than anything was to be among his own kind. It was a bit of a long shot, Auster taking him in, but the fellow seemed to have no doubt when Rod called his office from the vestibule of a convenience store three blocks north of Sylvio's. Not only had he said it would be OK for Rod to stay with him awhile, he had dropped whatever he was doing and driven all the way to Fremont to pick him up. The drive back over Queen Anne Hill was brief, with Auster constantly on the phone, so Rod had spent it mostly in silence, visibly appreciating the luxury of the attorney's Mercedes and watching their progress on the GPS display that held pride of place in the center of its dash.

The house to which Jim has brought him is just as impressive as his car, though considerably older. Perched on the face of Queen Anne Hill, on a street largely taken over by condominium and apartment buildings, it hugs the sidewalk with a wide veranda, above which a collection of bay windows and dormers describe spaciousness and variety which must have cost a fortune when it was first built. In the gap between the house and its neighbor Rod catches a glimpse of Seattle Center and downtown at the bottom of the hill, with South Seattle in the distance; its myriad lights just beginning to stand out against a sky darkening above the blue-black water of Elliot Bay.

"Very nice place you've got here," Rod offers in the entry, as Jim closes and locks the extra-wide door. The space in which the two men stand is broad enough and deep enough for half a dozen people to mill around in, and paneled on every surface with clear fir whose deep syrup patina and straight grain give testament to a quality of timber which disappeared several generations ago from all but the most remote pockets of the northwest forests. To one side a pair of sliding panels opens into a spacious parlor filled with deep velvet sofas and chairs, tables decorated with artful iron lamps and walls hung with paintings of sailing vessels plying rough waters. To the opposite side stands a stair of the same polished wood, its treads fitted with a thick oriental runner, its lowest three steps curved around a newel post as thick as a man's torso, and nearly as tall. Toward the rear, at the hallway's end, a half-open door allows a glimpse of a spacious kitchen, all stone countertops and stainless steel. A deep stillness fills the house, as of a museum not yet opened for the day, or a library overseen by a very stern mistress.

All in all, an environment very well suited to the attitudes Rod proclaims – a place where strength and objectivity are valued; where success rewards achievement, and the obvious correctness of things is not subject to question by every Tom, Dick or Harry who thinks he has a better way, or just doesn't like the old one. Auster has seen before how this house affects people - indeed, that is one of the reasons he chose it: to impress clients. And not-clients, as the case may be on any given evening. His attitude is similarly salubrious, as he politely urges his new guest up a flight of stairs which are generously wide, though their steepness challenges those still-weak and unsteady legs.

"Sorry about the climb," Auster says, in response to her slow progress, "but there isn't a bedroom on the ground floor. You can stay in the room right at the top of the stair; it's got a nice view, and its own bath. We could get you one of those little refrigerators if you have trouble with the stairs, maybe a coffee maker..."

"Oh, no," Rod insists, "You don't need to do anything like that. I'll manage the climbing - in fact, it will be good for me. Help me build my stamina. Agility. Tired of being treated like an invalid. You know what I mean, I'm sure."

Auster nods, makes a guttural noise of agreement. Reaching the upstairs hall, he proudly points out an 1827 mahogany breakfront topped with two stuffed prairie chickens, giving himself a moment to contemplate his visitor. It has been months since he spent a very few hours on her case, and the changes have not been kind to her. Chopped-off hair and rumpled clothes make her a far cry from pretty, but still, there is something intriguing about the bizarreness of it all. Calling her 'Rod' would be a total turn off, if not for the unmistakably female form beneath her suit coat. And those lips. Even without color they stand out against her fair skin, their edges crisply defined, their shape slightly puckered. In his mind he can picture them wrapped around all sorts of body parts. Those lips haven't changed a bit, no matter what name she uses.

"I was a little surprised that you chose to call me," he says, entering a small dim room and placing the bags on the bed. Christina – or 'Rod;' he'll get used to it eventually - settles into the corner chair with a sigh, the effort of climbing the stairs obviously a strain.

"I had to get out of there," she is saying as he switches on a floor lamp, revealing an antique sleigh-bed with heavy duvet, a tall oak dresser and subdued paintings on the walls. Her eyes take it all in with obvious satisfaction. "The filth, the clutter. Always some problem about money for this or that. Little things anybody else would just pay without thinking about it. I don't know how people can live like that. Especially a woman. I've had enough of women. Aubrey; that girl's mother…"

"Mrs. McKloskey?" Auster interrupts, at first legitimately confused by the multiple layers of denial going on before him, then intrigued, though he would almost certainly deny that particular twist, under questioning.

"Yes, her. And there's that lady doctor who's come around a few times. I'm sick of women, so I asked myself, who could I call on for help? A responsible, established fellow who might be able to take me in for a little while, till I can get my feet under me again. And that's how you landed the honor of my call." Rod stops for a moment, leaning forward, hands flat on the upholstered arm-rests, eyes fixed on Auster's own in universal man-to-man fashion. "The truth is, Jim, I don't have a lot of people I can turn to. I was never very social; my work has always been my life."

"I know how that is," Auster says, his eyes taking in how gracefully the smooth flesh of her neck curves down to disappear beneath the tightly-buttoned collar of her shirt. "Focusing on one's work can be both a refuge and a trap, if one hopes to sustain any relationships over the long term." Though there is no such conflict if all one seeks is pleasure and amusement. Jim Auster has learned over the years to be quite satisfied with those rewards, and this - a pretty young thing who appears to fully believe she is someone else - this is about as amusing as it gets.

"It was incredible," Rod tells Auster later that evening, as they sit in the study. The hearty steak-and-potato dinner left by the housekeeper has been amply shared between the two of them and its remains left on the table for her to deal with in the morning. Auster is in his customary leather armchair enjoying one more glass of Pinot, while his house guest has switched to single-malt and now sits crumpled in a corner of the sofa, glass cradled between her two hands and a look of disbelief on her face as she tells of her encounter with Jake.

"Did he actually hit you?"

"No," Rod insists, "No, he didn't hit me. Somebody came by, an elderly gentleman. He stepped in before it got to that."

"But you felt assaulted. Violated?"

"No," Rod dismisses the thought, then reconsiders. "Not exactly. No. What I felt was…helpless. He was so much larger than me. I couldn't fight him and I couldn't run away," Rod gestures to his legs, stretched limply before him. "So I was so grateful to that man, for helping me out. And I should have thanked him, but I have to admit I was too shocked and…disoriented, I guess. Not myself…the things I feel these days, they're…I guess this situation has had an effect on my mind, after all."

Auster looks into Christina's eyes and sees the emotion building there, the tension in her mouth as she tries to maintain control. There's something about a woman in distress, he thinks to himself. It brings out their most enticing qualities, and this girl has it in spades. So small and compact; it makes a man feel like he could just wrap his arms around her and hide her from the entire world. That soft face, with features so precise and perfect: a doll's face.

"And the girl you were living with…"

"Aubrey."

"Yes, Aubrey. I remember her from before. I don't imagine she was much help."

Rod snorts, takes another sip of his drink. "Help? She practically laughed about it. Says I asked for it, the way I led him on. She said he's in love with me. That we were engaged. But that…wasn't…" Auster hears Christina's voice begin to crack, sees around the corners of her eyes the wet glistening which he knows to indicate that a woman is about to cry; a sight which always brings out his strength; and also, his desire.

"That wasn't you," he suggests, "was it?" and those few words are all it takes to make her breakdown complete.

"No," Rod manages to say between sobs, then "I'm sorry. I don't know what is happening to me. Crying? I don't cry. It's just…I'm not really like this…but I can't seem to stop it."

412

As Rod is saying these words, Auster is moving. Quietly, without ever quite seeming to stand, he slips from his chair to the sofa. Setling close beside the girl he puts a hand on her back and begins to rub, a circular motion in time to the heaving of the sobs taking control of her body. The gesture is truly intended to sooth her, though it does offer an added benefit - confirming his suspicion that she is not wearing a bra. Pulling her close he presses her head onto his shoulder, feeling only slight resistance as her crying continues.

"It's all right," he says, patting her on the back with one hand as the other slides beneath the suit coat to encircle her waist. "It's all right. That stupid girl couldn't protect you; she didn't understand what you need. What you need is a friend." Rod's head moves, trying to rise, but Auster's is above it now, pressing it into his shoulder. "So you came here. To me..." His hand is on her back now, beneath the suit coat as, sliding the fabric of her shirts across her skin, he begins to explore, around the side toward the front. Searching, searching as she begins to wriggle and squirm, until he finds one of the soft mounds he knows are hiding there and molds his hand to its shape, feeling her squirming increase and with it, his own arousal. The scene is so familiar to him, her movements, sounds, even the scent of her tears. That moaning surprise as she realizes her own desire, a sound he has heard many times before, from sorority girls and secretaries, from a parade of evening dates and afternoon assignations. It is only when Rod manages to free a hand and rake Auster's face with the quick-trimmed edges of her fingernails that he realizes this encounter will not be a success.

"What the hell do you think you're doing?" the girl shouts as she squeezes out of his grasp and struggles to her feet, stumbling backwards into the corner of the coffee table then halfway across the room in an attempt to keep her balance.

"*You* called *me*," Auster reminds the girl, his tone making clear that, in his mind, those few words explain the entire situation.

"I asked if I could stay with you - be your *guest* for a few days," Rod shouts, her voice still cracking, but any trace of timidity long gone. "When a man comes to you, asking for hospitality you try to...try to..."

Listening to her words, Auster's body settles back into the sofa. Completely relaxed and in control, his laughter booms out through the house. "A man?" he cries. "I don't know what is going on inside that pretty little head of yours, kiddo, but there's no way in the world anyone is ever going to believe that *you* are a man."

Standing awkwardly in the center of the room, Rod opens his mouth as if to speak, then appears to think better of it. Shaking his head in disgust he makes his way across the room, through the entryway to the massive front door. The multiple locks take a bit of fumbling, but only a bit, and moments later he is gone, leaving Auster still slouched on the sofa as he shakes his head in disbelief, then reaches to the table where the girl's scotch still sits. Picking it up he examines the glass carefully, even sniffing at it a bit before bringing it to his lips and downing its contents in one swallow, followed by a shake of his head and a deep sigh of wonderment, his smile all the while growing wider and wider and wider until, finally, it consumes his entire face as he pours himself another.

Elaine has been walking for several hours, when finally she must admit the light has become simply too dim to continue safely. In steadfast denial of the growing probability that she will have to spend the night outside, and alone, she has not really been looking for a proper place to stop and so, when the time comes, finds nothing better than to huddle against the trunk of one tree slightly larger than the rest. Pulling her feet close she forms a tent with her skirt, aiming to hold against her legs and feet what little heat her body can produce. Her jacket already on, she drapes the light wool shawl over her head and around her shoulders, tucks hands beneath arms, and settles in to wait out the long darkness.

For a time it seems the spot she has chosen provides some shelter from the wind; allowing her to hear, rather than feel, how it rustles the branches above. As time goes by, however, the rustling becomes more insistent, and the air around her comes to life: first a soft caress, ever-so-slightly cooling her cheeks, then more briskly moving, tugging at the edges of her shawl, ruffling the draping fabric of her skirt.

'At least,' she finds herself thinking after some time, 'the wind drowns out the sound of any animals which might be lurking.' Does this landscape harbor tigers, she wonders, quickly deciding it is better to fill her mind with other thoughts. The night before, she reminds herself, their party stayed near a small hamlet, six or seven mud-and-rock houses, with low roofs and tiny doorways. Perhaps Beryl and the head man are in such a house right now. Carefully she constructs the picture in her mind: a smoky interior, oil lamps throwing out their amber light to be reflected off Beryl's remaining brass and silver ornaments; the muted crackling of a dung fire, the rippling sound of tea being poured into tiny cups. Conversation simmering around her in a language she cannot comprehend, with sly jokes and embarrassed whispers, the woman and girls of the household covering their faces with the back of a hand to hide their laughter.

'Cold,' Elaine's body interrupts her recollection. Temperature insists on being recognized, as her toes seem first to swell and tighten in her boots, then grow numb and heavy. Fingers, too, complain loudly until she begins working them against the fabric of her clothing, muscle action and friction combining to give some relief, though still she can feel them threatening to go numb, as the blood supply slows down, shepherding heat toward the body's core.

'Hungry as well,' says another part of her body. She feels her stomach churn, as if a bubble has escaped somewhere and is making its twisting way up through her viscera, searching for an exit.

'Sleep,' says her mind; that conscious and calculating mix of memories and reactions which purports to be in control of the rest. It is not in control, of course, not really, which is why - as much as she may recognize the need for rest and long for the escape it would provide - sleep does not come this night to Elaine Gimbal, not until nearly the last hour before the sun's light will be revealed once again by her planet's inexorable spinning, around and around and around.

A solitary figure makes her way down the block. Moving quickly at first, her pace slows as she puts more distance between herself and the big house. She carries no purse, no parcels - no visible baggage at all. At the first intersection she stops. For some time she stares up the avenue, toward the top of the hill over which lies the Fremont Bridge and beyond that the Wallingford neighborhood in which she has been living. Straight ahead, past the shoulder of Queen Anne Hill and across the Regrade, beyond the towering viaduct of I-5, are the Montlake neighborhood and the house she remembers, though who occupies it now, she can only guess. For some time she stares in each direction. Cars slow as they approach the painted crosswalk, their drivers assuming the shadowy figure wishes to cross. When she does not step off the curb they change gears and accelerate hard, up the hill or down it, tires hissing on damp pavement as the drivers grumble at being delayed for nothing.

It is several minutes before the girl moves from her spot, the slow tread of her heavy oxfords echoing off nearby building walls as she turns right and begins to make her way downhill toward the flatter geography of Belltown and the Center, where lights shine brightly and the city offers memories of fitting in. Of belonging. To something. Somewhere.

Robin Andrew

bluebirds fly

fourth movement

1

Night deepens, and a chill mist materializes out of thick air.

Settling on every surface, it amplifies the colors put out by artificial lights in their idiot's palette of photometric prejudice; halides flood parked cars in gimlet-green, halogens cast their yellowed pools along the I-90 off-ramp, peeling away the edge of Belltown in its mad dash toward Capitol Hill, while a Crayola collection of neons pinball themselves off any surface they can find, their random fonts announcing ground-floor businesses tight-shuttered for the night. On upper levels, the amber incandescences of draped and curtained windows signal apartment homes occupied by people who - presumably - know just who they are and where they belong.

Traffic, even after ten PM, flows in steady streams, up one street and down another. Signals change and drivers turn, as Rod wanders, idling, meandering. Not hurrying any more. Now that the adrenalin of his encounter with Auster has been burned off he has no idea, really, of where he is going. This part of the city has changed from what he remembers. Where once small industries occupied blank-walled boxes, now apartment and condominium buildings rise on random plots, even as some lots sit empty of anything but parked cars, giving the blocks a gap-toothed look, like something not completed, or already being destroyed - or maybe both at once. Workshops have been replaced by coffee shops, warehouses given way to bars and restaurants with names proclaiming their marketing strategies – Tres Fleurs, and Los Hermanos, Ho Palace and The Pig & Whistle.

He is not conscious of walking toward anything, only away. Away from Jim Auster's hands, from Aubrey's expectations and all their many names for him; from waking up in the middle of the long night of The Nothing to find his reliable dream-world gone and this fantastical one intact, himself misplaced in it.

Slicing across the city-planner's grid, the I-90 connector cuts off the street on which he has been walking, and with it, his momentum; the deep recess of its concrete canyon forcing a decision. Distantly aware that right leads toward the waterfront, he turns left, into the Regrade, with a vague thought that home lies beyond that, around the hill toward Portage Bay and Lake Washington. What *once* was home at least, though now no longer his, as the mist becomes more dense and begins to form droplets, accumulating on his face until it becomes necessary to wipe them off every few minutes.

The thought of his old home is displaced a few blocks later, after he's paralleled the recessed ramp for a while, and found a street that passes over it. Across the next intersection a Volkswagen dealership blares 'LOWEST PRICES!' and offers deals 'YOU CANNOT AFFORD TO MISS!' while opposite it, toward the middle of the block, a streamlined swipe of lemon neon rises up a pillar supporting a sign in the shape of a small orange building – gable-roofed and clapboard-sided, awakening a recollection. Reaching into his breast pocket, Rod pulls out the card, battered and dog-eared, but still legible. Scans the front, with its leathery-blue embossed logo and the number he once called, then flips it over to see the name printed there, in green felt-tip; a clear and steady hand. Looks up again, and wonders if what he sees might be a good thing, or just one more trick of this hallucination in which he finds himself. Beneath the 'DOGHOUSE' sign, long horizontal windows simmer with a buttery glow, granting fractured glimpses of an interior where hanging paper globes float above the heads of patrons nodding over their plates, or staring off toward the rear of the room, intent on something he can neither see nor hear from this remove, but finds himself imagining with a surprise of fondness.

Stevie notices the young transman as soon as he enters, though her hands play on and her eyes maintain contact with the crowd. Not a bad crowd, for a Thursday night; and a few are actually paying attention to the music, even beyond the handful of regulars like Don and Angie, Larry and Phyllis, and of course, the Sanger sisters in carefully coordinated shades, tonight of peach and mauve. She's been working the Nat King Cole songbook for an hour, to a smattering of applause, and finishes up *The Very Thought of You* as Alonzo deposits a cup of coffee on the boy's table. Taking a long sip from the glass of ice water she keeps handy, she avoids eye contact as some lobe or other of her brain ponders what might bring him here. He looks thoroughly wet, and equally tired, holding a dog-eared business card between thumb and forefingers like a talisman, forgotten but not discarded. The look of a lost puppy, very much in contrast to the self-possession of their phone conversation.

"I don't believe in coincidences," she says a few minutes later, approaching his table during her second break of the evening. "May I sit down?"

He nods, and she sits, caddie-corner on the chair so her crossed knees don't bump the table. Experience tells her there are vicious repairs hiding beneath these tabletops - screws and plates cobbling together aging particle-board – that can run a stocking in the flicker of an eyelash. Besides, she likes the way her legs look, and likes to keep them visible. Sets her half-empty glass on the table before her and traces a drip down the frost on its side to fill the time.

"I didn't actually plan on coming here," Rod states after a while.

It takes a conscious choice not to respond to the resentment in his voice, and so she's grateful when Angie stops by to say how much she enjoyed hearing *Route 66* - it brings back memories, she explains, but she has to go; 'work in the morning, you know.' Stevie rises for a diplomatic hug, and thanks the woman, sincerely. Angie knows who Stevie is of course, and doesn't seem the least bit bothered by it, any more than the rest of the Doghouse crowd, this mixed-grill assortment of music-loving seniors and campy cabaret-fans who have gravitated to the place in the ten or eleven months since she took over after June had to move into the care center.

"Lots of things happen that we didn't exactly plan on," she says after sitting back down. "But you're here." When the silence seems to go on too long, she takes a sip of water and starts to rise.

"No," the boy says, then abruptly softens his tone of command. "Please don't go. Not yet."

"Okay," Stevie agrees. "I've got a couple of minutes." She watches as the boy continues to sit, shoulders hunched over, eyes fixed on his coffee cup with the sort of bone-deep weariness that comes not from physical fatigue, but from one's inner journey; from living with dysfunction and no expectation of anything better beyond the horizon. How sad, she thinks, to see that much regret in one so young.

"Look," she says, after another minute passes vacantly. "I've got one more set to play. If you're still here when I'm done, we can talk. If not, it's good to see you. Rodney, wasn't it?"

The boy nods, and Stevie pats his hand, small beneath her own, and warm despite the dampness of his clothing, then takes her ice water and heads back to the organ bench. Kicking off satin pumps she runs her feet across the pedals, finds the proper place, then glances at her cheat sheet. "Okay, folks," she speaks toward the microphone, in a voice at once both sulky and cajoling. "Time to liven it up a bit." Her left hand pulses out the opening chords of '*At the Hop*,' and several lined faces broaden into smiles of recognition.

Lying in blackness, Elaine struggles to comprehend where she is, how she has gotten there. The sounds of this place are unfamiliar to her ears. Rain drumming overhead, not sharply, as on a metal roof, but muffled and deep. Now and then a gust of wind is audible, a shuffling of leaves perhaps, and a creaking which seems to come from all around her.

Her body feels leaden, as if all were still asleep except brain and eyes. When she swallows, her throat is dry and tight; her belly knotted and without knowing quite how, she quickly forms the conviction that no food has passed her mouth for a long time. Her eyes feel dry as well, lids scraping over eyeballs as she strains to make out any form in the sticky blackness around her, and remembers...

She was walking - again - after a nearly-sleepless night among the trees, and the path had taken her high into a realm of dried-out grass and angular rock, on the flanks of what were unquestionably no longer hills, but mountains. On the path to Beryl's village, she hoped. Separated from the rest of the group; moving forward only because there seemed no other choice. Late that afternoon she had found herself approaching a divide, the trail rising steadily for several miles toward a notch in an escarpment where towering granite drew a ragged line against the sky. She had no idea of the elevation, only that she had crossed above the tree line. Lonely country, though the trail was regularly-used, as evidenced by the stone cairns which marked it; pyramids of rock sometimes as tall as herself. There were piles of flat prayer stones as well, decorating every switchback, and several runs of tall rock steps laboriously placed to ease the steepest pitches. Climbing one set of steps she had tried to envision their construction; a pack of wiry men laboring in the sun and thin air, searching around for just the right stones, hoisting and selecting, hauling and setting them, chinking the gaps with smaller bits. Days of back-breaking labor, for what? There was no direct economic incentive for it; no toll to be collected. No Public Works Department paying them wages, no corporate sponsor to place its sign above the steps in exchange for footing the bill. No, the only purpose of all that labor was to ease the way for anyone who might come after - decades, perhaps even centuries, after. So much labor invested for such a distant benefit. By a people whose lives barely topped the level of pure subsistence. There must be something to learn in that, she remembers thinking as she climbed toward the divide, some idea about labor and reward, or perhaps labor without reward.

Or maybe not. Maybe it was just the effect of too many months travelling with Beryl, listening to her endless reflections on the sights and behaviors they encountered. Maybe this was just a trail, pure and simple.

3

The boy is still there at the end of Stevie's final set, as she shuts off her instrument and gathers up her music sheets. Several regulars stop by to thank her for the evening, and she takes time, as always, to listen to each comment and thank the giver in return, with the result that the room is nearly deserted and all the other tables empty by the time she picks up her tip bowl and makes her way across to where he sits. Setting herself down opposite him, she notes the coffee cup still full as she pulls a handful of crumpled bills from the bowl and begins to sort and flatten them, three enameled fingertips of one hand pinning down an end while she burnishes the heel of her other hand along the crinkled paper.

"I used to have a goldfish," she offers, as the stack of bills begins to grow. "She died, so now I use her bowl for tips."

"I don't know where to go," the boy responds, confirming Stevie's suspicion, born of listening to the stories told by dozens of young men and women who have passed through her support group over the years. If he were an ordinary boy, she'd steer clear, of course. But he is different, and the difference one with which she sympathizes. He's a little thing besides – hell, if most people knew anything about the two of them, they'd say it was he who had to be wary of her, wouldn't they? Besides, Stevie figures, she can protect herself a bit better than your average woman.

"Do I need to be afraid of you?" she asks, anyway.

"What?" the boy asks, and seems sincerely shocked at the question. "No," he answers after seeing she is serious. "Of course not. The way I was brought up - *when* I was brought up -a man protected a woman. That's the kind of man I am. You can count on it."

Even now, at 3:45 on a Wednesday afternoon, traffic flows through the doors of the Seafirst building like a mountain stream in spring runoff. Late arrivals fight for door space with early departures; well-tailored men and women whose days might have begun at 5:30 that morning and are already ending, or who are heading off to their next appointment in a day which may last past evening. The uniformed lobby attendants are far less attentive in late afternoon though, and Jake has found the hours between 3 and 5 are prime for catching those hapless figures who have suddenly remembered a birthday, anniversary or marital faux pas.

Adjusting the bundles in his hands he pauses for only a second in front of the building directory before stepping into an elevator between a UPS man wheeling a handcart and a short brunette carrying a cardboard tray of Starbucks's cups. He catches a whiff of scent upon her, and is momentarily energized, until her sideways glance reminds him of his own appearance – crumpled khakis rescued from the laundry pile and a raincoat which should have been retired years ago, face a testimony to sleepless nights, graying temples overdue for a trim, and beneath it all, the first signs of a gut, now that his membership at the gym has expired. In no shape to be making a pass, Jake is first to step out of the cab when its doors open. Scanning the corridor he avoids the glass-fronted reception area with its Seafirst logo and painted legend reading 'COMMERCIAL FINANCE DIVISION,' heading instead for a smaller door down the corridor, near the rest rooms. Opening this door he finds himself, as experience told him he would, in a narrow aisle between rows of eye-level office partitions cordoning off cubicles, each with its own desk and credenza, and its own wage-slave, tapping away at a keyboard or murmuring seriously into a telephone.

Back straight, face arranged in a confident smile, Jake Brindle approaches the nearest cubicle and raps his burly knuckles on the frame of its panel till the startled worker turns around, then launches into the pitch he has already delivered a dozen times this afternoon, speaking rapidly and without pause because - as he has been taught by Tommy, the towel boy at the gym who turned him on to this gig-the farther you get in your spiel, the better the odds of a hit.

"Hello friend, care to buy a fresh red rose for you wife, girlfriend or another lovely woman in your life? Fresh off the plane this morning and I got the best price in town. What do you say? Can I make it a dozen? Beautiful fresh red roses…"

'Dracula's Castle,' Mary dubs her destination, when she first glimpses it from across four jam-packed lanes of a Manhattan avenue as she waits for the traffic light to change. Like it should be perched on top of a hill in some Eastern-European, ex-Soviet Bloc semi-republic, at the end of a twisting carriage road in a raging downpour. She shivers slightly at the image.

The object of this disaffection is a co-op apartment building near the epicenter of this concrete island's real estate market. Only eight stories tall, it is a dwarf among its neighbors, but imposing nonetheless - all soot-stained gray stone with quoined corners and a massive water-table course of stones at its base which looks like it could hold off an army for decades. By contemporary standards, the windows are small, almost stingy, but they bear impressively-carved stone trim, evidence of a craftsman's attention to detail: deep sills and jambs which set the glass back into shadow, where it can sleep without reflection, while their heads are crowned with graceful arches on the lower levels, serious straight lintels on the upper ones. Stacked bays of these openings punctuate the facade at regular intervals to either side of the entry, their order and regularity intended no doubt to imply the same qualities in the occupants themselves. A false cornice marks the sixth floor, though, so that above it, the seventh - where she imagines her quarry lurks - sits back slightly, feigning discreet reserve. Higher still, the penultimate story inhabits a complex jumble of gables, turrets and projecting towers, a landscape more varied and mountainous than any offered by the actual topography of the island on which it resides, even in the remnant faux-natural contours of its signature Central Park.

Even without the purpose of her meeting, this building would have inspired apprehension in Mary. The whole idea of being in New York is intimidating; from the moment she filed through ticket-check at SeaTac and into the boarding tunnel she has noticed a different vibration among her fellow passengers. Despite smiles and conversation, she could feel an undertone of tension and wariness, as if they were headed not on a journey, but into battle. Voices grew harsh and insistent, movements more crisp and assertive. Stepping out of the plane and into the chaotic clamor of JFK airport had only upped the ante, with drivers shouting names of passengers, mothers calling after indifferent children, and the PA system mumbling unintelligibly over it all. For a moment she had considered turning right back onto the plane and letting it take her wherever it was going; anything to get away from what seemed a hostile place, and a hostile people. The memory of sleepless nights though, reminded her of why she had decided to come here: the need to put this thing to bed, to find herself a measure of peace, and maybe help another in the process.

It took twenty minutes to find an information counter and when she did, the woman behind it reacted as if her question were the dumbest she had ever heard.

"Well, lady," she said, with an over-polite tone and a shrug, dropping her eyes back to the newspaper in her lap after flicking them up just enough for the briefest glimpse of this fool who had interrupted her reading. "You could take a cab, you could hire a car service, you could take a bus, or you could rent a car. If ya' got too much money you could take the helicopter, or if you don't - like me - you could maybe walk; but it would take all day. So you're gonna to have to tell me *how* you want to get to where you're going before I can tell you *where* you want to go to get there. Right?" Only on that last syllable did her eyes return to Mary's face, with a glare which seemed to measure and account for every dollar the young doctor had earned in her life and the information clerk had not.

The cab ride, expensive as it was, had at least been a period of relative peace and privacy, her driver thankfully not one of those famous fast talkers, but a silent pilot over highways and bridges. When finally he pulled to a curb opposite her destination Mary found herself sad that the ride was over, that she must once again brave the energy of this city. Stepping out of the cab, she felt her body tense at the noise and the crowd; the crush of frosty-blank faces coming straight at her like an avalanche roaring down a mountain slope and she a single tree, not knowing whether her presence would part the flow or be swept away before it. Just as the information she had been gathering about the girl Christina's treatment seemed to be sweeping her into something strange and threatening, so every step she took on the sidewalk of this urgent and self-occupied city seemed to take her further from what she knew and understood.

It is in this mood that she ascends the front stoop, its dozen stone steps cupped with decades of wear, and lets herself into a spacious vestibule lined, unexpectedly, in pristine sheets of spirally-burnished stainless steel. The only interruption in its sheer surfaces is a small control pad with a dozen or so numbered buttons and a star-shaped arrangement of perforations, located well below her head height. With no idea which number represents her quarry, Mary steels herself and presses the topmost button. There is no feedback from her action, no clicking-on, no distant bell heard through untold tons of stone and concrete, only silence and the constant flow of traffic, visible now as a washed out dumb-show through the heavy glass of the entry door. After a time she presses a second button, only to be told, when she asks, that she has the wrong apartment, there is no Mrs. Seivers living in that apartment. Tries another, unresponsive, then a fourth – again 'No Mrs. Seivers here,' and a fifth, before her sixth foray brings another response from the ceiling above her.

"Who is it?" calls a gravelly voice, its attitude alone sufficient to raise her BP a full stage.

"I'm..." Mary's voice seems stuck in her throat and she has to cough to clear it before starting again. "Delivery for Mrs. Seivers."

"This is 7-D. You want E."

Before she can open her mouth to apologize for disturbing the unseen man, Mary hears a buzz from the door beside her, followed quickly by the dull click of hidden mechanisms shifting their positions. After a moment's confusion she realizes this is her cue for action; fumbling her purse and carry-on into one hand she scrambles to twist the heavy door lever and immediately finds herself admitted into the hushed elegance of a lobby large enough for a wedding reception, yet absolutely devoid of occupants. Across the space gleams the polished-brass door of an elevator older than her parents, which she hurries to enter before anyone can arrive to stop her. Its slow ascent and reluctant opening at the seventh floor are followed by a walk down crimson carpet until she finds herself standing before the glossy black door of apartment 7-E.

Before she can search for a doorbell, or rap her knuckles against the deeply molded wood, it opens to reveal a woman striking in both her slenderness and elegance. Jessica Seivers is dressed in a cashmere suit of the palest pearl-gray, her make-up, hair and nails as perfect as a magazine model's, and her face set in an expression of great irritation. She has clearly anticipated Mary's first question.

"Morey Feinstein's aide heard him buzz you in before she could stop him. She doesn't want the co-op board to get on the old bird's ass, so she called to warn me someone was coming up. You're lucky you look harmless or I'd be calling the day-man, who should have been in the lobby to stop you in the first place, if he knew what the hell he was doing." She stops long enough to give Mary a full body appraisal, then continues. "You have about thirty seconds to tell me who you are and why you're here; you're obviously not making a delivery, unless I left a cheap suitcase somewhere I don't recall."

It takes Mary only a few sentences to explain her mission and, to her great surprise, Mrs. Seivers seems to have anticipated that as well, though not without a certain pessimistic skepticism.

"You're not at all what I expected," she begins, as she leads the way through a marbled foyer into what appears to be the apartment's main sitting room. Mary's mouth nearly drops at the sight of the space, its ceiling a full two stories high, and gridded with golden-edged beams and coffers. The walls too, bear deep layers of paneling and moldings, their pickled white wood edged in gold and in the center of several panels are hung massive mirrors in deep frames. A dozen chairs and settees - souvenirs of some Louis or other - are laid out in semi-intimate groupings, crystal accessories occupying the elegant curve-legged tables positioned conveniently among them while a glittering white concert grand commands one corner. A bevy of French Empire courtesans would not seem out of place here, Mary imagines, but, like the lobby and hallway, the room has an eerie quiet, so empty with only herself and Mrs. Seivers, who leads the way through shafts of light cast by the overscaled windows, toward a pair of high-backed chairs, almost hidden in the shadows of the room's furthest corner. A stack of magazines beside the chair, a waste basket beneath the small round table, and a box of tissues - recognizable despite its gilded cover - identify this as the most lived-in sector of what is otherwise an imposing stage set. "I've always assumed someone would come around sooner or later, asking questions...but I thought it would be a couple of old men in rumpled suits and overcoats." Jessica tilts her head, twists her mouth into a wry little grin and studies Mary's face carefully before asking, as she settles her cashmere onto the matted silk of her favorite chair, "you're not an old man under there, are you?"

Elaine had felt surprisingly strong as she followed the trail that morning, and safe, despite the night spent outside and alone after being separated from her party. Over the months of travelling she had developed some satisfaction in her ability to walk for hours while subsisting on a minimal diet of fruit, rice and tea. Finding herself separated from the group was a shock, certainly, but in the light of day, the clarity of the path was reassuring, as was even its relentless climb. They had been headed for a pass, after all, which guarded access to Beryl's secret valley; every foot climbed, she reasoned, must be taking her closer to the summit and the relief of the descent. True, without map or guide she had no idea how much elevation she was gaining, but certainly it was substantial; her body told her in no uncertain terms that the air was becoming thinner as the trail snaked upward, her breaths deeper and yet less rewarding. 'Short steps,' she counseled herself, 'and slow. Find the pace which does not require you to stop to catch your breath – your cruising speed.'

It wasn't till afternoon, several hours after she had stopped and eaten the last bits of dried fruit from her daypack, that she realized the clouds were taking over. Where before she had walked beneath sunny skies, feeling sweat on her brow and inside the collar of her blouse, now those same regions of the flesh were growing chilly, the blue overhead no more than a few jagged windows in a heavens gone thick and wooly. As the trail climbed higher and more steeply, it had begun switching back and forth on itself as well, sometimes ducking into the shadow of the ridge above, and each time it did so she felt a shiver run up her spine. This mountain air had no substance to it, no mass in which to retain heat; its temperature dropped precipitously as soon as one left the sun's bright glare.

It was there - trail turning back upon itself, cloud overtaking sun, shadows stretching overhead through air too thin to hold the heat of day, that Elaine realized she might truly be in trouble.

"Jake, it's Aubrey."

"Oh, hi, Aub," Jake answers, jamming on his brakes, to the dismay of a line of cars behind him. "Listen, this isn't a good time. I'm, uh...I'm at work."

"You got a job?"

"Yeah." Jake switches the phone to his left hand so his right can toggle the shifter into reverse. Twisting his head around to see the curb and raking the steering wheel one-handed, he begins backing into the short gap he had just spotted before his phone began to sing its ringtone. "And it's...I'm kinda' busy."

"That's great," Aubrey says, sounding genuinely impressed, though clearly more interested in getting on with her news. "The thing is, Kim is gone."

Halfway into the space, front fender still hanging well out into the lane, Jake turns full attention to the phone, as Aubrey gives a brief explanation of the confrontation at Sylvio's and her roommate's subsequent disappearance. When finally she pauses, it's comforting to hear him speak once again in that solid, confident tone she remembers from the old days.

"I'll find her," he says, reaching into the mess of papers blanketing his dashboard as the car behind him honks its horn. Digging a pen out of the mess, he flips several pieces of paper over before finding one with a blank side. "I'll find her," he says, as he begins writing. "I'll make her come back. We're her life, after all."

Tossing the pen back into the mess, he switches the phone to his right hand once again, and uses his left to flip a finger out the window at the honking driver visible in his rear-view mirror.

'GET KIM,' reads the note in his lap, the letters scrawled and ragged as he cranks the wheel round and begins moving once again, till his bumper touches the parked car behind and he lets out an accusatory curse.

"She'll come back, Aubs," he speaks into the phone as he shifts once again, slapping the lever into position and hitting the gas sharply in frustration. With a lurch the car moves forward, and this time it's the front bumper that makes contact, waking the silver Volvo in front of him.

"I'll make sure of it," Aubrey hears, accompanied by a honking horn and screaming siren alarm. The flashing lights - and Jake's intense expression - she must imagine for herself.

Surprisingly, as Mary recounts her search for the facts about Christina McKloskey's treatment, Jessica Bagley Seivers seems to grow more receptive, at times even charming, nodding affirmatively at several critical junctures. By the time her story has been told, Mary is convinced she has found not an adversary but an ally in this woman who so graciously offers her coffee from an exquisitely-decorated porcelain service of two cups and two pots, brought - without being requested, as far as Mary can tell - by a small man in shirtsleeves and a manner of enforced anonymity. One cup handed over, sugar and cream offered and declined, her own cup in hand, finally it is Jessica's turn to speak.

"Sadly," she begins, with a decidedly-theatrical sigh, "I can't talk about a patient's treatment. To do so would be a violation of confidentiality. Not to mention my termination agreement with Medical Holdings. And my pre-nuptial with William – but that's another story." Jessica pauses, eyebrows raised, cup suspended delicately between two fingers, and Mary has the impression she is debating whether to continue. Only for a moment though, after which the hostess allows herself the smallest of smiles, and continues in a more somber tone. "But I can tell you – hypothetically - about how a certain situation might be dealt with, if it had ever occurred, which I am not saying it ever did." Taking a sip from that delicate cup, she sets it back down in its saucer, crosses her legs and lays her hands, clasped, in her lap. Mary notices great care and precision in this woman's every movement, a consuming self-consciousness, as if she were on stage, even here, in her own home.

"Let us say," Seivers begins, once she has positioned herself just so. "That on a certain day, a certain young woman was admitted, unconscious and unresponsive due to... overindulgence. And let us say that, not long after, another patient presented Hilltop's administration with an extraordinary medical and ethical dilemma, a situation so outside the bounds of normal events that a unique group of staff had been convened in my – excuse me, the Director's; we are being hypothetical here, after all – the Director's conference room, to discuss a possible course of action..."

Seivers' voice trails off and the room goes silent for a time. Mary sees the woman's eyes drift toward the windows, their views of gridded towers rendered surreal by multiple layers of heavy glazing which allow not even a suggestion of the avenue's cacophony to invade the lonely perfection of this salon.

"Two patients," Mary prods, in hope of bringing the woman back from wherever she has drifted. With a start, Seivers straightens, casts a glance at her guest, and continues, as if frustrated by the interruption.

"Two subjects," she corrects, as if that noun makes all the difference in the world. "One - well, we've talked about her already. The other - again, just for the sake of argument - whose mind, due to an unconscionable error on our part, is conscious and viable, but whose body has...given out."

"Given out?"

"Oh, come child, work with me on this. I'm trying to tell a story here. Given out means...quit. Resigned. Abdicated. Heart failure, kidneys... Total shutdown of life support, at least as nature intended it. Happens all the time; and we assume the person has to go with it."

"So this second patient is terminal?" Mary asks, less from lack of understanding, than a desire to pin Seivers down, get her to be more specific. The woman, though, is having none of that. Voice rising and falling dramatically, her words stretch at random into multisyllabic melodies of sarcasm as she presses on with her narrative.

"That would be the usual description, the unconsidered opinion which avoids the dilemma. If the body is dying, we simply assume the mind must die as well. In which case, we would be presented with two terminal outcomes. But we're not talking about the usual here are we?

"Because, assuming Hilltop had ever had these two subjects, along with them it would happen to have an absolutely world-class team of physicians, including specialists in all sorts of things - things like pediatric endocrinology, multi-phasic dialysis, complex multi-organ transplant procedures and trauma management, plus researchers on the cutting edge - so to speak - of neural regeneration. And on the other side of the ring, we had corporate attorneys, administrators and a major financial jackal which just happens to be in the process of taking over this marvelous institution we call - called - home. Well, you can imagine the kinds of things that would be said, I mean, can't you?"

435

At this point Jessica Seivers stops her performance to refill her own cup, carefully pouring not from the carafe she used to top-off Mary's coffee, but from the other. The liquid she pours is amber, and could well be tea, by its look, though the scent which comes vaguely to Mary's nose is more reminiscent of dimly-lit bars and sloppy dates. Whiskey is her guess, Bourbon perhaps, or a very fine Scotch, more likely, though she is no expert at distinguishing such subtleties.

"Not really," Mary replies, with great innocence, after the length of pause makes clear the question was not completely rhetorical. "I'm afraid I don't understand what you are getting at."

"My darling," Bagley drawls, standing and smoothing her skirt against her thighs. Restlessly, she strolls around the nearest settee, touching its back with one long finger, whose polished nail matches perfectly the red stems of the cherry blossoms embroidered into the fabric. "Do you really believe, if Hilltop had allowed an experimental procedure to be carried out on a patient, that they would admit it? Why...to do so would open the entire institution to liability, negative publicity and possible loss of their accreditations. Oh, no, no, no, no, no, no. If such a thing had happened - which of course, it most certainly did not - they would do everything in their power to cover it up.

"Such as erasing the medical records of a patient?" Mary asks, doing her best to sound vapid.

"Goodness, *that's* not even worth mentioning," Seivers answers, a look of careless innocence consuming her features for a moment, only to be replaced an instant later by a slightly-pouty deadpan. "I'm imagining something more like, say - transferring the participants in said officially-unauthorized experimental procedure to far away paces like South Korea. Fairbanks, Alaska. Or perhaps - if the particular participant's level of cooperation in the erasure was complete, and the commercial potential of their contributions astounding — giving them their own research laboratories with full staff and funding.

"Doesn't it seem peculiar to you?" Seivers asks, sitting back down and taking another sip from her cup, its saucer poised with the greatest delicacy in one hand as the other lifts the tiny handle to lips whose color is gradually paling as their pigment is transferred molecule by molecule to the cup's blushing rim - as the discussion has progressed her smiles have become more forced, and Mary has the sense of something coiling inside this woman, whose cashmere softness seems to conceal a bitterness aching to be released. "That our friends provided care for that girl, at her mother's home?"

"And even after her friends removed her," Mary offers, proud to have knowledge which Seivers might not. "Instead of calling the police and reporting a kidnapping, they negotiated to keep the whole thing quiet and provided her medication free of charge."

"Imagine, if you can," Seivers continues, with no indication of appreciating Mary's information, or her grasp of the situation, "the potential to make disabled persons able-bodied once again. To end decades of full-time attendants, nursing home care, expensive therapies and accommodations, but through a measure which raises unanswerable questions of medical ethics; a phenomenal advance, but one which cannot even be uttered without calling down on our heads all the hounds of righteousness. Between the political climate, and the fact that such a breakthrough came about as a result of unauthorized activity, it would be impossible to...to take one's well-earned commercial advantage of it."

"So," Mary picks up the thread, excited by this motive she had not even glimpsed before, "they would choose to cover up their breakthrough for the time being. Shuffle all the players around and let them develop each of their special contributions in isolation, and then recreate their 'discovery' later, within a proper clinical framework, so they could exploit it financially?"

Seivers smiles discretely, and takes another sip of her beverage, neither assenting, nor disagreeing.

"But the press release, about MH taking over Hilltop," Mary points out, mind working hard to call up its information. "It said Dr. Sen was leaving Hilltop to join an aid agency doing work in Cuba; what could that..."

"It is a little-known fact," Seivers offers, very softly, "that despite that nation's technological stasis and general destitution, the Cuban medical system has several very well-equipped research hospitals. Given their isolation from the US medical system, and their antipathy toward religious institutions and beliefs, if one wanted to pioneer a medical procedure which risked offending the moral oligarchy, one might consider Fidel and Raoul's unspoiled beaches just an added amenity of exile.

"Sen is not a US citizen," she adds with a look which suggests she takes personal pride in the knowledge. "He's Romanian born, though one would never guess it to look at him, or hear him speak. And since Romania is a former member of the Soviet Bloc..."

"There would be nothing to prevent him living and working in Cuba," Mary finishes, her enthusiasm overcoming her now, though even as she speaks, the impact of what Seivers is pretending not to suggest settles into place: if you accept that a bunch of medical experts - who tend to be independent-minded to the point of arrogance - could jointly agree to go rogue, for even the most humanitarian of reasons; and if you accept that even a team as good as Hilltop's could solve the technical challenges - two awfully-big 'ifs' there – it means all those outlandish claims which Rod has been making since waking up in Mrs. M's cottage, *could be true*. He just might actually be who he says he is: product of the physicians' desperate attempt to make up for a horrendous error by their own staff. In which case Hilltop's missing records and offer of continuing care make perfect sense - the obverse and reverse of an elaborate attempt to cover up their own astounding success.

"But wait, Mrs. Seivers," Mary implores, realizing a gap in her own understanding. "How could it have been an error, that the subject's brain was still viable, how could that be a bad thing?"

Jessica smiles once again, that self-possessed little movement of lips and brows which seems to signal a trap being sprung.

"Because, my little innocent, it violates one of those assumptions we make without even realizing it, " an assumption she proceeds to attack with a conviction that comes as one more surprise to her visitor. Run a car into the ground, Seivers proposes, and you would make sure it is not occupied, before sending the steel to the junkyard. Wear out a billfold, and you would certainly remove the bills before consigning the leather to a waste bin. But when a human body is worn out, the inherent expectation is that that the mind - that marvelous collection of memories and capabilities, as she puts it, taking another sip, that repository of personal history which we profess to believe makes each unique and irreplaceable – must go with it. It's absurd. Indefensible, really, this implicit presumption that the mind and the body are one and the same. And if one reconsiders that presumption? If one attempts to make one's way over that mountain of ignorance into the valley beyond, one is accused of 'playing God;' of doing what no man - or woman, heaven forbid – should do.

"Our greatest success," she effuses, apparently forgetting for the moment the hypothetical framework of her own presentation, "can't even be uttered out loud until a proper framework – can you

438

believe that formulation, *'a proper framework*?' – has been laid. Until a more suitable political climate exists, or can be bought from some petty dictator hungry for validation in the eyes of his peers, of which there are far too many these days. Oh yes, we can solve the technical problems; we can advance the science a generation or two by implanting a seed-crop of genetically-modified cells into somebody's brain stem - but sooner or later the dull old men in their black suits and their white shirts, with those dull, dark eyes that paint the world in their own black-and-white palette, will find their prejudices threatened and then where do we find ourselves, Mary, *where do we find ourselves*? Out of the picture. Bound and silenced by the ones we thought valued our contributions; buried in Regency splendor. *Co-opted* if you will – by our own golden parachutes; which sounded fine at one time, but is not, as one can see, tremendously stimulating."

Setting her cup onto the wooden table with a clatter, Seivers inhales deeply, craning her neck first to one side, and then to the other, as if to relieve herself of some pain. Only after this is done, and her hands clasped demurely in her lap, does she speak again.

"Of course," she says, in a voice of resignation, "none of this is true. Why if it were, think of what it would mean to that poor girl back there. Although she wouldn't *be* a girl, would she?"

In the pause that follows, Mary imagines briefly that Seivers has understood Rod's full dilemma, but her next words put a lie to that assumption.

"No, not a girl at all," she continues bitterly. "Just another subject, reduced to the proverbial vegetative state. That's it, isn't it? Some sort of cross-bred hybrid root-vegetable, to be stored away in the cellar of her mother's backyard bungalow and never heard from again."

"I think you should know…" Mary begins to interject, eager to share the extent of Rod's recovery and self-awareness, but the woman is having none of it.

"Know?" she fires back. "Knowing is the worst thing one can do. Knowing has nothing to do with any of this. Supposing is the operative word, my dear. It's all just supposition - on your part, that is - and if anyone were to suggest that I had said any of these things, I would certainly deny them."

Puzzled, Mary waits what seems a very long time, until Seivers continues, speaking very slowly, as if ashamed of her own words.

"This life, here. All of what you see," she says, gesturing at the lovely room, with its plethora of textures and reflections. "Sometimes when you admit what you want, it's...it becomes... a weapon... in the other person's hand. To have a dream come true? That's a powerful thing, even if there is a price attached to it...giving up my career was nothing, by the way; I was ready for that, believe me. Seventeen years of daily battles; dodging bullets from managers and accountants, lawyers and regulators. I was *so* ready when Charming Billy turned on his endorphinos. But part of the price is...convincing oneself to believe that certain things did not happen. No matter what some young resident who flew all the way here from the rain coast might think or say; they did not happen. Ever. I'm sorry to disappoint you, Miss..?"

"Antonias," Mary offers, for the third time, as her hostess stands unsteadily, her fiery glare ample indication that this audience is over.

Here, now, lying in the darkness, Elaine no longer feels the cold - or the fear. What she *is* feeling is the weight of bedding, warm and comforting, surrounding her body. Holding her in equilibrium. Just as her hunger and thirst seem balanced. Yes, she will need to eat something sometime, but not just yet. Her throat will need to be wetted, but there is no urgency. Rather, there is a sense that these things will be taken care of in due time; that she can wait until an opportunity presents itself, then deal with the necessity and move on. It is unimportant after all, this body of hers, so distant and foreign. A second home in another state, visited only for the season, then boarded up and left until the next time.

It had not seemed that way as she climbed toward the divide, though. When she encountered the first patches of snow beside the trail she could feel clearly each frozen mass reaching out, sucking warmth from her uncovered fingers, and her face, their flesh not nearly thick enough to protect the bones within. Above, a single ever-morphing window of bright sky still lingered, but all around it the clouds had thickened and, yes, that was snow falling, off to the left. Barely perceptible at first, like the streaks of a brush dragged across the nearly-dried paint of distant peaks until a fresh gust of breeze soon brought the first flakes around her; few and far between but unmistakable - magic-crystals sparkling in the brilliant light still pouring down on this one piece of earth, they brought the air to life even as their dusty presence stole her last glimpse of the valleys below. And when she gazed directly toward the sun –no longer dangerous to stare directly into, but glowing now, like a bulb seen through layers of sheer curtain; – the flakes nearest its brilliance were surrounded by halos of color. Individual circular rainbows that sprang into existence for a fragment of a second and disappeared as one flake fell to earth only to be replaced by another and another and another. It felt, as she trudged ever-upward in a swirling tea of sun and snow and rainbow hues, as if the very atmosphere were offering up a confidence, a glimpse of all the wonders it could manage. Above and beyond the everyday presumptions of rain or shine, the heavens were putting on a show just for her; to reward her effort, and encourage it.

Even as she felt that validation, there was also a sense of urgency. She was small in the face of such magnificence; tiny and vulnerable out among the elements, and her window to the sky was growing smaller all the time. For a moment she considered turning back, but it would take the rest of the day, and the next as well, to walk back to the hamlet where they had stayed two nights before. Assuming she could even find the way. The memory of that lonely clearing - how quickly she had become disoriented there - was a stern reminder that 'going back' is not without its own dangers. Surely, she told herself, she would find her companions sooner by going forward, or if not them, then at least some sort of shelter. This trail was too well-established to be a dead end, Elaine told herself.

The fabric of her blouse had become heavy on her breastbone, weighted with perspiration, her body's own emission turned cold and foreign. A gentle puff of breeze was followed by another, stronger puff - a gust in fact, that swirled the flakes into columns of visible energy and flung her hair into her eyes, and when she raised a hand to brush the hair away the motion made her dizzy, evidence of the altitude she had gained this day and perhaps, as well, of the little food she'd eaten,. Despite the short steps and slow pace, she realized her body was becoming exhausted. This climb was much harder for her than she wanted to admit, and yet there was that magnificence all around, that secret shared with the clouds, spurring her on. She was, it seemed clear, intended to be here; intended to be climbing this slope as the elements put on their show for her alone. She could not back down now, could not refuse their offer of the unknown and the impossible. She would reach this summit; if it was the last thing she did.

Hmmm.
Well, well.

The idea did not creep up on her, dawning slowly, but sprang fully to life, with all the clarity and presence of a familiar quote, a remembered lyric, a childhood prayer: she might actually die on this mountain. Today, within the next few hours even - for as she walked onward, she found the snow no longer lying only in shaded patches, but all around, even covering short stretches of trail several inches deep, as its patches grew larger and more frequent, before melding into fields whose distant reaches were lost in the shower of new flakes falling more and more heavily. Her lightweight boots were not meant for this; their low tops allowing moisture to reach and be sucked into her cotton socks. As the air thickened with more and larger flakes she became acutely aware of her ankles - of all body parts, one of the last to ever call attention to itself - colder now than either the dry legs above or the feet below which, even wet, benefitted from the warmth of boots and friction. "That's it," she voiced out loud, "I'm going to die of frozen ankles," the absurdity of such a fate striking her as unbelievably comical. 'What the hey,' she thought, to herself this time, in a phrase recalled from long ago and far away, and found surprising power in the attitude. To die today would be a very real, authentic experience. Not some polite euphemism, like 'passing away,' or 'moving on;' the end of her life hidden away in some institution as if a shameful secret must be kept. To end it all up here would be to *die*, out in the open, in full view of God and everybody, and that was not, by any means, inconceivable.

"What the hey," Elaine said out loud, and considered where the phrase had come from. Something her father used to say, tossing off whatever daily trouble had afflicted him or one of his family. She felt a smile growing, a warming burst of joy at the silly sound resurrected from a past which at this moment seemed so distant as to have happened to someone else altogether. What it really meant was 'what the heck,' but that was too frank for a father to say in front of his daughter, in the time and place where she had grown.

"What they hey, what the heck," she murmured as she gazed at the stretch of path before her, snow-covered and steeply side-sloped. A new marching song, a mantra to keep her going and on pace. And 'what the heck' itself? A transparent fudge, to avoid saying 'hell.'

That was it then. A stride on 'what the hey,' inhaling, another on 'what the heck,' and then exhale on 'what the hell,' and back again to the old familiar euphemism for a euphemism.

"What the hey, what the heck, what the hell," breathe, breathe. "What the hey, what the heck, what the hell," breathe, breathe. She was moving again; up the mountain, the snowy wind pressing her skirt against freezing shins and thighs, but its cold no longer held power over her. It was a nuisance and insignificance, no more to her than the flapping wings of a butterfly on the other side of the world, for she was moving toward a pass, from which she would see the other side. Moving slowly but steadily, the way all things got done really, on this side of the pass. It might be different over there, perhaps magical, with everything revealed and no effort required for anything. That would be nice, she thought, and so as her body marched and her brain chanted, her deeper mind imagined a place of ease and harmony.

She was very high now, could feel the air scraping her throat; so cold and dry as she sucked it in that it threatened to tear the fragile tissues hidden within her mouth and throat and chest. In the deep snow her steps came slower still, and her chanting stretched out along with them, fueling her muscles and regulating her pace. "What the hey, what the heck, what the hell, what the fuck."

The first time she spoke it, the word came as a shock. If her mother... But her mother was not here; had passed on years ago, and now rested...far, far from here. Father too, and Rodney, bless his pointed little head. And Beryl, lost somewhere on the trail. The guides? No, there was no one anymore to be shocked at the forbidden syllable passing her respectable lips. Again Elaine smiled, and the act of smiling warmed her just a bit. It was good to laugh a little at oneself. At the remnant prudery which made her ashamed of the impulse - even here, utterly alone and approaching death - to make a certain combination of sounds. It was only a word, after all, and certainly not one she had never heard of, or heard spoken, for that matter. A sound, a meaning, an intention, an attitude. That was it – the attitude. The reason that particular word had popped into her head at this particular moment. An attitude to hold onto; of strength and of defiance; that in this moment and in this circumstance, it could not possibly make any difference that she had uttered a certain word, or not.

"What the hey, what the heck. What the hell, what the fuck," Elaine repeated, as loud as her heaving chest would allow, and found her step stronger for it. Two lines on the in-breath, two lines on the out, two steps on each and that much farther toward the ultimate goal. The summit, the pass. Toward seeing what was on the other side.

"There are ground rules," Stevie says sternly, after greetings the next morning. Hair uncombed, face bare of make-up, she leans against the counter, crossed ankles and a hint of cleavage visible beneath the teal-colored velour of her bathrobe. She holds a drip-pot high in one hand, a bone-china teacup and saucer just as high in the other: totems of a domestic tranquility she holds quite dear. "Respect my place, my things, me; and I'll respect you. Do *not* steal from me; *do* put your dirty dishes in the dishwasher. Pick up your stuff and don't keep me awake at night. No drugs, no bringing strange men - or women – into this house, and no hurting yourself. Those OK with you?"

The boy considers for a time, as if pondering a question of national importance, then nods, without smiling. "Those are certainly reasonable things to ask."

Lowering her hands, she fills the cup, pleased with the exchange. It makes her comfortable with the situation, just as her decorating has made her comfortable with her home; the carefully-coordinated colors and surfaces, the precisely-arranged clutter she has evolved over the months of living here.

The boy is wearing the same suit as the night before, since none of the pajamas she'd offered him were to his taste; even her flannel shirt and warm-up pants being, apparently, too contaminated with the feminine to fit the image he feels compelled to project. Of course, Stevie imagines, she might be just as insistent, if the shoe were on the other foot. Besides, there *is* something dashing about a young man in a suit coat first thing in the morning, collar open, hair all rumpled, and the residue of sleep still lingering around his owlish young eyes. Stevie is only too aware that her own eyes are, by contrast, rather too small and deep-set, though that trace of yesterday's mascara which never seems to come off with the nightly scrub does give them a slightly winsome look in the mornings.

"It's very generous of you," he says, breaking her reverie. "Miss. And I really do appreciate your letting me stay here until I can come up with...some idea of what to do with myself. But I have to wonder, what is it you expect? In return, I mean."

There it is again. That hard edge to him. Underneath the confusion, underneath the painful tender reminders of the girl he used to be, she can feel something else. Like deep down he is absolutely certain of who he is and has already decided how everybody else should fit into place around him. Not a quality she admires in a man - or anyone, for that matter, but maybe a wrinkle she can help him iron out.

"No 'return,' " she says, keeping it plain in hopes of diffusing his suspicion. "Just because. You need a place to stay, I've got one. I think I have an idea what's going on inside that head of yours...."

"I doubt it." There's bitterness in the retort, she notices. More than a trace of self-pity. Another attitude she has come to believe will never lead to anything worthwhile. Already there is so much she'd love to teach this youthful creature, so much she'd love to say to him. That's going to be one of the challenges, actually, to avoid preaching; talking his ear off and sounding like she thinks she knows it all; far better to let him learn for himself what it means to finally become himself.

"OK, so look at it another way. There've been times in my life when I needed help and people went out of their way to help me, so now it's my turn." She opens a cupboard and removes a pack of English muffins. Begins to twist off the wire tie, then stops, reminded of something. "Actually there is one thing I want."

The boy doesn't respond, only waits, eyes narrowed. If anything, he seems reassured. The fact that kindness has a price is a better fit - in his world view - than simple generosity.

"Sing," she says. Seeing his eyes drop and his mouth tighten, she stops what she is doing and turns to lean, hands tucked behind her back, against the counter. This is a good sign, she realizes with satisfaction, that he can let his shields down to such an extent in her presence. So different than if she were still a man. They'd both be all hale and hearty, buddy-buddy, and neither of them would ever admit what he was truly thinking. But she's not a man, not in his eyes anyway, not at this moment, so his defenses are less active. "You've got a beautiful voice," she says, intending to leave it at that.

Turning back toward the counter, she pulls out a fork and begins to split two muffins, then stops in mid-motion to shake her head rapidly back and forth, tossing out another thought. "God..." she says softly, without turning toward him. "What I wouldn't give to have your voice."

High above the Midwest, Mary Antonias sips a V-8 and fingers a folder of notes, unopened since she pulled it from her tote at the start of the flight. In the window seat beside her a man juggles his own paperwork – stiff manila cards, stamped with dates and times, alongside rows and rows of signatures and notations in ragged scrawls. Around them both, the engines drone and a movie plays silently on screens every third row, as through the window Mary glimpses the patchwork shadows of suburban sprawl. Dark rectangular blocks of industrial buildings can be made out even from this height, surrounded by parking lots nested in a web of roadways, with a river twisting and glinting through it all. As she stares, the plane's progress pans her view a bit farther west and with surprising speed the buildings begin to change, gaining a visible third-dimension as a downtown comes into view, narrow spires of skyscrapers reflecting the lowering sun. A short time later, a lake's shoreline joins the picture, water's edge flashing silvery before the whole disappears into the blur of a maritime cloud layer. Oblivious, the man scans his cards, every so often stopping to type a few rapid, confident strokes on his laptop, then fiddle with the touchpad, switch to another card and in a few seconds, type again. His concentration seems total, his intensity so remarkable, that Mary finds her anger rising, just to watch him. How, she asks herself, can anyone care that much about a bunch of notes and dates and times?

The visit to Jessica Bagley has left her depressed, she realizes, worrying the worn and fuzzy edge of her file, on the rounded tab of which she initially wrote simply 'Jane,' then added several months ago 'Christina.' Pulling a mechanical pencil from her purse she clicks its cap to extend the lead and adds, in smaller characters to fit the space remaining, 'RG?'

On the movie screen in front of her, two men maneuver around the furniture of a fabulously luxurious living room, every so often gesturing at one another in what appears to be great anger. A woman enters, dressed for an evening out, and the men stop - surprised, perhaps, or embarrassed maybe, their mugging expressions difficult to read on so small a screen. She doesn't even know the movie's title, Mary realizes, and yet her attention is drawn to its action, movement alone creating the impression of drama, and a desire to know how it will end. Is that, she wonders, really all that captivated her that morning in the ICU ; the drama of an unknown victim, and wanting to see how the story would end? Her mind recoils a bit at the thought. She is a physician, after all, her interest not only in getting to the end of a patient's treatment, but in shaping that ending, improving the outcome to the greatest extent possible. And with the Jane not being her patient, how could she help, except perhaps by shedding some light on the mystery of why this girl seems to have been shunted and shifted out of the light and into the darkness?

"Take that for you?" a flight attendant asks, reaching out for her beverage can. With a shake of the head Mary moves it a few inches away from him, the spell of her thoughts broken. Beside her, the man's concentration is broken as well. Setting his cards on the tray table he shifts, stretches a bit and seems to notice Mary for the first time.

"Not much to see out there," he offers, with a nod toward the window, now revealing only the uniform gray of cold and moisture-laden air. His voice is deep, deeper than she'd have expected from his size, and pale soft hands on the keyboard. Turning just enough to observe out of the corner of her eye, but not so much as might appear to be too interested, she sees his face is also soft and pale. An indoor face, but intelligent, with sharp brown eyes beneath a heavy brow. The mouth is crisp as well, as his chin rests on an open hand.

"No," Mary answers back. "You seem plenty busy though." Her hands feel awkward now, idle and obvious on the folder she has not even opened. Down the aisle another attendant comes, gathering up the empties and trash of the meager snacks she had so recently offered to the passengers filed neatly into their seats. What does this man see when he looks at me, Mary wonders, and instantly rebukes herself for caring. Better to just be yourself with a man - unconscious and impulsive - and let him decide how he feels, instead of always editing your actions to what you think will make a good impression. What she really wants right now is something, anything, to distract her from wondering about Christina McKloskey and Jessica Bagley Seivers and all the rest of the characters who've been keeping her up through the early morning hours. "So what is it," she ventures, "that's got you so absorbed in your little cards and numbers?"

Her companion laughs a bit, the kind of muted chuckle that says 'don't take me too seriously,' and Mary is pleasantly reminded of Jason, her funky young geek, the one unquestionably good thing which has come out of this whole business. The recollection softens her frustration a bit, and she finds herself looking forward to getting back home, to seeing Jase again, as her seatmate clears his throat, then speaks. "This," he begins, "is my little detective story."

He's a mechanical engineer, he goes on to explain, who designed the plumbing systems for a hotel over in Redmond. The hotel was completed several months ago, and everything is fine except for an unexplained water problem. Down in the basement, where guests park and the staff have their lockers, the concrete is sometimes damp; damp enough to see, to feel, and to give the air a musty smell. It's apparent that water is seeping in from somewhere, despite a spell of weather as dry as it has been for years.

"We put in a drain system, to take care of any underground water," he assures her, and all the piping checks out. "We pressure tested it to show up any leaks and there aren't any." With that possibility discounted, the hotel staff, the architect and the contractor all turned to him to figure out where the water could be coming from. What he's working on now are records of measurements: ground-water levels in a hole drilled outside the hotel, logs of water use by staff – running loads in the big commercial washing machines, hosing down the shuttle vans, watering the gardens, topping-off the swimming pool - anything that consumes or discharges a lot of water. "I'm plotting all that data against a time line." He shifts his laptop, opens the screen to a better angle and taps a few keys, and on the screen Mary sees a graphic, dozens of diamonds, colored red and blue and orange, all scattered across a grid of lines.

"I'm looking for a relationship," he explains, then gives another of those small laughs and corrects himself. "Not that kind of relationship. A correlation. Between the moisture in the floor and something else."

For a while more the fellow talks, explaining his theories and how he's shot them all down himself, and Mary finds herself envying his quiet methodical approach. Even though he doesn't know where his investigation is going, Terry, as he identifies himself, seems dead clear on how to proceed. Eventually, he falls silent and Mary, unable to think of anything worthwhile to add, nods her head, thanks him for the explanation, and allows her attention to drift toward the in-flight entertainment. The movie seems particularly unappealing; washed-out images of transient celebrities, flashing across a plastic screen hinged down from a luggage bin. And yet she knows the sensation of losing yourself in entertainment; how your mind can disregard its surroundings and choose to believe that a bunch of electronically-generated pixels and vibrations are actual; emotions aroused just as truly by words and actions you know for a fact to be faked, as by those of flesh and blood people in the same room with you. They're all the same, if you let yourself believe them, and maybe that is a little bit of an explanation for how an intelligent person like Jessica Seivers could convince herself that something as monstrous and implausible as what she's claiming – implanting the brain of a dying man into the body of a brain-damaged young woman - could actually have happened. And then been covered up.

Ever since leaving Dracula's Castle, Mary's been trying to figure out how the whole of Hilltop could conspire to hide whatever happened to Christina McKloskey, when it's at least equally plausible that Jennifer herself could be the one doing the deceiving. The woman is certainly bitter enough that it could warp her interpretation of the facts, if not her recollections themselves. What proof is there, after all, that any of what she has said is true? A few missing records? That happens all the time; a page misplaced, or pulled out of the copier with another sheet and so put back inside the wrong file where it seems to disappear forever - just as the Jane might have done, if her mother hadn't glimpsed a photo in a newspaper.

Such little things, then, that can decide our fate. A tiny dose of chemicals in the wrong hands, an inch-square grainy image in a hundred pages of newsprint. These thoughts are drifting through Mary's head as she finds herself turning again to her own folder, reviewing in her mind the skimpy notes she's been able to assemble in the absence of Christina's actual records. Meager milestones in the journey of her subject, from unidentified emergency, to arbitrarily-named patient, to a real person with a name, then two, and maybe even more. Events that happened months ago and yet here she is, traipsing across a continent trying to put it together, and all out of envy. That's what it is, she realizes with a start, looking again at the movie screen where the blond – clad now in a metallic-gold bikini - is being pursued around a swimming pool by the same two men from that earlier living-room scene. Envy. The simplest definition for how she was affected by the Jane's face that morning; the face of a pretty girl who'd always get the guy while Mary got the work, the caring-for and worrying-about.

Opening the folder, Mary scans its pages as if for the first time, wondering just how she could have thought it all so important, could have wasted so much time and sleep over petty jealousy. Could even for a moment have believed the ramblings of a bitter alcoholic like Jessica Bagley Seivers. Lost deep in those thoughts, she is unaware of the change in the sound of the plane's four engines - their drone interrupted, their overtones and harmonics muted for a moment - but quite aware of the compression in spine and the forward-tipping motion of her head as the seat seems to rise beneath her, before the plane drops back down in the next instant. Aware, too, of the split-second's horror at falling from the sky before those slender wings catch a fresh cushion of compressed atmosphere and all is back to normal.

All, that is, except the large splott of tomato juice cocktail which has extracted itself from the can in her hand and is now spreading across several sheets from her folder. Printouts which Jason brought her, from the one backup file he *was* able to access. Documenting Dr. Gimbal's final stay at Hilltop.

Grabbing a napkin, Mary wipes the wet spot into a pale shadow and stuffs the soggy mess into the opening of the juice can.

"The captain has advised us," comes an attendant's voice through the crackle of the plane's audio system, "that we may experience a bit of turbulence for the next few minutes. So we're going to turn on the seatbelt sign and ask you to stay in your seats for the time being."

While other passengers are checking their seat belts, or retrieving them from beneath lap blankets and scrunched sweaters, magazines and laptops, the passenger in 26D is busy flipping through her file folder, eyes suddenly narrowed, one damp sheet of paper clutched in her left hand as her right rifles the other sheets, knowing that the page she wants must be somewhere. Flipping, flipping again until there it is, in front of her eyes – a duplicate of the final page of Rod Gimbal's chart, Hilltop's terse recording of the care and treatment afforded one of its own. A tightly-written history of events and actions, of medications administered, procedures tried, resuscitation and defibrillation attempted, but halfway down the page it all abruptly ends, with Irv Keleher's terse notation: 'Unsuccess.' and on the next line, 'Pron. Dec. 2:56 PM, 3/20'.

Her eyes oscillate between this and the sheet she holds in the air, a standard Record of Procedure for the extraction of a 'Viable Donor Organ' from the remains of patient Dr. Rodney Gimbal, with the time of removal printed clearly: '10:42 AM, 3/21.' The physician's signature is illegible, as so many of them are, but the location noted beside it is clear as day - 'ApDL.' Which might sound reasonable to another observer – kidneys go with dialysis, after all, as shampoo goes with hair - except that anyone who's ever observed a kidney transplant, as Mary did nearly four years ago during her internship, knows that a kidney must be harvested immediately after death, and, once harvested, need only be kept cold to remain viable; you would no more run dialysis on a cadaver kidney harvested for transplant than you would on one from the grocery meat counter. So why was *any* part of Dr. Gimbal up in the Applied Dialysis Lab, eighteen hours after he was pronounced, and what *was* it that left there, to be transplanted into Christina McKloskey?

It may have been a few minutes later, or it may have been an hour, as Elaine continued placing one foot in front of the other and chanting her newly acquired mantra, that some logical, rational, segment of gray matter which still observed the impulses of its neighboring regions was taken to remark on the absence of memory. A dying person, after all, is supposed to relive their life, aren't they? Shouldn't she be thinking of a perfect summer day somewhere, or recalling the instant in which she had first fallen for a boy. Or dreaming the taste of a perfect soufflé; her mind seeking that one perfect instant of pure sensual escape to distract it from the terrifying. Instead, tainted by months in the East (or trained, perhaps?), she found herself far more interested in the present than even the most attractive of memories. In the concrete presence of air within her lungs, entering and departing with each rasping breath; in the cold and wet which had taken over her feet, legs and face, making them feel like foreign objects somehow appended to her true self, while beneath her blouse her chest was sweaty and hot and heavingly present; these were the things which demonstrated that she was alive. Still alive; still striving for a summit which was sure to appear one of those times when her eyes lifted from their task of following the faint trail and instead allowed themselves the luxury of imagining its end.

There. A shallow curvature of drifted snow between two stacked pillars of rock, marking the end of her journey. There she would be able to sit, finally, and rest legs which burned within, even as they froze from without. There she would be free of the need to keep moving and could see, once and for all, whatever there was to see from the end of her trail.

"What the hey, what the heck, what the hell, what the fuck."

"You said you thought you had some idea what's going on inside my head?" Rod asks, a little later. He and Stevie are sitting now at the small wooden table in a corner of the kitchen. Through sliding glass doors they gaze across the terrace toward a narrow slice of Lake Washington, its ebony surface fine-textured by choppy waves beneath a sodden sky. On the table plates sit, empty but for a few crumbs and one glossy round droplet of melted butter hell-bent on returning to a solid state. The coffee pot has been drained as well, and soon it will be time for Stevie to launch herself into another day. This conversation might be better held another time, she thinks, a little irritably. But then again, there's really never a good time.

"Because of who I am," she answers. "How I got to be ... me."

"I am not like you Miss..."

"Stevie," she suggests, for at least the third time this morning.

"Stevie," he pronounces, though not without effort.

"You make it sound like something to be ashamed of. My name, I mean."

"I'm not a...," he begins, then stops, the word apparently too great an obstacle for those taut lips to pronounce.

"Transsexual?" she offers. The kid's struggle with the word makes it all the more satisfying to form with her own mouth. "Look," she says, allowing her voice its old weight, coming up from the diaphragm, rather than the head-voice she has trained herself to favor. These are ideas she has phrased and rephrased a thousand times, occasionally out loud, but mostly hiding in her head. Ideas she has dissected and worried-at in the middle of endless nights and in the silent subtext of conversations about anything and everything but what was really pre-occupying her. Ideas to be spoken with her full self, not tailored to another's ear. "I'm not going to tell you how to live your life, but I can tell you that the day I announced to the world that I was no longer going to hide who I am, was the most...in a very real sense, it may as well have been the first day of my life."

"But I'm not..." he insists, rising from the table in agitation. Stepping around, restless, he shakes his shoulders and wrings his hands, then settles for standing behind a chair, fingers wrapped tightly around its bentwood back. "I have no explanation for why I look the way I look, but I know I'm not...what you are. I don't believe in it, for one thing. I'm a physician, and the purpose of medicine is to cure and to heal. It's against everything I stand for, to use medicine – surgery, in particular - to enable people to pretend to be something they are not…"

"First of all," Stevie interrupts, even as she ponders just how deep his self-delusion goes, "gender reassignment surgery is not about pretending, *Doctor* Gimbal. It's about making the package fit the contents. And second, if you must know: I haven't had surgery." As she expected, that sets the cocky kid on his side a bit, though she finds herself regretting it for just that reason; this is supposed to be about understanding, after all, not scoring points. "I am who I am, and it's nobody's business what's inside my pants. On the rare day when I actually wear pants, that is," a joke which seems lost on him.

"But…everybody believes you're a woman. You look like a woman; you act like a woman…"

"Well there. You've answered your own question."

"But… Isn't there a law against that?"

"Rodney, Rodney, Rodney," she chuckles, reaching out a hand, which he takes only after much consideration – and, even then, very tentatively, their fingers barely touching as she urges him back into his seat. "Look, Rodney, I've got to get ready for my day, so here's what it all comes down to. You and I are alike, not because of any label people put on what I am, or because I have made any conclusion about who *you* are or how you got there, but because we're both people who want to be accepted for who we are inside, regardless of our outsides; *that's* what makes us alike. As for what that's called…well, you don't have to accept any labels, from me or anyone else. You get to define yourself however you want to."

She stops, waiting for response. When none is forthcoming, she gazes off a bit, until an idea comes. "If I could give you a gift," she says, "this is what it would be." Bringing both hands up in front of her, she shapes them into a sort of bowl, the fingers pressed tight against one another, as if afraid to lose a drop of some precious liquid.

"Here's your life," she says, thrusting the imaginary bowl toward Christina's face, hardened as it is into Rodney Gimbal's customary skepticism. "It's brand new and no one can see it but you. Take your life and make it what you want it to be."

Setting her ghostly gift on the table before him, she rises, cinching the belt of her robe tighter around her waist, and starts across the room, only to stop, unable to resist divulging one more piece of information to her new pupil.

"And no," she says, turning back. "There's no law against being me. Not that I'd obey it, if there was. People may try to put us in their boxes, Rodney, but we don't have to go along with them. Ever."

The memory comes back gradually, the rememberer drifting between waking and a sort of dozing state, not quite sleep, but out of touch with the physical world around her. After one such doze she finds the darkness noticeably less dense. The rain has stopped sometime in the night, and now a window is visible, covered with a tight cloth, its small square shape a shade lighter than the black of walls surrounding her. Swiveling her eyes, she begins to make out other features; a glint of light off the far wall, an indistinct plane of ceiling above, before her thoughts resume their reconstruction.

Despair had overtaken Elaine as she watched the sun settle from her perch upon the divide, a viewpoint purchased so dearly that she could not imagine leaving it, any more than she could imagine staying. Through a distant crease of open sky, she had seen that indispensable neighborhood star diminish from glow to disc to semicircle to sliver and finally, to a pinprick of brilliance framed by a notch in the distant ridge, its beam flaring like a searchlight for one glorious moment before being sucked back into itself and vanishing. Though the sun's progress made no sound, its disappearance left behind a silence: a stillness as of death, over a landscape whose already-meager store of latent heat was rapidly being sucked up and out toward the darkening sky and the snow covered slopes which stretched in every direction; shadowy ranks of ridges and pinnacles as far as the eye could make out.

Gazing down the far side of the saddle Elaine thought she could perhaps make out a few traces of trail switching back and forth across the slope below, but no hint of any destination. Perhaps there was a village down there, only a few miles farther, perhaps not. Perhaps the nearest habitation was a full days' walk away, down where the rivers ran like thunder, or two days, where the air was moist and thick and verdant forest carpeted widening valleys. She would never know, she concluded, sitting on a cairn and feeling her breath settle slower and slower, for she had not the energy to start down that trail.

There was a small construction to one side of the summit trail; an angled wall of stacked stones, each flat slab inscribed with prayers. A weathered post protruded from the ground as well, guyed with dozens of strings of prayer flags, each string alternating the colors of blue, white, red, green and yellow, symbols of the sky, the air, fire, water and earth; all the elements which make up our world. Fluttering and snapping in the wind they made this a fitting place, she thought, to stop. To lay down care and worry and effort, and to wait, for whatever might come.

"Enough moping around."

It is still morning, Rod still sitting at the kitchen table, staring at the soiled dishes and his own hands, and Stevie has come out of her bedroom fully-dressed, hair and face done up for a day of visiting clients, but one more thing to do before leaving. "Let me hear that voice of yours."

Taking the boy's hand in her own she pulls him gently up from his seat, then heads off, through an open doorway beyond which lies the living room: a cozy parlor, with walls of pale sage outlined by white-painted trim. Floor-length curtains cover the windows, their sheer fabric allowing just the faintest glimpse of the neighborhood outside, where dated brick ranch houses sit next to six-story apartment blocks sandwiched along streets lined with parked cars. On the walls are prints and photographs of urban scenes, all narrow sidewalks and strolling couples.   A wrought-iron stand full of plants sits in front of one window sill, while nearly every other surface is cluttered with ceramic cats, stuffed plush cats, and silver framed pictures of cats, a preoccupation Stevie acknowledges with a laugh before her guest can even ask.

"I love cats," she says, petting one member of the artificial pack and shrugging her shoulders in resignation. "Unfortunately, I'm highly allergic, so this is as close as I can get to having one."

Against one wall is an upright piano, its pearly-white lacquer sparkling and dust free, its music ledge filled with books and sheets, its bench padded with dark-blue velour - mashed and crumpled from frequent use. Settling on the bench, Stevie shifts its position several times to get it just so, then rubs her hands together, lacing the fingers and squeezing, then pulling and massaging one hand with the other, in what seems a practiced sequence. After a minute of this she reaches out her left hand, almost warily, and flutters its fingers across several keys. A deep rich tattoo works its way out of the instrument, muffled by foot pedal and closed lid, but still filling the room with sonic sunshine. With her right hand, then, she reaches out in the other direction as if uncertain, testing what will happen, and flutters once again. The same notes, but this time higher in pitch, cutting across the space with more insistence.

From across the room, Rod watches and listens as his hostess runs through several arpeggios, breaking now and then into a bit of rhythm, then stopping in mid-phrase, only to begin an entirely different piece. His face is stern, apprehensive.

"Come on over," Stevie calls to him, hands still roving apparently at random, though the sounds they render are anything but.

"I'm no singer," Rod cautions. "Not since my voice changed."

For a moment Stevie is taken aback, until she realizes he must be referring to this history he claims as Rodney. Not for the first time she is blown away by the lengths to which the human mind can go in rationalizing what it wants, especially when that desire flies in the face of what others tell it. "Don't give me that," she answers, sliding into a ragtime number, left hand pumping as the right roves up and down. "I've heard you. That night at the club."

"That was just a fluke. It wasn't me; it was..."

"Rodney," she says to the crash of a brassy chord, followed by a cascade of notes that run down the keyboard in rippling succession, before stopping abruptly, so the silence which follows cannot be ignored. "Don't give me that. Don't do that to yourself. As long as you are here with me, let's just agree it doesn't matter who it is that does something beautiful. Or who it was, or wants to be. You are who you are, you do what you do. Now come over here and I'll show you what you sound like."

Reluctantly, the boy moves closer, hands stuffed into jacket pockets, head slouched forward in determination to be defeated.

"OK," Stevie says when he has reached her side. For the briefest instant her hands hover over the keyboard, wondering, then shift themselves into position and begin again, left hand pumping a simple two-fingered rhythm, right hand poised, a single finger outstretched. Her face shines with a secret joke as she starts to play and sing a melody as straightforward as the rungs of a ladder, in that same unsteady falsetto he heard at the club. "*Let's start at the very beginning,*" she sings, and the right hand taps out exactly the notes she is voicing. "*That's a very good place to start. Doe, a deer, a female deer, re, a drop of golden sun...*"

At first the boy is reluctant, tossing his head in denial, though he does manage to mouth the words '*Me, a name I call myself;*' to show he recognizes them. Punching the rhythm like a metronome, Stevie speaks the next line as clear and definite as she can, "*Fa, a long, long way to run,*" and is rewarded by Christina's voice, soft, but unmistakable.

"So, a needle pulling thread," comes out right on pitch, as does *"La, a note to follow so,"* and from there on in, the song takes over, Rodney relaxing into the melody like a homecoming warrior sinking into his favorite old chair, as the verse winds back toward where it started.

I hear the words coming from my mouth, and can't believe they're mine. It is not my voice, any more than this is my body, and yet...I know I am producing these sounds. For a moment, I feel like this is true and everything else which has gone before is the lie. But in my mind I know that cannot be. It cannot.

"What is it?" Stevie asks, stopping her playing as suddenly as his voice has shut itself off. "That was beautiful."

The boy does not answer, his lips pursed tight against some invasion she cannot perceive. His face - that lovely smooth face; eyes as warm and gently-drawn as in a Spanish portrait - is locked in a mask of disapproval. His hand, where it rests upon the wooden bolster at keyboard's end, is clenched tightly in a fist, and she can hear his breathing, each slow inward draw followed by a powerful expulsion, as if his body is trying to rid itself of something vile. Once again she is struck by the sense that there is way too much going on inside this young person, too many selves vying for control of what should be a smooth and seamless life. In this moment Stevie Margulies wishes with all her heart she could make it right for this child; could take away his contradictions and get him to see that half the world would thrill to have the talent he does, and that he so distrusts.

"OK," she offers instead. "That's enough for now. We'll try again another time."

16

Aubrey slouches against the wall, arms locked across her chest, smoldering cigarette held six inches in front of her own face, yet somehow it's too much work to pull the thing to her lips and take another drag. A few feet away the open door bleeds the racket of Sylvio's' kitchen in full swing – dishes clattering into the Hobart, the cooler door slamming shut with a puff of air, Sylvio himself barking complaints at everyone in sight as plates she can see in her dreams slide across the counter and are shuffled onto trays to make their way out into the dining room. Any minute one of the other staff people will miss her, but whoever it is will be too busy to come looking, so her tables will just have to stew for a bit longer. Right now she needs to listen to the rain dripping. To hear the hiss of traffic and the trace of music radiating through the back wall of the Black Hole bar across the alley. To feel like something is happening somewhere that isn't just more of the same.

Ever since Rod disappeared it's been like this. Work and sleep, work and sleep, and in the moments in between, just stupid waiting. Wishing for something - anything - to happen. Empty space and time stretching out with no end in sight.

It was so different, those first few months after they rescued Kim. Hard work, of course, *fucking* hard work and all, but at least it was...something. Oh, there's a bit of guilt along with that recollection, as if the whole thing was as much about feeding off the excitement of what they were doing as it was for Kim's benefit. Mark especially - she knew damn well all along that he was really just in it for the story – snatching Sleeping Beauty from the clutches of the Evil queen, and all. For herself though, she had really tried to believe it was all about Kim; about helping her regain her life. Seeing how hard her friend struggled to communicate with those eye-blinks; the horror when she first saw herself all made up into her mother's idea of perfection; there'd been no question then that someone had to do something - and if not her Best Girl Friend, then who else?

Only later, when this Rod character took over the whole scene, did she begin to wonder if they had done the right thing. Like, maybe Kim *was* really-really sick inside her head and needed more help than they could ever give her. The thought of that - that her bud might need to go away somewhere for a very long time - had woken Aubrey up in the middle of more than one night, and kept her up, sucking cigs and staring at the door behind which her ex-best-friend/new-biggest-headache was sleeping. And now that Rod has taken off and the work part is all over, instead of being a relief, what she's ended up with is a shitload of worry and guilt and going back to Sylvio's every afternoon and evening to stick food under people's faces; food that more and more makes her sick to her stomach just to see it, coming out of the kitchen all hot and pretty – 'presentation' Sylvio calls it, the way he insists on stuff being placed just so on his plates – only to end up a bunch of smears and lumps on plates the diners can't wait to get rid of. Everybody busting their ass and it all ends up as armloads of dirty dishes and a trash can worth of scrapings. 'That's life,' Aubrey thinks, as she manages to get her fingers to her lips and take another drag; 'from presentation to garbage in one easy lesson.'

"You OK?" she hears a voice ask. Twisting around just enough to catch a glimpse, she sees Felicia, the new girl, poking her beauty-shop-blonde head out the door. Still perky and upbeat after three days. Give her a few more shifts and she'll lose that, Aubrey thinks. Give her a few weeks and she'll be just as bored and pissed off as the rest of us.

"No," she answers, making it clear by her tone that her distress should be totally obvious to any sentient being and then - as so often happens - feeling immediately sorry for her attitude. Not that she's worried about hurting the puppy's feelings - like there was any chance of that! Rather, she can tell from that look that the kid is now about to ask her *what's* wrong; to want to hear about her troubles, sympathize, lift her out of her despair. Which is the last thing Aubrey wants right now. What she really wants is to see Kim, hear her laugh, be close to her again. Barring that, she just wants to be left alone.

"Boy trouble?" Felicia asks, and though her voice swoops up in the right way to sound sympathetic, her face is just as bright as ever, giving the unfortunate impression that she is actually thrilled to find a person in misery; it makes her feel so much more...perky. Kind of like that old lady - Kim's mom. The worse things got for her daughter, the more she seemed to thrive on it. Made her feel needed maybe. Which, if you thought of it, was part of what made Aubrey herself so ready to dip into hot water for her friend. The idea that for once Kim needed her.

So much for that shit, she reminds herself. She'll never see Mrs. M. again, never sink into another granny-chair in that god-awful house, crammed full of family photos and scrapbooks and hot tea and cookies. Tea and cookies, for god's sake! It was such a joke all that, although, right now, slouching in this dirty fucking alley with fuck-all to go home to but silence, there's actually something appealing – no, not appealing, Aubrey isn't about to go there, not even in her own mind; but maybe seductive, that's it, seductive - about the memory of that time, when for once she felt almost like a part of a family, there in that goopy old lady's house.

'Shit,' she admonishes herself, coming back to the now and here. 'That's a pisser.'

Tossing her cig to the watery pavement, Aubrey grinds it with the toe of a boot and coughs twice into the end of a balled-up fist.

"No," she tosses at Felicia, effectively shutting the door on any possible heart-to-heart. "Not boy trouble. Just trouble. Just real, plain, fucking trouble." Squeezing through the doorway past Felicia's despicably perfect body in her perfectly pressed skirt-and-blouse ensemble, she feels compelled to toss one more dart. "The kind you wouldn't ever know about," she says, and finds herself back in the kitchen's chaos which is, suddenly, a welcome distraction.

Within a few days of Rod's arrival a routine settles in. Rising early, Stevie makes sure she has time to shower, dress and do her face before he emerges from the spare room to settle like a heap of old fabric on a chair at the end of her table. From the start, it is she who does most of the talking there, as the two share the ritual of morning coffee before she heads out to the office or meetings with clients. In the evenings he's willing to consume whatever she's brought home – pre-cooked this-or-that from the market, or salads in clear-plastic clamshells; or sometimes takeout from the Rose Café, picked up on the drive home. After she's eaten and he's picked at it with little interest, a freshened drink is sufficient enticement to bring him back to the piano where the two scour Stevie's songbook collection for old acquaintances he's willing to admit. With every new arrangement a brick of the wall comes down; he grows a bit more human, though still, it's Stevie who takes the lead, decanting her own history in hopes of unlocking his.

Over time she shares her tale of growing up in difference: how from an early age she (or rather he, back then) felt drawn to try on the trappings of femininity, to sway his hips when walking alone, or read out loud to himself the girl's role in a class play, to see how it would feel to say those words and for a time be that character. He'd see a teacher's paisley dress, and yearn to experience the grace it gave as it flowed and draped; the way it set her apart from the male teachers in their gunny-sack sport coats and follow-the-leader neckties, their cold, judgmental voices emanating from razor-ravaged sandpaper faces perpetually set on scowl-mode. Without putting it into words, he saw how being female or male branded every person with a set of preconceptions, and just as wordlessly knew which brand he would prefer. It felt, Stevie puts it to Rodney in one of her mon-versations, as if all the world had chosen sides for some never-ending, omnipresent playground game, and all the people he wanted to be with, the people he looked up to and wished to emulate, were on the other team. Not only wasn't he allowed to join them, but once adolescence arrived, his teammates laid down the party line - those female creatures were adversaries: distant, inferior figures to be put down, complained about and folded into jokes which illustrated their inconsequence, proclaiming the superiority of the male gender in all the myriad ways boys and men compel one another to do.

Feeling as he did, it was inevitable that relationships with other boys became a sort of espionage, in which he constantly observed their behaviors and strove to imitate them, all the while secretly envying passing girls their luxuriant hair, burgeoning bodies, and the care with which they chose from an entire rainbow to create unique identities. The few female friendships he dared to venture were like flashes of sunshine, when for a few words or minutes he was allowed to share their interests, was granted a glimpse into their thoughts; but dating was a belittling failure, as he found it impossible to adopt the expected attitude of dominance, the confident male superiority that the rituals seemed to require, and all the girls to expect.

In college, she recounted to Rodney, the young man who still went by Steve had found a niche in software engineering, and eventually a woman, Sarah, who seemed to want a friend more than a conqueror. Their courtship and marriage he dealt with briefly, saying only that they had a lot in common until, two years into their marriage, she discovered his hidden wardrobe - silks and satins and skirts purchased on the sly, for trying-on when their differing schedules left him alone for an evening, a weekend. There was a child by then, in diapers, and Sarah felt betrayed, let down and shamed. Counseling didn't work, at least not in the sense of keeping them together - though it did lead Stevie to accept that she would never again settle for being just Steve. The divorce was brutal for all concerned, with Sarah demanding not only support, but sole custody, so their young boy would not be infected with his father's mental illness, as she could only describe it.

Since then, Stevie had carved out a life for herself, including providing financially for a family she never saw. Not that she's complaining, she points out repeatedly. There are friendships, mostly made through her consulting business, an arena in which her 'change' was accepted with astounding aplomb. One of the less-widely touted benefits of capitalism, she points out, is that making profits for others can be a powerful antidote to their personal aversions. There's also a support group she attends regularly, for transgender persons of all shapes and descriptions. All in all, the waters of the world have parted rather graciously to reveal a place in which she may exist, something she had for many years believed impossible - not even worth considering.

"But you haven't had surgery," Rod remarked, when she made a point of putting the topic on the table again one evening, about a week after he'd arrived. His manner was skeptical, interested but uninvolved; as if it were understood the issue under discussion in no way related to himself.

"It's expensive, and painful, and potentially life-threatening," Stevie points out, beginning a speech she has made more than once before. "And when you look at it objectively, it's not much more than a really-invasive form of face-lift. I mean there are people dying every day for want of less expensive health care. Besides, ninety-nine percent of life as a man or a woman isn't about sex, it's about gender, and I can be the gender I am, regardless. In fact, living as myself without doing that proves my point all the more. I am who I am. As long as I know that, what's under my skirt doesn't matter."

"But..."

"But isn't that dishonest?" she breaks in, anticipating the question, based on past experience. "To go around looking like a woman when you're not a woman?" The stolid look on Rodney's face is enough to confirm that her guess was correct.

"I accept who you are, Rodney, not because you do or do not resemble some picture I've got stored away in my brain, but because that is who *you* tell me you are. I expect no more and no less from the world - and from you, if you're going to live here: I am a person who looks like this and sounds like this and does the things I do. Period. End of sentence, end of story, capeesh?"

With some prodding she even gets Rod to relate, as best he can, his own story, beginning with awakening to what he calls 'my Nothing;' a netherworld which, he guiltily admits, was in its way so peaceful, so uneventful and undemanding, that even now it beckons as a refuge from the inescapable illogic of present reality. What comes across most strongly is the young t-man's conviction - despite all evidence to the contrary - that this is not *his* body, not *his* life; and the tremendous frustration of trying to live with that conviction. With a clear sense of shame, he describes how, for a time, he tried to deny it all, to simply refuse to participate, in hope the uncomfortable reality would go away. But gradually, as his capabilities returned, he found he could not do that. Life, it seems, has an allure, even when it makes no sense. It's difficult to stay on the sidelines, even if you don't believe you have any place in the game.

For Stevie, with her own history to refer to - and that of all the unique personalities she has encountered in support groups and books and counselors as she came to grips with her life - it would be easy enough to offer her own explanation for what he's describing, but that, she knows, is not the way to help him grow. "My job," she explains, when Rod seems to want to hear her view of him, "is to accept, not to explain. Only you know what's going on inside that pretty little head of yours," she says with a devilish grin, amused at how he squirms under even such a gentle entendre, "so only you can say what's really true in there."

Somewhere a cock crows, and Elaine has a memory of voices in the
darkness - two, three, or more perhaps, she has no idea really -
chattering in an unfamiliar tongue. She has no mental picture to go
with the voices, only the sound and the feeling of being raised,
bundled about the shoulders and head and picked up from some
hard place which had imprinted itself in her flesh, and then this:
waking in this room, whose earth and timber walls are appearing
now in dawn's early light, whose rough-planked roof is gradually
being made visible by the essence of a new day flowing in through
the small opening, its curtain now drawn, to reveal, as the light
grows, a patch of sky, and beyond it the pointed oval leaves of some
sparse shrubs and limbs. A trace of greenery outside the walls of a
room; outside the wall of her not knowing where she is or how she
has gotten here.

  Once again, there is a voice, coming from outside the room.
A single voice this time, raised in payer-like chanting. Tuneless yet
musical, rising and falling over and over again, it sends a great
comfort running through Elaine's bones, a confident well-being
replacing the tension which had threatened to take over as her
consciousness struggled to make sense of darkness and memory.
'Everything is fine,' she is given to believe as she listens to that voice.
All is well.

"In London today," a newswoman in a somber suit relates just after eleven one Tuesday night, "The House of Commons debated creating a separate court system to enforce Sharia law for the nation's mushrooming Islamic population, and a mosque in Cheapside was vandalized in apparent protest."

"You're troubled," Stevie remarks, pressing a button on the remote. On screen, the muted anchor continues mouthing her story as the room settles into silence, anticipating. Rather than filling the void, Stevie chooses simply to wait, eyes on her guest, who swallows, works his mouth in twisting motion, and waves a hand as if searching the air for something not found inside his head.

"I just..." he begins, then stops. "You've been very good to me, Miss Margulies..."

"I've told you," she interjects with a scolding finger and broad smile.

"I know. *Stevie.* But... you see, that's just one of the differences between us. It doesn't feel right to me. You're so much younger than I."

It is late, Stevie thinks to herself; at this hour she'd normally be getting on with the comforting rituals of nighttime. Brushing teeth and hair, cleaning off her makeup, moisturizing. Slipping into a nightgown and settling among her pillows. One part of her would like to rise up and leave the boy to his moroseness - let the kid figure it out for himself - but another part - and one she values much more highly - says no, this is a time to reach out and do what she can to help.

"You know," she says, careful to place her voice in the higher register, where it will sound most gentle and supportive. "There is a moment, when I first wake up in the morning. It's still dark, and I haven't begun to think about what I have to do that day, and for once, in that moment, I am only me. Not a woman who was once a man, not somebody's software optimizer, or their weirdo neighbor. Not someone's husband or son or daughter - that's a hard one, by the way - not a radical or conservative or any other 'ive.' In that moment there, in the dark, in my own head, I'm just me. Do you ever have a moment like that?"

Rod thinks for a bit, his young face scowling for all it's worth, and Stevie catches herself thinking what a shame it is - that smooth skin, that virgin canvas, is going to be rutted and creased before its time if this kid does not learn to be at peace with his selves.

"As much as I..." he begins, then stops himself, something he does so often it is practically a tick. "You know," he begins again, with the sound of one who has found his trail, after much searching. "First of all, I don't want to offend, but I would never, never in a million years, have believed I could be sitting here, talking to a... a person like you."

Stevie gives a hearty laugh, relieved at least to hear a little honesty. "Point taken," she says, and is rewarded with a bit of a smile. "For what it's worth, there were many years when I could not have believed I even *was* a person like me. So let's just stipulate that. I'm a freak, and you're a person who doesn't do freaks very well. Except, of course, that you are one."

This time Rod does not smile, and she feels compelled to go on. Though the entire point of staying up at this moment is to get him to talk, sometimes you've got to prime the pump.

"We're all freaks, Rodney. People; when you get to know them. Every one of us is different. Every. One. And...this is something I sincerely believe, though I'm sure I could get an argument in some quarters ...but I believe that any person who has the honesty to do a little self-examination will find something 'odd' inside themselves. Some thing which doesn't fit their other notions of who they should be or how they should behave. It's called character. It's what makes us unpredictable, creative. For goodness sake, it's what makes us human."

"But not like this," the kid jumps in, engaged now, excited by his disagreement. "Not like me. Inside, I know who I am, what I believe, and I've known it for longer than you've been alive, young lady..."

"Thank you, for that..." Stevie quips, immediately regretting the interruption, but fortunately his flow is no longer so easily stopped.

"But outside, there's this whole other person that I seem to be, that everyone else sees, and I see too, when I look at myself, touch myself. When I do so much as lift an ordinary object and realize how weak this body is. Every moment I'm being reminded that something is totally wrong with me, and the world around me."

"Except?" Stevie asks, more certain than ever that she knows the answer to her question. "Isn't there ever a time when you feel it all come together. When the differences don't matter?"

"When I sing," he says, and that answer, at least, is quick and effortless, which is reassuring. As intelligent as he clearly is, she'd been afraid his denial might go so deep he would not be able to admit even this, which is so obvious to her. "When I sing, it's as if all the confusion drops away. Who I am, and who I was, doesn't matter anymore; I'm only me, a person doing what I was meant to do. I've analyzed it, and I believe it is because my mind is too busy following the music, concentrating on doing my best. It's so busy that it can't be bothered with those other things."

"Or maybe..." Stevie points out, fatigue creeping over her like fog rolling off of a lake, "it's because 'that' is who you really are; a person who feels like Rodney, and chooses to look like him, but who sings like Christina - and doesn't ever have to apologize to anyone *for any of it*! Maybe...or maybe not. It's up to you, because right now, who *I* am, is a person who's going...to bed."

"*You may be right,*" the singer calls, repeated through speakers secreted among the wooden sleds, fishing creels, woven-willow pack-baskets, replicas of old traffic signs and a hundred other knick-knacks studding the walls and shelves of the restaurant's interior. "*I may be crazy,*" he continues, as patrons queue up in the vestibule, leaving names with a hostess who hands them electronic placeholders which will harass them as soon as their table is available. There's no waiting for Aubrey though, as she spots Jake immediately, hunched on a stool at the rectangular bar that occupies the middle of the space, lit from above by hanging lamps in the shape of trout and by a half-dozen TV sets, all tuned to the Sonics' game, their sound submerged beneath the general hubbub so that the athletes and commentators on their screens move like automata, wound up and running about for no discernable reason. "*But it just may be a lunatic we're looking for.*"

"Hey, Aubs," the hostess greets her, with a toss of dimpled chin, then continues talking into her headset as she scrubs grease-pencil markings off the seating chart and adds new ones.

"How's it goin', Steph?" is sufficient answer to acknowledge the couple of months the two women worked together at another restaurant, nearly two years ago, and Aubrey continues on past without waiting for a response, aware of several pairs of eyes from the bar monitoring her approach. Defiantly she returns their glances, one by one, and is pleased to see each face cast quickly down, or turn away in sudden play of innocence. Her head is high and her mood upbeat as she sets herself on the stool next to Jake's and orders a Pink Lady.

"Not what I would have guessed," Jake says, his ham hands cradling a mug of beer. Her first impression is that this cannot be the same guy Kim dated less than a year ago. Gone is the tailored suit and the crisp, almost military, haircut; this guy has two days of stubble shading his face and his hair could use a wash. The nap of his suede jacket is matted, glossy and dark around the collar and cuffs, and underneath it his polo shirt bears more wrinkles than a bulldog's snout. His shoulders are still broad as a beam, but there's a definite gut visible as he leans against the bar, and his droopy eyes give the impression there's been way to much drink in his life lately, or too little sleep, or maybe both.

"It's a joke," she answers, watching as the bartender hoses

ingredients into a tall glass. "Kim's joke, actually. She said I should make it my 'signature' drink; it's so *not* me." The bartender, a grad student from the looks of him, and unfazed by Aubrey's selection, sets a napkin before her, pops the glass down and hurries on to his next customer. Jake's hands remain steadfast around his mug and he doesn't offer to put her drink on his tab, so Aubrey begins fishing through her purse for the tip money she stuffed in at the end of her last shift.

"So how's it going for you?" she asks as she separates two fives from the rest of the wad, drops them on the bar and reaches for her drink. Odd, to find herself somehow holding the upper hand. Sylvio's might not be much, and Kim is gone, but from what she can see up close, it still looks like her life is going better these days than Jake's is, and not by just a little.

Sure enough, as they make conversation, the man readily admits to being broke and 'kind of desperate.' DigiBank shut down, he explains, without ever turning a profit and Colin disappeared somewhere overseas, leaving Jake to answer for back rent, office equipment and attorney's fees, which will pretty well consume what's left of his inheritance. His condo is up for sale, job interviews are sparse and unpromising, and the rose-selling gig barely covers food and gas for the Beemer, which, he is quick to point out, is paid-for.

"One thing no one is going to take away from me," he says morosely, grabbing another handful of pretzels from the bowl on the bar beside him. "Dinner," he remarks, seeing her eyes follow his hand.

It isn't long before the conversation turns to Kim - the whole reason Aubs agreed to meet him here. It seems Jake has been searching for her, without success. When Aubrey asks how one searches for a person in a city as large as Seattle, his answer is hardly encouraging.

"I hang around," he explains, in the tone of one explaining a very tricky technical problem. "Places I know she might go. The U., her old studio building. Places she'd hang out. I saw that movie guy...what's his name?"

"Mark Peterson?"

"Yeah, that's the guy. He was a friend of Kim's, wasn't he?" Aubrey nods, and Jake shakes his head with enthusiasm: one of life's great mysteries solved, it seems. "I saw him coming out of the Good Cup one night. Followed him for hours. He went to that second hand clothes shop over there. Took his time checking stuff out, shirts and shoes mostly. Didn't buy anything though. Then he ducked into this big arcade – with the dragon lit up on the outside? They've got computers set up for people to play against a whole room of other people - and it all shows up on these giant screens on the wall, you know? I had a good feeling about that, like maybe Kim would be there, because of her art; like all that stuff she used to do with old TV sets? Hanging them upside down and shit, playing the channels where there wasn't anything to watch, all static and fuzz?"

"Yeah," Aubrey agrees, remembering her friend's fascination with video. What once had been so impressive – cutting edge artistic inspiration – now seems a distant, cozy oddity, like an eccentric aunt you never really appreciated until she was gone. "She said that static had a special power; like if you looked at it long enough it would drag up images from way down inside your head to fill up the void. That was how she got ideas for some of her pieces. Least that was what she said."

"Bunch of creeps in there, playing video games all night in the dark," Jake continues, making Aubrey wonder if he even heard her reminiscence. "Went home to his fucking mother's house, if you can believe that. 'Nother time, I'm pretty sure I actually saw her, walking with two other chicks, up on Capitol Hill, near the Deluxe. It took me a minute to find a place to leave my car, and by the time I got back to where I saw them, they were gone. Searched all along Broadway for over an hour, but she must have seen me and split, 'cause I couldn't find her anywhere, and when I got back to my car it had been towed. Cost me seventy bucks to get it out - goddamn the fuckers - plus the cab ride. I went back up there a couple of times, only I never saw them again, so I think she must be livin' somewhere else, and just came up there for a movie or something."

The big man downs the last of his beer and motions to the bartender for another, then turns to Aubrey with renewed seriousness.

"This is killing me, Aubrey; knowing she's out there somewhere, all by herself. Ever since Kim went away, my life is falling apart. She's the only good thing I've ever had in my life, and you've gotta' help me find her."

In his eyes she can see tiny twin reflections of the TV behind her, flickering flames of color dancing in unison on the damp orbs. The intensity of his words is beginning to concern her, so she makes it clear as possible there is nothing she can do, a protest he seems to take as a personal affront.

"Bullshit," he challenges, and the word rings out, even over the noise of the bar's crowd reacting to a play. He leans closer, locking eyes. "You know her as well as anyone Aubrey. You'd know where she'd go, who she'd hang out with..."

"She just walked, Jake. I don't have any idea..."

"I don't believe you," he spits, grabbing her near arm in his great fist. "I know you've got a thing for her - that's why you don't want me and her to get back together - but you don't understand how important this is to me. I mean...I'll do anything I have to, to get her back. Anything, understand?"

Try as she may, Aubrey cannot pull her wrist free. She looks around for help, but all eyes now are elsewhere. Fifteen feet away, the bartender is engrossed in conversation with two cocktail waitresses, while around the counter all eyes are upturned to the TV sets, where the basketball game is in its final minutes, its flock of players oscillating furiously from side to side within the frame, approaching climax. Alarmed now, she tries to pry apart Jake's fingers, only to have him grip her other hand as well, flattening it with no apparent effort, so that she finds herself squirming in her seat, purse crashing down to spill its contents across the floor. Still no one seems to notice as the announcer's voice rises and comments percolate in response to the on-screen action.

"Am I hurting you?" Jake asks, without sympathy. " 'Cause this is hurting me, you know. Goddamn it, girl, I've got no money left, no job worth talking about. I'm gonna' lose my home and the only thing I've got left is Kim and if I find out you know where she is and you didn't tell me..."

"Let go," Aubrey spits between teeth clamped shut. His grip is really hurting now, and she can't believe that not a single person in this entire stupid hole has noticed. A cheer erupts all around as Seattle's bench swarm onto the court, high-five-ing and butt-slapping one another. Drinkers raise their glasses in relief or turn to their neighbors to remark on the outcome. "Let go," she says again, almost a shout, and is rewarded when several heads finally turn in their direction.

Abruptly, Jake releases her, bringing his hands up above his shoulders, palms forward in a gesture of surrender, though the look in his eyes is unchanged.

"Fine," he says, loud enough for half the bar to hear, then drops his voice to near a whisper. "Have it your way. But don't fuck with me little girl, 'cause I love her and I'm gonna' get her back if it's the last thing I do." As if a spell has been broken he stops and glances around, chasing half a dozen grown men away with just his eyes and his size. "I'm gonna," he says again, as if the words answer any possible questions, then turns, striding out through the crowd, defiantly tall and unapologetic.

Gathering the contents of her purse from the floor, Aubrey regains her stool and sits, composing herself. Gradually, the thumping in her chest dies down enough that she can take a sip of the elaborate drink before her. Only then does the bartender approach, a bit sheepishly.

"Your friend?" he suggests, with a nod in the direction of Jake's departure.

"Yeah, right," Aubrey mutters, taking another sip of Pink Lady, relishing the sweet juice and the knowledge that beneath it there is a bit of relaxation coming.

"He didn't pay for his beers," the 'tender explains, in a hopefully off-hand way. Astonished, Aubrey fixes his innocent eyes in hers, willing him to recognize the blackness of her mood, her hair, her clothes, wondering just how much balls this bleached-out kid has got.

"I gotta' ask you to pick them up," he adds, in answer to her look. A bit apologetic perhaps, a teeny bit sympathetic, maybe, but not backing down an inch. "Seeing he's you're friend and all."

Another evening, another song. Stevie at the keyboard as Rod stands nearby, one hand on the baby grand, one hand in his pocket.

"I'm not trying to change who you are, Rodney," she says. "I'm just reacting to what I hear."

"And that is?" he asks, reaching for the nearby glass of scotch.

"I hear you resisting. Pushing your voice down where it doesn't go naturally, instead of letting it soar."

"And you're the authority on that are you? The way you talk, trying to sound female. It's fake and forced, it's..."

"OK," Stevie cuts in. "If this is what it takes to get you to see your own gift, here we go. I'll be Steve, if you'll be Eydie."

With that she flips through the pile of music books on top of the piano, finding the one she wants near the bottom, and sending several others falling to the floor as she tugs it out. Checking the back cover index, she thumbs to a page, then flattens the book roughly in her lap before setting it on the music stand with a flourish. "You know this one?" she asks, and Rod nods.

"From *Ella in Hollywood*," he offers proudly, "Nineteen sixty-...uh...-one, I think; or maybe -two. A great performance; not many people know, but it was actually written by..."

"Steve Allen," Stevie interrupts, flashing a cheater's smile as she reads the credit at the top of the sheet. "In fifty-six. So: I take a line, you take a line," and her hands begin moving, slowly at first, picking out the chords, then gathering speed and finding the rhythm as the patterns come clear. "*You're walkin'*," she sings, then stops. "Sorry," she offers, shifting her hands down the keyboard an inch or so to begin again in a lower key. "*You're walkin*," she sings again, her voice deeper and more full, yet still gentle. "*Down the street*," and the music jumps a bit, hammering home the next few words, "*or you're at a party*." With a nod she indicates it is Rodney's turn.

"*Or else*," he sings, still rounding his belly and pushing from way below the belt.

"No, not like that," Stevie corrects, "*Or else*," she sings, chin raised to the ceiling as her voice strains to put the notes up where she wants them. "Back-up and take it again," she says, as her fingers tromp two chords out of rhythm before resuming the song in an earlier measure.

Rodney takes a breath and swallows, waiting for the line to

come, then opens up his mouth and sings again. *"Or else,"* comes out a little tentatively, but sweet and high, one hundred percent Christina's voice, to be answered by Stevie's glowing smile.

"That's it," she urges, interrupting the music for a beat before continuing, and mouthing along as he continues.

"You're alone," he sings, a sly satisfaction beginning to take over his face. *"And then you suddenly dig,"*

"You're looking in someone's eyes," Stevie's baritone answers, as the music flows on uninterrupted. A tiny toss of her head gives him the next line.

"You suddenly realize," he sings, the smile growing.

"Now both of us," Stevie injects beneath the beat, and in the next instant two voices join, one high, one low, but both in sync to the rhythm and working together as one.

"That this could be the start of something big."

Lying in this unfamiliar bed, Elaine is initially dismayed by just how weak she feels; her body and mind drained not only by the exertions which took her to that mountain pass, and whatever brought her to this new place, but by so much that went before. In the twilight of a morning she had given up hope of reaching, she is struck by a vision of herself, of how the months and years and decades of her life had chipped away at what was once an abundance of youthful optimism and opportunity, till there was little left but a bleak core of weary obligation. This perception comes not with sadness though, or bitterness, for the simple reason that the person it concerns seems far away now; left behind on that rock near the top of the trail perhaps, or even earlier; in the clearing where she discovered herself alone. Instead, as she sleeps and wakes, slowly gathering the strength to explore her circumstances, what seems to be arising is a *new* energy, a new approach, which she understands could come about only after the old concessions had been forcibly stripped away, leaving raw and open ground on which a new seed could take root and grow.

This impression forms slowly, over several days during which she does not leave that small room, and during that same time, she also discovers a few facts about the place in which she finds herself. A family home apparently, judging by the child she catches looking in on her, its round head peeking past the door jamb. Eyes wide, it scampers away as soon as she turns to look, its delighted cry as clear and bright as the ringing of a bell. There is a woman too, who brings her a starchy porridge in the morning, and milky-fragrant herbal tea several times throughout the day, and takes away the copper bowl she indicates should be used as bedpan. Small and wiry, this figure seems to move without a sound, her mahogany-hued face at once both young and old; as if the features of a child have been overlaid with the unquestioning seriousness of great responsibility. Her skin is strikingly rich, shining with an inner moisture, and her almond eyes brace a nose which is both wide and flat, and aimed straight as an arrow at the pair of full dark lips which utter barely a sound while she goes about her work. Over a white linen shirt she wears a tunic of tightly-woven wool, each sleeve highlighted by a single narrow stripe of delicate embroidery. Her long full, skirt is black as night, its hem frayed and fringed with soil, and around her waist she wears several fabric belts, woven in many hues, to which are attached various ornaments, including two large brass keys. Her head is topped with a multi-layered cap from which a single long, black braid runs down her back, and her neck, wrists and ankles jingle with silver, brass and copper, the pieces simply-wrought and burnished from rubbing against one another, her clothes and her flesh. This woman Elaine chooses to call Petal, from a yellow flower tucked into her cap one afternoon, and the single petal which drops from it as she turns to go. Rising stiffly from her bed once she is sure she is alone, Elaine plucks the tiny fragment from the floor and blows it free of dust, savoring its rich color, feeling with a fingertip its velvety soft surface and the hint of moisture it gives off, like a promise of continuing life.

For some days Elaine remains in this place, spending the time drifting between sleep and wakefulness, during the latter of which she has ample time to catalog her surroundings. On one short wall of the room is centered the window: chest high and less than two feet square. Unglazed, it is covered by an oiled cloth, with a hinged wooden shutter at the ready as well. Opposite that, the door consists of four wide planks fastened to three smaller cross-pieces, the whole hung on heavy hammered-iron hinges, with a crudely-carved wooden handle and a latch – also of wood - which extends through a hole from the other side. The narrow bed on which she lies fills one of the room's long walls; a simple wooden cupboard anchors the opposite, its top piled high with folded quilts and rugs. Much of the floor is filled as well, with rush baskets, and bundles wrapped in animal hides or woven woolen blankets. On a shelf pegged into the outside log wall sits an earthenware lamp, colorfully decorated, which smells of burning butter when Petal lights it for a few hours each evening.

Gradually, Elaine finds herself aware for longer periods, and growing curious about the life around her. In addition to Petal's comings and goings in the room, she hears outside the sound of chores being done: chopping, pots banging, the sizzle of cooking. Infrequent muted conversations and the noise of children are deeply comforting, despite the incomprehensible language. Beyond the walls there is also the clucking of some sort of fowl, a snorting and snuffling which she guesses might be pigs, and once even the chuffing breath of a horse, its hooves scraping and stomping, their beats resonating right through the earthen floor of her abode.

That there are *children* - not just one child, but several - she discerns as the surreptitious visits continue. A scraping on the packed-earth floor will typically alert her, and turning toward the door she'll catch just a glimpse of a small face and several dirty-nailed fingertips before the visitor disappears with a wail, footsteps diminishing as he or she moves farther off. Soon after that she catches another, the head and hands higher or lower on the jamb, the laughter noticeably different in pitch and timbre. Eventually she learns that, if she lies with head at the foot of the pallet and is very careful not to move, she can observe them out of the corner of her eye as they observe her. In this way she identifies four unique visitors, of four different sizes, but all with dark, round heads, darker eyes and shaggy jet-black hair, which tumbles and curtains in front of their faces, though they seem never to notice it.

One morning, after several days of this cat-and-mouse, she wakes from dozing to find one of the larger children standing squarely in the doorway, his eyes fixed upon her. Keeping her head still on the bundle of cloth which serves as pillow, she studies this boy of perhaps eleven or twelve years. Wearing baggy black trousers over bare feet, with a jacket in the same muted red, brown and amber as Petal's tunic, he stands with shoulders back, hands stiffly at his side and the determined expression of one facing a notorious foe. A muffled giggle from beyond suggests he is not alone, and memories of her own childhood instill in Elaine the conviction that he must be operating on a dare. Sliding one hand slowly out from underneath her rugs and blankets to wave a finger toward the far inside corner of the space, she casts the boy a smile and a wink. Without changing his expression, he moves, pressing his back against the wall as Elaine, silently as she can, slides her feet out and down to the floor, then creeps to the doorway. The instant her head passes its plane, a trio of shrieks pierce the air and she sees three small backs, six pumping legs and an equal number of flailing arms, tangling over and under one another as they compete to run away as fast as possible.

Collapsing back upon the bed and gathering its layers around her, Elaine studies the now-smiling figure across from her.

"What is your name?" she asks him, only to realize immediately the folly of her question, for she has not heard a word of English since her last conversation with Beryl, which must be several days ago by now, and miles from this place. Her surprise is all the greater then, when he answers.

"Dore-eh," is the name he pronounces, and the connection that comes with that word is like the opening of a new world to them both. Within a few minutes she has determined that he is the son of the woman she knows as Petal; his 'Ama,' as he calls her. Schooled 'a little time,' he has picked up most of his words during travels with a person he calls 'Ootay,' though he does not seem to have the words to specify whether that is his father, or someone else. The other youngsters she has seen are his 'brother children' he tells her, rattling off their names so fast she cannot catch them. Elaine finds herself vastly disappointed when, after only a few minutes of struggling conversation, Dore-eh begins to move toward the door.

"Go now," he tells her, with a certainty which belies his years and the playfulness of moments before.

"Wait," she urges him. "I haven't told you my name." Placing a hand upon her chest she is careful to enunciate. "I am Elaine," she says, then again, "Eeee-lane."

"No, no," Dore-eh replies, without a moment's hesitation. "You Ber-eel. Zhe-Khong Ber-eel," and with a crisp and beaming bow, is out the door and gone, leaving her - once again - alone.

23

A Monday evening in Stevie's dimly-lit living room. Dinner long over, the two singers drained by forty minutes of trying out new material, and twenty more of listening to the world's events disgorged by the network news. Heels kicked off and stockinged-feet tucked beneath her, Stevie sits on the sofa, a formal-looking piece with a curved back and narrow piped arms that seem designed more for display than for comfort. As they talk she twines a lock of hair around a finger, twisting it and releasing it, twisting and releasing. Rodney occupies a cinnamon-colored velveteen armchair, suit coat unbuttoned but still on, shoes planted squarely on the floor. Stevie's wine glass is only a few sips shy of full, the kid's third scotch-on-the-rocks half gone, his body-language suggesting that 'half-gone' might be an apt description for his mental state as well, and that this is, perhaps, an opportune moment for Stevie to pursue some questions she has been mulling.

"So look, Rodney," she begins, then interrupts herself. "That seems so formal, now that we've gotten to know each other. Would you consider it terribly familiar if I were to call you Rod from now on?" The boy shakes his head, smiling bit shyly, pleased to be asked. "Rod. I just wanted to tell you...I mean, I understand that you don't relate to who you were - who other people tell you you should be - what did you say her name was?"

"Christina. McKloskey."

"Christina," Stevie pronounces, trying the name on her lips. "No, you don't seem at all like a Christina to me."

The boy smiles again, as if even that small tease eases something gnawing at his insides, and Stevie feels her affection for him tightening another notch.

"The thing is Rod, I've had to learn to accept some rather unlikely things in my own life. Things I never wanted, didn't think I could live with, but finally decided I couldn't deny. So I try not to be concerned with whether all the pieces fit together in the way some other people might say they ought to. And I'm thinking, maybe you could do that as well. Be the person you know you are, but also keep the good parts of who you were." A slight sound comes from the boy, an unintentional inhalation suggesting primal reflex tensing against a threat, and Stevie sees suspicion gather in his eyes, the faintest hint of a wrinkle between those finely drawn brows.

"Who *they say* you were?" she ventures, with a nod and a flapping of hands in the air beside her face. Rod seems to accept the apology, and she can see by his face that this line of questioning has promise; might just open up a door to some of what troubles him so. When she presses, his response is slow in coming - even for him - and its halting delivery gives evidence of the discomfort the subject causes.

"There is one thing," he begins. "About...this...person, that I look like."

Stevie waits, prompts him with her eyes to go on, then waits again while he considers, swallows deeply, and continues, the words parsed out like steps across very thin ice.

"It happened while I was staying at that girl's. Aubrey. Happened for the first time, I mean, but not the only time. I'd gone to the library, to catch up on my journals, and I was sitting at one of the tables in the periodical section, next to a window. It was a beautiful day, the sun breaking through here and there, and..."

Again the boy pauses, his eyes examining hers. Stevie has the feeling he's asking for permission, so she nods, just the slightest movement of her own head, so as not to break the spell, whatever that may be. He turns his eyes away then, as if intensely interested in the far wall.

"And as I was reading, I became aware of...this feeling. Warmth. Down...there. And I realized the sun had broken through and was shining in the window, and just between the table, and the wall, and the shadows and all, it was falling on my lap. Only what I felt was more than just the sun, it was...inside my head. Not a picture, not an image but maybe...a feeling - and more - of ...of having this...I suddenly felt like I had this...place... inside me. That needed to be...touched, somehow. And as much as I know inside here" - he reaches up and touches Christina's close-cropped head - "who I am, I have to admit that I was feeling something else, that I would have thought only...a woman, could feel."

The words out, Rod settles even deeper into his chair, kneading his hands together, the fingers wrestling one another in tight little circles. After a moment he huffs out a breath and turns back to Stevie, eyes meeting hers for just a second, then pulling away from them, to settle on some other aspect of the room. Without looking, he reaches out for his glass and drains the liquid until the ice cubes topple and bump against lips, then pulls it a few inches away and proceeds to examine the shining cubes, tilting and swirling them around several times before setting the glass back down on the coaster he is always so careful to use.

"And that scares you?" Stevie asks.

"Not scares," the youngster answers, though it sounds to Stevie more like an argument than a statement. "Confuses. Frustrates. And..."

Rod looks up at her; Christina McKloskey's lovely eyes so sad and worried that for a moment they make the woman in Stevie wonder if she should have stayed a man.

"Thank you," she offers, after the silence has run its course. "For trusting me enough to share that." Now it is her turn to pause, debate whether what she's just thought of would be the right thing to do or the worst thing in the world, to which she concludes that there is, really, only ever one way to find out. But not now; what she has in mind will take some preparation; some laying out of groundwork, so to speak. And for the boy to be more ready, which suggests another question.

"When you sing, Rodney, and you hear that voice, coming from who you are, does that confuse you too?"

The boy nods, but then stops, and in the stopping she fancies she is witnessing a fracture; a further chink in the wall he has erected around himself.

"At first it did," he says very softly. "But then I realized how good it is, this voice. I don't say 'my' voice, because it's not anything I can take the credit for; it just is. And sometimes, when I let it come out, it's like everything else doesn't matter. For that time, for as long as I let that feeling take over, I'm just me and this is my voice and the whole damned thing may as well never have happened, because it's all alright."

Stevie has sat through enough group sessions to know gold when she hears it, so she lets that wisdom hang about them both for a while. You don't applaud moments like this; you quietly let them linger until just maybe they sink in. And when they've sunk as far as they're going to, when you can see by the way the speaker sighs and shakes out his tension that he's ready to move on, you move with him, careful to make space for that new reality.

"Alright then," Stevie says when that moment has come, "let's do it." Rising from her seat and moving across the room, she gathers her skirt beneath her in a practiced motion, to settle onto the piano bench and pass manicured fingers just above its keyboard, as if imagining herself playing.

"It's such a beautiful voice," she says as those fingers descend and begin to strike the keys. "I was struck by it that first night at the club. One shouldn't have to hide one part of one's self, just because it doesn't fit with some other part." Seeing him still in his chair she pats the bench with one hand, as the other keeps tapping, the notes seemingly random, but harmonious just the same. "Come on. Sit here with Stevie, and we'll work on something familiar, something comfortable." Her hands continue to move, caressing the keyboard until it too, in its own way, is singing. "You're so good - who knows, maybe we could even do an act together sometime."

24

Cruising slowly, the BMW makes its way along the intermittent line of parked cars. Halfway up the block it finds a long empty stretch between a red minivan and a Honda - dull green, with a tacky after-market spoiler on its tail. As he backs in, it makes Jake think of Kim's old Honda, with that freaky paint job she insisted on giving it. Makes him wonder where that little car is these days; if Mrs. M. sold it, or maybe has got it sitting in her garage all this time. 'Yeah,' he thinks, as he steps out, catching a glimpse of himself in the door glass - hardly the stud he used to be, but hell, that's not his fault, is it? - 'that's probably where it is: sitting in Kim's mother's garage, gathering dust.' He'll have to ask about that, but only after he's learned whether she's had any more luck locating Kim than he has.

The sidewalk is familiar as he makes his way to her front door. Feels like old times, from when he used to come here to visit Kim, tucked away in her little guest house. Bizarre, Jake thinks to himself as he rings the bell and waits. Even though he and Kim never got to get married - never really even got 'formally' engaged, though he's not about to admit that to anyone else - her mother's house feels kind of like home. Like going back to someplace safe and reliable. Funny how those things happen, whether you're looking for them or not.

"Jake," Anne McKloskey gushes as she opens the door. "What a wonderful surprise."

Over the next several days, with Dore-eh's help, Elaine begins to understand her situation. This house in which she finds herself is home to a substantial family: in addition to Petal, and Dore-eh, of course, there is someone else he calls Lahtso - apparently a greatly respected figure from how he says her name - plus a younger brother, and three sisters. Each of these children seems to have several names, both in Dore-eh's explanations, and in the banter which erupts whenever he coaxes one or more of them to venture into Elaine's room and linger for as long as their courage will sustain. They must be nicknames, Elaine imagines, or titles for the place they hold in the family, or even childish epithets, and so, since she cannot be sure which descriptors are most correct, she develops her own, christening the eldest girl Tulip, because she seems a blooming young version of her mother. The next, a girl of around ten, she christens Thin, for that is what she seems beside her younger brother, five or six year old Pooh, round as the story-bear, and with the same slow and gentle composure. The final child, a toddler, she deems Little One.

There is a village somewhere nearby, she gathers from Dore-eh's remarks, and other homesteads too, and beyond those, what he calls the 'hard mountains;' presumably the range whose pass she had reached when caught by the snowstorm. The 'hard mountains' can only be crossed for part of each year, she is given to understand, and even then it is many days journey to any town with 'stinking carts,' which she takes to indicate cars, buses, trains, or all of the above.

The question of what country they are in elicits the strangest answer of all, for whether she asks 'Are we in China,' or 'in Tibet,' or Sri Lanka, Burma, Kashmir, India, Pakistan, Laos or even Argentina, the answer is always the same. 'No way boss," Dore-eh replies, to every nation she names, his broad smile suggesting she must surely be aware of the joke she is making.

"*My Way?*"

"Oh, God no," Stevie answers, another evening, delivering the words in campy outrage, as appalled as she can make herself sound. "It's such a cliché."

"*Ain't misbehavin'?*" Rod offers, flipping pages at random in the immense 'fake book' Stevie has brought home from Capitol Music.

"Maybe. Kind of puts a damper on the crowd, though."

"*Exactly like you?*"

"Yes, that's perfect." Stevie's hands scan the keyboard, find a position and attempt several dissonant chords as she parses words in search of a melody. "*My mother… made me… for someone…*" Finding the key, her hands accelerate and their voices rise together, Stevie's falsetto sounding strained and tight in contrast to Christina's silky ease. "*Exactly like you.*"

Rod's hand is warm on her shoulder as the room fills with satisfied laughter. Another late evening exploring songs which were popular before she was born. Trying out keys and running through lyrics, most of which Rod seems, improbably, to already know by heart. It has been several weeks since he arrived at the Doghouse, wet and weary as a lost puppy and, to Stevie at least, the arrangement is beginning to show signs of possibility.

"It's nice" she says, reaching around to place her hand on top of his. "Having you here." To her surprise, she feels his hand pull away, going, as it so often does, to the glass nearby.

"You're not worried…" he begins, and in the hesitation she sees his mouth working, chewing on some thought he is not sure he wants to let out. "About me being here," he explains. "About what people might think?"

Amazed, Stevie studies this person who appears to be younger than her, yet acts sometimes so much older; all full of worries and preconceptions that don't jive with her – his, she reminds herself, because even a person like Stevie can slip sometimes, seeing what she sees – that don't seem to go along with his body, his face, his eyes.

"Let me be sure I understand this, *Rodney,*" she begins, turning sideways and draping one leg deliberately across the bench, where her confidence can benefit from its exposed slenderness, from the graceful shape her foot forms, secured in its strapped lilac pump.

"You're worried about what the neighbors might think? Because I've got this pretty young boy," she reaches out and grabs his free hand, holding it at arm's length to capture and examine him from head to toe, "staying in my home?"

A bit sheepishly Rod ducks his head, making a halfhearted effort to pull his hand out of hers, to which Stevie responds by taking-up his other hand as well, gazing into his eyes with the disappointed look of a prim schoolteacher, or even a mother.

"What do *you* think about it? You and me, living under the same roof, un-chaperoned. Is Dr. Gimbal offended?"

"No," he answers, unconvincingly. "Not offended...exactly."

"Intrigued then?" Stevie asks, then watches him squirm, torn between wanting to keep his distance, and something else she now suspects has been on his mind for a while. Using her greater strength she pulls him closer, at the same time rotating them both, so Rodney ends up sitting on the bench between her legs with her arms wrapped around his chest and her lips behind his ear, where she can whisper confidentially as she moves ever so slightly against the soft contours of Christina's body. "It seems to me, *young man...*that in order to be concerned about an arrangement such as ours, one must have been imagining what terrible things might happen in such an arrangement. You haven't been having bad thoughts about this old girl, now have you?"

His silence is answer enough, as she feels him first stiffen, then relax into her embrace, but Stevie knows from experience how delicate a process it can be, coming out of one's cocoon. There's no hurry, she reminds herself, even good reason on her part to delay; to let things simmer until they're truly ready before adding anything else to the stew of emotions he must be feeling. For a moment she continues holding, pressing, enjoying the feel of her own body as well as his, the satisfaction of being found attractive, even if it is unspoken. Then, with a playful nip at the irresistibly soft ear right in front of her face, she pushes herself away, returning to the keyboard, to waggle her fingers silently above it.

"Come on, you evil thing," she says, voice full of joy and possibility. "We've got work to do." Once again fingers touch ivory and muted notes fill the room as Rodney slides around to sit beside her, their elbows and shoulders touching now and then as her hands move left and right.

"*I know why I've waited,*" Stevie begins, and is rewarded by that liquid warble, close beside here own ear.

"Know why I've been blue," Rod sings, confident and comfortable. More comfortable in this than anything else she has seen or heard in their time together, as she brings the song to full tempo and joins in, allowing her voice again to drop to where it used to live, to serve as foundation for his.

"I've been waiting each day," they sing together. A shiver runs down her spine and she finds herself hoping he is feeling the same thing. *"For someone, Exactly like you."*

It is a change in the spirit of the house that finally draws Elaine out of her room; an unaccustomed urgency to Petal's early morning ministrations, an increase in the number of times one or another of the children race past her doorway, and heavier freights of emotion in the voices scolding or cajoling one another in words she cannot begin to understand. After an hour or so of this, curiosity overcomes lethargy and fear of being left out trumps fear of the unknown. Pulling herself to unsteady feet in the thin homespun tunic which has served as nightdress, she looks around for her clothes, but finds them nowhere, and so settles on a bolt of reddish-brown cloth which has been serving as her pillow. Wrapping it around as best she can, she creeps through the doorway and finds herself in a narrow passage, with identical plank doors opening off on either side. Ignoring these, she makes her way to where the hall ends, and finds herself in what must be the house's main room. Roughly square, with two walls of layered flat stones and two of stacked rough-hewn timbers, it is about the size of a two-car garage, its low ceiling framed in logs which still bear patches of bark. On one wall, a long bench is piled with bulging water-bladders and baskets of earthy-looking patties, along the opposite wall stand several handmade wooden trunks and cupboards. Across every surface are strewn or hung a collection of well-worn tools and harness gear, cooking utensils and bowls and plates decorated in brilliant patterns, and bronze objects of purposes undecipherable to her American eyes. In the center of the space a modest fire burns in the hollow of a large rock slab, the rising smoke illuminated by a shaft of light from a square hole above, which seems inadequate to the job of exhaust. Indeed, the atmosphere is thick, and close, full of the smells of people, smoke and meals gone by. Dim, as well; the walls and ceiling absorbing what little light exists into surfaces darkened and unreflective thanks to their coating of accumulated soot.

Her arrival creates a flurry of activity, as five children scatter back against the walls and Petal, who had been busy near the fire, scrambles toward a low platform beneath the big room's single window. Pushing aside several large sacks of foodstuffs and a goatskin of unknown liquid, she motions for the new arrival to take what seems to be a place of honor. It is only when she has seated herself in the warmth of the sunbeam there that Elaine realizes she is not alone, for close beside her, among the grain sacks, covered pots, goatskins and other household goods, sits a woman who looks to be far older than herself. Removing a long white pipe from her mouth, this gnarled and wizened figure pulls closer the layers of clothing which wrap her, flashes a toothless smile and bows her head in greeting.

"Ber-eel," the milky-eyed elder says, dipping her head in recognition. "Yao, zhe-Khong-Ber-eel."

"Lahtso?" Elaine asks, pointing and mimicking as closely as she can the name she has heard from Dore-eh. Seeing the woman's head bob in agreement, she goes on, placing her hand on her chest and pronouncing "I am Elaine," then pointing at the old woman and repeating "Lahtso." Back and forth, she indicates; "Elaine, Lahtso. Elaine, Lahtso."

"Eee-lane, Lah-tso" the old woman mimics back at her, first smiling, then giggling, as her eyes dance round the room, sometimes in the general direction of Petal, sometimes toward one of the children, sometimes into empty space, but repeatedly coming back to settle decisively on Elaine. "Eee-lane, Lah-tso," she repeats, her girlish giggling swelling into a joyful cackle as the others join in. "Eee-lane, Lah-tso," she says a final time, feigning exhaustion and placing the pipe back between her thin lips for just a moment before pulling it out again, a look of great seriousness suddenly upon her features.

"Ber-eel," she says quite sternly, jabbing the stem of the pipe toward where Elaine's hand rests upon her own chest. "Zhe-Khong Ber-eel," and clamps the pipe back into place with a look which assures all present that the matter is settled.

"No, no, no. After the coda the key changes. Up, not down. Let's try it again."

It begins with the feel of a song. The muscular pull of massed voices, a cappella and ecstatic; familiar but indistinct. Heard through a wall perhaps; a thick solid wall and the competition of other sounds as well, layered over and in front of the song I am trying to reclaim, from back before The Nothing.

I am standing in a line of children, feet squared on a narrow riser. My head barely reaches above the shoulder of the child in the row in front of me. On my neck I can feel the rustle and breath of the row behind. Back straight, hands clasped in front of my chest, it feels as though we have been practicing forever - stopping and starting, repeating and refining, and nothing I do is ever right. Voices rise around me and I cannot find their pitch, cannot make myself one with them.

I am off the riser now, the chorus dispersing noisily, children smiling and laughing, moving on to the next moment of their lives as the teacher, a rotund man in a purple sweater, with shiny pink fingernails and orange-brown eyebrows whose ends twist like mustaches, is coaxing me through yet another passage.

"Flat," he pronounces, and I hear in his voice the same frustration which has been echoing through my head for weeks now. "Let the note come from your diaphragm, not your throat."

Again I sing the note, knowing it will not be right.

"You're pushing too hard," Mr. Farley pronounces, his words issuing between tight lips in a face all jowls and cheeks, and eyes eternally disappointed. "You cannot sing with your head, you must sing from your heart. First you have to hear the music, then you can sing it."

"But I do hear it," I say to him, my own eyes beginning to burn. "I hear it perfectly, I just can't find the notes. I..."

Before I can finish, the pressure inside my chest becomes too great to fight and I hear myself sobbing. I know the other children will be staring at me, the younger ones worried, the older ones amused. Still there is nothing I can do to control it. I want so desperately to make my voice do what I hear inside my head. That liquid clarity I hear from others' mouths, the perfect piercing notes flowing from ovalled lips, effortless and powerful. It used to happen naturally, and I was one with the sound, a single key on an instrument without boundary. The teacher's hands would move through the air, pulsing us forward, pulling us higher into the range of angels, and then softly letting us down into the quiet of deepest thought. For three years I have sung in this choir and loved every moment of it but now it is turning to rust and dirt, my voice the grinding of coarse sand beneath my shoes, and I feel a failure at eleven years old.

Mr. Farley's arm reaches around my shoulder as he pulls me close, patting my back. The room is quiet; everyone else has snuck away, fleeing the fetid fragrance of my failure.

"It happens," he says softly across the top of my head. His hand touches my hair, strokes gently down the back of my skull and neck, pats several times between my shoulder blades. "Voices change. All voices- boys...girls - you're growing up, and your bodies are changing, in lots of ways. I think maybe we should try you on a different part, find out what your new voice is trying to tell you."

"I don't want a new voice," I say through the heaving in my body. "I want the one I had before. My voice." Face pressed against his chest, I smell a trace of cigarette smoke coming from his sweater. The fine cashmere, clutched now in both my hands, is as smooth and cool as a puppy's coat in early morning. I am terrified of this growing up, terrified of losing what I've known and loved, and of new challenges which erupt out of nowhere, out of my own body, my self. I want to hide here in this moment forever, to feel his hands patting my head, my back; never to grow older - but then I feel my teacher's body stiffen and his chest rise.

Looking up I see his gaze directed toward the door behind me. Turning inside the circle of his arms I look to see my father standing in the door, topcoat buttoned close to his throat, hat in hand, its crown shining wet and black with the dust of an evening snow. Ashen-faced, his jaw hangs open and those dark eyes are weapons aimed to pierce us both as he takes in the scene. I have never known that look before and it brings something hard and large rising up into my throat. Hot tears are in my eyes and yet, without knowing why, I am certain I must not cry, now that my father is here. I cannot hear the words his lips are mouthing, but I know it is time to go, and that I will never return to this room, this chorus; to this music that I loved so dearly.

"I had a dream last night," Rod says one morning, cradling a steaming mug between his fingertips.

"Is that a good thing, or bad?"

"I don't know. I just...got me thinking about...things. The way they were."

At the sink, Stevie continues scrubbing the breakfast pan, day-glo-orange gloves shielding her tender skin from the scalding water. Truth be told, she's not been listening very much to his comments, or the morning show playing softly on the TV perched on its corner shelf. Her day is more-than-typically pressing - meeting a prospective new client at nine, then a feedback session on some recent revisions to another client's point-of-sale application, the kind of thing which experience tells her will probably devolve into a bitch session about the idiosyncrasies of customers and vendors, issues which software can address only so far. She hasn't slept much either, one of those nights where waking up to pee turns into three hours staring at the darkness mulling over worries and regrets which seem to come to mind only at the precise moment there is nothing one can possibly do about them.

"I don't put much stock in that myself," she says, taking a certain pleasure in being coldly dismissive as she rinses the pan. "Old news is no news." Immediately sorry for being unsympathetic, she turns sideways, braces a hip against the counter, fixes him with eyes narrowed and adds, more gently, "We decide what is going to hurt us, Rodney - and how much - so my advice is: put it to bed. Get on with your life." Wiping hands on her flowered apron she reaches behind to untie it, pulls it overhead - careful not to muss her hair - and carries on, cheered by the lightness of being herself. "Whatever it was, find a way to say goodbye to it. That's Aunt Stevie's advice for this Tuesday morning. And now, I'm off, to slay us a dragon for supper."

For some time Elaine sits and watches as Petal goes about her chores, cutting hunks of dried meat into a large iron pot hung above the fire, prying bits from a brick of dried tea and placing them into an enameled pot of boiling water, grinding handfuls of grain in a stone mortar with a well-worn hardwood pestle. From time to time one of the children assists in some small way, fetching more sticks for the fire, or hauling a sack to her mother's side, and each time Elaine is unable to discern any orders or direction given. It is as if, having performed the same tasks so many times, they communicate without words. This habit of silent contemplation, she realizes, must account for the uncanny quiet she has felt when Petal attended her in her sick-room, and the lack of adult conversation she has heard for long periods around the household. She is thus surprised when, an hour or so after her entering the large room, the joyful barking of several dogs is heard outside, first moving away, then coming close again. When the sound of a man's voice is added to the din, all the children jump up and run out the doorway, pushing aside the heavy felt curtain which hangs there. Petal, too, seems excited by what is going on, following them with buoyant steps as she pats her hair and smoothes her clothes. Only Lahtso ignores the activity, sucking her unlit pipe and staring in the general direction of the slender vine of smoke which dances up from the fire to spread across the ceiling.

Rising from her seat and pushing aside the door-curtain, Elaine makes her own way out, to find her senses overwhelmed, after so many days indoors, by the bright sunlight, the brisk air and the commotion of animals and people. It is only as her eyes grow accustomed to the brightness that she can fully comprehend her setting: a sloping expanse of rutted earth, one side bounded by the large room and the other, longer, sides by two wings of the house, the timber wall of the wing to the left punctuated with three small windows, one of which must be her own. The other wing contains a larger opening, giving way to what appears to be a stable. At one corner of the courtyard, a pen has been constructed of closely-spaced branches, inside which several goats tangle over and around one another, while half a dozen chickens strut and dance about, barely missing both the goats and the two small pigs lying in one corner. The fourth side of the yard is bounded by a wall of stacked rock, interrupted by a sagging wooden gate. From the top of this wall, and from the corners of the house as well, crooked limbs jut upward, long white banners fluttering from their tips in the chill breeze which blows steadily, though none of the other persons seem to notice it. Beyond the courtyard she glimpses a wide plane of earth, tilted to one side like a tray propped up to drain, but otherwise smooth and nearly featureless: a gray-brown emptiness of earth and rock, dried-out scrub and grasses. No road mars its surface, no fence or power line interrupts the eye's inspection of what seems the grandest - and most humbling - shard of globe she has ever encountered.

The prime attractions though, and certainly the reason for all this activity, are a dusty red horse and its rider, a man perhaps in his thirties, in khaki slacks with their knees torn open, a coarse and heavy high-necked sweater and a puffy down vest, its emerald nylon shell as foreign to this setting as a water buffalo set down on a Paris sidewalk. Only a few inches taller than Petal, his body and limbs are visibly thicker than hers, and as he dismounts and goes about the other animals, his movements have an almost dance-like precision: as if he knows beforehand each move they will make, or has by force of thought caused them to come to him, as much as he to them.

Cheerfully extricating himself from the press of children and trailing them behind, the man makes his way over to where Elaine stands. Cupping his hands in front of his chest, the fingers spread wide with the tip of each touching its opposite, he makes a small bow and pronounces the same name she has heard from Dore-eh and Lahtso. "Zhe-Khong Ber-eel," he says. "I am Oo-tay. The 'oncle' of these children."

From the way he speaks the words, and the attention he is receiving, she quickly suspects this man is more than uncle to the little ones who knot themselves about his arms and legs. Petal's behavior, too, seems different than a sister's: blushing laughter at some of his remarks, the playful swatting of a wooden spoon upon his shoulders in response to another and, over all of it, a smile so wide it seems about to split her cheeks.

Above the walls and beyond the plain, Elaine can see Dore-eh's 'hard mountains,' innumerable jagged peaks that rise like walls. On the West, toward the soon-to-be-setting sun, they appear to be a great distance away, while to the right and left of that they are more near, and in the direction opposite - the East - where their ridges and chutes are bathed in amber light, they are quite close, and even under that softening glow their slopes are uniformly steep and stony, with no sign of tree or trail to soften what is certainly the most intimidating landscape she has ever seen. Gazing up, it seems incomprehensible that, somehow, she has come through those mountains to arrive here.

Incomprehensible, too, that in the midst of all this desolation she should find herself sharing the glee of this warm homecoming, with a family who seem already to consider her one of their own.

"I was thinking of doing some shopping on my way home tonight," Stevie suggests, as Rod reaches inside his jacket to pull back a shirt sleeve which has once again slid down to puddle several inches of itself around his wrist. To eyes such as hers - always wary for the silent messages we communicate through our clothing - the few items with which he showed up are a constant contradiction to the growing self-assurance projected by his words and voice. "I think it's time we got you something a little more...elegant."

"I will pick out my own clothes," Rod responds, the measured and uninflected tone a clear indication that he will breach no disagreement on the topic. "I am not an invalid. Or a child."

And pick them out he does, only two days later, when she finds her Thursday afternoon open, with no clients to meet and no pressing projects to complete. He is quiet at first, as her car pulls away from her building, eyes wide at the unfamiliar neighborhood, and disoriented perhaps, but once they crest Capitol Hill he directs with conviction, as if he were the one in control and she a neophyte with a learner's permit. 'Turn here,' 'you need to be in the other lane,' and 'there's a space three cars up you can pull into,' are the mileposts by which she finds herself arriving at Martin's Menswear, a bright-brass-hardware and mahogany-paneling enclave of the sort she thought she had left behind for life, but within which Rod insists he will be greeted with the courtesy and respect due a customer of long standing. With mounting concern she listens as he introduces himself to the impeccably-suited salesman who greets them at the door.

"Arthur," Rod exclaims jovially, Christina's reedy voice nearly disappearing as racks of jackets and slacks soak up its soprano sonority. "Good to see you again. It's been a long time."

The salesman's head gives a slight tilt and Stevie sees his brows settle unevenly as he scans the two women who have invaded his masculine realm. "Yes," he agrees, "It has been a long time. And I'm afraid my memory is...Afraid I'm not quite so good with names as I once..."

"Dr. Gimbal," Rod offers, reaching out a small and slender hand. "Dr. Rod Gimbal. Been shopping here since sixty-three."

"Of course." Grasping the very end of the offered fingers, the salesman gives them a timid shake, his head nodding rapidly to indicate agreement even as his eyes implore Stevie for an explanation, to which she simply shrugs and offers her most demure smile. Of the three, only Rod seems unperturbed as he launches into seemingly-effortless banter.

"Arthur is from Suffolk, Stevie. Suffolk, England, that is – not the one in Massachusetts. Or New York. Came here right after the war, if I remember correctly?" to which Arthur nods politely. "I believe you told me your father was lost in North Africa, and your mother remarried - to a GI. A southerner?"

"That's correct...Miss. We settled in Mobile..."

"But the heat in Alabama was not to your liking," Rod cuts in, apparently oblivious to the offending pronoun. "So when you came of age, you decided to relocate here, to a more familiar climate?" Arthur makes no reply, his mouth hanging slightly open as his eyes widen.

"How's the wife, these days?" Rod continues, offhandedly studying a nubby gray swatch clipped to one of the hangers nearby. Browsing along an aisle between numbered racks of business suits – 40, 40 Long, 42 Short, 42 - he appears to be settling in for a long peruse, completely at home in this world of gabardine and worsted. "Seems like last time I was in, you were asking my opinion on the applicability of indefinite-term hormone replacement therapy for a woman with a mixed family history of diabetes and cardiac arrhythmia."

"Well yes," the salesman's face twitches slightly at this, settling into a look of befuddled obedience as he follows along behind Christina's shuffling feet. "My, uh, my wife... Or rather, I may have discussed something like that with a customer once. One of my more...*senior* customers, who happened to be a doctor. As I recall it, I believe he suggested she consider herbal remedies as an alternative."

"Red clover," Rod agrees, fingering the lapels of a chalk-striped blue number. The entire time he speaks, his eyes are on the clothes, alerting Stevie to another aspect of her new charge's personality; his unwillingness to hold eye contact. Whether afraid of confrontation or simply saving the salesman the difficulty of correlating words with speaker, she cannot tell, but clearly, beneath the apparent ease, Rod is not unaware of the disconsonant impression he is making. "It moderates many of the symptoms of menopause without the added cardiac stress of true estrogen. Made *your* life a hell of a lot more pleasant I'll bet?"

Arthur flashes the tight smile of one amused by a joke, but

unwilling to admit it, as Rod continues down the rack, separating the hangers here and there to examine the front of a jacket, all with the casual yet critical attitude of an expert in tailoring as well as pharmacology. '44,' '44 Long,' '46,' the tags read as Rod passes them by, coming to a stop finally at a rack marked '46 Long.'

"Went through the same thing when my wife had the change. Of course it was Ellie who came up with the herbal approach. I was never much for any of that 'alternative' mumbo jumbo, but she said it worked wonders, and who are we to argue with the women about a thing like that, eh, Arthur?"

"Yes...sir. Who *are* we...indeed."

"A couple of these should do me nicely," Rod continues cheerfully, fingers lifting and caressing the lapel of a single-breasted selection in a charcoal wool flecked with tiny curlicues of mohair. Pulling it off the rack, he stands behind the suit, its jacket reaching nearly to his knees, the shoulders extending inches to each side of his own.

"I think perhaps a slightly smaller size," Arthur intones dryly, his posture more erect than ever, a passive declaration of deep offense at the trick being played here, and the proud refusal to allow it to compromise his professional composure. For a moment he fixes Rod with a glare, then turns crisply and strides off, footfalls audible despite the carpet. Stevie sees the disappointment in Christina's features, then watches them harden into determination as Rod drapes his selection across the rack and follows Arthur to a bank marked '38 Short.'

"I'm afraid this is the smallest size we carry," the salesman declares, lifting a similarly-colored but far less luxurious looking number from the rack, and removing the jacket from its hanger. His face assumes a mask of tolerance as he holds the jacket open, inviting Rod to drop his own coat and slip his arms inside. This done, Arthur looses his grasp and the garment settles into place, shoulder seams drooping as they shelter thin air. The tips of Rod's fingers peak woefully from the cuffs as Arthur pulls the lapels together, their fabric overlapping a good four inches across Christina's stomach, though somewhat less ample across her bosom.

There is silence for a moment, as the subject studies himself in a nearby mirrored column and Stevie feels her insides turn, for the image none of them can avoid is not that of a mature and successful gentleman, as Rod seemed to be expecting, but of a young woman, rendered childlike by dressing up in someone else's clothes. A

Halloween figure, actually - pretending and assuming, but hardly convincing. Gone now is the Doctor's glib banter, replaced by silence as the subject studies his reflection for a moment, then walks briskly to a three-paneled mirror outside the changing rooms. There he stands, one hand clasping the overlapping coat front, the other slipped with deliberate casualness into a pants pocket. With little shifts to left and right he works to view the effect from front, from side, from behind; expressions flashing the whole while across his face - anger, concern, lip-curling distaste. It is the first time Stevie has seen Rod confront head-on the incongruity between what he professes to believe and what the rest of the world sees, and having fought her own battles on that field, she finds herself impelled to help him out. No one but he can *solve* his dilemma, she knows, but there is something she might do to soften it a bit.

Crisply clearing her throat to draw his attention, she steps in her most hip-swaying feminine stride to the end of a nearby line of racks and strikes a Vanna White beside the shiny black sign announcing 'Formal Wear.' Removing the smallest item, she holds it up for him to see, satin lapels gleaming as the matching side-stripes of the slacks peek out from underneath.

"A gentleman does *not* wear a rented tux," she suggests, putting on a pouty sternness. "Not if he's part of *my* act."

As hoped, the look on the kid's face brightens. Once again those slender fingers reach out to rub the fabric between their tips. Finding it satisfactory, he takes the hanger from her outstretched hand and turns to confront the salesman, whose eyes now register, if anything, even more confusion than before.

"Well, Arthur," Christina's voice pronounces loudly, but with all of Rodney's command. "I'd say your tailor's got some work cut out for him."

Over dinner that evening of boiled chicken and balls of barley dough with milk curd, Ootay explains to Elaine a little more about her refuge. Just as she suspected, he is not actually the uncle of the children, but the father of three out of the five. The other two, Thin and Pooh, have a different father, who left two years ago on a caravan with his own brother and son – who is not Petal's child at all; this family apparently having more extensions than a reality-TV clan – and has not been heard from since. Ootay himself is about to head off on a similar journey, joining a handful of other men from the valley to cross the mountains with a load of hides and herbs, musk, poppy and ponies, which they hope to trade for tools, salt, cloth and kitchen goods to bring back to the valley. This, it seems, is the way of life for those who live in this region, the men away for long periods of time, either tending herds or trading, the women planting and tilling fields of soybean and barley, caring for the children and the livestock. As Ootay tells her this - in surprisingly serviceable English he explains he has acquired on his travels - it is clear that he is more visitor than authority; the family, and indeed the home in which they sit, are always mentioned as Petal's, never 'mine' or 'ours.' This fits with what Elaine has observed already: that it is Petal who runs the household and decides what goes or not. In their conversation, Ootay also sometimes refers to her the 'dabu,' which he translates a bit hesitantly to mean 'leader of the house.' Where normally this would be the oldest woman in the family, it seems Petal assumed the mantle some seasons back when Lahtso's lameness and cataracts led her to choose something akin to retirement on her platform beneath the window of what he refers to as 'the Mother Room.' It is doubly unusual that Petal ever reached this status, as she has an older sister who was first in line, but Gudelema was captivated by a pair of Christian missionaries who passed through the valley when she was young, and left when they did, to become the wife of one of their pale-skinned blue-eyed sons.

Perched on the long bench as they sip steaming cups of butter-tea following the meal, Ootay explains that the people of the valley are mostly descendants of an ethnic group known as the Moso. Scandalized by the people's matriarchal and marriage-less way of life, the Han authorities had tried to assimilate them, using economic and punitive measures to induce women to marry and become subservient to the 'uncles' who visited them and gave them children.

In the same ways, they pressured the men to abandon their extended trading journeys and take jobs in communal workshops, or to till the small fields in their mountain communities. About the time of Ootay's grandparents – or perhaps earlier, chronology seeming somewhat elastic in his telling – several hundred Moso left their homes in western China to escape the government. Heading west, in the general direction of Tibet, these refugees endured tremendous hardship, including attacks from bandits and local residents alike, until they found this valley, too high to appeal to lowland farmers, too remote for industry, and cut off from the rest of the world for several months every year by deep mountain snows. Here they settled, their numbers augmented over time by other wanderers from various directions, especially nearby Tibet. Far more loyal to their clan and tribal origins, they had never accepted the title of 'Chinese,' nor could they call themselves Tibetan (although he admits they have adopted many Tibetan ways), as the true Tibetans were of totally different ethnic origin. They describe themselves instead as the 'azhe-Moso,' meaning 'little Moso,' or sometimes just 'Azhe.' As for any of the surrounding nations and governments, the azhe Moso avoid contact whenever possible, and closely guard the secret of their valley and the few paths which lead in and out of it.

As Ootay talks, Petal sits quietly by his side, picking lice from the head of Thin, while Pooh plays with a wooden antelope, and Little One a doll made out of yak tails, both gifts from their uncle's saddle sacks. Tulip mends one of his thick felt leggings by lamplight, as the sounds of the livestock taper into nighttime quiet. Off in the distance a dog barks, chasing some wild animal perhaps, or fending off an evil spirit, but in this cozy room all is safety and belonging.

Some years ago, Ootay continues, when he was still a young man, an elderly trekker found her way to the valley, asking about the missing brother she believed might have travelled to the region long before, when the peoples outside were fighting one of their many wars. Despite finding no trace of her lost brother, this woman stayed for some time, living with various families, becoming close with their women, and captivating the children with fanciful tales of flying through the sky and all around the world. When finally she left, it was with a promise to return, a promise which she had kept every two or three years since, each time bringing with her a quantity of medical supplies, books and shoes, plus treats for the children. This woman they have come to call 'zhe-khong Ber-eel,' as much a title as a name; signifying great honor, and an association also with the god of earth who made this valley and who brought her to it. When Elaine arrived, the Azhe immediately noted her resemblance to the Ber-eel, and when, during the next break in the weather, three exhausted porters arrived carrying crates of rubber running shoes, Tibetan-language textbooks and powdered infant formula, they concluded firmly that Elaine must truly be the Ber-eel, her form rejuvenated so she could be with them once again. This semi-mystical interpretation was aided by the fact that no one quite understood how she had arrived in the valley in the middle of a late-autumn storm. Gatusa, the son of a family from the far end of the valley, was attempting to retrieve several of his sheep who had wandered across a high and snow-covered shelf when he happened upon her sodden form lying unconscious in the lee of a large boulder, with but a single trail of footprints leading out of a nearby snowpatch at the base of a tall cliff, far from any of the usual paths. The porters offered no answers either, professing no idea how Elaine had made her way after becoming separated from them. Nor could Elaine question them about Beryl's fate or what had cause the break-up, for by the time of Ootay's arrival, they were long gone, eager to get home before the passes closed again.

Lying in her bed that night, hearing the giggles and grunts of Petal and Ootay, Elaine cannot help but picture the eager pleasure they take in making, quite possibly, another mouth to feed. Although she has yet to truly connect with the woman who leads this household, she has developed a great admiration for Petal. In this inhospitable landscape, surrounded by a continent which barely knows of her existence and would probably not approve of it if they did, she sustains her children, cares for her mother (and a virtually-helpless stranger), and seems to find more joy with her cavalier horseman than any number of secure and settled women Elaine can recall back home. Having Ootay around promises to be a blessing for Elaine as well, for finally she has someone to talk with and through whom she can communicate more fully with the others.

"And now, Ladies and Germs, I'd like to introduce a good friend of mine. A living demonstration of the old adage that good things come in small packages, please give a warm Doghouse welcome to...the Doctor, *Miss-terrr* Rodney Gimbal."

The crowd watches as a person rises from one of the front tables. Most of them had not even noticed him, sitting hunched with folded hands, his dark suit manufacturing a shadow in which to hide. Now they see he is quite small, a bit pudgy perhaps, and with a youthful cast to the complexion, as if his beard has not yet come in, though he moves stiffly, and almost as slowly as some of the older folks among the audience. An odd person, the uninformed observer might be forgiven for thinking, but still, this is Stevie bringing him on, and they trust her judgment, so the applause is polite, the questions kept to themselves. It is well into the evening; they've been listening and talking for hours, many of them; drinking and eating and enjoying themselves. This is not some high-priced nightclub, after all, where the audience demands their money's worth out of every second; this is Thursday night at The Doghouse, and most of the crowd is ready to give the benefit of the doubt.

Thanks to its main function as a diner, the Dog doesn't have a real stage, just a raised plywood platform in a back corner, where the organ was installed so long ago no one can remember a time when it wasn't there. A plug-in desk lamp allows the player to see her music, while an electric candelabrum to one side splashes enough light on her face for the audience to catch her expressions. Sitting at the organ as Rod makes his way over, Stevie wonders again whether he is ready for this - not to mention whether *they* are ready for *him*. Reaching her side, he sets his glass on a coaster, gives his tie an unnecessary tug, and nods in her direction, his face as serious as one about to perform major surgery.

Out among the tables, bits of conversation continue and menus rustle, the sound of silverware on dishes mixing with her music, and after sixteen bars of intro Stevie knows there's nothing for it but to toss out the first lyric. *"I'm not the guy,"* she sings and, as expected, there are a few friendly snickers from the regulars who know her back-story. *"Who cared about love,"* settles them down, delivered as it is with earnest sincerity and a phrasing borrowed from the Bobby Darin recording. Stevie's heart holds its breath as the music flows on, until finally, at just the right moment, she hears that liquid begin to flow, a bit timid right now, but magic none the less.

"*And I'm not the guy who cared about fortunes and such,*" Rod sings, bringing the room to silence as the crowd try to square Christina's voice with the figure before them. "*I never cared much,*" provides just enough time for most of them to put together whatever explanation they like, so that, by the time the two voices come together for the tag, there are satisfied smiles gleaming up at them from all corners of the room. "*Oh, look at me now,*" Stevie and Rod sing together, and anyone who hadn't caught on before, knows now that it's OK to be amused at the irony of this odd couple. Flowing easily into the next verse, Stevie feels the music lifting her on its strong arms, and sees her friend also, buoyed by the audience's appreciation for his unexpected gift.

Time draws itself into a thread, weaving in and out of events. First The Nothing, then so much confusion, and now this. Standing here, singing this song: in one way it's as familiar and natural as can be, like breathing and walking, and at the same time, it is clearly impossible. Nothing about anything makes sense anymore, and yet there is no denying it - to hear the music beside me, surrounding me, and to open my mouth and be one with it, feels like a dream come true.

Dream, memory, reflection, illusion, I have no idea any more. Facts, convictions, all the things I thought I knew, are useless, as - true or false - this feeling, this be-ing, is just... Here, now; this is so right, it must be real.

Or true.

Or something.

The number ends with a flourish, arpeggios piling up against one another like clouds against a steepening coast, and Stevie is gratified that the applause lasts longer than it ever has for her alone. Sees Rodney basking; though his down-turned eyes and hunched shoulders might fool those unfamiliar with him, her guess is that he is very much affected. This is what he needs, she thinks, as her hands introduce the next selection in their carefully arranged playlist. To be out in the world as himself, to feel the acceptance. To understand the value of his gift and know that there are plenty of people - hundreds, thousands, millions even, if you stretch the net far enough - who do not care how the parts and pieces of him fit together, or not.

Back when I was in The Nothing, I tried to figure out what was dream and what reality, and now again I strain to decide. Running through the numbers Stevie has arranged for us is solid, real. There are mistakes, and when they happen, my own reactions tell me they exist outside of my imagination, and yet there is this place, this run-down shack hung with the most awful collection of cheap gimcracks and gewgaws. Dirty and dreary, if they ever turned the lights up enough to see it as it really is. Not a dive even, but a dead-end, filled with old codgers and young weirdoes, half of them queer, by the look of them. Losers and loners who probably don't count for anything except to their own nutty crowd. Never in a million years would I have chosen to be here, in real life – the life I remember having lived for so long - and so it must be a dream.

But there are none of the signs of a dream. No sudden shifts of context, nothing coming in out of left field to instantly challenge continuity; nothing at all to dispute the authenticity of what I am experiencing – unless you count myself, but even that seems to amount to less and less anymore...can it be I'm getting used to it? Despite logic, despite intellect, when the music begins and wraps its magic all around, I find myself creeping close to accepting that this leaky vessel - with all its unfamiliar attributes, the trembling neediness that scares me half to death, and this one great virtue - is me.

Forty minutes later, sitting at a two-top counting their tip money, Stevie lets the silence go on even longer than usual. With Rod, she has learned, prolonged silence is a necessary prelude to meaningful conversation. It is only when all the bills are sorted and straightened, the few pointless quarters tallied, that she settles back, takes a sip of mineral water, and ventures to ask, "So how did that feel?"

As usual, the kid takes his time, filling it up with those little movements of his jaw, as if he's chewing over the words before he lets them escape.

"Good," he answers, though the smile spreading across his features proves the word unequal to the emotion. "It felt...very good," he adds, and in that moment, as the two burst into laughter at the confounding variety of their world, Stevie knows she would go anywhere and do anything to make that smile a regular feature on the kid's face.

So warmly has the family wrapped itself around Ootay, that it comes as a shock when, only two short days after his arrival, Elaine wakes to the sound of horses stamping beyond her window. Hurrying outside, she finds the smaller children sobbing as he struggles to secure a squealing squirming goat across the haunches of his horse, all the while enduring staccato jibes from four other men already in their saddles and itching to set out. Off to one side, Dore-eh sits astride a smaller pony, his face alight with the excitement of the coming journey even as Petal chatters orders at him, sounding very much like any mother anywhere, sending her son off for the first time.

"Wait," Elaine cries out, racing to Ootay's side, only to find that he has anticipated her request. "No, no, Ber-eel," he explains with a beaming smile. "Too soon for you. Snow is still many deep, and you not so many strong." Despite her pleas he will not budge, and in minutes the horsemen are off, raising dust toward the distant southern mountains, leaving Elaine to the company of Petal and Lahtso and the children.

Without even Dore-eh's few words, she finds herself now totally unable to communicate or contribute, no more than a spectator to the domestic routine going on around her. Her attempts at joining in are met with laughter, even from the children, or rapid-fire admonitions from Lahtso in her place upon the platform, the implication being that 'zhe-khong-Ber-eel' is not to humble herself with chores. When visitors arrive, as they do every few days, she finds herself an object of respect and curiosity, but mostly a spectator to their exchange of simple gifts and the sometimes raucous conversations they share over tea - which she is allowed to drink, but never to brew or to serve.

Despite the unbroken good humor and generosity of her hostesses, as the days turn into weeks, and the weeks into months, Elaine comes to feel herself as much a prisoner as a guest, trapped in the silence of her own thoughts, divorced from the occupations of those around her.

Gas-fired flames flicker in the dimly-lit room, flashing off fireplace glass. The wall behind the sofa bears outsized shadows of two heads as Stevie and Rod unwind from another evening at 'the Dog.' The black satin lapels of his tuxedo jacket shine softly, as does his bow tie, which Stevie wound carefully tight several hours ago.

"I can't believe you don't know how to do this yourself," she'd teased, careful not to brush her hands against his face as she worked , so close.

"Never had to," he grunted. "Elaine always…" and stopped.

"You miss her?"

Tie tied, Rod turned away, busied himself picking up the tux coat, then putting it down to straighten his cummerbund, fastened loosely so as not to call attention to Christina's narrow waist or the awkward chest above it. Picked up the jacket again.

"Sometimes I hear her voice in my mind. Like she was right here, right now, and it makes me wonder if I ever really heard it before. All those years we were together, and I don't think I ever considered how her voice sounded, or what it meant that she was always there. Tying my tie. Pouring coffee. Other things she must have been doing all the time, that I never even realized.

"I tried to call her, you know," he added, and Stevie felt herself inhale abruptly. Flashed first on a picture of Rod stepping into the arms of some woman who claimed him, and herself standing by like a stupid statue - before realizing with a start that she had actually fallen into his fantasy, been taken up for a moment with his story, from which realization her thoughts quickly segued into just what it would mean if there really *was* an Elaine Gimbal out there somewhere, and Rod - *this* Rod, the one who Stevie knows - were to show up at her door claiming…

"I never got any answer," he continued, and she breathed normally again. "We don't - didn't - have a machine. Partly just too old-fashioned to get one, but then we never needed it anyway, because Elaine was always at home. That's the kind of woman she was. Is. So I went by the old house." Stevie feels the fear rising again. "It was…not what I expected. Or, not what I wanted it to be. The house was just like I remembered it, but different…not mine anymore. It had changed somehow…moved on…while I've been away. As if even the sidewalk had moved on from where it was - to being something new."

'As if maybe *you* had moved on,' Stevie thought. 'Toward becoming who you really are and leaving behind this old story you made up to fit yourself into the way you thought the world had to work.' That's what she was thinking as he dressed, but not what she said.

"We're the ones who've got to be moving on now," she had quipped instead, letting him off the hook. "We've got people waiting for us. Real people."

On Stevie there is satin also, as the room steeps now in after-hours fire glow. A dress the color of aged-merlot, with precious tiny buttons down the front, and sleeves that pouf about her shoulders then narrow, sheathing her arms and slithering past her wrists to pool against the heels of her hands and lap over their backs, ending just in time not to be a problem at her keyboard . A romantic dress from another era, the skirt so slender she has to walk in tiny steps, which she doesn't mind; treasures actually, not to mention the way people treat her when she's wearing it.

"We made quite an entrance tonight," she recalls, breaking the silence.

Thursdays are becoming events, now that Stevie and Rod are an act at the Doghouse. The crowds are a bit larger, nearly very table filled at the peak hour, but it's not the numbers so much as the attitude. More and more it seems they've come for the music, not just to get out of their houses. Applause is more sustained and focused. There are fewer requests too; as if it's less about reclaiming memories than making new ones. Certainly it is for Stevie. It's about being up front, exactly who she is, and having folks accept – no embrace – that...and all because of Rodney, and who he is. There are times lately, when the urge to thank him, to make him understand just what a gift he is giving her, becomes overwhelming. Words, she has convinced herself, are no longer enough.

An afternoon, and much like every other afternoon since the men departed, the homestead humming softly with familiar activities as Elaine sits on the platform, drinks her tea, and watches. Lahtso has been gone for several days, following a visit by another old woman who was greeted like a close relative. After sharing tea and conversation, the visitor's two strapping boys had loaded their mother and Lahtso into a two-wheeled cart pulled by a hungry-looking yak. Petal too, is out; morning meal and chores accomplished, she has gone off to deliver a freshly-baked sweet-cake somewhere, perhaps to one of the other families nearby, perhaps to another village. Even after several months, Elaine has managed only a few words of the language around her, so rapidly and casually is it spoken, and so mostly she sits and watches the action, like a play performed for her alone. She senses no resentment of her presence, or her eating from the communal pot, only a slightly amused acceptance, as if she were some dotty aunt who had always been around. Still, she feels a twinge of guilt each time Petal or Tulip ladles food onto her plate.

Turning, she glances out the window at the courtyard, where Pooh and the other children busy themselves with a strip of ragged harness leather. In the span of moments it is a streamer, a whip, a harness to pull Little One, and again a streamer, flapping about in the sun and the breeze of a spring noon as the children disappear around the end of the stable wing. For a time, the sounds of their play still reach her, then suddenly, nothing. In the interval she can hear the fire's silence as it smolders between meals, the scraping of a branch where a shrub has grown up tight against the house, thirsty for what moisture drips from the eave when rain comes, or even a heavy dew. The silence is remarkable, in fact, for though there is little actual conversation, never in the daytime is this homestead quite so still, and Elaine feels the hair on her neck rise, her apprehension rewarded almost as soon as she recognizes it with a new sound: of Little One crying. Something in the toddler's tone brings Elaine up off the platform, unfolding stiff legs to take her toward the door where she sees Pooh come staggering into view, to fall heavily on his backside and gaze around him, as if lost in his own front yard.

Running now, her progress impossibly slow in light of the certainty that something is truly wrong, she ignores the child and rounds the corner of the stable, to see the other children all clustered before the pile of branches and sticks stored to feed their precious fire. There, among the fuel, Petal sits, one leg beneath her, the other, outstretched, the bottom of its foot smeared with a deep red mud of blood and dust. Her face is contorted as she holds the leg with both hands, but no cry of pain escapes her lips, only a terrified gaze as Elaine reaches her and takes in the thick splinters of wood protruding from swollen flesh.

"Back," Elaine commands Tulip, Thin and Little One, brushing them aside as she kneels to study the injury, for once grateful that she cannot understand the words around her, for they would only distract. The situation is clear enough; Petal, coming home from wherever she had gone visiting, must have stopped at the wood pile for some sticks to brew the mid-day tea. Perhaps she was careless, perhaps distracted by the children and stumbled, but one way or another she stepped bare-footed on a broken stick and jammed its jagged end deep into the bottom of her foot. The dust, the flies, the animals meandering and defecating all around, only heighten Elaine's concern that this is not a minor injury. Indeed, as soon as she begins to tug on the larger splinter's exposed end, she feels Petal shudder, and sees the skin stretch, caught by ragged edges deep within.

"Better to leave it in for now," Elaine says in a voice which comes out more panicked and less soothing than she intended. With a few quick gestures, she manages to push the children away again and persuade Petal to place an arm around her shoulder. Feeling herself shaky beneath even this small woman's weight, Elaine hoists her up and leads her, stumping along on one leg, back around and into the house. Here she sets Petal upon the platform, her outstretched foot dripping dark onto the earthen floor.

"I need water," she explains, holding an enamelware basin out to Tulip who - quickly understanding the object, if not the word - takes the basin and disappears out the door. "And I need cloth," she commands the others, who only look on in bafflement, eyes wide in tear-streaked faces, glancing between the stranger who has never spoken in such a tone to them before, and their mother, whose silence now terrifies them.

Indeed, Petal's face is taut, her body rigid as she staves off the pain of her injury. In those features Elaine sees something else as well, an unaccustomed look which is more than simple attention, but not exactly fear. What it is, she realizes, as her eyes cast about the room for a source of cloth to clean the wound, is worry. For the first time since arriving here she is seeing her guardian worried about how to cope with this new situation. That, in turn, brings home just how much she has come to rely on Petal's ability to provide not only for her, but for all of them.   The rhythm of this household has been so natural, eternal almost, that she has taken it far more for granted than she should have, for without Petal's constant work and direction, none of them would be secure.

Tulip's return, the pot brimming with water from the cistern, brings Elaine back to her purpose.   With a few gestures she is able to communicate to the girl that the fire must be stoked, a process which takes long minutes as the other children try to help. By the time the flames are tall, the room is thick with smoke, but eventually the pot is heating, as Elaine searches the hooks and ledges, discarding every rag, garment or piece of bedding as too filthy for her purposes. The cleanest cloth for miles, she realizes, is upon her, preserved from the soiling which afflicts everything else in the house by her own indolence - lying about recovering while all the rest were working. The thought increases her sense of guilt sufficiently to overcome the embarrassment she feels as, standing there in the center of the Mother Room, she removes the embroidered vest she's been given to wear, unties the three knots at the side of the long-sleeved shirt beneath, and shrugs it off. Pulling the vest quickly back on, she takes a cooking knife to the linen. The smoky air lends a chill to her now-bare arms as she cuts and tears several strips from the shirt and stuffs three of them into the water, which is at last beginning to steam.

After dipping her own hands into the pot, and holding them there as long as she can stand, Elaine takes one of the cloths and begins to squeeze it over the wound. Her patient stiffens even more, breathing in sharply between clenched teeth, but without so much as a moan. As vapor rises off the wound, Elaine begins to see better what she is up against. Two large splinters of cedar project from the center of the sole, right beneath the arch. One is slender and straight, and indeed, it yields to the first pull, drawing out with only a slight tug of the flesh, rich red blood oozing in its absence, but not gushing, as the torn skin closes neatly. That will still require cleaning out, Elaine reminds herself, no doubt there is dirt and maybe small fragments of wood left behind, but it is the larger shard that concerns her the most. Half-obscured by dirt and callous, it is jagged and misshapen, the portion trapped beneath the skin thicker than what protrudes.

Dipping the cloth back into the pot, she feels her own skin on the edge of scalding and welcomes the pain, for it suggests perhaps she can achieve some level of cleanliness in what must come. Carrying the pot closer to her patient and gesturing to Tulip to set another one to boiling, she employs a cooking spoon stick to dunk and swirl the cloth before pulling it out again, nearly searing her hands as she twists and wrings to run the steaming fluid down Petal's skin, carrying dust and dirt with it. Close-up, Elaine can see the way that labor has shaped her flesh, the heel and ball areas and the bottoms of the toes all thickened into hard, dry pads, fissured by cracks black with ground-in soil, though the skin at the height of the arch is soft and thin. It is this vulnerable region, the result of a healthy musculature, which allowed the splinters to do their damage. The irony holds no fascination for Elaine, as she turns and twists the foot to cleanse all around the margins of the wound. Several times she feels the leg jerk slightly, as if wanting to pull back from the pain of her exploring, but that is the nearest thing to protest as she swabs and rinses for several minutes before the field of battle seems as clear as it is likely to get.

The shard has penetrated toward the ball of Petal's left foot, driven in no doubt by the force of her energetic stride, and still projects a finger's breadth. Its other end can be felt and but not seen, nearly two inches forward of the entry, the skin stretched tight by its bulk. Tugging at the exposed end has no effect, it is too short to get a grip, and the concealed portion's shape forms an effective barb against extraction, even if she could. With sinking heart, Elaine realizes what she must do, if Petal is to walk again on this foot.

A quick pantomime sets Thin to work tearing the rest of Elaine's blouse into strips as she steps around little Pooh to retrieve the narrow-bladed skinning knife from its peg on the wall among the other tools. A crude and evil-looking thing this, hardly more than a fragment of sheet steel, its wide end sandwiched and riveted between two strips of hardwood burnished smooth by long use. The wood proves a useful insulator though, as she holds the blade deep inside the fire's flames, and crude as the knife's assembly may be, she knows from observation that its business end is effective, the slender tip just right for slicing flesh precisely - which is what Elaine commences to do, once it has glowed red and then cooled to a dull black. Resisting the urge to avert her eyes, she inserts the steel tip on top of the splinter and presses forward, feeling the already-stretched flesh tighten further and strain against her push then finally give way, tearing forward as Petal's leg winces once and the thick lump of wood can be pulled free, to join the muddy bloody patch which has accumulated on the floor below her foot.

Heart beating faster than she has ever felt before, Elaine casts a smile at her patient, whose own eyes are tightly shut, her lower lip sucked in between yellowed teeth. Swabbing and dipping she cleanses the wound as best she can, alternately squeezing the surrounding tissue so the flow of blood will help, then blotting and dabbing, and picking out with her fingers or the tip of the knife the smaller bits of splinter left behind. Reassuringly, the flow of blood slows as she does all this, and beneath the flap the smoky shadows of deep-blue veins and silver-gleaming tendons are uncut. "You'll live," she hears a voice saying - only belatedly realizing it is her own - and though the joke can mean nothing, clearly her tone communicates something, as Pooh and the other children begin again to talk among themselves.

"I need a needle," she urges as they press close, butting curious heads to examine their mother's foot more closely. "And thread," she adds, miming the act of sewing. Tulip comprehends immediately, scampering across the room to rummage in a rush basket and return holding a roll of silken cloth which Elaine unravels to reveal several shiny needles and a spool of dark silk thread.

"Perfect," she remarks, and the girl's face beams with satisfaction. Shortly, a needle and a length of thread are boiled and retrieved, Petal's position adjusted for best light on the work and Elaine prepares herself again. "This will hurt," she warns the woman, who cannot possibly comprehend her words but whose face seems marvelously free of concern, given what is being done to her, and by whom. "A lot," she adds, touched by an intuition that it is not her - Elaine Gimbal - in whom the mother has such confidence, but zhe-Khong-Bereel. "But it's the last of the hurting. I promise."

With a deep breath she presses the needle's end into the skin, her stomach turning as the sooty point drives in and disappears, then becomes visible in the crimson gulf between flaps, then vanishes again, only to reappear once more as it punches through the other side, sending a shudder through Elaine's core. Trembling fingers switch places to grab the tip and tug until the knot catches and the jagged edges of the wound are pulled together. Shaking her head to clear the fog which threatens to engulf it, she glimpses the eyes of all upon her, astonished and curious, and yet, it seems, completely trusting of this stranger and her unusual ways.

Stabbing and pulling, she seals the wound until only a ragged

'Y' remain, counting seventeen stitches in all before she is done and can knot the thread slice off the excess with the knife. Gathering a shorter piece of thread, she does the same for the other splinter-wound, comparatively minor at only three stitches. Looking up at her patient, she finds Petal's eyes closed, her breathing deep. Whether passed-out or asleep, her face again projects the placid self-assurance it has borne since Elaine first glimpsed it, standing over her own sick-bed, long months ago. Settling back, Elaine straightens her shoulders with a sigh, then begins to bandage the foot with the remaining strips of dry cloth, gesturing to Tulip to do something about the mess beneath their feet as she dips her own hands into the still-hot water to wash away the already-congealing evidence of their efforts.

Doug Hrastnik flips carelessly through the pages of the Weekly, the city's self-described alternative newspaper, where left-leaning politics, social issues and new-brow culture share equal billing with ads for sex shops, head shops and escort services. He's settled into a booth at the Cambridge Pub, an optimistically-upscale name for what is actually a rather down-market bar, sandwiched between a wholesale paint distributor and a mobile phone retailer in a neglected commercial block on Highway 99 north of town. At ten PM, the evening is old already, the few customers scattered around the dim and slightly damp interior sit mostly staring into their beers, hoping for something interesting to walk in the door or to flash across the TV behind the bar, currently tuned to a tennis match between two unknown Europeans. The paper was lying on a bench when Doug and his friend wandered in, and he picked it up as much for something to eep his hands occupied as for its content. He's nearly all the way through the rag when a small but well-composed photo catches his eye.

"Hey, Jake," he mutters, his tone suggesting a barely amusing throw-away as he folds over the page and holds it up for his companion to see. "See anything familiar?"

On the page, under a small header reading 'Duo at Doghouse," is a photo of a middle-aged woman at the keyboard of an electronic organ. Beside her stands a younger person, dressed in a tux, but clearly female in her features, mouth open in song. 'Stevie Margulies and Rodney Gimbal wow their fans every Thursday night at the organ,' reads the caption. 'Playing all your favorites from the fifties, sixties and beyond. No cover, no minimum.'

"For a second I thought that was your old girlfriend," Doug prompts as Jake stares, wide-eyed. "What was her name?"

"Kim," Jake answers, grabbing the paper from his friend's hand.

"Yeah. What ever happened to her?" Doug asks, pulling a long swallow of beer from his mug. "Didn't she, like..."

"She got sick," Jake answers irritably, his real attention still on the paper. "She got real sick. But she's gonna' get better, if I have anything to say about it." Grabbing his mug, he drains the contents in one gulp, then rises from his bench, fumbles a couple of bills out of his wallet and tosses them on the table. "I gotta' go," is all the farewell he offers, before turning and walking, a bit unsteadily, toward the bar's door, the parking lot, the street, and beyond.

'Facilities Management - Storage – 053-42'

A simple sign, its digits routed into laminated plastic, so they read as white against a crimson background. Dusty and unimpressive in the basement hallway, as Mary waits for Jason to find the correct key. This is at least the fifteenth storeroom they have visited since he borrowed a ring of keys from some guy he knows in Operations. Jase, as she has taken to calling her friend, has absolutely no idea what they are looking for, and Mary not much more; just that once upon a time there was a lab called Applied Dialysis and no one seems to know what went on there, or if they do, to be willing to talk about it. But if there was a lab, then there was equipment, and Hilltop never throws anything away, as anyone who has ever requisitioned a chair or a stapler quickly finds out; fill out a form, wait a ridiculous length of time, and when the big day comes - what you get is someone else's old chair or stapler that's been in storage since that person didn't need it anymore, and now it's yours. (Mary herself once put in through Admin for some manila files to keep her registration paperwork straight, and what she got was a box of well-used folders plus a page of sticky-back labels to go over the ones that were already on their tabs, sometimes two or three deep.) So somewhere around the Center, there's bound to be a remnant left of Dr. Resor's A.D. lab, and Jason has taken it up as his quest: to find that missing grail for his new damsel - a role to which Mary feels herself ill-suited, but not enough to protest the elevation.

"Got it," Jase mutters, as the key turns and the door groans back to reveal yet another darkened room, this one extending beneath the bustling halls and brilliantly-lit examining rooms of the Doris Lessing Cardiovascular Care Center. From the hall all that can be seen are the ends of several tall metal racks bolted together in perpendicular uniformity. To one side an aging steel desk seems to personify bureaucracy, the blotter on its surface being several generations past its purpose. Jason finds a light switch on the wall, and as they have in each of the other such rooms they've visited, the two squeeze inside and close the door before he flicks it on, bringing to life four rows of wire-caged fixtures above four long aisles lined with shelves, stuffed to the ceiling.

"All right then," says the triumphant explorer with a squeeze of his hand on Mary's arm, "let's see what we've got here," and he sets off down the farthest aisle to the left. Mary heads to the right, pondering the realization that, after so many of these little outings, it is not so much the thought of what they might find that keeps her going, so much as the chance to be doing something – anything – with Jason. Certainly that was not the case at the start of their search, just after her visit with Jessica Bagley; Mary had been worked up then, quick to anger at the thought of anyone departing so radically from the rules of practice as the woman suggested. Which, in fact, was how she presented it to Jason; that what she suspected happened in ADL was a clear case of malpractice - physicians performing untested and unauthorized treatments on patients whose consent, whatever its legal documentation, had never anticipated where their fates were taking them.

To her dismay, her high-tech wizard seemed not the least bit surprised at any of it.

"Like you didn't know doctors make their own rules?" he asked at one point, discounting her moral outrage with a careless wave of his cafeteria latte. "You're one of them, my dear lady. You see it from the same side of the looking glass. The rest of the world?" he took a long slurp of caffeinated milk, "We just stand back and watch them, running around like they're saving the world. They're people Mare, with lives of their own. They get pissed off at things and take it out on their wives. They worry about their mortgages and how their kids are doing at school, just like auto mechanics and accountants. And sometimes they get too full of themselves and think they know more than anyone else. The difference is, if your mechanic gets a wild hair, maybe your car engine idles a little too high. Your accountant plays fast and loose? You end up paying less taxes, and if you're smart enough to know about it - and still dumb enough to care - you might lose a little sleep every April. But docs? They get too enthusiastic and you've got a vegetable in her mother's spare bedroom, like your little girl. And even that's better than what it could have been. I mean, did you hear about that lab back in DC, where they were studying Ebola and one of the techs. ended up getting infected? That's like the most contagious thing there is in the whole entire world? I'll take computer viruses any day over that shit."

Over time, Jason's cavalier attitude has hijacked their little expeditions, to the point where they seem now to be as much a chance for the two of them to hang together – a weirdly personalized form of dating – as about anything they might actually find. It is this thought which is on Mary's mind as she wanders down the aisle, surveying its contents. The upper shelves tend toward cardboard boxes, neatly labeled in fat black marker. 'GLASSWARE, Lab – ASTMD: 105 – 08/06' is typical of the labeling. Maddeningly prominent, and at the same time, almost totally inscrutable.

The lower shelves are more interesting, generally, for that is where the big bulky stuff resides. An old fashioned cardiac monitor - the kind she learned to use in first-year internship - stands on wheels which may never roll again. Superseded by newer machines with more chips and fewer ways to fail, it gathers dust next to some sort of specialized examination chair, its arms and legs festooned with slots and eyelets to secure...it's difficult to imagine *what* would be secured to all that hardware, or for what purpose. Remnant of the apex of medical knowledge at one particular date, it looks now like something out of a horror film, no more useful than those old bone-saws and cauterizing-irons you find in museums of the Revolution. Or the Civil War. Or the last war, for that matter. How long, she wonders, before the very treatments students are learning about today – individualized meds and neo-natal micro-surgery and narrowly-targeted chemotherapy– how long till someone looks back at those things and asks "Chemotherapy for God's sake! What were they thinking?"

Fortunately for her professional confidence, that line of thought is interrupted by a yelp from Jason. Poking his head around the far end of the aisle, his broad face is consumed by a grin as he waves excitedly.

"You need to see this," he urges, somewhere between a whisper and a shout. Seeing her muted reaction, he repeats, nodding to confirm his own conclusion. "Seriously, Mare, you *need* to see this.

An hour after Petal's surgery, all traces have been cleared away and Elaine is just beginning to settle the jumble of emotions engendered by the accident and its treatment, when she hears a rustling from the platform, and sees Petal sitting up, examining her bandaged foot as if it were a foreign object. With a slight bow of gratitude toward Elaine, she sets her good foot upon the floor and makes to stand.

"No, no," Elaine shouts, dashing over to press her patient back down. She knows her words mean nothing as she explains the need to keep the wound clean to prevent infection, to keep her weight off of it to avoid pulling the stitches, all so it can heal properly and avoid permanent disability; still she knows no other way to communicate. Nor does Petal, who replies with her own barrage of syllables and gestures, beginning gently enough, as perhaps she thanks the Ber-eel for her help, then turning stern as she makes the case for her need to get back to work, and ultimately growing quite angry, as she struggles to rise and is held back. Marveling at the tiny matriarch's strength, and realizing she is about to lose a battle which must be won, Elaine is as surprised as anyone when her right hand swings out, wide and swift, to come slapping down square on the sole of the injured foot. Petal's scream tears at her heart, and the fire in her eyes is a fearful thing to see, but the gesture has its effect; the flood of words ceases, and in the void Elaine assumes what she hopes will be seen as an attitude of humble pleading.

"Tell me what to do," she says, several times, hands cupped before her chest and head held low. Pointing at Tulip, Thin, Pooh and Little One, huddled against the far wall and crying in terror of what zhe Khong Ber-eel has just done, she continues. "Have the children show me and I will do it; all the things you do. *Please*, let me help you; after all you've done for me."

Whether her words have gotten through, or her gestures of obeisance, or just the power of pain, Elaine will never know, but whichever it may be, she sees a new expression come across Petal's face as, with a single syllable, the mother calls her children to her, then scolds and reprimands them until, one by one, their composure returns. Singling out Tulip, she then speaks at some length in a tone that is serious and commanding. Satisfied by her eldest daughter's nodding reply, she addresses Elaine in almost as much detail, all the while gesturing toward Tulip, the fire, the food stores all around the Mother Room, and herself. Only after speaking for several minutes to put the new regime in place, does she settle herself against a sack of barley, the injured leg stretched out before her, and cross her arms, a gesture Elaine has never seen her make before. 'Show me,' her expression is clearly challenging Elaine, facial features fluently bridging the vast linguistic gulf between them.

Over the coming days a new routine is established, Elaine rising early and Tulip leading her through the many tasks which must be done to keep this household humming, starting by breathing the fire back to life with a bellows, fetching in more fuel, and hauling water in skins when the cistern has been drained. She learns to make a dough of barley and milk curd, and to place it in one side of a cup, then fill the rest with hot tea so the family can breakfast by licking the solid and the liquid together, without utensils. Learns also to fry thick fritters in yak butter, for which she must first milk a yak and then stir the milk forever with a long pole, churning it to draw out the butter and curds, a chore which leaves her in awe of the women who have done such work all their lives and seem to think nothing of it. Though she takes to wearing Petal's long knife at her waist, she draws the line at killing a chicken, and so for a time their diet is vegetarian, until a neighbor woman happens by and discovers their situation. The next morning, the neighbor returns with a cloth-covered bowl of something akin to stew, and nearly every day after that someone else looks in upon them, bringing barley cookies or firewood, or slaughtering one of the family's own animals at Petal's instruction, and butchering it so Elaine can use it for their meals. With Petal confined to her place on the platform and limited to directing others, these visitors seem emboldened to interact with Elaine, and she learns from them many small tricks and techniques, helping her grow more efficient in her efforts. Despite their lack of common language, she feels a kinship growing as well, its currency no more than shared giggles, grunts of reassurance and crisp bowing at the doorway, but in such small ways are friendships forged, and it pleases Elaine no end to feel herself accepted by these capable strangers.

Examining Petal's wounds each morning, Elaine grows proud of her handiwork. Although the larger gash glows red and hot for several days, it eventually settles down once she removes the bandages and convinces Petal to position it toward the one small window, its shutter opened in the midday hours so the strong high-altitude sun can warm it and encourage circulation. Recovery is aided also when Elaine, rummaging for more cloth to make clean bandages, comes upon the clothes she had been wearing on the trail before arriving here, well-washed and mended, and rolled-up inside a clearly-precious silken cloth. In a deep skirt-pocket, whoever took such care with her belongings has placed the small bottle of hand-sanitizer, still partway full. With no better antiseptic available, she takes to squeezing a small amount of it on the wounds each morning and each evening.

As tasks become familiar, Elaine feels her spirits rise. After months of helpless dependence, it is wonderfully satisfying to learn new things, and experience her own competence once again. Tiny gestures of respect from people she hardly knows feel like triumphs, and every time she presents a bowl of food or a cup of tea to Petal it feels as if she is making an offering, not to some superior being, but to a deserving equal. Of it all, though, the most rewarding is how her relationship with the children changes, now that she has become a functioning member of the family. Tulip's instructions, delivered at first with an almost trembling tentativeness, grow gradually more matter-of-fact, and Elaine's failures cease to be cause for frustration, but elicit instead a baffled amusement, shared laughter, and a girlish conspiracy to get it right the next time. Thin is, as always, overshadowed by the first daughter, but as Elaine's education progresses, the child seems also to be learning, the three of them at times achieving a level of cooperation not unlike that wordless efficiency Elaine had noticed when first she got to know the household. Not since her school days, she realizes with chagrin, has she spent so much time in effort with other women, or experienced the warm glow of confidence it can produce. This is reinforced a hundred-fold when, several weeks into her convalescence, Petal calls her over and presents to her one of the multi-colored sashes she keeps in a wooden box. Elaine thanks her profusely as she wraps it round and round her own waist and ties it just as she has seen visiting dabu do when presented with such a gift. When Petal reaches out and hangs upon it the key to the grain storeroom, Elaine feels herself near tears.

As for the smallest children - Little One and Pooh – they spend the first two days of Elaine's reign huddled with their mother, but are soon thrust away to resume their usual pastimes of scurrying underfoot and sowing disorder wherever they can create it. With time they learn to understand Elaine's admonitions to stop this or that, to come when their nick-names are called, or to shoo away when necessary. Familiarity may breed contempt in some circumstances, but for these two it seems to breed affection, as Elaine realizes one cool evening, when Little One climbs into her lap to toy with a necklace of beads which Petal has presented to her. Feeling the child's weight on her tired limbs, breathing in the sagebrush-dust and sunshine embedded in her clothes and hair, the goat and pig and dinner smells on her hands, Elaine relaxes as the beads lose their fascination and the child snuggles down to drift into a deep sleep, causing her adopted 'ami' to rechristen her from 'Little One' to 'Little Love.' The fire takes its time dying out that evening, and it has been a long day of what she might once have called 'back-breaking' labor, yet zhe-Khong Ber-eel feels no urgency at all to move to her own bed.

Dallas Volmer glances up from straightening a comforter in the front bedroom, her eye caught by the mustard yellow of a taxicab, not a common sight in this neighborhood. Sees a smallish person, in some sort of gray pantsuit and a baseball cap, climb out of the cab, stand staring for a while, then head up the Gimbals' front walk. Notices the awkward step-stop-step rhythm of her stride through the intervening foggy drizzle, and judges her harmless. Still, it bears watching, given how long the place next door has been empty.

Her suspicions rise a bit when the figure approaches the front door and, rather than ringing the bell, grabs the door handle, only to find it securely locked. She tries the bell then, which Dallas knows to be pointless, waits a bit, tries again, then begins wandering around the front lawn, looking in windows and casting about as if in search of something. When the figure disappears around the side, Dallas finds herself in a quandary; to go out there and talk to the woman, tell her there's been no one home for months, or to call the police and report her. Or, perhaps, to pour herself a cup of tea and forget the whole thing. 'None of our business,' Henry would certainly say, if he were still here. 'You're too doggone quick to stick your finger into other people's affairs,' he'd told her more than once. It used to make her cheeks burn when he said things like that, and there were moments she almost hated him for it, only now she wishes to heaven she could hear his voice again, no matter the words, so out of respect she does what he would have wanted her to.

Folding laundry in the back room she has almost forgotten the whole thing when the doorbell sounds. Checking her hair in the mirror as she passes through the hall, she fluffs the back with stiff fingers, then opens the door as far as the chain allows, to find the same woman standing on her doorstep, much younger up close than she had expected from that stiff-legged walk.

"Good morning, Mrs. Vollmer," the youngster greets her, pulling the cap off and clasping it in both hands, exposing a head shorn almost to stubble. She delivers the greeting with a sort of reticence, a distance kept, which suits Dallas just fine, as she ponders whether maybe the child has cancer or something, which would explain why her hair looks just grown-in, and why she walks that way. "I wonder if you know where Elaine is. Or when she might be back?"

"Oh, goodness," Dallas answers. "No idea. She's been gone

for…" she is about to explain that Mrs. Gimbal's been out of the country so long it seems unlikely she'll ever come back, when Henry's admonitions return in all their careful wariness. Strangers are dangers; even this wistful young girl could be a criminal, scoping out houses to rob. 'The less said the better,' was Henry's way of dealing with strangers, and it must be hers too.

"I don't know," she corrects herself, and feels her back straighten a bit for it. "But if you leave your name, I'll let her know you called. If I see her, that is."

There is real sadness in the girl's eyes at this. Like she'd gotten her hopes up very high, and Dallas' sympathy must show too, because in the next moment the look of despair disappears and the stranger seems to take control of the conversation, reassuring with her tone, just the way Henry might have done.

"Of course," she says, giving a knowing look, and again Dallas has that sense of the familiar. "You wouldn't give out information to a stranger. That wouldn't be right would it?" Dallas nods, and the girl smiles a bit haughtily. "In that case, just tell her that Rodney came by," she concludes and begins to turn away, then swivels back again, a bit of hope returning to her face. Fishing in the pocket of her jacket – which looks, Dallas notes in a flash of loss, very much like one of Henry's from before he retired and delivered every single suit, sport coat and necktie in his closet to the Goodwill - she pulls out a dog-eared business card and hands it over. "If Elaine…Mrs. Gimbal, comes back, please tell her she can reach me at this number."

Dallas looks at the card. 'REALITY BYTES,' she reads. 'Customized Software Solutions for POS, COP, ICS and MPE' - none of which means anything to her, although, as she ponders the odd abbreviations, she realizes the name Rodney does.

"That's so funny," she calls, as the figure starts down the steps. "That was Dr. Gimbal's name too - Rodney. He passed away, you know." To her surprise, this seems to amuse the stranger. Not rude funny - like on TV where they make light of the saddest things - but in a quiet way; like it means something more to her than Dallas can quite grasp.

"I know," the girl says, placing the cap back on her head. "I was there," and as she makes her careful way down the steps, tightly grasping the rail, Dallas notices the nails of her fingers, cut short and unpolished, but meticulously tended, their narrow whites as crisp and even as the pinstripe lines of her coat and slacks.

As the weeks pass, and Petal's wounds heal, Elaine finds her own strength returning as well. Muscles which had grown lean and firm in the months she wandered with Beryl, then soft and dull in her enforced idleness, are now revitalized as she lifts and carries, milks and churns, mixes and kneads and digs at the soil with a pointed stick to pull up the roots which grow there. Several times she walks for miles with one of the neighbor women to where a stretch of forest remains, hauling a bundle of branches on her back as they make their way home under the summer sun.

From what she can observe about these other households, it is clear that they are, for the most part, similar to Petal's; families headed by women, the adult men continually off either on trading journeys, or herding animals in search of decent grazing. In each household, brothers and sisters live together with their parents, grandparents and children. When a woman chooses to take a man into her bed, it is for only as long as she wishes and he a welcome visitor to her family, but still resident in his own mother's house. In this way inheritance and history are passed down from grandmother to mother to daughter, and both male and female typically reside their entire lives in the house in which they are born.

The days have reached their peak and are in fact growing shorter - the midday sun not rising so nearly toward vertical - by the time Elaine acquiesces to her patient's desire to get up and begin moving about with the aid of a makeshift crutch. Petal gives little evidence of pain as she hobbles around the homestead on the bandaged foot, but dives right back into her role, directing the children, creating the meals. For the first few days, Elaine is still allowed to fetch firewood and perform a few other of the heavier chores, but soon even those are taken back over and she feels, once again, superfluous, if honored even more for her actions than before.

Visits to some of the other homesteads serve to alleviate the tedium, as does a trip to the 'village,' which turns out to be no more than half a dozen homesteads in relatively close proximity to the crossing of two of the more well-travelled footpaths, with a one-room shop appended to one of the homes. A dozen yards of cheap cloth and some second-hand clothes constitute the core of the shop's stock, along with baskets of locally-produced vegetables and obscure pieces of mountaineering gear which look to have been discarded by some outside visitors. With words and pantomime Elaine asks the woman in charge for a variety of simple necessities – first aid supplies and basic medicines, needles, thread and buttons, scissors, paper and something with which to write on it, to all of which the woman shakes her head and puffs her pipe. 'No,' her attitude is clearly indicating, the shop has none of those.

It is no wonder, Elaine thinks, walking back to Petal's homestead across a plain whose dimension is matched only by the towering peaks which surround it, her feet kicking up little swirls of dust as a trio of vultures carve their interconnected circles high overhead. No wonder at all, that Beryl returned again and again. So little, in this place, could go such a long, long way.

The black coupe is one in a block-long line of parked cars; notable perhaps for its filthiness, but actually more curious for its windows, cracked open against the fog of exhalation. Nearly invisible in the comingled reflections and shadows of those windows, a man slumps against the driver's side door, cardboard cup of coffee in his hand, the music turned down so low it's barely more than a buzz. Can't have it heard outside, he knows. Not when you're hiding in plain sight.

Across the street and halfway down the block, a front door opens, its chromed frame and tall oval-shaped glass flashing and flaring as they capture momentary reflections of street and headlights, only to release them immediately in their sideways sweep. A man in an overcoat exits, and with him, a woman. The watcher in the black coupe leans forward, trying to make them out. Could that be her? – no, too tall. And the man? Old. Very old. Feeble old. Definitely not the people in the photo.

Sits back, sips his coffee. Java this late could keep him up all night, but then again, he's not sleeping well enough these days to worry. Funny expression that, 'not sleeping well enough to worry,' when it's worry that keeps him up at night. Ha, ha. Kim would have picked that up, riffing on for five minutes about how it reflected his 'preoccupation with artificial constructs of achievement and attainment' or some other bullshit. Jesus, if he could see her now. If she could see him now. If...

The door opens again, two women this time. That could be her: small, hair cut short, though not as short as in the newspaper photo. Man, that was a shock, but now that he's had a chance to think about it, he understands that doesn't really matter – how she looked in that picture. She'll grow her hair out again, for him. The other one coming out with her is blond, and not bad. No, not bad at all. The way her head tips back as she laughs. Got that walk, too, the kind that says she's all girl, always has been, always will be. Kim has that walk; when she wants to. She's a chameleon, his girl Kim. Be whatever she wants to be. Like in that picture - the short hair, the bow tie. All dressed up for a performance with some crusty-looking chick with a big nose. Doing another act. It's all an act for her, except when they're alone. That's the real Kim, alone with her fiancée. Not this diner-musical act, and not that sick 'Doctor' bullshit she spelled out at her mother's place. Maybe that was what made her so crazy -

being stuck in her mother's place. Some psycho-shrink thing, like she was back being a kid again and couldn't do anything she wanted to, so she went all wacko instead. This time he'll be the one to set the rules, decide how to take care of her. You can be sure of that.

No, that's not them either; he's certain of it, as the two women head around the side of the diner and make their way through the lot to a red compact. Before they open the door the tall blond kicks her head back again, laughing at something the other one said. Next thing he sees, they're hugging each other, like girls do sometimes, only this hug goes on too long and then they're kissing. Heads bent together and moving around like it's midnight on New Years Eve, right there in plain view and Jake lets out a moan despite himself. So that's the kind of place this is: fucking lesbies and queers? Jake grubs around on the seat beside him and finds the paper with the picture. 'Stevie and the Doctor.' Well, Kim's no doctor, and now that he knows what to look for, that Stevie's no woman either, and now he's more pissed than ever at the whole fucking world, which is just not right anymore. Just. Not. Right.

A car comes down the street and something tells Jake to slouch a little lower. There's a shadow up above its roof line, blocking out the lights in the distance as it approaches. Light bar alright; yeah, it's a cop, but it passes by without event and he sits a little straighter. The coffee cup is empty and he tosses it over his shoulder into the growing mess. He could go inside, he could. Check them out from the back of the room, but then she might see him and then what would he have? Better to wait right here; they've got to come out sometime - paper said they're here every Thursday night - and when they do, he'll follow them. Find out what they drive, where she lives. That's the key -where she's living these days. Once he knows that he's back in control. Plan. Decide. Prepare.

It's only a matter of time, he remembers Colin saying. 'Only a matter of time, Jakey boy.' That was such a fucking train wreck. Colin and all his bullshit. That's the reason this is all so fucking piss poor. Living in this fucking car. Come down so far, anyplace in the world looks like up these days; but that's all history now. Colin's gone - somewhere overseas probably, no one seems to know - so there's no getting back at him; that's what the lawyer said - fucking lawyer. No damned help at all. One more bill to pay. Or not.

Jake laughs, the sound barely escaping taut lips beneath squinted eyes in a face beginning to show its age; going downhill fast, in fact. 'Or not.' No fucking way he's going to pay a guy three-twenty-five an hour to say 'I can't help you.' No fucking way, and besides, it wasn't Colin started it all. It was her. Kimmie. She got herself messed up and that's when his life went down the tubes.

That morning in the hospital with Aubrey, talking to that hospital guy - Jake can't remember his name, but it doesn't matter; nothing matters, not since Kim got herself all jacked up and sick - ever since that, not a single fucking thing has gone his way, so here he is, sitting and waiting. Just like on TV. Stakeout. Surveillance. Sooner or later they've gotta' come out of that place, and when they do, he'll be here. Watch and wait. Observe. Find out what they're driving, where they go. Where she's living these days. Damn well better be living alone.

'If she's living with that fucking queer in the picture I'm gonna' shit my pants,' he thinks. 'Or worse.'

It doesn't matter though. Doesn't really matter, because he's going to get her back. One way or the other, Kim belongs with him.

'We belong together,' Jake's weary brain repeats. 'Whatever it takes.'

Summer is short in the valley of the azhe-Moso, and it seems at most a few weeks after Petal is up and about that Elaine begins to feel the wind growing chill. The dabu is back in full command now, Elaine allowed to help in a few small ways, but spending most of her time on the bench beside Lahtso. Mother and children spend less time cultivating their small fields, and more time digging them up; hanging the produce from the rafters of the Mother Room, or locking it away in the granary. Other hours are spent in gathering dung from fields where yaks have been grazing, and shaping it into patties which are baked in the sun, to be used for winter fires. One day a brother of Petal's - whom Elaine has never met but recognizes instantly by their common features and familiar-yet-not-quite-intimate ways with one another - returns from some far-off grazing land, leading eleven bleating sheep, their coats full and dense, ripe for shearing into the wool which will be spun and woven through the shut-in months of winter. As the family feasts that evening on mutton from a freshly-slaughtered sheep, Elaine finds herself almost blissfully happy to be part of the homecoming, yet simultaneously recoiling at the thought of passing another season with nothing to do, so little ability to communicate, and no way to contribute to these people who saved her life and have taken her in as if it were the most natural act in the world.

It is with some relief then, that she hears one afternoon the children's shouts and the sound of horses outside the courtyard wall. Her heart is full as Oo-tay and Dore-eh and another young man lead their horses through the gate and begin to unload.

Setting her wineglass down on the end table, Stevie stands.
Smoothes dress against legs to reinforce her courage, then twists and
bends to undo the straps of her tall sandals, kicking each with a
flourish into a different corner of the room. As she'd hoped, that
draws a smile, relaxing the atmosphere as she sets herself back onto
the sofa, close by the boy now, legs tucked up beneath her, and
stares into his eyes for only a moment before leaning forward to kiss
him on the lips. A short kiss, but full and warm as she makes a point
to press his mouth open just a bit, her hand behind his head pulling
them together then releasing. Settling back a little, she lets her
hands linger on him, waits another short moment, then speaks very
softly and slowly.

"So tell me," she asks, "what you felt when I did that?"

"I felt...." Rod starts, then stops, his concentrated expression
so dour Stevie has to break in.

"That proves it," she says teasingly. "Can't even figure out
how to say you enjoyed a kiss? You're male, all right."

"I guess... I'm just not used to talking about things like that.
How I feel."

"So I'll talk for both of us." Stevie shifts a little, sliding one
leg out to rest against his, one hand dawdling across his chest, their
faces very near. "You're wondering what I have in mind. You're
worried that I'm going to mess up this nice friendship we seem to
have. You're also worried that you find me attractive. Not because
I'm a woman - you're a man and it feels natural and right for you to
be attracted to women - no, you're worried because somehow you
have this body you have, and being attracted to a woman, even
though it's the most natural thing in the world for you, you're afraid
of what that makes you. Am I right?"

Rod shifts uneasily, takes another sip from his ever-present
drink. "Something like that."

"Well, just for tonight," Stevie says, picking up the boy's hand
and beginning to massage it, her sturdy fingers cushioning its back
while her thumb presses into the center of his palm, pushing the
fleshy muscles this way and that in slow relaxing rhythm, "just this
once, let's pretend there is no one else in the whole entire world,
and then we won't need to put any name at all on who we are or
what we are doing."

With that she leans forward and kisses him again, feeling her painted lips the slightest bit waxy against Christina's, so full and smooth and bare. Tentatively, Rod reciprocates, reaching an arm around her back to lay his hand between her shoulder blades. After a moment she feels his flattened palm move ever so slightly, the fabric of her dress sliding smoothly over her skin.

For several long moments they kiss, even as Stevie reaches out and switches off the one small table lamp, plunging the room into darkness, save only the fire's glow and a faint glimmer of street lamps filtering in past drawn curtains.

"When you sang that first night, at the club," she begins, after their mouths finally part, "I had this surge of feeling. Like pride, but more than that. To witness you discovering yourself, this voice that you were so afraid to admit you had..."

"You'd never even met me before."

"Oh, but I could see it all." Without announcement Stevie's hand has gravitated to Rod's chest where it circles very lightly, fingertips tracing one of the mounds bound beneath his layered shirts. "Women... some people are more tuned in to those kinds of things than others; and when I saw you breaking through like that, it made my heart sing. It was like a part of me was breaking free too."

"I don't know why you would have cared about how I was feeling. A total stranger?"

"I always care what you're feeling, Rodney. Like now. I know that you are feeling something new, and maybe kind of scary. Tingling just a tiny bit, maybe?" Rod clamps a hand on top of Stevie's, damping her fingers' motion.

"No," she says, moving her entire hand beneath his, which resists, but not enough to stop them both sliding slightly across the surface, friction teasing the projection which has risen there. "We don't need to stop."

Stevie watches as Rod's eyes examine hers, seeming to search for something. She feels his decision as, face still dead-serious, he reaches out and slides a fingertip softly across one of her own breasts, sending a shudder running up her spine and into her scalp. Their lips meet again, this time forcefully, her tongue entering his mouth to roam across lips and teeth until it finds the tip of his. For a few flickers the two joust until, falling backwards and pulling him on top of her, she opens her lips more fully and allows him to penetrate her in clear imitation of that other act.

"So," she whispers, pulling her head aside and addressing her tongue now to one small ear, its surface soft as velvet, its archaic piercing barely noticeable as, at the same time, her hands move here and there upon his body. "Was I right this time, too? Are you feeling what I think you're feeling?"

"I don't know," Rod whispers back, head bowing down until his face is pressed against her neck, his breath hot on that tender flesh. His hand is on her leg now, rubbing up and down, sliding slippery layers over her stockinged thigh in smooth circles, making a slight rustling sound. "You're a lovely woman. And if things were different...if it wasn't for all of this...confusion, I could imagine..."

"You don't have to imagine." Stevie is all over Rod's face now, nibbling and caressing as one hand works to undo her own buttons and guide him toward her, urging Christina's subtle fingers to trace the gentle curve from neck down to shoulder, the slight indentation above her collarbone, the smooth arc from there to the swell of her own small breasts. As she kisses and nuzzles she feels his awkwardness releasing, a welcome reassurance that this evening might turn out as she has planned it.

"But...I'm only me on the inside. Outside, I'm..."

"I know what you are outside." Stevie's hand slides between Rods legs, pressing against the warmth trapped between them. "You're beautiful. To me, all of you is beautiful...that there's Rodney inside you, quiet and solid. And that there's this other part of you outside, innocent and beautifully awkward. It all works for me."

Rod's legs part, ever so slightly, and Stevie feels her way up against his crotch, maneuvering the back of her hand against his mound. At first she simply presses, letting him feel that sense of safety, of being held. Then, slowly and gently, she begins to move her hand a fraction of an inch, protruding knuckles oscillating against him.

I never would have imagined it could be this powerful. With nothing outward to signal it, this body is aroused as surely as anything in my memories. Electric tingles radiate from its center to its surface, echoing all around my mind, making me want to melt against her, to press us into one, and yet....

"This isn't right," Rod protests, raising himself up on stiff arms to look into her eyes. Though his expression is pained, she hears his words in Christina's voice, clear and musical. "I still am who I always have been, I'm..."

"You're thinking too much," Stevie answers cheerily, rolling him toward the wall and sliding out from under. "This isn't a time for thinking, it's a time for *feeling* and *doing*, so you just stop worrying and let old Stevie show you how it all works." Standing up from the couch, dress half open and twisted round her hips, she reaches out ruby-tipped fingers, and when, after a long hesitation, he takes them, she leads her slender young part-man-part-woman, all somber-faced and unsure of himself, on the long walk down the short hall and into her own room.

Stopping just shy of the bed, she lets go his hand to throw open the bedclothes, then stands before him, their two forms no more than shadows in the lampless dim. Undoes another half-dozen buttons and offers him her sleeves to tug, till the dress slides down her arms and pools upon the floor. In smooth and practiced motion she pulls the camisole up and over to expose bare skin from waist to face, careful to retain the lace-edged half-slip below. Leaning forward, she brushes her swaying breasts across his chest before her hands move efficiently to slip off his jacket and cummerbund and undo the belt and button of his trousers, then the zipper, so they too drop, even as his hands rise up to cup her. With a catching in her breath at their touch, she stiffens, then goes to work on first his shirt, then the two t-shirts beneath, exposing Christina's surface just in time for their mouths to come together again before they fall onto the bed, arms working around and among one another. Rod is cooperating fully now, climbing on top and hungrily mouthing Stevie as she wriggles and squirms, pushing pillows to the floor.

I feel her flesh against mine, familiar sense of warmth against warmth, but unfamiliar things as well. Between my legs not the heavy swelling I know should be, but something hot and yielding, a longing deep inside of me that is not weak at all, but powerfully hungry. She's touching me again and like that sunbeam her touch calls up an urgency unlike any other. I know I am not this person; this body is not mine, but still it overpowers. I want, I want, I want to be myself again...

"You just relax," I hear her say, all giddy playfulness as she rolls us over and straddles me, then pulls her face from mine and disappears, to where I feel her cheeks brush against the inside of my thighs, and I erupt with the heat of her mouth. My body is in full flood, these foreign sensations crying out inside my mind.

"Imagine I am you," I hear her speak down there, as her hands come up to my chest, her fingertips sliding back and forth to generate a sensation all out of proportion to the act. "And you are me. Imagine you are doing this to me, and this is what it feels like for me, this is the pleasure you give to me." She brushes her lips across my abdomen and I feel myself stiffen, arching in pleasure on the edge of pain, pressing myself upward, offering myself without decision. "Whatever you feel, I feel. Whatever I feel, you feel. That's what making love is all about, Rodney - erasing the boundaries between two people, making two bodies into one. It's the closest thing to being someone else that there is, and if you let yourself experience that, then it doesn't matter which side of the coin you're on. Inside is outside and outside is inside."

I am aware of my hands now, moving all around - on her, on the bed, behind my head - trying to relieve the tension which swells from head to toe as she does what she is doing; trying, testing, changing her motions and rhythms until I cannot help but move my pelvis underneath her. Up and down and round and round; the base of my spine takes on a mind of its own, as natural at this moment as walking or breathing. Somehow, somewhere along the line, she appears again before my face, eyes lost behind the wild curtain of her hair, but her excitement unmistakable. Our lips meet and now our mouths are as one, working and exploring, tasting the other, dissolving the boundary in yet another way. I feel her hand removed amid a complex rustle of fabric as she shifts position once again, adjusting something in between us; a momentary distraction, then back at it again. Propped above, she has me under her spell, a willing captive as she slides her knees forward, splaying me upon the bed. Exposed beneath her, still I want to reveal even more; I want to turn myself inside-out and be exposed in all my strength and weakness, and this she somehow seems to know.

"What's inside is outside," she whispers, in a voice at once both gentle and insistent. "What's mine is yours, what's yours is mine."

Together we are moving, rocking and pressing as I feel myself split in two, completely vulnerable yet urgently embracing that vulnerability. Her hand is working at me and I feel the buzzing in my brain rise beyond a fever pitch. Distant sounds emerge from my own lips and they are Christina's sounds and mine, Stevie's sounds and Elaine's and in the midst of it all there is a new sensation, part pleasure and part pain, as with a jolt I realize...

"What..." Rod begins to exclaim, but Stevie's mouth is upon his before another sound can escape. Far away and below their mouths, her motions continue, pelvis against pelvis, thumb against clit, her now-open secret pressing its cause a little longer before she finds herself thrust away; flung across the bed as Christina's slender form erupts in abject horror.

"No," Rod wails. "That's not..." he stumbles, scraping at the covers and pulling them around himself as he backs away.

"Yes," Stevie counters even as she crumples to a far corner of the bed, folding arms across her odd assortment of body parts. "What's mine is yours, what's yours is mine. That's what I want to show you," though as she speaks the words, her voice is breaking, cracking into a sob at what she suddenly knows is coming.

For a time the room is still - only the ragged sound of anxious breathing disturbs its airless quiet, two uneven rhythms, choppy and strained and totally out of sync with one another - until Stevie shifts, pulling a pillow from the floor to clasp it tightly against her chest. Shifts her legs as well, tugging at the slip that barely covers the awkward bulge at the base of her abdomen; not large to start with, and now rapidly diminishing. Reaching up she pushes hair from her face, smoothing it a bit, comforting herself. Mere feet away, Rodney sits huddled, covers pulled tight to his chin, eventually reaching out to turn on the bedside lamp, its glow a flare that blinds both sets of eyes for seconds, till, squinting, they adjust and fix upon one another, then flash away, return. Waiting, their gasps trailing off now, and settling, as the heat of their two bodies occupies the space between.

"How..." Rod begins after a while, his question stillborn in confusion and disbelief.

Stevie's first answer - that she had conceived the idea after Rod confessed his sun-beamed imagining, had planned it and prepared for it ever since - elicits only more disbelief, Christina's head shaking 'no, no, no,' and so she switches tacks, addressing the deeper explanation.

"I thought," she begins again, her voice drained and broken, begging for reassurance, "that I knew how you were feeling." When no agreement comes she presses on. "When you talked about that empty place inside, that wants to be touched? I feel that same longing, only I can't get at my place because there's all this other... stuff... in the way. So I thought I understood what you were feeling and I wanted to see if I could do that for you... I'm sorry. It's not...it's not what I'm about; what I imagine for myself - I just thought, maybe for the two of us, because of who we are..."

"You mean because we're two freaks whose bodies happen to fit together?" Rod's anger is still palpable, Christina's eyes wide but dry, her lips tight as a bud before its time. He sits with the duvet wrapped round her slight form as if warding off a winter's chill, though the room is warm and close.

'That isn't what I meant,' Stevie imagines shouting back. Yes, in that other world - out there - the way two bodies fit is all the rage; what makes one couple blessed and another cursed. It's *all about* how the bodies fit together, not their hearts, or their minds or their hopes or their dreams. 'That is not me,' she wants to tell him, but at this moment, who she is seems less certain than it has for a long time. She's gotten on the wrong side of her own arguments, and only he can let her come back.

"Because our *selves* fit together," she answers, as gently as possible. Without her actually deciding to, a hand reaches out toward his arm, but before it even makes contact he flinches and she pulls back, stuffing both hands in her own armpits, safe where they will not try to touch anything, not reach for anything that might cause even more trouble. "Rodney, my dear, it's not that I'm dying to get laid. *Believe* me; that's not what I'm about. I want to touch you because it can connect us in a way that's very difficult to do without touching. Because it breaks down the barriers that say *you* have to be all alone in *your* world, and *I* have to be all alone in *mine*. When we touch, our worlds touch. If we made love, I thought our worlds could be one for a few moments; I thought I could help you feel filled, and at the same time I could feel like I was...holding you. The way other women hold their men." Stevie pauses, eyes welling up, voice cracking and breaking as she hears her words falling on deaf ears, sees Rodney pulling himself up from the bed, retrieving his clothing from the floor; gathering underwear, t-shirt, pants and all the rest into his arms like a shield, even as she meanders on. "When I was...when I tried to...I was imagining that it was you doing that to me... I know that sounds weird. Maybe it's even freaky to you, maybe I'm just making things worse by talking too much..."

The frozen glare on his features, the wad of clothing clamped tight across his chest, tell Stevie it is pointless to go on; whatever he is hearing as he turns toward the door, it is not what she is trying to say, and yet she cannot stop the words, or their rising volume as she pleads. "I wasn't trying to hurt you, Rodney; I'm not... I mean - look at me," she cries out, as he reaches the door and rounds it, disappearing without a backward glance at the sorry creature clutching a pillow to her breast. "How could anyone feel threatened by *this*?"

Five days after Ootay's return, Elaine sits on her bed with the door closed and a bundle clutched in her lap, its few contents wrapped in a threadbare quilt and tied with strings of twisted yak hair. Through the window she watches as the men load their horses. All through the homestead an atmosphere of great excitement prevails, adults attending to details and shouting directions, youngsters following at their elders' heels. Already Little Love has had his hand stepped on, broken into tears and only moments later been distracted into awed silence when a toothless uncle placed him high upon the saddle of a pony and led them around the courtyard. By the second lap the boy was smiling as broadly as ever, only to burst into tears again when it came time for him to be hoisted down. At the moment he sits nearby, sifting powdery dirt thru the fingers of one hand into the other, in imminent danger of being stepped on again as the horses tap-dance their eagerness to be off before the moist cool of morning is burned away by that orange glow which is just now arising from its hiding place, beyond the eastern ridges.

Petal and the girls are busy, of course; for two hours already they have been stoking fires, brewing tea and boiling curd, and baking loaves which they have stuffed, steamy and moist, into saddle sacks which hang now across the animals flanks. Elaine has been helping them as much as they allow, only slipping away a few minutes ago to gather what few things she owns here and to steel herself against the emotions of the moment. A thousand thoughts collide: excitement and dread, enthusiasm and guilt, and over it all the impossibility of explaining exactly where she is going and why.

As expected, her basic intention is known the instant she sets foot outside the Mother Room. Thin, coming round the corner with a bladder of water, begins to wail as her eyes - which she had barely opened to accomplish chores she knows so well - widen into full attention. Oo-tay, by contrast, gives Elaine his trademark grin, as if hauling an aging and endlessly ignorant pale-woman over the mountains is the most joyous treat he could imagine this fine morning.

In a moment she is surrounded, Petal and the girls chattering, Pooh and Little Love jammed between their knees. It takes all Elaine's patience not to try to explain, but she knows from the last few months that her words will be inadequate. Nor does she wish this message to be interpreted by one of the men, for it is a truth she must convey herself, and so, with gestures and sounds she carves a space out of the crush then kneels to stab a finger in the dust, just as she imagined, late in the sleepless night, that she would do.

"Look," she commands, drawing a circle and beginning to stab around it, as she repeats their names. "Petal, Lahtso. Tulip, Thin, and Pooh. Little Love." For each name she stabs a dimple into the dust and meets the subject's eye, then after listing them all, ends with a sweeping of her hand, to take in the entire homestead, the village and the valley. Captivated, her audience is silent, as she repeats again, "Here," and then "Me. zhe-Khong Beryl," pressing the tips of two fingers near the diagram she has drawn and beginning to walk them away from it. Immediately the wailing and imploring begin again but Elaine quiets them with a sharp clap of her hands. Confused eyes watch as she walks her two fingers to the edge of the open space at their feet, then swipes them in a great arc, spraying dust between the array of ankles and out, into the void beyond their little circle. Another clap stills the first sounds of reaction as Elaine holds her hand upward toward the sun, still barely a glow beyond the eastern ridge. Straight-armed, she swings her hand across the sky to the west, then quickly back to east and across again. This she does several times, each arc tighter and faster than the last, until her motion is a rapid circling, indicating the passage of many suns, at which she sees tears forming upon Tulip's worried features.

Squatting down again, Elaine thrusts her hand out between the girl's dirty ankles, tickling one in the process, and begins walking her two fingers back again, into the open space, and toward the dimpled circle. "Me," she announces, "Ber-eel." As her digits approach the points which represent her newfound family, she feels her own face growing warm with emotion and the urgent need to be certain. "Me," she says again, thumping a fist against the hardness of her breastbone, then pressing it down into the circle which represents this family. At this, the children's gestures indicate understanding, their rapid explanations to one another unintelligible, yet music to Elaine's ears. Ootay's bobbing head and broad grin tell her she has made her point; the Ber-eel will return.

Within minutes the men have redistributed the loads between their packhorses, freeing up space for a passenger. There are hugs and bows, and more hugs all around as Elaine finishes her goodbyes, only to be struck with a flush of sweaty heat when she notices that Petal has disappeared. That the dabu would refuse to see her off is a heavy blow; a confirmation that she has indeed resented having another mouth to feed, or maybe the way she was treated when injured, or perhaps the very degree to which Elaine allowed herself to believe she belonged to what is, when all is said and done, not really her family.

The guilty realization brings a touch of bile to Elaine's throat as she mounts up, suddenly eager to be off. Oo-tay is on his own horse, the lead rope in his hand when Petal bursts through the doorway, shouting "Ber-eel," and holding an object in her clenched fist. Her face is radiant as she reaches up and hands it to Elaine, though there are tears in her eyes as they narrow and tighten in concentration.

"T-h-ank. Yu," she says, mouth working hard to embrace those foreign words as she presses into Elaine's hand a small wooden amulet, crude likeness of a female form. Girdled with silver wire and threaded onto a leathern thong, closer inspection reveals it to be that same chunk of cedar-wood which was extracted from the young matriarch's foot months before, still bearing at its un-worked end the dried and blackened traces of her own life force.

"Th-ank you, zhe-Khong Ber-eel."

For some time Stevie lies in fetal curl around her pillow, eyes wide to the darkness as she deciphers faint sounds from the next room. Pictures Rod carefully hanging up the satin-trimmed slacks and jacket she so proudly picked out for him. Placing the pleated white shirt in the laundry basket in his closet before pulling on pajamas and preparing to climb into the single bed she'd initially purchased in hopes her own son might someday be allowed to visit – another great plan that never came to fruit. It is only when she hears the front door open, that she realizes the sounds were of Rod putting clothes *on*, not taking them off, and only when she hears the door slam closed behind him that she understands how truly wrong her actions have been, and what their price might be.

It is late in the day when the horsemen pull to a stop near the bottom of a broad and grassy bowl. The weakening sun's rays cast Giacometti shadows in the valley far below, as cascading water gurgles among the rocks of an eroded gully to a small pool where the men allow their animals a drink. After the comfortable months of summer, Elaine is struck by the cold which rises up from this little rivulet, sucking at her skin and calling up a memory of another day's cold. Tall grass glows under the glancing rays, a broad emerald carpet stretching toward rocky walls that have the look of burnished steel. Beneath one of those walls, the dark intrusion of a tent is visible and on the slope above it, the pale puffs of several dozen grazing sheep. Noting Elaine's gaze in that direction, Oo-tay informs her that it is the camp of Gatusa, the very herder who brought her to Petal's house half a year before.

"I must see him," Elaine insists, surprised by her own conviction. It is as if the rightness of her impulse is inherent to this setting, arising from the same source as the overwhelming beauty which surrounds them.

"Our journey is long," Ootay responds, in his deliberate way. Fearing him impatient to be on, she is already opening her mouth to protest when he concludes the thought; "and there will be many lonely nights."

With no more persuasion than that, their journey is ended for the day, and soon enough they are gathered around a fire, sharing tales with Gatusa, a robust young man dressed in threadbare rags, with a lambskin hat and wild hair that hangs in front of his eyes. His gaze takes in all the party, but returns repeatedly to Elaine as he slices meat from what remains of a whole salted pig, placing the pieces in a pot to boil among grain the travelers have contributed, augmented by scrapings from several of the roots that hang outside his tent, which must account for the delicious aroma which soon rises with the steam. Despite his wild appearance, Gatusa turns out to have almost as good a command of English as his brother-in-law. In his youth, he explains, he had fallen under the spell of the same missionaries who converted Gudelema, and had travelled with them to a city many days to the west, where he began learning to read their scriptures in their language. For nearly two years he lived with them, but then they told him he must become a missionary himself, and make strange promises to their God. The vow of poverty was no obstacle, for once he saw the city he realized the Azhe had always been poor, at least in the way the missionaries meant it. Their other demands, though, eventually collided against his Azhe ways, and the mash of Buddhist, Daoist, Confucian and Animist beliefs with which he had grown up. When they insisted he subject what he *knew* to what they *said*, Gatusa had left, making his way back to the valley of his origin where he slipped into a more natural role, gathering the sheep of several families to tend through the seasons. After a few years he became beloved of a woman from the family of his distant cousin, Howeii, and walked down every now and then to visit her in her own home. He has been doing so for many summers now, and this woman has born him three beautiful children.

Not much later, as the party sit cross-legged, scooping food with fingers from one communal platter, Elaine asks Gatusa to tell how he found her. This he does, with great pride, and at some length, as Ootay translates their conversation for the other men's benefit.

"And you did not see anyone else around?" she asks, as he describes discovering her at the bottom of the snowfield.

"No," Gatusa replies,

"The last thing I remember," she tells him, "is voices. Several voices; of men, I'm certain, but speaking a language I did not recognize. It might have been the language of the azhe-Moso, or one of the languages of the porters who had been travelling with us before I became separated, but I'm not sure."

Gatusa is certain, he tells her, that there was no one else around for a very long way. No animals, no tracks, no sounds. No tent or shelter. He is, in fact, much more adamant about this than she can be about having heard the voices, given her state at the time.

"Is it possible," she asks, realizing that the question she is about to ask has come to be of intense importance to her, "that I made my way down from the pass, alone, in those conditions, without even being aware of what I was doing?"

"If you can fly," Gatusa answers quickly, his offhand delivery and Ootay's translation drawing knowing chuckles from the others. Elaine resists the urge to rise to this jibe, allowing silence to emphasize the seriousness of her question, and for a time the fire's crackling is the only sound, as Gatusa seems to study her face. Staring directly into her eyes, his own orbs glow yellow-white against the deep amber skin of his face, while above and around it a universe of stars are visible in the dome of blackness which surrounds their little circle. Slowly the herder forms his words, and she imagines this is how he might have sounded had he chosen to stay with his earlier vocation, delivering sage counsel to a congregation who hung upon his every word. No wonder the missionaries wanted him.

"It would be difficult," Gatusa suggests, the words rising fluidly from deep within his chest. "Even for a young person. But for a wise one, such as yourself?" Elaine notes with amusement the polite euphemism, as he shakes his head from side to side. "Difficult. Very, very difficult."

"I didn't ask if it would be difficult," Elaine insists, struck with a sudden, and certain, comprehension that 'difficult' and 'impossible' are as distant from one another as the stars are from the earth on which she sits. "I asked if it would be possible."

"Yes," Gatusa answers slowly, pulling a stick from the fire, its end flaming brightly as he gazes into her eyes. "It is possible."

Then, bringing the stick near to his face, with a single puff he extinguishes it, and adds, "but it would be a miracle."

At daybreak the next morning, the train of horses sets off, and by early afternoon has crossed the pass, taking Elaine out of the valley of the azhe-Moso under a perfectly clear blue sky, its one and only sun calling forth beads of sweat upon her brow and a wondrous, raging, fullness in her heart.

bluebirds fly

fifth movement - chorale

1

A single sphere of moisture on the farthest leaf of a holly branch, in the misty dim disguisement of the hour before dawn. Perched upon the pricking point it lingers, surface tension barely holding shape; its skin a silvered miniature of everything around; capturing the scene and reflecting it in tiny tableau - a faerie's vision, if only there were one around, to take it in.

Past the corner of the house a person creeps, no faerie, but real. Girl by her eyes and the shape of her nose, boy by the way he holds his shoulders and the cut of his clothes. Tousled hair spiked with wet she creeps, the tension beneath his own surface evident in the way her eyes scan the yard. There is wariness in them, along with recognition, as he takes in the darkened kitchen windows, faint glow of a lamp from the downstairs hallway, and another in the upstairs, its light sneaking out through the window of the hall bath whose door has been left slightly ajar. In her mind's eye he can picture it, just as if she were inside.

Assured no one is watching, he moves a little farther into the pool of moonlight left between overhanging crowns of alder, spruce and madrona. Her pace is slow and careful, his footsteps practically inaudible, their impacts on the flagstones muffled by a smattering of damp leaves and needles. In deepest shadow beside the tool shed, she reaches out to touch its aluminum siding, to brace and guide as he rounds its corner. Two more steps and her fingers discover the padlock, hanging right where it should be. Finding it fastened, a trace of satisfaction puckers the corner of his mouth.

Relaxing a bit, she leans back to study the shed's exterior, searching for something, then steps toward the corner, crouches, and stretches three fingers into a gap between the bottom of the shed wall and the concrete pad on which it sits, drawing back a second later with a chromed-steel key between two finger tips. Damp, and rusted round the edges, still it does the job when inserted into the padlock, and carefully the young man slides the door to one side, its plastic roller giving only small complaint. Almost without looking she reaches into the darkness to the right of the door where he finds a wood-and-canvas chair folded against the wall, just below a shelf of herbicides and soil conditioners, whose labels confess them long out of date.

Bolder now, as if something has been decided, she take his prize to a far corner of the yard, where branches of a huge spruce have been trimmed up, leaving a canopy above a flag-stoned alcove, and sets it down, unfolding its arms with practiced confidence. Settling in, her elbows find the chair's arms, hands come together in a pyramid to support a delicate chin as he scans the panorama before her; a rough rectangle of lawn edged by narrow gardens. Even in moonlight it is clear the shrubs are ragged, in need of a good prune, the beds mulched carelessly with their own detritus, but still there is a composition to it all, evidence that once this was a lovely yard. Directly across from her the house rises, overhanging eaves casting moon-shadow down walls buttressed by the kitchen bay's projection. To the left a stone chimney peeks between overhanging branches, anchoring the whole and giving it an air - though no smoke rises at this hour - of safe refuge in a cold world.

Dropping her hands once again, the new arrival settles into his chair, crosses one leg at right angle above the other, and exhales deeply, the weariness upon her features diminished a little as his head settles back against the curve of canvas, and their eyes begin to droop.

A breeze rustles the holly, choosing droplets at random and tossing them into the air, to crash against one another, or a leaf, or a branch, or just to arc out and down until they to impact on the flagstone surface, dying in darkened splatters which linger a while then fade, blending into the surrounding damp as the brightening day tries to decide just how much moisture it will bestow upon the already sopping ground.

Inside the house the timers have switched-off, and in the yard the sleeping figure stirs, first a small shudder, then a shift of the weight, relieving the slight ache of muscles whose flow of precious blood has been constricted by the pressure of her posture. A moment later she moves again, hand rising to brush a drop of dew which has fallen on his forehead, and then she is awake. Instantly his eyes go to the upstairs windows, and she imagines what will soon occur. Pictures a woman - not so young as she once was - awakening to stretch and yawn and tug at the covers even as she remains warmly beneath them. How carefully she then folds back the upper right-hand corner, slides her legs from under them and settles feet into the pair of slippers waiting there. Stands up and stretches again, before making her way down to the kitchen to put the kettle on. After living in the same house for all those years, this watcher is sure he knows how that woman's morning will go, unless she intervenes.

For a while he lingers, considering. Studying the distance across the lawn to the back door of this house she knows so well. Thirty feet perhaps, thirty five at the most, and yet a gulf between them, yawning wider every time he imagines what she might possibly say to bridge across the changes and events which have so separated their lives.

With a sigh the figure rises, stiff and slow but committed. Begins to fold the chair, then stops, smiles and presses it back open, shifting its position just a bit before leaving, so it faces squarely at the kitchen window, where he knows, as she steps carefully around the edge of the grass to where a narrow path leads to the street, it will be seen as soon as the kitchen blinds are raised.

A minute later he is at the sidewalk, walking purposefully for several blocks until, abruptly, she stops at a street corner. Looking one way, then the other, he stands, fidgeting with the pieces of change in a pants pocket, a look of disappointment across her tender features. Looks again to the left and to the right, then back the way he has come, and her head dips down, swings a bit to one side as a heavy sigh escapes his mouth. In all four directions stretch streets lined on both sides with houses, in a multitude of shapes and colors: some brick, some stucco, others wood-planked or stone-clad, with gabled roofs or flat ones, dormers and bays and garages that tuck neatly inside or jut out or sit detached completely - every house different, yet all recognizable as houses, despite their idiosyncrasies. A house is a house is a house; allowed – even encouraged, the realtors will tell you, if you want to maximize its value - to be different, to be itself.

Down the side street to the left, a car pulls out of a driveway, backing into the street and away, its headlights first a glow in the foggy air, and then a pair of slivers growing into crescent moons, then more nearly-full as they swing in her direction. Before their beams can sweep her up she turns as well, so her back is to the car, and begins to walk, hands in trouser pockets, shoulders and head thrust forward in pale impersonation of a person with a purpose.

"Mrs. Gimbal? Mrs. Gimbal?"

It takes a moment to realize that that name refers to her, with the result that Elaine is feeling guilty, and a little bit disoriented, as she rolls down the window of what still feels rather more her husband's car than hers. The rush of fog-thickened air brings it all back though; the mixed fragrances of spruce and rhododendron and distant seawater arousing in her a powerful sense of history, of being back where things were once so constant and familiar; this street where she spent the better part of 23 years. She'd only meant to drop in; to leave a list of instructions for the movers, coming to put her things in storage so the new buyers could have the house re-painted. She was just pulling out of the garage when she heard the knock on her passenger-side window and looked up to hear that name which still seems to refer to someone else, though she has been back in the states for nearly a month.

"Mrs. Volmer," she replies to the bright-eyed woman standing in her robe and slippers beside the driveway.

"I thought that was you," the other woman exclaims, quite pleased with herself. "I saw the lights on last evening, and wondered who was in that house and then this morning I looked over from my kitchen and there you were in yours, and I said to myself, 'If I didn't know better, I'd say that was Elaine Gimbal in there,' and wouldn't you know, I was right."

Despite her pleas, Elaine finds herself, a few minutes later, following her old neighbor into her house for a cup of tea and a scone. Entering Dallas and Henry's home she is struck by how strange it feels after all her time abroad. Dark walnut cabinets brace the entry hall, stuffed to their gills with porcelain figurines and silver serving pieces, all carefully composed behind beveled glass. In the front parlor, pristine glass-topped tables hover before brocaded chairs and a sofa long enough for four persons to share it without learning anything they don't want to know about each other, while on every surface are photographs in fancy frames, vases with fresh flowers from the well-tended gardens which surround the house, and more colorful knick-knacks and souvenirs of the Volmers' past life. 'So much,' Elaine finds herself thinking, 'so much...everything.'

In truth, the décor is not all that different from her old home next door. A different color scheme perhaps, and Rodney would never have put up with her collecting Lladro, but the same obsessive attention to quality and coordination, the precise arrangement of items which lack any real function. The same abundance of excess, striving to conceal the vacuum of days and weeks with nothing, really, to do. How foreign it seems now, how pointless - the same feelings which drove her out of her own house the day after she arrived back in town; sent her scurrying to find a room somewhere and to interview half a dozen realtors till she found one who didn't look at her like she was absolutely crazy for wanting to pull her roots up so completely. And yet, somewhat to her own surprise, Elaine finds herself still quite capable of polite conversation; accepting Dallas' condolences on her husband's passing, offering a very abridged version of her travels, and explaining that yes, indeed, she has sold her home, including much of the furniture, and is placing all its other contents in storage. For a few more days she will be staying at the Elderhostel near the university, cleaning up loose ends and making contacts for a vaguely-described aid organization with which she's begun working, but very soon she will be heading back overseas. "To do some more exploring," she hears herself suggest, though the reality is considerably more focused and, even unspoken, fills her heart with eagerness and joy.

Mrs. Volmer, too, is the picture of polity, topping off her guest's cup and pressing her to take just one more scone with an expression that suggests she appears to need it. Fills her in also on all the local news – how Mrs. Gillespie's chemotherapy has dragged on, that business with the Timroth's teenage daughter getting pregnant and how typical it is that the young father's parents have not insisted he stay involved. Apparently crime is up in the neighborhood, or maybe just the awareness of it; in either case she is oh, so grateful Henry had a security system installed before he passed away, with motion detectors and outside cameras, in addition to the double deadbolts they already had on all their doors, and key-locks on every window. It is the crime in fact, that has Dallas looking out her windows all the time, which was the reason she first noticed the young woman prowling around that morning some time ago, even before the girl came right up to the door and rang.

"I have it here somewhere," she says, rising from her seat and casting about the living room as if seeing her own furnishings for the very first time. "I had no idea where to send it, so I just put it in one of these drawers…" As if oblivious to her visitor, Mrs. Volmer proceeds to search the drawers of both end tables, the semicircular console and then the large hutch against the entry wall, before disappearing through a doorway toward the kitchen. "Such a strange little girl," her voice projects from around the corner. "Dressed like... like one of those 'hobos' who come around on Halloween, in their father's clothes? Oh, here," she exclaims from somewhere in the next room, only to reappear a moment later holding a crumpled and creased piece of card stock in her hand.

"She told me she used to live there, and of course I told her that wasn't possible, because Dr. and Mrs. Gimbal had lived there for... well, almost as long as she'd been alive, by the look of her, and then..."

Elaine's eyes follow the scrap of paper as Dallas's hand flutters about in accompaniment of her tale; how odd the young woman's appearance was, and yet how familiar some aspect of her manner. How knowledgeable she seemed about the Gimbals' home. It is only when Dallas has put off the climax as long as her vivid recollection seems capable of, that the card stops moving and her voice assumes a girlish tone which must once have been its habit but now appears only in imitation of others.

" 'If Mrs. Gimbal comes back,' she started to say to me, and then she corrected herself. 'W*hen Elaine* comes back, please tell her she can reach me at this number.' I have to say, I didn't know what she was going to suggest I give you, she was searching around in all the pockets of that old suit coat like a magician in a vaudeville. I half expected a silk handkerchief or a rabbit to come out of one of them, but no, it was just this old business card, and I looked at it and it didn't make any sense, because this says 'Stevie somebody,' but she'd already told me her name was Rodney, and when I said that was a coincidence, because your husband was a Rodney too, though he had passed away, she gave me the strangest look. 'I know,' she answered me, rather rudely, I thought. 'I was there.' "

A long white shed extends out into Lake Union. Projecting from its side, a regiment of floating docks shelter a collection of wooden boats, each one a different size and shape, each a testament to its creator's choices and prejudices. Pocket-sized catboats with their fore-mounted masts, longboats with lapped strakes and sterns rounded to take the seas from behind. Tugs with their prows high and sturdy to push through whatever waters they may meet, and at the furthest end, an aging schooner, her paint peeling and her spars stripped of their rigging, yet still graceful enough to make a tourist's heart sing.

Along the sidewalk that lines this waterfront, on a bench which misses the full force of the modest cold front currently oozing eastward through the Straight of Juan de Fuca, Rod Gimbal sits, hands in pockets, feet planted squarely on the concrete before him. He gives no notice as a skateboarder glides past, wheels rattling on the weathered concrete, nor when a yacht glides by two hundred yards offshore, to disappear behind the pier's end as it heads for its own home berth. He could be listening to something, it seems, taking in a lecture in the space before his eyes, though there is nothing out there except night air full of moisture and distant rotting wood.

It's been hours since he took up this spot, arriving from the east with the weary stride and vacant eyes of one who has been walking aimlessly for a very long time. That he ended up on this particular bench, on this particular stretch of bare space between the Wooden Boat Museum and a pier full of yacht brokers and seafood restaurants, is pretty much an accident; a by-product of the psychological truth that walking uphill takes more will than not, and the geographic reality that if you're not going uphill in this town, sooner or later you find yourself at some water's edge.

The morning has gone, and afternoon as well; evening giving way now to a night which might be dark but for the low-hanging clouds which gather light from every building and headlight around the lake, diffusing and reflecting them back again, so the world seems ceilinged with glowing cotton batting. Not far away, tires hiss and hum, engines rise and fall as they do throughout the city, ignored by most of its inhabitants - the ambient noise of modern life, familiar to the point of nonexistence.

Rustling a bit, Rod's hands search around and then dive back into the pockets of his jacket, seeking warmth and finding also a folded packet of bills and several pieces of change. His share of the tip jar, from one of those evenings at the Doghouse, which now seem so much more complicated than they felt at the time. Another pleasure boat comes gliding by, red and green running lights casting Christmasy reflections off the ridges of her bow wave. Music plays inside her cabin - more sensible than audible, as only the occasional note rises above her engine's idle, but those few notes are enough, along with the scraping of silverware and clinking of glasses and bottles, to form an idea. Idly his fingers wander the folded paper notes, ponder the weight of the coins, as an image forms, of a destination. Someplace to get in out of the weather perhaps, and to pursue the process of not thinking about it - any of it - which is his current highest aspiration.

'Six, seven, eight,' Stevie counts, her lips barely moving as she slaps the bills onto her stack and the busboy clears tables around her. 'Nine, ten, eleven,' she's saying to herself when she becomes aware of someone nearby. Looking up she sees at her elbow a gentleman who looks to be well into his sixties, his face so earnest and polite she figures he might just stand there forever with his coat draped over his arm if she doesn't break the ice first.

"Hi," she offers with her sweetest smile. Focusing on him, she recognizes a regular; one of those faces she's noticed before, not because it's worth noticing, but just because it's been there often enough to become a part of the scene she sees, looking out from her perch on the organ bench. "I thought everyone had gone."

"I...had to make a stop," he says, with a nod in the direction of the rest rooms. Stevie gives an agreeing tip of her own head. Goodness, she thinks. To be so careful, about everything you say and do. So worried about being proper that you can't even say 'I was in the rest room.' What a chore it must be to be that careful all the time. And how wary it makes you, like this poor fellow. Clearly has something to say, but he just doesn't know how to get it out.

"I hope you enjoyed the music tonight," she offers, shaping the pile of bills with her fingertips. Of course he enjoys the music, or he wouldn't come back here every week, sitting at his two-top over by the wall, sipping something tall and cola-colored. A quiet little man who favors brownish slacks, and sweater vests in muddled earth tones - like he's trying to disappear into the woodwork. Applauds politely. She tries to remember if he's ever made a request, but doesn't come up with anything. In fact, she's pretty certain they've never spoken before this.

"Oh, yes," the little man assures her. "You play very nicely," he says, then looks at his watch, as if his time is being metered out, even at this hour. "Only," he says, like he's introducing the most delicate of topics. "I hope you won't mind my saying this, but I wonder... about the kind of music you've been playing tonight?"

Stevie thinks back over her choices: there was *Cry Me a River*, and *Hit the Road Jack* for the oldies fans and, later, *You Ain't Nothing But a Hound Dog*. *Rainy Days and Mondays* should have satisfied the romantics, and if not that, then *Tears in Heaven* hits everybody where it hurts, even if they don't know the back-story. Tom Waits' *Ol' 55* might not be familiar, but that swaying, loping, gospel rhythm has got to touch anyone with ears. Maybe he's more of a Broadway fan – she recalls throwing in *Wishing You* from Phantom of the Opera, and *Send In the Clowns* is Broadway as well - at least that's where it originated, before it went pop and started showing up everywhere. Yes, *Total Eclipse of the Heart* is probably obscure to this crowd, but then there was *God Bless the Child* - every generation's got their own version to claim of that one, haven't they? Hell, there's a whole world of great material out there, if you've got the fake-books.

"It's music," she answers instead. "Just music."

"Well," the man says, apparently considering very deeply the sounds he has been listening to for the last couple of hours. "I like it better when you play things that are more...upbeat. We tend to...it's just more fun; for us." He gives a sort of shrug, which she takes to indicate that 'us' means persons of his generation, which covers a lot of the people who've been showing up lately. Ever since she and Rod had started singing his old selections, though the crowd got bigger and more enthusiastic, they'd also gotten older; blue hair and bald heads the norm, beaming smiles at stuff that was published and laid down a couple of generations ago. Leading up to a night like tonight, when she chose to play the songs that sang to her, and felt the whole time like she was sending the music out into nothing, for no one.

The man is still there, one hand fiddling with the hem of his folded coat as she ponders this. He has something more he needs to say.

"I was just wondering," he offers, still more embarrassed. "You haven't got a cold or something, have you?" Stevie shakes her head, the conversation turning perilously close to the underlying truth; that she knows full well the reason the crowd was so unresponsive tonight, the tips so short, and so does he.

"No," the man agrees, beginning to unfold his coat, tugging at a shirtsleeve before he aims it into an armhole. "But, you used to sing; when that other girl was here."

It's not pronounced as a question, so Stevie does not answer. Like her visitor, she's thinking back, remembering the nights when she and Rod were here together, and how that felt; her range for once an asset, instead of an embarrassment.

"I liked it better when you did. Sing, I mean. You play very well and all, but...the best was when the two of you did it together."

For a moment Stevie wonders if the guy is making some kind of a crack. She's got a pretty good radar for people slipping verbal knives at her or her kind, but this fellow doesn't seem like he'd ever be that bold, even if his mind ran in that direction, which she suspects it does not. Dead honest is what he seems to be. Just an old music lover.

"When's she gonna' come back?" he asks, then remembers something important to him. In fact, judging by the way he lays the words out, it may even be the whole reason he worked up the courage to come talk to a stranger. "She's not really a doctor, is she - so young?"

"No," Stevie answers, enjoying the honesty with which she can respond to that last part. His first question is more difficult, though, calling up an unpleasant truth upon which she has avoided dwelling, in the time since their little scene together. "And no, I don't think The Doctor is ever coming back. I just...don't think so."

"Too bad," says the little man, one arm already inside his coat as he reaches around to grab the other lapel. "She's got quite a voice, that one. Even if she is a little odd."

Wavelets lap at the base of a concrete wall, its cementitious matrix eroded to expose the rounded pebbles inside, their wetted curves capturing fragments of mid-morning sunlight through a threadbare overcast and sending them out again, in tiny glitters and glints. The glossy surface of Lake Union is opaque, allowing no glimpse of what lies beneath, as a slight frame wanders by, hair and clothes in disarray after a night spent curled inside a playground tunnel, her rhymed and drooping eyes fixed earthward, oblivious to the effects of sun and shade, the chiaroscuro of broken clouds, the towering pipes and chimneys of the old gasworks just over a knoll.

On a bench nearby, two men sit slouched, the handles of their fishing poles wedged between the bench's slats, a cooler tucked out of sight, the beers in their hands wrapped in foam covers for disguise. Curious, they eye the young woman as she approaches, her steps slow and aimless, though her feet never stray beyond the concrete path. A smile passes between the two, tacit acknowledgement that the fishing has not been all that great this day, the beer is almost gone, the wind is getting bitter and something has got to give or they may just die of boredom.

"Hey, Miss," one calls out as the young woman gets closer. His words get no reaction, and he casts a questioning glance at his friend, whose smile only widens.

"You look like you could use a drink, Miss," the second offers, rising to his feet and joining step beside her. "I know someplace nice and warm...."

"So basically you tried to rape him."

Others may have been thinking it, but Jeena is the girl with the balls to say it out loud. "Come *on*," she says, driving right over Stevie's hemming and hawing, "any person tries to do any other person without getting their clear consent, that's rape."

Up till this, the group has been quiet while Stevie explained what she'd intended as her 'gift' – how she'd stopped taking her hormones; suffering the effects of pseudo-menopause as she substituted the little blue pills ordered on the net, hoping they'd help her rise to the moment. How the encounter has ended up bringing not the effect she expected, but another outcome altogether.

"I thought it was what she wanted," she answers Jeena now, looking her straight in the eye. "It wasn't an angry thing, or being desperate for sex, but it wasn't true to me either; to who I am inside. So I've come to a decision." She pauses, savoring their hungry silence. "I'm scheduled for surgery," she announces, and watches with satisfaction as her friends' faces light up, each with its own private recipe – disbelief, envy, or just plain delight.

This is Stevie, after all, who for almost three years has been the group's leading exponent of the irrelevance of 'having it off.' Of the greater importance of being yourself, with all its complexities and contradictions. Stevie - who has succeeded as fully as any of them in defining a new identity for herself without denying who she had once been. Yet here she is, cheerily abandoning all those reasoned, logical arguments, to make the journey so many of them contemplate, some in wonder, some in anger, some in fear and some, as apparently she does now, in raw, burning hunger for resolution.

Laurie, a rangy t-girl with bad teeth and a pronounced lisp, is the first to overcome her surprise. "You go, girl," she says, reaching across to slap Stevie on the back in a gesture at once affectionate and also inadvertently revealing of her own private history.

"And what about your ex?" challenges Herb, the group's resident authority on spousal conflict, his expertise grounded in a protracted and painful divorce when, still known as Jeanine, she had admitted to her first husband that she was fundamentally attracted to other women. After that divorce, and multiple unsatisfying hook-ups with *both* sexes, Jeanine very nearly married another man who seemed wonderfully tolerant of her occasional digressions, until it became clear that he was actually quite infatuated with the vision of his wife and another woman - the group had closed an amusing session once speculating on how likely it was that a man who fantasized about two women together was really a closet T-woman, still stuck in self-denial. Then, after Jeanine had her revelation and began living as Herb, he had found himself blissfully happy with a sweet young thing named Elise until, one shocking Christmas Eve, she announced that she, too, was transgendered and was about to start the process of becoming Eddie, leaving Herb - the former heterosexual woman, then tentative lesbian, now contented heterosexual man - to figure out how he felt about becoming one half of a gay couple. Those who know this history give Herb more latitude than most to comment on other people's marital issues.

"She doesn't need to know," he answers his own question with a wry smile. "What's inside your drawers is no longer her business," to which the group readily agrees, with uncharacteristic unanimity.

There follows some discussion about the mechanics of getting a doctor's referral for surgery (Stevie explains that she already has the precious letter from a shrink she's been seeing for longer than the required two years), where to go (right there in Seattle, with a doctor trained at the famous Minneapolis clinic that practically invented modern gender-reassignment surgery), and how soon it all will happen. This last elicits a fair amount of envy when Stevie explains that the surgeon had had a cancellation shortly before she called this morning, allowing her to avoid the typical year-long backlog which has led more than one person they know to travel as far as Morocco or Thailand for their surgery.

"That's how it works," suggests a superbly confident group member who goes by the name of Genda Warria and refuses to be identified in any more specific way. "Once you are true to your own spirit, the universe lines up to help you. Like this experiment we did once in high school science, with a magnet and a pile of metal shavings on a piece of cardboard. The shavings are all in a mess, but when you pass a magnet underneath the cardboard, then suddenly they're all standing there in perfect rows, every one aligned. Just like that magnet, a heart that is true to itself gives off a force that can make everything else come into line. A true heart can change the world, if you let it."

Another evening, another stakeout and another coffee. Bigger cup
this time, though, and black. Talk-radio, too; something to keep him
agitated through the long ours ahead. Can't hurt.

Two nights ago, he fell asleep - no way of knowing for how
long, god damn it. They could have come and gone right in front of
him and he'd never have known.

So then last night, Jake had put the window down a ways to
let the night air seep in, help him stay alert. Got rewarded with a
glimpse of it - the drag queen from the photo in the paper -
wandering out after midnight and climbing into a white Toyota. New
and boring; nothing like that wild little Honda Kim used to drive.

Jake followed him that night and saw where he parked, the
open garage beneath a four-story building at the end of Madison, a
decent-enough place, though you'd never notice it unless someone
you knew lived there. Which he does, judging by what Jake's seen
since of his comings and goings – dressed in full drag all the time,
even in broad daylight, if you can believe that.

So now it's a Wednesday, he still hasn't seen Kim, but this is
the best he's got, trailing this freak to some run-down County social-
services-center on Capital Hill to see if maybe it leads him to her. A
long shot, admittedly, but long shots are where you get the big
payoffs, aren't they? The lobby door opens and there he is, breezing
out like it was the most normal thing in the world. Chatting it up and
trading hugs with the rattiest bunch of men and women Jake has
seen in a long time, before he goes around the corner into the
parking lot. Couple of minutes later, and out comes the little white
car.

Firing up the Beamer, Jake scans traffic, picks a gap and
moves out, two cars behind it. Turns the radio up louder now that
he's moving, not really paying any attention to the ranting, but it
keeps him company, and he's starting to get a good feeling about
tonight. Yeah, something's gonna' happen tonight, he can feel it in
his bones. Something's gonna' happen - and it's about time.

Two hours after the end of group, Stevie is alone in a booth at the
Be-Hive, a t-friendly night spot up on Broadway. The place is
jammed, as it is every Tuesday thru Saturday, with a clientele who
call it second home. The décor is Victorian Brothel - tastefully
executed - and the music techno/disco/eclectic. There isn't a sports
channel in sight, and the crowd is meeting and greeting and mixing
and matching like they believe any minute a buzzer is going to go off
and anyone still flying solo will be SOL – Shit-Outta-Luck: a term
which might very well describe Stevie at this moment; last occupant -
unless you count the dirties and the empties waiting for a bus to the
kitchen - of a booth built for six. Herb stopped in for a while, but he
doesn't drink so he never stays long. Laurie showed as well; always
up for going out after group, but she's drifted off, standing at the bar
now with a guy-couple she seems to know pretty well, judging by the
body language the three of them are exhibiting for each other. Jeena
stayed the longest, and ate a full dinner once it was clear Stevie was
paying. Sweet as she is, the girl can't hold a job; she's been broke as
long as she's been coming to group. She left about ten-forty, headed
to meet her sister somewhere, still hoping to reconcile and maybe
connect with the rest of their family again, though the odds have
never been good, and sounded no better tonight.

Filling out the credit slip, calculating a tip, Stevie feels her
earlier euphoria drooping. Finds herself wishing her life were more
like Laurie's over there, who always seems to find someone to make
the evening hum, despite being not exactly the prettiest pumpkin in
the patch. Or like when Rod was around, for that matter. Odd as he
was – is - it was certainly nice knowing he would be there all the
time. Mornings over a cup of coffee together, evenings working up
songs. Even when she was off visiting clients, the knowledge that he
was back at home gave her something more to look forward to than
her own thoughts.

Maybe it's the wine - too much but not quite enough – that's
dumped her in this big fat tub of 'would'a, could'a, should'a'. The
realization that her mind is going in that direction is followed by a
resolve to find a brighter side. Yes, she screwed up, drove Rod off
just as she was trying to give him all she could of herself. She's got to
own that, live with it, and move on. After all, it's not like she *meant*
to hurt him, and besides, the boy chose to react the way he did. It
was not the only way to play that scene. 'There are always options,'

Stevie reminds herself, a line learned from her first therapist, back in the days she and Evelyn were still trying to figure out whether they had a future together.

Maybe he'll be back, Stevie tells herself as she gathers up her purse and coat; or maybe there'll be someone else. An open-minded woman-who-loves-women perhaps, so the two of them can share their appreciation of the finer things this life has to offer. Especially now that she's going to be all of a piece, self-contradictions sliced away and stitched up tight. But she's not going to find that someone at home, scrubbing off make-up in the silence of her own bathroom. There's room at the bar, one more glass of wine would be an OK thing right now, and maybe Laurie will introduce her to those two friends. This is a big evening after all, with her announcement, and Stevie Margulies is not ready for it to be over just yet.

Minutes later, she is standing by the bar, sharing break-up stories with Laurie and the couple – Jerry and Jim, it turns out - Jim is in tears telling them how he and Jerry once broke up - for all of four hours. Stevie can see Laurie rolling her eyes and guesses she's heard this story more than once before.

"I get it," Stevie breaks in, "really, I do; but this isn't like that - I mean, yes, I feel honestly bad about Rodney leaving and all, and I worry about what he's doing now, but I'm not going to let it turn my life around." Jerry nods approvingly as he reaches across and blots Jim's eyes with his napkin. "I'm moving forward. I'm having this done and I'm going to start a whole new phase and it's going to be great. I can feel it in my…"

"We don't want to know where you feel it, girl," Jim interrupts through his own emotions, and the three burst into laughter as Stevie blushes. Just then the bartender arrives with four Honey-shots – the Hive's signature lemon-and-brown-sugar gelatin made with tequila instead of water – giving a nod to Jerry who had quietly ordered them a short while ago. Laurie reacts with mock horror as Jerry thrusts a glass toward each of them and Stevie explains that she's not about to do shots on a weekday.

"It's a party," Jerry insists. "You're off on a great adventure; Jim and I are back together again…"

"That was two years ago," Laurie points out.

"Yes. And we're *still* back together again," Jerry says, raising his glass in toast before sucking the Jell-O into his mouth in several tiny pulses, like a hamster at its water tube.

"And still celebrating," Jim adds, before downing his own shot in one gulp and wiping the back of a hand across his mouth in a pseudo tough-guy gesture.

Amid the laughter, Stevie's shot sits untouched on the bar, while Laurie examines her own with wary curiosity. Lifting it to the light she squints through the golden semi-solid with exaggerated concern.

"Is this really..?" she begins, only to be interrupted by a nudge from behind. All turn, and three faces erupt with glee at the sight of an outrageously buxom woman in white spandex, a profusion of orange curls billowing round her head.

"Oh yeah," the newcomer growls, making no attempt to hide her baritone. "It's real Jell-O, trademark and all." She pauses for a second, as her very presence induces Laurie to action, tossing back the glass and swallowing its contents. "And real tequila," the big woman concludes, though Laurie's grimace left no doubt of that.

"Stevie, *this* is Jolene," Jim explains off-handedly, as the newcomer proceeds to give great warm hugs to Jerry and Laurie and finally to him.

"I heard there was a party going on," Jolene gushes, as the surrounding crowd shifts to make room for the growth of their little knot. "And I never miss a party. You gonna' drink that honey?" she adds, indicating Stevie's shot, "or am I gonna' have to do it for you?"

Moments later Stevie is the one with a twisted-up face, Jolene is reaching out to capture the bartender's attention and two more friends have drifted over to join what suddenly has all the earmarks of a real party.

"Buy you a drink?" Brady Josephs asks, sliding his butt onto a wooden stool whose gouges and splinters have been polished into harmlessness by years of similar approaches. The girl next to him is cute enough for the price of a drink, if a bit odd. Short hair and a gloomy scowl cannot hide the softness of her skin, the pert little upturned nose, or the suggestive way the corners of her mouth pucker when she sucks the last melt-water from between cubes frosted together at the bottom of an otherwise empty rocks glass.

Wordlessly, her head turns a few degrees in his direction, then back again, to stare directly forward, eyes fixed somewhere in the distance beyond the back bar mirror. The glass there is dusty, and the room it reflects is dimly lit, which is merciful, given how worn-out the space and everything in it is. Despite the fact it's nearing midnight, there are not more than a dozen bodies occupying booths and tables which could hold four times that number, and the flicker of one TV at the other end of the bar is the brightest sign of life among them all, not excluding the morose George Jones tune leaking out of an underpowered stereo somewhere. So it's not like she's staring at anything of great interest as she avoids looking his way. No, this chick is either very full of herself, Brady imagines, or very full of whatever she's drinking. Either way it's late, he's just blown into town and there is no one else in this shit-hole of a bar to whom he would give the time of day, so what they hell, as they say.

The equally-bored man behind the bar responds to Brady's hand signals by plopping a fresh glass of scotch in front of the girl, whose hand slips out like a snake on the hunt, wraps carefully around, and pulls it to her lips, where a goodly portion of the amber liquid disappears in the first sip. Returning the glass to the counter her stare and her silence resume as if nothing had happened at all. There's no 'Thanks;' no practiced launch into a hooker's ritual banter; but also no wary word of denial - as some women will do to set the ground rules before a guy gets his hopes up. This one is just...there, which means Brady has got to do all the work himself. Take his chances or walk away; and walking away is definitely not Brady's strong suit.

"You know something?" he begins, reaching out so the tips of two fingers can caress the knuckles of her other hand where it lies inert on the plasticized wood of the bar-top. Her skin is soft to the touch, though oddly cold, despite the warmth of this place. Now that it looks like he may be here for a while, he'd like to take off his windbreaker, but having just made contact he's reluctant to pull his hand away, so instead he raises the stakes a bit, spreading out his fingers to cover hers, gathering up the small extremity and squeezing it gently. "You got real nice hands," he says softly.

"These?" the girl asks, sounding somewhat shocked as her free hand floats up in front of her face. Twisting in the air, it curls into a fist, opens, then curls again as she seems to examine it for the very first time. "Oh, no," she says finally. "These are not my hands."

Nearly two AM, and what had been rain has given way to a dank drizzle, eager to penetrate the bones of those few late night wanderers who brave the darkness. Here, a couple straggle from a movie theater, having stood in the aisle to read every last credit and song title, long after the rest of the audience had departed. Here, a lone panhandler stands on the median at an empty intersection with his cardboard sign, still hoping for a few more coins from sympathetic drivers heading to their homes, before he returns to his overpass. And over there, around the corner and down the way from the Be-Hive, a pair of men with the heavy clothes and weathered faces of those who perform physical labor for low wages fiddle under the hood of a great old slab of Detroit metal, its roof and trunk-lid mapped with peeling paint, wheel wells lacy with rust spreading out from beneath battered chrome trim. Tired and disoriented after several hours in a bar, they curse and fume at their machine's refusal to start. If not for this rotting beast's intransigence, they would be asleep now, crashing at a boat-mate's place in Burien before setting off tomorrow on the first leg of their long return trip, from a season of work on a crab boat out of Ballard harbor, back to their homes near Galveston; back to the same depressed and depressing shrimping industry that drove them north for four months in hopes of making a killing, only to find the crabs had other ideas.

"Fucking piece of shit," says one, tall and dark haired, with haunted eyes and a Chinese pictogram tattooed crudely on the tendon-stranded flesh of his neck. Turning away from the car, he hauls off and kicks a concrete-filled pipe bollard, its battered surface thick with layers of red enamel to ensure its effectiveness in separating the drug store's parking from the sidewalk. "Fucking Detroit piece of fucking shit gotta' die on me right fucking now."

"Go ahead, Bawdy," suggests a man lying in the back of the car, his legs draped over the end of the seat to rest thick-soled engineer boots on the door-sill. Not quite as tall, this man is heavier, with shaggy hair in a mix of dirty gray and cinnamon. A fat white cat sits on the mound of his stomach, licking at a spot on the man's coat as he strokes her matted back repeatedly with the thumb protruding from a heavy bandage which encases his abbreviated right hand, memento of a stormy night, hauling traps over the rail in heaving seas. One second's inattention by a fellow crewmember and his middle two fingers the price to pay. "Bust your foot why don't you?

That'd make the night a total fucking success."

"I'll bust my goddamned foot if I want to," growls the first, stepping away from the offending steel. Arms swinging out to the sides he lurches forward, landing the thick sole of one boot flat against the bollard again with a slapping thud which provides little satisfaction.

"Here," says the sleeper, tossing the cat off as he rises from his berth on the back seat. His face and head seem large even for his big body, which bulges and sags over a wide leather belt. The effect is exaggerated by the full beard which covers his jaw, billowing out as he casts his eyes around the empty lot till they settle on a nearby dumpster filled with broken-down cardboard boxes. "You wanna' kick something, kick this." In three running steps he has flung himself nearly horizontal, foot smashing into the center of the dumpster's steel front panel, sending out a hollow toneless boom which fills the parking lot and escapes down the street, leaving a greater stillness in its wake as the bearded man's body settles to the pavement with a heavy grunt of exhalation.

"Fucking A, Jimbo," calls the smallest of the three men, still poised at the open hood, and his eager voice indicates gratitude at the distraction from his mechanical frustration. Matching his friend's performance he runs and flings himself at the dumpster, producing a decidedly smaller noise as he falls to the dark pavement beside his friend.

"You sorry sons of bitches," moans the tattooed man, the only one still standing. "Sorry fucking sons of bitches lying in the fucking rain..."

"You must have a hollow leg, girl,"   Brady says as he sets another
glass before his new acquaintance. He knows it's a cliché, but hell,
it's just something to fill the air; this kid doesn't seem to care what
he says one way or the other. Tell her his name? Nothing. What he
does for a living? Nothing. Could probably tell her his whole life
story – the short version only, he's not really interested in giving
anyone the whole history – and still he'd get no reaction. Offer to
buy her another drink though, and at least you get a nod for your
trouble, plus, you can use the drink as bait to lure her away from the
bar to a booth in the dark end of the room, which is where the two
are sitting now, side by side, their backs to the rest of the crowd. The
only people who can see them here are the ones passing back and
forth to the toilets, and given as most of those are at least half drunk,
there is really no one going to notice as he slides an arm across her
shoulder.

     Another thing about luring her down off that bar stool is, he's
gotten to see more than just her face; and what he's seen, he likes.
Despite the baggy slacks and shirt, this is not a girl he'd kick out of
bed. Put her in some real clothes and girlie shoes, she might even
walk like a grown-up woman, instead of the dockworker's roll she did
across the floor, though that might be excused by the peanut shells
lying around, or the Scotch she seems so fond of. Not that it matters
all that much what she would look like cleaned up, as she is clearly
female and clearly alone, and any woman drinking alone in a dump
like this is clearly looking for action.

     "So you don't believe in names," Brady offers, between swigs
of his own beer. "You believe in politics maybe? Want to talk about
what's happening in the Middle East these days? I got my money on
the A-rabs. I figure there's way more of them than there is of the
Jews, plus they got more money. I remember, when my grandfather
was still around, he used to talk like the Jews had all the money in
the world, you know? But today... I mean, I hauled a load of stuff
once for this A-rab who was moving into a new house up near
Bellingham, and that truckload was insured for two-million bucks.
You believe that? Two-million bucks for one truckload of stuff they
invoiced as 'household goods'! Oughta' be a helluva lot better than
'good' for that kinda' money, you ask me. Oughta' be damned
great!"

Robin Andrew

A mournful steel guitar plays on in the background as the girl continues to stare straight ahead, and Brady begins to feel a little uneasy. The best way to start a conversation, he's always found, is to say something out of line; that way a person either agrees with you, and you know where you stand, or they don't, so ditto; and that story <u>always</u> gets him a reaction; the whole A-rab/Jew thing - custom made to get anyone going, whether they agree or disagree. But this character? No balls, no strikes, no game. Like pouring liquor down a crack in a fucking stump. Which means there's really only one more way to go about it.

"Look," Brady says, when the girl has reached the bottom of her glass. "This place charges an arm and a leg for a decent drink. What'a you say we go someplace else, hunh? I can get us a bottle, and then we can find someplace warm. Get you ouughta those wet clothes, maybe a hot shower, and we can see what happens from there, OK?"

A couple of chicks sashay past on their way from the pool table to the ladies room, one hanging on to the other like they were hiking through a hurricane, and still he can hardly tell if this girl has even heard what he said, which leads Brady to remember something a Sergeant told him twenty-five years ago, when he was learning to drive big-rigs at Fort Leonard Wood, a few months after he'd enlisted. One of the other trainees had climbed into the cab of a tractor-trailer loaded with two howitzers and he did a great job with the clutch and the gears and the gas, only when he pulled out, the trailer stayed put. 'Ya' gott'a hitch 'em before you can tow 'em,' the instructor had sung out, like he'd been listening to too many country songs, but there were very few useful thing Brady'd learned from four years of boredom mixed with hell, and good advice was good advice no matter where you picked it up.

Sliding his ass off the bench, Brady stands to chug the last of his beer and plop the mug down with a clear thunk. Reaching back across, he motions toward the girl's glass and watches as she downs the last of it, before placing his hand around her upper arm and guiding her out of the booth.

"Come on, little lady," he says, as the girl stumbles down the aisle past a pool table where two bearded old coots are happily knocking balls together, oblivious to how long their women are taking to powder their noses. "I think it's time we got you out of this place. A pretty little girl like you deserves better, don't you think?"

"No. Well, yes, actually. There is ...someone."

"I thought so," says the man in the black turtleneck, his smile broad as a six-lane highway at three AM, and just as vacant. Clearly a man who prides himself on his sensitivity, delights in demonstrating his 'understanding' side, even when he's just been shot down. "You OK? To drive, I mean?"

Stevie looks at the guy, something like pity in her eyes. He's so...earnest. Like he's in any better shape then she is? If he was, he probably wouldn't have been hitting on *her* for the last half hour. Either that or he's just desperate. It is closing time after all, and there's a buzz of desperation all around the Hive. Guys and girls and every increment between; all making one last attempt to connect before the lights come up and show them out the door. Alone. Again.

Oh well, Stevie thinks, her earlier moroseness washed away by the good vibe of the past two hours. In a couple of months her secret will be gone. Snip and stitch, a week or two of bed rest and Percoset, and she'll be a new woman. She might just come back here and try her luck then. Find out how it feels to take it all the way - this heady experience of being stalked by the predators of the night. After two Jell-O shots and who-knows-how-many glasses of Chablis, the prospect is nothing if not intriguing; the way they eye her down the bar, then sidle up so carefully-subtle they might as well be shouting. 'Hello,' they start in, and every word that follows is a fingertip playing on her ego.

'I should have done this long ago,' she's thinking, as she says goodbye to mister black turtleneck and gathers up her coat and purse. All those years of imprecision, lingering between one thing and another, are soon to be swept away now by the clarity of it all. No more 'this and that,' no more 'neither here not there.' Though she really did believe all those arguments for living on the edge of in-between. Still does believe them, in a lot of ways: intellectually, politically, morally. But just not for her, not anymore.

Stepping out the front door, she pauses a moment to draw in the night air. Cool, but not cold. A little damp, which is OK; it's good for the skin. Feeling tall on her heels, slim and straight and put-together, a happy shiver runs up her spine and she hugs her arms around herself as she takes a moment trying to recall where she parked. Things look different at this hour, but God, it's good to be alive and on the way to being one with herself; finally and fully.

"So," Brady calls, early next morning, dragging the word out to several seconds in length as he stands in the bathroom doorway, fanning yesterday's folded-up sports section in front of his face while staring at the girl staring at the ceiling of his motel room. Reaching back inside the door, he flips a switch and hears the vent fan's motor grind uneasily into motion. "You interested in some coffee?"

In the big bed the girl gives no sign that she has heard. Just lies, flat on her back, same as she did through all of last night's exertions.

Coming out of the bar she had stumbled, a good excuse for Brady to put an arm around her, itself a good excuse for him to verify the narrow place above her hips and the way her shoulder fit just beneath his. She didn't exactly melt against him, like they did when they were really asking for it. This one was just...there. When he asked if she had to call anyone, to tell them she wouldn't be coming home tonight, or anything, he could detect no reaction at all. The girl just stared out across Aurora Highway, mesmerized – not surprising, if she was anywhere near as drunk as he was - by the fast-moving lights and shearing noises zipping by a few yards from their noses as, above it all, the bar's sign flickered on its pole, pulsing purple glow out across the asphalt. Brady could see his tractor parked in front of the motel a hundred yards or so down the other side of the highway, past a darkened tire store and a boarded up upholsterer's shop. Easy enough then, to guide his prize along, half carrying her when a break in traffic allowed them to cross, and in a few minutes make it to the door, where they had to pause while he dug in a pocket for the plastic fob and its bright brass key.

"For such a little thing," he remarked as he worked the door with one hand, holding her up with the other, "you sure are an armful."

"I'm really much bigger," was the girl's response, not so much disagreeing, as disappointed, which brought a laugh from Brady.

"All right," he said as he hip-bumped her through the door into the darkness beyond, "you got a sense of humor after all."

Once inside it was easy as pie: the girl standing in the middle of the room while he began to kiss her, the head snapping away at first, then going still, though she never really returned anything, just let him go at her without any sign of enjoying it. Getting her back to nature was a bit more work than usual, what with shirt buttons and friggin' cuff links, then not just one but two t-shirts to strip off; but at least after that there were no funky women's bits to figure out, just plain old belt and trousers and - the big surprise - fucking boxer shorts underneath it all. Through the whole process the kid stood there and took it; even as he pushed her down onto the bed and piled on top of her, she barely seemed to notice what was happening.

"God damn," Brady muttered into the side of her neck, his lips brushing across the soft skin, feeling her youth before he grabbed a bit of it in his teeth and shook his head playfully back and forth, like a predator on a kill. Not enough to leave a mark, just enough to confirm to himself that he was in control, could do whatever he wanted with her. "You're the quietest fuck I've ever had."

"This isn't me," the girl replied, in a voice that seemed to come from a lot farther away than even the widest motel bed could account for. "You. Being here. Whatever happens – none of this is real."

Maybe it was the way she said those words, or maybe he was too drunk, or just burned-out from the length of the day that had come before the night. Most likely, it was those god-damned boxer shorts, but whatever the reason, right about then the momentum began draining away from his critical component and about all he could really manage was to roll off to one side and pull the covers over the both of them before he fell into a deep and dreamless sleep.

When he woke up it was already light, several sharp shards of sunshine streaming past bent slats in the blinds; the peephole a brilliant star against the deep brown universe of its door. He came-to on his side and it was only when he rolled onto his back and started to stretch that he remembered there was somebody else in the bed. Looking over he saw this little slip of a thing, barely a lump under the bunched-up spread, and for one horrible second he thought something was really wrong with her; those eyes wide open and staring straight up at the ceiling, that neck and bristled head held straight and rigid, but when he slid a hand beneath the covers he could feel warmth coming off of her naked skin, and when he listened hard he could hear breathing. Deep, slow breathing, like she was actually a lot more relaxed than she looked.

It took some serious rubbing of his eyes and shaking of his head to bring the whole thing into focus, but eventually he got the events of last night put into something like the right order, and even figured out that it had been the sound of a newspaper dropping outside the door that woke him, then the conflicting demands of a full bladder and an empty stomach that kept him awake, and it was on the basis of those few facts that he dragged himself up from the bed, kicked his way through the pile of clothes beside it, and headed to the john.

Now, keeping an eye on the motionless figure as he moves back across the room, a frown comes over his features. It's not about the embarrassment a guy'd naturally feel after a failure like he had; in fact he's actually kind of grateful that he *didn't* manage the deed, given how things look in the light of day. There's just too many things about this chick that are simply not right. Pawing through the pile of clothes to retrieve his shorts, he comes across hers; smaller yes, but otherwise way too similar.

"That's it," he calls out, moving closer and grabbing a foot, to shake it roughly. "You're just a little too weird for me, so let's get this over with OK?" The tone of his voice seems to get through to her, as those freaky eyes come rolling over to focus hard on his face, not that that makes him feel any better about having her there, in a room rented in his own name, on his company card. Gathering up her clothes he tosses them into the bathroom, where the fan has finally gotten up to speed, its crusty-loud whirring nearly drowning out the ascending whine of the toilet valve as its flush comes to an end.

"You go on in there and do what you need to do; then get your clothes on. I'm gonna be here, doing the same, and when we're both dressed, I'll buy you a cup of coffee and figure out what the hell to do with you." Turning his back he hears a rustling of bedclothes, then soft footfalls before the door closes and he is left to pull a clean shirt from his bag and wonder what the hell it is with kids these days.

"Well," Brady remarks when the girl finally emerges from the bathroom, clothes more or less arranged, hair still ragged as when her head came off the pillow. "You sure do a good job of hiding your best assets. If I didn't know how much we both had to drink, I'd be asking myself what the hell I was doing with a weirdo like you."

For a moment she seems about to reply, then swallows deeply and turns toward the door, moving more forcefully than any time since he first glimpsed her on that bar stool.

"Wait a minute kid," Brady urges, stepping between her and the way out. "You got a car out there?"

Her silent stare confirms his suspicions.

"You live around here?" he asks next, to no more reward.

"So, what - you just go out the door and start walking?" Still no shake of her head, no reaction at all, just those deep eyes staring right through him. Scary eyes, Brady realizes, in their emptiness and how slowly they move. Unnatural eyes, that make you wonder if there's anyone at home behind them.

"Look," he says after a moment. "I've got to get out of here myself. Pick up a load in Tukwilla. It'll only take me a minute to pack up, then I can take you wherever you've got to go. Like home?" he offers, but sees no sign she has heard him. "School then, you in school maybe, you want me to drop you off there?" Still nothing, and this is beginning to get a little bit old. "All right then," he says, picking up his travel bag and heading into the bathroom to collect the few things he's got laid out on the counter there. "You won't tell me anyplace else, I'll drop you at some store with a pay phone and plenty of people hanging around, you like that? Some kids your own age? Maybe they'll know what to do with you, ya' friggin' nutcase. Maybe your own kind'll know what to do with you, 'cause I sure as fuck don't."

Startled out of sleep by the sound, it takes Aubrey a minute to understand. Nobody ever rings her doorbell; the few friends who come round her place tend more toward raucous laughter and the pounding of fists, than to extending a genteel finger at that button, which is pretty hard to find, seeing as how it's been painted over more times than a Texas cheerleader's face. Finally, though, she puts one and one together and, with a resentful shout of "Coming," hauls her sorry ass out of bed, wraps the spread around it and stumbles through darkened rooms to investigate.

"Aubrey Maturin?" asks a uniformed policewoman, as soon as the door is wide enough for eye contact. Something in her look tells Aubs this is no ordinary hassle, jumping her heart into a faster rhythm and her stomach into a twis - like when you take a swig from the milk jug only to find it has gone old and thick and lumpy.

"Yeah," she says, and steps back into her living room, letting go of the door as the cop enters, followed by another, this one in suit and tie, his hangdog face a vision of compassion compared to the woman's narrowed eyes and tight-set mouth.

"You know a person named Stevie Margulies?" the suit pronounces, in a manner that manages to be at once both a question and a warning, that there's something more important about to come.

"I know a Stevie," Aubrey responds quickly, then stops herself, wondering if she really wants to be so cooperative at whatever hour this is. Glancing toward the kitchen she makes out the numbers on the microwave - 5:12 - god damn it! Five fucking AM and they're waking her up about someone she hardly knows? "Don' know her last name," she continues, thinking this just might be serious and if the shit's gonna' get serious, there's no advantage letting a cop know how pissed off you really are at him. Or her. "Just Stevie."

The uniform moves farther into the house, her eyes darting here and there, taking in the sweaters and jackets on pegs behind the door, the stack of newspapers beside the TV on its rickety stand. Without asking she flips a switch and the overhead fixture comes on, its light harsh and uncomfortable at this hour, as if the stretches of bare wall and uncovered windows are private flesh, exposed without warning or consent. A threadbare spot in the carpet by the bathroom doorway seems to occupy the cop for a moment, before she reaches in and turns on the bathroom light too, disappearing for a moment to return with a shake of the head toward her partner.

"There's a cell phone account in your name," he suggests to Aubrey, then turns deliberately to where a shoulder-bag slumps on the seat of a chair beside the table, its surface still crowned with last night's dirty dishes and several empty Miller bottles. "Can we see your phone?"

Shuffling her feet, and pulling the comforter tighter across her chest, Aubrey wonders what this could be about. There were those ring tones she downloaded for free, and plenty of bootlegged music, but those sites were right out in the open; it's not like she was doing anything there to rate an early-bird visit from the cops. Something about the atmosphere in the room is making her way more uneasy those petty crimes would merit.

"I'm pretty sure my bill's paid up," she jokes. "Hell, it's probably the only bill I'm not late on - and anyway it's not like you guys come and arrest people for a phone bill, is it? I mean..."

"Mr. Margulies' phone is evidence in a crime, Miss," the woman interrupts. "And the last call made with it was to your phone. We want to listen to that message. Are you OK with letting us do that? If not, we can take the phone as evidence and get a warrant to examine it."

"That'd take a lot more of your time," the plainclothes officer interjects. His tone is softer, sympatheticevn, and Aubrey discovers she wants to please him somehow. Like one of those distant relatives you don't really know until you meet them once at some holiday meal, and the fact that you're related means you have to find things to talk about so you make all the right noises and lo-and-behold, you actually find you've got something in common; go figure. "Plus," the cop continues, with what sounds like real concern, "you'd be without it for...could be quite a while."

With a twitch of one shoulder and a tilt of the head Aubrey admits defeat. "Inside pocket, with the zipper."

The woman moves and picks up the bag as the man waves a hand to suggest Aubrey have a seat on her own couch. Legs and arms tangled among the comforter she settles with a thud, then lolls her head back against the wall to watch as the woman flips the phone open, studies it for half a second, then quickly punches all the correct keys for speaker and voice mail. Impressed, Aubs listens as she hears first the canned voice telling them all that she has six unheard messages, then the playback. Message number one is a call from Mark about seeing a movie on Thursday; two is Lisa, asking if she can trade shifts on Friday. The next few are more of the same, typical and familiar, the little details of keeping her life afloat, and Aubrey finds herself making notes of who to call back and what to tell them when the sixth call begins, a less familiar voice.

"Hello, Aubrey?" Stevie announces, voice shifted a bit by the crappy speaker, but still recognizable from that night at the Social Club. The attitude of her greeting is buoyant, almost too upbeat. Like she's either putting on an act, or maybe had a bit too much to drink, which seems likely, given the amount of background noise coming through along with the words. "This is Stevie, and I was wondering…" There's a pause - a distraction maybe, or second thoughts, but then the voice returns. "Look," it says, more certain of itself. "I'm really worried about Rod. He left my place a few days ago. We had kind of a row about… Anyway, you know how he can be sometimes and I need to tell him that I'm sorry, and that I've made a decision and I'm really very happy about it. He helped me realize some things about myself, and, like I said, I'm really happy now with where I'm going, and I'd like for him to be happy too and… anyway, I was wondering if maybe he'd moved back in with you? Like I said, I'm really worried about him and…." but whatever else Stevie was going to say is lost as the automated voice intones "message duration exceeded," and the apartment goes quiet once again.

Reaching a hand out from beneath her comforter, Aubrey adjusts the folds to wrap more tightly around her throat. Shifts her weight to one side so she can pull her feet up underneath her on the sofa, as the uniformed officer settles on the other end and locks eyes with her.

"This person Rod," she asks. "Is he, in your opinion, dangerous?"

"*Dangerous*?" Aubrey snorts, the somber moment terminated by such an offbeat suggestion. The seated officer gives no reaction though, while the other one begins jotting in a small notebook he has pulled from among his pockets as she continues. "Rod is the last person in the world I'd call 'dangerous;' she's…" She looks from cop to cop and feels the amusement sucked out of her once again. Seizing on the woman, a sense of urgency impels her voice. "What's going on anyway? You said that was her 'last call.' You've never said what…"

"Approximately two-thirty this morning," the uniformed man interjects, "Stevie Margulies was assaulted."

"An especially brutal assault," adds the woman without emotion, her eyes still locked on Aubrey's, waiting to observe her reaction. The girl gives no satisfaction though, hiking the comforter a little closer, sniffing her nose to one side, so the officer continues. "She's at Hilltop Medical Center now. Intensive Care." Waits again, glances at the suited detective, his hand still poised above his notebook. "She's on life support, Miss Maturin, and we wondered what you could tell us about her. And now, about this guy Rod."

"Rod's not a guy," Aubrey blurts out quickly, then stops, mouth agape as the female cop issues a snort, so like her own. Something in that sound, and the smug smile which accompanies it, drives her eyes away from the uniform and the badge and the tightly-gathered ponytail, to wander in tighter and tighter circles until they discover a corner of the comforter where the seam has burst, exposing the stuffing inside. Distracted, she reaches out a hand to finger the brilliant white batting, its edge cut so square, so sharp, at exactly ninety-degrees. The newest, freshest, most perfect thing in the entire room.

"Not such a big surprise," the detective adds, in a tone of grave agreement. "This Stevie person is no woman."

"And closer to home…"

The voice from the clock-radio is thin and crackly with static. Half-asleep, Doug Taylor makes a mental note to replace the old thing with a newer model, one with digital tuning, so the cleaning lady who comes in every Wednesday won't have a dial to bump and mess up the station every time she dusts, but the mental post-it doesn't stick as he drifts back down in hope of a few more minutes of sleep. Those blissful extra minutes, when he knows he should be getting up and starting in on his day, but manages to squeeze just a little more peace out of the pillow. Three or four minutes, and yet somehow more precious than all the hours that went before.

"Seattle Police were called last night to an alley off Boren Avenue, where an anonymous caller reported finding an assault victim. The woman was rushed to Hilltop Medical Center where she is listed in very critical condition due to unspecified injuries. We'll have more details as they are available, but first, here's April with your forecast for the day…"

Downtown. Pike's Place Market. Broadway and Capitol Hill. The University District. Anne has seen them all. Been over to Belleview even, several times. The malls. Every morning she scans the paper and tries to imagine what Christina might find of interest among all the events going on around town, then climbs into her Accord and heads out. She's wandered through art openings at galleries and stood outside the doors of obscure clubs scanning the faces people going in.

It was so much easier when her daughter was at school, she recalls in her weaker moments. The little red Civic so handy to spot; Christina's schedule of classes more or less consistent after the first week of each semester. Even after the whole disaster, once Anne knew she was staying with Aubrey there was at least a connection. And when Aubrey started coming to visit, well, things were just fine there for a while. Checking in every week or two, Anne had been able to feel in touch, but this, this is just impossible; not knowing where your own daughter is living, how she is getting by. There has to be a way to find her.

Not surprisingly, those men at the hospital were no help at all. 'Confidential information,' they claimed, though she knows it's not that. Everybody talks about everything these days, just look at what they can find out about people on the news. Somebody gets into trouble and suddenly, there they are on the TV because she bought some Bufferin at a 7-Eleven store three weeks ago, and somehow the reporters have gotten their hands on the tape. An unhappy landowner claims a city councilman has a conflict of interest, and suddenly the newspapers seem to know the details of every business transaction he's made for the last fifteen years. They get the information somehow, so don't tell Anne it's all confidential. No, the truth is, those men just don't take her seriously. 'Little old lady,' they think, and that's as far as it goes. All the rules about how you are supposed to treat everybody equally these days, the one person you can still ignore is a mother trying to keep an eye on her daughter.

"The court ruled your daughter competent to make her own decisions," that Mr. Taylor said. "Therefore we cannot release any information we might have about her treatment without her consent. Written consent, Mrs. McKloskey, not your word that she'd want us to tell you."

"You don't have to give me her address or anything," Anne suggested with a wink. "Just a general idea of where she is. I know there was some sort of an arrangement for the hospital to keep providing her the medications that she needs, so surely you can tell me how she's been getting them?" But it was no good. You'd think from the cut of his suit that he was a gentleman, but when it came down to it that Mr. Taylor was no better than any of them, all hiding behind their tall counters and the plastic name cards hanging around their necks.

Not to worry, though. Sean McKloskey's wife is nothing if not persistent, and she'd know her daughter's face anywhere, so this morning, as so many mornings before, she is going to fold herself into her car and make her way around to the all places she thinks Christina might be found. Looking, looking, always looking.

"Breaking news," a young woman announces, with unconcealed enthusiasm, though in the next instant her toothy smile disappears, replaced by an expression of the most sincere concern, with just a twinkle of amusement visible beneath long dark lashes and brows which arch like souvenirs of St. Louis. Behind the newswoman, a larger than life video image erupts; a police cruiser with roof-bar pulsing in the half-light of early morning as a variety of uniformed and non-uniformed personnel mill about a crime scene roped off with yellow tape and wooden barriers.

"Returning to our earlier report of a transvestite prostitute brutally assaulted near downtown, sources tell CONSTANT NEWS that the victim of last night's attack in the Regrade has been identified as Stephen F. Margulies, one of several Tacoma-based entrepreneurs who founded Decent Technologies, an early innovator in point-of-sale and retail end-user application software." Shuffling the papers on the desk before her, the anchor gives a little toss of her head and a flicker of her eyes toward someone on her left before continuing, in a tone that makes clear she is only now getting to the good part. "Decent Technologies was in the news three years ago when it was purchased by Microsoft for an eight-figure price. Since that time, CONSTANT NEWS has learned, Margulies has apparently been living here in Seattle, *as a woman,* 'Stevie' Margulies, who has been a quiet supporter of gay and lesbian organizations, as well as the Seattle Symphony and other musical organizations around the Pacific Northwest."

During this last, the display image changes, the crime scene giving way to a stock shot of one of the buildings at Hilltop Medical Center, where a deeply overhanging roof shelters extra-wide sliding glass doors bearing an 'H' shaped logo and a red letter 'E' nearly as tall as the doors themselves.

"Margulies was taken to Hilltop Medical Center's Level One Trauma unit where his condition is currently unknown."

At this point the graphic display behind her changes once again. Quick clips of war, disaster and nature's fury jump and flash against a blue and red background which seems to shrink away from the viewer until the final photo flares out and the colors are revealed to be those of the show's logo, telescoping in as if from some alternate universe till it proudly fills the screen as the anchor's expression morphs once again, this time to one of eager anticipation, as she continues.

"To learn more about this horrific assault and the bizarre story emerging about its victim, stay with us right here on CONSTANT NEWS; your source for reporting that goes beyond the headlines and beyond the facts, to get you," – the rhythm of her words breaks, just enough to allow a slight conspiratorial nod of that beautiful, hair-encased head – "the story *beneath* the story."

Jeena stands in the doorway of her kitchen, a purple-terry robe falling open over shabby flannel pajamas, cereal bowl in one hand, spoon stopped short of her open mouth as a commercial swells to fill the screen opposite. What is normally a mildly aggravating diversion while eating a quick breakfast has become, today, a personal shock. Despite the lack of a photo, there is no doubt in her mind that this Stevie must be the same girl she knows from group.

They've all heard stories, of course, about t-girls who get careless, letting some guy believe for too long before explaining their origins, and paying the price in blood. And yeah, there are girls who use their bodies for income; what else to do if who you are makes you unemployable and there's rent to be paid, clothes to be bought, therapists and treatments to be paid for? *And* no shortage of men intrigued by the prospect, or just too blind-set on a piece of ass to care that it's a product of remodelling. But Stevie? Straight-laced, zipped-up Stevie who was like a kind old aunt to everyone – Stevie, out turning tricks just days after she was crying about how she'd mishandled things with that t-boy? No way. Jeena knows next to nothing about this 'assault,' but she knows in her heart – the one organ she trusts at this stage of life – that whatever happened out there in the darkness, the fact there was a penis under a dress is enough for most of the public to write the victim off and say she deserved whatever she got.

Through two and a half commercials Jeena stares, her vivid imagination running in a whole host of directions, adrenaline and other potions coursing around her brain like some mad scientist's late night concoction. It is only when the CONSTANT NEWS logo begins forming once again that she sets her unfinished cereal on the coffee table and digs her phone out of the purse she tossed there last night. Thumbing a speed-dial, she's already into the bedroom and pawing through a pile of unfolded laundry by the time she hears Genda pick up.

"Have you seen the news?" Jeena snaps without introduction. As much as these two are on the phone to one another, there's little need for ritual, and yes, it turns out, Genda has seen the same story on another channel. On several of them in fact; apparently it's a slow morning for traffic accidents and mudslides. "We've got to do something," Jeena cuts in, pulling a bra from the pile and flailing it about to untangle the straps, as she feels herself begin to tremble with the realization of what her friend Stevie must have gone through, barely hours after they saw her at group - is *still* going through, even as they talk and walk and breathe. The girl's fate could just as well be hers. Or Genda's, or Herb, Amy, Les, Patricia – any of the dozens Jeena has met over the years of trying to figure herself out. Any one of those bruised souls cursed and blessed by having non-standard equipment in a standard-issue world; searching for a way to fit their round-peg selves into the square holes the world seems to prefer.

"We've got to do something, Genda," she says, as she feels her legs go weak and suddenly finds herself sitting on the pile of clothes, "or else they're gonna' make it out like this whole thing is her own goddamned fault. Like she's just one more sicko-pervert-tranny-queer who got what she deserved. Like we all are," she continues, no longer even hearing Genda's attempts to calm her down. "Like we all deserve to be beaten to a pulp and dumped in some back alley…."

"I mean, it just seems..." Aubrey pauses, finding herself at a loss for words, which gives Mrs. M. the opportunity she has been waiting for.

"You feel responsible?" she suggests, though with that gentle air of amusement which seems sometimes to allow her to speak her mind without giving offense. "That somehow this happened because you and Christina had a fight, and so it's your fault that this Stevie person was hurt?"

The line is quiet as Aubrey considers, oblivious to the intrusion of passing traffic into her bedroom: drone of a truck climbing the ramp to Aurora, wet shoos-ing of a car turning through the virtual pond which lingers in the corner gutter just down from her place. The cold gray morning barely glows the window shade but she hasn't even managed to turn on another lamp since the cops left. This is the only thing she could think to do: to call Mrs. M. and see if by some strange chance she had any idea where Kim – no, Rod – no, *Christina*, damn it; it always had to be Christina when you talked to Mrs. M. – might be. As much as she knows Rod wants to avoid the old bird, there's something about Anne and her total commitment to what she believes, that makes Aubs think the woman might be able to find him, if anyone can. And, on top of that, there is something comforting in hearing her voice. Like the grandmothers Aubrey never knew but other girls told her about: older, wiser and able to see past a young woman's troubles. 'The voice of experience,' and yes, the old bird is right: at this moment Aubrey *is* feeling like somehow she screwed up, even though all she ever wanted was to be Kim's friend. Her best, best, best, best friend. And, oh yeah; quite a bit more than a friend, she has to admit, though only to herself, and only in the instant before Mrs. M. offers her own prescription.

"When my Sean was taken from me so suddenly - there was no warning, you know, we had spoken on the phone only a few hours earlier. We spoke as often as we could when he was travelling, although it wasn't as easy in those days. There were no cell phones, e-mail; none of those things you people take for granted nowadays. He'd place a call through a hotel operator, and he might have to wait forever for the call to be put through, especially from some of the places he visited. Oh goodness, Sean went everywhere. Europe, South America. Jerusalem, India, Japan. He'd be gone for weeks sometimes, and all I had was letters and phone calls. We talked that morning; it was quite a long call and everything was just as it should be, and then a few hours later I got another phone call from a very polite man in Manila." The flow of Anne's words halts for just a moment, and her voice when it resumes is so buoyant, so full of good cheer, that Aubrey has the odd sensation she is about to hear a punch line. "He was so polite, the way he put it, although his English wasn't at all good. He said, 'Missus, I am considered to tell you...' I remember that exactly, 'I am considered to tell you,' and suddenly my whole world came crashing down."

There's another pause, and Aubrey wonders whether she's supposed to laugh at the joke, or say something to comfort the old woman. One of those smart, caring things she hears people say in movies, except the things that come to her mind all sound stupid and pointless, like 'holy shit, that sucks.' Fortunately, Mrs. M. is not finished.

"But the thing was, you see, my Sean had been away so much, that after a little while it began to seem as if nothing had really changed. As if, at any minute the phone could ring again, and it would be him, telling me it had all been a mistake and...well, I don't know if I should be telling you this, especially right now, when you've had a bit of a shock yourself, but I really do feel that he is out there somewhere. He's not gone, he's just...traveling. In different circles, I mean. And one day he'll come home to me, or I'll fly off somewhere to meet him; and that's why, when Christina ran away to be on her own - or even when she got sick and couldn't speak to me for all that time, or now that she's pretending to be this Rodney person - I don't get upset. It's all the same, don't you see? People are each their own persons, travelling around and around and around; and sometimes we're together, but most of the time we're going our own ways and yet we're never really alone because we know the ones we love are out there, and that's how we get through it all, my dear. Knowing that the ones we love are never really gone, just out there somewhere, and they will be calling us again. Like you called me now, which is really very nice you know, that you would think to call me...."

More than once Aubrey has the impulse to interrupt this flood of words, to remind Mrs. M. of the reason she called - that the person she suspects Rod had been staying with was beaten up and is maybe about to die. That the cops have called twice more since they left, reminding her to contact them immediately if she hears from Rod and implying - as much as they avoid a straight answer when asked - that they think he might have had something to do with the assault.

The words hang in her mouth though, stillborn by her picturing that white haired woman's face, smiling so sweetly as she talks. Aubs imagines her in a spacious bedroom with matching furniture, sitting up against a satin-padded headboard with a perfect little night lamp turned on. She'd be wearing a 'nightie,' the girl imagines, flannel, with a bit of lace trim and a prissy satin ribbon to tie it closed around her neck. Jesus, she can just imagine the whole scene and Mrs. M. smiling as sweetly into the shadows around her as when they'd sit for tea in her living room in that house with the plants all drying up and the outside paint peeling off, and she just doesn't have the heart. At this hour, on this day, she just doesn't have the heart to remind an old lady that people really do die, that sooner or later they really do go away for forever and you never see them again, like Aubrey has never seen the man who's supposed to be her fucking father (but how can you be a fucking father in the first place if you were never there?) and that's what it must have meant to Christina when her father died, and that's what it might have meant when the cops came to her apartment and told her that Stevie could be dying any minute, and the last thing she wants to do is to make Mrs. M. feel the way *she* is feeling right now, so she makes a conscious choice and she lies like the dog she is, despite Stevie being epically fucked-up and Kim out who-knows-where.

"I get what you mean, Anne," she says, realizing as she does so, that it's the first time she's ever addressed the old gal by that name. Like this is the first time it's ever been the two of them as friends, rather than her and her girlfriend's mother, which is so totally different. "I didn't know Stevie very well, but it sounds like she was a good person, so I know she's…it will be OK, I guess, is what I know. Some way, it will be OK."

"That's right, dear," Mrs. M. responds, and from the certain joy in the woman's voice, Aubrey is assured that she has said the right words. "That's exactly right. And Christina is all right too; you'll see. I will get in my car and I'll go looking, and sooner than you can imagine, I bet I'll find her; just sitting on a park bench somewhere, and then we can go see your policemen and get this business straightened out and then we can all have tea together, and won't *that* be nice?"

"Hello?" The voice over the phone line is tentative, like one roused out of a deep sleep, or interrupted in even deeper thought. The thin timber suggests youth, or that the person producing it is small, perhaps even tiny.

"Herb," Genda prompts. Very gently, very patiently. "Herb Bunting?"

"Who's asking?" she hears back, that almost frail voice filling with a wary defensiveness, as if accustomed to unpleasant outcomes from unexpected phone calls.

"It's me, Herb. Genda from Group."

"Oh yeah," He's recognized the name now, put it together with the voice and the group so he knows it's not a threat, and with that returns his confidence, the breathing from the diaphragm and speaking from the chest; all the things Jeanine taught herself to do when she became Herb. "What can I do for you?"

"I'm afraid I have some bad new. Stevie was attacked last night..."

"Oh no," Herb interrupts, pitch rising once again as vocal lessons are forgotten. "No, no..." he erupts, in a flood of denial prompted by his certain understanding, even before the details come out, that an attack on Stevie is likely to have only one cause and that the outcome is certain to be ugly.

Genda is good at this though; she's played den-mother before, and within a couple of minutes she's turned Herb's sadness and anger into desire for action. It's he who tells her about a neighbor of Stevie's named Alice, a big-hearted southern gal who has an emergency key to her condo. In minutes Herb is on his way to pick up Jeena and head over to the condo, where they somehow convince Alice to let them in for long enough to search around and find an old address book, neglected by the police when they impounded all of Stevie's computers to scour them for evidence. Half an hour later they're both back at Genda's place using their cell phones to make their way through Stevie's book, as Genda uses the land line to work the names from her own list of contacts.

"I know you don't want to make a splash," Genda agrees with one of the first she catches, turning over in her mind's eye the image she remembers of Edna, an elderly woman with thinning hair and very tired eyes. Recently married, if she recalls correctly, to a retired military man, which hardly seemed a good match when she announced it, but she said the fellow was OK with her past, though he never chose to come to group with her. Understandable, then, that she doesn't want to be part of what they're planning, but still, Genda presses on. Something has to happen to make clear that Stevie is not as alone as the things they've been hearing from the media suggest. "Maybe it's not going to change what they put on the news or anything, but at least we'll know we didn't just forget about her. Let her disappear without … something."

"Yeah, this is Judy," answers another name pulled from Stevie's book, after a run of 'no longer in service' and numbers apparently so old they've been reassigned, leading to confused conversations with people who say they don't know why Herb is calling them. "What can I do for you?"
"I'm afraid I've got some bad news. About Stevie Margulies…"

"Hi. This is Elise," announces a machine on her next attempt. "Always has been, always will be, despite what anyone might tell you. Life is good, so leave a message and if it's nice I'll call you back."
With a machine Jeena doesn't want to say too much, just 'a friend of Stevie's, please call as soon as you can.' Tries to hide her emotions too; take all the suggestion out of what she says and how she says it. Not even to hint at tragedy until she's got an actual person on the line in real time and even then to deliver the news gently, and soften it by listening and commiserating. Every time she leaves one of those empty messages though, it feels like she's somehow erasing Stevie - denying what's happened and how it makes her feel, which in turn leaves her feeling like a traitor.

"Jesus," says Claudine, an acquaintance from a QueerPac fundraiser several years ago, when Genda reaches her, farther down the list. "I saw her last night at the Hive and she was just fine. Except maybe…she seemed to be working really hard at being…well, I mean she was saying how happy she was, but you could feel there was something she wasn't talking about. Real excited about the future though; telling everybody she had an appointment with Doctor Maggie. She's pretty good, you know, but I went to Dr. Carstairs in Minneapolis because he …Oh, you don't want to hear about that right now, do you?"

Claudine pauses, the line quiet for long seconds, and Genda is just about to thank her, end the call and extend the search in some other direction, when she speaks again.

"She was asking for trouble, if you ask me. Making herself too visible, you know what I mean? People like us, we've got to keep a low profile. It's just... it's safer that way. So uh, no. I don't think it's a good idea for us to go make a big scene right now..."

Another phone call, by Herb this time, ringing a listing for someone named Annika, who turns out to be a dermatologist with a private practice where Stevie visited once to consult on a skin growth and ended up managing the network of laptops and bookkeeping stations for next to nothing in fees.

"I was afraid something like this would happen," Annika admits, after she's heard the basics. "I warned her to be more careful, but she was so proud of who she had become. So glad to be out of hiding," she finishes up, then adds, as almost an afterthought. "Is anybody with her? Has she got any, you know, any family?"

"None that she kept much contact with, as far as I can tell," Herb explains. "We all knew she used to be married, but it doesn't seem like she had much to do with any of her relations, if you know what I mean...."

"Yeah," Annika interrupts, not anxious to hear any more. "I can imagine."

"Some of the folks are going to set up a vigil, at the hospital, you know? Where they've got her?" Herb continues. "Just to be there. We don't know that we'll get in to see her or anything, but at least we can be close by and...I don't know. Maybe somehow she'll sense that we're there. And we can put a face on the story, for the rest of the world. So she's...at least she's not just...you know..."

"Yes," Dr. Annika says. "I do know."

Genda's up to the Gs now. Sunshine "Sunny" Gershorn, with two phone numbers noted as old, and a question mark in front of the third. Clearly someone who moves around a lot.

"Genda? You one of the guys from that 'Transitions' group?"

"Girl, actually,"

"Oh, sorry. Yeah, I think I heard Stevie mention your name, a while back. What's up?"

"In his address book, hunh? All that 'high-tech' talk and he still uses an address book?" This from one 'Scoobie' Reynolds, whose name is written in a hand which, while distinct and large enough to fill out its line, seems hurriedly scrawled; not cared-for like many of the other entries. By this point in the alphabet, Herb can make a pretty good guess about the people just by how they are written. The least legible names, all in blue or black ink and a messy hand, are the older ones, from when Stevie was Stephen. The ones in an Easter basket of different color inks and pencil, scribed with obvious care in a hand grown smaller and more precise, but with an abundance of erasures and cross-outs - those seem to be the more-recent entries, from after Stephen became Stevie, and those are the ones that include people from group. The reactions don't break down that simply though; both old and new acquaintances seem to contain a proportion of people who are devastated to hear that something so horrible has happened to their friend, and a nearly equal number whose reaction is some variation on a deep sigh; followed by a resigned thought along the lines of 'I told him (or her) so.'

"Well, yeah," Scoobie says, and Herb notes with pleasure that there's none of the tentative hemming and hawing he gets when someone hears his name and his voice and stumbles, wondering if he's a man or a woman. He's passing just fine with this dude, who's giving all the auditory signals of being a total 'man's man.' "We were friends, yeah. But it was kind of a long time ago. Before he... you know, all that jazz. So we haven't really been in touch for a while. You know how that is, right?"

Yeah, Herb admits. He knows how tempting it is to avoid those who stand out in the wrong ways. He's felt it himself actually, now that he's able to pass pretty much all the time; that reflexive urge to stay away from people who don't pass yet - if they ever will. Whose differences make being with them a constant risk of his own history coming into question. For Herb though, it is a point of honor not to succumb to that desire for correctness. He resolved long ago, that no matter how well he himself may pass, he would never use that as an excuse to abandon those who cannot, or *do* not.

"If he asked you to call me, it won't work," says Susan Margulies, one of several listings with that surname. "I've made it abundantly clear I'm not interested in talking to him until he comes to his senses."

"No," Jeena interjects, before the woman can go on any

further. Between the name, the achingly familiar timbre of her voice, and the clear open-wound of her reaction, she figures this must be a sister, and so proceeds with extra care. "Stevie didn't ask me to call. I'm going through her old address book," and right about there, she hears a quick intake of breath from Susan. Jeena pauses a moment, thinking Stevie's sibling has realized something bad is coming, and it might be kind to give her a moment to prepare herself, but breathing room is not what this woman needs.

"Well, whatever happened to him," she points out, in a tone that says she will brook no disagreement, "he made it clear years ago he didn't care how much he hurt any of *us*, so I guess the feeling is mutual." A clacking 'thunk,' and the line goes dead; the righteous voice of Stevie's sister replaced by the electronic drone of an anonymous switching station somewhere between here and there.

By the time of that call, Jeena and Herb's determination is waning. Genda, on the other hand, is only more incensed, when she considers what they've all been running into. "Enough of calling the people who knew Stevie," she says. The people who should care, but half the time don't even want to be identified with her. It's time to cast the net a little wider. The Gay Alliance maybe, and the Sapho Society. Folks who've been on the outside themselves, and might be willing to stand up for a fellow outsider. And surely there must be some sort of community group for the neighborhood where she was hurt; people who'd want to cast some light on the crime itself; because after all, if someone is out there taking advantage of Stevie, couldn't it be any one of them that gets hit the next time? Some elderly woman maybe, or a teenager, or a little kid? "It's not just our problem, you know? If it's not safe to be on the street after dark, that's *everybody's* problem. Or at least it should be."

The more she talks about it, the more they all like the idea. There are lots of people out there, Herb agrees, who know what it is to take a public stand on something they believe. Surely some of them will believe that Stevie's right to be Stevie is worth standing up for, and if they get the word out as widely as they can, that should be enough to make some kind of a showing. To make it at least *look* like the world cares what happens to a good and gentle person, no matter what pronoun she wants them to attach to her.

Putting down the phone, Herb wakes up his own laptop and begins searching. In seconds he has a neighborhood merchant's association phone number for Jeena to call, then a website he'll contact himself and a blogger's address for Genda to follow up, and after those, another, and another, and another. Facebook and Twitter follow, and there's an immediate response when Herb connects with a software chat room where Stevie was apparently quite a regular, and soon there are almost as many messages coming in as going out. It's hours after noon when finally the trio break for something to eat, but the ball is rolling. Connections made, and promises, too, that e-mails will be blasted and blog-posts published.

"The guy was dressed as a woman, for crying out loud," an over-nourished man in a brown suit and rep tie exclaims. Regular viewers know him as Dan Allard, sometimes called 'The Conscience of the Country' (though that is mostly in his own press releases). Frown lines run deep across his forehead as a hand slaps down on the surface before him to emphasize the depth of his conviction. "He deserves whatever he gets, running around in public like that..."

Even as he speaks those words the camera pulls back, allowing the shot to include another commentator sitting beside him.

"All right," Livie Thornton concedes, though her head is shaking in denial, her own hand rising up as if searching for someone to slap. "You've got a guy in a dress, apparently making some kind of advances – *maybe* commercial, but maybe not..."

"Innocent until proven guilty?" another voice interjects sarcastically, as the camera angle switches to catch Judy Babbett's heavy-lidded look of disdain.

"Yes, actually," Thornton shoots back before continuing, as the camera intersperses quick shots of several other panel members, gathered round the table in obvious enjoyment of the argument they are witnessing. "Even admitting he was wearing a dress..."

"In public," Allard reminds the entire group. "Where anyone could be exposed to his fetish – women. Children. Mothers."

"Pregnant mothers," Babbettt adds darkly.

"Does a pregnant woman actually count as a mother yet?" jokes Tony DaVilla, the third man at the table, who has yet to get a foothold in the discussion.

"How many children are out on a dark street at three in the morning, Dan?" Thornton asks, pointedly ignoring DaVilla's attempt to lighten things up. "How many..."

Before she can continue she's interrupted again, as the camera settles on a bright-eyed fellow in a bow-tie, his blazer a shade of bluish gray that catches the studio lights more than most, his pocket handkerchief striped with red, white, and blue to match the flag pin on his lapel.

"It's not just the dress, Olivia," Will Brown points out with satisfaction. "This guy was wearing," and here he lifts a piece of paper to make it clear he is reading someone else's words; words apparently so foreign to his tongue that he has difficulty pronouncing them. "A turquoise silk dress with...'pencil' skirt...'scoop' neck...and...'renaissance' sleeves...and matching...high-heeled strapless sandals. I mean, is that what our public life has come to; middle-aged men in strapless sandals?"

In an instant the entire table is alive, the men and women shouting their opinions over one another as the camera moves in on the woman seated in their center. Judy Babbett gives the camera a wink and a wry twist of her mouth.

"Time for a commercial break," she offers, eyeing the uproar proudly, as an image appears on the screen behind her: a daylight shot of several awkward-looking figures standing on a concrete plaza beside a bank of glass doors set in a substantial stone façade. Heads bowed against a slight drizzle, the figures hold sheets of poster board before them, their legends obscured by the super-imposed headline: 'RADICAL FRINGE SUPPORTS MIDNIGHT STREET-WALKER.'

"We'll be right back ,though, with more on what this breaking story says about the decline of our community's values. This is *Judy Babbett and The Truth Table*, where we're not afraid to tell you the truth behind the so-called facts." At the table around her, the argument roils as music swells and the image fades to one of an ambulance pulling to a stop, lights flashing and doors opening, over which multi-colored text seems to fly in from off-screen. 'ASSAULT IN DARK OF NIGHT,' the letters spell out, streaming in from one side as a loaded stretcher is unfolded out the back of the ambulance and wheeled toward glass doors which slide apart to admit it, the title now swelling and fading, to be replaced by another. 'JUST ANOTHER CRIME, OR JUST DESSERTS?' asks the final line of text, lingering several seconds as the ambulance lights pulse, before the entire image dissolves, its place taken by the distraught face of a housewife staring at a streak of grape juice across her fluffy white carpet.

Turning away from the TV, Doug Taylor picks up the phone and punches a number from memory, scowling deeply as he waits for the call to be picked up. Scanning the news stations has only reinforced the impression that this thing is growing legs of its own; legs which will do nothing good for the institution he is supposed to be managing.

"It's Doug," he says curtly when the call goes through. "I'm seeing our PR problem all over the TV, and I'd like to know what the bloody hell is going on." The few seconds which follow do nothing for his expression, which only grows tighter as he answers back, "and how the hell could they get that organized so quickly? It's barely been a day." Whatever the answer to his question, its effect is to take some wind out of his sails. "Well, make sure security sets up a rope line and keeps them out of the way," he responds in measured tones as one hand grabs a silver pen off the desk and begins clicking it repeatedly, something like resignation creeping into his face and voice. "No one's quite sure *where* Bill is; in the air somewhere. I've already e-mailed, text-messaged and left VMs in Atlanta, San Diego *and* Phoenix, but till I hear back, we're on our own. And for God's sake don't let them inside. At least we've got the right to keep them out of our buildings."

Setting the handset into its base, Taylor picks up the remote, then thinks better of it. Dropping the device onto the credenza behind him he gathers up a stack of papers from the desk's surface, shuffles their edges into line and slips them into a drawer before folding his laptop shut. Grabbing his suit coat from its place on the arm of a leather sofa he is still pulling it on as he heads out the door.

"ADL / Support VESSSEL #2," read the label to which Jason led Mary ,his hand warm and slightly sweaty on her forearm, days before most of the world had even heard of Stevie Margulies. The characters were scribbled in permanent marker, and gave the impression that the person who made them was thinking of larger issues than labeling. That, in Jason's quick summary, suggested they dated from when the object was still in use, as compared to the compulsively careful categorizing that happens when surplus items are being archived. The rest of the markings on this particular object were similarly loose and to the point.   Next to a large toggle switch was scrawled, in red: "DO NOT SHUT OFF WITHOUT WRITTEN DIRECTIVE," followed by three exclamation points, a poorly rendered skull and crossbones, and a smaller remark, in blue; "UNDER PAIN OF FLOGGING." Seeing that, Mary found herself wondering who, among all the interns, techs. and even residents she has known, would have had the temerity to add that particular grace note in a recognizable hand.

　　"It's so...g-roovy," Jason quipped, and as usual his irreverence brought a smile to her heart. Indeed the object had the look of something out of first-generation TV sci-fi: a stainless steel cylinder, tapered like a high-tech conga drum - but with several small access plates screwed into its sides, and a plexiglass-dome-top sitting slightly askew - cradled in some very impressive rubbery-looking mountings; vibration isolators, he suggested as he studied them. A manifold of plastic tubing jutted out from one side, each tube with its own adjustable valve mounted just before it disappeared into the vessel's side. The base of the thing was a gray steel box, almost three feet square and two high, from which projected a variety of pipe fittings and other connectors.

　　"Whatever this was, it took a ton of electronics," he continued, stepping aside so she could move around to where the neighboring crate cast deep shadows. Held off the drum by metal brackets was a panel arrayed with computer connections - the kind of rectangular plastic pieces that receive a plug with twenty or thirty tiny electrical conductors down each side - only here, there were dozens of those plugs, and from the back of the array, what must have been several-hundred very fine wires looping out in carefully-choreographed sweeps to a series of grommets just below the top of the cylinder, through which they disappeared inside it. "This is, like, enough connectivity to monitor a whole city," Jase muttered, lifting the dome to reach inside and pull up one bundle of wires from where it draped into the unseen interior. That remark was followed by a soft "whoa," as the ends of the wires came into sight, each one a slightly different length, each bearing a tiny, numbered, stainless tag, and each one terminating in a shiny needle so fine they caught the light like fresh-cut hairs, gleaming silver against the shadowy darkness beyond.

The rim of the vessel was above her eye-level, but even so, Mary found she had a clear picture of what must be inside it – a stainless mesh grid, hand-moldable to the contours of the precious object which was to rest on it, probably cushioned with a layer of silicone-gel padding to ensure an even distribution of pressure, though at around three pounds, there wouldn't have been a lot of pressure to deal with. This was it, then: the grail of Jessica Bagley's waking dream, David Resor's intended contribution to the body of science - and the science of body repair – and Dr. Rodney Gimbal's final resting place before he became someone else entirely.

Well, not quite *entirely*.

Gazing down from the skybridge between Hilltop buildings 6 and 9, Doug Taylor studies the knots of people scattered across the red-and gray granite of Hilltop's formal entry plaza. Above them a banner sways from ropes strung between a light pole and an equally spindly street-tree.

'END ANTI-GLBT VIOLENCE,' its purple letters read, hurriedly brushed onto what may recently have been a couple of bed sheets. Twenty-two people - Taylor knows, because he has counted every one of them - stand stiffly beneath it, hands clasping poster-board signs or thrust into jacket pockets against the morning's light rain. Five more mill about with stacks of paper in their hands, pressing flyers on anyone unwary or unwise enough to pass close by. At least three other groups are visible as well, flanking each side of the wide plaza separating the building from Broadway, and holding up signs of their own. Even as he watches, a car pulls up to the curb, disgorging two black-clad persons who rush up to the main group and burst into rapid conversation punctuated by hands flailing and hugs all around. As the car pulls away, a bulky white van sweeps into its place, satellite dish perched on its roof, a local TV station's logo slashed diagonally across its side.

"Think of it as free advertising," Bob Baker suggests casually, as he arrives by Taylor's side.

Twisting his head just enough to meet the public relations man's eyes, Taylor takes his time sizing up the remark. "Just the demographic we want to reach with all our campaigns," he offers after assuring himself of the other's facetiousness. "The un-tapped revenue potential of welfare queers and pre-ops."

For a few moments the two observe the scene outside their window. In the foreground a new cluster coalesces, their movements, from this vertical angle, like pieces on a game-board. Three black umbrellas arrive from different directions, confer, then scatter, only to return leading strings of smaller figures, obediently trailing in slickers and rain boots. As if directed by a single mind they form up into a line with their backs against a concrete planter-wall, directly opposite and parallel to the large banner, whose attendants seem to be closely-watching this new development. From one end of the line a figure splits off and moves to the center of the space between the two factions; a sturdy man in long overcoat, his hand flashes bright as he doffs his hat, then kneels to face his battery of followers. As if upon a signal, the entire line kneels to the ground and bows their heads.

"Takes two sides to make a game," Baker offers grimly. "And it looks like the away-team has just arrived."

"Oh yeah," Taylor remarks offhandedly, as if the thought has only now occurred to him, though it has actually been at the forefront of his mind for some time. "Security got a call from some detective working the hooker's case."

Baker answers with a grunt as the two men pull away from the window, striding side-by-side toward Bldg. 6, nodding now and then to acknowledge the crisp greetings of various staff, all visibly hurrying as soon as they notice the presence of these two pillars of the hierarchy. Just inside the building the two separate momentarily to give way to a passing wheelchair, then weave easily back together.

"Cop wanted background on one of our doctors; seems his name came up in their investigations."

Several steps farther down the corridor, when Taylor has not elaborated further, Baker steers him into an alcove and stops. "OK," he says, quite softly, as a pair of nurses pass out of earshot. "I'll bite. Which of our doctors?"

Taylor does not meet his subordinate's eye, but gives a furtive glance toward the floor, as if Baker's footwear has suddenly become quite interesting. "Gimbal," he answers softly, and only then does he look directly into his PR man's face. "Doctor Rodney Gimbal."

"Shit," Baker mutters, the word expelled between teeth nearly clenched, the syllable more exploded than pronounced. For a moment the two are motionless, each examining the other's eyes. Then, with a shrug, Taylor turns and walks away, disappearing quickly among the flow of white coats and blue scrubs, leaving Baker to consider this newest revelation in silence – but for the bustling hum of conversation, creaking wheels and barely intelligible PA system announcements.

Sean McKloskey is dressing, taking his garments one at a time from the rosewood stand. Slacks perfectly creased, the satin stripe down each leg flashing glimmers of his dressing mirror lights as he pulls them on, one leg at a time. Anne watches as if from above, her perspective changing, circling so that she sees him first from one side, then the other, back then front. A hand disappears into a sleeve of his starched white shirt, then pops out the cuff, bending up to grab the lapel as the other hand reaches back and finds an opening to stretch into its own sleeve. With practiced motions he gathers studs from a velvet-covered jeweler's box and pins the shirt-front together, its pleats as straight and parallel as the strings on a harp – or a bass, a cello, viola or violin; any instrument will do.

She has always loved to watch her husband dressing for performance. There is a ritual aspect to how he goes about it, always showering beforehand, so he will be completely awake; the performance effectively the start of a new day, divorced from all that has gone on before it. Drying his hair with an extra towel and combing it straight back from his forehead – a lovely forehead, she muses. High and smooth, it catches the light, such a contrast to the inky black of his hair which still - as he prepares for this December thirty-first gala at Benaroya Hall with the astonishing young alto from Israel - has not yet shown its first streak of gray. Anne's own hair is already going, if she let it show, but Sean's… 'Well,' she thinks, as he inserts a pair of square onyx links through his cuffs and sits on the edge of a chair to slip his feet into black dress pumps, 'he *is* younger by two years; we've always known that. For all we know, he may even outlive me.'

She's sliding away from him now, out of the line of sight as his attention turns to the mirror. Taking up a brush, he begins to smooth his hair with slow rhythmic strokes, over and over again as she finds herself first at the door and then outside it, looking in, her view diminished by the aperture, then growing smaller and smaller; cut off as the wall seems to shift and slide, blocking one shoulder, his back, then most of him, until all she can see is the rosewood dressing stand empty and silent with a wet towel crumpled beside it, and there, leading up to the crumpled fabric, a line of footprints, their wetness darkening the crimson carpet to blood red as the light fades down and down, red turning to brown and brown turning to black until there is nothing left to see and then, with a start, she is awake.

Robin Andrew

The bedroom is still dark, this second day after Aubrey alerted her, the curtains admitting only the faintest sunrise glow, and the lime-green letters of her bedside clock agree it is still early, but Anne is fully-alert and keenly aware there is something she must do. Unsure what it might be, her mind wanders for several moments. The dream of Sean has left her warm and contented – they always do – but with a tender longing. Something else is calling her, something familiar and comforting, and then it comes to her - Christina. *Today* may be the day she finds Christina. Her daughter is out there somewhere, in this town, in this same darkness that surrounds her house - their house – and that, she realizes as the sleep clears from her head, is why she had to leave her Sean just now. He's busy, he has a concert to perform, and she is busy too; she has to find Christina.

Satisfied, she stretches out a hand and switches on the bedside lamp. Stepping into its pool of light a smile comes to her pale mouth. Yes, she is thinking as she pads across to the bathroom, this is the day I will find my daughter. This is the day.

Swinging the nose of his Escalade into the entrance of Lot 7A, Bill Seivers cannot help but notice how full the nearby sidewalks seem. Pulling into a space marked 'Visitor,' the Chairman of Medical Holdings LLC does not immediately leave his car, but cracks the window an inch to avoid fogging as he listens to several messages on the hands-free and returns two calls, his conversations far more abrupt than the subjects deserve. Still calm and effective, of course - Three-Dollar-Bill is not the man to let emotion affect his interactions - but since receiving Doug Taylor's text, he's had a hard time focusing on any issue other than this Seattle thing, which is why he was on a flight out of San Diego barely an hour after touching-down there. When finally he steps out of the car, gathering-up briefcase and overcoat, his manner is carefully neutral - until he notices several new signs, stapled to the tops of thin wooden slats held high among the crowd.   Unlike the hand-made slogans which showed up in the first 36 hours or so, these are professionally printed, with well-chosen typography, easily legible from a distance - or on a video playback. 'VIGIL FOR STEVIE' they read, in crimson letters across a pink and purple logo.   His expression sours even further as he watches a technician in a blue rain jacket scoot crisply into place, camera perched on his shoulder and outstretched hand flashing a thumbs-up to a stylish young reporter sidling up next to one sign-bearer to thrust a microphone in her face.

Seivers watches with growing concern as his steps skirt the fringe of the scene. The reporter has been interviewing the woman for a minute or so before her attention is abruptly pulled away by a loud electronic screech from the far side of the plaza, where another twenty or so men and women have arrayed themselves in ranks, with children of all sizes in front, beside, or in their arms. Protesters, TV crew, and Seivers turn in unison as a young man in blazer and sharply-pressed slacks steps forward of the line, raising a bullhorn to his mouth and his free hand high into the air, pointer finger aimed heavenward.

"Cleanse our community," the fresh-faced youth intones, each beat emphasized with a thrust of his pointer-finger toward heaven. He is immediately answered by his companions, chanting in response, *"Cleanse our community!"*

"Wash away the filth," the amplified voice implores next, the speaker crouching slightly, then springing up to reinforce his pointing. Once again, his call is echoed, with even more passion, even more enthusiasm as he begins to move to the rhythm. *"Wash away the filth!"*

Several more young people and adults arrive to join them by the time Seivers reaches the plaza, which he must cross to enter the building. Falling into what seems a practiced choreography, tallest in the back, shorter in the front, they look for all the world like happy family members gathering on the front walk to have their picture taken. A middle aged man in wool overcoat is the clear head of this faction, nodding to the young cheerleader, waving new participants into line. Some hold their hands clasped before their chests, others clutch black-bound books like talismans, or hold aloft hand-printed sheets of poster-board. 'AS YOU SOW,' reads a sign held chest-high by a girl of about fourteen. 'SO SHALL YOU REAP,' reads the next, wobbly in the hands of a boy who could not be more than eleven.

With urgent gestures the reporter waves her cameraman to focus on the new tableau, where the leader immediately recognizes his advantage. Signaling to the blazer-clad youngster, this older man raises his own bullhorn to his lips and instantly the electronically enhanced voice of authority begins to echo off the walls of buildings and across the parking lot, to the street beyond.

"Homosexual acts are an abomination in the eyes of God," he begins. "And he will have his punishment." The cameraman moves closer, half-squatting to get the most imposing angle while the reporter speaks softly into her microphone and the leader eyes them with satisfaction, clearly waiting for a pause in her narration. "Witness God's judgment," he intones then, stretching a hand majestically out toward the hospital before him. "Witness God's judgment," repeat his companions in unison, to a roar of reaction from the vigil's supporters, ringing the other three sides of the plaza.

Right about then Bill Seivers decides he has seen enough. Briefcase in hand, overcoat draped across the opposite forearm, he turns away, reaching the building's entrance in a few broad strides. No huffing or fussing marks his departure, no muttered curses under his breath, but only that row of lines which crease his brow, noticeably deeper now than when he arrived, the lips a bit more pursed. It is as if he has aged a decade since turning his car in off the street; someone - some person among all those persons he pays so well to keep Hilltop functioning smoothly - has got some explaining to do. And very shortly.

It is getting more difficult, Anne realizes, as she makes a tight right away from a narrow lane which would have taken her winding down the hill into Ballard. So much more difficult, to keep track of all the things she needs to keep track of. Listening to the radio, in case there should be any news about Christina - like when she had that episode and ended up in the hospital. Watching the traffic signs and lights – one doesn't want to get pulled over, because the police can be so hard on older drivers. She's read about that in the newsletter from the Magnussen Senior Center, which, by the way, she would rather not get, but it's been coming every month since Lorraine Walsh talked her into going over there one Wednesday evening to register for bridge classes, which she never actually attended.

      Silly thing that; why on earth Lorraine thought she had time to take up something like bridge, with all that counting and remembering who played what suit? There is not enough room in one's head, to add a card game to all the important things. Things like dinner, for example - what to prepare, and does she have all the ingredients already, or will she need to stop off for, say, a potato. Or some fresh parsley, if she's going to roast that chicken, and yes, she is certain she put it out this morning to defrost - or was that two weeks ago? And wasn't it a Cornish game hen? Game hen is just the right size when dinner is only just for one, but if she did put a chicken out, then what to do with all those leftovers? Perhaps a soup; Christina would probably benefit from some homemade chicken soup, if she's been out in the damp.

      Dinner, unlike bridge, is an important issue. One which comes up every single day, and requires planning.

      Radio. Meals. Pedestrians. Traffic signs. Traffic itself; the cars coming up so quickly from behind and pressing on her, as if she weren't already going close to the speed limit most of the time. So many people in such a hurry. Even on the sidewalks. When she gets into some of these streets with lots of shops, like around Green Lake, or the University, there are so many people trying to cross from all directions that it is sometimes hard to decide who to look at first. And you have to look at them, because the looking is the most important part after all. To keep one's mind focused on looking; searching each person, each doorway, each window, bus stop and parking lot, for a glimpse of Christina.

Robin Andrew

All these things to keep track of at once, and then too, life goes on inside one's head. How is the shoulder feeling, is it still morning-stiff, or has turning and turning the steering wheel warmed it up enough to drive the pain away? Some days it works out like that, walking out to the garage is all stiffness and aches, but then after a couple of hours of driving around looking, she realizes the aches have gone away and she's forgotten her body completely for a while. Other days, it's just the opposite, From the moment she gets out of bed, every movement brings a new voice, a new place in her body registering its disapproval, telling her to sit down, drink a cup of tea. 'Take it easy,' as Lorraine would say. Easy? As if taking it easy were anything to be proud of, when all the really important things in life come through hard work and concentration, as her Sean would be the first to remind that silly old Lorraine Walsh.

Radio. Meals. Traffic signals. Traffic. People. Body.

Weather is another thing to be aware of. One does not want to be caught far from home if the weather closes in. Clouds can thicken up so quickly; sometimes it seems as dark as twilight in the middle of the day. It is less easy to make things out in that kind of weather, one must admit, and the roads can get quite treacherous, and when the rain is serious – not just misting like today, but seriously raining down so you have to run the windshield wipers on the high speed and it feels like you're watching one of your brother's slide shows in between the sheets of water being squeegee-ed off,well...then the reflections can get so confusing. A car over to the left could be an actual car, or it could be your own car, reflected in the window of a florist's shop. One sorts these things out quickly enough, of course, but in the moment when that reflection jumps into the side of one's vision, it can be quite startling. The heart starts to race and the mind starts to wonder what in the world to do, and then one notices that the car is not moving in the way one would expect and so deduces that it is a reflection, by which time something *else* is going on that has to be paid attention to.

Radio. Meals. Traffic signals. Traffic. People. Body. Weather.

So much to do, and on top of it all, watching for Christina. Because at any moment, one could spot her. Over there, among that knot of people waiting to cross – but no, those are school children. Middle school age, or maybe even high school; but either way, still younger than her Christina. Coming up on the other side of the road, inside that red car driven by the bearded man...but no, the girl in the passenger seat is much taller than her Christina. A couple climbing

614

out of a brand new black station wagon, very sharp and clean, with two children bobbing in the back seat – perhaps someday that <u>will</u> be Christina; with a husband and babies - oh, wouldn't that be nice; but not today. Or over to the right, just as Anne is passing, a door opens, of a blocky little apartment building. That might be Christina coming out, but by the time Anne can round the block and pass again, the figure is gone and Anne is no longer certain it was her daughter. Is certain, in fact, that it was not.

No matter. Anne McKloskey is not one to give up easily. There it is again. Easiness. Not a concept to which one should aspire. The most valuable things in life are often the least 'easy'. Sean understood that, he never shrank from a difficult score, or stepping into a performance at the last minute with hardly any preparation. Hardly. 'Hardly' is much better than 'easily,' Anne agrees to herself with amusement as she comes to a sharp stop. It certainly seems as if the people who manage traffic signals are making the yellow lights shorter and shorter. Perhaps there is someone she could call to tell them about that. At the triple A, perhaps, or the City. That new man who's running for mayor said on the radio that he wants to make the city better, after all. Like it used to be, he said. Before so many people moved in from other places - other countries, he said - bringing their problems with them.

Light change. Green. Go. Weather still reasonably clear, no cars coming from the left so it's OK for Anne to turn right; see what is down another block. Check each passing car, each doorway, each figure walking down the sidewalk, because it is always possible, at any minute. That person in the brown slacks and white shirt, who was very nearly hit by a car pulling into the parking lot of Payless Drugs over there; who's still walking along without even noticing the close call, sloshing right through a deep puddle of standing water without paying any attention; that person...

A truck horn blares and its tires chirp asphalt as the driver makes an emergency stop. "Son of a bitch," Royal Roberts mutters out loud to no one but himself. "Pull over like that with no warning, or anything?"' His estimation of the other driver's intellectual capacity doesn't rise any higher when he sees the sedan's door pop open and a woman as old as his own mother struggle awkwardly out of the driver's seat, the tail end of her Accord still sticking a couple of feet out into the traffic lane, its nose directly beneath a "NO PARKING – TOW AWAY ZONE' sign. Shaking his head he watches the fancy-dressed granny scoot across three more lanes of traffic, hands and purse waving to ward off the oncoming vehicles. 'People say the kids these days are crazy, but hell, no,' he thinks as he swings his Fed Ex van around the semi-parked car and gets underway again. 'It's goddamn *everyone* that's going crazy, when even little old ladies jump out of their cars with no warning and race across traffic to grab some punk and hug it as if it was their long lost love.'

"You're shitting me," Doug Taylor answers, eyes turning from the phone as his fingers tap harshly at the keyboard slid out from underneath his desk. In a few seconds he's looking at the same website Seivers is. 'MAYORAL HOPEFUL WEIGHS IN ON SEX ASSAULT,' reads a banner headline just below an advertisement for male enhancement. Scanning down the text, Doug finds the paragraph and reads.

"Law is law, of course," candidate Norm Fergus stated, when asked about the recent brutal attack on a street-walking transvestite, "But there's also a thing called personal responsibility. People who engage in illegal and immoral acts create a danger to the community as well as to themselves. So, if, in the act of committing a repulsive crime, they get hurt? Well, we have got to remember that our public safety personnel have plenty of good, law-abiding people to protect, and they have to come first. In my administration...."

"It's campaign season," Taylor cautions Three-dollar Bill over the intercom after he's read the snippet. "Everybody's got to satisfy their base, even if it means hanging the odd queer out to dry."

"On our front sidewalk?" Seivers reminds his Head of Administration. "Not good PR Doug, just when we're about to lock-down a major capital commitment."

"Actually," Taylor begins, immediately regretting what he's about to say, but knowing it's too late to stop. "It's not *our* front sidewalk."

The ferocity of Seivers's response suggests to Doug that it might be best to continue this discussion face to face.

"Look, Boss," Aubrey pleads as Sylvio stands in the kitchen doorway, thick fingers gathering and twisting the fabric of his apron the way they always seem to do when he's forced to pay attention to anything other than his beloved food. "She's my bud, OK? And she's like...actually, sometimes even *I* don't know what she is, but that's not the point...I mean, we haven't seen her for days, and now the freakin' cops are looking for her but her old lady found her first and if I can just talk to her for a minute I could maybe, you know, help her to explain herself and...I mean, you remember; from when she was here? It's not that she's a bad person, she's just sort of screwed up in her head and besides, man – look around! We've got two fucking tables! Laurie can handle that and she'll be happy to have my tips, so you gotta' give me a break here, just this once..."

To which Laurie, who only started two days ago and is still learning the ropes and yet has somehow managed to arrive behind Aubs at just this moment, agrees enthusiastically, with the result that Sylvio huffs as loudly as he can, while making a show of tossing the crumpled end of his apron away from himself. "Fine," he bursts out, in the voice of a man who's lost everything, before elbowing his way back through the kitchen to thrust his hands gratefully into a lump of dough in the middle of a floured stretch of counter.

"I owe you," Aubrey whispers, giving Laurie a quick hug and a peck on the back of her neck as the waitress gathers plates from beneath the heat lamps onto her tray.

"So what's new?" comes the reply, barely registering as Aubrey tugs off her own apron and grabs her coat and bag, determined to be out the door and down the alley before her boss can possibly change his mind.

As always, it's cold in Three-dollar Bill's office, two doors down from Taylor's own, and the cold is making Doug feel...exposed. He's just finished explaining to the Chairman how that expensive plaza out front was actually deeded to the Parks Department before it was even constructed, making it legally public property and so a guaranteed pulpit for all kinds of free speech; one of several concessions which had been necessary to receive City Council approval to build an extra four floors on the new Oncology tower. The reminder of those concessions has left the frustrated entrepreneur standing cross-armed at the corner window as evening's approach casts its shadow over the commotion below. More than a hundred and fifty people according to Security's last count, and reinforcements arriving all the time; streaming in from the cars now filling his Visitor Parking at an hour when he'd expect it to be three-quarters empty, and lining up in one another's faces like opposing armies. On the far side of the space the protesters have now set up several folding canopies over portable tables holding water jugs and plastic tubs of food; like something you'd see on the sidelines of a high school football game. Closer to the building, a woman in a bulky cinnamon-colored coverall has climbed onto one wall of the central fountain, and is shouting something, shaking both fists and getting the rest of the sign-holders to shout back at her. Thankfully, the double-paned windows of Hilltop's climate-sealed tower mean the men don't have to listen, though a stack of boxy amplifiers and several coils of cables being unloaded from a double-parked mini-van suggest they may not have the luxury of silence very much longer. Even without audio, the signs say it all.

'PROSECUTE KILLERS, NOT VICTIMS,' reads one; 'END HATE CRIME,' another, both neat and professionally printed from the look of them. 'FREE TO BE YOU AND BE ME,' says the one bobbing in between, its letters loose and uneven, alternating between red, blue and purple, against a pink background.

Most of the time the executives can't read the signs held by the other side; the better-dressed and more-orderly crew with their backs to the building, but every now and then someone turns around to check in with their compatriots and Doug catches a glimpse. 'GOD HATES FAGGOTS,' says one. 'SNUFF OUT IMMORALITY,' reads another, with some numbers at the bottom which he can guess to be a scriptural reference, in case anyone wants to look it up in the Bibles some of them periodically brandish above their heads.

The ranks of these counter-demonstrators have been growing almost as quickly as the patient's supporters. Families, many of them, recognizable by their graduated sizes and the casual way the adults have of reigning the kids back into their places. An assortment of unattached men as well; some skinny young kids in suits and ties, but a lot more middle-aged and tough looking. In thick utility jackets over heavy plaid shirts, they mill about the edges and talk among themselves. Clearly on the families' side but just as clearly different from them, these men form a new force, vibrating around the fringe of the disturbance, as if their energy cannot stand for all this talking and waiting; as if they need something more to do, and soon.

Two sides, facing off across the sprawling plaza – the City's plaza, Taylor reminds himself, rubbing salt into his own wound. At least the fountain's dry this time of year; he doesn't need some kid drowning in sight of the Center's front door while its parents are chanting to change the world, and all right under the watchful eye of the beloved media. They're up to three news-trucks now, telescoping antennae rising out of their roofs like slender steel erections, as soon as each one parks. Fashion-plate reporters and jeans-and-black-windbreaker techies spreading out like juice from a smashed melon; one reporter interviewing a cop beside his cruiser on the side street while another two of them are talking together, microphones almost touching - leading him to wonder if they've finally descended to interviewing each other. Any minute the local stations will be breaking in on their own programs to make sure the public is fully informed on *that* new angle.

'Wonderful,' Doug Taylor thinks, as he turns away from the window. If the crazies are this worked up now, what will they do when that vegetable in ICU actually kicks. Or worse, if it doesn't? And then there's that detective, asking about Rod Gimbal. Probably not a good moment to tell Bill about that one, he imagines, but then, will there ever be a better time?

Making her way down the block and around the corner, Aubrey holds a newspaper over her head to fend off a rain which has recently matured from drizzle to downpour. She has barely arrived in front of the consignment store when Anne's pale Honda creeps into sight and eases to a stop right in the traffic lane, Rod's form barely recognizable in the front passenger seat what with all the reflections on the car's glass and Aubrey's attention being focused mostly on getting herself inside before someone rams the car for blocking traffic. Climbing into the back seat she can tell immediately that something is not right about her friend; shoulders slumped, his head does not turn to acknowledge her arrival, but stares down in the direction of the dashboard, bobbing loosely as the vehicle lurches forward. The air inside the car is thick with Anne's perfume and beneath it, a musty smell of damp clothes, sweat and cigarettes. Even craning around from behind, Aubrey can see that Rod's face is smudged with dirt, his shirt all matted and soiled.

"Jesus F. Christ, Rod," she greets him, whatever composure she'd managed in the weeks since his disappearance crumbling at the sight of that fuzzy round dome; so familiar and yet so baffling. Though she hates the tone of accusation in her own voice, still she finds herself unable to stop the words - echoes of some confrontation long ago in which she played quite the opposite role. "Do you have any idea how worried we've all been?"

"It doesn't matter," is Rod's reply, without even turning to meet her eyes. "You're no more real than any of this."

"The fuck I'm not," Aubrey blurts out, then winces at the thought of Mrs. M. overhearing, though a glance reveals her to be thankfully oblivious of the remark, totally absorbed in the complexities of a left hand turn. "I'm as f'ing real as the way you walked out on me. You just....Kim, you didn't even...."

"This is all some sort of dream I'm having," Rod interrupts bluntly. "Hallucinations; voices in my head; and sooner or later I'll wake up and it will all be gone."

"You..." Aubrey begins, then realizes the futility of argument under these circumstances. "So, Anne," she asks instead, as the car swings around the corner onto Forty-fifth St., heading toward the freeway. "How do you think this is all going?"

"Just wonderfully," Anne replies, as Rod makes no sign he has even heard the question. "It was so lucky I happened to see

Christina," she continues, turning nearly around to catch Aubrey's eyes as one hand flies up from the wheel to make a micro-adjustment to the position of the rear-view mirror. All the time she is talking in fact, her hands are moving; from wheel to hair, to mirror, to the bright yellow cell phone sitting prominently on the dashboard, practically in front of the diminutive woman's eyes, which barely crest the top of the steering wheel.

"I was just thinking about turning back for the day, because of the weather, you know, but my little feeling was very strong, and I promised myself I would keep on for just a few more minutes and then I saw a car with the nicest family; a young woman and a man and two children. That wasn't Christina, of course - I have a feeling whatever friends she's been making lately are not that sort of people at all - but it made me think of what might be – someday; if only I *did* find her – and so I went on a few blocks more and then there she was; walking along right in front of that big drug store – getting her feet soaked in the puddles. I always had to remind her to watch where she was putting her feet, and I guess some things never change – but anyway, I knew it was my Christina as soon as I saw her, so I didn't take my eyes off her and now here we all are."

Where they 'all are' at this point is the I-5 freeway, poking along in the right-hand lane, and Aubrey's hand is gripping the door handle for all it is worth; Mrs. M's. driving leaving a lot to be desired, especially when she is this excited and distracted. The gunning of a diesel is clearly audible as a giant dual-cab/dual-wheel pick-up pulls out from behind to pass them, then drops back into the lane just feet from the Accord's front bumper, its non-verbal expression of the driver's irritation lost on Anne, who continues her monologue.

"Of course, once I got her into the car I was not about to leave her, not for a moment, but fortunately I have this new telephone Jake gave me. That's how I called you, and I've been trying to reach him too, but I can't remember his number; we haven't spoken nearly as much lately as we used to. He said there's a memory somewhere inside it with his phone number, but I don't see anything that says 'memory,' so I wasn't sure what to do about calling."

By this time they are buried in traffic on the lower level of the Portage Bay causeway, concrete barriers beside them blocking out all but a horizontal slot of view into the thick gray air, more concrete lanes overhead, and the wipers grating across a now-dry windshield. Anne is only too happy to hand over the phone, a special

geriatric model with oversized buttons and minimal features. Aubrey
navigates its simplified menus without much difficulty, only to hear
Jake's outgoing voicemail message once the call goes thru.

"Jake," she begins after the beep, "this is Aubrey. I'm with
Anne – Mrs. McKloskey, I mean - and we've got Rod – I mean Kim.
Anyway, Anne found her up on Phinney Ridge somewhere and, well, I
don't know the whole story, but we're going..." It is at this point that
she realizes she has no idea where Mrs. M. is taking them, since
they've passed the exit that would have taken them to the
McKloskey house in Madison Park. "Where are we going?"

"To the hospital dear," is her pilot's cheery answer. "We're
going to pay a visit to Christina's friend Stevie - the one you told me
about; who's been in all the papers? It sounds like he's in a very a
bad way so I thought we really should visit while...while we have the
chance, if you know what I mean. Or else Christina would never
forgive herself...Then once we've done that, we're headed back
home to get her cleaned up and fed - I doubt she's had a decent meal
in days, judging by the state of her clothes."

The car is on the ramp to Madison Street by the time Aubrey
completes a second call to tell Jake where they're headed, and
Christina hasn't said a word since denying the reality of everything
around her. As they exit the freeway and make their way into the
southern reaches of Capitol Hill the mélange which is Hilltop presents
itself; obsessively maintained brick and stone and steel in a dozen
colors and configurations. Blocky towers dominate one street, their
upper levels connected by skybridges, while just around the corner
an old merchant's mansion survives to serve as headquarters for the
Someone-Something Institute of Something-Something – too many
syllables for Aubs to catch between the busses and delivery trucks
crowding this part of town. It's to the main building, though, that
they're headed; the former veteran's hospital which was re-titled
'Hilltop Central' when MH decided to christen their newly acquired
campus more grandly, as 'The Institutes at Hilltop Medical Center.'
The largest edifice in the whole bunch, 'The Center' as it is familiarly
called, rises twelve stories in its central tower, six in the wings that
flank each side; a cascading wedding cake of pale limestone
surrounded by newer, smaller, structures, and a few remaining
parking lots - vast extravagances of precious real estate this close to
downtown; and one which MH fully intends to replace with more
towers as soon as Bill Seivers' silver tongue can round-up the capital.
Eyes studying every sign to find her way, Anne takes a meandering

journey around two blocks and past several 'FULL' signs before a car pulls away from the curb half a block ahead and she manages to insert the her own vehicle - on the third attempt - into the space it has vacated.

Unfolding herself as quickly as possible from the rear seat, Aubrey opens the front door to get a hand on her friend's arm before she has any opportunity to bolt, and feels a shiver as she gazes into eyes which seem vacant, above a mouth which hangs just short of closed, the lips loose and dry and unconcerned with anything. There's a swelling on one side of her lower lip; maybe the start of a cold sore, or maybe from an injury, which seems more likely as Aubs notices also a darkening near the hairline which could be a bruise starting to show. When she asks about these the only response is silence, her friend's expression still stuck midway between waking and sleep, her attention elsewhere, if anywhere.

"I don't know, Anne," Aubrey suggests as she virtually drags Christina from the vehicle, thankful that the rain seems to have stopped, at least for the moment. "Maybe we should go to your house first, get her straightened out and cleaned up and all, and come back here some other time."

"First things first," is Anne's reply as she takes her daughter's other elbow and urges her forward between the cars. "If this Stevie is as ill as it sounds, we owe it to him to come now. A visit can do wonders for someone who's been under the weather, you know. *And,* it will do Christina good as well. Seeing someone with real troubles is just the sort of thing to snap her out of herself."

Surprisingly, this motherly optimism seems rewarded as they make their way across the side street and find a path through the packed lot on the other side. Or maybe it is the fragments of music drifting from up ahead, keyboard arpeggios and a woodwind whistling, supported by a complex aboriginal drumbeat, that begin to awaken something in Christina, pulling her eyes away from the ground and quickening her steps just a bit.

"It looks like some sort of carnival," Anne suggests with glee as they reach the first huddled groups. Indeed, if Aubrey suspends what she knows of the circumstances, she can find a hint of festivity in the scene: the assorted banners whipping in the growing breeze, the colorful logos on the news trucks. Off to the left two police cars idle, red and blue lights rotating slowly as they block an aisle, though no one seems to be trying to leave. On the contrary, in fact: a steady trickle of people are still arriving, adding to the couple of hundred already spread across the plaza's multiple levels and wide stone steps. Their attention is focused on the central feature, a complex arrangement of walls and ledges, layered like the facets of a mountain cascade. A water feature in the summer time, with geysers and cataracts pouring over its many surfaces, it is dry now, and the largest ledge has been taken over as a makeshift stage, jammed with people and equipment. A woman with a guitar slung over her shoulder stands center-front, hunched around a microphone stand, and behind her are squeezed in another woman at an electric keyboard, a banjo-wielding lumberjack, a fiddler, a female percussionist pounding what looks to be about a dozen simple wooden drums of different shapes and sizes, and two small men blowing into clusters of wooden pipes, with an assortment of others pipes in a rack beside them. The various amplifiers, keyboards, control boards and microphones are tied together by a tripping tangle of cords and junction boxes, from which several larger cables snake away to where a generator throbs on the open bed of a truck bearing the name "Grizzly Excavation" on its door, over a picture of a dancing bear in pink tutu and bikini top.

Hilltop Central - just now beginning to glow from within as the sky darkens and lights come on - seems far away across this crowd; in order to reach their destination, the women must pass through it all, and though they skirt the thickest gathering, still their progress slows. At one cross-aisle a battered minivan is stopped with two wheels up on the curb and a swarm of young men and women have formed a bucket-brigade to unload its extensive contents. Cardboard boxes with various logos are pulled from the rear, while the sliding side door disgorges red and white plastic toolboxes and kits, all of which are quickly stacked beneath one of several nylon canopies they've erected. Beneath a second fabric roof, two men in white t-shirts emblazoned with large red crosses are setting out first aid supplies on a table.

"How silly is that?" Mrs. M remarks to Aubrey as they sidestep a woman with a large carton in her arms. "Setting up a first aid station, right in front of a hospital?"

"It's not like *they're* gonna' take care of us," answers a man passing by, his arm around his grim-faced partner's waist. "The shit hits the fan, they'll be hiding behind the cops, so we've got to be ready to take care of our own." Without seeming to notice Mrs. M.'s astonished reaction, the couple melt into the mass, pressing toward the stage which Rod suddenly seems intent upon reaching.

By now Aubrey has read enough of the signs to recognize this is no carnival, but a protest; a gathering of the City's queer community in all its many varieties, to express their outrage at what has happened to Stevie. Accompanied, as such expressions must be these days, by the requisite counter-protest - in this case from those who believe her way of life to be an affront to their own values - and those who've just come out to watch, whether idly or professionally. Where at first the various constituencies may have been separated by distance, the press of more and more bodies filling the available space has pushed them closer, so that now they face one another at close range. The mass directly in front of the stage though, is of one mind, their signs and slogans all in agreement, and their faces - some teary–eyed, some hardened in anger - all turned toward the performers as a song slides into its final coda, to a stirring tide of applause and hoots, whistles and cheers.

I hear the music and, though it's not my music, still I feel it resonating; pulling me, urging me forward like gravity on a downhill slope. Rhythm and harmony, like cool water on my overheated thoughts

"Rodney!" calls a voice. Swiveling her head, Aubrey sees a tall woman with remarkably crooked teeth waving frantically in their direction. "Over here, Rodney, it's me Tammy." Christina shows no sign of recognizing the woman, her own eyes fixed on the stage, though her posture has changed. Gone is the limp slouch Aubrey observed in the car and when the three women first exited it, replaced now by a posture almost of excitement - head high, hands touching, fingers working among themselves as if to puzzle something out. Her animation is unbroken even when a pair of strangers squeeze out of the crowd and greet him like an old friend.
"Rodney, right?" says the first. "We met at group, the night you came with Stevie, remember?

Vaguely, I recall it; being dragged off one evening to some group-hugging self-help sort of session, with a bunch of misfit weirdoes she called her friends. Losers and malingerers; I doubt most of them ever contributed a thing to the world in all their years; there was no way I belonged among those people. Any more than she did; I made her take me home as soon as possible.

626

"I never forget anyone who comes to group - not that I'd call them out on the street, you know, not unless I know they're in the open and all but here...well, I'm just so glad you came and – Oh," she interrupts herself, turning to Aubrey and Anne. "I'm sorry. Tammy Hill."

The hand she offers is so large it could easily encompass Aubrey's, but surprisingly soft, and the greeting it offers is gentle; beefy fingers barely wrapping around Aubrey's own in a reassuring embrace, rather than diving deep for a palm-to-palm squeeze-challenge. Over the din of the crowd the introductions continue, and as soon as Anne identifies herself as Christina's mother, this Tammy reacts with a gush of sympathy.

"Oh god," she says, enfolding the elderly woman's narrow shoulders in a hug, then holding her and patting her back as she continues. "I really <u>can</u> imagine what you've been going through, you know. My own mother, when I told her - about myself? - well, it took her years and years to accept me as I am."

In a moment the two are chatting excitedly about what it means to be the mother of someone 'different.' Not for the first time, Aubrey is astonished to see how Mrs. M. manages to roll with whatever comes at her; that sometimes feeble-seeming mind dodging and weaving to fashion a commodious truth out of the most disparate information. Around them the crowd is pressing tighter, some voices soft and mournful, some urgently agitated, still others energized and elevated by the energy around them. On the platform the musicians have started up another tune, the rapid-fire strumming suggesting something angry and emphatic.

People I don't know, but they all act as if we're long lost friends! The mother still calling me Christina, the girl acting like I'm her best friend whatever-her-name-was; everywhere I turn somebody wants me to be somebody else for them, and still nothing makes sense - except maybe the music. When I would sing with that...with her... The music at least, felt right; out of everything.

"I didn't even realize," Anne is explaining. "Until Aubrey told me they had met once, at some sort of night club; I had no idea Christina even knew him."

"Her," corrects the dread-locked person who's arrived next to Tammy. Tall and slender, with narrow hips and a flat chest, but a hairless complexion of the smoothest chocolate-milk tone, he - or she; Aubs can't decide what she thinks about that, given this crowd - exudes an easy confidence that suggests one who has never doubted their identity, whatever it is. "Stevie lived as a woman, so that's how we think of her."

For a moment Anne is clearly taken aback, embarrassed even. Yet another first in Aubrey's experience, on this day which is turning out to be full of surprises. The revelations continue as this young person identifies herself as Rose Budd – 'Budd, with two Ds because everyone called me Buddy when I was little, and Rose because I'm a beautiful flower, but if you aren't careful, you might get pricked.'

Another song I don't recognize, played by this make-shift gypsy orchestra, and yet I cannot help but feel its call - an urgency, a swelling beneath my sternum, a pressure that must be let out. The rest of what I'm seeing and hearing - these women, this place, this celebration – its just more nonsense playing in my head; but the music feels so right, so real. More solid than touch itself.

Introductions are completed as the crowd presses closer and Aubrey is jostled by a shoulder here, a hip there. The music swells and she has to lean forward, bend her head down to be a part of the conversation with these new others who are looking to her and Anne to fill in the blanks of their own understanding.

"I didn't know Stevie all that well," she admits, in answer to a question from Rose, and immediately Tammy's focus jumps to a more promising avenue.

"Rodney knew her though," she says eagerly, "Hell, he was living with her, wasn't he?"

Aubrey, of course, has expected as much. Had pretty well assumed the message on her phone was the sign of a lover left behind, and yet the confirmation hits her deeply. The image that comes to mind is one of Kim; the *old* Kim, many months ago, flopped on the sofa in Aubrey's place, shoes off and legs tucked beneath her, a bottle of green tea in one hand, an art magazine in the other and a look of total peace on her face, if only for that one moment.

'I wouldn't know,' Aubrey is about to say, when she realizes the subject of their wondering is nowhere to be seen. "Where'd she go?" she calls out instead, feeling panic at the thought of Christina, in her disoriented state, alone among this mob. "Rod?" she shouts more loudly, as all four heads begin swiveling, searching for

Christina's cropped hair and diminutive form among the horde of taller people all around. It is Tammy who makes the discovery, calling out for them to stop looking, and listen.

"Such a pretty voice," Anne says, with a nod. "I do believe I've heard that voice before, somewhere."

"It's her," Aubrey exclaims, craning her head to see. "It's Kim...I mean Christina."

Thank goodness for choruses. Verses can be anything, but a chorus...you hear it once and know it as if it's been part of your life forever.
"Come to my window..." *I sing along, and the words are a command aimed directly at me, to move toward the light, the sound, the very rightness of opening my mouth and having this unfamiliar yet somehow correct sound come pouring out of me.*

"Bless me, no," Anne exclaims in a tone of genteel astonishment. "You must be mistaken. Oh, I know you said she was going to get voice lessons and all, but then Jake explained it was just something you made up because you knew I wouldn't give you money for beer and cigarettes and *I* said that was very mean and probably you were both just too embarrassed about having to ask..."

"No, really; it is," Aubs implores, grabbing Anne by the hand and pulling her to where she can glimpse, between the intervening heads and shoulders, Christina's profile, right there at the edge of the stage, head held high, tipped back and swaying a little as her mouth moves along with those of the singers up there, whose attention, too, is upon her and the sound she is producing.

"Wait by the light of the moon..." and as that note hangs in the air a piece of me hangs also, projected up and out where everyone can know it. Like tearing off some outer wrapper to reveal the contents within; debriding charred tissue to reveal the burn beneath it; when I use this voice I strip off what is outside me and expose a bare and naked truth, though it makes no sense at all. "Come to my window...I'll be home soon..."
If only that were true. If only home was even a possibility any longer.

"Damn, that kid's got pipes," Rose comments, with a disbelieving shake of her head as she pulls Tammy close with an arm around her waist. The two melt against one another as the musicians extend the song, repeating the chorus twice, three times, with broad smiles on their faces while the newcomer repeats with them, each time gaining confidence, even experimenting a little with the notes.

A nod of the guitarist's head signals the others that the time has finally come; in the next measure she swings her instrument's neck toward the sky and brings it down, chopping the song to a close amid cheers and applause, not the least of which is Aubrey's, her hands clapping madly as she sees her best friend Kim, first reaching a hand up to shake that offered by the guitarist, then held there, as others move closer, crowding round and speaking all at once. In a moment Kim has both arms raised above her and then Rod's soiled suit coat rises as she is pulled bodily up onto the ledge and disappears among the people assembled there.

Mrs. M. is excited now, disbelieving what she has seen and heard, though Aubrey reassures her. Yes, that was Christina, her daughter, and yes, she was singing; and damn well, too. With Tammy and Rose, the women crowd forward, but the bodies are thick and progress is slow to impossible. From the fragmentary remarks they can make out around them, it is clear that Rod's unorthodox appearance does not confuse this audience, but resonates with many of them, predisposing them to support her and appreciate even more the talent she has shown.

All these people, talking so close to my face. 'What do you know?' they ask me, 'Have you got any favorites we can jam on?'

More strangers, acting like old friends, this time not because they recognize my face, but just because they like the way I sing. Crowding close - too close - and yet it is exciting too, to be wanted in this way. Not for titles and degrees – achievements, bureaucratic accolades – but for this voice that springs from so far down it feels a part of me, despite everything.   Being wanted - in this way - it feels...as if I've been hacking and chopping forever through the deepest, darkest forest and suddenly a path reveals itself before me; a wide open avenue to light and air and cool blue water, glimmering in the sunlight. And what am I supposed to make of that, damn it?

'Old things,' I answer their questioning, as I glance at a dog-eared sheet of paper thrust before my eyes. 'Before your time; you wouldn't know...' Song titles, they must be, the words on that page, but unfamiliar and odd-sounding. 'No, I've never heard of that....no,

not any of those. No, no...wait – What a Wonderful World, isn't that Louis Armstrong?' I ask.

'No, dude, it's K. D. Laing,' someone tells me, 'and Tony Bennett.'

'The Tony Bennett?'

'Yeah. The old guy.'

'Not that old,' I point out. 'Only a few years older than I am;' and their expressions tell me I'm some kind of crazy, but it doesn't matter because I can hear the tune inside this head I'm wearing and as I vamp the first line these kids around me - this misfit band of outcasts - are nodding and shaking their heads that yes, that's the song, and yes, they know the changes and let's go already, so I stop and the girl who seems to be their leader gives me a little push toward the front of the stage

'I'm Evie Lee,' she tells me, brushing the top of my head with her hand in a way that makes me feel like a little boy again, after all these years. 'And over there on the keyboard, that's Ashton Ford, and the girl with the drums, she's just Lady.' The others are introduced as well, the burly banjo man with one of those fey British-sounding names, the dark little natives with their aboriginal flutes, and the fiddler, but I cannot hold any of it in my head with all this excitement and then I see Evie nodding to the keyboard player; the music starts and I close my eyes so I won't think about who I am or where I am, but only hear the music making its own kind of sense.

"We're gonna' have another one," Evie pronounces into the mic as, behind her on the keyboard, Ashton lays down a series of rippling arpeggios. "And this time we've got a new friend is gonna' join us. His name..." Stopping in mid-sentence she steps over and locks heads for a moment with the stranger, then returns to her audience. "His name is Rod," at which a few cheers and several friendly hoots can be heard around the audience. "Rod Gimbal," repeats the band leader, "And he's gonna' sing this one out for Stevie and for all the freaks and queers here today and everywhere else, who just want to be left alone to appreciate this great big wonderful world we live in."

"*I see trees of green,*" Rod and Evie sing together after the first introductory bars, and the assembled crowd recognizes Satchmo's old number, ubiquitous these days in movies, commercials and cover recordings. "*Red roses too...*" and by the end of the second line, Evie drops back, allowing Rod the center stage so she and the band can just groove on sharing the language they live on with a total stranger.

"*And I think to myself,*" the new kid sings as a hundred voices and more join in to raise up the key line, "*What a wonderful world.*"

A pale-green sedan sits far from the curb in a jumbled block of Northlake Ave., its front wheels angled for a quick getaway. Behind it, a Mitsubishi bob-tail truck bears the logo of Lake Union Prop Works; in front of it, a space large enough for two cars is taken up with several large wooden crates stamped in Chinese characters, while across the street sits the black car which has occupied Officer Lon Pinoy's attention for the last forty minutes.

It's been a day and a half since the 911 call from the alley off Boren Street, and in that time Seattle's finest have been on alert for any information on the assailant or assailants responsible. Pinoy isn't up on every detail - like any cop on patrol he's got a lot of action to keep track of and Wallingford/Lake Union breeds its own unique mix; shipyards tend to attract some pretty hard customers, while the fancy condos that have crowded up against them over the last few years are ripe for burglary and domestic calls. A big park like Gasworks generates its share of action, too: underage drinkers, homeless sleepers, runaways, drug deals and even back-seat lovers, and Fremont has the bars and the hookers – not that most residents would ever guess that last, but there you have it. What Pinoy *does* know about the Boren Street story, is that there's a bulletin out for make, model and plate, and that the ones across the street match up, so he gets to spend the next however-long sitting here, waiting to see when - and if - someone comes back to it.

He's already done a casual walk-by; glancing inside to see the back seat jumbled high with clothes and duffles, and a single running shoe on the rear shelf, along with one of those heavy black kidney belts like warehouse workers wear, or delivery crews. Bunch of tall square cardboard boxes jammed upright between the back of the front seats and the front of the back, dashboard littered with what looks like weeks worth of mail - envelopes and advertising flyers jammed into where the insect-caked windshield meets bleached leatherette. All of which fit with the thick layer of dirt on the exterior, Lon thought, as he walked back to his own vehicle; the owner either too busy or too out of it to take care of what is still a valuable automobile.

After three-thirty now, and Pinoy is beginning to wonder if he'll have to stay past the end of his shift, when a movement down the block catches his eye. The figure which has rounded the corner is big, and moving with confidence; making no effort to hide himself. Jacket hanging open, hands in its pockets, he gives the impression of someone out for a stroll. From the neck up, though, the cues are all negative – thick stubble across his jaw, dark pools around his eyes and a deep-creased scowl that looks to be settling in for a life sentence. Now that he's moving down a straight sidewalk, Pinoy catches a slightly seasick waver in his walk, a not-quite-bee line that suggests substance abuse, illness, or extreme introspection. As the distance decreases, he can see accordion creases at the knees and crotch of the slacks, and the leather jacket fitting like a second skin; these clothes have been worn for days on end. The hair, too, is matted on one side, and spiked up on the other - bedhead or intentional; it does not go with the guy's age and build, nor does it suggest your typical quiet citizen, as the guy leaves the sidewalk and comes around to the driver's door of the Beemer.

Pinoy calls in his location again, lets dispatch know he's got someone approaching the car, and in turn is advised of the nearest back-up, which will re-route and be on scene in about two minutes. He's out of his seat now, door opened slowly and quietly, as the subject pulls something from his pocket. That gives the officer pause, till he measures the size of the hand closed round it, and concludes the object is too small to be a piece. Sure enough, after punching the remote fob several times and then tossing his head in frustration, the man proceeds to insert its hard-key in the door lock and set his other hand on the handle. His movements are slow, like his mind is really elsewhere, and he does not seem to hear as Pinoy approaches, moving quick but quietly, and stopping far enough away to anticipate if the guy tries to rush him.

"Seattle Police Department," Pinoy announces, careful to make the words sound serious but not threatening. Loud enough that he can't be ignored, but not so loud it sounds like he's trying to cause a scene. Policing is about community after all; a cop is the eyes and ears of the public, and its arms too when necessary, but keeping the peace means not disturbing it unnecessarily along the way and as usual, his measured tone seems to do its job. There's no sudden movement, no freaky jerk to the broad shoulders as the man twists around, still gripping the handle so the door opens partway, allowing light into the car's interior. His face, now that Pinoy can see it up close, is more tired than anything else; resigned would fit it, too, like maybe he's even been expecting someone to come looking for him. Trained to observe, the officer doesn't let his eyes linger there, but takes in the hands as well, black lines beneath fingernails in need of a trim and, on the driver's seat, a brown streak which experience tells him was red and wet when it got there, maybe just about 36 hours before. Same vital substance as caused those deposits dotting the jacket cuffs, he'd be willing to bet. It all goes together, and he's glad to see the back-up approaching two blocks away as his eye takes in one more piece of this derelict's puzzle; now that the door is open, he can see those boxes standing upright between the seats *are full of flowers*. They, too, were red at one time - deep red - but they're not red any more; they're dried out now, shrunken and shriveled into sorry parody of their former glory. Dozens and dozens of long-stemmed roses, as black and as dead as can be in the back of a car registered to a man wanted for questioning in what may by now have become - if the medical report reviewed during roll-out this morning was any kind of accurate - a murder.

"You are beautiful," the musicians sing, and Rodney with them. *"No matter what they say."* After exhausting the only selection they have in common, they've turned to other material, Evie singing the first verse and chorus of each selection, after which he joins in as she places her face close to his ear to feed the next lyric. Like a seasoned pro, he fits the words together with the music as it comes, anticipating the progressions, feeling the geometry of rhythm and song structure. *"Words can't bring you down..."*

The sound sends a chill up Aubrey's spine, almost as thrilling as if she herself were up there. Kim's features, locked in sullen denial only a few minutes ago, are relaxed now, with even the trace of a smile peeking out beneath her concentration. So wonderful to see and hear; all the hassling about whether this is Kim or Christina or Rod - and now it's clear that *this* is who she really is: this voice, this singer. Like, maybe, the whole Rodney trip was just something she had to do to be able to find herself – the only way she could get out from under being the daughter of some famous music guy was to turn herself into Kim, who rejected everything her father stood for including music, but then somewhere along the way she realized she had the music in her, and she couldn't keep it shut up there forever, so she invented this character of Rod, the same way she invented her street lady and her frustrated housewife and her porn star for those performance pieces, and her little school girl for the clubs.

Aubrey is trying to explain all this to the others, as they work their way closer to the stage while the musicians wrap up this latest number and the crowd applauds enthusiastically. Anne, for her part, seems blissfully unconcerned with the how and why of it, just happy to see her daughter connecting with something which was once so much a part of her family, as the guitarist announces a break in the music, " 'cause we're overdue for some more speech-making."

"Your father would be so proud," she sighs, touching a hand to Christina's face as Rod is hoisted down from the stage. "To hear..."

'My father would be livid,' I tell her, this crazy woman. 'My father couldn't have cared less for music or musicians.' He believed that men do real work, not prancing around singing and dancing. As always, she looks at me as if I were wishing her happy birthday, like nothing I ever say can cut through that membrane of good cheer she

wears like a body bandage. Lord - the difference; one minute I'm inside the music, natural as breathing, the next I'm back here again, in never-never land where nothing makes any sense.

'I understand,' that crazy Aubrey tells me, and starts to spout some theory about how I've made up a character named Rod, for God's sake! Pseudo-scientific pop-psychology, does she get that from the TV, I wonder or what? And then another one attacks me.

"Hey, listen," Tammy interjects, placing a hand on Rodney's arm to direct his attention toward the stage, where a local club-celebrity who uses the stage name of Brandy Alexander has come forward. His campy manner – shrink-wrapped even now into shiny spandex and perched on four inch platforms – is so obviously opposite of Stevie's shy discretion, that those who really knew her are unsurprised at the tale of how he once heard Stevie play the piano, and counted her as a friend - even if her act was kind of 'retro-Kansas-City.' "You should go back up there and tell them what Stevie was really all about."

"Yeah," agrees Rose, "You and her; when I saw you doing your act, dog, it was so tight. Tell them what that was like."

"I have nothing to say to these people," is Rod's reply, and layered into his stiff-backed 'these people' is a clear suggestion that he would have plenty to say *about* them, given half a chance, which only adds to Aubrey's impression of some turmoil going on inside her friend; of forces pulling in multiple directions – because of being back at this hospital maybe, or in this crowd of strange strangers with all their voices and music and whatever memories they call up. It's obvious Kim's attention is not in the moment, not focused on Tammy and the others who continue to plead, nor on Anne, urging her daughter to do the right thing, to honor her friend with a few well-chosen words.

Whatever the interior debate, the force of all these women appears to win out, as Aubrey watches Kim disappear into the crowd, then reappear a moment later being raised up onto the platform once again by Tammy's broad shoulders and half a dozen other hands. A stout figure has taken over from the musicians, acting as a sort of MC, and Aubrey experiences a moment of disorientation until she realizes it is the same woman who introduced festivities at the Swedish Social Club the night she and Rod met Stevie; the night Christina's gift first made itself known. This woman - Aubrey recalls her name now as Carol - squats down to confer with the instigators,

637

then eagerly nods and rises to bring Rod to the front, where they join a tight knot of people waiting as the sequined queen stumbles to the end of his remarks.

"OK," Carol says, as that under-whelming speech tapers off to small applause. "We've got another of Stevie's friends here. What's your name again, honey?" she asks, thrusting the mic in front of Christina's vacant features.

I look out and there are all these people staring up at me. Boys and girls mostly, decades younger than me, and dressed accordingly. Miss-fits and outcasts, non-conformists and self-styled rebels, I wonder if any of them is contributing a thing to their upkeep - if any one of them has a real job - and then my own thoughts remind me what is real *and what imagination.*

Receiving no response, Carol tries again, the effort greeted by several snarky calls from the crowd, impatient for something to sustain its energy. Casting them a wary glance, she tucks the mic into its nearby stand so she can grab Christina by both shoulders and speak intently into her face. A moment later, a scattering of claps and hoots peppers the crowd as the youngster is ushered sheepishly to the stand, which Carol adjusts until the silver ball is level with her lips.

"My name is Rodney Gimbal," a wary voice pronounces, and the hoots lessen, replaced by shouts of support. "<u>Dr.</u> Rodney Gimbal," she repeats, a little more confidently. The shouts and applause continue, though fewer. Around her, Aubrey catches people exchanging skeptical glances, wondering how that name and title jive with the speaker's appearance. Undaunted, the figure on the stage continues, seeming to draw confidence and energy from the crowd's response. "I don't know how I got here," she says next, though there is no uncertainty in the words. Indeed, as she says them her shoulders pull back and her spine straightens, showcasing Christina's full five-feet-three inch stature; alert and focused. Grabbing the stand in both hands she casts her eyes first to one side then the other, takes a deep in-breath and pulls the mic tight to her face, which is now composed in a determined scowl. "But I do know one thing..." she declares defiantly, and the crowd is in her court, their cheers louder than ever.

"All you people here; all worked up about whatever you think has happened? And all those people over there, telling you you're wrong and you're going to go to hell for being different from them? It doesn't matter what any of you have to say," she continues, much of the audience still registering their approval, though some among them begin to show confusion. On the stage, heads turn to one another in concern, as they hear "because I don't believe in you. I don't believe in them. None of you are real, none of this exists at all..."

A multitude of shouts erupt, as the crowd reacts in shock. On stage, Carol rushes forward and tears the mic from Rod's hands. Others swarm around and Aubrey loses sight of her friend as she hears someone nearby shout "No denial," and farther away, boos and curses erupt.

"We _are_ real," Carol shouts into the microphone, her fist upraised as chaos ensues all around. Hands grab Rod and roughly hustle him down from the ledge as others swarm upward.

"We are real," a buzz-cut person in biker leathers shouts into the microphone she has torn from Carol's hand. "And we fight back!" adds another, in heavy canvas overalls and a jacket with torn elbows and frayed cuffs. "We've had enough of this crap...right?"

Across the plaza another point of view turns up the volume on their own megaphones; the Reverend Lucius and his flock only too happy to agree with Rod. "That's right, brothers and sisters," he advises, addressing his flock while directing them with a wave of the hand to observe the chaos, "All these evils are as the smoke from a dying fire, and will be blown away by the fresh breeze of faith; will _disappear_ before the Lord's truth, that he made us all men and women, to serve his purposes, and anyone who denies that will perish..."

From somewhere in the crowd a yellow object comes flying: a banana, rolling and twisting in the air as it heads toward the Reverend, only to thump against a sign held by one of his young followers. Over the past hour, as each contingent has grown, the space between the two has shrunk, so that now only a few yards of open pavement remain to separate them as the bodies begin to surge. Despite the insults being hurled back and forth, despite being outnumbered, the Reverend and his crew stand their ground, variations of pride and resignation on their faces.

"You are one fucked-up kid, kid," Carol growls, putting her face right in Rod's as soon as they both are down from the stage. Around them bodies press and swirl, some climbing up in hopes of a chance to speak their own minds, some heading off purposefully to join the confrontation, more than a few pressing close to voice their anger at this interloper who has threatened to derail their movement. The blank look on Christina's face seems only to enflame their anger as behind them the musicians strike up a song in hopes of regaining the positive mood.

"*I won't let you down,*" they sing. "*I will not give you up.*"

"I thought you were Stevie's friend," demands Herb, his furious face appearing over Carol's shoulder just as Aubrey and Anne manage to force their way through the crush. "But I guess not. I guess you don't give a shit about her, or anyone else except yourself."

Frantically, Aubrey struggles to the side of the small figure and wraps an arm around her shoulder to ward off all these others. "The fuck, Chris?" she asks, locking on to eyes which once again seem totally alien to her. Before she can say any more, though, a familiar voice breaks in, and she turns to find the squared-off glare-shield of a professional-sized video camera inches from her shoulder.

"Beautiful!" Mark Peterson is shouting, flashing a thumbs-up as his face comes out from behind the big machine. "That was so fucking real," he enthuses to Rod. "Singing along like you're part of the whole scene, then you just, like, flip it around right in their faces. Talk about balls, Kim; you got 'em!"

It takes a few minutes for Aubrey and the others to convince Mark that Rod's remarks are not, as he has supposed, part of some new performance piece Kim is enacting. Even when he accepts that, the filmmaker's excitement is hardly dimmed.

"I'm on retainer now," he explains. "For the Orlando Foundation? They're all about, like...diversity and stuff, and we've got three cameras - Riley's over there covering the Jesus freaks, and Dook Kim is around somewhere. They pay us per diem and we shoot anything we hear about and then we cut it into this documentary they're making."

Mark's enthusiasm wanes a bit as Aubrey brings him up to speed on Rod's escapades, but blossoms again when he's introduced to Tammy and Rose. In an instant his camera is back at work as the pair begin explaining how many different groups make up the protesters, vamping their impressions of each faction as the music continues behind them.

"*All we have to do now,*" the musicians sing, "*is take these lies and make them true somehow.*"

From over by the wall a louder shout bursts through, a cry of pain, followed quickly by exhortations, to 'Move!' to 'Stop!' and to 'Go! Go! Go!'

"All we have to see; is that I don't belong to you... "

Grabbing a handset from his pocket, Peterson calls out for Riley, asking what the hell is going on over there.

"And you don't belong to me."

"It's crazy, man," comes the barely intelligible reply, Riley's voice garbled up with screams and cries, thumps and scrapes. "It's fucking chaos and it's fucking beautiful. You're gonna love it..."

"Freedom,
"You've gotta give for what you take,
"Freedom,
"You've gotta give for what you take."

"Hey, Mare," the voice on the phone is excited, almost incoherent. Or perhaps it's Mary's own mind that is garbled. Five-seventeen, says the bedside clock, and she got off shift at two, home around three after stopping to pick up a few groceries; so either she's had all of two hours sleep following a thirty-four hour shift, or she's been asleep for fourteen hours straight. Whichever it is, her head feels like it's filled with cotton balls and her mind is moving slow.

"Did you hear?" the voice continues, the easy familiarity of Jason's voice summoning up a warm fuzzy glow to spice-up her fatigue. "All that hoopla goin' on out front? Some kid just stood up to sing, and they introduced her as Rod Gimbal. That's our guy, isn't it?"

Gimbal's name cuts through the cotton in her head like a scalpel through adipose tissue, and in a few moments she hears the gist of Jason's story: the injured person in ICU, her queer friends all showing up, and then the anti-queers; the scene turning from vigil to protest to simmering national-news material. How Jason and the rest of the gotta-know-it-now freaks in IT have been following the demonstration by keeping their favorite news feeds windowed-in on their monitors, and how it had caught Jason's attention when this young chick identifying herself as Dr. Gimbal told them they were all just figments of her imagination.

"It was, outrageous," he enthusiases. "All the queer crowd, they were like, 'don't tell us we don't exist!' I mean, they were ready to start tearing the place down, and the preacher's posse were like 'rah, rah! right on; Disappear the Queers! God will disappear them all!' She managed to piss off both sides at the same time, and then she just disappeared herself; got swallowed up…"

"Get the thing," Mary urges, as she scrambles out of bed, searching among the clothes littering her floor for something to pull on. "The, the, the …"

"Vessel?" Jason offers, and she can just imagine the impish grin which must be taking over his entire face.

"Yes. Right," she laughs, finding two similar socks and setting her butt down in the center of the pile, cradling the phone to her shoulder as she tugs them onto her feet. "Get the 'vessel' and bring it to…" For a moment she is at a loss. Where to go? Admin; someone's office? Or Community Relations maybe, the Center's publicity department. Turning over the possibilities, she is not even aware that she is talking the whole time, downloading her thoughts directly to Jason just as they come to her own consciousness.

"Building 6," he interrupts conclusively, and to Mary the effect is as if he has read her mind. Not for the first time, she is struck by just how close she and Jase have become, and how quickly. By the surprising reality that she, who had pretty much accepted the idea of being alone, now has this puppy-cute geeky-smart guy practically hard-wired into her life. "That's where the victim is," his voice continues in her ear as she goes to the dresser for a clean sweatshirt so at least she won't be totally pitted-out when they meet up. "ICU; on Seven. But the cops have been all over the place for two days – they've got, like, a swat headquarters or something they've set up downstairs, and I'll bet the bigwigs have the whole event wired, they'll be on everything she said too, so I'll meet you in the lobby, as soon as I can get it there."

Taking the phone away from her ear, Mary hits the speaker button and sets it on the dresser so she can sort out her shirt's sleeves. "Thank you," she says out loud, as if he were right there in the room with her. "Thank you for doing this,"

"Oh hey, babe..." he answers back, and Mary has another flash of disconnection - where it feels at once so absolutely natural for Jase to be calling call her 'babe,' and at the same moment, so inconceivable that anyone would ever call her their 'babe;' and somehow both of those thoughts are flaring up together in her head at the same time that it is practically exploding with the need to get over to Hilltop *right now* and make them all understand that something absolutely momentous is going on with Dr. Gimbal. Which thought is also coexisting with a sonorous strain of 'Where the heck – and why don't I say the f-word like everybody else seems to do, but I just don't and actually, all together, I'm good with that – where the *heck* are my Nikes?' all of which messages shoot by in only the fraction of a second it takes for Jase to resume streaming across the telecom universe and out her phone's tiny speaker into her waiting ears.

"It's nothing any other guy wouldn't do, for his... you know, my..."

"Yeah,' Mary interrupts, catching a glimpse of herself in the mirror, a full-frontal smile consuming the space where her face should be. Jason is normally so confident, so sure of himself, so full of facts and figures and how to do whatever it is that needs to be done, that hearing him stumble for words is incredibly charming; so little-boy-in-a-big-boy's-body that it makes her heart sing; and other parts of her positively tingle.

"I know," she says, spotting the sole of one sneaker peeking out from beneath a chair. "I know what you mean. And it goes for me, too."

Compared to Dallas and Henry Volmer's home, or her own to which she has so recently bid goodbye, the hostel room is bare. Anonymous.

A bed, a wardrobe, a small table-cum-desk with a hard wooden chair; and in the corner a faded wingback, perfect for reading and contemplation. It is, nevertheless, everything Elaine has required these couple of weeks. She sits now upon the bed, near where her two suitcases lie, open-faced and halfway packed, eager to accept the rest of her small collection. In her hand the receiver hangs loosely.

"If you'd like to make a call…"

Yes, she'd like to make a call, but there are no numbers to dial for the people she'd like to call right now. Her mother, or her father, for example; both passed-away and lain to rest for years. An assortment of best friends in whom she once confided, back when years were longer and emotions more resilient. Or that latest in her line of confidants and presumed to be the last - for by now Elaine has accepted that she is the captain of her own flight; at some point in life it ceases to be possible that any but one's own self can truly comprehend the context and meaning of even the smallest event. Too much has been invested, too much wagered, lost, borrowed and spent for any newcomer to understand, she feels, as the hand holding the receiver flops back, its wrist at this moment the weakest link in her survival.

Still, even the impulse to share what she has just heard must, at this point in life, bring thought back to her Beryl; in this case to a conversation along the trail from Laos into China and Myanmar and beyond. Eating sticky rice from a shared bowl, their fingers like burled and gnarly twigs as each in turn reached in to grasp a clump of grain.

Perhaps, Elaine was admitting, she should have gone back right away, when the news of Rodney's passing had first reached them. Yes, at the time it had seemed an imposition, a typically inconsiderate act on his part that would interrupt her personal growth - her 're-birth', as she had later come to see it – but without having gone back, she felt something unresolved. There was a lingering anger, a hurt that required treatment. "Not a hurt, actually," she realized, as she swallowed hard to down the unsalted rice. Their water was in short supply that day, the previous night's stop affording only local pond water which was not safe for her and Beryl to drink, and so the morning had been hot and thirsty. A minor hardship, Elaine knew, but perhaps enough to explain her somber state. "It's like an ache. A muscle that needs to be stretched and relaxed before it can do its job again."

"You need 'closure'?" Beryl asked, the word pronounced around her food in a way that made abundantly clear the low regard in which she held that new-age ideal.

"I loved him," Elaine insisted, then elaborated, expressing how it had felt in those early years, when it was still conceivable that she and Rodney might be right for one another. It was only later, she emphasized as the rice was finished and she began gathering up their bowls and the few other things from lunch, that she understood the depth of disconnect between them.

"When I didn't become pregnant," she goes on, venturing into terra which is somewhat incognita, for herself as well as Beryl. "When *we* did not become pregnant..."

They had never determined, in fact, whose biology was amiss. Elaine's periods came with clockwork regularity and showed every evidence of full reproductive health, and Rodney's body certainly acted up to the task, but he was never willing to try the treatments which might have made a difference, or even to have the tests to find out what was not working. 'Medicine is for the truly ill,' he said, in various different phrasings on various occasions, 'not a magic wand to make our lives turn out the way we'd like them to.' 'Some things are meant to be,' he always concluded, 'and some are not.'

"What it really was, I think, with the benefit of hindsight..."

"And distance, dear," Beryl interrupted. "Don't forget the benefit of physical distance in changing one's perspective."

"With the benefit of distance then – real or cosmic." The two women shared a small laugh, their long days together having equalized their status, giving the student license to tease her instructor a bit. "Is think what the truth is, he was actually...relieved. At not having to deal with what a child would have meant. At not having to divide his attention in that way, perhaps."

"I don't think - from what you have told me - that your Rodney would have been the kind of father who spent a lot of time with his children, in any case."

Loading packs onto their shoulders, the two stretched and stalled a bit, bodies not quite ready to resume their exertions. From up the trail the lead porter emerged, spoke briefly with Beryl, then departed again with, for once, a smile on his face.

"Not time, so much." Elaine struggled to frame the thought in her mind, as they set off along the trail. "Energy. Some sort of energy he would have had to spend on...the whole business of it. My being pregnant, for a start; we'd seen what that demanded of other couples. The planning, the impact on what the parents do with their lives; how they do it. 'It's very disruptive,' he once said to me. But there was something more. Something I never saw in Rodney in any other way. He was afraid," she realized as they stopped in the middle of a rickety footbridge to gaze at the small stream beneath it - one more flowing course of water unavailable to their thirsty throats - "Of all the questions it would raise. About him; and us. About the world and what sort of place it is. It was as if he really was relieved at not having to ask himself what kind of a father he would be."

The stream, in that season, was narrow - a large man's arms could have stretched from bank to bank - and its flow sluggish, nearly stagnant. From either side thick grasses hung over, shading banks of slick black mud fragrant with decay; the sort of muck in which might lurk any number of venomous reptiles, or insects bearing strange and exotic diseases. Beyond the grassy verge lay tangled shrubs, taller than either of the two women, their stalks and foliage thick and impenetrable, their interior dark and humid. Secretive.

"And for that he denied you what you wanted more than anything else in the world? Prevented you from experiencing what may just be the greatest joy this world of ours has to offer?" Beryl mused.

Not ready to concede the criticism of her husband, Elaine was on the verge of responding, of insisting that no, she had not really wanted a family more than *anything* else in the entire world, when inside her head she was already hearing her friend's retort. 'You may have hidden this from yourself for all these years,' the voice instructed without rancor, 'but do not ask me to play the fool as well.'

The slightest touch upon her shoulder informed Elaine that it was time to start moving once again.

"Yes," Beryl belatedly answered her own question, as they left the small patch of light that the stream's interruption had admitted through the overhead canopy and re-entered the shadowed uncertainty that seemed to surround it without end. "That might leave a bit of a scar."

"...please hang up and dial again," the disembodied voice repeats. With a start, Elaine sets the phone back on its cradle. Talking to that detective has upset her more than she would have predicted. Assuming, that is, that she could ever have predicted such a conversation. More than it 'should' have, then. More than she would like to admit it could. Has.

Staring round the room, she is amazed by its tidiness. Such simplicity; such order. 'If only life could be so tidy,' she thinks.

If only.

"Sorry," Jase mutters as he backs into the elevator, forcing a couple of frowning residents to the corners as he tugs and jerks the dolly carrying Resor's vessel across the threshold gap. "This thing is f'ing heavy."

The residents show no sympathy as the cab doors close, only resume their unselfconscious debate over the efficacy of Thorozine therapy in a case of pernicious and persistent hiccoughing. The dolly's load is not exactly well-balanced; the car's first jerk of upward motion causes the vessel to sway heavily to one side, and Jason has to insert himself between it and the nearest resident to avoid a topple.

"My bad," he offers again, with his best submissive grin, but the other only glares, as the doors open once again, revealing a ground level corridor of E Building, Hilltop's pediatric facility. The basement in which they found the vessel had been quiet, almost deserted; this is a busy thoroughfare, with orderlies pushing children in chairs, med and support staff moving in every direction, and clusters of family members, all of who seem to exist either in a state of extreme good humor as they endeavor to distract a child from the reality of where they are, or a state of equally extreme seriousness, as the adults struggle with that same reality. Jason feels absurdly conspicuous manhandling his heavy load out into the stream, scanning the walls for a sign which will point him toward the west lobby, from which he will have to roll this B-movie-looking object outside, across a staff parking lot, and then either through or around G and L buildings, in order to reach #6, where Mary has told him to meet her.

"Mommy, what's that?" asks a boy in a green gown and fuzzy blue slippers whose toes are molded into bunny-rabbit heads, complete with floppy ears. The boy's up-stretched arm is held tight in the grip of his mother's hand and his speech is a bit slurred, but his curiosity is that of any normal kid, despite the gauze wrapping one side of his head and covering one eye. Just your ordinary, everyday, normal kid walking along trailing an IV stand, and Jason would like to give him a clever answer, but all he can think about right now is that this place is too damn crowded and there is way too much likelihood of running into someone who knows him and knows he has no business moving Center hardware around like this, so instead of making some quip about it being a Klingon Death Ray – no that would be bad taste here, how about a Vulcan Life Ray? – he just casts his eyes down and gives the dolly another shove, aiming as best he can down the center of the crowded hallway and hoping everyone will get out of his way.

By the time he exits L, visions of his girlfriend staring baffled and fuming at her watch are in his head. As the door closes behind him he takes a moment to wipe away the hair plastered to his forehead by the exertion of shoving and stopping and turning his heavy load through the seemingly-endless succession of corridors and lobbies, vestibules and doorways, and in that moment recognizes the sounds of voices raised in song, interlaced with others, chanting dirge-like, as they try to overwhelm the music. It's coming from nearby, around the corner of Bldg. 6, and putting that sound together with the visual of news-clips he's caught, makes very clear that route is out of the question. Fortunately though, he doesn't have to go to the front, for just as he'd envisioned it, the big building's receiving entrance is directly ahead. With a few well-placed shoulder-hits he steers the dolly across the dirty asphalt, swiveling and changing direction each time its wheels get hung up on a pebble or the nascent edge of a pothole beginning to form. A concrete ramp leads up to the door landing and he is just about to congratulate himself on conquering its slope when the door opens of its own accord to reveal one of Hilltop's best, her starched white shirt lumpy over body armor, her heavy black belt bristling with nifty security gadgets.

"No access today," says the guard, waving a hand whose fingertips are barbed with brilliant blue nails at least half an inch in length. Her plastic sunglasses are decorated with rhinestones, but still effective in preventing him from having any idea of her mood, or how much interest she's taking in his burden. "We got ourselves a *situation* here, ya' see," she goes on. "No one gets into the building without proper authorization."

Despite the dark glasses, Jason has no doubt she's scanned the ID hanging around his neck, its blue border signifying Info Tech, a department whose brief even the most sleepy guard is bound to realize does not extend to moving heavy equipment between buildings. Quickly, he improvises a story about an urgent call for this 'specialized incubation sterilizer,' tossing in a 'Code Red' and a 'Stat' for good measure, but the woman isn't buying what he's got to sell.

"Wait here while I check with my supervisor," she says, raising a hand to the radio-piece clipped to her shirt.

"Ah…that's OK," Jason advises. "I'll… I'll check back myself. With my own boss. I don't want to bother you."

"It's no bother," the guard is saying, but Jason is gone already, headed back where he came from, with maps of Hilltop in his mind, trying to recall another way to get into The Center.

"So you're Dr. Rodney Gimbal?" a new voice inquires, practically shouting to be heard over the din. Two men materialize out of the nearby crowd, moving against the flow as the human mass shifts toward the new commotion, and take up positions on either side of Christina, their attitudes alert, hands poised as if expecting her to run at any moment. It's the larger of the two who's speaking, a hang-dog sort of fellow, with stooped shoulders and a face that looks as if it's seen several lifetime's worth of disappointment. "We've been looking for you, *Doctor,* so it's mighty nice of you to stand up there and identify yourself to us."

"Detective Bannerjee," announces the smaller of the two, his tone managing to convey both a greeting and a threat. "Special Vice Task Force. And this is investigator Kallispell," he adds, indicating the other, who Aubrey recognizes as one of the visitors to her own apartment, the morning after Stevie was attacked. "We're investigating Mr. Margulies - the person who was assaulted? We've been following up a lead that a woman who called herself Rod was among the last persons to have contact with him. Haven't had much success locating her, though, so the fact that she's showed up right here...well, it is mightily convenient. For us, that is. Not necessarily for her." Pausing to allow his little joke to sink in, the detective seems only now to notice the crowd of friends tightening protectively around Rod. "And you all are?"

It is Anne who responds, slipping easily into her old role as the maestro's social director: graciously introducing everyone, then proceeding right into an explanation of Christina's recent adventures, which would seem - from her telling - to have nothing whatsoever to do with Stevie Margulies. All of which gives Aubrey a chance to consider this new policeman, a species of which she's suddenly seeing way too much. Little older than her from the looks of him, he's also little like all those weary, weathered detectives she's used to from TV and movies. A long way from tall, and lean as a punker, in a suit that fits like it was borrowed from an elder brother. A little bit like Rod there, she realizes, except the shadow on Bannerjee's cheeks and chin is nearly as dark as the skim of buzzed hair that outlines his oversized head, and he's just about brimming-over with energy. His small, dark, hands seem always active; one second they're scratching at the back of his neck, the next they're waving to dismiss some concern in Anne's words, then back to itch first an ear and then the tip of his nose, before diving through various pockets to pop back out holding a pad and pen. For an instant, he glances toward the distant conflict, as if measuring its possible impact on his efforts, then turns back to focus on Christina as Peterson's camera jockeys into position for a mid/close two-shot.

"Tell me how you knew the victim," he suggests, over Anne's continuing pleasantries. His tone is matter of fact, but with a hard center that makes it clear he is dead serious, and as he speaks he moves a little closer, so that his body is positioned directly in front of Christina, feet planted wide. His eyes, dark and hooded, continue to dart between Anne's face, Aubrey's and Christina's with a quickness which suggests there is a lot going on behind them, but they get no response from Rod, who seems oblivious to the questions, his attention fixed on the stage where the musicians play on.

"*I think there's something you should know,*" they sing. "*I think it's time I stopped the show,*"

"Let's get her out of this commotion," suggests Kallispell, and with a nod to all, Bannerjee sets off through the crowd, his slight form parting the bodies as if by sheer force of will. Behind him, Aubrey leads Chris by a hand, Kallispell taking position right behind, as if he expects her to bolt at any moment.

They're still six feet from the wide bank of doors when one leaf swings partway open, revealing a uniformed cop standing just inside. With a nod to Bannerjee he steps aside just far enough to allow one person at a time to pass, all the while eyeing the rest of the crowd for any interlopers who might make a dash to join them. At the narrow gap Christina hesitates, head craning back toward where the musicians still play; Aubrey has to grab her by the elbow and tug to get her through. Doing so, she feels once again just how little of her friend there is to pull, the baggy suit coat draping an arm which seems hardly more than sticks of bone inside it.

Behind their small party the door shuts, and the bustle and noise of the plaza gives way to a thick hush, like an airport terminal in the middle of the night. Building 6's lobby does, indeed, resemble some transit terminal, or perhaps a museum gallery, its generous height and wide dimensions a surprising contrast to the small windows and intricate details of the building's façade. Two horizontal rows of windows above the entry explain the contradiction: the space has been carved out by cutting thru what were once the second and third floors, linking their volumes to the first to create a space nearly thirty-feet tall, and some seventy feet in each direction. At this afternoon hour, the last gasps of daylight penetrate deeply from those high windows, supplemented by the glow emanating between several overlapping planes of ceiling that step down toward the sides, focusing the space upon its central feature, a grand stairway leading up to a mezzanine, whose glass and chrome balustrade extends across the entire rear of the space.

On the far wall, a multi-layered frosted glass display is alive with slowly changing images; gorgeous Pacific Northwest nature scenes alternate with shots of Hilltop's buildings, intercutting and cross-fading over happy, healthy-looking people as four-foot-high letters stream across it all, spelling out words like 'CARING,' and 'RESPONSIVE,' 'COMMTTED,' and 'UNCOMPROMISING.' The synthesized movement mesmerizes Aubrey for a moment, even as a whiff of antiseptic cleanser recalls a different morning – herself and Jake, Kim's photo in the paper; hospital people telling them where to go, and then the bandaged figure lying in its motorized bed amid a welter of wires and tubes. The memories bring with them a rush of gratitude, that her good friend has survived it all, but when Aubs turns to hug that cherished companion, what she encounters is Rod: disheveled and mis-fit, his face still smudged with dirt and damp from his days of wandering. A face which, no matter how hard or long she stares at it, she can no longer convince herself is that of the girl she knew as Kim.

Pushing the dolly ahead of him, Jason Privet makes his way along the narrow sidewalk fronting Harris House, a tiny brick box which started life as carriage house to some long-gone mansion and now serves as a meeting room for briefings and lectures by visiting authorities on medical arcana. He's headed for another entrance to Bldg. 6, this time approaching from the east. The walkway around Harris is narrow and winding, bordered on each side by decorative plant beds, with brass plaques on little posts identifying each of the specimen shrubs and trees. Between them the soil is bare and carefully raked; its surface picked-over until every speck of alien material has been removed, leaving it monochromatic, uniform and oddly lifeless, even as it sustains the cultivated life above and below. The events on the other side of the looming main medical building seem far away as he sets his hands lower on the vessel and one foot against the edge of the dolly to start it up another concrete ramp. It is only when he has reached the top of the slope and is almost in reach of his goal, an aluminum-framed rectangle of mirrored glass, that Jase is reminded of the action back there, for even before his hand can touch the handle the door is opened from inside.

"Sorry," says another uniformed security staffer. "This building's secured. No entry unless it's specifically authorized by Admin." The man's glare confirms to Jason how completely at odds his baggy khakis and faded blue bowling shirt are with his current activity of hauling freight around the complex, and he feels his face begin to flush. Once again he tries to claim his load is needed upstairs and like the other guard before him this one reaches for his radio set, politely offering to check the story.

"That's OK," Jason insists, already turning to slow his load as he allows gravity to take it back down the ramp. "You don't have to mess with it. I'll go back and check with my department. I probably got the wrong building."

"Yeah," the guard says a few seconds later, two fingers holding down the 'TALK' button of his radio set as he watches Jason moving off through the gardens, his image drained of color by the glass door's heavy tinting. "Sounds like the same kid Stevens reported. Soon's I said I'd check, he turned 'round and headed back where he came from." A muffled squawk emerges from the radio and the guard shakes his head, though there's no one else at his station to see it. "Yeah," he answers. "Wouldn't be surprised. He seemed pretty anxious to get wherever he was going." Conversation over, he drops his hand to the belt around his ample waist, idly fingering the many tools and devices holstered there, and leans heavily against the wall. He's done his job, after all, manned his post and reported in. It's up to someone else to figure out why a kid from Info Tech would be dragging a piece of lab equipment around Hilltop when he should be punching a keyboard. 'Gotta' make you suspicious,' Security Officer Anthony Morse is thinking as he settles back against the wall. 'Anybody working that hard at something that is clearly not a part of his job description...'

The lobby of Building 6, Aubrey and the others find once they are inside, has been turned into an outpost of the Seattle Police Department, which has set up operations amidst the comfortable cluster of lounge furniture that occupies one corner. Anti-bacterial-vinyl upholstered sofas face suck-you-in recliners around a coffee table denuded of its usual magazines and outreach flyers, their place taken now by a scattering of file folders, weatherproof steel clipboards, days-old newspapers and several identically-battered radio handsets standing in a neat line - each mini-monolith buzzing with a different strain of hails and conversations from the outer world.

"So you knew the victim?" Bannerjee asks of Christina once they have settled her into a chair with her back to the entry doors. Watching the two cops watch her, Aubrey has little trouble imagining their evaluations. 'Dirty clothes, weird haircut, needs a shower.' 'Uncommunicative and detached.' Any second now they'll be asking for a blood sample, especially if Kim starts in again with her talk about nothing being real.

"It's been a big shock to her," Aubrey interjects, hoping to avoid that particular awkwardness. "She...she feels like what happened to Stevie could happen to her, to anyone..."

"Yeah," suggests a new voice. Turning Aubrey sees a uniformed officer has separated herself from a group of persons clustered near the security counter and made her way over. Her face, too, is familiar: Officer Dominguez – Marie is just too gentle a name to use, though that's what her badge says when she comes close enough for Aubrey to check it and confirm that this is indeed the cop she recalls from the early morning she and Kallispell showed up unannounced at the apartment to listen to Stevie's last voice message. Recalls also the lady cop's lack of sympathy, on full display once again as soon as she opens her mouth. "Could happen to anyone who goes around in drag. Is that what's got you worried?" she asks, jabbing a finger at Rod, who rewards her with nothing more than an empty stare. "What's she on," the cop asks Aubrey.

"Nothing. She's just tired..."

"She's been out on the street," Rose adds, her even tone cutting through the officer's antagonism like an esteemed professor through a kindergarten class. Aubs is taken by surprise that the two T-girls managed to attach themselves to the little group that fled inside, but she is instantly grateful, for Rose's genially-ambiguous persona draws at least a little attention away from Kim. "*Living* on the streets, that is. Homeless. Not like what you people have been saying about poor Stevie, when she can't even defend herself."

"I'm sure Christina doesn't know anything about what happened," Anne chimes in, as the uniformed officer visibly struggles to take stock of this odd assortment of women who suddenly seem to have surrounded her.

"She's just upset," Tammy puts in, in a sweet-as-can-be way that suggests these things happen all the time. Stepping closer she smiles wide to show those crooked teeth right in the policewoman's face and throws back a question in a tone grown suddenly cold and hard. "You'd be upset, too, if a friend of yours'd had her balls cut off?"

There's no chance for the officer to respond to this oxymoron, as all eyes turn to Rod, who's shot up from his seat and is standing now, a little unsteadily, with one hand on the chair's back. Christina' face is paler than ever: what little color her skin had gained from the cold and damp drained now, but there is energy in her eyes, which glare at Tammy with unconcealed horror. "Is that what they did to her?"

"Mr. Margulies was the victim of a sexual assault," Bannerjee replies, placing himself once again directly in front of Rod.

"What they did to that girl wasn't about sex, you fool," Tammy interrupts, clearly incensed. "Any more than that riot outside is. It's about..."

" 'Genital mutilation' is how the report reads..." Dominguez insists.

"Well <u>that</u> *certainly* isn't about sex," Rose adds, and instantly the conversation becomes a shouting match, as the two T-girls question why this assault is being handled by Vice when anyone who knew Stevie could tell in a second she was no hooker, and Kallispell defends that they don't choose their cases, and Dominguez adds that if they did they certainly wouldn't choose to investigate 'a drag-queen in an alley with his crotch slit open,' at which point Anne screams and Aubrey finds herself with one arm around the older woman and the other stiff-arming Rod to keep him from striking anyone. Several Hilltop staffers in scrubs are now staring at them from the reception desk across the lobby, while the cop at the front door looks about to rush over, hand poised above his firearm, and Mark Peterson is flashing a thumbs-up from behind his jet-black mega-cam, it's single red eye confirming he's getting this all down for posterity.

It is Bannerjee who eventually calms things down, asking everyone to remember that a crime has been committed.

"The point is," he says, "that we've got several good pieces of physical evidence on the perpetrators, and a number of leads to follow up. For example, there was cat hair all over the victim's coat, and as far as we can tell, the victim didn't..."

"Stevie was allergic to cats," Rod spits out, then adds, as if angry with himself. "Is."

"And I don't have one either," Aubrey adds, "So there's no way that came from Kim."

"Who the fuck is Kim?" ask Dominguez and Kallispell, simultaneously. Bannerjee, too, looks at her as if she's just come from Mars, while Tammy and Rose seem simply surprised and Rod shakes his head in apparent disgust.

I must not allow myself to fall into believing any of this. What they say about Stevie – that could not happen. Not in this day and age, not in this country. Just one more proof that none of this is real and there's nothing to be gained by trying to respond.

"No problem," the security guard at the second-floor skybridge advises Mary, handing back her ID as she opens the door no more than half its swing. "Not gonna' let those loonies out there stop you from taking care of folks who need it, are we?"

Dropping the lanyard back down to hang before her chest, the young doctor mutters something agreeable as she squeezes through the narrow gap and into a hallway which seems unnaturally quiet after the commotion she has witnessed first-hand, looking down through the skybridge's glazed walls as she crossed over from the Oncology tower. Here in 6 there are no patients exercising, no orderlies transporting, no families milling about with anguished faces, only potted plants in need of water and a few idle carts of equipment. With so little going on the corridor seems wider than it should be, its floor a little too shiny, the sound of her footsteps just a touch too loud; every sensation a reminder that she doesn't really belong here. There is no patient in Rm. 6-123, or if there is, it isn't one of hers. There is no 'contamination isolation study' going on, with a review convening in fifteen minutes which requires her check-in on that imaginary patient to be done within the next ten so she can make it back in time, like she told the guard. All lies, those things she said. Little lies; innocuous in themselves, but lies nonetheless, and all the more uncomfortable, considering that the whole idea of coming over here is to find some sort of truth.

Reaching an intersection she pauses for a moment to get her bearings. It all seems so unbelievable; but Bagley - bless her pickled heart - was certainly convincing, even for a drunken, bitter stay-at-home who clearly had a grudge against the Center. Looking at the passages branching out in front of her, Mary studies the signs and wonders one more time what really constitutes doing the right thing. Turn left, where the sign says she will find 'Admitting' and 'Patient Information' and possibly destroy her career with a wild story no one is likely to believe, or continue in a straight line, toward 'Physician Services' and 'Clinical Specialties;' the direction she's been heading ever since choosing her profession at age four.

"I want to be a doctor," little Mary Antonias told the preschool teacher, a woman she can still picture though not name. Paisley scarf draped carefully over a pale blue turtleneck sweater, long full skirt that swished audibly to ears which stood below the level of her hip, and strong arms that picked you up if you skinned a knee or wandered off in the wrong direction. Sitting in a circle talking about what they liked to do and little Mary announcing to the bunch of them that she wanted to be a doctor, for no specific reason she can remember, but certain from that day to this that there was nothing else worth doing and now here she is about to maybe screw it all up because – why? Is it really about telling Bagley's story and getting the truth out, or is it about that face in the ICU that night and all the people fretting more than they would if it had been an old woman, a fat man, or just a plain girl – a girl like Mary Antonias, for example - rather than 'that pretty little thing in there,' or 'such a beautiful child.' All this obsession of hers, the questions asked of baffled-looking strangers, the searching through records and sneaking around storerooms, the flying all the way to New York, for goodness sake, which she certainly cannot afford – is it really about searching for the truth, or just some way of getting back at that mysterious Jane for being so special, so damned pretty that everyone rates her tragedy higher than all the other tragedies that unfold every day in a place like this?

No, Mary concludes as she heads to the left. It might have been about that at one time, long ago. But that was before she started discovering odd facts, and putting them together. And it was before Jason; if nothing else good comes out of this, the fact that she met quirky, funny little Jason makes it all worth while. Thanks to him she could hardly care less how the world regards that girl, or what name they give her. Now it really is about truth. And medical science too; for if what she is about to claim is true, it could point the way to any number of new treatments, breathtaking possibilities for patients with no other hope of recovery.

Of course, she is reminded, as a pair of double doors looms closer ahead, it all depends on Jason in another way as well. So far, that vessel is the only concrete proof of what she has to tell them; without that, it's all just words.

Outside, the October night has fallen, deep and chilly, and music has given way to talk. Umbrellas have been opened and jackets hoisted overhead as a suggestion of rain whips about: on-shore breezes desperately seeking passage through the surrounding maze of buildings, and tearing themselves to gusts in the process. In the wake of Rod's denial and the ensuing scuffle, the vigil's leaders have managed to restore some semblance of order, and to bring a more substantive tone to things. Above, they've strung a new banner - "RAINBOW WORLD UNITED" it proclaims under the surgical glare of borrowed spotlights, as Carol introduces a speaker of a different sort.

"All right y'all, I know it's getting wet out here," she says, in a voice hoarse from the long day. "We asked the folks that run this place to let us in out of the rain but you know how that goes, so let's just make the best of it, and listen up to our next speaker: an author and a lecturer, she's travelled all the way from Des Moines, Iowa, to be with us here today, so give her all your attention please – Doctor and Professor...Lynn Jameson."

True to her mid-west departure point, the person who steps up to the microphone has all the flash of a Sunday school teacher. Dressed in long paisley skirt and low-heeled pumps, with a woolen jacket over high-necked white blouse, her rigidly-set hair would not look out of place at a bingo parlor or small-town library reference counter. Her posture exudes formality, and an air of chilly self-importance, yet despite this, the crowd reacts with warmth, a murmur of recognition running beneath the smattering of applause as she approaches the microphone.

"We are here tonight," she begins with all the authority of a senior faculty member addressing the first session of an introductory class, "to bear witness for Stevie Margulies. In doing so, it is critical that we focus our thoughts not on the terrible act which has been committed, but on the life which it has threatened. Not the murder of a cross dresser – as some are trying to call ir - but the life of an explorer. For Stevie was that, a person willing to explore all the possibilities of the cultural space in which e found irself."

A murmur ripples through the crowd as those familiar with Jameson's revisionist grammar explain it to those to whom her gender-free pronouns are new.

"Now there are those," she continues, "in the press, in the law, in the narrow sanctuaries of religionism..." A cry from the

Reverend's crew by the wall confirms that her amplified words are reaching them too. Bullhorns blaring they begin to shout her down, but Jameson is undeterred, even gaining energy from their opposition. "There are those who will tell you that Stevie asked for what e got. That e should have accepted the biology to which e was born, and used 'will power' to silence the voice within irself. And there are those among our own number, maybe even some of you here tonight, who will say that ir sin was in trying to be two things at once. If Stevie had simply made irself a woman, this reasoning goes, and forgotten e had once been a man, if e had hidden ir memories and obliterated all traces of that previous life, e could have slipped beneath the radar, gone stealth. E could have *survived*."

There's a brief moment of quiet, as Jameson pauses for effect, then comes back in a voice loud and emphatic enough that it could reach a crowd this size with no electronic aid at all. "Well, I'm here to call 'bullshit' on both of those rationalizations," she shouts, expertly playing to her crowd's enthusiasm. "There is a *person* lying in that bed up there. Not a man or a woman, a tranny or a crosser, not a hooker or a queer, but a *person* - with a capitol 'P'. And the reason e is up there, the reason e may be dying as we speak, is that there are people among us who hate anything with which they are not familiar - anything they cannot put in neat categories and therefore choose not to understand." At this the audience positively roars, pumping signs up and down, some even waving fists to express their common desire to move; to act on the sentiments they are hearing. "E is up there hooked to a machine because even in this great nation and this wonderful city – even in this modern-day time - there is ignorance; and prejudice; and jealousy; and fear; and the lesson of Stevie's life is not that we should try to fit ourselves into the two or three categories other people wish us all to fit into, but that we must strive to create a world which is *free* of categories. A world where every person is allowed to be irself, in all the glorious variety that implies."

The instant Jameson pauses, the voice of the crowd rushes in to fill the void, cheering and chanting. Suddenly, the stage is being stormed by three dark-clad figures scrambling up the stony ledges to jostle her out of the way and grab the microphone.

"That's all very nice," one of the figures announces. "We all want to make the world a better place, but we didn't all come here tonight for a class on gender-speak."

"Yeah," agrees another, pulling the mic away for herself.

"The important thing is, what do we really know about what's going on up there - what they're doing to Stevie? When they won't let any of us in to see her. They say she was a hooker – does anyone believe that?" Holding the mic out to the crowd she captures their shouts of 'no, no, no,' and feeds them back, amplified ten times or more.

Now all three are shouting, faces jammed together, shadows and highlights mingling them into one vibrating image.

"And how do we know what they're doing to her? Remember what they do to babies who don't fit into their boxes!" Again the woman holds out the mic, picking up shouts of 'they cut them' and 'they make them fit,' as the mob surges right up against the front ledges of the fountain.

"That's right," she says, the mike now pressed against her sneering lips. "They slice 'em and dice 'em and make them over in their own image. Well, we're gonna find out what they're up to with our Stevie, and if they won't let us in, we'll *find* a way in, to see what's really going on up there!"

"We want in," chants one of her companions into the mic, and immediately the call is taken up by the crowd.

"We want in," they shout in response. "We want in."

With that, two of the three leap down from the stage and begin to press their way through the now-fluid crowd, its massed bodies eddying aside to make way for the ring-leaders, then sweeping in behind to join the charge. With bobbing heads the human river flows toward the base of The Center, where soon a multitude of hands are tugging and pulling against the polished chrome doors, to no avail. With more shouting and swirling, the current sweeps to either side, searching along the building's walls for any opening, as off to one side the Reverend and his crowd maintain what decorum they can, singing out their verses and bowing their heads.

At very nearly the same moment a sweaty young man passes through a doorway into yet another corridor, less spacious than those in which Mary has been travelling; less sanitary as well, and far less well lit. Built as separate structures, in separate eras, each of Hilltop's buildings seems to have its own idea of a proper floor level, so the service tunnels which have been constructed over the years to tie their basements together are a maze of twists and turns, ups and downs. Still, he's grateful they exist, since there seems to be a security guard at every other entrance, or at least all three of those he tried above-grade before heading back to where he started: this institutional underworld. From the service level of K building, he's travelled through a tunnel that connects to a gallery alongside Bldg. #9, where an auxiliary cooling plant has been tucked below the courtyard between M and K. From there it was a short trek past the cafeteria kitchen, its service hallway a tight fit as he steered between pallets of crated vegetables waiting to be chopped into the salad bar, its damp atmosphere smelling of stale milk and barbequed pork even as he glanced in at the dishwashers in their steamy purgatory. After that came a series of mechanical rooms, with giant fans squeezing wind around humming doors and through an entire wall of louvers, then a blast of cold, wet air as he passed beneath a grating open to the world above, allowing a brief taste of the music and chanting from that horde assembled on the plaza above, welcome sign that he must be getting close, very close. Stepping backwards now, he maneuvers the dolly, wheels squeaking loudly, down a sloping concrete floor toward a door labeled 'Bldg. 6 – East Wing.' If his memory is correct, that door will lead into a corridor on the second sub-level of 6, and from there he can catch an elevator and then...

Reaching for the door, Jason holds the dolly with one hand, the floor's slope doing its best to drag them both back where they have come from. The tarnished knob is stiff, and turns only reluctantly, taking all the strength of his hand to move it just a fraction of a rotation, and as he struggles with it Jason finds himself stretched farther and farther, the vessel's weight urging it back down, away from him. Chuckling at the absurdity of his predicament, he heaves the dolly uphill and, in the instant of relief its forward momentum provides, is able to apply his full strength to the doorknob. Sure enough, it twists the rest of the way and he's able to transfer the weight of the dolly through outstretched arms and shoulders to the door, pulling its screeching hinges out of their long slumber and opening a portal to the light ahead.

"Nice work," admits a voice from the corridor on the other side, where his squinting eyes recognize the security guard from the West entrance. It's not the guard who's congratulating him though, but the person standing just behind him: a gray-haired, triumphant-looking dude in a crumpled brown suit and neck tags bearing the gold border that denotes membership in the Executive Administrative Department. "You don't take 'No' for an answer, do you, young man?"

"Kim was my best friend," Aubrey begins, then proceeds to explain how Christina assumed a new name when she fled her parents' house, eventually to attend the University and find her true self as a performance artist. Glossing over the exact reason Kim ended up as a Jane Doe at Hilltop, she recounts how she and Jake came to this very building and saw their friend comatose and not expected to survive the night, only to find out the next day that her condition had miraculously stabilized, leading to her convalescence at Anne's guesthouse where she regained consciousness – everyone's joy tempered to varying degrees by the minor complication of her believing herself, from that time on, to be one Dr. Rodney Gimbal. The reaction of the three stooges – 'her court-appointed physicians,' Anne hastens to correct – and her subsequent relapse into a drug-induced coma are touched upon, although at the point where Aubrey and friends rescued Rod, the account again becomes sketchy. All eyes are upon her as she describes Rod's de-tox and awakening at the apartment, and the tedious months of re-learning; to speak, to eat, to dress and do all the daily tasks which other adults take so much for granted. Recounting their eventual arguments, Aubrey finds the telling less easy as she explains their parting.

"It was my fault really," she admits, relieved to notice the two detectives have been distracted by their radios as she turns to look her former BFF directly in the eyes. "I couldn't take the act any more, Kim. You always picking on how I live, what I do, who I am. It was like, you were always telling *me* to grow up and take care of *myself* - when you're so fucking into your own shit you don't even know it's an act anymore."

I know this is not real. It is not possible for any of this to be real, and yet it feels so ...it is all I have, and if I do not engage in it, what else is there for me?

"Who I am is not an act," Rod begins, but gets no farther.
"God damn it, girl, it is. It's just like your bag lady and your fucked-up housewife; and the time you pretended to be a substitute teacher for a Lit class and gave those poor kids a snap quiz on shit they'd never even fucking heard of before. I know how much you enjoyed that, because you told me all about it while we got stoned together at Kristal's place after. You got off on the power of that,

just like you're getting off now, making everyone call you Rod and all that shit. I mean...Kim, I love you, girl - I really do fucking love you more than I ever wanted to admit to myself, much less to all these people who are hearing me make a fucking fool of myself - but it's time for this to end."

'I am not Kim,' I say, as clearly and evenly as possible. 'I am not Christina, or a bag lady or any kind of an artist." For the umpteenth time I find myself defending what is completely clear to me: that I am who I am and it is they who need to explain themselves, their continued trespass in my thoughts.

"Whoa," exclaims Tammy, head shaking in agreement, eyes roving the group from face to face in search of aid as she attempts to defuse the confrontation between Aubrey and Rod. "I know what this is; it's like, imagine if you lived one life; and then you died? But then you were, like, reincarnated as someone else, only you remembered who you had been? I mean, wouldn't that mess with your head! One minute you're yourself, the next minute everyone thinks you're someone else completely?

"No," Rose corrects her. "That's not the way reincarnation works. There's time in between it somehow; like, you die in one life, and then there's this place you go to..."

Superstitious mumbo-jumbo. Spirits and past lives. Junk philosophy for junked up minds.

"Limbo?" Aubrey offers, rubbing the tears from her eyes, and Tammy readily accepts the aid.

"Yeah, that's it. Your spirit goes to Limbo until there's a right time for you to come back."

"But wait," Rose jumps in, excited by the possibility. "What if there was, like, a perfect host waiting right there?" Before she can complete her speculation, the group's attention is pulled away by a commotion at the front door, a sudden surge in the arguments of those clustered outside it as the lone officer argues with them, eventually allowing through one man, his exhausted expression well in keeping with his matted slacks and the shabby leather jacket he wears, open and dripping as he cautiously crosses toward the officers and their mixed bag of witnesses.

"Jake, dear," Mrs. M. calls out, cheerfully, then stops, with a sharp little inhalation that suggests she wonders if somehow she's made a great mistake.

For a long moment he stands, five paces away, as if unsure whether to approach them or run away. With tight little dips of his head he acknowledges Aubrey and Anne, then settles his eyes on Christina, whose features show clearly that she is familiar with this newcomer.

I should have guessed he would be wrapped up in all this. A hot-head and a trouble-maker; I haven't trusted him since that first time he tried to force his way into that girl's apartment.

"What's he doing here?" Rod asks grimly, rising from his seat.

"So you two know each other," Dominguez replies, in the tone of one whose worst suspicions have just been confirmed. "Mr. Brindle was our first suspect…" Before she can say any more, Rod is moving across the floor, winding up a roundhouse punch. As quickly as the young woman's body can move, though, Kalispell's tired frame is quicker, catching her by the shoulders and stopping her forward momentum enough that the blow just brushes by Jake's already bruised cheek.

"You son-of-a-bitch," Rod cries out, struggling as the two cops work to restrain him.

"He must have seen Stevie and me together, and thought there was something between us and…I don't even want to think about what he did to her…" I no longer have any idea how much of what I'm saying is out loud; what is inside my head and what is outside it – not that I ever know that difference these days; not really…. not since the beginning of my Nothing.

"Wait a minute there, tiger," Bannerjee is saying softly into Christina's face. The depth of his brown eyes seems to calm her a bit as he continues. "The Officer said Mr. Brindle was our <u>first</u> suspect, and that's true. He was our first suspect because he's the one who called 911 to report a woman assaulted in an alley, but then refused to give his name. We traced the call to his cell phone but couldn't locate the guy until his car was spotted a couple of hours ago, and when the stakeout caught up with him, they found blood stains on his jacket and a bloody shirt and slacks in his car."

"You did this to her? The one person that took me for who I am, and you try to kill her?" This is too much. Even in a nightmare,

my mind would not make this up and yet, if my mind is not making it up, if I am not willing to take credit for it, then it must be real. And if it is real...

Again Rod struggles against the officers holding him, and Bannerjee hurries to complete his explanation. Yes, he tells them all, initial signs pointed to Jake as the perpetrator, except that his story checked out. During questioning after he was brought in, Brindle admitted he'd been following Stevie, but claimed he had been some distance away when he saw her strike up a conversation with several other men on the sidewalk in front of a deserted parking lot.

Though the pavement was wet, it was not actually raining any longer, a fact of which Bawdy and his two companions were only dimly aware, what with the amount of beer they'd consumed since evening. What they *were* aware of though, despite addled vision and a very real need for sleep, was the woman who had just appeared around the corner of the shuttered supermarket building. Walking slowly, heels clacking unashamedly against the damp concrete and eyes fixed straight ahead, she gave no sign of having noticed the bodies reclining in the parking lot, their denim, canvas and black leather so opposite to her own textures; nylons and a soft knit skirt, feather-light rayon blouse beneath a satin-lined overcoat left unbuttoned and loose-flowing, to allow the cool night to clear her head as she searched for her car.

She had thought it was out the door of the Hive and just to the right, but did not find it there, and so she's been making her way all around the block - not really worried; just a little disappointed with herself, and if she walks at all warily, it is not from fear of what may lurk in the night so much as caution. In shoes like these, even a small inconsistency can trip one up.

"Hey, Babe," the small man calls out, still lying in front of the dumpster as she passes. "I fell down and I can't get up."

"Yeah," adds the bearded one, as the cat winds itself around his feet, paying no attention to the stranger. "Can you help us get up?"

Stevie is careful to show no reaction as she makes her way steadily onward. She's had her party, let them have theirs. Besides, she's spotted her car now, tucked behind a large van, halfway down the block. A dark block, she realizes with a bit of chagrin; darker at this hour of the night than she would like, but in another ten steps she will be in the pool of a streetlight. A truck is coming down the street as well, a block and a half away, giving her the warm assurance that there will soon be other eyes watching the scene.

She continues walking. One pace, two, three, four; their length constrained by the slim sheath of her skirt and the geometry of three-inch heels. She is almost to the light when she hears footsteps behind her, accompanied by soft chuckling and a muffled belch. Stevie increases her pace, the short steps ringing in quick staccato. She has just entered the brighter glow when she hears herself addressed again.

"Where you goin' in such a hurry, lady?" the skinny, tattooed man wheedles. "Why you running away from old Bawdy?"

"Maybe it's your face she's scared of Bawd," taunts the bearded man, who has pulled himself up from the pavement and is brushing gravel from his sleeves and bottom. Ahead, the truck is signaling for a turn, yellow blinker flicking on, off, on, then off for good, as it sweeps left onto the avenue, the beam of its headlights never even reaching Stevie on this street where every door is closed and locked, every window dark. Blind. Not a person present but her and the three men now clearly fixed upon raising a response from her.

"That it, girl?" Bawdy asks, his voice full of mocking sympathy. "You a'scared of my face?"

Stevie says nothing, but continues walking, head high, eyes straight ahead, as the man catches up and matches her pace a half stride ahead, face turned sideways to insert himself into her field of view. "You a'scared of this?" he leers, eyebrows high, cheeks sucked in to make potholes of their stubbled skin.

Still walking, she has almost exhausted the pool of light now. Re-entering the darkness feels like a step into danger, but her car is only a few spaces away. To carry on toward that safe refuge, she wonders, to open it with her key and slide into the seat, closing and locking the steel door behind her? Or to stop here, in the light, where any driver who comes down the street must see them? Or to make a run for it, kicking off shoes and dashing barefoot across the concrete towards the brightly lighted intersection three blocks away, where a steady stream of traffic promises other eyes to shame her pursuers into civility. Considering this last alternative, she can readily imagine the impact of soft heels against hard pavement, the awkward hobbling skirt and counter-flapping coat, and knows that she will not get far enough, fast enough. Not against their boot-shod heavy stepping.

At the edge of the light she stops. Turns. Gives her followers a gentle looking over, careful to smile pleasantly. To be every inch a lady.

"I'm just going to my car," she says, voice in high register, soft enough to avoid sounding confrontational, but firm enough to avoid invitation - she hopes. In one hand she displays her key chain, as if to validate her purpose. In the other she clutches the small red purse she has carried all evening, its velvety kid leather reassuringly soft to the touch.

Warm as living flesh, the glove-tanned leather flexes between her fingers without creasing, and through its membrane she receives abundant reassurance of the items inside: lipstick - a bottomless crimson, which gives her lips a life of their own; the flying-saucer disk of a compact, its blue plastic as dark as a night sky, safekeeping a glistening mirror, baby-soft pad and pink powder ground to flyaway fineness so that it disappears into the skin; a small plastic sleeve from an old pocket calculator, just the right size to hold the state-issued driver's license showing Stevie Margulies - face washed ambiguously clean, hair pulled back in gender-neutral pony-tail. Along with the license are two credit cards and a bit of cash, the bills folded in fourths. How much cash, Stevie asks herself, in case that's what they want? Maybe forty dollars or so - this late in the evening it's difficult to recall. These few items clutched through soft leather, and a key chain - her shield and her sword.

"Why don't you let me help you then?" Bawdy asks, and in a flash he reaches out and tears the keys from her hand.

"Please," she says, shaking the pain out of her fingertips. "Give them back."

"I'm just gonna' open the door for you," the man explains, oozing consideration with every word. "A gentleman always opens the door for a lady." His smile has grown now, spreading across his face like an idea assembling itself from bits of information, gleaning clues and intuition as the keys dangle daintily between his fingertip and thumb. Held high in front of his face they catch the light, vibrating and swaying without a sound. "And we're gentlemen. Isn't that right Jimbo?"

The bearded man with the giant head chuckles his agreement, confident and unhurried, as Stevie calculates: two men, both more powerful than her, and powerfully inebriated. The third one over there is smaller and quiet so far, he doesn't seem to be a threat. Might even turn out to be an asset, as he looks a bit more susceptible to reason; or begging. If he were to take her side - speak up and tell his friends to leave her alone - it'd be an even...no, even in numbers perhaps, but still no even match.

Making a conscious choice for trust above suspicion, Stevie nods in the direction of her car, so tantalizingly close, in front of a darkened paint store, and yet so far. "There," she says. "The white Toyota," and begins walking toward it.

The men move with her. When Bawdy reaches the white

Toyota he stops, bending his string-bean frame into a graceful 'S' and extending the key at arm's length toward the chromed keyhole, a swashbuckling swordsman planting the coup de grace. Stevie is momentarily charmed as this dark wraith of a man pretends a dancer's grace, turning the key with an elaborate flourish, then pivots from the hips to move himself aside as he swings the door wide open. Only then, as the car's interior stands waiting in the icy glow of the dome light, does he pause and turn back toward her. The relaxing of his body is a slow motion sequence, as it settles, half sitting, half leaning, against the door jamb, long limbs barricading the welcoming cocoon of her car.

"How about a kiss first?" he asks, the very model of polite gentility. In the quiet which follows, Stevie hears the other two chuckling behind her, distracting her attention from sensations that would otherwise be notable – an invisible something tickling her throat, the slight increase of pressure deep inside her sinus.

"Please, give me my keys and let me go home."

"Just one kiss for old Bawdy?" He holds the keys high; a lion-tamer now, urging his captive animal to do its trick. "A pretty girl like you, you can afford one kiss for me."

Stevie studies his face, considers the situation. It has been a long day, a journey all its own: from the work-a-day hours to the familial reinforcement of being at group, then the barren solitude as she paid the dinner tab in an empty booth, followed by that lucky culmination with Laurie and Jolene and the boys and a whole bunch of others, who managed to make it, in the end, a warm and happy evening. A level of acceptance that makes all her old doubts and fears seem foolish and misguided. On this night, the world has shown itself a widely welcoming place, and even if these guys are a little rough around the edges, it's not fair to assume they mean any real harm.

"And then you'll give me my keys?" she asks, suppressing a sniffle that has come, it seems, out of nowhere. "You'll let me go home?"

"Of course I will. What kind of a man you take me for anyway?"

"What kind of a girl do you take *me* for?" Stevie answers, drawn in by his playful flirting, and only then does it come together - the late hour, the dark street, their obvious intoxication - *these guys have not read her at all!* These men are from another world, where people like her do not exist, and suddenly alarms are going off, screaming out from every corner of her mind. The worst thing a girl like Stevie can do with men is lead them on: being fooled brings their own sexuality into question, and re-establishing it requires a public demonstration of masculinity, which is unlikely to be pleasant. She makes a quick calculation – the product of which is that there's no way she's going to just walk out of this, so she'd better get her cards on the table.

"I need to tell you," she begins, all seriousness now, voice dropped halfway down, into what should be eyebrow-raising territory. "There's more to me than meets the eye."

According to the interview they recorded at the station, Jake watched the scene for some time before he realized something truly bad was going down. When he finally decided to intervene, he took the three men on all by himself; finding the one holding a knife to be less interested in a fight than in running, and the one with the bandage to be the most trouble despite that handicap. Still, Jake managed to scare them off, and caught a glimpse of them climbing into a big old whale of a car and peeling-out, the rumble of its cracked exhaust ripping the night. That part checked out with a report from a bus driver on the swing shift who'd been cut off about that hour by an old beater running a red light at an intersection six blocks from the scene. He described the car that nearly cost him his job as a seventies sedan with a vinyl top that had peeled half off, only one headlight on, and a muffler in serious need of repair.

The first officer who reached the scene supported another part of Jake's story, too, that the guy he found there was holding the victim's head up and trying to clear her airway as she gagged and coughed. He couldn't have avoided getting blood all over himself just trying to help out, though the officer was too busy checking the victim for vitals to question him, and by the time the paramedics arrived and took over, the mystery man was nowhere to be found. It was only when Jake Brindle was picked up earlier this afternoon that the cops even heard his side of the story.

By the end of this explanation, Rod's energy has waned, and the officers are able to relax their hold on him. With serious faces the two study one another; Jake still tall and handsome, but far less confident than back in the days when he and Kim were talking of marriage; and Rod, with Kim's face and features, but all of her enthusiasm lost, replaced by suspicion and mistrust. To Aubrey they are like a pair of fighters injected into the ring against their will, each one wary of the other, waiting for the first blow, instead of which Jake offers what is, for him, an apology.

"I was afraid," Brindle admits sheepishly, addressing Rod directly.

"Scared?" Christina's voice shoots back. "You don't look to me like the kind of person who scares easily."

"Listen, please. I know I did some things I shouldn't of, but the truth is...I understand a lot more now. These last few months...and then seeing what they had done to... Look; I'm not the same person I was back when Kim and I were together, or even after, when you were… you. That person doesn't exist anymore, and I understand now, that Kim…the Kim I loved…she's not here either, so…bottom line, you have nothing to fear from me, Christina. Or Rod or whoever. I won't bother you anymore. You have my word on it." With that his great, flat slab of a hand stretches out, waiting, until, very slowly, Christina's hand ventures out across the gulf between them,

"OK," Tammy says brightly, when the moment seems to have gone on long enough. "I'll bite. If this guy is no longer a suspect, why is he here; and why the f... -'scuse my English - are you asking us all so many questions?"

Bannerjee turns to Brindle, with a shrug of his shoulders.

"So you confirm it; this is the Rod person you told us about?" When Jake's nod confirms the identification, the cop thanks him, adding that he's free to leave, though he shows no sign of wanting to do so. Across the lobby the door cracks open again as the officer there questions someone else wanting to be admitted. Through the narrow opening, the sound from the sidewalk arrives with full force, a ragged, roaring cheer followed by a percolation of screeches and instruments. Over it all a new note is audible, slightly distorted, as from an overdriven speaker, repeating a refrain, 'God hates faggots, God hates queers,' over and over.

"Sorry," says Kallispell, gathering up one of the radios as he moves away toward the door. "I've got to keep an eye on this." From inside the building, a steady trickle of staff and visitors flow and eb, drifting in ones and twos toward the darkened windows, which give them a perfect view of the makeshift stage, a hundred feet away across the crowd. Hands full of paperwork or cradling paper cups of coffee, they populate the space as the two remaining cops continue to face Rod, though it is Banerjee who does nearly all the talking.

"Perhaps I'm searching for enlightenment," he offers in belated answer to Tammy's question, though the words seem directed toward all of their small grouping. "Isn't that what my people are supposed to do? And besides that, you see, it has been my experience that people don't attack other people for no reason, and they do not usually attack random strangers. I want to understand why those men picked this particular person; did they know her, or were they put up to it? Was there someone else involved? And in order to move a little closer to those answers, Miss,

677

I'd like *you* to tell us where *you* were the night this person was attacked."

Incredible! He actually thinks I could have had anything to do with...that! Of course I tell them I couldn't possibly - but it has no effect. This interfering foreigner acts as if he's heard my every word before I speak it. To no avail, I explain how I wandered after leaving the Maturin girl's apartment. How I bought myself a drink or two – maybe more, I admit it - and then it all gets muddy; nights, people, sleeping somewhere – with someone?! - drinking more. "The truth is," I end, "I have no idea when it even was that she got hurt, much less where I was at that particular moment."

"No idea? Really," asks Bannerjee, his obvious disbelief more of an accusation than if he came out and said he thought Rod had done the deed. "Let's try another moment then. How about the night you started a fist fight at the Swedish Social Club – do you remember that?"

Remember it? Of course I remember it; that was the night I found my voice. The one good thing which has come out of this hallucination. "Yes, officer, I remember that night. Quite clearly."

With falling spirits Aubrey listens as Rod admits to participating in what was almost, but not ever quite, a fight.

"So you're a belligerent little girl?" Dominguez prods, sounding like she wants a fight herself.

Outrageous! As much as I know she's trying to get a rise out of me, as much as I'd hate to give her the satisfaction... to be stuck here in this form, listening to...

"My daughter has had a serious illness." Anne protests. "She's going through an identity crisis - isn't that what they call it? The sort of thing that happens to lots of young people these days, but that doesn't make her a criminal..."

"Is that it, girl?" the uniformed officer continues, pressing her face close as she sees Christina seethe. "Are you having an identity crisis?"

"*I* don't have any problem with my identity," I shout. "It's all of *you* who have the problem. *I* know *exactly* who I am!"

"Woo-oof," hoots the smallest of the men, the one who has hung back behind the others, and now has the cat in his arms, stroking between her ears as he watches eagerly. "She thinks she's too much woman for you, Bawdy."

"Let's just say I'm not your average girl..."

"And I'm not your average fucking guy," Bawdy interrupts before Stevie can finish her warning. Reaching out he grabs her arms above the elbows and pulls her toward him. Surprised and out of balance, she falls against his chest and finds her face on his. Harsh dry lips press themselves upon her mouth, first gently, and then with growing impatience. Swiveling and opening, his mouth works at her, insistent tongue testing the film of her lipstick. His hands are on her back now, rubbing and circling from shoulders to waist as his tongue probes harder and Stevie feels her mouth forced open, the foreign organ darting across her teeth accompanied by a stale mingling of cigarettes and beer as a hand reaches her buttocks and begins squeezing. That familiar tickling sensation has grown now, to fill her nose and throat, and with it comes real dread. The sense of suffocation gives new strength as, wriggling her arms free she pushes herself away, stands and smoothes her hair.

"There, you've had your kiss," she manages, eyes squeezing hard to fight back the sneeze coiling-up within her airway. "Now give me back my keys."

"I don't know," says the other man, the bearded one called Jimbo, moving very close and grabbing her arm with his good hand. "I think it's my turn now."

"Is that your cat," Stevie interjects, voice breaking as the urge to convulse causes her breath to catch. Fighting it down she tries to explain. "I'm...allergic. To cats...you see...."

"You don't like Little Pussie?" asks the tattooed man, taking the cat from his friend and thrusting it, legs flailing and eye's wide, at Stevie's face. His tone feels like an accusation, and Stevie turns her head aside, scrunching her eyes against their itchy watering, as she wonders just how much this guy has figured out; whether his words are chosen in slyness or in ignorance. In the distance a siren sounds, racing along the interstate. Six blocks over and elevated a hundred feet up a hillside, it might as well be on another planet as she fights back the need to expel offending particles from membranes already swelling in resistance to what they register as a deadly assault.

"Answer him, girl," comes the big man's voice, the heavy hand on her arm twisting her around to face him. "My friend Bawdy's askin' if you don't like Little Pussy there."

"Ahh...ahhh...tzhooo," comes the sneeze, full-throated and round, from the very bottom of her diaphragm and about as feminine as a Mack truck. As it echoes off the nearby brick walls Stevie sees the eyes of all three men gone wide, their mouths, for once, silent.

"I'd like my keys back," she says softly, and as humbly as she can, eyes squeezed tight in hopes of avoiding another eruption. Hand held out to receive what is hers, she hears instead a sound of fabric rustling, of air rent in movement, and then the keys clattering to the pavement, somewhere far down in the street. She tries to record the direction and the distance, but the thought is interrupted by a hand grasping her head from behind, snapping it back as another pulls her toward the big man. She can feel the heat and smell the odor of his body, as the fingers on the back of her head tug the roots of her hair and other hands grip her arms much tighter than necessary to keep her from moving.

"You a woman or a man?" Bawdy demands, all the playfulness gone from his leaden tone.

"Not *or*," Stevie replies, "*and*." Immediately she feels the slap which that reflexive attempt at intellectual distinction has earned her.

"You just kissed a guy!" taunts the small man, his rising laugh cut short by the glare which Bawdy directs his way. For a long moment they examine one another, measuring and challenging, while Stevie hangs in the two men's grip, aware of the moisture draining from her nose but unable to do a thing about it.

"Let me see," Bawdy demands, breaking the spell as he tears open the front of Stevie's dress to probe beneath its surface. "It's got real tits," he remarks as she struggles beneath his fondling.

"Son of a fucking bitch," announces Jimbo, "Let's see what it's hiding down below."

"Not here," warns Bawdy, whose face has taken on the eager look of a hungry hound as he jerks his head to indicate a narrow gap between two buildings, a leftover space even darker than the rest of the street. "In there."

Despite Rod's declaration, Bannerjee remains unruffled. "All right then," he says, with exaggerated politeness, "why don't you tell us - *Doctor* Gimbal - how it is that a highly-credentialed surgeon who's well past retirement age is appearing today in the body of a twenty-one year old girl. Why don't you do that doctor?"

"I have no idea," I reply, feeling just how weak that sounds, and speaking all the louder and more forcefully for it. "I'd like to understand it as much as you would. No," I correct myself, "actually, I'd say my interest in finding an explanation is actually a whole lot more visceral than yours. Detective."

"I think perhaps I can help with that."

All heads turn as one to see the source of this new voice, a woman just arrived via the building's interior corridor, face flushed and damp with perspiration, hair pulled haphazardly back above jeans and sweatshirt which look as though they may have been slept in. A fat manila folder is clamped tightly in her outstretched hand and a Hilltop ID badge swings on its lanyard in counterpoint to her purposeful steps.

"Mary Antonias," she introduces herself, the syllables broken-up and halting due to the exertion of racing through Hilltop's labyrinthine halls. Fixing Christina's eyes with her own, she takes several deep breaths and composes herself, as if hoping the interval will impress them all with her dead seriousness. When she speaks again it is with the level tone one might use to deliver devastating news to a patient or a family: the crisp vice of expertise.

"Dr. Mary Antonias, second year Resident. Ccurrently in 'neonatal.' I used to be in...well, that doesn't really matter. But I was on shift the night she," Mary turns to Christina and her voice softens. "The night you were brought in. I heard people talking, and then, I saw you, up in ICU, and...there was something about you, lying there, with all these people making a fuss about what a beautiful young girl you were." At that, Rod snorts, the tiniest sound of disagreement.

"But that's what they were all saying. That this perfectly innocent, beautiful little girl had been brought in, and 'Wasn't it such a tragedy?' It didn't stop, either, even when they did a work-up and realized you weren't really a little girl, but a young woman, it was still all about, 'Ooh, she looks so innocent' and 'Such a shame that should happen to a girl with everything to look forward to.' As if, if you hadn't been so pretty you wouldn't have such a wonderful life ahead of you, and then it wouldn't matter so much; and when I heard that talk, it made me angry, and later, when you had this totally counter-predictive outcome, I couldn't get it out of my mind, wondering...and ever since that day, I've been trying to understand who you are, and what happened, and I've been finding things that don't make sense. But now, I think I understand it, and the truth is, I believe that you are Dr. Gimbal."

If Mary expects her revelation to be met with rejoicing, she will not get it from Christina, whose look of skepticism would wither a weaker spirit.   It is the others who react most visibly; Anne McKloskey blanching and placing a hand on the arm of Aubrey who looks, herself, totally confounded.   Detective Bannerjee rocks back on his heels, as if to say 'this better be good,' exactly the words which *do* issue beneath the breath of Office Dominguez, while Tammy and Rose look on with the wide eyes of kids at a Saturday matinee, eager to hear what will come next, a desire which Mary immediately obliges.

"Some months ago you - Dr. Rodney Gimbal - collapsed while performing a surgical procedure. Because the team in the OR had to attend to the patient first, and because the other physician on the team was somewhat out of practice..." Here Mary's story is overlain with a knowing grunt from Rod, which she acknowledges but does not allow to interrupt her flow. "There were some shortcomings in the response to your crisis, and, on top of that, the staff...well, they had some personal feelings; about a man they'd known as...you were not particularly...

"It was never my goal in life to be liked" I cut in, saving her the difficulty of putting into words what she has already made so obvious.

"On top of that there was a problem with one of the monitors. It showed a complete cessation of brain activity, so that when an On-Call made it up there and tried to resuscitate you, he thought your episode had already gone on longer, and done more damage, than it really had, and so you were pronounced and entered into the system as a donor-candidate for transplant and for research, per your organ donor registration. Which is how one organ was determined to be appropriate for use in an ongoing study; a thinly-funded track aimed at improving the ability to support organs outside the body for longer periods. It was called the Applied Dialysis Project.

"David Resor's group?" I offer, the name coming back from
far away, accompanied not by a face though, but by a sign beside a
doorway on a corridor I know like the back of my hand - well, not
either of these hands, but that is beside the point. I see the surprise
on her face, and realize she barely believes her own tale, but has
willed her mind to wrap around it, forcing old logic to retreat in the
face of facts. I like that; this one is actually intelligent. Objective. A
more reassuring figment than most.

"Yes," Mary answers, thrilled at the confirmation Rod's
response has given her. "It was hours before they noticed, before
they realized that the organ in their apparatus was more alive than
they ever suspected. A living functioning human brain trapped
outside its body."

My Nothing!

Looking around her, Mary sees the fascination her
explanation is generating. Anne and Aubrey, the two strange
women with them, the uniformed cop and the suited one, who must
be a detective; not one of them has the medical background that
would compel them to contradict her, and so they listen as she
continues the tale she has pieced together from Jessica Bagley and a
few conflicting file entries. How Resor's team realized the horrible
mistake that had been made, and how Hilltop's automatic tissue
matching software alerted them to a possible match with an
overdose victim brought in early the next morning.

"There was a group of doctors back then - they've all been
transferred away now, one of them is even dead - but they were
working on different tracks and it all came together beautifully. I
mean, in a scientific sense, it was – a kind of beauty."

With that she goes on to relate the events alluded to in
Bagley's penthouse prison; how, over a period of hours, Resor and
several other senior staff had pondered the moral and ethical aspects
of an act which was more or less permissible under the terms of
broadly-worded donor agreements, but still beyond the pale of any
normal standard of care. Given the limited options available to them,
they had eventually approached Bagley for authorization, only to find
her own position compromised by the impending takeover of Hilltop
by Medical Holdings, an event which was taking place that very day.

*Endless agony! All that I have experienced – the Nothing,
these people, this incomprehensible universe I find myself in – all of
that is nothing compared to what this child is trying to make us
believe. And yet, the brilliance of her lie is, it fits. Of all the crazy*

ideas, what she describes is exactly what it feels like to me. Exactly. Impossibly.

An indecipherable grunt issues from Rod, as Christina's features suggest some inner struggle. On the other faces, a mix of confusion and skepticism, despite which – or perhaps more *because* of which - Mary plows on; recounting Jessica Bagley's tale of discussions with Hilltop's in-house legal staff over what she presented as a hypothetical teaching problem on the limits of the Compassionate Use Doctrine; and how Legal in turn made carefully-veiled inquiries with their indemnity's actuarial department - 'to understand the comparative liabilities in either situation,' as Bagley had put it - and what they found out: that if the Hilltop staff was liable for the negligent death of an aspiring artist whose work had already sold for as much as twenty-thousand dollars a pop, with perhaps fifty productive years ahead of her, the amount could be quite staggering. Dr. Gimbal, on the other hand, was at the end of his career, and suffering inoperable cancer. Even before they learned that he had been self-medicating like crazy and could be accused of bringing on his own coronary, the foreseeable monetary damages were…well, from an institutional-liability standpoint, it would be much better if Christina survived than if Dr. Gimbal did. And, unlike the thing in their fancy petri dish, there was no doubt about the young woman's state. Here Mary turns to Mrs. Mckloskey, who has not moved a muscle through all this telling. Reaching out a hand, she touches the older woman's arm very gently, a small human contact to leaven the complex history she has been recounting.

"Your daughter, Mrs. McKloskey, suffered massive brain damage due to impaired oxygen supply after she passed out at the club. I believe it was probably caused by a ruptured aneurism, a tiny imperfection in her cerebral circulation that had been lurking there for, well possibly since birth. By the time the paramedics had arrived the damage was irreversible. I'm sorry."

As Anne's eyes rise up to meet Mary's, it is clear to all that, for once, she has grasped the gravity of what is being said to her. To Aubrey, it is as if this woman, who often seems so out of touch and yet still manages to be one of her warmest friends, has aged decades in an instant, has shrunk by half her size with the knowledge that her beloved daughter is not, in truth, standing beside her. A great sadness comes over Aubrey, a desperate urge to go back in time, to put this horrible mistake right, and with it, a growing sense that just because this Antonias woman has a fancy ID badge, that does not make everything she says the gospel truth. Even a waitress knows there are some things these guys in their white coats can't do. Isn't that what Aubrey learned back at the other place where she had to deal with hordes of doctors; where her own mother lay in a room that stank of her body's breakdown? 'There are some things we just can't do,' they told her then.

"So you're saying," she begins, "that Dr. Gimbal's brain was taken out of his body and transplanted into Kim's?"

"Transplanting a human brain from one body to another? The hurdles would be...unbelievable. Simple antigen compatibility – with over 50 variants of HLA-A, and even more for each of HLA-B and –DR – and that would be the least of it; what about the mechanics? The cranium is absolutely individualized; close-fitting and solid. Not like the thoracic cavity, with its flexible perimeter and plenty of soft tissues to adapt to a transplanted heart or lungs. It boggles the mind, even without considering the number of neural connections to be re-established – countless connections between brain and body at an almost cellular level of complexity? It takes nature nine months of gestation to assemble their physical form, and over a decade of maturation to establish their functions – doing that in a procedure would be like programming the world's largest supercomputer while it is operating at full speed..." This entire line of thought is so bizarre, so disorienting, it is only when the woman responds that I realize I have been speaking out loud.

But Rod *has* been voicing his thoughts, and with such clarity and energy, such absolute confidence in his knowledge that all are taken aback. If Christina's appearance belies the tale they are being told, the words issuing from her mouth are the surest reason yet to listen further to Mary's counter argument.

"First of all, the people who proposed this, they never expected any of those things to work out that way. They fully expected that Dr. Gimbal's brain, transplanted into Christina's skull, would not survive. But they knew they had to do something. These are ethical people remember; the idea of letting a viable human brain sit in a maintenance vessel, possibly conscious at some level - trapped in what would seem to it like total sensory deprivation - that was simply not acceptable. And to just turn off the support, to shut it down..."

For the life of me, I can imagine their nightmare. To be faced with that situation, that responsibility. Of course, they have only themselves to blame; there are no accidents in a surgery.

"But they do that all the time," Tammy chimes in. "I've seen it on TV. Someone gets so sick they can't ever get better, they shut off the machines..."

Mistakes were made; procedures ignored. None of this could have happened, damn it, if that fool Jorgendern hadn't insisted on assisting a procedure which was beyond his skills. If there had been proper supervision, if...

"That's not the same," Rose points out. "It's not the same thing at all; I mean, the person is already dead when they do that; it's just the body that's being kept alive. Breathing and pumping like one of those oil things you see by the road in the middle of the desert; pumping away for years and years and there's not a soul around."

"That's right," Mary agrees, thankful for any semblance of support. Glancing at her watch she wonders what is keeping Jason. That vessel would be so convincing, such clear proof that someone invested thousands of hours - and hundreds of thousands of dollars - in at least one part of what she is describing. Without it...still, there is no way out but forward and so she resumes her tale of minimized expectations. How Resor and the others thought they would, at best, give biology a chance to take its course to a more complete death.

"They grafted cultivated bone into Christina's skull where it had been opened, to add volume; inserted silicone to modify its shape. That's why she has all those lumps and scars underneath her hair."

Aubrey recalls how odd her friend had looked before her hair grew in, how even now, beneath the buzz-cut fuzz, the flesh is fissured with pale and jagged lines.

"They did their level best to make it work, and if it didn't - if after they had honestly given it the best efforts of their collective experience, the patient expired - then that was an outcome they could live with." As it was, she continues, a fairly standard roster of immunosuppressants addressed the possibility of rejection, and Lembec and Rosen used a modified dialysis processor to institute a hematomic bypass, maintaining the brain stem in a fluidic environment manipulated to resemble that of a gestating embryo. The theory was that this would trigger sells to organize themselves and connect the brain stem to Christina's spinal nerve bundle. After that, it was terra-incognita, as they had no idea whether the adaptive capacity of the patient's own neural net could manage the degree of self-re-programming required to sort out the proper connections. When they actually saw some resumption of autonomous function they were overjoyed, but still, the very best they thought might occur was some sort of prolonged vegetative state. Hardly desirable, but a far better expression of the oaths they had taken and the reasons they had gotten into medicine in the first place, than simply throwing up their hands and flipping-off a switch.

Can it possibly be possible: that they succeeded far beyond their expectations? Despite my stake in the outcome, "I have a hard time believing that. I knew David Resor, after all. Didn't respect him terribly, but yes, there was intelligence there. And Lembec, with his pie-in-the-sky attempts to regenerate spinal tissue and cure paraplegia? Another dreamer, sucking up resources that could have been used on treatable conditions. He and Rosen might cook up something like this, but only if there were funding involved."

"No, Doctor Gimbal," Mary defends. "This wasn't about funding, in fact they did everything they could to keep it all a secret." It was, after all, an unprecedented and highly experimental procedure. Had Jenifer Bagley not despised the idea of MH taking over her beloved Hilltop, had she expected to be on the premises to deal with the consequences of her decision, there is little chance she would have gone along. As it was, one price of her acquiescence was that the team take no credit for their breakthrough, not publish or teach or make any other move to capitalize on what was, as it turned out, prize-worthy work.

"There has to be another explanation." Oh yes, my emotions would like to believe this girl's story; to have this clear and simple – if such a thing could possibly be considered simple! – explanation for what I feel, see and hear, but my intellect tells me it cannot be. All my training, experience and knowledge tell me such a thing is beyond reach. There must be another explanation for these things she is describing.

"All any of the original team ever knew was that the subject had resumed breathing on her own. As soon as she – I'm sorry Doctor Gimbal - as soon as *you* were stable, they were all transferred away, and not long after that the patient was shipped off to exile in her mother's guest house, watched over by a hand-picked team who could be counted on to keep their mouths shut."

"Bravo, my dear," announces a stout, gray-haired man, addressing Mary across the little group. "A fascinating tale," he continues, with a glare toward the larger man who has arrived along with him. "It has intrigue, suspense. Bad guys in suits, and good guys in white coats riding to the rescue. Type it up, send it in, and we can watch it next week on the television. All very well, except - it has nothing to do with reality."

Before the intruder can say any more, a non-descript door tucked beneath the landing of the lobby stair bursts open. Surging through it, a stream of protesters carrying cardboard signs begin fanning out across the lobby. 'Let us see her,' they cry in a dozen variations, and 'We want the truth,' as the officer who had been manning the main door races over to intercept them.

"Bastards found another way in!" Officer Dominquez cries, racing to assist him, while Bannerjee turns calmly aside, radio held close and cupped by a hand to muffle the commotion as he reports this latest development. From their place by the windows several staffers rush to help as well, but one of the intruders has already made it to the now-unguarded entrance and hit the crash bars on a pair of doors, allowing her compatriots the access they've been seeking. Almost immediately, there are bodies surging all around, pressing Rod and Aubrey together, as Jake offers an arm to Mrs. McKloskey to keep her from being bowled over. Amidst the confusion the stout man continues to smile confidently, impressive in a close-cut suit of deepest blue, its fine gray chalk lines and azure pocket-handkerchief perfectly complimenting the striped satin of his necktie.

"A very interesting tale, young lady," he continues, as more security and police arrive from deeper inside the building and the noises around them blend into a new and louder background level. "A very serious accusation against this Center; if you had any evidence."

"And you are?" Bannerjee prompts, setting his radio down and picking up another.

"Mr. William J. Seivers," is the reply from the second man, taller than Seivers, and equally well-turned-out, if not quite as composed. Though he is addressing the detective, his eyes seem fixed upon the emotion-filled faces of the protesters, some still outside, hands pressing against the glass, but a steady stream of them now entering the lobby, where the security forces appear to have settled for keeping them from penetrating past its grand confines. "Mr. Seivers is President and CEO of Medical Holdings LLC."

"He owns Hilltop," Mary explains, with little attempt to conceal her distaste.

"Hardly," Seivers corrects, with a modest chuckle. "I'm simply a representative of the various entities which have the privilege of participating in the management of this fine institution. Here to protect their interests from idle speculation and character assassination. And this is Jim Auster, Staff Counsel to MH."

"Our attorney," I point out, only to be told in the most patronizing manner that he is very sorry he can no longer represent me, us, since in his new position that would pose a conflict of interest. Sorry, my Aunt Fanny; I don't believe this ambulance-chaser has ever been sorry for a thing in his entire life, but of course there's nothing to be gained by arguing. It's clear from their manner that these two believe they know everything worth knowing about us - and many other things as well.

Aubrey, too, is torn, for though the hair is longer, and the designer-eyeglasses more flamboyant, there is no doubt that this is indeed the same Auster who represented Christina's interests those months ago, but before she can speak she feels Jake's hand on her arm, and sees his subtle shake of the head, urging her to hold her comment. Instead she nods in turn as introductions are completed. Amidst the increasingly-congested lobby, the group is pressed closer together as Seivers again professes to being fascinated by what Mary has told them, which apparently he has been overhearing for some time. An intriguing tale, he admits, and inspiring - the thought of such a breakthrough happening under his very nose! One they might truly wish to believe, and he might too, if only there were some shred of proof, some tiny bit of physical evidence which could back it up. How convenient it is for her that all the physicians she has accused of this renegade act are no longer available to respond to her allegations.

"There is proof," Mary interjects defiantly. "We've got a... my friend is bringing it right here, any minute now...I guess he's been delayed; by all this...you know; the crowd out there, all this security."

"You don't mean Mr. Privet, do you?" suggests Auster, whose smug expression makes clear that he is quite certain of whom she is speaking. "I have it on good authority," he continues, "that Mr. Privet will not be joining us. In point of fact, he no longer works for this institution, having been terminated a short while ago, and as for the item to which you were referring, we've verified its purpose - an obsolete device for neutralizing infectious biological waste. It's being disposed of as we speak. In accordance, of course, with federal mandates for handling biologically-hazardous materials."

Hearing the sentence his words pronounce, Mary feels her world slipping out of control. It had all seemed so clear when Jessica Bagley told it; so obvious when she and Jason found the vessel with its tags and markings, and now... Helpless, she listens as Seivers piles back on, telling Bannerjee how these two – indicating Aubrey and Rod with a nod – have been claiming since her recovery that there was some sort of conspiracy and now they've managed to drag a promising young physician into their crazy plot. For a time, he says sadly, it appeared that Miss McKloskey was suffering some after-effects due to damage from her overdose. Later it seemed the motive was money, Miss Maturin using her sick friend to milk Hilltop so she could improve her tenuous economic position. Indeed, Auster admits as he joins the tag-team, MH did enter into a settlement with them some time ago, for a small sum, but now, by being here and by this one claiming to be some sort of reincarnation of Dr. Gimbal, they've violated the terms of that agreement. If they persist, he will have no alternative but to take legal action against them, though the prospect truly saddens him, knowing it might only increase suspicions about the girl's possible involvement in the tragedy playing out upstairs.

As much as I want to respond, what is there that I can say? Of all the people in the room, these men are the ones with whom I most identify – mature, responsible, objective... I want to be like them; I am, for God's sake! I think like them, I work like them. The thoughts they voice support everything I believe and have believed, and yet where they would lead me, I cannot go.

"And you," Seivers challenges, turning back to confront Mary. "You, of all people should know better than to cooperate with their little extortion. Brain transplant? Rubbish and science fiction, and whose word do you have for any of it? A lonely woman suffering from multiple neuroses, whom you tricked into allowing you into her sick room, just the same way you once tricked your way into Miss McKloskey's – do we see a pattern here?"

It takes a moment for Mary to realize whom Seivers is speaking of, and even as her mind races to catch up, he continues, generously filling in details for the rest of his audience.

"My wife, Jessica Bagley Seivers, used to work at Hilltop. We met during the negotiations for her institution to become part of our corporate family, and very soon realized we wanted to be family as well. Little did I know then, that my new love was hiding a dark secret; her alcoholism had been well concealed, but once the acquisition was completed and her work schedule eased, Jessica found herself somewhat – adrift, shall we say?" Turning back to Mary, 'Three-Dollar Bill' wears the weary expression of one who has been dealing with a tragedy for longer than he cares to admit. "My wife is a very sick woman, Miss Antonias. Like a lot of people with dependency problems, she suffers also from paranoia and delusions – hell, she's even been known to accuse me of keeping her locked up in our co-op; a pretty nice prison, if you ask me – so I would not put too much store by whatever she may have told you."

Mary's mind races. Has she really been deceiving herself, allowing her own insecurities, her obsession over that first glimpse of the Jane, to lead her down a garden path? For a moment it seems absurd that she could even listen to Jessica Bagley, her illness so obvious in retrospect. In a flood she is aware of all the rules she has broken, the trouble she has gotten Jason into – 'borrowing' keys, searching secured areas. Her wonderful Jason, who should have been here long ago, and herself, too, her own career in question now, her job in jeopardy and most of her meager savings spent to travel to New York, how gullible she's been, convinced by what, by...

"Wait," she sputters, "wait," as from the pocket of her lab coat she pulls a palm-sized black device, the Physicians Portable Reference that MH requires Hilltop to issue to every Resident, an electronic library filled with data and protocols.

"It's not just me..." she stutters, as from another pocket she pulls her car key, its fob a tiny, fuzzy bear whose eyes strobe in embarrassing multi-colors when her fumbling fingers happen to press its belly. Split-rings on the fob hold other necessities as well - apartment key, emergency whistle, a grocery discount card and a metallic-blue lozenge shape, no larger than her pinkie. "A friend of mine found this," Mary explains, careful not to identify Jason, as she slides back the shell of the object to expose a silvered plug-end, which she inserts into a socket on the side of her PPR before touching its the screen several times. "On the internet...it wasn't hard; but he thought it was... interesting. And maybe you will, too."

A click of static, a split second of rustling, and a sound emerges from the device, thin and artificial through its tiny speaker, but clearly recognizable as she taps the device, jumping back and forth several times before finding the section she wants.

"Impossible?" a voice asks after the last jump. Clearly

recognizable as that of Bill Seivers, its delivery is energetic, and utterly confident - downright charismatic. "Who are we to say what is possible or not? You say all this is impossible? Tell me then, if you know so much, tell me - anybody: what day was October 11, 1492?"

The tape is silent for a few seconds, during which Mary explains that this recording is an excerpt from Seivers' address at last year's annual meeting of the Association for Corporate Medical Research, the entire speech available for download off the ACMR website, for a small fee.

"Public relations," the corporeal Seivers dismisses. "Window dressing to hide how bad the food..." but his protest is cut short as the recording continues.

"The day Columbus discovered the new world," someone chimes in, sounding muffled and remote, apparently shouted up from the audience.

"Wrong," Seivers' recorded voice announces with carnivorous glee. "The day *before* his crew sighted land. The *last* day on which the existence of the New World could be claimed by his adversaries to be *impossible*. What day was April eleventh, nineteen sixty-one?"

This time there are a number of responses, none of them intelligible, and a bit of a chuckle from Seivers before he corrects them all.

"That was the day *before* the day Yuri Gagarin made the first manned space flight. The last day on which most of the world believed such a thing *was not possible*. How about December second, nineteen-sixty-seven?"

Again multiple answers shouted out, as Mary reminds her own audience. "This is what he says when he's raising money for all the things he just told you I made up in my head."

"I'll tell you what day it was," the recorded Seivers responds. "December second, nineteen-sixty-seven was the day *before* Christiaan Barnard performed the first human heart transplant. The last day on which much of the medical establishment and virtually all of the general populace would have said such a thing *was not possible*. Every day my friends - every single day of our lives - is the day *before* tomorrow." Here the recorded voice changes tone, taking on an attitude of confident declaration not unlike that of the Reverend in the plaza outside. "Any day we live could be the last day before aliens make contact with earth, or someone announces cold fusion – for real this time – or it could be the last day before a paraplegic walks again, thanks to MH's Embryonic Hormonal Environment technology. Medical Holdings; dedicated to using the power of private capitol, leveraged through the mechanism of the free market, to turn yesterday's 'impossibilities' into tomorrow's reality."

With another touch of the screen Mary shuts off the recording and glances around her. The faces are all serious, their owners deep in thought - except Seivers, whose expression is, characteristically, a mix of great amusement, satisfaction, and eagerness. "He does talk a good game," he admits, as if speaking of someone other than himself.

Before any of the assembled group can say more, an electronic alarm erupts from Bannerjee's radio. Raising a hand to his ear he listens for a moment, grunts his acknowledgement and turns back to the group. The situation is getting more complex, he advises them. Hilltop Security managed to stop the protesters from penetrating farther than this lobby, but has decided it's not feasible to push them back out. There's going to be some sort of a press conference shortly, which may change the situation, and he's got to go upstairs for that. Warily eyeing the protesters now milling about the lobby, he takes Christina by the arm and directs the others to follow, leading them back and around the L-shaped reception counter, into the space between it and the rear wall. Interrupting the security man at his console there and flashing a badge in the fellow's face, the detective instructs him not to let the 'suspect' leave, then disappears into the crowd in the direction of the grand stair.

Suspect! After all that's been said, how can anyone believe I would have anything to do with such a thing?

Looking around their new refuge, Aubrey sees Jake pull out one of the bucket chairs facing the counter and settle Mrs. M into it. The woman is distracted, paying no attention to the multiple images filling a bank of monitors tucked beneath this side of the tall counter; one large screen filled with a view of the courtyard and stage outside, a grouping of eight smaller ones focused on various exterior entrances to the building and interior views of the lobby and grand stair, and another large one aimed from somewhere in front of and above this very station, showing in full digital clarity, Anne, Aubrey and Jake, Rose and Tammy, the lanky young guard at his post, and

Christina, her back against the wall as Auster and Seivers move closer, corralling her away from the hearing of the others, their voices low.

And now that he's gone, here come Tweedle-Dee and Tweedle-Dum to tell me everything I know is wrong.

"Doctor Gimbal," the fellow Seivers begins, and I feel my heart jump until he goes on. "We haven't got a lot of time, and we've got to get a few things understood between us before that Keystone cop comes back and makes this whole thing more complicated than it already is. Just between us girls - and totally, permanently off the record - if I were ever required to testify, I'd have to say there is a grain of truth to what my wife told that girl; there were mistakes made in your care. The massive medication applied in their attempt to reduce cerebral swelling led to an acute and sudden kidney failure. With the extra urgency due to change of ownership, and a new administrator coming in, my wife authorized an emergency transplant, skirting the usual administrative procedures. That's why our girl Mary was unable to find the proper documentation, and the reason for the conflicting time references she's all hopped up about, and that's what has been blown all out of proportion to fuel my poor wife's paranoid delusions."

Not far away, her back turned for a modicum of privacy, that very Mary punches the same speed-dial she has punched so many times over the last few weeks, and places her phone to her ear. Listening to the familiar sequence of dialing tones, she feels her hopes rise as a connection is made, then fall again as the ringing goes on: two, three, four, five - six times in all, before Jason's recorded voice kicks in, his jovial greeting only increasing her worry and her guilt.

"I can't talk right now," it says, " 'cause the Klingons stole my com-badge, so leave a dispatch and I'll get back to you in the next episode."

"What Mr. Seivers is getting at," Auster jumps in, placing a dead-weight arm across Rod's shoulder, "is that no matter how much you may believe something, that does not mean it is in your best interest to keep repeating it. There are always other theories, other explanations, and I assure you we can produce enough evidence to guarantee that any rational observer will prefer our explanation to yours; especially when your tale flies so much in the face of – well – your face. Bottom line? Whatever you believe about who you are, it is disadvantageous for you to try to get the rest of the world to go along."

Is this it then, their end-run around the truth? 'Forget what you know, expedience is all.' Reality defined by the limits of what the unschooled world will accept?

"Now," Seivers resumes in my other ear, his breath hot and wet as he leans close to avoid the others overhearing. "You are an obviously intelligent person, with a highly-developed sense of purpose, so I'm thinking there might just be a win/win for us here. If you give up this whole story about brain transplants and past lives or whatever flavor it's taking today, I'm prepared to offer you a position with one of our research institutions."

For a moment I'm taken aback at what seems like an admission. Certainly there would be no place for an untrained art student in medical research, so...but just as I suspected, the plan has been well-rehearsed.

"Here in the states," the lawyer chimes in, his face as close as when he had me cornered that evening in his house. The smell of Old Spice comes back, familiar as my own, yet sickening on another man; so close, so viscerally personal. I can see the stubble of his cheek, the sharp ends of cut hairs at the top of his sideburns, the shining ends of still others protruding from his nostrils. Just to stand up against this masculine presence is exhausting. "There would be no place for someone like you – no resume, no credentials, obviously too young to have the experience you claim. But there are places overseas, under other systems of...regulation...where enterprises are trusted to take their own precautions. Where you would be free to work with brilliant minds, your contributions limited only by your own abilities. This Dr. Gimbal, he was a cardiologist, right?"

"Thoracic surgeon," I correct, and feel a shiver race up my spine as those familiar words roll off this borrowed tongue. The possibility is thrilling, that maybe they do understand; do recognize the skills and experience I have to offer, even like this.

"Yes," Three Dollar Bill agrees. "We could arrange for you to put your intelligence to work as part of our research efforts. Lembec's Plegia work, perhaps. Or with Resor, on the frontier of transplant technology. All that stuff your girlfriend is spouting? Crazy as it is right now, it will happen someday, and then what? Who

knows, it might even be possible to do what she's been suggesting; get you a new body that matches your image of yourself. Now isn't that worth working toward?"

It is only then that any of us realize the young man, Jake, has been listening in. "I've heard this kind of crap before," he says, and for a moment it looks like he may take a punch at Dollar Bill, so fierce is his expression; the contused eye livid, the scratches on his face scabbed and black, shirt collar smudged and the shoulders of his coat dark with sweat and rain. Despite his appearance, though, it is words he uses now not fists. "I lost everything I owned to a couple of guys who talked just like you do, and somehow they're still driving great cars and wearing great suits, and it's the people like me, people like Kim, who end up living on the streets..."

As much as I distrust this young tough - am still not sure I believe he had nothing to do with Stevie's assault – on this I do agree with him; there is no way Seivers and Auster are offering me anything but what <u>they</u> want. Sure they might ship me overseas somewhere. I've heard that North Korea is happy to overlook loose credentials, they're so desperate for medical knowledge, and any trickle of foreign currency. But once these two have me there, I can well imagine myself ending up in some tumble-down 'research' lab with a bunch of military guards, and disappearing forever.

"It's your choice," Seivers tells Rod out the side of his mouth as he stands to confront Jake. A muffled buzzing interrupts the confrontation, however, sending the executive's hand diving into his breast pocket. "Doug," he tells Auster, identifying the caller by a quick glance at the display before bringing the phone to his ear. For a few seconds he listens, then grunts agreement to something and stares at the device for a moment before punching it once with a finger and stowing it back in its resting place as he turns toward Auster. "Time for us to go," he says. "End game is beginning, upstairs."

"Think about what we've said," the attorney suggests to Rod as the two turn to leave. "You won't get a better offer."

The expression on Rod's face as the attorney and executive head up the stairs rekindles Mary's concern. Glaring at the phone in her hand, she wonders if maybe somehow the speed dial is not working. After punching the digits from memory, her breathing stops as she listens to their musical notes, then the distant ringing and the voice she longs to hear in person.

"I can't talk right now," it says, the rest of the message aborted as Mary hits the red cut-off button and slaps the device closed, folding her hand around it with a deep, deep sigh, only to open it up again a moment later and stare, for long seconds, at its impassive face.

One floor above the airy lobby, Detective Vivek Bannerjee watches several news crews attaching logo-clad microphones to a podium. In a corner of the conference room Doug Taylor confers with a woman of perhaps thirty-five years, her face drawn and tired behind its fringe of auburn curls. The full sleeves of her dress flutter as her hands tremble, the fingers twining and untwining in a flutter of shiny pink nails, though her posture is straight and tall - unnaturally so, as she struggles for self-control.

This, Bannerjee learned as soon as he arrived upstairs, is Evelyn Margulies - divorced, but still using her married name; raising their child largely on the alimony Stevie has been sending out like clockwork. Initially she wanted nothing to do with the circumstances of her ex's injury, but the legalities have made it impossible for her to avoid becoming involved.

Bannerjee looks around himself at the people assembled to hear the latest. The usual local news organizations are represented, of course, but there are others as well. Out-of-town vultures in designer suits, flown in to pluck some easy characterizations their networks can broadcast on the hour or the half, and then forget when a better tidbit comes along.

At least the investigator can take satisfaction in one thing; the call that came in just as he arrived upstairs - informing him that Colorado State Patrol has three suspects in custody, picked up at a rest stop in some nowhere burg called Fruita. Car they were driving matches the one reported near the scene, and one of them has an injured hand, which explains the second blood type found on the victim's clothes. Patrol even found a cat lurking on the back window shelf; no one doubts that its hair will match what was on the victim's coat. No more need to dig into that crazy kid downstairs, Bannerjee thinks with relief as he watches one of the doctors testing out a riser they've put behind the podium. Weird as she is, he'd never quite believed her able to participate in such a dirty deed; but there are too many crazy kids on the streets these days for him to give it any more thought; by now there's probably another reckless woman getting beaten-up somewhere, another kid buying his first snort, or a door being tested to see if someone forgot to lock-up before they went out for the evening. Plenty to keep a detective awake at night, even if this particular case appears to be wrapping itself up.

Everywhere I look, another hare-brained accusation, another reason not to believe my own eyes and ears – if they even are mine anymore. My own memories then…but, 'no' to that as well; memories lie as easily as attorneys and CEOs. My own whatever-it-is that tells me I am who I am even when it makes no sense even to me. Endless maze of contradiction and impossibility, and for an instant I find myself longing for the certainty of the Nothing. The peace of it, like lying on the table as the anesthesiologist twists a valve and liquid slumber runs down the tube into a vein. 'To sleep, perchance to dream,' isn't that how it goes? Words from a lifetime ago, two lifetimes, calling more sweetly than anything else in all this confusion.

At his console nearby, Herman Miller, the muscular young Hilltop guard tapped to keep Christina from leaving, is finding this new assignment a blast as he demonstrates features of the security console to Tammy and Rose, one young woman pressing close against each of his uniformed shoulders. "You can swivel any way you want," he explains, to which Tammy replies with a suggestive 'hmmm,' and Rose reaches across to thwap the back of her head.

"He's talking about the camera, smut-brain."

Herman's face reddens a little more as he glances at the characters on either side of him, then back to his monitor. "Select any camera," he offers, tapping the touch-screen embedded in the counter's surface to select a new image for one of the small monitors, then sliding his finger slowly across another part of the screen, which sends the image zooming into giant magnification, then mini, then giant again.

"In and out," Tammy enthuses, "in and out and in…," ruffling the short hair on Herman's head until the guard squirms with embarrassment and Rose thrusts a fist against her. "What?" she fires back. "I'm not bothering him. Am I, Hermie?"

The young man tosses his head happily, delighted at the attention, and taps the screen a few times more, calling up images to flash across the monitors; the motley crew idling around the lobby, among them one of the musicians who is tapping out a rhythm on wooden drums clasped between her knees as Mark Peterson crouches nearby, filming; a very normal-looking corridor somewhere up above, with scrub-clad techs and lab-coated docs going about their everyday business; a weakly lit utility corridor on some lower level, where two uniformed maintenance men wheel a dolly down a ramp, its cargo nearly toppling off one side until a hand steadies it; a scuffle out in the forecourt, demonstrators and counter-demonstrators slashing at one another with signs and fists until several heads jerk off in the same direction and the camera swivels and zooms to follow their eyes to where a squad of officers clad in heavy vests and face-guarded helmets pour out of a van and dive into the crowd in the direction of the ruckus; a close-up image of Christina, her face blank and slack as she sits alone where Seivers and Auster have left her.

Life is not supposed to be like this. A man knows himself, knows who he is and what he does. Decisions made decades ago set you on your course, you follow through, you persevere, and when you find yourself at the end of your life, either you've succeeded at what you set out to do or you've failed, but you're still the person you started out to be. That's how I've always understood it, that's how the world has always worked, and now instead I find this hall of mirrors, where everyone has their own idea of who I am, and even in my own mind I cannot be sure of what is real and what is...not.

"Anne," Aubrey begins, gliding her swivel chair close to where the mother sits at the open end of the counter, as far as she can be from Rod and Seivers and Auster and the commotion outside the station. To Aubs it is apparent that the day has drained her; those bony shoulders sloping steeply beneath the pilled and shabby cardigan, the curved spine drooping her head forward even more than usual. "Are you OK?"

Of course she is OK, Mrs. M. informs her. Why wouldn't she be?

"Well, it's just..." but in mid-sentence Aubrey finds the words dissolving in her mouth, as she realizes the degree to which she herself has been disrupted by what they have been hearing, and wonders why on earth that should be the case. It has been months, after all, since she was told her friend was gone. First by Mrs. M., informing her that 'Kim' was just a fabrication; then the doctors, saying Christina would never recover, and then more recently, straight from the horse's mouth, steadfastly maintaining he was and always had been Rodney Gimbal. None of those tales had affected her like this though - like hearing that young doctor-woman explain that he might really be telling the truth, in which case...

"It's…I guess I never really believed Kim was gone. I always thought that someday, somehow, she would be back. Even with all this Rod business…but now, after hearing that doctor-lady explain it all…"

"Oh, my dear," Mrs. M. replies softly. Despite her tired appearance, she manages a humoring smile as she raises her eyes to meet Aubrey's. "You're not worried about that, are you? Didn't you hear that nice Mr. Seivers? He said there's nothing to any of that, and his word is good enough for me. I only wish…" Her voice trails off and she pulls her eyes away, looking out toward the front wall of the lobby where the glass of doors and windows offer edited reflections of the interior, layering its sharp white planes over the filtered scene outside: a scrim of fallen evening and charcoal sky above a crowd still thick and restive.

"What, Mrs. McKloskey? You can talk to me, you know; I mean, these last few months, I feel kind of like you're… well, like, my Aunt or something. Like family, only not so close it has to be this big deal or anything, and so…anyway…I'd really like to hear. To help, I mean. If I can. Even if it's only just listening."

"Well," the older woman begins, placing one hand on top of Aubrey's then the other on top of that. "Sometimes I do feel that, perhaps Sean and I made things a little too difficult for Christina. Her father was so capable, you know. Not just in his music, but – my goodness, I can't remember anything he ever set out to do that he didn't accomplish. And very well, too. Creating and leading an ensemble like my Sean did is quite a complex business you know: organizing, scheduling; auditioning and selecting musicians - it's not like hiring any other sort of staff. And when he became successful - financially, I mean - Sean managed all of that as well. That's how I've been able to be so comfortable, you know, although I have to admit, it's not what it was. I'm afraid I don't have the kind of mind for that sort of thing."

Seeing those featherweight hands begin to tremble the tiniest little bit, Aubrey takes them in her own, offering what reassurance she can as the woman continues. 'Little Christina' always resisted being taught how to do things, she explains. Always insisted she could do them before even knowing what the task entailed. Ride a bike? She'd hop on the seat as if she'd been riding all her life, fall off, then announce she had never wanted to ride in the first place. Learn the piano? She'd climb up on the bench, feet dangling far above the pedals, and plunk out two bars of some nursery tune, then announce to her frustrated papa that she had proven she knew how to play. No amount of discipline, no withholding rewards or enforcing practice times, could convince her to make the effort required to excel at anything she sensed her parents valued, and so, eventually, her father had given up, throwing that much more effort into his own work.

"I just wonder," Anne concludes, "what might have happened if we hadn't set such a high bar for her, if maybe then she wouldn't have felt the need to...escape. Leaving home, changing her name, inventing this Rodney character. I just..."

As the voice trails off it seems to Aubrey that something else is ebbing as well, and she catches a fleeting image of what it must be like to be old and alone. Living in a house decorated with someone else's achievements, the photographs fading, the clippings yellowing and everything around you slowly – or not so slowly – wearing out, devolving from treasure into junk. From the first time she met Christina's mother, Aubs has taken her for granted, really, assuming those bubbling good spirits were a natural state; something that had always been there, and would always be. Only now does she consider how much it might cost to maintain that attitude in the face of all that has gone on, and how critical it is to Anne to do so. 'Having a positive attitude' has always been a joke to Aubrey and the people she hangs with; a cliché spouted by dorky youth-ministers and creepy guidance-geeks trying to get you to buy into their world, only now it seems like maybe her own cynicism is the real luxury – a careless bullshit that only works if someone else is paying the bills, or if you're ready to write off everyone and everything, including yourself. Losing Kim is proof enough, if Aubrey ever really needed it, that there are some things worth caring about, and maybe some truths worth believing in, despite the evidence against them.

"It's not..." she begins, searching for a right way to say what she is thinking; trying on a new perspective as she fumbles and discards thoughts that don't ring true. "It's...like that Bill guy said? That what the doctor lady said is just plain impossible. Christina is your daughter. The whole thing when she was sick, that's just got her confused, and if you...if we, take good care of her, I think maybe she could get better. Remember how when she was in the hospital - this same hospital, isn't that a weird thing? – they said she'd never be able to walk or talk, or any of that?"

When Anne's eyes rise to meet hers once again, Aubrey can see the thoughts dawning in them. A question first; the surrounding flesh tightening, deepening the furrows of experience; and then an answer, the muscles relaxing and the eyes themselves capturing the brightness of the lights shining down on them and reflecting it back out, as her hands - still clasped within Aubrey's - clench just a little tighter.

"Yes," Anne recalls firmly, the slender voice resuming something like its usual vigor as her head too, rises to embrace the image they are sharing. "Yes. They said she would never even become conscious."

"And look what happened?" Aubrey feels the excitement now, the power of her own words to shape the thoughts that follow. "She proved them all wrong. And maybe, you know, if we believe in her as much now as we did back then, maybe we can help her get over this...thing she's doing, and be herself again. I mean, I don't care if she never remembers being Kim; I've like, grown out of that myself. I'm ready to be...to live a kind of...a different life than we had back then anyway. I mean, school is *so* over... But Christina and me, I think we could be real good friends. And maybe after she's gone through all of this, maybe she'd be able to see how much she needs you too."

Perhaps it's only natural, having convinced themselves of the possibilities, that the two women would choose this moment to glance at the subject of their imaginings - the prodigal daughter - and would take note of her sudden stillness. Not the sullen withdrawal of denial; that heavy-lidded expression that says her thoughts have gone away to who-knows-where-they-go, but another type of stillness. Alert and focused, and perhaps a little skeptical, Christina's eyes are on a woman who has materialized out of the demonstrators, her wide broomstick skirt and pleated blouse like a costume from another place, another time even. A patterned scarf encircles her head and a dozen silver bracelets jangle, as she thanks Officer Dominguez for escorting her this far, then strides easily across the floor, into the security station and right up to Christina, amber eyes focusing like a laser on that youthful face, examining its contours.

"So you're Rodney Gimbal?" she asks, in a voice that seems to quiet the noise around them, just as oil stills choppy waters. Like oil and water they look, too: Christina in her dreary gray suit and chopped-off hair, face locked in a mask of disapproval, and this new arrival, all color and texture and sparkling metals, her features aglow with ruddy sunshine and poised in eager anticipation. Ready, it

703

seems to Aubrey, to burst into a smile or a laugh at any moment. Polar opposites, they could be, each one the counter to the other's truths.

"Yes, I am," Rod answers, a little resentfully, though the question has been asked in the nicest possible way. "Thank you for allowing me that. And you are?"

The new arrival continues to study Christina, looking her over from head to toe, even reaching a hand out to touch her face, very softly, with just the tips of two fingers, which are quickly pulled away as their owner looks her straight in the eye.

"You really don't know me?" she asks sadly.

"No," Rod answers, giving her a thorough looking-over. "You look like...for a moment I thought you were...but no. I don't think we would ever have met, you and I."

"No," the woman admits. "I don't suppose we would. Not now. But perhaps a long time ago?" She casts a conspiring look at Anne, and in fact the two are of similar vintage. What few wisps of hair project beneath the stranger's head-scarf are ghostly-white, and the laugh lines around her eyes are deeply carved, as are the creases which map the rest of her face like veins on a leaf, and cover the soft flesh which drapes beneath her chin. "But perhaps our paths have crossed before. Perhaps we have some acquaintances in common. Lizzie Blakely, for example, do you know Lizzie Blakely?"

"My wife's roommate," Rod answers immediately, ever the honor student looking to excel. "In New York, back in about....sixty five."

Sucking in her cheeks, the woman pauses, considering. For a moment her head seems to totter, but it recovers quickly, clear blue eyes locking once again on their target – Christina's haughty expression and the stiff-backed posture she has adopted.

"No," she says softly, as if a trifle disappointed. "That isn't it. Perhaps we met at a function. The funeral of a..."

"I don't go to funerals..." Rod interjects, only to have his own words overridden just as imperiously.

"Damned waste of time," the woman pronounces mechanically, clearly repeating a familiar line, at the end of which she waits, lips pursed, breath still.

"And I don't like being interrupted," Rod points out harshly, the words hardly necessary as the angle of his head and the rising of his shoulders make that personality trait clear to everyone watching.

"I'll second that," Aubrey puts in, eager to break the spell these two seem to have cast on one another. Behind her Herman and his two new groupies join in to offer their own wisecracks but the colorful interloper ignores them all, her attention fixed on this one person with so many different names. Unperturbed by his irritation, perhaps even a bit reassured, the woman takes her time before responding. She has, it seems, all the time in the world for this examination.

"You never liked being disagreed with either," she suggests. "For as long as I can remember. Not when you were living in the little house in Brooklyn, with Mr. and Mrs. - what were their names?"

"Kapinsky," Rod answers quickly, his suspicion rising in response to these questions which seem aimed less at finding answers than as some sort of test.

"That's right," the woman agrees, much as a gentle teacher might encourage a valued pupil. "And not when your future wife's father quizzed you about your prospects. What was it he used to say, when he wasn't satisfied with your answers, he'd say...."

A faint haze of humor lapses over Christina's features as her voice jumps in to fill the void. "Shoot straight, cowboy," she offers, pronouncing the words in imitation of a gravelly Brooklyn accent. "Shoot quick, and shoot straight..."

"And you'll be all right with me," the newcomer joins in, so the two voices finish in unison, with very nearly the same accent and manner. In that instant they could be a pair of old vaudevillians revisiting an ancient routine, except that Christina's eyes are wide now, in expression of Rod's confusion and irritation, with a slight overtone of something Aubrey has not seen in him before. It might be worry, or perhaps apprehension, but mostly what it looks like is fear – as if for once he has encountered something for which his regular reflexes of anger, disapproval and denial have not prepared him.

"How?" he asks the stranger. "How do you...?"

"You really don't recognize me," the woman says sadly, verbalizing what is obvious to all around them. "It's me, Rodney. I'm Elaine. Your wife."

Their conversation till now has been halting, but this pause is longer than any before, as Rod's gaze travels down and up. Silver bracelets silent, silken skirt-pleats still, even the stranger's breathing all but ceases as she is subjected to Rod's clinical analysis and found, finally, to be correct.

"You've changed," is how he puts it, the disapproval unmistakable.

"As have you," Elaine points out, a gentle smile upon her own features. "As have you."

"Listen up," Tammy cries into the silence which follows, catching them all by surprise from her seat at the security console. "I've been watching the bulletins," she explains, "and there's a press conference getting ready to start upstairs. 'Bout our girl Stevie." One of her hands is pointing to the center monitor, where a podium bristling with microphones has come into view, while the other is squeezing Herman's shoulder, encouraging as his fingers tap across the touch screen that controls his system. "There," she shouts with satisfaction, directing attention now out and across the lobby, to where the words and pictures which had been crawling across the display wall have been replaced by that same podium image, larger than life-size above a sea of heads beginning to turn in its direction. Seconds later, a new sound begins emanating from speakers in the walls and ceiling: the softly innocuous music of a telephone call on hold. Immediately the crowd quiets, all eyes on the giant image, where men and women mill around, their faces grim, awaiting some event.

"Hey, everybody…" Tammy says into the console's gooseneck microphone, then stops when it becomes obvious her voice is not going out as she had hoped. A glance at Herman leads to several more taps of the screen before he rises with a sigh to full height and leans out across the counter.

"They're gonna' have a press conference," he booms, as in the distance Mark's camera turns to catch him.

"About Stevie," Rose adds in a commanding tone. "And…and…well, just wait and see."

"I must admit I did not believe it myself," Elaine is telling the others, though she seems mostly to be speaking to Anne. "When Mrs. Volmer said there'd been a girl coming round the house, claiming she was Dr. Gimbal. I thought it was a joke perhaps, or a hoax; some kind of con-artist who'd learned that Rodney had passed away and that I was out of the country. I probably wouldn't have paid any more attention, except the sheer absurdity of it - a young *woman* claiming to be Rodney? How could she possibly imagine anyone would believe that? But then, as my friend Beryl once said, 'there's often more to learn from the unbelievable, than from what seems to make perfect sense.' And when I called the number on the card, I found myself talking to some police-person who said they had been monitoring that number ever since the poor thing was beaten up. When I explained how I got the card she said that Rodney's name had come up before in their investigation, and asked me to come here to answer some questions and give them the card, and now," she continues, turning again to Christina, "seeing you, hearing you...I have no idea how, or why, but I must admit that when I look into your eyes..." Despite her good humor, there is a weariness in her weathered features as both hands reach out to touch Rod's shoulders. "How difficult this must be for you."

"You're his wife then, right?" Aubrey asks. "This doctor guy she thinks she is?"

"That's correct. I am Elaine Gimbal, and this...in some way I cannot explain or defend, is Dr. Rodney Gimbal, who was my husband, a lifetime or so ago."

On the giant screen a man appears. Stepping in front of the podium he reaches out to tap one of the microphones and a loud thump startles the lobby's listeners.

"I'm Robert Baker," the man announces. "Director of Family Relations for The Institutes at Hilltop Medical. Here beside me..." All eyes are on the screen as he proceeds to introduce Hilltop Chief Legal Counsel Tyrone Lee, SPD Assistant Chief Marianne Pogue and finally, Doctor Andra D'Aousta, the lead physician who's been attending to Stevie Margulies. An ascetic-looking woman with a caramel complexion, tightly-curled reddish-black hair and eyes that look to have seen no pillow in a very long time, it is she who takes over the podium to explain the patient's condition.

"The injuries sustained in this case," she tells those in the conference room, and by electronic extension, those in the lobby and wherever else the multiple video feeds will eventually lead, "included several lacerations in the genital area, one of which penetrated the femoral sheath, causing arterial bleeding. This Class Four Hemorrhage amounted to approximately 55% of total blood volume, and was accompanied by significant blockage of the airway, probably occurring after the lacerations." Taking a deep breath, she glances down at the podium but, finding no escape there, continues. "Aggressive resuscitation was applied at the scene and successive transfusions both during and after transport - a, uh...a total of three and one-half liters whole blood were required before pressure was stabilized. These measures were clinically effective but due to the circumstances of the assault and response, were not applied soon enough after the onset of trauma to prevent extensive soft tissue damage due to HAI. That's hypoxic/anoxic injury," she explains, then pauses once again, looking out across the room and sweeping her head from side to side, before taking a deep in-breath and continuing. "It is the unanimous conclusion of our consulting team that the subject is, as a consequence, unlikely to survive for any length of time without external life support and, if surviving, the most positive outcome which can be responsibly predicted is a persistent vegetative state with no hope of recovery or improvement."

The sound which comes over the lobby after these words is a complex mix of sighs and groans, of obscenities spat down toward the floor and cries raised to the ceiling and beyond, all blending into one carnal gasp; as if two-hundred and more individuals had somehow melded into one living, breathing organism. Only for an instant, though, does this effect persist; for almost immediately that unanimity dissolves into cacophony, the loudest strand of which are cries of denial and demands for someone, anyone, to be held accountable.

"Let me go," Stevie demands, but the men pay no heed as they gather her up between them, one pinning her arms around her chest, another pulling her feet out from under her. Horizontal and squirming she is carried, sees the storefront sliding by only to be eclipsed by blank wall as the men carry her into the garbage-strewn space beside it. An empty can is kicked, the sound sharp and painful in the tight confines. Stevie works a leg free and struggles to reach the ground, discovers her shoe already gone, the earth wet and gritty as a bottle rolls away, tinkling cheerfully till it hits the wall and stops. Deep between these buildings the air is colder; it's a place never touched by sunshine, never quite completely dry. She smells soured milk, rot and beery breath in her face as she is dropped on the uneven surface, head hitting hard. Ears ringing, lungs struggling to breathe in against the stench and cold and allergy, she feels something wrenching at her skirt, then hands scrabbling to explore between her legs, pulling and tearing the layers, until they find her flesh.

"Son of a bitch," Bawdy's voice exclaims. He gives a hard squeeze on the organs he has found tucked inside her panties, and Stevie gasps at the pain which flashes through her. Shutting her eyes tighter she imagines screaming for help, but finds her mouth will not open. Despite the darkness, the three against one, the presence of the city all around, she cannot bring herself to do that. A judgment comes to mind then, that this is all her own fault, and she must solve it herself, not cry for help from strangers. Whether this is some intrinsic male characteristic, or just the fossil remains of a stereotype beyond which she thought she had evolved, there it is. This embedded voice, telling her she must do as a man does: be solitary and self-sufficient.

"You one of those boys wants to be a girl?" asks the bearded man. "That it?"

Opening her eyes, Stevie makes out only a round mass hanging over her, the features lost in shadow. Searching, she locks on to where the eyes should be, certain that she must not avoid them, must not flinch, for in that is some salvation. To meet with dignity whatever comes.

"I'm just a person," she manages, softly. "Who looks like this, and sounds like..."

"You made me fucking kiss you," interrupts the voice,

accompanied by a fist landing straight against her face, sending the back of her head slamming against the ground again. Echoing pain erupts throughout her skull, yet not quite obscuring the warm wetness of blood erupting in a spurt from her nose. "That the way you get your rocks off?" the man asks, though Stevie hears the words only distantly, filtered through the pulsing sensation which is filling her head. "Making me want to kiss you? You're a fucking freak; a fucking queer little freak piece of shit."

"He wants to be a girl," offers Jimbo, sounding - for once - slow and thoughtful. "Serve him right if we helped him along."

"Yeah," Bawdy agrees, turning the idea over in his mind. "Hey, Booger," he challenges the small man who's been hanging off to one side. "You ever fish for prairie oysters on that ranch you grew up on?"

"Shit," comes the answer, wary and unsure, as if defending against something unspoken. "I don't care if it is a queer..."

"You *owe* me, Booger," Jimbo says, the words full of menace as he raises his bandaged hand toward the other's face. "I'd have all my fucking fingers if it weren't for you."

The smaller man cowers, eyes wandering over the moaning figure on the ground. "I never actually..."

"Well, what the fuck good are you then, hunh?"

"I seen it done, though," Booger immediately corrects himself, voice assuming a veneer of confidence. "Lots'a times." Shrugs his shoulders, then adds, as if unsatisfied with himself, "it ain't no big deal."

Bawdy turns back to the figure beneath him, no longer struggling, except for breath. "That what you want freak?" he growls. "You want us to help you be a girl?" Hearing no answer he reaches out his good hand and slaps Stevie's chin from side to side and back again. "Answer me freak. Is that what you want?"

"No," she answers, the sound barely more than a moan.

"Then why you dressed like a girl, unless you want to be one?"

The sound of a car approaches and for a few seconds the wash of its headlights threatens to illuminate the scene, but they pass perpendicular, never casting more than a pale glow into the alleyway, the driver's eyes wholly on the road he is travelling, not theirs. Eyes clamped tightly shut, Stevie does not see even that faint light as her mind searches for a thought, for a place to go that is not here, not now. Again she feels hands pulling, shifting her body, tearing away clothing while in her mind she conjures up a theater lobby, tall and grand, glittering with people. Legs pulled apart, spread wide in the chill air, and still she does not scream. There are men in the lobby crowd, uniformed in dark jackets and black bow-ties, but her attention is on the women, sheathed in brilliant colors. Pale, cool blues, sparkling gold and silver; rich maroon and dazzling white with sequins. And black of course - when all else fails, there's always black. The women's arms and shoulders are bare and smooth, their hair lustrous in piles atop their heads or draping their backs as they stand. Tall, slender, full of grace. Elegance abounds, trumping all else as a click is heard, signature of a folding knife being opened, but Stevie ignores it, listening instead for the murmur of that lobby crowd. To their hundred-and-one conversations, soft and intimate, reveling in all that such an evening has to offer. Something else is happening somewhere, but Stevie wills herself to ignore it, to not imagine what accounts for that spreading warmth she feels, to concentrate instead upon the image in her mind so that everything else will disappear, and for a moment she can hear the clink of glasses, orders called across the crystalline surface of the lobby bar as cool jazz plays above it all. Clatter of change on the counter, rattling of bottles stuffed back into tubs of ice, then all is interrupted by an electronic bell, signal that patrons must return to their seats; the curtain is about to rise. The bell sounds just as it should, but then it does not stop, instead ringing and ringing and rising in volume as its pitch seems to be all over the scale; low and high and indescribable. Louder and louder it rings inside her head, a thundering rush of discordant sound she cannot possibly withstand and then the sound is her pain and it wipes out all other sense, washing over her and through her until it is the whole world; a world of pain intensified by fear and by the dead-weight realization that there is no going back from where she has come to be right now - that all is pain and pain is all, and that is all there is.

Dr. D'Aousta's announcement subdues the crowd, both inside the lobby and those still gathered outside, where the rain has again slackened to a chill mist and the news has travelled via pocket electronica and old fashioned word of mouth. Around the Reverend, his followers cluster, the men dropping to one knee, the women and children tenting hands before their hearts, as he leads them in a prayer for the victim's soul.

"Beloved Father," he begins, taking on the requisite tone of thoughtful anticipation to signify words addressed not to those visibly present, but to The One who listens from outside and above, from another plane and another reality. His words are softly echoed by dozens of voices issuing from bowed heads, their eyes tightly shut as they concentrate not on the here-and-now, but on their visions of the eternal and omniscient; the ultimate authority. "We ask you to look down upon this poor sinner..."

In the conference room upstairs, the audience remains composed as Bob Baker takes over the podium once again. Given that prognosis, he explains, Hilltop's legal staff have been going over various documents and conferring with outside authorities. Their research, in the time since Stephen Margulies was admitted, has confirmed that although he and his wife Evelyn were divorced more than two years ago, she is still named in a Medical Durable Power of Attorney that was drafted along with their Living Will prior to their separation.

"That Living Will," Baker notes, eyes directly on the camera, "is of legal effect, and specifically states Mr. Margulies' wish that artificial means of life support not be continued in the event there is deemed to be no reasonable possibility of his ever regaining consciousness. As Agent under the Power of Attorney, Evelyn Margulies is the person who will make the determination whether such measures should be discontinued."

Miss Margulies, he informs them all, is in the building at this time and reviewing her options with Hilltop's legal staff and chaplain. With that, and without taking any questions, the press conference is adjourned until further notice.

Out on the plaza, beside the makeshift stage, Herb and Genda are locked in one another's arms, as tears flow freely from both. Nearby Carol and a few others confer with leaders the various groups who've been part of the vigil. Grim faces abound, and what remarks are made are soto voce; embarrassed admissions that 'I thought it would come to this,' angry outrage that 'It took two days for them to figure that out?' or simple words of helplessness: 'What a goddamned shame.' Beneath a canopy still dripping its accumulated moisture, tarps drape amplifiers, keyboard and drums – equipment ready to rock but sadly out of place now, in what was once a demonstration, then a vigil and a celebration of shared apartness, and could now perhaps be best described as a wake-in-waiting. At the sparse edges of the gathering a few individuals turn and begin to walk away, but for the most part, everyone stays, expecting more; some finality to the tragedy which has been unfolding here.

So many words for such a simple truth: a person is dead, and all that's left is housekeeping. I have to admit, it saddens me. Even in the midst of all the rest – the cops, this place, Elaine – still it affects me more than I would have believed. Strange, that she could seem so genuine and caring, and all the time be living a lie.

"I'm sorry," the boy Jake says, and in his eyes I still see longing, but no longer any threat.

One of the weird ones too, with the dirty hair, is offering condolences. "I guess you two had something good," she says, as if those feeble words could possibly be sufficient to sum up a life.

"Somehow she managed to rationalize it all," I tell them. "To make sense out of the pieces of herself, and in the process, she made it seem for a while that I could do the same. That finding this new voice was more important than figuring out where it came from. And now..." I look across at this stranger who claims to be my wife. Who is my Elaine, but different; so different that at first I didn't even recognize her. These others, too, trying to convince me with their stories about reincarnations and transplants. "None of your explanations is enough. Nothing comes close to convincing me how I can be here, like this."

"I can't explain it either," Elaine responds. "But then, does any of us really know how we come to be the persons we are? I know that I loved a man once, but over many years I changed, and he changed, and we became...other people. And then I met a stranger in an airport, and now I am who I am today. But I can't explain *why* any of those things happened; I only know that I have to live the life I've been given and not allow what I don't know to tie me up in knots. There's a freedom to it, Rodney, when you let go of the need to figure out everything and simply live what is before you. Surely you've felt that too? Sometime, in all your years?"

"When I sing," she hears Christina's voice answer, haltingly, carefully. "When Stevie used to play and we'd sing together. Or today, when I was singing with those people up there...when I feel the music coming out of my mouth like it has its own life, then I don't care who I am or how I came to be, I am just myself and the music I can make."

"Then that's what you need to do, my dear. That's where your heart is telling you to go. Just as my heart is telling me I have to go on with my life. Do new things. Not try to go back to what once was."

"But..." Christina's voice cracks, the look of joy and optimism which had consumed her face for a moment replaced by one approaching terror. "Now that we're together...you said you believe who I am..."

Gently, Elaine takes up Rod's hand; Christina's pastel flesh so full and round and ripe against her own, where lumpy bones and blued veins stand-out in deep relief beneath spotted, fissured skin. Pulling it to her cheek she holds it there and closes her eyes, as if drifting far away.

"Life is about making choices," she says after a moment, her eyes still closed, her voice soft as a whisper, and thin - as if there exists inside her barely enough energy to blow the words past her own thin lips. "And whenever we make a choice, even for the best of reasons, we reject a thousand other futures, leaving them stillborn in the womb of possibility. It's all a guessing game, my dear, and anyone who tells you otherwise is blowing smoke. About the only thing I know for sure is that I made a choice that morning I stepped out of our house and onto an airplane; before I had *any* idea what it would lead to. I chose to go forward then, and I can't go back now. And neither should you."

With security focused on the conference room, and on preventing the crowd from penetrating further into Hilltop's recesses than they already have, it's no longer a problem to wander from the courtyard to the lobby. More and more people pass through the main doors, propped open now by rolled-up newspapers jammed into hinges and under door bottoms. They seek the relative warmth of the lobby and its huddled mass, united in their determination to stay until the drama's end. With all the furniture long since claimed, these new arrivals settle on the stone floor, some spreading damp coats to sit or lie upon, some resting heads down on folded arms or the lap of another. Old friends take the opportunity to catch up, new acquaintances to share what the events of these hours mean to them, why they felt compelled to leave their homes and bars and clubs and spend their evenings in the rain without even a glimpse of the subject of it all. Some of the voices which emanate from these conversations are angry, some pleading, but many just plain weary.

On the landing of the stair Ellie and the fiddler pick up their instruments and begin to play in herky-jerky fragments, working out chord changes to some new tune, just loud enough for them to hear themselves. In another corner, Lady sits with a double conga clasped between her knees, tapping its two heads sporadically, almost idly; less a rhythm than a reminder of the possibility of a rhythm - keeping a musical avenue open, despite the overwhelming sense of momentum lost.

Behind the counter Herman sits, zooming cameras in and out on various faces as he explains to Mark Peterson the capabilities of his system. The filmmaker's equipment is idle for the time being, but close by, ready for whatever may come. Behind the guard's chair, Rose stands close, thumbs hooked in the epaulets of his uniform as she listens to the two geeks dissect the merits of wireless inputs and coaxial outputs. Now and then she leans in even closer, whispering some private comment to turn Herman's eager ears a brighter shade of pink.

"It's not like that at all," Tammy is insisting to Aubrey. "It's like, he's got Christina's vocal chords and lungs and all, so the sound is the same way she would sound, but this guy Rod is at the controls, so it's not one or the other of them, it's like ... what do you call that thing when two people play the piano - with one hand for each of them? *Chopsticks?*"

"A duet," Mary suggests without much interest, her eyes still on the screen of the phone which has not left her hand for the past hour. Seivers' veiled threats have left her apprehensive and confused, and the snatches which she has caught of Rod and Elaine's conversation have only added to the sense that there is something else she must be doing; something other than hanging out here listening to theories about events that may or may not have happened months ago, and will play-out in their own way and in their own time regardless. Lurching from her perch against the counter, she moves a few steps away, punches the #1 speed-dial, and places the device against her ear.

"Yeah, that's it," Tammy continues, oblivious. "It's like, when she sings, she's singing a duet with these other pieces of herself."

With a guilty smile toward the young doctor's turned back, Aubrey chimes in softly, saying she doesn't believe any of Mary's talk about secret surgery and body transplants. The suits would never have the balls, she says, to step that far outside the lines they draw for themselves. Deep down inside, she admits, a part of her still believes that Kim is punking them all, and if that's not it, then there's got to be some other explanation besides a medical one.

"I saw a thing on TV once," Rose interjects. "On *Ghost Hunters?* This guy was a college professor; and he said that when somebody dies with something left that they didn't finish in their life, then sometimes their spirit just hangs around, looking for a way to finish it up..."

Pulling the phone away from her ear, Mary stabs the 'end call' button in frustration. Looking around at the compatriots gathered behind the security counter her expression slides through several settings, from worry and fatigue to something rather angry and then, a look of quiet decision. Stuffing the phone into the pocket of her hoodie, and without a word to any of them, she begins walking; first out of the security station, then across the lobby, threading her way around loitering figures, toward the main entry doors. With a few soft 'excuse me's she passes through the tangle there, to find herself outside. Night mist gives the scene an eerie glow, and the cold sends a shiver up her spine, but weather does nothing to dissuade her as she turns and begins to prowl along the outside of the building, seeking another entrance, some little-used back or side door where she can show her credentials and convince Security to admit her back into the world of Hilltop. Jason is somewhere in that world, she knows, and finding him is more important - *more real* - to her than anything she might learn from hanging with Christina McKloskey and her odd assortment of friends and family. It is her own story she must unlock now and, for this moment at least, Jason Privet is its key.

"So, maybe that doctor's spirit was still hanging around like that," Aubrey continues rose's thought, "and then when Kim was brought in, maybe his spirit went into her body, and that's why she's acting like she is?"

"An outer-body experience," Rose agrees, wholeheartedly.

As the young women thrill to their new understanding, Jake listens idly, his large frame propped against an inside-corner of the counter, eyes wary on the milling crowd, as if he expects at any moment they will threaten his adopted clan. Now and then he does allow a glance toward where Christina sits, motionless and withdrawn, even as, beside her, the new woman who calls herself Elaine has stuck up with Mrs. M., the two of them chatting away like a pair of long-lost sisters.

He's just about to go for coffee when a call from Herman signals some new information has come in over his headphones. Like a fast-moving virus the message spreads across the lobby as he and Mark alternate taps at the control screen, and in a few seconds the video display is up on the wall again, all eyes turning to watch as the imposing figure of Tyrone Lee steps forward, his thick black hair gleaming under the lights, his stolid features calm and composed above a necktie knotted tightly and with perfect symmetry. With one raised arm he gently brings to his side the same auburn-haired woman whom Bannerjee had observed when he first arrived upstairs. Tired face devoid of make-up, her v-necked dress a deep and somber gray; this, it is immediately clear to all, must be the grieving ex.

"At eight-forty three this evening," Lee intones, his voice a rolling rumble, "Evelyn Margulies directed the trauma team to discontinue mechanical means of life support for Mr. Margulies. Her instructions were implemented at eight-fifty, and as of this time the patient's condition is unstable and critical." The two seem about to turn away, when Evelyn reaches out and tugs at Lee's sleeve. Bending down he listens as she whispers something in his ear, then turns, thrusting his face close to the clustered microphones.

"There will be no public service," he adds with a glare, and then the moment is over, attorney and presumptive-widow turning as one and heading out of the picture. Bob Baker's closing remarks are lost to those in the lobby, overwhelmed by cries and shouts, voices raised in prayer and signs tossed dejectedly to the floor.

"Hmmph," Rod grunts, only to catch the startled looks on Anne's and Elaine's faces. "Patient isn't even gone and they make an announcement about services. It's disrespectful."

When neither of the women responds, he continues, fidgeting Christina's hands in her lap, then letting them rise to sweep the air in emphasis.

"As if there isn't still a whole team back there doing their best to improve her condition. It disrespects their efforts..."

"Perhaps," Anne offers carefully as around them the crowd hums with whispered comments and embarrassed conversations, "that poor woman just needed some sort of closure."

"Closure?" Rod harrumphs again, and to Elaine his attitude says it all. Closure means giving up. No 'one more treatment' to try, no endless new avenues to consider. 'Closure,' she can hear Rodney's old voice saying inside her, 'is for quitters.' Anne must have understood it, too, for Elaine can see her features fallen, his blunt dismissal taken as comment on her emotion.

There is another way to look at it, Elaine knows. Through Petal's eyes, and those of her clan, who regularly watch their loved ones go off on trips of months or even years, with the very real possibility that they might never return. Through the eyes of Azhe women, who enjoy their 'visitors' for a night or two or twenty, then watch them leave without ever knowing when - or if - they will be back.

"When I first heard about you, Rodney – about you being who you claimed to be and all... well, odd as it seemed, it occurred to me that, perhaps, it was meant to be. To give me an opportunity to say the things I never had a chance to say...about your passing. About how I walked out and left you. I feel terrible that I wasn't there when you needed me..."

"Wouldn't have made any difference," Rod interjects, and in that instant it is as if he has answered all her doubts; every question Elaine has addressed to herself since receiving word back in that Thai hotel room. "I already had the best of care, if there was anything that could have been done..."

"Yes dear, I know," she answers, fully aware of how the interruption will be received. "You didn't need me. You haven't needed anybody in a very long time."

Far across the lobby, Lady has resumed her tapping. Still slowly, still softly, her fingers hit the drawn skins. The left hand seems to be in command, striking the larger circle like a metronome, calling out a slow and mournful time. In between and around these her right hand dances, sometimes echoing the beat, sometimes doubling it, the fingertips striking now at the center of the taut membrane, now at its upper edge, now on the side of the drum itself, each location resulting in a clearly different voice from the same instrument. After a few minutes of this, but still before the sound can be called by any more specific name, another tapping joins in; an angular boy with a cobalt Mohawk has stripped a wooden dowel from one of the signs and broken it in two. Holding them like the bar-band drummer he is and bouncing them on the glass top of the very coffee table where Detective Bannerjee's paperwork and radios were lying not long ago, Spyder Hawkins beats out a counterpoint to Lady's pulse. Before long, they are joined by a serious-looking woman in serious shoes, a drum-circle regular who goes by the name of Dusty Rainbow, tapping her own fingers on the bottom of an upended trash receptacle, a triplet timed to every fourth of Lady's beats.

Mark Peterson is one of the first to notice these developments, looking up from the control board as the assortment of improvised percussions popcorn around the crowded space. In the span of several minutes he listens as independent taps and slaps solidify into something more substantial; a scrim of skipping, smattering accents hovering in the air above Lady's steady time, which gathers and supports them as she shifts the emphasis to the after-beats; the second and the fourth instead of the more traditional first or third. It is an outside rhythm, a tempo for the dispossessed and unexpected, and has been growing for five minutes or more, swelling in numbers and power, by the time Evie joins in, stepping backwards up to the third tread of the staircase with an old acoustic six-string strapped around her neck as she begins a steady drag across its tightly-wound strings. The simplest strum of all, fingers holding the pick lightly, letting it flex and angle so the six notes sound in gentle succession - each tone given its due, but close enough on one another's tail to suggest a chord.

Even as more of the crowd are joining in, tapping feet or slapping hands on some convenient surface, Mark observes a dark quartet emerging from the guarded hallway that leads to the elevator bank. Seivers, Auster, Doug Taylor and Bannerjee cross the floor easily, the now-somber crowd making way for them, like townspeople parting for a band of gunslingers marching to the show—down. From the opposite direction, opened doors admit the sound of the Reverend's supporters in the plaza, closing a prayer with shouted 'Amen's,' followed by a single voice calling an instruction.

"A Mighty Fortress," it declares, then "two, three, four..." and is joined by a chorus of voices high and low in what must be a hymn familiar to them all, its ancient, borrowed melody plodding and relentless - no celebration, but a dirge.

"A mighty for-tress...is our God," they affirm. *"A bul-wark ne-ver fail-ing."*

Alert for serendipity, Peterson hears as Evie's guitar gradually fits itself around this distant rhythm, adjusting her strums in millisecond intervals until they conform to its meter, yet with a different accent. Sees Lady take notice as well, gathering her drum under one arm while with the opposite hand she maintains her heartbeat rhythm in sync with the guitar. Rising and making her way across the space she settles in on the second stair, from which she can make eye contact with the rest of her impromptu orchestra, nodding as their beats interact, tying disparate individuals together on a level without words, yet clearly understood. Feeling a familiar tingle in his spine, Mark gathers up his camera, checks its battery status and settings, and then begins to move; searching for the angle, the light, the visible gap in the forest of people around him through which he can capture that unknown something which his filmmaker's instinct tells him is about to happen, even as, behind him, Bannerjee speaks softly to the guard Miller, and the three MH functionaries crowd closer around Christina's corner.

"So, my dear," Seivers oozes, as he reaches the young woman. "Have you decided what you're going to do?"

"For still our ancient foe," the voices sing outside, *"doth seek to work us woe..."*

"She's not your dear," Aubrey shoots back, one hand on Mrs. M's shoulder, where the older woman's hand rises to cover it.

"Whatever you've offered her," Jake chimes in, "it's only for your own good, and we'll fight you every inch of the way before we let you get hold of her."

"You'd better be careful there, Jacko." This comment comes from Auster, his thick forefinger cocked close to Jake's face, as he speaks just loud enough for those close-by to hear. "Your friend keeps on claiming to be Rod Gimbal and she's going to end up institutionalized, tranquilized and dead to the world."

The crowded station erupts then, as Tammy and Rose and Jake and Aubrey and Mrs. McKloskey all jump to defend their vision of the figure in question. Voices rise, and gestures flash, Auster and Seivers laying down the law while Taylor watches, superfluous in this institution of which he is supposed to be in charge.

'On earth is not his equal,' sing the voices outside, less audible now as Evie and Lady and the rest gather confidence in their common inspiration.

I hear them all talking, gesturing. The expressions on their faces are like one of those awful foreign movies - a jumble of images, each one different and each one replacing the last in such rapid succession they make no sense at all, only impressions - Confusion. Anger. Desperation.

In the larger crowd there is not only sound, but movement as well; a random scattering of people rising to stand, shoulders squared toward the stairs and the musicians' unspoken leadership. A blanket-wrapped young woman pulls out a cigarette lighter, flicks it on and holds it high, drawing eyes upon her accidental tableau of a latter-day Lady Liberty. Rubbing weary faces and shaking fog out of their heads, still more rise in slow succession, their eyes gravitating toward Evie as her strums become more purposeful and the drummers gain confidence, a dozen different voices hammering sonic stones into one secure foundation.

"*I remember,*" Evie begins, more shouting than singing at this point, and though the words are distantly familiar to many in the gathering, it takes them several lines to recognize where she is heading and why, though by the time she reaches the line "*Good friends we've had,*" a first few voices are cautiously joining in.

"*Good friends we've lost along the way...*" they mouth, searching for confidence as outside the open doors, that other chorus is strong on its own lyric: *"...and though this world, with devils filled..."*

Where a few moments ago I was the center of attention, now I am only in the way; an object they all talk around, over, across. Every one of them thinks they know who I am and what to do about me. The girl Aubrey, for one: convinced I am her old friend Kim...but if that were true, then everything I remember and believe about myself would be a fabrication – a silly art-school project taken too far. Such total self-delusion would surely be insanity, and even if not, to accept the history she claims for me would be to deny everything that is real and true within myself – no; that way lies a madness squared.

"In this bright future," the interior voices sing, *"you can't forget your past,"* countered from outside with *"...his truth to triumph through us."*

If Mrs. McKloskey is the one who sees most clearly, then still I am lost, for as much as I sympathize with the old loon, there is no way I can call myself her child. I had a mother once, decades ago, who I remember - and think I may have loved - and I cannot accept that she and all that goes along with her are just a fabrication built up to protect me from the loss of a some unremembered musician-father of whom I have exactly zero recollection.

And then there is Elaine. This new Elaine, recognizable as my dear wife and yet not recognizable. Aged by decades on her surface, but apparently oblivious to all that; and brimming instead with the cock-eyed self-delusion of someone half our years. A world of change has happened in the months since I last saw her, that morning we argued. Leaving the house afterwards, I counted myself successful, in launching her toward the next phase of her life. Now I see only a misfit eccentric wanderer and dabbler in mystic mumbo-jumbo. Oh, there was a moment after she'd identified herself, a moment of assurance there that – yes! - the self I hold in my mind is real. That was the greatest relief I've had since waking from my Nothing. For a brief time, hope and certainty washed over me, only to be dashed almost as soon as she spoke again. 'Things as they are meant to be,' my ass! The words smell of pre-destination, invisible hands moving us like pieces on some infernal chessboard. And 'simultaneous contradiction'... Mumbo-jumbo of the highest order, when the only true reality is that she intends to go traipsing off again and I will remain here, trapped in this body - and this world - which are not mine. Which can never be mine.

"*No woman, no cry,*" Evie is singing now, and with the start of this chorus, the crowd has fully caught on. To a person they have risen to their feet and turned toward the center of the room, a sea of faces opening themselves to the healing power of shared performance, some holding aloft flaming lighters, some the paper flyers which had brought them here – rolled-up into batons - a few clenched fists.

"*Oh my little sister,*" they sing, gaining power with every word. "*Don't shed no tears.   No woman…no cry.*"

Which leaves me only strangers. That young girl who calls herself a doctor, but behaves like a Hollywood actress in a made-up movie, boasting she's found some mysterious bit of equipment that proves her theory - as precious as if it were the holy grail. The only reason I give any credence to her preposterous story is the look on Jim Auster's face when she showed up. I may be a poor judge of human nature, but I know guilt when I see it, and there was guilt writ large across not only his face but that shyster boss of his as well, this Seivers character.

But even if she's right - if all I believe about my self is true – it still leaves me trapped; stuck for another thirty, forty, fifty years in the form of this woman child, to be seen by all around me in light of her body, her face, her past. Somehow to reconcile that with the 'me' I know I am. To give up my memories and skills, all the authority I worked for decades to win, only to be stalked forever by the Jakes and the drunkards and whoever else fixes their hungry eyes upon these buttocks or these…Who could stand to live like that?

Capturing developments, Peterson's excitement is growing, when a new thought strikes him. Without taking the camera from his eye he asks Herman if his system has a dial-up connection, for remote troubleshooting and testing. For a minute or two the pair scurry, Mark patching a cable from camera to his cell phone as Herman digs into a deep drawer full of cables and jacks, then both scrambling to find another phone with the proper capabilities.

"It's a form of beaming," Mark explains to Jake, as he takes the offered phone.

"Like Bluetooth," the big man agrees, sounding downright grateful for the opportunity to contribute.

"Well...yeah," the filmmaker admits as he plugs the cord into the device. "Only this is to Bluetooth, like, uh...like Starbucks is to Dunkin' Donuts,"

At his control board, Herman taps the screen a few times more and the layered wall opposite erupts in an image of the gathering. Ill-composed and steeply angled from its camera hidden in the ceiling, still it serves to remind the multitude of themselves; their number and their strength. Scores of eyes widen a moment later, when that static image is replaced with the one from Peterson's camera; panning, and zooming as he heads back out among the singing mass, catching first one beaming face and then another till the image reaches the bottom of the stairs. Another guitarist has arrived to join Evie, and in the bottom corner of the frame two figures bend and scurry; Elliot Silverman, geeky technical director from the Swedish Social Club, helping Ashton setup his electric organ and amplifier, then running off in search of an outlet in which to plug its cord.

"*Everything's gonna be all right,*" the leaders sing, extending the choral break to fill time until this last bit of business can be accomplished.

"*Everything's gonna be all right,*" a hundred voices answer, bodies swaying to the captivating rhythm which has by now completely drowned out the competing hymn from which it sprang.

"*Everything's gonna be all right, yeah,*

"*Everything's gonna be all right,*

Repetition bestows confidence on this amateur choir; each instance louder and more clear as finally the organ's connection is made and its rippling tonal waters join in, swelling the community of sound that much wider and stronger.

"*Everything's gonna be all right,*" Evie mouths for one last time, swinging her guitar and head to tell all those eager others that the time has come to launch back into the chorus.

"*No woman, no cry...*"

Or Seivers' offer. 'Suspiciously generous,' does not even begin to describe it. Will not admit for a moment to anything the girl has claimed, yet he offers me a chance to explore exactly that possibility. Offers me opportunity and respect consistent with who I am. Was.

Am I to take that as tacit admission, or just a ruse to get me out of the way? Ship me off to North Korea where I will disappear... and maybe my disappearing would be the best thing for all of them! Relive Elaine of the burden of returning to me in this form. Relieve Mrs. McKloskey of believing her lost daughter will ever return, and this 'Jake' person of his misdirected lust. Even Aubrey - that strange little thing for whom, I must admit, I have developed some affection – might be relieved of pining for the friend I can never be, the same way I pine for the life I once had: the life I can only glimpse when music guides me to myself. That's it really, the only reason I can even consider any of this, let myself believe for a moment that any of it is real, is that: the music. They're all singing now, out there in that big crowd. An unfamiliar tune, with words I've never heard before and an awkward, unfamiliar beat. It seems to stutter and almost stop on every measure, and yet it manages to keep going.

> *"My fear is my only courage,*
> *So I've got to push on through."*

Absurd words – 'fear is courage?' But powerful, in some unfathomable way. Especially when all those voices are pushing the lyrics out, laying one person's will on top of another and another. Creating a sound that wants to pull you out of yourself and into the very air; empowered with the possibility of leaving all this confusion behind, to inhabit, instead, that world of order and belonging that happens when rhythm and harmony come together.

Eyes on the larger scene, Aubrey sees that Carol has joined Evie and the others on the stair steps, bringing with her the man who was introduced outside as Herb and another woman she credited in her speech as having ignited the vigil, who've dragged along the 'RAINBOW world UNITED' banner and are enlisting bystanders to rig it across the stair. Surprisingly, one of the Reverend's flock is making his way over as well, trailed close by two others who argue heatedly about their errand, and soon the whole mixed-up posse are bending heads together in conference as the last chords of Bob Marley's anthem sound. A smattering of self-conscious applause begins to rise but is immediately cut off as the young church-man - a fresh-faced boy of barely twenty, in immaculate suit and skinny gray tie knotted tight against his tender neck – turns out toward the waiting faces and bursts into a new song, one hand stirring the air above his head to keep the beat alive.

"*This land is your land,*" he sings in brightly confident tenor, "*this land is my land,*" and is answered with a cluster of derogatory shouts from the crowd, a crumpled sheet of newsprint flying toward his face. At the same time though, they can all see Carol and Herb and the new woman rising to a higher step and linking arm in arm with him beneath the banner to join the song, as Evie raises her guitar to accompany the boy with a school-book simple chord progression.

"*From California, to the New York island.*" All around the majestic staircase expressions change yet again as they realize what is happening; musical hands reaching across the divide between factions to seek a common thread; a neutral meeting place in the shadow of their common mortality.

"*From the redwood forest, to the gulf stream waters...*"

Now these lyrics sound familiar. One of those 'folk' songs the kids sang back in the sixties, before they got all sidetracked in riots and revolutions. Steinbeck? No, he wrote books, I think. Woody, then; Woody-somebody-or other - and notorious, if I recall correctly; people called him a communist, but he could certainly write a catchy tune. Must have done, because I remember it now, despite myself.

"*This land - was made for you and me,*" *I sing, straining to catch the thread of meaning and anticipate the next word, latching on to the life-preserving melody so I can feel the song run through my soul – ha! Did I really say 'my soul?' Another form of mumbo-jumbo, no better than the rest of the superstitions I have been subjected to. We are our bodies: our organs and cells and enzymes down to the last molecule, and no amount of endorphin-response physiology can change that.*

"*As I was walking', the words continue and I want to sing them out with all my heart – yes, I will admit to having one of those – so I can be carried into the air along with the words. In this one act I am freed from contradiction, free to be the self that I alone can know, whose truth is confirmed just by the knowing. You can have your reality and I can have mine, and still we can join in this one thing.*

"I saw before me – an endless skyway."

From all around the space, eyes turn to find the source of this new contribution, though to a few it is familiar.

"That's her," shouts a voice from the crowd, and instantly half a dozen stricken faces are turning in Rod's direction. "The one that dumped on Stevie. It's all because of her that she was out there."

"It's not like that," Tammy protests, as several persons appear at the open end of the counter. But it doesn't matter, because the musicians and their compatriots on the staircase have latched on to the beautiful serendipity of Stevie's one-time stage partner headlining at her wake. Seeing her struggle and stumble over the unfamiliar lyrics, they lean together and chatter for a moment before sliding smoothly into another song they hope perhaps she'll know, and one more suited by custom to the occasion.

"*Oh when the saints,*" Carol nearly shouts, to be rewarded by that sweet soprano on "*Come marching in...*"

"We have to get her back on the right medication," Auster is urging in a back corner of the station, his body carefully positioned to block Mrs. McKloskey's view of her daughter as he and Three Dollar Bill labor to control the situation.

"*We are trav-ling,*" Carol calls out, moving into the first verse of this newest selection, only to see Rod shake Christina's head in frustration, ignorant of the lines. Sensing an opportunity, Elliot signals the musicians to keep playing, grabs up his backpack from among the sound equipment and scrambles through the crowd into the security station. Squeezing in behind the counter, he drags a laptop from the backpack, searches out a USB port and, in the time it takes his machine to come out of hibernation, begins feeding lyrics from his karaoke software onto one of the monitors where he points them out to Rod, who quickly catches on. Relieved of the need to search his memory for words, the talent passed down from Sean McKloskey and the years of childhood exposure to great music become more apparent than ever, causing members of the crowd to shift their attention, one by one, away from the assorted musicians jammed upon the staircase and onto this singular figure who has risen to her feet behind the security counter and is belting as if his life depended on it.

"*We are trav-lling,*
"*in the footsteps,*"

"Mr. Seivers," Anne interrupts, her voice small but steady against the rising volume of singers joining in the song. Her words compete,3 too, with the sound of Rose and Tammy arguing with Stevie's supporters and, closer at hand, Herman and Aubrey shooting ideas back and forth about how best to arrange the lyric feed on the big wall among all the different camera angles available, now that Mark's partners Riley and Dook Kim have gotten their own equipment connected to the system as well. Craning her head past Seivers' bulk to track her daughter's image on the giant display, Anne's eyes are alight as she continues most politely: "I want to thank you for all you've done, but..."

"o-f those who've,
"gone before,"

I hear myself cry out these words, and they are certainly true enough. Footsteps of the writers who have written these songs and the singers who have sung them, who have given us the avenue to voice what cannot be said with words alone. This music takes me back, to when that person and I performed; the almost blissful pleasure we had of sharing what we'd been given. Back farther, too, to what seems like centuries ago, before any of these strange people, and their baffling stories. A time when everything was clear. Old I might have been, and sick and even bitter, but at least I knew myself; I knew my place in the world. Now...to start again, amidst all these competing voices, every one screaming for my attention, every one selling a different opinion..."

"Oh when the saints," *the chorus begins again, and these words I know without looking at the screen, so I take the chance and let them fly, jumping up some interval whose name I could not guess, but know instinctively will harmonize with all around it, then flattening the steps of the next line, putting it all on one note that hangs above the others, calling them to rise to its power.* "Come marching in." *In the pause before the next line, my attention drifts off to glance at my Elaine over there. Not mine though, anymore. Her own, her self, a woman on a trajectory to places I will never know, as are the girl, and the mother, and all these others. Only in the music can I believe that I am not alone.*

"Oh lord, I want,"

'I want, I want, I wa-ant,' I vamp into the interval, torqueing the words out of my chest so they carry twice as much emotion - three times as much - as they fly up over the others.

"To be in that number,"

'Yea-ah-h-h'
"Oh when the saints go marching in."

Astonished, Aubrey listens as the old woman thanks Seivers
for his help, for knowing all along that her daughter needed care.
"But wait," she tries to break in, only to be dragged aside by Auster,
whose breath smells of breath mints and too much coffee. One hand
clasped tightly around her upper arm, he reminds her of the trouble
that awaits if she and Christina continue to violate the settlement
reached months ago, when he himself was generous enough to act as
their attorney: critical medical services no longer provided for free,
kidnapping charges reconsidered by the DA, his own fees billed
retroactively in one throat-clogging lump sum. If, however, Aubrey
will only convince Christina to sign-away any claims against MH, he
can assure her...

Through several verses Christina's voice leads the crowd,
growing more and more confident as it plays with the melody in
imitation of his beloved jazz artists, throwing in a bluesy grace note
here, a bit of gospel counterpoint there, while Peterson scrambles to
get his camera into the best position to beam this story from phone
to phone to console to wall.
"Unbroken Circle," Carol shouts, announcing the musicians'
newest selection over the trailing tones of the last chorus. There's a
moment of confusion as Rod shakes Christina's head once again and
Elliot scrambles to pull up his index, but only a few bars of
introductory instrumental are necessary before the words appear on
monitor and wall for all to see and follow.
"*I was standing, by my window*," Jake hears Christina sing,
and finds himself choking up as she takes charge of yet another song,
the entire gathering focused in rapt attention on her voice and face
as they feel themselves uplifted by her vocal pyrotechnics.

"*On a cold and, cloudy day*," the assembled voices sing, many
now swaying in time as they lock arms or embrace, tears flowing on a
good percentage of their faces.
Of all Rod's and Christina's assorted friends and family, it is
Elaine who reaches out as that marvelous voice soars over their
heads. Places her hand on Christina's soft shoulder, so much lower
and smaller than her husband's had been, and speaks to those eyes

so fixed upon the streaming monitor before them, that face so intent on using music to hold the world at bay.

"Listen to yourself, my dear: there are scads of people who would give up everything to have a voice like that. Whatever else this life so far has done to you, whatever the pains and frustrations, it's given you this beautiful voice, and that's a gift you should not turn away from. Listen to that voice, regardless of anything else, and follow it where it takes you."

"Will the circle..." I sing, the melody of this old war-horse warmly familiar from somewhere in my own pre-history, "be unbroken..." Closing my eyes, I am reminded of what it was like inside The Nothing: the un-noticed and under-appreciated peace of truly knowing and believing who I was. A peace I was beginning to believe I had lost forever after this ridiculous world began creeping in, only to find it again in this gift of my own voice.

Nearby, Herman's arm has wrapped itself around the waist of Rose, herself entangled with Tammy in chaste embrace as they listen to the multitude mourn the passing of one of their own: a misfit-oddball-dreaming-freak, who managed to find the joy in who she was, and bring a bit of it into the lives of those around her.

"*Well I told the...undertaker,*" they all hear the wondrous voice sing out, every note strong and clear and perfectly in tune. Sure and true, it jumps an octave for the next phrase. "*Undertaker... please drive slow.*" Hearing a lyric he can support, the Reverend has come inside, and brought the rest of his troops as well. Gathered in front of the security counter, they've formed up into their habitual ranks, hands clasped in front of chests, and are singing out their faith, bodies swaying like saplings in a gusty wind, faces bright with the glory of belief.

'To a physicist,' Elaine recalls her gypsy mentor saying one day - the voice popping into her awareness unbidden, but nevertheless welcome - 'there is no such thing as cold. There is only heat and the absence of heat. And in the same way, to a person who looks at the world with innocent eyes, there is no such thing as death, there is only life and the absence of it, so if you must believe in something, believe in Life – in its power and its majesty and its all-pervading mystery. *Believe in Life.*'

Across the lobby Ellie and the other musicians beam too; they are playing hard now, each instrument reinforcing the others into a rushing surf of sound, the rhythm insistent, the tempo growing faster – 'keep up or drop out' it tells the world – emotions running higher and higher. Evie's fingers fly as she shifts familiar chords up and down the neck to give them different voicings that keep each repeat sounding fresh and new. Ashton's hands evidence a split personality, the left pulsing out a walking bass while the right runs up and down, casting rippling arpeggios around the melody; rainbows of sonic light that reach into his listeners' heads and hook onto processing centers in their brains, triggering chemical releases and stimulating neural clusters dedicated to memory, to excitement, to pure pleasure despite the grief that lingers still in other regions currently subdued. All the while, Lady continues to hammer at her drum-heads, fingers a ragged blur as she finds ever more ways to subdivide and multiply the beat, geometrically enhancing it without ever losing its cardiac progression – one, *two*, three, *four*; one, *two*, three, *four* - and the fiddler's bow flies faster than them all as it carves out variations and polyphonies in the highest octaves, sixteenth and thirty-second notes slicing through the vibrating atmosphere like flickering points of sunlight dancing through the leaves of a wind-whipped oak. Grinning like idiots, or crumpling their features in concentration, each musician grooves in his or her own way to this almost orgiastic payoff for their years of work and dedication to their craft. Throughout the lobby there are smiles on the faces of the multitude and tears even, of joy and reassurance as the power of song binds friends and enemies together, swelling their hearts and crowding out every other sense, but before the next line can be sung, there comes a sudden shift in the young woman behind the counter.

The slightest movement of the eyes - my God! The product of a lesser effort even than that other blink that reconnected me to this world....

An instant of distraction - of devilish curiosity - leads me to lift my eyes from the words on my TV screen to the room beyond, and in that instant I am captured by a face upon the wall. Taller than the tallest man, in crisply focused Technicolor projection, it is a stranger's face - except that when I mouth a word she mouths it too. When I blink incomprehension, she blinks as well and I feel my mind splitting in two or three or four to follow the tune and read the words, and struggle to make sense of what I am seeing even as I scream at myself not to allow my attention to be drawn by that face which looms so large above me and about me, upon me and within me as the song presses on, relentless.

"For the body...that you're a hauling," *I sing, boring my eyes into the lyrics on the screen in hope that they can bring back that unity I felt so effortlessly a heartbeat before, but it is gone. Shattered by the recognition that this is what I have become. This and that, before and after; positive and negative of myself and never the twain shall meet.* "Lord I hate...to see her go," *I hear, but the shining image across from me does* not *go. It stays there, larger than life, filling my mind with disappointment and frustration and impossible longing for what can never again be.*

"Will the circle, be unbroken," Aubrey and Anne and Elaine hear Christina's voice ring out, still clear and strong, though the expression on her face has gone from one of joy to something indecipherable; unstable and disturbed. Around them all, the crowd continues obliviously; clapping and stamping, swaying and beaming with the ecstasy of shared emotion.

Part and parcel of my world, it is - this face, this other person it belongs to – and the only way to make it go away would be to lose that world completely. Return to my Nothing, which, now that I've escaped it and seen what lies outside, seems less a prison than a refuge. There was no anger in the Nothing, no regret, no one to satisfy. Not these freakish strangers who plague me, not this doppelganger-Elaine who is so different than I remember; none of them were there to try to tell me that everything I know is wrong, and in this moment I know that if I choose I can go back there in an instant. Shut my mouth and my eyes...

Her shoulders slump, her head lolls back, and in the interval between one line and the next her lips settle into stillness, pursed just the slightest bit, the air flowing softly in and out.

"By and by Lord, by and by," the accidental choir sings, voice less numerous by one, than only a measure before.

But then I'd have no voice!
For in the instant I stop singing I feel its loss like a clot inside my throat, blocking up the passage that links my inside to my outside,

to the space and voices all around me. In my Nothing there is nothing, but out there, with this voice that should never have been mine yet is, I feel a part of something greater than myself, something worth following, even if I have to ignore what my eyes tell me and to armor my mind against all I hear - except this one unaccountable voice.

"There's a better, home awaiting," the lyrics claim as the women hear their young friend's voice rise again, strong and proud, defiant even, though her face bears an expression not of anger, but of peace as she sings on, eyes gently closed, corners of her lips drawn up in perhaps the nearest thing to a smile they have seen there since before that May morning they each remember so differently.

Focus only on my voice and let that be who I am; to me, to them, to whoever and whatever, for as long as it may last. I know one day the Nothing will come again for me, as it does for every living person, and on that day I will have no choice but to fall into it, once and for all and forever.
But not today.

Robin Andrew

grace notes

Nearly ten years have elapsed since the events described above, and in that time, there have been many changes in the lives of those involved.

Following the removal of life-support, Stevie Margulies labored for nearly an hour before succumbing to the effects of her injuries. The announcement of her passing brought an end to the vigil at Hilltop Center and within forty minutes virtually all of the demonstrators and counter-demonstrators had dispersed, leaving in their wake a tidal wash of trash and memories.

The three men accused in the attack on Stevie were held for several months in Colorado while their court-appointed attorneys fought extradition to Washington and, in the case of Jimbo and Bawdy, to Mississippi as well, where the two were wanted on prior charges. Their original assault charges in Seattle were changed, after Stevie's passing, to Homicide, Second Degree. All three eventually pled guilty to lesser charges to avoid trial, and are now free.

Evelyn Margulies and her son now live in American Fork, Utah and have joined the Church of Jesus Christ of Latter Day Saints. An application for posthumous baptism of Stephen Margulies has been filed with the Church elders and is currently under consideration.

After many lengthy delays, the Patient Care Review Board of Hilltop Medical Center issued its final finding that Christina McKloskey's continuing erratic behavior and delusional belief that she was actually someone else were long-term effects of her drug overdose, not caused by anything which occurred during the period of time she was under the institution's care. Despite this evidence that the Center was not responsible for her condition, Hilltop and MH continue to provide full and free medical services for Christina, as a demonstration of corporate generosity and commitment to their patients.

Jim Auster, now In-House Counsel to Medical Holdings, LLC, recently filed an extensive amicus brief in the Federal Appellate Court case of Organic Engineering, LLC vs. Riker-McCoy Derivative Industries, supporting the right of medical researchers to receive patent protection for a new development in surgico-pharmaceutical treatment of an obscure motor-function-disjunction syndrome. The case is considered likely to go before the U. S. Supreme Court in its upcoming session and will likely set the standard for ownership of medical advances for years to come.

'Three Dollar Bill' Seivers was forced to sell off significant portions of Medical Holdings LLC during the 2009 recession. He is currently under investigation by the SEC for allegedly understating the number of shares outstanding at the time of those sales.

Jessica Bagley Seivers left the couple's New York co-op in 2010 and checked into the Betty Ford Center for treatment of her alcoholism. She graduated several months later, clean and sober, but is currently back at Ford for follow-up treatment, her second such return.

Mary Antonias and Jason Privet recently celebrated their eighth wedding anniversary and now reside in Annapolis, Maryland, where Mary completed her Residency in pediatric endocrinology at a hospital not affiliated with MH, and Jason has joined NeuroSecurityConsultInc, a start-up company dedicated to ensuring that hackers such as himself do not disrupt the operations of next-generation wireless prosthetics and other implantable medical devices.

Elaine Gimbal used part of the proceeds from the sale of her home to establish a charitable foundation, which currently has a clinic (named in honor of her late husband) and two schools under construction or planned in a remote region of southeast Tibet. She spends most of her time traveling, interspersed with brief visits to Seattle to renew friendships and raise funds for her endeavors.

Jake Brindle, having sold his beloved Beemer and used the proceeds to enroll himself in Seattle Central Community College, is now an independent Professional Financial Adviser, helping others to avoid the sort of mistakes which obliterated his inheritance.

With Jake's assistance, Anne McKloskey has been able to retain ownership of the family home and offer support to her daughter. She is currently at work on an expanded edition of her husband's papers.

Aubrey Maturin lives in the guesthouse of Mrs. McKloskey's home, along with Christina, who has legally changed her name to Rodney and is studying voice and composition at Cornish College of The Arts and vocalizing frequently with several local jazz combos.

Of Beryl Nathanson, nothing has been heard since she started up the trail ahead of Elaine, and she is presumed - by those who remember her at all - to have re-united at last with her long-lost brother.

Robin Andrew

bluebirds fly

coda

Beneath a sky as wide and open as...well...as only a Tibetan-plateau sky can be, a woman walks, unhurried and unworried, her compliment of bracelets, anklets, earrings and ornaments tinkling softly. Behind her a train of colorful figures follow, their backs piled high with loads they have been hauling now for many days. In every step and on every face is evident their relief at having reached the end of a long journey, the prospect of setting down their burdens and, for a few, reunion. The landscape through which they walk might seem barren to an unschooled eye, but to one familiar with its scale and textures, everywhere there are signs of community. Here, a cairn of flat stones stacked shoulder-high to mark the way through winter's heavy blanket of snow - thankfully only a memory on this afternoon in early June - here, a trio of slender logs lain parallel across a wash, providing passage during spring rains - like the one this party endured two nights ago on the other side of the pass - and there, in the distance, the square block of a house, its color one with the dun of the surrounding earth, its presence discernible only by the unnatural straightness of wall and roof lines rising above the faint shadows cast by outbuildings and stone fences; shadows which serve to blend homestead into landscape, as if its entire composition were no more than an extrusion, drawn upward out of the earth itself.

Gradually, impatiently, their pace quickening despite themselves, the party comes closer to this small enclave, eyes eagerly taking in the few small fruit trees huddled in its lee, the garden plots grown leafy and promising. By the time they are near enough to make out a string of fluttering prayer flags or the head of a goat poking through the gate, their arrival has been heralded by the barking of a mongrel horde and, soon thereafter, the squealing cries of several children. Small - as children tend to be - but not *as* small as they once were.

"Ama," they shout, charging from house to gate, to house again, then out once more and through the gate, with all the exuberance that other children, worlds away, might show on Christmas morning. "Ama, de-sho! Zhe-Khong Ber-eel young-ua! Ama!"

Even before Petal has emerged from the house, the long sliver of the skinning knife gripped in her graceful fingers, Little Love is in The Ber-eel's arms. Stubby fingers dislodge the paisley scarf around her head, toying with the white hair tucked beneath it as he giggles at the words she speaks - foreign words, entirely unintelligible to the child, and just as entirely superfluous, because all the meaning they are intended to convey comes clearly through in the energetic way she bounces him upon her hip and the buoyant gestures of her free hand; in the arching of her back and the bobbing of her head, and in the beaming smile which lights up not just her creased and dusty face, but her entire person.

The End

bluebirds fly

Robin Andrew

bluebirds fly

Acknowledgments

This is a work of fiction, and I hope unique in enough aspects that there is no question about its originality, however its creation certainly drew upon many sources. *Only The Eyes Say Yes*, by Phillipe and Stephane Wigand, and *The Diving Bell and The Butterfly*, by Jean-Dominique Bauby, each provided some inspiration for Rod's experience of Locked-In Syndrome, while *Mutant Message Down Under*, by Marlo Morgan, encouraged me to consider that a woman of advanced years might have a physically-challenging adventure such as Elaine's. *Leaving Mother Lake*, by Yang Erche Namu, opened my eyes to the extraordinary (and real) Moso people, while Xinran's *Sky Burial: An Epic Love Story*, lent further detail to the (fictional) azhe-Moso people, and the isolating effect of living among those with whom one shares no language. *West With The Night*, by Beryl Markham, was the source for some of Beryl Nathanson's backstory, as well as her first name, the appropriation of which I hope will be seen as a tribute, for that is how it is intended. Similarly, Patrick O'Brian's astounding Napoleonic-era naval saga (in twenty and one-third volumes!) was the source for another character's name, though there is no other connection to that opus except that I sought refuge in it during one stage of the writing. The conceit of the body transplant (a more apt term, in the author's opinion, than 'brain transplant'), has been around at least since 1818 (Mary Shelley's *Frankenstein, or The Modern Prometheus*) but my own encounter began with Robert A. Heinlein's 1970 *I Will Fear No Evil*, which layered a new issue of gender-flopping onto the already-present themes of reincarnation, identity and outlaw technology. For the character and thoughts of Stevie Margulies, I am indebted to all who have journeyed through gender and had the courage to be public about it; you are greater in number than commonly-believed, and your forthright insistence on being yourselves has changed the world in which we live - for the better. For anyone who finds irself along that spectrum, or encounters one who is, a good starting resource is *Transgender 101: A Simple Guide to a Complex Issue*, by Nicholas M. Teich, beyond which today's Internet offers a world of further information and support.

To all those and many more, I offer my thanks and admiration, and hope I have not done them an injustice.

Robin Andrew

Lyric Credits

Opening Quote

Galileo - Emily Ann Saliers, © EMI Music Publishing, Universal Music PUblishing

Third Movement

Chicago – Frank Sinatra, Chicago lyrics © Sony/ATV Music Publishing LLC, Warner/Chappell Music, Inc., Universal Music Publishing Group, IMAGEM U.S. LLC, Ultra Tunes

Gimme Mo' Bling - (not found; made up?)

Turning the Beat Around - Peter Jackson Jr/Gerald Jackson, lyrics © Warner/Chappell Music., Inc.

Heartbreak Hotel - Mae Axton, Arthur Crudup, Tommy Durden, elvis Presley, © Unichappell Music Inc., Sony/ATV Publishing, Durden Breyer Publishing, Crudup Music

Somewhere Over the Rainbow - Bob Thiele, George David Weiss, George Douglas, Harold Arlen, E. Harburg, © Larry Spier Music LLD O.B.O Abilene Music LLC, Emi Feist Catalogh Inc., Range Road Music, Ind.

Fourth Movement

Do-Re-Mi - Earl King Johnson © Sony/ATV Music Publishing LLC, Imagem U.S. LLC

You May Be Right, I May be Crazy - Christian Simon, Billy Joel © Impulsive Music

This Could Be the Start of Something Big -

Steve Allen © Meadowlane Music Inc.

Exactly Like You - Jimmy McHugh, Dorothy L. Fields © EMI Music Publishing, Shapiro Bernstein & Co. Inc.

Oh, Look at Me Now -; John M DeVries, Joe Bushkin, John Devries © Hampshire House Publishing, Embassy Music Corp.

Fifth movement

Come to My Window – Melissa L. Ethridge © M L E Music

What a Wonderful World – George Douglas, Howard Dietz, Bob Thiele, Robert Thiele, Arthur Schwartz, Axel Christofer Hedfors, George David Weiss, Bob Thiele Jr. © Chappell & Co. Inc., Quartet Music, Range Road Music Inc., Imagem Sounds O.B.O. Abilene Music LLC, Universal Music Publishing AB, Quartet Music Inc.

Beautiful - Calvin Broadus, Daniel Powter, Aliaune Thiam, Linda Perry, John Eugene Wesley, Giorgio Tuinfort, Chad Hugo, Pharrell Williams, Colby O'donis © Jada Loves Daddys Musik, Sony/ATV Songs LLC, 360 Music, Stuck In The Throat Music, Songs Mp O.B.O. Pharrell Williams, Sony/ATV Tunes LLC, Sony/ATV Harmony, Song 6 Music, Byefall Productions Inc.

Freedom – George Michael; © Warner/Chappell Music Inc.

A Mighty Fortress is Our God - Martin Luther, trans. Frederic H. Hedge, Public Domain

bluebirds fly